Great Stories of
Mystery
and
Suspense

Great Stories of
Mystery
and
Suspense

Selected and condensed by the editors of
The Reader's Digest

VOLUME
2

The Reader's Digest Association
Montreal, Sydney, Cape Town
Pleasantville, New York

CONTENTS

The Maltese Falcon

A CONDENSATION OF
THE BOOK BY

Dashiell Hammett

ILLUSTRATED BY OSCAR LIEBMAN

It was only a small statuette—
the golden figure of a falcon, a foot high
and enameled over. In four hundred years
it had been the possession of emperors,
knights, soldiers and adventurers.
A number of people had already died
because of it, and several very unpleasant
characters were now trying desperately
to get their hands on it. Why? Sam
Spade wondered. And what possible
connection could the beautiful girl called
Miss Wonderly have with this
storied and priceless relic?

Once a Pinkerton detective, Dashiell Hammett
is credited with the founding of
the "hard-boiled" school of American
detective fiction—a reputation established
in 1930 with *The Maltese Falcon*
and later confirmed by such landmark novels
as *The Glass Key* and *The Thin Man*.

Chapter 1

SAMUEL SPADE's jaw was long and bony, his chin a jutting V under the more flexible V of his mouth. His nostrils curved back to make another, smaller, V. His yellow-gray eyes were horizontal. The V motif was picked up again by thickish brows rising outward from twin creases above a hooked nose, and his pale brown hair grew down—from high flat temples—in a point on his forehead. He looked rather pleasantly like a blond Satan.

He said to Effie Perine, "Yes, sweetheart?"

She was a lanky sunburned girl whose eyes were brown and playful in a shiny boyish face. She finished shutting the door behind her, leaned against it, and said, "There's a girl wants to see you. Her name's Wonderly."

"A customer?"

"I guess so. You'll want to see her anyway; she's a knockout."

"Shoo her in, darling," said Spade. "Shoo her in."

Effie Perine opened the door again, following it back into the outer office, standing with a hand on the knob while saying, "Will you come in, Miss Wonderly?"

A voice said, "Thank you," so softly that only the purest articulation made the words intelligible, and a young woman came through the doorway. She advanced slowly, with tentative steps, looking at Spade with cobalt-blue eyes that were both shy and probing.

She was tall and pliantly slender, without angularity anywhere. Her body was erect and high-breasted, her legs long, her hands and feet narrow. She wore blue, and the hair curling from under her blue hat was darkly red, her full lips more brightly red. White teeth glistened in the crescent her timid smile made.

Spade rose bowing and indicating with a thick-fingered hand the oaken armchair beside his desk. He was quite six feet tall.

Miss Wonderly murmured, "Thank you," softly as before and sat down on the edge of the chair's wooden seat.

Spade sank into his swivel chair, made a quarter turn to face her, smiled politely. "Now what can I do for you, Miss Wonderly?"

She caught her breath and looked at him. She swallowed and said hurriedly, "Could you—? I thought—I—that is—" Then she tortured her lower lip with glistening teeth and said nothing. Only her eyes spoke now, pleading.

Spade smiled and nodded as if he understood her, but pleasantly, as if nothing serious were involved. He said, "Suppose you tell me about it, from the beginning, and then we'll know what needs doing. Better begin as far back as you can."

"That was in New York."

"Yes."

"I don't know where she met him. I mean I don't know where in New York. She's five years younger than I—only seventeen—and we didn't have the same friends. I don't suppose we've ever been as close as sisters should be. Mama and Papa are in Europe. It would kill them. I've got to get her back before they come home."

"Yes," he said.

"They're coming home the first of the month."

Spade's eyes brightened. "Then we've two weeks," he said.

"I didn't know what she had done until her letter came. I was frantic." Her lips trembled. Her hands mashed the dark handbag in her lap. "I was too afraid she had done something like this to go to the police, and the fear that something had happened to her kept urging me to go. What could I do?"

"Nothing, of course," Spade said, "but then her letter came?"

"Yes, and I sent her a telegram asking her to come home. I sent it to General Delivery here. That was the only address she gave me. I waited a whole week, but no answer came, not another word from her. So I came to San Francisco to get her. I wrote her I was coming, that I would go to the St. Mark, and I begged her to come and let me talk to her even if she didn't intend to go home with me. But she didn't come. I waited three days, and she didn't come, didn't even send me a message of any sort."

Spade nodded his blond Satan's head, frowned sympathetically, and tightened his lips together.

"It was horrible," Miss Wonderly said. She shuddered. "I wrote her another letter, and yesterday afternoon I went to the post office. I stayed there until after dark, but I didn't see her. I went again this morning, and still didn't see Corinne, but I saw Floyd Thursby."

Spade nodded again. His frown went away. In its place came a look of sharp attentiveness.

"He wouldn't tell me where Corinne was," she went on, hopelessly. "He wouldn't tell me anything, except that she was well and happy. He wouldn't take me to her. He promised to tell her he had seen me, and to bring her to see me—if she would come—this evening at the hotel. He said he knew she wouldn't. He promised to come himself if she wouldn't. He—" She broke off with a startled hand to her mouth as the door opened.

The man who had opened the door came in a step, said, "Oh, excuse me!" hastily took his brown hat from his head, and backed out.

"It's all right, Miles," Spade told him. "Come in. Miss Wonderly, this is Mr. Archer, my partner."

Miles Archer came into the office again, shutting the door behind him, ducking his head and smiling at Miss Wonderly, making a vaguely polite gesture with the hat in his hand. He was of medium height, solidly built, wide in the shoulders, thick in the neck, with a jovial heavy-jawed red face and some gray in his close-trimmed hair. He was apparently as many years past forty as Spade was past thirty.

Spade said, "Miss Wonderly's sister ran away from New York with a fellow named Floyd Thursby. They're here. Miss Wonderly has seen Thursby and has a date with him tonight. Maybe he'll bring the sister with him. The chances are he won't. Miss Wonderly wants us to find the sister and get her away from him and back home." He looked at Miss Wonderly. "Right?"

"Yes," she said indistinctly. Spade winked at his partner.

Miles Archer came forward to stand at a corner of the desk. While the girl looked at her bag he looked at her. His little brown eyes ran their bold appraising gaze from her lowered face to her feet and up to her face again. Then he looked at Spade and made a silent whistling mouth of appreciation.

Spade lifted two fingers from the arm of his chair in a brief warning gesture and said, "We shouldn't have any trouble with it. It's simply a matter of having a man at the hotel this evening to shadow Thursby when he leaves, and until he leads us to your sister. If she doesn't want to leave him after we've found her—well, we'll find a way of managing that."

Miss Wonderly looked up at Spade, quickly, puckering her forehead. "Oh, but you must be careful!" Her voice shook a little. "I'm deathly afraid of him, of what he might do to her."

Spade smiled and patted the arms of his chair. "Just leave that to us. We'll know how to handle him," he said. "You can trust us."

"I do trust you," she said earnestly, "but I want you to know that he's a dangerous man. I honestly don't think he'd stop at anything. I don't believe he'd hesitate to—to kill Corinne if he thought it would save him."

"You didn't threaten him, did you?"

"I told him that all I wanted was to get her home before Mama and Papa came so they'd never know what she had done. I promised him I'd never say a word to them about it if he helped me, but if he didn't Papa would certainly see that he was punished."

"Can he cover up by marrying her?" Archer said.

The girl blushed and replied in a confused voice, "He has a wife and three children in England. Corinne wrote me that, to explain why she had gone off with him."

"They usually do," Spade said, "though not always in England." He leaned forward to reach for pencil and pad of paper. "What does he look like?"

"Oh, he's thirty-five years old, perhaps, and as tall as you, and either naturally dark or quite sunburned. His hair is dark too, and he has thick eyebrows. He talks in a rather loud, blustery way and has a nervous, irritable manner. He gives the impression of being—of violence."

Spade, scribbling on the pad, asked without looking up, "Thin, medium, or heavy build?"

"Quite athletic. He's broad-shouldered and carries himself erect, has what could be called a decidedly military carriage. He was wearing a light gray suit and a gray hat when I saw him."

"What time is he coming to see you?"

"After eight o'clock."

"All right, Miss Wonderly, we'll have a man there."

"Mr. Spade, could either you or Mr. Archer"—she made an appealing gesture with both hands—"could either of you look after it personally? I'd be—I'd expect to be charged more, of course." She opened her handbag with nervous fingers and put two hundred-dollar bills on Spade's desk. "Would that be enough?"

"Yeh," Archer said, "and I'll look after it myself."

Miss Wonderly stood up, impulsively holding a hand out to him. "Thank you! Thank you!" she exclaimed, and then gave Spade her hand, repeating, "Thank you!"

"Not at all," Spade said over it. "Glad to. It'll help some if you either meet Thursby downstairs or let yourself be seen in the lobby with him at some time."

"I will," she promised, and thanked the partners again.

"And don't look for me," Archer cautioned her. "I'll see you all right."

Spade went to the corridor door with Miss Wonderly. When he returned to his desk Archer nodded at the hundred-dollar bills there, growled complacently, "They're right enough," picked one up, folded it, and tucked it into a vest pocket. "And they had brothers in her bag."

A TELEPHONE BELL RANG in darkness. When it had rung three times a man's voice said, "Hello. . . . Yes, speaking. . . . Dead? . . . Yes. . . . Fifteen minutes. Thanks."

A switch clicked and a white bowl hung on three gilded chains from the ceiling's center filled the room with light. Spade, barefooted, in green-and-white checked pajamas, sat on the side of his bed, his hands working with a packet of brown cigarette papers and a sack of Bull Durham tobacco. He lit the cigarette, stood up, and began to dress. A tinny alarm clock, insecurely mounted on a corner of Duke's *Celebrated Criminal Cases of America*—face down on the table—held its hands at five minutes past two.

When he had fastened his shoes he picked up the telephone, called Graystone 4500, and ordered a taxicab. He put on a green-striped white shirt, a soft white collar, a green necktie, a gray suit, a loose tweed overcoat, and a dark gray hat. The street-door bell rang as he stuffed tobacco, keys, and money into his pockets.

WHERE Bush Street roofed Stockton before slipping downhill to Chinatown, Spade paid his fare and left the taxicab. A few yards away a small group of men stood looking up an alley. Two women stood with a man on the other side of Bush Street, looking at the alley. There were faces at windows.

Spade crossed the sidewalk between iron-railed hatchways that opened above bare ugly stairs, went to the parapet, and, resting his hands on the damp coping, looked down into Stockton Street. An automobile popped out of the tunnel beneath him with a roar.

Not far from the tunnel's mouth a man was hunkered on his heels before a billboard across the front of a gap between two store buildings. The hunkered man's head was bent almost to the sidewalk so he could look under the billboard. A hand flat on the paving, a hand clenched on the billboard's green frame, held him in this grotesque position.

Spade turned from the parapet and walked up Bush Street to the alley where men were grouped. A uniformed policeman under an enameled sign that said BURRITT ST. put out an arm and asked, "What do you want here?"

"I'm Sam Spade. Tom Polhaus phoned me."

"Sure you are." The policeman's arm went down. "I didn't know you at first. Well, they're back there." He jerked a thumb over his shoulder. "Bad business."

"Bad enough," Spade agreed, and went up the alley.

Halfway up it, not far from the entrance, a dark ambulance stood. Behind the ambulance, to the left, the alley was bounded by a waist-high fence, horizontal strips of rough boarding. From the fence dark ground fell away steeply to the billboard on Stockton Street below.

A ten-foot length of the fence's top rail had been torn from a post at one end and hung dangling from the other. Fifteen feet down the slope a flat boulder stuck out. In the notch between boulder and slope Miles Archer lay on his back. Two men stood over him. One of them held the beam of an electric torch on the dead man. Other men with lights moved up and down the slope.

One of them hailed Spade, "Hello, Sam," and clambered up to the alley, his shadow running up the slope before him. He was a barrel-bellied tall man with shrewd small eyes, a thick mouth, and carelessly shaven dark jowls. His shoes, knees, hands, and chin were daubed with loam. "I figured you'd want to see it before we took him away," he said as he stepped over the broken fence.

"Thanks, Tom," Spade said. "What happened?" He put an elbow on a fence post and looked down at the men below, nodding to those who nodded to him.

Tom Polhaus poked his own left breast with a dirty finger. "Got him right through the pump—with this." He took a fat revolver from his coat pocket and held it out to Spade. "A Webley. English, ain't it?"

Spade took his elbow from the fence post and leaned down to look at the weapon, but he did not touch it. "Yes," he said, "Webley-Fosbery automatic revolver. That's it. Thirty-eight, eight shot. They don't make them anymore. How many gone out of it?"

"One pill." Tom poked his breast again. "He must've been dead when he cracked the fence." He raised the revolver. "Ever seen this before?"

Spade nodded. "I've seen Webley-Fosberys," he said without interest, and then spoke rapidly. "He was shot up here, huh? Standing where you are, with his back to the fence. The man that shot him stands here." He went around in front of Tom and raised a hand breast-high with leveled forefinger. "Lets him have it and Miles goes back, taking the top off the fence and going on through and down till the rock catches him. That it?"

"That's it," Tom replied slowly, working his brows together. "The blast burned his coat."

"Who found him?"

"The man on the beat, Shilling. He was coming down Bush, and just as he got here a machine turning threw headlights up here, and he saw the top off the fence. So he came up to look at it, and found him."

"What about the machine that was turning around?"

"Not a damned thing about it, Sam. Shilling didn't pay any attention to it, not knowing anything was wrong then." Tom turned and put a leg over the fence. "Coming down for a look at him before he's moved?"

Spade said, "No."

Tom halted astride the fence and looked back at Spade with surprise.

Spade said, "You've seen him. You'd see everything I could."

Tom, still looking at Spade, nodded doubtfully and withdrew his leg over the fence.

"His gun was tucked away on his hip," he said. "It hadn't been fired. His overcoat was buttoned. There's a hundred and sixty-some bucks in his clothes. Was he working, Sam?"

Spade, after a moment's hesitation, nodded.

Tom asked, "Well?"

"He was tailing a fellow named Floyd Thursby," Spade said, and described Thursby as Miss Wonderly had described him.

"What for?"

"He was an Englishman, maybe. I don't know what his game was, exactly. We were trying to find out where he lived." Spade grinned faintly and patted Tom's shoulder. "Don't crowd me. I'm going out to break the news to Miles's wife." He turned away and went out of the alley.

In an all-night drugstore on the corner of Bush and Taylor streets, Spade used a telephone. "Precious," he said into it a little while after he had given a number, "Miles has been shot. . . . Yes, he's dead. . . . Now don't get excited. . . . Yes. . . . You'll have to break it to Iva. . . . No, I'm damned if I will. You've got to do it. . . . And keep her away from the office. . . . Tell her I'll see her—uh—sometime. . . . Yes, but don't tie me up to anything. . . . That's the stuff. You're an angel. By."

Spade's tinny alarm clock said 3:40 when he turned on the light in the suspended bowl again. He dropped his hat and overcoat on the bed and went into his kitchen, returning to the bedroom with a wineglass and a tall bottle of Bacardi rum. He had drunk his third glass and was lighting his fifth cigarette when the street-door bell rang. The hands of the alarm clock registered 4:30.

Spade sighed, rose from the bed, and went to the telephone box beside his bathroom door. He pressed the button that released the street-door lock. He muttered, "Damn her," and stood scowling at the black telephone box, while a dull flush grew in his cheeks.

The grating and rattling of the elevator door opening and closing came from the corridor. Spade sighed again and moved towards the corridor door. Soft heavy footsteps sounded on the carpeted floor outside, the footsteps of two men. Spade's face brightened. His eyes were no longer harassed. He opened the door quickly.

"Hello, Tom," he said to the barrel-bellied tall detective with whom he had talked in Burritt Street, and, "Hello, Lieutenant," to the man beside Tom. "Come in."

They nodded together, neither saying anything, and came in. Spade shut the door and ushered them into his bedroom. Tom sat on an end of the sofa by the windows. The lieutenant sat on a chair beside the table.

Spade brought two wineglasses in from the kitchen, filled them and his own with Bacardi, gave one to each of his visitors, and sat down with his on the side of the bed. His face was placid and uncurious. He raised his glass, and said, "Success to crime," and drank it down.

Tom emptied his glass, set it on the floor beside his feet, and wiped his mouth with a muddy forefinger. He stared at the foot of the bed as if trying to remember something of which it vaguely reminded him.

The lieutenant looked at his glass for a dozen seconds, took a very small sip of its contents, and put the glass on the table at his elbow. He examined the room with hard deliberate eyes, and then looked at Tom.

Tom moved uncomfortably on the sofa and, not looking up, asked, "Did you break the news to Miles's wife, Sam?"

Spade said, "Uh-huh."

"How'd she take it?"

Spade shook his head. "I don't know anything about women."

Tom said softly, "The hell you don't."

The lieutenant put his hands on his knees and leaned forward. His greenish eyes were fixed on Spade in a peculiarly rigid stare. "What kind of gun do you carry?" he asked.

"None. I don't like them much. Of course there are some in the office."

"I'd like to see one of them," the lieutenant said. "You don't happen to have one here?"

"No."

"You sure of that?"

Spade set his glass on the table and stood up facing the lieutenant. "What do you want, Dundy?" he asked in a voice hard and cold as his eyes.

Lieutenant Dundy's eyes had moved to maintain their focus on Spade's. Only his eyes had moved.

Tom shifted his weight on the sofa again and growled plaintively, "We're not wanting to make any trouble, Sam."

Spade, ignoring Tom, said to Dundy, "Well, what do you want? Talk turkey. Who in hell do you think you are, coming in here trying to rope me?"

"All right," Dundy said in his chest, "sit down and listen."

"I'll sit or stand as I damned please," said Spade, not moving.

"For God's sake be reasonable," Tom begged. "What's the use of us having a row? If you want to know why we didn't talk turkey it's because when I asked you who this Thursby was you as good as told me it was none of my business. You can't treat us that way, Sam. It ain't right and it won't get you anywheres. We got our work to do."

Lieutenant Dundy jumped up, stood close to Spade, and thrust his square face up at the taller man's. "I've warned you your foot was going to slip one of these days," he said.

Spade made a depreciative mouth, raising his eyebrows. "Everybody's foot slips sometime," he replied with derisive mildness.

"Who's Thursby?" Dundy demanded.

"I told Tom what I knew about him."

"You told Tom damned little."

"I knew damned little."

"Why were you tailing him?"

"I wasn't. Miles was—for the swell reason that we had a client who was paying good United States money to have him tailed."

"Who's the client?"

Spade said reprovingly, "You know I can't tell you that until I've talked it over with the client."

"You'll tell it to me or you'll tell it in court," Dundy said hotly. "This is murder and don't you forget it."

"Maybe. And here's something for you to not forget, sweetheart. I'll tell it or not as I damned please. It's a long while since I burst out crying because policemen didn't like me."

"Be reasonable, Sam," Tom pleaded. "Give us a chance. How can we turn up anything on Miles's killing if you won't give us what you've got?"

"You needn't get a headache over that," Spade told him. "I'll bury my own dead."

Lieutenant Dundy sat down and put his hands on his knees again. His eyes were warm green discs.

"I thought you would," he said. He smiled with grim content. "That's just exactly why we came to see you."

The wariness went out of Spade's eyes. He made his eyes dull with boredom. He turned his face around to Tom and asked with great carelessness, "What's itching your boy friend now?"

Dundy jumped up and tapped Spade's chest with the ends of two bent fingers. "Just this," he said, taking pains to make each word distinct, emphasizing them with his tapping finger ends. "Thursby was shot down in front of his hotel just thirty-five minutes after you left Burritt Street."

Spade spoke, taking equal pains with his words. "Keep your damned paws off me."

Dundy withdrew the tapping fingers, but there was no change in his voice. "Tom says you were in too much of a hurry to even stop for a look at your partner."

Tom growled apologetically, "Well, damn it, Sam, you did run off like that."

"And you didn't go to Archer's house to tell his wife," the lieutenant said. "We called up and that girl in your office was there, and she said you sent her."

Spade nodded. His face was stupid in its calmness.

Lieutenant Dundy raised his two bent fingers towards Spade's chest, quickly lowered them, and said, "I give you ten minutes to get to a phone and do your talking to the girl. I give you ten minutes to get to Thursby's joint—Geary near Leavenworth—you could do it easy in that time, or fifteen at the most. And that gives you ten or fifteen minutes of waiting before he showed up."

"I knew where he lived?" Spade asked.

"You knew what you knew," Dundy replied stubbornly. "What time did you get home?"

"Twenty minutes to four. I walked around thinking things over."

The lieutenant wagged his round head up and down. "We knew you weren't home at three thirty. We tried to get you on the phone. Where'd you do your walking?"

"Out Bush Street a way and back."

"Did you see anybody that—"

"No, no witnesses," Spade said and laughed pleasantly. "Sit down, Dundy. You haven't finished your drink."

Dundy sat down, but paid no attention to his glass of rum.

Spade filled his own glass, drank, and set the empty glass on the table. "I know where I stand now," he said, looking with friendly eyes from one of the police detectives to the other. "I'm sorry I got up on my hind legs, but you birds coming in and trying to put the work on me made me nervous. Having Miles knocked off bothered me, and then you birds cracking foxy. That's all right now, though, now that I know what you're up to."

Tom said, "Forget it."

The lieutenant said nothing.

Spade asked, "Thursby die?"

While the lieutenant hesitated Tom said, "Yes."

Then Dundy said angrily, "And you might just as well know it—if you don't—that he died before he could tell anybody anything."

Spade was rolling a cigarette. He asked, not looking up, "What do you mean by that? You think I did know it?"

"I meant what I said," Dundy replied bluntly.

Spade looked up at him and smiled, holding the finished cigarette in one hand, his lighter in the other.

"You're not ready to pinch me yet, are you, Dundy?" he asked. He put the cigarette in his mouth, set fire to it, and laughed smoke out. "How did I kill this Thursby?" he said. "I've forgotten."

Dundy said, "He was shot four times in the back, with a forty-four or forty-five, from across the street, when he started to go in the hotel. Nobody saw it, but that's the way it figures."

"And he was wearing a Luger in a shoulder holster," Tom added. "It hadn't been fired."

"What else did you find on him, or in his room?"

"What'd you think we'd find?" Dundy asked.

Spade made a careless circle with his limp cigarette. "Something to tell you who he was, what his store was. Did you?"

"We thought you could tell us that."

Spade looked at the lieutenant with exaggerated candor. "I've never seen Thursby, dead or alive."

Lieutenant Dundy stood up looking dissatisfied. Tom rose yawning and stretching.

"We've asked what we came to ask," Dundy said, frowning. "We've told you more than you've told us. That's fair enough. You know me, Spade. If you did or you didn't you'll get a square deal out of me, and most of the breaks."

"Fair enough," Spade replied evenly. "But I'd feel better about it if you'd drink your drink."

Lieutenant Dundy turned to the table, picked up his glass, and slowly emptied it. Then he said, "Good night," and held out his hand. They shook hands ceremoniously. Tom and Spade shook hands ceremoniously. Spade let them out. Then he undressed, turned off the lights, and went to bed.

Chapter 2

WHEN Spade reached his office at ten o'clock that morning Effie Perine was at her desk opening the mail. She put down the handful of envelopes and the brass paper knife she held and said, "She's in there." Her voice was low and warning.

"I asked you to keep her away," Spade complained. He too kept his voice low.

Effie Perine's brown eyes opened wide and her voice was as irritable as his. "Don't be cranky, Sam," she said wearily. "I had her all night."

Spade stood beside the girl and put a hand on her head. "Sorry, angel, I haven't—" He broke off as the inner door opened. "Hello, Iva," he said to the woman who had opened it.

"Oh, Sam!" she said.

She was a blond woman of a few more years than thirty. Her facial prettiness was perhaps five years past its best moment. Her body for all its sturdiness was finely modeled and exquisite. She wore black clothes from hat to shoes.

Spade took his hand from Effie Perine's head and entered the inner office, shutting the door. Iva came quickly to him, raising her sad face for his kiss. Her arms were around him before his held her. When they had kissed he made a little movement to release her, but she pressed her face to his chest and began sobbing.

He stroked her round back, saying, "Poor darling." His voice was tender. His eyes, squinting at the desk that had been his partner's, across the room from his own, were angry. "Did you send for Miles's brother?" he asked.

"Yes, he came over this morning." The words were blurred by her sobbing and his coat against her mouth, "Oh, Sam," she moaned, "did you kill him?"

Spade laughed a harsh syllable, "Ha!" He stepped back out of her arms, went to his desk, and sat down. His yellowish eyes glittered between narrowed lids.

"Who," he asked coldly, "put that bright idea in your head?"

"I thought—" She lifted a hand to her mouth and fresh tears came to her eyes. "Be kind to me, Sam," she said humbly.

He laughed at her, his eyes still glittering. "You killed my husband, Sam, be kind to me." He clapped his palms together and said, "My God!"

She began to cry audibly, holding a handkerchief to her face.

He got up and stood close behind her. He said, "Now, Iva, don't." His face was expressionless. When she had stopped crying he put his mouth to her ear and murmured, "You shouldn't have come here today, precious. It wasn't wise. You can't stay. You ought to be home."

She turned around to face him and asked, "You'll come tonight?"

He shook his head gently. "Not tonight."

"Soon?"

"Yes."

"How soon?"

"As soon as I can."

He kissed her, led her to the door, opened it, said, "Good-by, Iva," bowed her out, shut the door, and returned to his desk.

Effie Perine opened the door and came in. Her brown eyes were uneasy. Her voice was careless. She asked, "Well, how did you and the widow make out?"

"She thinks I shot Miles," he said. Only his lips moved.

"So you could marry her?"

Spade made no reply to that.

The girl took his hat from his head and put it on his desk.

"The police think I shot Thursby," he said.

"Who is he?" she asked.

"Thursby's the guy Miles was supposed to be tailing for the Wonderly girl."

"Are you going to marry Iva?" she asked.

"Don't be silly," he muttered.

"She doesn't think it's silly. Why should she—the way you've played around with her?"

He sighed and said, "I wish to God I'd never seen her."

"Maybe you do now." A trace of spitefulness came into her voice. "But there was a time." She wrinkled her forehead and asked, "Do you suppose she could have killed him?"

Spade took the girl's hand and patted it. "She didn't kill him."

Effie Perine snatched her hand away. "That louse wants to marry you, Sam," she said bitterly.

He made an impatient gesture with his head and one hand.

She frowned at him and demanded, "Did you see her last night?"

"No."

"Honestly?"

"Honestly. Don't act like Dundy, sweetheart. It ill becomes you."

"Has Dundy been after you?"

"Uh-huh. He and Tom Polhaus dropped in at four o'clock."

"Do they really think you shot this what's-his-name?"

"Thursby."

"Do they?" she insisted.

"God knows. They did have some such notion. I don't know how far I talked them out of it."

"You worry me," she said. "You always think you know what you're doing, but you're too slick for your own good, and some day you're going to find it out."

He sighed mockingly and rubbed his cheek against her arm. "That's what Dundy says, but you keep Iva away from me, sweet, and I'll manage to survive the rest of my troubles." He stood up and put on his hat. "Have the SPADE & ARCHER taken off the door and SAMUEL SPADE put on. I'll be back in an hour, or phone you."

Spade went through the St. Mark's long purplish lobby to the desk and asked a red-haired dandy whether Miss Wonderly was in. The red-haired dandy turned away, and then back shaking his head. "She checked out this morning, Mr. Spade."

"Thanks."

Spade walked past the desk to an alcove off the lobby where a plump young-middle-aged man in dark clothes sat at a flat-topped mahogany desk. On the edge of the desk facing the lobby was a triangular prism of mahogany and brass inscribed MR. FREED.

The plump man got up and came around the desk holding out his hand. "I was awfully sorry to hear about Archer, Spade," he said in the tone of one trained to sympathize readily without intrusiveness. "I've just seen it in the *Call*. He was in here last night, you know."

"Thanks, Freed. Can you give me some dope on an ex-guest, and then forget that I asked for it?"

"Surely."

"A Miss Wonderly checked out this morning. I'd like to know the details."

Freed said, "I'll see what I can learn," and went out of the alcove. Fifteen minutes later he returned.

"She arrived last Tuesday, registering from New York. There were no phone calls charged to her room, and she doesn't seem to have received much, if any, mail. The only one anybody remembers having seen her with was a tall dark man of thirty-six or so. She went out at half past nine this morning, came back an hour later, paid her bill, and had her bags carried out to a car. The boy who carried them says it was a Nash touring car, probably a hired one. She left a forwarding address—the Ambassador, Los Angeles."

Spade said, "Thanks a lot, Freed," and left the St. Mark.

When Spade returned to his office Effie Perine stopped typing a letter to tell him, "Your friend Dundy was in. He wanted to look at your guns. I told him to come back when you were here."

"Good girl. If he comes back again let him look at them."

"And Miss Wonderly called up."

"It's about time. What did she say?"

"She wants to see you." The girl picked up a slip of paper. "She's at the Coronet, on California Street, apartment 1001. You're to ask for Miss Leblanc."

Spade said, "Give me," and held out his hand. When she had given him the memorandum he took out his lighter, snapped on the flame, set it to the slip of paper, held the paper until all but one corner was curling black ash, dropped it on the linoleum floor, and mashed it under his shoe sole.

The girl watched him with disapproving eyes.

He grinned at her, said, "That's just the way it is, dear," and went out again.

Miss Wonderly, in a belted green crêpe silk dress, opened the door of apartment 1001 at the Coronet. Her dark red hair, parted on the left, was swept back in loose waves over her right temple.

Spade took off his hat and said, "Good morning."

His smile brought a fainter smile to her face. Her eyes, of blue that was almost violet, did not lose their troubled look. She said in a hushed, timid voice, "Come in, Mr. Spade."

She led him past open kitchen, bathroom, and bedroom doors into a cream and red living room, apologizing for its confusion. "Everything is upside down. I haven't even finished unpacking."

She laid his hat on a table and sat down on a walnut settee. He sat on a brocaded oval-backed chair facing her.

She looked at her fingers, working them together, and said, "Mr. Spade, I've a terrible, terrible confession to make."

Spade smiled a polite smile and said nothing.

"That—that story I told you yesterday was all—a story," she stammered, and looked at him with miserable frightened eyes.

"Oh, that," Spade said lightly. "We didn't exactly believe your story. You paid us more than if you'd been telling the truth, and enough more to make it all right."

She leaned forward and spoke eagerly. "And even now you'd be willing to—"

Spade stopped her with a palm-up motion of one hand. "That depends," he said. "The hell of it is, Miss— Is your name Wonderly or Leblanc?"

She blushed and murmured, "It's really O'Shaughnessy—Brigid O'Shaughnessy."

"The hell of it is, Miss O'Shaughnessy, that two murders"—she winced—"coming together like this get everybody stirred up, make the police think they can go the limit, make everybody hard to handle and expensive. It's not—"

"Mr. Spade, tell me the truth." Her voice quivered on the verge of hysteria. Her face had become haggard around desperate eyes. "Am I to blame for—for last night?"

Spade shook his head. "Not unless there are things I don't know about," he said. "You warned us that Thursby was dangerous. Of course you lied to us about your sister and all, but that doesn't count; we didn't believe you." He shrugged his sloping shoulders. "I wouldn't say it was your fault."

She said, "Thank you," very softly, and then moved her head from side to side. "But I'll always blame myself." She put a hand to her throat. "Mr. Archer was so—so alive yesterday afternoon, so solid and hearty and—"

"Stop it," Spade commanded. "He knew what he was doing. They're the chances we take."

"Was—was he married?"

"Yes, with ten thousand insurance, no children, and a wife who didn't like him."

"Oh, please don't!" she whispered.

Spade shrugged again. "That's the way it was." He glanced at his watch and moved from his chair to the settee beside her. "Out there a flock of policemen and assistant district attorneys and reporters are running around with their noses to the ground. What do you want me to do?"

"I want you to save me from—from it all," she replied in a thin tremulous voice. She put a timid hand on his sleeve. "Mr. Spade, you don't think I had anything to do with the—the murders—do you?"

Spade grinned and said, "I forgot to ask you that. Did you?"

"No."

"That's good. Now what are we going to tell the police?"

She squirmed on her end of the settee and her eyes wavered between heavy lashes, as if trying and failing to free their gaze from his. She seemed smaller, and very young and oppressed.

"Must they know about me at all?" she asked. "I think I'd rather die than that, Mr. Spade. I can't explain now, but can't you somehow manage so that you can shield me from them, so I won't have to answer their questions?"

"Maybe," he said, "but I'll have to know what it's all about."

She went down on her knees at his knees. She held her face up to him. Her face was wan and fearful over tight-clasped hands.

"I haven't lived a good life," she cried. "I've been bad—worse than you could know—but I'm not all bad. Look at me, Mr. Spade. You know I'm not all bad, don't you? You can see that, can't you? Oh, I'm so alone and afraid, and I've got nobody to help me if you won't help me. I know I've no right to ask you to trust me if I won't trust you. I do trust you, but I can't tell you now. Later I will, when I can. I trusted Floyd and—I've nobody else. Be generous, Mr. Spade. You can help me."

Spade, who had held his breath through much of this speech, now emptied his lungs with a long sighing exhalation between pursed lips and said, "You won't need much of anybody's help. You're good. You're very good. It's chiefly your eyes, I think, and that throb you get into your voice when you say things like 'Be generous, Mr. Spade.'"

She jumped up on her feet. Her face crimsoned painfully, but she held her head erect and she looked Spade straight in the eyes. "I deserve that," she said. "I deserve it, but—oh!—I did want your help so much. I do want it, and need it, so much." She turned away, no longer holding herself erect. "It is my own fault that you can't believe me now."

Spade's face reddened and he looked down at the floor, muttering, "Now you are dangerous."

Brigid O'Shaughnessy went to the table and picked up his hat.

She came back and stood in front of him holding the hat, not offering it to him, but holding it for him to take if he wished. Her face was white and thin.

Spade looked at his hat and asked, "What happened last night?"

"Floyd came to the hotel at nine o'clock, and we went out for a walk. I suggested that so Mr. Archer could see him. We stopped at a restaurant, in Geary Street, I think it was, for supper and to dance, and came back to the hotel at about half past twelve. Floyd left me at the door and I stood inside and watched Mr. Archer follow him down the street, on the other side."

"Well, what did you do after they had gone?"

"I went to bed. And this morning when I went out for breakfast I saw the headlines in the papers and read about—you know. Then I went up to Union Square, where I had seen automobiles for hire, and got one and went to the hotel for my luggage. After I found my room had been searched yesterday I knew I would have to move, and I had found this place yesterday afternoon. So I came up here and then telephoned your office."

"Your room at the St. Mark was searched?" he asked.

"Yes, while I was at your office." She bit her lip. "I didn't mean to tell you that."

"That means I'm not supposed to question you about it?"

She nodded shyly, returned the hat to the table, and sat beside him on the settee again.

He said, "I've got nothing against trusting you blindly except that I won't be able to do you much good if I haven't some idea of what it's all about. For instance, I've got to have some sort of a line on your Floyd Thursby."

"I met him in the Orient." She spoke slowly, looking down at a pointed finger tracing eights on the settee between them. "We came here from Hong Kong last week. He was—he had promised to help me. He took advantage of my helplessness to betray me."

"Betray you how?"

She shook her head and said nothing.

Spade, frowning with impatience, asked, "Why did you want him shadowed?"

"I wanted to learn how far he had gone. He wouldn't even let me know where he was staying. I wanted to find out what he was doing, whom he was meeting, things like that."

"Did he kill Archer?"

She looked up at him, surprised. "Yes, certainly," she said.

"He had a Luger in a shoulder holster. Archer wasn't shot with a Luger."

"He had a revolver in his overcoat pocket," she said.

"You saw it?"

"Oh, I've seen it often. He always carried one there."

"Why all the guns?"

"He lived by them. There was a story in Hong Kong that he had come out there, to the Orient, as bodyguard to a gambler who had to leave the States, and that the gambler had since disappeared. They said Floyd knew about his disappearing. I don't know. I do know that he always went heavily armed and that he never went to sleep without covering the floor around his bed with crumpled newspaper so nobody could come silently into his room."

"You picked a nice sort of playmate."

"Only that sort could have helped me," she said simply, "if he had been loyal."

"Yes, if." Spade pinched his lower lip between finger and thumb and looked gloomily at her. "How bad a hole are you actually in?"

"As bad," she said, "as could be. I don't think there's anything worse than death."

"Then it's that?"

"It's that as surely as we're sitting here"—she shivered—"unless you help me."

"I can't work miracles," he said irritably. He looked at his watch. "The day's going and you're giving me nothing to work with. Who killed Thursby?"

She put a wrinkled handkerchief to her mouth and said, "I don't know."

Spade stood up. "This is hopeless," he said savagely. "I can't do anything for you. I don't know what you want done. I don't even know if you know what you want." He went to the table for his hat.

"You won't," she begged in a small choked voice, not looking up, "go to the police?"

"Go to them!" he exclaimed, his voice loud with rage. "They've been running me ragged since four o'clock this morning. I've made myself God knows how much trouble standing them off. For what? For some crazy notion that I could help you. I can't. I won't try." He put his hat on his head and pulled it down tight. "Go to them? All I've got to do is stand still and they'll be swarming all over me. Well, I'll tell them what I know and you'll have to take your chances."

She rose from the settee and held herself straight in front of him though her knees were trembling. She said, "You've been patient. You've tried to help me. It is hopeless, and useless, I suppose." She stretched out her right hand. "I thank you for what you have done. I—I'll have to take my chances."

Spade made a growling animal noise in his throat and sat down on the settee. "How much money have you got?" he asked.

The question startled her. Then she pinched her lower lip between her teeth and answered reluctantly, "I've about five hundred dollars left."

"Give it to me."

She hesitated, looking timidly at him. He made angry gestures with mouth, eyebrows, hands, and shoulders. She went into her bedroom and returned with a sheaf of paper money.

He took the money from her, counted it, and said, "There's only four hundred here."

"I had to keep some to live on," she explained meekly.

"Can't you get any more?"

"No."

"You must have something you can raise money on," he said.

"I've some rings, a little jewelry."

"You'll have to hock them," he said, and held out his hand.

She looked pleadingly at him. His eyes were hard and implacable. Slowly she put her hand inside the neck of her dress, brought out a slender roll of bills, and put them in his waiting hand.

He smoothed the bills out and counted them—four twenties,

four tens, and a five. He returned two of the tens and the five to her. The others he put in his pocket. Then he stood up and said, "I'm going out and see what I can do for you. I'll be back as soon as I can with the best news I can manage. I'll ring four times—long, short, long, short—so you'll know it's me. You needn't go to the door with me. I can let myself out."

He left her standing in the center of the floor looking after him with dazed blue eyes.

SPADE went into a reception room whose door bore the legend WISE, MERICAN & WISE. The girl at the switchboard said, "Oh, hello, Mr. Spade."

"Hello, darling," he replied. "Is Sid in?"

He stood beside her with a hand on her plump shoulder while she manipulated a plug and spoke into the mouthpiece. "Mr. Spade to see you, Mr. Wise." She looked up at Spade. "Go right in."

He squeezed her shoulder by way of acknowledgment and went into an office where a small olive-skinned man sat behind an immense desk on which bales of paper were heaped.

The small man flourished a cold cigar stub at Spade and said, "Pull a chair around. So Miles got the big one last night?" Neither his tired face nor his rather shrill voice held any emotion.

"Uh-huh, that's what I came in about." Spade frowned and cleared his throat. "I think I'm going to have to tell a coroner to go to hell, Sid. Can I hide behind the sanctity of my clients' secrets and identities and whatnot, all the same priest or lawyer?"

Sid Wise lifted his shoulders and lowered the ends of his mouth. "Why not? An inquest is not a court trial. You can try, anyway. You've gotten away with more than that before this."

"I know, but Dundy's getting snotty, and maybe it is a little bit thick this time. Get your hat, Sid, and we'll go see the right people. I want to be safe."

Sid Wise looked at the papers massed on his desk and groaned, but he got up from his chair and went to the closet by the window. "You're a son of a gun, Sammy," he said as he took his hat from its hook.

Chapter 3

SPADE RETURNED to his office at ten minutes past five that evening. Effie Perine was sitting at his desk reading *Time*. He grinned. "I think we've got a future. I always had an idea that if Miles would go off and die somewhere we'd stand a better chance of thriving. Will you take care of sending flowers for me?"

"I did."

"You're an angel. How's your woman's intuition today?"

"Why?"

"What do you think of Wonderly?"

"I'm for her," the girl replied without hesitation.

"She's got too many names," Spade mused. "Wonderly, Leblanc, and she says the right one's O'Shaughnessy."

Effie Perine sat up straight and said, "Sam, if that girl's in trouble and you let her down, or take advantage of it to bleed her, I'll never forgive you as long as I live."

Spade smiled unnaturally. Then he frowned. He opened his mouth to speak, but the sound of someone's entrance through the corridor door stopped him.

Effie Perine rose and went into the outer office. Spade took off his hat and sat in his chair. The girl returned with an engraved card—MR. JOEL CAIRO.

"This guy is queer," she said.

"In with him, then, darling," said Spade.

Mr. Joel Cairo was a small-boned dark man of medium height. His hair was black and smooth and very glossy. His features were Levantine. A square-cut ruby, its sides paralleled by four baguette diamonds, gleamed against the deep green of his cravat. His black coat, cut tight to narrow shoulders, flared a little over slightly plump hips. He held a black derby hat in a chamois-gloved hand and came towards Spade with short, mincing, bobbing steps. The fragrance of chypre came with him.

Spade inclined his head at his visitor and then at a chair, saying, "Sit down, Mr. Cairo."

Cairo bowed elaborately over his hat, said, "I thank you," in a high-pitched thin voice, and sat down. He sat down primly, crossing his ankles, placing his hat on his knees, and began to draw off his yellow gloves.

Spade rocked back in his chair and asked, "Now what can I do for you, Mr. Cairo?"

Cairo turned his hat over, dropping his gloves into it, and placed it bottom up on the corner of the desk nearest him. Diamonds twinkled on the second and fourth fingers of his left hand. He rubbed his palms together and said over the whispering sound they made, "May a stranger offer condolences for your partner's unfortunate death?"

"Thanks."

"May I ask, Mr. Spade, if there was, as the newspapers inferred, a certain—ah—relationship between that unfortunate happening and the death a little later of the man Thursby?"

Spade said nothing in a blank-faced definite way.

Cairo rose and bowed. "I beg your pardon." He sat down again and placed his hands side by side, palms down, on the corner of the desk. "More than idle curiosity made me ask that, Mr. Spade. I am trying to recover an—ah—ornament that has been—shall we say—mislaid. I thought, and hoped, you could assist me."

Spade nodded with eyebrows lifted to indicate attentiveness.

"The ornament is a statuette," Cairo went on, selecting and mouthing his words carefully, "the black figure of a bird."

Spade nodded again, with courteous interest.

"I am prepared to pay, on behalf of the figure's rightful owner, the sum of five thousand dollars for its recovery. I am prepared to promise that no questions will be asked."

"Five thousand is a lot of money," Spade commented, looking thoughtfully at Cairo. "It—"

Fingers drummed lightly on the door.

When Spade had called, "Come in," the door opened far enough to admit Effie Perine's head and shoulders.

"Is there anything else?" she asked.

"No. Good night. Lock the door when you go, will you?"

"Good night," she said and disappeared behind the closing door.

Spade turned in his chair to face Cairo again, saying, "It's an interesting figure."

The sound of the corridor door's closing behind Effie Perine came to them.

Cairo smiled and took a short compact flat black pistol out of an inner pocket. "You will please," he said, "clasp your hands together at the back of your neck."

Spade did not look at the pistol. He raised his arms and, leaning back in his chair, intertwined the fingers of his two hands behind his head. His eyes, holding no particular expression, remained focused on Cairo's dark face.

Cairo smiled nervously. His dark eyes were humid and bashful and very earnest. "I intend to search your offices, Mr. Spade. If you attempt to prevent me I shall certainly shoot you."

"Go ahead." Spade's voice was as empty of expression as his face.

"You will please stand," the man with the pistol instructed him. "I shall have to make sure that you are not armed."

Spade stood up, pushing his chair back with his calves as he straightened his legs.

Cairo went around behind him. He transferred the pistol from his right hand to his left. He lifted Spade's coattail and looked under it. Holding the pistol close to Spade's back, he put his right hand around Spade's side and patted his chest. The Levantine face was then just six inches below and behind Spade's right elbow.

Spade's elbow dropped as he spun to the right. Cairo's face jerked back not far enough; Spade's right heel on the patent-leathered toes anchored the smaller man in the elbow's path. The elbow struck him beneath the cheekbone, staggering him so that he must have fallen had he not been held by Spade's foot on his foot. Spade's elbow went on past the astonished dark face and straightened when Spade's hand struck down at the pistol. Cairo let the pistol go the instant that Spade's fingers touched it. The pistol was small in Spade's hand. Cairo's face was twisted by pain and chagrin.

Spade turned the Levantine slowly and pushed him back until

he was standing close in front of the chair he had lately occupied. Then Spade smiled. His smile was gentle, even dreamy. His fist struck Cairo's face, covering for a moment one side of his chin, a corner of his mouth, and most of his cheek between cheekbone and jawbone. Cairo shut his eyes and was unconscious.

Spade lowered the limp body into the chair, where it lay with sprawled arms and legs, the head lolling against the chair's back, the mouth open.

Spade emptied the unconscious man's pockets one by one, working methodically, moving the lax body when necessary, making a pile of the pockets' contents on the desk. There was a large wallet of dark soft leather. The wallet contained $365 in United States bills of several denominations; three five-pound notes; a much visaed Greek passport bearing Cairo's name and portrait; five folded sheets of pinkish onionskin paper covered with what seemed to be Arabic writing; a raggedly clipped newspaper account of the finding of Archer's and Thursby's bodies; a large silk handkerchief, yellow with age and somewhat cracked along its folds; a thin sheaf of Mr. Joel Cairo's engraved cards; and a ticket for an orchestra seat at the Geary Theatre that evening.

Besides the wallet and its contents there were three gaily colored silk handkerchiefs fragrant of chypre; a platinum Longines watch on a platinum and red gold chain; a handful of United States, British, French, and Chinese coins; a ring holding half a dozen keys; a small street guide to San Francisco; a Southern Pacific baggage check; a half-filled package of violet pastilles; a Shanghai insurance broker's business card; and four sheets of Hotel Belvedere writing paper, on one of which was written in small precise letters Samuel Spade's name and the addresses of his office and his apartment.

Having examined these articles carefully—he even opened the back of the watchcase to see that nothing was hidden inside—Spade leaned over and took the unconscious man's wrist between finger and thumb, feeling his pulse. Then he dropped the wrist, settled back in his chair, and rolled and lighted a cigarette. When Cairo presently moaned and fluttered his eyelids Spade's face became bland, and he put the beginning of a friendly smile into his eyes and mouth.

Joel Cairo awakened slowly. His eyes opened first, but a full minute passed before they fixed their gaze on any definite part of the ceiling. Then he raised his head from the chair back, looked around the office in confusion, saw Spade, and sat up. He opened his mouth to speak, started, clapped a hand to his face where Spade's fist had struck and where there was now a florid bruise.

Cairo said through his teeth, painfully, "I could have shot you, Mr. Spade."

"You could have tried," Spade conceded.

"I did not try."

"I know."

"Then why did you strike me after I was disarmed?"

"Sorry," Spade said, "but imagine my embarrassment when I found that five-thousand-dollar offer was just hooey."

"You are mistaken, Mr. Spade. That was, and is, a genuine offer. I am prepared to pay five thousand dollars for the figure's return." Cairo took his hand away from his bruised face and sat up prim and businesslike again. "You have it?"

"No."

"If it is not here why should you have risked serious injury to prevent my searching for it?"

"I should sit around and let people come in and stick me up?" Spade flicked a finger at Cairo's possessions on the desk. "You've got my apartment address. Been up there yet?"

"Yes, Mr. Spade. I am ready to pay five thousand dollars for the figure's return, but surely it is natural enough that I should try first to spare the owner that expense if possible."

"Who is he?"

Cairo shook his head and smiled. "You will have to forgive my not answering that question."

Spade thumped Cairo's wallet with the backs of his fingers and said, "There's nothing like five thousand dollars here. You could come in and say you'd pay me a million for a purple elephant, but what in hell would that mean?"

"I see, I see," Cairo said thoughtfully, screwing up his eyes. "You wish some assurance of my sincerity." He brushed his red lower lip with a fingertip. "A retainer, would that serve?"

"It might."

Cairo put his hand out towards his wallet, hesitated, withdrew the hand, and said, "You will take, say, a hundred dollars?"

Spade picked up the wallet and took out a hundred dollars. Then he frowned, said, "Better make it two hundred," and did.

Cairo said nothing.

"Your first guess was that I had the bird," Spade said in a crisp voice when he had put the two hundred dollars into his pocket and had dropped the wallet on the desk again. "There's nothing in that. What's your second?"

"That you know where it is, or, if not exactly that, that you know it is where you can get it."

Spade neither denied nor affirmed that; he seemed hardly to have heard it. He asked, "What sort of proof can you give me that your man is the owner?"

"Very little, unfortunately. There is this, though: nobody else can give you any authentic evidence of ownership at all."

Spade blinked his eyes sleepily and suggested, "It might be better all around if we put our cards on the table."

"I do not think it would be better." Cairo's voice was suave. "If you know more than I, I shall profit by your knowledge, and so will you to the extent of five thousand dollars. If you do not then I have made a mistake in coming to you, and to do as you suggest would be simply to make that mistake worse."

Spade nodded indifferently and waved his hand at the articles on the desk, saying, "There's your stuff"; and then, when Cairo was returning them to his pockets, "It's understood that you're to pay my expenses while I'm getting this black bird for you, and five thousand dollars when it's done?"

"Yes, Mr. Spade; that is, five thousand dollars less whatever moneys have been advanced to you—five thousand in all."

"Right. And it's a legitimate proposition." Spade's face was solemn except for wrinkles at the corners of his eyes. "You're not hiring me to do any murders or burglaries for you, but simply to get it back if possible in an honest and lawful way."

"If possible," Cairo agreed. His face also was solemn except for the eyes. "And in any event with discretion." He rose and picked up his hat. "I am at the Hotel Belvedere when you wish to communicate with me—room 635. I confidently expect the greatest mutual benefit from our association, Mr. Spade." He hesitated. "May I have my pistol?"

"Sure. I'd forgotten it."

Spade took the pistol out of his coat pocket and handed it to Cairo.

Cairo pointed the pistol at Spade's chest.

"You will please keep your hands on the top of the desk," Cairo said earnestly. "I intend to search your offices."

Spade said, "I'll be damned." Then he laughed in his throat and said, "All right. Go ahead. I won't stop you."

AFTER Joel Cairo had gone Spade put on his hat and overcoat, turned off the lights, and went down to the night-lit street.

An undersized youth of about twenty in neat gray cap and overcoat was standing idly on the corner below Spade's building.

Spade walked up Sutter Street to Kearny, where he entered a cigar store to buy two sacks of Bull Durham. When he came out the youth was one of four people waiting for a streetcar on the opposite corner.

Spade ate dinner at Herbert's Grill in Powell Street. When he left the grill, at a quarter to eight, the youth was looking into a nearby haberdasher's window. Spade went to the Geary Theatre and posted himself on the curb in front, facing the theater. The youth loitered with other loiterers before Marquard's restaurant below.

At ten minutes past eight Joel Cairo appeared, walking up Geary Street with his little mincing bobbing steps. Apparently he did not see Spade until the private detective touched his shoulder. He seemed moderately surprised for a moment, and then said, "Oh, yes, of course you saw the ticket."

"Uh-huh. I've got something I want to show you." Spade drew Cairo back towards the curb a little away from the other waiting theatergoers. "The kid in the cap down by Marquard's."

Cairo murmured, "I'll see," and looked at his watch. He looked up Geary Street. And then his dark eyes crawled sidewise in their sockets until they were looking at the kid in the cap, at his cool pale face with curling lashes hiding lowered eyes.

"Who is he?" Spade asked.

Cairo smiled up at Spade. "I do not know him."

"He's been tailing me around town."

Cairo said with every appearance of candor, "I give you my word I do not know him, Mr. Spade. I give you my word I have nothing to do with him. I have asked nobody's assistance except yours, on my word of honor."

"Then he's one of the others?"

"That may be."

"I just wanted to know, because if he gets to be a nuisance I may have to hurt him."

"Do as you think best. He is not a friend of mine."

"That's good. There goes the curtain bell. Good night," Spade said, and crossed the street to board a westbound streetcar.

The youth in the cap boarded the same car.

Spade left the car at Hyde Street and went up to his apartment. His rooms were not greatly upset, but showed unmistakable signs of having been searched. When Spade had washed and had put on a fresh shirt and collar he went out again, walked up to Sutter Street, and boarded a westbound car. The youth boarded it also.

Within half a dozen blocks of the Coronet, Spade left the car and went into the vestibule of a tall apartment building. He pressed three bell buttons. The street-door lock buzzed. He entered, passed the elevator and stairs, went down a long yellow-walled corridor to the rear of the building, found a back door, and let himself out into a narrow court. The court led to a dark back street, up which Spade walked for two blocks. Then he crossed over to California Street and went to the Coronet. It was not quite half past nine o'clock.

THE EAGERNESS WITH WHICH Brigid O'Shaughnessy welcomed Spade suggested that she had been not entirely certain of his coming. She had put on a blue satin evening gown with chalcedony shoulder straps, and her stockings and slippers were blue. "Do you bring me good news?" she asked. Anxiety looked through her smile, and she held her breath.

"We won't have to make anything public that hasn't already been made public."

"The police won't have to know about me?"

"No."

She sighed happily and sat on the walnut settee. Her face relaxed and her body relaxed. She smiled up at him with admiration.

Spade stood beside the fireplace and looked at her with eyes that studied, weighed, judged her without pretense that they were not studying, weighing, judging her. Then he crossed to the settee. "You aren't," he asked as he sat down beside her, "exactly the sort of person you pretend to be, are you?"

"I'm not sure I know what you mean," she said quietly.

"Schoolgirl manner," he explained. "Stammering and blushing and all that."

She blushed and replied hurriedly, not looking at him, "I told you that I've been bad—worse than you could know."

"That's what I mean," he said. "You told me that this afternoon in the same words, same tone. It's a speech you've practiced." Then, "I saw Joel Cairo tonight," he said in the manner of one making polite conversation.

Her eyes, focused on his profile, became frightened, then cautious. There was a long pause before she asked uneasily, "You— you know him?"

"I saw him tonight." Spade maintained his light conversational tone. "He was going to the theater."

"You mean you talked to him?"

"Only for a minute or two, till the curtain bell rang."

She got up from the settee and went to the fireplace to poke the fire. When she returned to her seat her face was unworried.

Spade grinned at her and said, "You're good. You're very good."

Her face did not change. She asked quietly, "What did he say about me?"

"Nothing. He offered me five thousand dollars for the black bird."

She started, and her eyes, after a swift alarmed glance at Spade, turned away from him. "And what did you say?"

"Five thousand dollars is a lot of money."

"But, Mr. Spade, you promised to help me." Her hands were on his arm. "I trusted you. You can't—" She broke off, took her hands from his sleeve and worked them together.

Spade smiled gently. "Don't let's try to figure out how much you've trusted me," he said. "I promised to help you—sure—but you didn't say anything about any black birds."

"But you must've known or—or you wouldn't have mentioned it to me. You do know now. You won't—you can't—treat me like that."

"Five thousand dollars," he said again, "is a lot of money."

"I've given you all the money I have." Her voice was hoarse, vibrant. "I've thrown myself on your mercy, told you that without your help I'm utterly lost. What else is there?" She suddenly moved close to him on the settee and cried angrily, "Can I buy you with my body?"

Their faces were few inches apart. Spade took her face between his hands, and he kissed her mouth roughly and contemptuously. Then he sat back and said, "I'll think it over." His face was hard and furious. "I don't give a damn about your honesty," he told her, trying to make himself speak calmly. "I don't care what kind of tricks you're up to, what your secrets are, but I've got to have something to show that you know what you're doing."

"Can't you trust me just a little longer?"

"How much is a little? And what are you waiting for?"

She bit her lip and looked down. "I must talk to Joel Cairo," she said almost inaudibly.

"You can see him tonight," Spade said, looking at his watch. "His show will be out soon. We can phone him at his hotel."

She raised her eyes, alarmed. "But he can't come here. I can't let him know where I am. I'm afraid."

"My place," Spade suggested.

"All right," she exclaimed, jumping up, her eyes large and bright. "Shall we go now?"

THEIR taxicab drew up behind a dark sedan that stood directly in front of Spade's street door. Iva Archer was sitting at the wheel of the sedan. Spade lifted his hat to her and went indoors with Brigid O'Shaughnessy. In the lobby he asked, "Do you mind waiting here a moment? I won't be long."

"That's perfectly all right," Brigid O'Shaughnessy said, sitting down on one of the benches. "You needn't hurry."

Spade went out to the sedan. When he had opened the sedan's door Iva spoke quickly. "I've got to talk to you, Sam. Can't I come in?" Her face was pale and nervous.

"Not now."

"Who is she?" Iva asked sharply.

"I've only a minute, Iva," Spade said patiently. "What is it?"

"Who is she?" she repeated, nodding at the street door.

He looked away from her, down the street. In front of a garage on the next corner an undersized youth of about twenty in neat gray cap and overcoat loafed with his back against a wall. Spade frowned and returned his gaze to Iva's insistent face. "What is the matter?" he asked. "Has anything happened? You oughtn't to be here at this time of night."

"I'm beginning to believe that," she complained. "You told me I oughtn't to come to the office, and now I oughtn't to come here. Do you mean I oughtn't to chase after you?"

"Now, Iva, you've got no right to take that attitude."

"I know I haven't. I haven't any rights at all, it seems, where you're concerned. I thought I did. I thought your pretending to love me gave me—"

Spade said wearily, "This is no time to be arguing about that, precious. What was it you wanted to see me about?"

"I can't talk to you here, Sam. Can't I come in?"

"Not now."

She made a thin line of her mouth, squirmed around straight

behind the wheel, and started the engine, staring angrily ahead.

When the sedan began to move Spade said, "Good night, Iva," shut the door, and stood at the curb with his hat in his hand until the sedan had been driven away. Then he went indoors again.

Brigid O'Shaughnessy, smiling cheerfully, rose from the bench and they went up to his apartment.

IN HIS bedroom that was a living room now the wall bed was up. Spade took Brigid O'Shaughnessy's coat, made her comfortable in a padded rocking chair, and telephoned the Hotel Belvedere. Cairo had not returned from the theater. Spade left his telephone number with the request that Cairo call him as soon as he came in. He sat down in an armchair beside the table.

There was silence between them for a while until Brigid O'Shaughnessy left her chair and stood in front of him, close. Her eyes were wide and deep. "I don't have to tell you how utterly at a disadvantage you'll have me, with him here, if you choose."

Spade smiled slightly. "No, you don't have to tell me," he agreed.

"And you know I'd never have placed myself in this position if I hadn't trusted you completely." Her thumb and forefinger twisted a black button on his blue coat.

Spade said, "That again!" with mock resignation.

"But you know it's so," she insisted.

"No, I don't know it." He patted the hand that was twisting the button. "My asking for reasons why I should trust you brought us here. Don't let's confuse things. You don't have to trust me, anyhow, as long as you can persuade me to trust you."

The telephone bell rang.

"Hello," Spade said into the instrument. "Mr. Cairo? . . . This is Spade. Can you come up to my place—Post Street—now? Miss O'Shaughnessy is here and wants to see you."

Spade put the telephone down and patted her hand again. "He'll be here in a moment. Get your business with him over, and then we'll see how we'll stand."

"And you'll let me go about it—with him—in my own way?"

"Sure."

She turned her hand under his so that her fingers pressed his. She said softly, "You're a godsend."

Spade said, "Don't overdo it."

She looked reproachfully at him, though smiling, and returned to the padded rocker.

JOEL CAIRO was excited. His high-pitched thin-voiced words were tumbling out before Spade had the door half open.

"That boy is out there watching the house, Mr. Spade, that boy you showed me, or to whom you showed me, in front of the theater. What am I to understand from that, Mr. Spade? I came here in good faith, with no thought of tricks or traps."

"You were asked in good faith." Spade frowned thoughtfully.

Brigid O'Shaughnessy came into the passageway behind Spade and asked anxiously, "What boy? What is it?"

Cairo removed his black hat from his head, bowed stiffly, and said in a prim voice, "If you do not know, ask Mr. Spade. I know nothing about it except through him."

"A kid who's been trying to tail me around town all evening," Spade said carelessly over his shoulder. "Come on in, Cairo. There's no use standing here talking for all the neighbors."

Cairo, holding his black hat to his belly with both hands, came into the passageway. Spade shut the corridor door behind him and they went into the living room. There Cairo bowed stiffly over his hat once more and said, "I am delighted to see you again, Miss O'Shaughnessy."

"I was sure you would be, Joe," she replied, giving him her hand.

He made a formal bow over her hand and released it quickly.

She sat in the padded rocker she had occupied before. Cairo sat in the armchair by the table. Spade, when he had hung Cairo's hat and coat in the closet, sat on an end of the sofa in front of the windows and began to roll a cigarette.

Brigid O'Shaughnessy said to Cairo, "Sam told me about your offer for the falcon. How soon can you have the money ready?"

Cairo's eyebrows twitched. He smiled. "It is ready."

She frowned, put her tongue between her lips, withdrew it,

and asked, "You are ready to give us five thousand dollars, now, if we give you the falcon?"

Cairo held up a wriggling hand. "Excuse me," he said. "I expressed myself badly. I did not mean to say that I have the money in my pockets, but that I am prepared to get it on a very few minutes' notice at any time during banking hours." Eagerness showed in his eyes and voice. "I can be quite prepared to give you the money at, say, half past ten in the morning. Eh?"

Brigid O'Shaughnessy smiled at him and said, "But I haven't got the falcon."

Cairo's face was darkened by a flush of annoyance. His eyes were angry. He did not say anything.

The girl made a mock-placatory face at him. "I'll have it in a week at the most, though," she said.

"Where is it?" He used politeness of mien to express skepticism.

"Where Floyd hid it."

"And you know where that is?" he asked.

"I think I do. Whom are you buying it for, Joe?"

Cairo raised his eyebrows. "I told Mr. Spade. For its owner."

Surprise lit up the girl's face. "So you went back to him?"

Cairo shrugged. "That was the logical development." He rubbed the back of one hand with the palm of the other. His upper lids came down to shade his eyes. "Why, if I in turn may ask a question, are you willing to sell to me?"

"I'm afraid," she said simply, "after what happened to Floyd. That's why I haven't it now. I'm afraid to touch it except to turn it over to somebody else right away."

"Exactly what," Cairo asked in a low voice, "happened to Floyd?"

The tip of Brigid O'Shaughnessy's right forefinger traced a swift G in the air.

Cairo said, "I see," but there was something doubting in his smile. "Is he here?"

"I don't know." She spoke impatiently. "What difference does it make?"

The doubt in Cairo's smile deepened. "It might make a world

of difference," he said, and rearranged his hands in his lap so that, intentionally or not, a blunt forefinger pointed at Spade.

The girl glanced at the pointing finger and made an impatient motion with her head. "Or me," she said, "or you."

"Exactly, and shall we add more certainly the boy outside?"

"Yes," she agreed and laughed. "Yes, unless he's the one you had in Constantinople."

Sudden blood mottled Cairo's face. In a shrill enraged voice he cried, "The one you couldn't make?"

Brigid O'Shaughnessy jumped up from her chair. She took two quick steps towards Cairo. He started to rise. Her right hand went out and cracked sharply against his cheek, leaving the imprint of fingers there.

Cairo grunted and slapped her cheek, staggering her sidewise, bringing from her mouth a brief muffled scream.

Spade was up from the sofa and close to them by then. He caught Cairo by the throat and shook him. Cairo gurgled and put a hand inside his coat. Spade grasped the Levantine's wrist, wrenched it away from the coat, forced it straight out to the side, and twisted it until the clumsy flaccid fingers opened to let the black pistol fall down on the rug.

Brigid O'Shaughnessy quickly picked up the pistol.

The doorbell rang.

"Who is it?" the girl whispered, coming close to Spade; and Cairo's eyes jerked back to ask the same question.

Spade gave his answer irritably. "I don't know."

The bell rang again, more insistently.

"Well, keep quiet," Spade said, and went out of the room, shutting the door behind him.

Spade turned on the light in the passageway and opened the door to the corridor. Lieutenant Dundy and Tom Polhaus were there. Dundy spoke quietly. "We want to talk to you, Spade."

"Well?" Spade stood in the doorway, blocking it. "Go ahead and talk."

Tom Polhaus advanced, saying, "We don't have to do it standing here, do we?"

Spade stood in the doorway and said, "You can't come in." His tone was very slightly apologetic.

Tom's thick-featured face took on an expression of friendly scorn, though there was a bright gleam in his small shrewd eyes. "What the hell, Sam?" he protested and put a big hand playfully on Spade's chest.

Spade leaned against the pushing hand, grinned wolfishly, and asked, "Going to strong-arm me, Tom?"

Tom grumbled, "Aw, for God's sake," and took his hand away.

Dundy clicked his teeth together and said through them, "Let us in."

"You're not coming in," Spade said. "What do you want to do about it? Try to get in? Or do your talking here?"

Tom groaned.

Dundy put his hands behind him and thrust his hard face up towards the private detective's. "There's talk going around that you and Archer's wife were cheating on him."

Spade laughed. "That sounds like something you thought up yourself."

"Then there's not anything to it?"

"Not anything."

"The talk is," Dundy said, "that she tried to get a divorce out of him so's she could put in with you, but he wouldn't give it to her. Anything to that?"

"No."

"There's even talk," Dundy went on stolidly, "that that's why he was put on the spot."

Spade seemed mildly amused. "Don't be a hog," he said. "You oughtn't try to pin more than one murder at a time on me. Your first idea that I knocked Thursby off because he'd killed Miles falls apart if you blame me for killing Miles too."

Dundy looked him straight in the eyes. "If you say there was nothing between you and Archer's wife," he said, "you're a liar, and I'm telling you so."

Spade moistened his lips with the tip of his tongue and asked, "Is that the hot tip that brought you here at this ungodly hour?"

"That's one of them."

"And the others?"

Dundy pulled down the corners of his mouth. "Let us in." He nodded significantly at the doorway in which Spade stood.

Spade frowned and shook his head.

"All right, Spade, we're going." Dundy buttoned his overcoat. "We'll be in to see you now and then. Think it over."

"Uh-huh," Spade said, grinning. "Glad to see you anytime, Lieutenant, and whenever I'm not busy I'll let you in."

A voice in Spade's living room screamed, "Help! Help! Police! Help!" The voice, high and thin and shrill, was Joel Cairo's.

Lieutenant Dundy stopped turning away from the door, confronted Spade again, and said decisively, "I guess we're going in."

The sounds of a brief struggle, of a blow, of a subdued cry, came to them.

Spade's face twisted into a smile that held little joy. He said, "I guess you are," and stood out of the way.

When the police detectives had entered he shut the corridor door and followed them back to the living room.

Chapter 4

BRIGID O'SHAUGHNESSY was huddled in the armchair by the table. Joel Cairo stood in front of her, bending over her, holding in one hand the pistol Spade had twisted out of his hand. His other hand was clapped to his forehead. Blood ran through the fingers of that hand and down under them to his eyes. A smaller trickle from his cut lip made three wavy lines across his chin.

Cairo did not heed the detectives. He was glaring at the girl huddled in front of him.

Dundy, the first of the three into the living room, moved swiftly to Cairo's side, put one hand on his own hip under his overcoat, the other on the Levantine's wrist, and growled, "What are you up to here?"

Cairo took the red-smeared hand from his head and flourished it close to the lieutenant's face. Uncovered, his forehead showed a three-inch ragged tear. "This is what she has done," he cried. "Look at it."

"Did you do that?" Dundy asked the girl, nodding at Cairo's cut head.

She looked at Spade. He did not in any way respond to the appeal in her eyes.

The girl turned her eyes up to Dundy's. "I had to," she said in a low throbbing voice. "I was all alone in here with him when he attacked me. I couldn't—I tried to keep him off. I—I couldn't make myself shoot him."

"Oh, you liar!" Cairo cried. "Oh, you dirty filthy liar!" He twisted himself around to face Dundy. "She's lying awfully. I came here in good faith and was attacked by both of them, and when you came he went out to talk to you, leaving her here with this pistol, and then she said they were going to kill me after you left, and I called for help, so you wouldn't leave me here to be murdered, and then she struck me with the pistol."

"Here, give me this thing," Dundy said, and took the pistol from Cairo's hand. "Now let's get this straight. What'd you come here for?"

"He sent for me." Cairo twisted his head around to stare defiantly at Spade. "He phoned me and asked me to come."

Dundy asked, "What'd he want you for?"

Cairo withheld his reply until he had mopped his bloody forehead and chin with a lavender-barred silk handkerchief. "He said he wanted—they wanted—to see me. I didn't know what about."

Dundy asked, "Well, what happened then?"

"Then they attacked me. She struck me first, and then he choked me and took the pistol out of my pocket. I don't know what they would have done next if you hadn't arrived at that moment. I daresay they would have murdered me. When he went to answer the bell he left her here with the pistol to watch over me."

Brigid O'Shaughnessy jumped out of the armchair crying, "Why don't you make him tell the truth?" and slapped Cairo on the cheek.

Cairo yelled inarticulately, and Dundy pushed the girl back into the chair.

Spade, lighting a cigarette, grinned softly through smoke and told Tom, "She's impulsive."

Dundy scowled down at the girl and asked, "What do you want us to think the truth is?"

"Not what he said," she replied. "Not anything he said. Make him tell the truth," she added defiantly.

"We'll do that all right," he promised. He turned to his subordinate. "Well, Tom, I don't guess we'll go wrong pulling the lot of them in."

Tom nodded gloomily.

Spade left the door and advanced to the center of the room. His smile and manner were amiably composed. "Don't be in a hurry," he said. "Everything can be explained."

"I bet you," Dundy agreed, sneering.

Spade bowed to the girl. "Miss O'Shaughnessy," he said, "may I present Lieutenant Dundy and Detective-sergeant Polhaus." He bowed to Dundy. "Miss O'Shaughnessy is an operative in my employ. I hired her just recently, yesterday. This is Mr. Joel Cairo, a friend—an acquaintance, at any rate—of Thursby's. He came to me this afternoon and tried to hire me to find something Thursby was supposed to have on him when he was bumped off. It looked funny so I wouldn't touch it. Then he pulled a gun—well, never mind that unless it comes to a point of laying charges against each other. Anyway, after talking it over with Miss O'Shaughnessy, I thought maybe I could get something out of him about Miles's and Thursby's killings, so I asked him to come up here tonight."

Dundy confronted Cairo and brusquely demanded, "Well, what've you got to say to that?"

Cairo's eyes were shy and wary. "I don't know what I should say," he murmured.

"All you've got to do," said Dundy, "is swear to a complaint that they took a poke at you and the warrant clerk will believe you enough to issue a warrant that'll let us throw them in the can."

Spade spoke in an amused tone. "Go ahead, Cairo. Make him happy. Tell him you'll do it, and then we'll swear to one against you, and he'll have the lot of us."

Cairo cleared his throat and looked nervously around the room, not into the eyes of anyone there.

Dundy blew breath through his nose in a puff that was not quite a snort and said, "Get your hats."

Spade winked at Cairo and sat on the arm of the padded rocking chair. "Don't you know when you're being kidded?" he asked Dundy.

Tom Polhaus's face became red and shiny.

Dundy's face was immobile except for lips moving stiffly to say, "No, but we'll let that wait till we get down to the Hall."

Spade rose and put his hands in his trouser pockets. His grin was a taunt, and self-certainty spoke in every line of his posture. "I dare you to take us in, Dundy," he said. "We'll laugh at you in every newspaper in San Francisco. You don't think any of us is going to swear to any complaints against the others, do you? You've been kidded. When the bell rang I said to Miss O'Shaughnessy and Cairo, 'It's those damned bulls again. They're getting to be nuisances. Let's play a joke on them. When you hear them one of you scream, and then we'll see how far we can string them along before they tumble.' And—"

Brigid O'Shaughnessy bent forward in her chair and began to laugh hysterically.

"And the cut on his head and mouth?" Dundy asked scornfully. "Where'd they come from?"

"Ask him," Spade suggested. "Maybe he cut himself shaving."

Cairo spoke quickly. "I fell. We intended to be struggling for the pistol when you came in, but I fell. I tripped on the end of the rug and fell while we were pretending to struggle."

Dundy said, "Horsefeathers."

Spade said, "That's all right, Dundy, believe it or not. The point is that that's our story and we'll stick to it. The newspapers will print it whether they believe it or not, and it'll be just as funny one way as the other, or more so. What are you going to do about it?"

Dundy gripped Cairo by the shoulders. "You can't get away with that," he snarled, shaking the Levantine. "You screamed for help and you've got to take it."

"No, sir," Cairo sputtered. "It was a joke. He said you were friends of his and would understand."

Dundy pulled Cairo roughly around, holding him now by one wrist and the nape of his neck. "I'll take you along for packing the gun, anyway," he said. "And I'll take the rest of you along to see who laughs at the joke."

Spade said, "Don't be a sap, Dundy. The gun was part of the plant. It's one of mine." He laughed. "Too bad it's only a thirty-two, or maybe you could find it was the one Thursby and Miles were shot with."

Dundy released Cairo, spun on his heel, and his right fist clicked on Spade's chin.

Brigid O'Shaughnessy uttered a short cry.

Spade's smile flickered out at the instant of the impact. Before his fist could come up Tom Polhaus had pushed himself between the two men, facing Spade, encumbering Spade's arms with the closeness of his barrellike belly and his own arms.

"No, no, for God's sake!" Tom begged.

After a long moment of motionlessness Spade's muscles relaxed. "Then get him out of here quick," he said.

Tom looked at Spade's eyes—hard and glittering—and mumbled, "Take it easy, Sam." He buttoned his coat and turned to Dundy, asking, in a voice that aped casualness, "Well, is that all?"

Dundy's scowl failed to conceal indecision.

Cairo moved suddenly towards the door, saying, "I'm going too, if Mr. Spade will be kind enough to give me my hat and coat."

Dundy put his lips together firmly and said nothing. A light was glinting in his green eyes.

Spade went to the closet in the passageway and fetched Cairo's hat and coat. He said to Tom, "Tell him to leave the gun."

Dundy took Cairo's pistol from his overcoat pocket and put it on the table. He went out first, with Cairo at his heels. Tom halted in front of Spade, muttering, "I hope to God you know what you're doing," got no response, sighed, and followed the others out. Spade went after them as far as the bend in the passageway, where he stood until Tom had closed the corridor door.

SPADE RETURNED TO THE living room and sat on an end of the sofa, elbows on knees, cheeks in hands, looking at the floor and not at Brigid O'Shaughnessy smiling weakly at him from the armchair. Red rage came suddenly into his face and he began to talk. He cursed Dundy for five minutes without break, cursed him obscenely, blasphemously, repetitiously, in a harsh guttural voice.

Then he took his face out of his hands, looked at the girl, grinned sheepishly, and said, "Childish, huh? I know, but, by God, I do hate being hit without hitting back. Not that it was so much of a sock at that." He laughed and lounged back on the sofa, crossing his legs. "A cheap enough price to pay for winning." His brows came together in a fleeting scowl. "Though I'll remember it."

The girl, smiling again, left her chair and sat on the sofa beside him. "You're absolutely the wildest person I've ever known," she said. "Do you always carry on so high-handed?"

"I let him hit me, didn't I?"

"Oh, yes, but a police official."

"It wasn't that," Spade explained. "It was that in losing his head and slugging me he overplayed his hand. If I'd mixed it with him then he couldn't've backed down. He'd've had to go through with it, and we'd've had to tell that goofy story at headquarters." He stared thoughtfully at the girl, and said, "Now you've had your talk with Cairo. Now you can talk to me."

"But I didn't," she said, "have time to finish talking to him." She looked at Spade with clear candid eyes. "We were interrupted almost before we had begun."

Spade lighted a cigarette and laughed his mouth empty of smoke. "Want me to phone him and ask him to come back?"

She shook her head, not smiling.

He said amiably, "I'm still listening."

"Look at the time!" she exclaimed, wriggling a finger at the alarm clock saying 2:50 with its clumsily shaped hands. "It would take hours to tell you."

"It'll have to take them then."

"Am I a prisoner?" she asked gaily.

"Besides, there's the kid outside."

Her gaiety vanished. "Do you think he's still there?"

"It's likely."

She shivered. "Could you find out?"

"I could go down and see."

"Oh, that's—will you?"

Spade studied her anxious face for a moment and then got up from the sofa, saying, "Sure." He got a hat and overcoat from the closet. "I'll be gone about ten minutes."

"Do be careful," she begged.

He said, "I will," and went out.

WHEN he came back Brigid O'Shaughnessy was standing at the bend in the passageway, waiting.

"He's still there," Spade said.

She bit the inside of her lip and turned slowly, going back into the living room. Spade followed her in, put his hat and overcoat on a chair, and went into the kitchen.

He had put the coffeepot on the stove when she came to the door, and was slicing a slender loaf of French bread. She stood in the doorway and watched him with preoccupied eyes.

"The tablecloth's in there," he said, pointing the bread knife at a cupboard that was one breakfast-nook partition.

She set the table while he spread liverwurst on, or put cold corned beef between, the small ovals of bread he had sliced. Then he poured the coffee, added brandy to it from a squat bottle, and they sat at the table. They sat side by side on one of the benches.

"You can start talking now, between bites," he said. "What's this bird, this falcon, that everybody's all steamed up about?"

She picked up a slice of bread encrusted with gray liverwurst. She put it down on her plate. She wrinkled her forehead and said, "It's a black figure, smooth and shiny, of a bird, a hawk or falcon, about that high." She held her hands a foot apart.

"What makes it important?"

She sipped coffee and brandy before she shook her head. "I don't know," she said. "They'd never tell me. They promised me five hundred pounds if I helped them get it. Then Floyd said, after we'd left Joe, that he'd give me seven hundred and fifty."

"So it must be worth more than seventy-five hundred dollars?"

"Oh, much more than that," she said. "They didn't pretend that they were sharing equally with me. They were simply hiring me to help them."

"To help them how?"

"To help them get it from the man who had it," she said slowly when she had lowered her cup, "a Russian named Kemidov."

"How?"

"Oh, but that's not important, and wouldn't help you"—she smiled impudently—"and is certainly none of your business."

"This was in Constantinople?"

She hesitated, nodded, and said, "Marmora."

He said, "Go ahead, what happened then?"

"But that's all. I've told you. They promised me five hundred pounds to help them and I did and then we found that Joe Cairo meant to desert us, taking the falcon with him and leaving us nothing. So we did exactly that to him, first. But then I wasn't any better off than I had been before, because Floyd hadn't any intention at all of paying me the seven hundred and fifty pounds he had promised me. I had learned that by the time we got here. He said we would go to New York, where he would sell it and give me my share, but I could see he wasn't telling me the truth." Indignation had darkened her eyes to violet. "And that's why I came to you to get you to help me learn where the falcon was."

"And suppose you'd got it? What then?"

"Then I could have talked terms with Mr. Floyd Thursby."

Spade scowled at the ashes he had dumped on his plate. "What makes it worth all that money?" he demanded. "You must have some idea, at least be able to guess."

"I haven't the slightest idea."

He directed the scowl at her. "What's it made of?"

"Porcelain or black stone. I don't know. I've never touched it. I've only seen it once, for a few minutes. Floyd showed it to me when we'd first got hold of it."

Spade mashed the end of his cigarette in his plate and made one draught of the coffee and brandy in his cup. His scowl had gone away. He wiped his lips with his napkin, dropped it crumpled on the table, and spoke casually. "You *are* a liar."

She got up and stood at the end of the table, looking down at him with dark abashed eyes in a pinkening face. "I am a liar," she said. "I have always been a liar."

"Don't brag about it. It's childish." His voice was good-humored. He came out from between table and bench. "Was there any truth at all in that yarn?"

She hung her head. "Some," she whispered.

Spade put a hand under her chin and lifted her head. He laughed and said, "We've got all night before us. I'll put some more brandy in some more coffee and we'll try again."

Her eyelids drooped. "Oh, I'm so tired," she said tremulously, "so tired of it all, of myself, of lying and thinking up lies, and of not knowing what is a lie and what is the truth. I wish I—"

She put her hands up to Spade's cheeks, put her open mouth hard against his mouth, her body flat against his body.

Spade's arms went around her, holding her to him, muscles bulging his blue sleeves, a hand cradling her head, its fingers half lost among red hair, a hand moving groping fingers over her slim back. His eyes burned yellowly.

BEGINNING day had reduced night to a thin smokiness when Spade sat up. At his side Brigid O'Shaughnessy's soft breathing had the regularity of utter sleep. Spade was quiet leaving bed and bedroom and shutting the bedroom door. He dressed in the bathroom. Then he examined the sleeping girl's clothes, took a flat brass key from the pocket of her coat, and went out.

He went to the Coronet, letting himself into the building and into her apartment with the key. He switched on all the lights and searched the place from wall to wall with expert certainty. Every drawer, cupboard, cubbyhole, box, bag—locked or unlocked—was opened and its contents subjected to examination by eyes and fingers. He did not find the black bird. He found nothing that seemed to have any connection with a black bird. The only thing he found that interested him was a double handful of rather fine jewelry in a polychrome box in a locked dressing-table drawer.

When he had finished he unlocked the kitchen window, scarred the edge of its lock a little with his pocketknife, opened the window—over a fire escape—got his hat and overcoat from the settee in the living room, and left the apartment as he had come.

On his way home he stopped at a store that was being opened by a puffy-eyed shivering plump grocer and bought oranges, eggs, rolls, butter, and cream.

Spade went quietly into his apartment, but before he had shut the corridor door behind him Brigid O'Shaughnessy cried, "Who is that?"

"Young Spade bearing breakfast."

"Oh, you frightened me!"

The bedroom door he had shut was open. The girl sat on the side of the bed, trembling, with her right hand out of sight under a pillow.

Spade put his packages on the kitchen table and went into the bedroom. He sat on the bed beside the girl, kissed her smooth shoulder, and said, "I wanted to see if that kid was still on the job, and to get stuff for breakfast."

"Is he?"

"No."

She sighed and leaned against him. "I awakened and you weren't here and then I heard someone coming in. I was terrified."

Spade combed her red hair back from her face with his fingers and said, "I'm sorry, angel. I thought you'd sleep through it. Did you have that gun under your pillow all night?"

"No. You know I didn't. I jumped up and got it when I was frightened."

He cooked breakfast—and slipped the flat brass key back into her coat pocket—while she bathed and dressed.

She came out of the bathroom whistling. "Shall I make the bed?" she asked.

"That'd be swell. The eggs need a couple of minutes more."

Their breakfast was on the table when she returned to the kitchen. They sat where they had sat the night before and ate heartily.

"Now about the bird?" Spade suggested presently as they ate.

She put her fork down and looked at him. She drew her eyebrows together and made her mouth small and tight. "You can't ask me to talk about that this morning of all mornings," she protested. "I don't want to and I won't."

"It's a stubborn damned hussy," he said sadly and put a piece of roll into his mouth.

BRIGID O'SHAUGHNESSY would not let Spade go in with her. "It's bad enough to be coming home in evening dress at this hour without bringing company. I hope I don't meet anybody."

"Dinner tonight?"

"Yes."

They kissed. She went into the Coronet. He hailed a taxi and told the chauffeur, "Hotel Belvedere."

When he reached the Belvedere he saw the youth who had shadowed him sitting in the lobby on a divan from which the elevators could be seen.

At the desk Spade learned that Cairo was not in. He frowned and pinched his lower lip. Points of yellow light began to dance in his eyes. "Thanks," he said softly to the clerk and turned away.

Sauntering, he crossed the lobby to the divan from which the elevators could be seen and sat down beside—not more than a foot from—the young man who was apparently reading a newspaper.

The young man did not look up from his newspaper. Seen at this scant distance, he seemed certainly less than twenty years old. His features were small, in keeping with his stature, and regular. His clothing was neither new nor of more than ordinary quality, but it, and his manner of wearing it, was marked by a hard masculine neatness.

Spade asked casually, "Where is he?" while shaking tobacco down into a brown paper curved to catch it.

The boy lowered his paper and looked around. He said, in a voice as colorless and composed as his young face, "What?"

"Where is he?" Spade was busy with his cigarette.

"Who?"

"Cairo."

The hazel eyes' gaze went up Spade's chest to the knot of his maroon tie and rested there. "What do you think you're doing, Jack?" the boy demanded. "Kidding me?"

"I'll tell you when I am." Spade licked his cigarette and smiled amiably at the boy. "New York, aren't you?"

The boy stared at Spade's tie for a moment longer, then raised his newspaper and returned his attention to it.

Spade inhaled cigarette smoke and said, "You'll have to talk to me before you're through, sonny—some of you will—and you can tell G. I said so."

"Shove off," the boy said from the side of his mouth.

"People lose teeth talking like that." Spade's voice was still amiable though his face had become wooden. He dropped his cigarette into a tall stone jar beside the divan and with a lifted hand caught the attention of a man who had been standing at an end of the cigar stand for several minutes. The man nodded and came towards them. He was a middle-aged man of medium height, compactly built, tidily dressed in dark clothes.

"Hello, Sam," he said as he came up.

"Hello, Luke."

They shook hands and Luke said, "Too bad about Miles."

"Uh-huh, a bad break." Spade jerked his head to indicate the boy on the divan beside him. "What do you let these cheap gunmen hang out in your lobby for, with their tools bulging their clothes?"

"Yes?" Luke examined the boy with crafty brown eyes set in a suddenly hard face. "What do you want here?" he asked.

The boy stood up. He looked like a schoolboy standing in front of them.

Luke said, "Well, if you don't want anything, beat it, and don't come back."

The boy said, "I won't forget you guys," and went out.

They watched him go out. Spade took off his hat and wiped his damp forehead with a handkerchief.

The hotel detective asked, "What is it?"

"Damned if I know," Spade replied. "I just happened to spot him. Know anything about Joel Cairo—635?"

"Oh, that one!" The hotel detective leered.

"How long's he been here?"

"Four days. This is the fifth."

"What about him?"

"Search me, Sam. I got nothing against him but his looks."

"I'm doing a little work for him."

"Want me to kind of keep an eye on him?"

"Thanks, Luke. It wouldn't hurt. You can't know too much about the men you're working for these days."

It was twenty-one minutes past eleven by the clock over the elevator doors when Joel Cairo came in from the street. His forehead was bandaged. His face was pasty, with sagging mouth and eyelids.

Spade met him in front of the desk. "Good morning," Spade said easily.

"Good morning," Cairo responded without enthusiasm.

There was a pause.

Spade said, "Let's go someplace where we can talk." He led the way to the divan. When they were seated he asked, "Dundy take you down to the Hall?"

"Yes."

"How long did they work on you?"

"Until a very little while ago, and very much against my will." Pain and indignation were mixed in Cairo's face and voice. "I shall certainly take the matter up with the consulate general of Greece and with an attorney."

"Go ahead, and see what it gets you. What did you let the police shake out of you?"

There was prim satisfaction in Cairo's smile. "Not a single thing. I adhered to the course you indicated earlier in your rooms." His smile went away. "Though I certainly wished you had devised a more reasonable story. I felt decidedly ridiculous repeating it."

Spade drummed with his fingers on the leather seat between them. "You'll be hearing from Dundy again. Stay dummied up on him and you'll be all right. Don't worry about the story's goofiness. A sensible one would've had us all in the cooler." He rose to his feet. "You'll want sleep if you've been standing up under a police storm all night. See you later."

EFFIE PERINE was saying, "No, not yet," into the telephone when Spade entered his outer office. She looked around at him and her lips shaped a silent word: Iva. He shook his head. "Yes, I'll have him call you as soon as he comes in," she said aloud and replaced the receiver on its prong. "That's the third time she's called up this morning," she told Spade.

He made an impatient growling noise.

The girl moved her brown eyes to indicate the inner office. "Your Miss O'Shaughnessy's in there. She's been waiting since a few minutes after nine."

Spade nodded and asked, "What else?"

"Sergeant Polhaus called up. He didn't leave any message."

"Get him for me."

"And G. called up."

Spade's eyes brightened. He asked, "Who?"

"G. That's what he said." Her air of personal indifference to the subject was flawless. "When I told him you weren't in he said, 'When he comes in, will you please tell him that G. phoned and will phone again?' "

Spade worked his lips together as if tasting something he liked. "Thanks, darling," he said. "See if you can get Tom Polhaus." He opened the inner door and went into his private office, pulling the door to behind him.

Brigid O'Shaughnessy, dressed as on her first visit to the office, rose from a chair beside his desk and came quickly towards him. "Somebody has been in my apartment," she exclaimed. "Locks have been jimmied and it is all upside down, every which way."

He seemed moderately surprised. "Anything taken?"

"I don't think so. I don't know. I was afraid to stay. I changed as fast as I could and came down here."

Spade frowned. "I wonder if it could have been Cairo. He wasn't at his hotel all night, didn't get in till a few minutes ago. He told me he had been standing up under a police grilling all night."

She looked at him with cloudy eyes. "You went to see Joe this morning?" she asked.

"Yes."

She hesitated. "Why?"

"Why?" He smiled down at her. "Because, my own true love, I've got to keep in some sort of touch with all the loose ends of this dizzy affair if I'm ever going to make heads or tails of it." He kissed the tip of her nose lightly and set her down in the chair. He sat on the desk in front of her. He said, "Now we've got to find a new home for you, haven't we?"

She nodded with emphasis. "I won't go back there."

He looked thoughtful. "I've got it," he said presently. "Wait a minute." He went into the outer office, shutting the door.

"Effie," he said, "does your woman's intuition still tell you that she's a Madonna or something?"

She looked sharply up at him. "I still believe that no matter what kind of trouble she's gotten into she's all right, if that's what you mean."

"That's what I mean," he said. "Are you strong enough for her to give her a lift?"

"How?"

"Could you put her up for a few days?"

"You mean at home?"

"Yes. Her joint's been broken into. That's the second burglary she's had this week. It'd be better for her if she wasn't alone. It would help a lot if you could take her in."

She scratched her lip with a fingernail. "That would scare Ma into a green hemorrhage. I'll have to tell her she's a surprise witness that you're keeping under cover till the last minute."

"You're a darling," Spade said. "Better take her out there now.

I'll get her key from her and bring whatever she needs over from her apartment. Let's see. You oughtn't to be seen leaving here together. You go home now. Take a taxi, but make sure you aren't followed. I'll send her out in another cab in a little while, making sure she isn't followed."

Chapter 5

THE telephone bell was ringing when Spade returned to his office after sending Brigid O'Shaughnessy off to Effie Perine's house. He went to the telephone.

"Hello. . . . Yes, this is Spade. . . . Yes, I got it. I've been waiting to hear from you. . . . Mr. Gutman? Oh, yes, sure! . . . Now—the sooner the better. . . . Twelve C. . . . Right. Say fifteen minutes."

Spade sat on the corner of his desk beside the telephone and rolled a cigarette. His mouth was a hard complacent V. His eyes, watching his fingers make the cigarette, smoldered.

The door opened and Iva Archer came in.

Spade said, "Hello, honey," in a voice as lightly amiable as his face had suddenly become.

"Oh, Sam, forgive me! Forgive me!" she cried in a choked voice. She stood just inside the door, peering into his face with frightened red and swollen eyes.

He did not get up from his seat on the desk corner. He said, "Sure. That's all right. Forget it."

"But, Sam," she wailed, "I sent those policemen to your apartment. I was mad, crazy with jealousy, and I phoned them that if they'd go there they'd learn something about Miles's murder."

"What made you think that?"

"Oh, I didn't! But I was mad, Sam, and I wanted to hurt you. You weren't nice to me last night. You were cold and distant and wanted to get rid of me, when I had come down there and waited so long to warn you, and you—"

"Warn me about what?"

"About Phil. He's found out about—about you being in love with me, and Miles had told him about my wanting a divorce, and now Phil thinks we—you killed his brother because he wouldn't give me the divorce so we could get married. He told me he believed that, and yesterday he went and told the police."

"That's nice," Spade said softly. "And you came to warn me, and because I was busy you got up on your ear and helped this damned Phil Archer stir things up."

"I'm sorry," she whimpered. "I know you won't forgive me. I— I'm sorry, sorry, sorry."

"You ought to be," he agreed, "on your own account as well as mine. Did you tell them who you were when you phoned?"

"Oh, no! I simply told them that if they'd go to your apartment right away they'd learn something about the murder and hung up."

He patted her shoulder and said pleasantly, "It was a dumb trick, all right, but it's done now. You'd better run along home and think up things to tell the police. You'll be hearing from them. Maybe you'd better see Sid Wise first." He took a card out of his pocket, scribbled three lines on its back, and gave it to her. "You can tell Sid everything." He frowned. "Or almost everything. Where were you the night Miles was shot?"

"Home," she replied without hesitating.

He shook his head, grinning at her, then looked at the watch on his wrist. "You'll have to trot along, precious. I'm late for an appointment now. You do what you want, but if I were you I'd tell Sid the truth."

She put her arms around him. "Won't you go with me to see Mr. Wise?"

"I can't, and I'd only be in the way." He put his hands on her shoulders, turned her to face the door, and released her with a little push. "Beat it," he ordered.

THE mahogany door of suite 12 C at the Alexandria Hotel was opened by the boy Spade had talked to in the Belvedere lobby. Spade said, "Hello," good-naturedly. The boy did not say anything. He stood aside holding the door open.

Spade went in. A fat man came to meet him.

The fat man was flabbily fat with bulbous pink cheeks and lips and chins and neck, with a great soft egg of a belly that was all his torso, and pendant cones for arms and legs. His eyes, made small by fat puffs around them, were dark and sleek. Dark ringlets thinly covered his broad scalp. He wore a black cutaway coat, black vest, black satin ascot tie holding a pinkish pearl, striped gray worsted trousers, and patent-leather shoes.

His voice was a throaty purr. "Ah, Mr. Spade," he said with enthusiasm and held out a hand like a fat pink star.

Spade took the hand and smiled and said, "How do you do, Mr. Gutman?"

Holding Spade's hand, the fat man turned beside him, put his other hand to Spade's elbow, and guided him across a green rug to a green plush chair beside a table that held a siphon, some glasses, and a bottle of Johnnie Walker whisky on a tray, a box of cigars—Coronas del Ritz—two newspapers, and a small and plain yellow soapstone box.

Spade sat in the green chair. The fat man began to fill two glasses from bottle and siphon. The boy had disappeared.

"We begin well, sir," the fat man purred, turning with a proffered glass in his hand. "I distrust a man who says when. If he's got to be careful not to drink too much it's because he's not to be trusted when he does."

Spade took the glass and, smiling, made the beginning of a bow over it.

The fat man raised his glass and held it against a window's light. "Well, sir, here's to plain speaking and clear understanding."

They drank and lowered their glasses.

The fat man looked shrewdly at Spade and asked, "You're a closemouthed man?"

Spade shook his head. "I like to talk."

"Better and better!" the fat man exclaimed. "I distrust a closemouthed man. He generally picks the wrong time to talk and says the wrong things. And I'll tell you right out that I'm a man who likes talking to a man who likes to talk."

"Swell. Will we talk about the black bird?"

The fat man laughed. "Will we?" he asked and, "We will," he replied. His pink face was shiny with delight. "Let us talk about the black bird by all means, but first, sir, answer me a question, please. You're here as Miss O'Shaughnessy's representative?"

Spade replied deliberately, "I can't say yes or no. There's nothing certain about it either way, yet." He looked up at the fat man. "It depends."

The fat man sat down, took a mouthful from his glass, and suggested, "Maybe it depends on Joel Cairo?"

Spade's prompt "Maybe" was noncommittal. He drank.

The fat man leaned forward until his belly stopped him. His smile was ingratiating and so was his purring voice. "You could say, then, that the question is which one of them you'll represent?"

"You could put it that way."

The fat man's eyes glistened. His voice sank to a throaty whisper asking, "Who else is there?"

"There's me," Spade said.

The fat man sank back in his chair. "That's wonderful, sir," he purred. "That's wonderful. I do like a man who tells you right out he's looking out for himself."

Spade said, "Uh-huh. Now let's talk about the black bird."

The fat man smiled. "Mr. Spade, have you any conception of how much money can be made out of that black bird?"

"No."

The fat man leaned forward again and put a bloated pink hand on the arm of Spade's chair. "Well, sir, if I told you—by Gad, if I told you half!—you'd call me a liar."

Spade smiled. "No," he said, "not even if I thought it. But if you won't take the risk just tell me what it is and I'll figure out the profits."

The fat man laughed. "You couldn't do it, sir. Nobody could do it who hadn't had a world of experience with things of that sort, and"—he paused impressively—"there aren't any other things of that sort." He stopped laughing, abruptly. He stared at Spade with an intentness that suggested myopia. He asked, "You mean you don't know what it is?"

Spade made a careless gesture with his cigar. "Oh, hell," he said lightly, "I know what it's supposed to look like. I don't know what it is."

"She didn't tell you?"

"Miss O'Shaughnessy?"

"Yes. A lovely girl, sir."

"Uh-huh. No."

The fat man's eyes were dark gleams in ambush behind pink puffs of flesh. He said indistinctly, "She must know," and then, "And Cairo didn't either?"

"Cairo is cagey. He's willing to buy it, but he won't risk telling me anything I don't know already."

The fat man moistened his lips with his tongue. "How much is he willing to buy it for?" he asked.

"Ten thousand dollars."

The fat man laughed scornfully. "Ten thousand, and dollars, mind you, not even pounds. That's the Greek for you. Humph! And what did you say to that?"

"I said if I turned it over to him I'd expect the ten thousand."

"Ah, yes, *if!* Nicely put, sir." The fat man's forehead squirmed in a flesh-blurred frown. "They must know," he said only partly aloud, then, "Do they? Do they know what the bird is, sir? What was your impression?"

"I can't help you there," Spade confessed. "There's not much to go by. Cairo didn't say he did and he didn't say he didn't. She said she didn't, but I took it for granted that she was lying."

The fat man shut his eyes, opened them suddenly—wide—and said to Spade, "Maybe they don't." His bulbous pink face took on an expression of ineffable happiness. "If they don't," he cried, and again, "If they don't I'm the only one in the whole wide sweet world who does!"

Spade drew his lips back in a tight smile. "I'm glad I came to the right place," he said.

The fat man smiled too, but somewhat vaguely. His eyes, avoiding Spade's, shifted to the glass at Spade's elbow. His face brightened. "By Gad, sir," he said, "your glass is empty." He got up and went to the table and clattered glasses and siphon and bottle mixing two drinks.

Spade was immobile in his chair until the fat man, with a flourish and a bow, had handed him his refilled glass. Then Spade rose and stood close to the fat man, looking down at him. He raised his glass. His voice was deliberate, challenging. "Here's to plain speaking and clear understanding."

The fat man smiled up at Spade. He said, "Well, sir, it's surprising, but it well may be a fact that neither of them does know exactly what that bird is, and that nobody in all this wide sweet world knows what it is, saving and excepting only your humble servant, Casper Gutman, Esquire."

"Swell." Spade stood with legs apart, one hand in his trouser pocket, the other holding his glass. "When you've told me there'll only be two of us who know."

"Mathematically correct, sir"—the fat man's eyes twinkled—"but"—his smile spread—"I don't know for certain that I'm going to tell you."

"Don't be a damned fool," Spade said patiently. "You know what it is. I know where it is. That's why we're here."

"Well, sir, where is it?"

Spade ignored the question.

The fat man bunched his lips, raised his eyebrows, and cocked his head a little to the left. "You see," he said blandly, "I must tell you what I know, but you will not tell me what you know. That is hardly equitable, sir. No, no, I do not think we can do business along those lines."

Spade's face became pale and hard. He spoke rapidly in a low furious voice. "Think again and think fast. I told that punk of yours that you'd have to talk to me before you got through. I'll tell you now that you'll do your talking today or you are through. What are you wasting my time for?"

He turned and with angry heedlessness tossed his glass at the table. The glass struck the wood, burst apart, and splashed its contents and glittering fragments over table and floor.

Spade, still furious, said, "And another thing, I don't want—"

The door to Spade's left opened. The boy who had admitted Spade came in. He shut the door and stood in front of it with his hands flat against his flanks.

"Another thing," Spade repeated, glaring at the boy. "Keep that gunsel away from me while you're making up your mind. I'll kill him. I don't like him. He makes me nervous. I'll kill him the first time he gets in my way. I won't give him an even break. I won't give him a chance. I'll kill him."

The boy's lips twitched in a shadowy smile. He neither raised his eyes nor spoke.

The fat man said tolerantly, "Well, sir, I must say you have a most violent temper."

"Temper?" Spade laughed crazily. He held out a long arm that ended in a thick forefinger pointing at the fat man's belly. His angry voice filled the room. "Think it over and think like hell. You've got till five thirty. Then you're either in or out, for keeps." He let his arm drop, scowled at the bland fat man for a moment, scowled at the boy. Then he crossed to the chair on which he had dropped his hat, picked up the hat, set it on his head, and went to the door through which he had entered. When he opened the door he turned and said harshly, "Five thirty—then the curtain."

Spade went out and slammed the door.

Spade walked down Geary Street to the Palace Hotel, where he ate luncheon. His face had lost its pallor, his lips their dryness, and his hand its trembling by the time he had sat down. He ate hungrily without haste, and then went to Sid Wise's office.

When Spade entered, Wise screwed his chair around to face him, and said, "'Lo. Push a chair up."

Spade moved a chair to the side of the big paper-laden desk and sat down. "Mrs. Archer come in?" he asked.

"Yes." The faintest of lights flickered in Wise's eyes. "Going to marry the lady, Sammy?"

Spade sighed irritably. "Now you start that!" he grumbled.

A brief tired smile lifted the corners of the lawyer's mouth. "If you don't," he said, "you're going to have a job on your hands."

Spade looked up from the cigarette he was making and spoke sourly. "Did she tell you where she was the night he was killed?"

"Yes."

"Where?"

"Following him."

Spade sat up straight and blinked. He exclaimed incredulously, "Lord, these women!" Then he laughed, relaxed, and asked, "Well, what did she see?"

Wise shook his head. "Nothing much. When he came home for dinner that evening he told her he had a date with a girl at the St. Mark, ragging her, telling her that was her chance to get the divorce she wanted. After he had gone out she began to think that maybe he might have had that date. So she got their car from the garage and drove down to the St. Mark, sitting in the car across the street. She saw him come out of the hotel, and she saw that he was shadowing a man and a girl—she says she saw the same girl with you last night—who had come out just ahead of him. She followed Miles long enough to make sure he was shadowing the pair, and then she went up to your apartment. You weren't home."

"What time was that?" Spade asked.

"When she got to your place? Between half past nine and ten the first time."

"The first time?"

"Yes. She drove around for half an hour or so and then tried again. That would make it, say, ten thirty. You were still out, so she drove back downtown and went to a movie to kill time until after midnight, when she thought she'd be more likely to find you in. She stayed in the movie till it closed." Wise's words came out slower now and there was a sardonic glint in his eye. "She says she had decided by then not to go back to your place again. She says she didn't know whether you'd like having her drop in that late. So she went to Tait's—the one on Ellis Street—had something to eat, and then went home—alone."

"Well, what then? Miles wasn't home. It was at least two o'clock by then—must've been—and he was dead."

"Miles wasn't home," Wise said. "That seems to have made her mad again—his not being home first to be made mad by her not being home. So she took the car out of the garage again and went back to your place."

"And I wasn't home. I was down looking at Miles's corpse. What a swell lot of merry-go-round riding. Then what?"

"She went home, and her husband still wasn't there, and while she was undressing your messenger came with the news of his death."

Spade didn't speak until he had with great care rolled and lighted another cigarette. Then he said, "I think that's an all-right spread. It seems to click with most of the known facts. It ought to hold."

Wise studied Spade's face with curious eyes and asked, "But you don't believe it?"

Spade plucked his cigarette from between his lips. "I don't believe it or disbelieve it, Sid. I don't know a damned thing about it."

EFFIE PERINE was standing in the center of Spade's outer office when he entered. She looked at him with worried brown eyes and asked, "What happened?"

Spade's face grew stiff. "What happened where?" he demanded.

"Why didn't she come?"

Spade took two long steps and caught Effie Perine by the shoulders. "She didn't get there?" he bawled into her frightened face.

She shook her head. "I waited and waited and she didn't come, and I couldn't get you on the phone, so I came down."

Spade jerked his hands away from her shoulders, thrust them far down in his trouser pockets, said, "Another merry-go-round," in a loud enraged voice, and strode into his private office. He came out again. "Phone your mother," he commanded. "See if she's come yet."

He walked up and down the office while the girl used the telephone. "No," she said when she had finished. "Could—could somebody have followed her taxi?"

Spade stopped pacing the floor and glared at the girl. "Nobody followed her. Do you think I'm a damned schoolboy? I made sure of it before I put her in the cab and I rode a dozen blocks with her to be more sure." He made a harsh noise in his throat and went to the corridor door. "I'm going out and find her if I have to dig up sewers," he said. "Stay here till I'm back or you hear from me. For God's sake let's do something right."

He went out, walked half the distance to the elevators, and re-traced his steps. Effie Perine was sitting at her desk when he opened the door. He said, "You ought to know better than to pay any attention to me when I talk like that." He grinned humbly, said, "I'm no damned good, darling," made an exaggerated bow, and went out again.

Two yellow taxicabs were at the corner stand to which Spade went. Their chauffeurs were standing talking. Spade asked, "Where's the red-faced blond driver that was here at noon?"

"Got a load," one of the chauffeurs said.

"Will he be back here?"

"I guess so."

The other chauffeur ducked his head to the east. "Here he comes now."

Spade walked down to the corner and stood by the curb until the red-faced blond chauffeur had parked his cab and got out. Then Spade went up to him and said, "I got into your cab with a lady at noontime. We went out Stockton Street and up Sacramento to Jones, where I got out."

"Sure," the red-faced man said, "I remember that."

"I told you to take her to a Ninth Avenue number. You didn't take her there. Where did you take her?"

"I took her to the Ferry Building."

"Didn't take her anywhere else first?"

"No. It was like this: After we dropped you I went on out Sacramento, and when we got to Polk she rapped on the glass and said she wanted to get a newspaper, so I stopped at the corner and whistled for a kid, and she got her paper."

"Which paper?"

"The *Call*. Then I went on out Sacramento some more, and just after we'd crossed Van Ness she knocked on the glass again and said take her to the Ferry Building."

"Was she excited or anything?"

"Not so's I noticed."

"And when you got to the Ferry Building?"

"She paid me off, and that was all."

"Anybody waiting for her there?"

"I didn't see them if they was."

"Which way did she go?"

"At the Ferry? I don't know. Maybe upstairs."

"Take the newspaper with her?"

"Yeah, she had it tucked under her arm when she paid me."

Spade thanked the chauffeur, said, "Get yourself a smoke," and gave him a dollar.

SPADE bought a copy of the *Call* and carried it into an office-building vestibule to examine it out of the wind.

His eyes ran swiftly over the front-page headlines and over those on the second and third pages, but nothing held his attention. He continued until he reached the thirty-fifth page, which held news of the weather, shipping, produce, finance, divorce, births, marriages, and deaths. He read the list of dead, passed over pages thirty-six and thirty-seven—financial news—found nothing to stop his eyes on the thirty-eighth and last page, sighed, folded the newspaper, put it in his coat pocket, and rolled a cigarette.

For five minutes he stood there in the vestibule smoking and staring sulkily at nothing. Then he walked up to Stockton Street, hailed a taxi, and had himself driven back to his office.

In the doorway of his office building he came face-to-face with the boy he had left at Gutman's. The boy put himself in Spade's path, blocking the entrance, and said, "Come on. He wants to see you." The boy's hands were in his overcoat pockets. His pockets bulged more than his hands need have made them bulge.

"Well, let's go," Spade said cheerfully.

They walked up Sutter Street side by side. The boy kept his

hands in his overcoat pockets. They went into the Alexandria, rode up to the twelfth floor, and went down the corridor towards Gutman's suite. Nobody else was in the corridor.

Spade lagged a little, so that, when they were within fifteen feet of Gutman's door, he was perhaps a foot and a half behind the boy. He leaned sidewise suddenly and grasped the boy from behind by both arms, just beneath the elbows. The boy struggled and squirmed, but he was impotent in the big man's grip. The boy kicked back, but his feet went between Spade's spread legs.

Spade lifted the boy straight up from the floor and brought him down hard on his feet again. The boy's teeth ground together audibly, making a noise that mingled with the noise of Spade's breathing as Spade crushed the boy's hands.

They were tense and motionless for a long moment. Then the boy's arms became limp. Spade released the boy and stepped back. In each of Spade's hands, when they came out of the boy's overcoat pockets, there was a heavy automatic pistol.

Spade put the pistols in his own pockets and grinned derisively. "Come on," he said. "This will put you in solid with your boss."

They went to Gutman's door and Spade knocked.

Gutman opened the door. A glad smile lighted his fat face. He held out a hand and said, "Come in, sir! Thank you for coming."

Spade shook the hand and entered. The boy went in behind him. The fat man shut the door. Spade took the boy's pistols from his pockets and held them out to Gutman. "Here. You shouldn't let him run around with these. He'll get himself hurt."

The fat man laughed merrily and took the pistols. "Well, well," he said, "what's this?" He looked from Spade to the boy.

Spade said, "A crippled newsie took them away from him, but I made him give them back."

The white-faced boy took the pistols out of Gutman's hands and pocketed them. The boy did not speak.

Gutman laughed again. "By Gad, sir," he told Spade, "you're a chap worth knowing. Come in. Sit down. Give me your hat."

The boy left the room by the door to the right of the entrance.

The fat man installed Spade in the green plush chair by the

table, pressed a cigar upon him, held a light to it, mixed whiskey and carbonated water, put one glass in Spade's hand, and, holding the other, sat down facing Spade.

"Now, sir," he said, "I hope you'll let me apologize for—"

"Never mind that. Let's talk about the black bird."

The fat man cocked his head to the left and regarded Spade with fond eyes. "All right, sir," he agreed. "Let's." He took a sip from the glass in his hand. "This is going to be the most astounding thing you've ever heard of, sir, and I say that knowing that a man of your caliber in your profession must have known some astounding things in his time."

Spade nodded politely.

The fat man screwed up his eyes and asked, "What do you know, sir, about the Order of the Hospital of Saint John of Jerusalem, later called the Knights of Rhodes and other things?"

Spade waved his cigar. "Not much—only what I remember from history in school—Crusaders or something."

"Very good. Now you don't remember that Suleiman the Magnificent chased them out of Rhodes in 1523?"

"No."

"Well, sir, he did, and they settled in Crete. And they stayed there for seven years, until 1530 when they persuaded the Emperor Charles V to give them Malta, Gozo, and Tripoli."

"Yes?"

"Yes, sir, but with these conditions: They were to pay the emperor each year the tribute of one"—he held up a finger—"falcon in acknowledgment that Malta was still under Spain, and if they ever left the island it was to revert to Spain. Understand?"

"Yes."

The fat man hunched his chair a few inches nearer Spade's and reduced his voice to a husky whisper. "Have you any conception of the extreme, the immeasurable wealth of the order at that time?"

"If I remember," Spade said, "they were pretty well fixed."

Gutman smiled indulgently. "Pretty well, sir, is putting it mildly." His whisper became lower and more purring. "They were rolling in wealth, sir. For years they had preyed on the Saracens, had taken nobody-knows-what spoils of gems, precious metals, silks, ivories—the cream of the cream of the East. That is history, sir. We all know that the Holy Wars to them, as to the Templars, were largely a matter of loot.

"Well, now, the Emperor Charles has given them Malta, and all the rent he asks is one insignificant bird per annum, just as a matter of form. What could be more natural than for these immeasurably wealthy knights to look around for some way of expressing their gratitude? Well, sir, that's exactly what they did, and they hit on the happy thought of sending Charles for the first year's tribute, not a live bird, but a glorious golden falcon encrusted from head to foot with the finest jewels in their coffers." Gutman stopped whispering and asked, "Well, sir, what do you think of that?"

"I don't know."

The fat man smiled complacently. "These are facts, historical facts, not schoolbook history, but history nevertheless." He leaned forward. "The archives of the order from the twelfth century on are still at Malta, with a clear and unmistakable statement of the facts I am telling you."

"All right," Spade said.

"All right, sir. Grand Master Villiers de l'Isle d'Adam had this foot-high jeweled bird made by Turkish slaves in the castle of St. Angelo and sent it to Charles, who was in Spain. He sent it in a galley commanded by a French knight, a member of the order." His voice dropped to a whisper again. "It never reached Spain. A famous admiral of buccaneers sailing out of Algiers took the knight's galley and he took the bird. The bird went to Algiers, and it was there for more than a hundred years, until it was carried away by Sir Francis Verney, the English adventurer who was with the Algerian buccaneers for a while.

"It's pretty certain that Sir Francis didn't have the bird when he died in a Messina hospital in 1615. He was stony broke. But the bird *did* go to Sicily. It was there and it came into the possession there of Victor Amadeus II sometime after he became king of Sicily in 1713, and it was one of his gifts to his wife when he married in Chambéry after abdicating.

"Maybe they—Amadeo and his wife—took it along with them to Turin when he tried to revoke his abdication. Be that as it may, it turned up next in the possession of a Spaniard who had been with the army that took Naples in 1734—the father of Don José Moñino y Redondo, Count of Floridablanca, who was Charles III's chief minister. There's nothing to show that it didn't stay in that family until at least the end of the Carlist War in 1840. Then it appeared in Paris at just about the time that Paris was full of Carlists who had had to get out of Spain. One of them must have brought it with him, but, whoever he was, it's likely he knew nothing about its real value. It had been—no doubt as a precaution during the Carlist trouble in Spain—painted or enameled over to look like nothing more than a fairly interesting black statuette. And in that disguise, sir, it was, you might say, kicked around for seventy years by private owners and dealers too stupid to see what it was under the skin."

The fat man paused to smile and shake his head regretfully. Then he went on: "For seventy years, sir, this marvelous item was, as you might say, a football in the gutters of Paris—until 1911 when a Greek dealer named Charilaos Konstantinides found it in an obscure shop. It didn't take Charilaos long to learn what it was and to acquire it. No thickness of enamel could conceal value from his eyes and nose. Well, sir, Charilaos was the man who traced most of its history and who identified it as what it actually was. I got wind of it and finally forced most of the history out of him, though I've been able to add a few details since.

"Charilaos was in no hurry to convert his find into money at once. He knew that—enormous as its intrinsic value was—a far higher, a terrific price could be obtained for it once its authenticity was established beyond doubt. Well, sir, to hold it safe while pursuing his researches into its history, Charilaos had re-enameled the bird, apparently just as it is now. One year to the very day after he had acquired it I picked up *The Times* in London and read that his establishment had been burglarized and him murdered. I was in Paris the next day." He shook his head sadly. "The bird was gone. By Gad, sir, I was wild. I didn't believe anybody else knew what it was. I didn't believe he had told anybody but me. A great quantity of stuff had been stolen. That made me think that the thief had simply taken the bird along with the rest of his plunder, not knowing what it was. Because I assure you that a thief who knew its value would not burden himself with anything else—no, sir—at least not anything less than crown jewels."

He shut his eyes and smiled complacently at an inner thought. He opened his eyes and said, "That was seventeen years ago. Well, sir, it took me seventeen years to locate that bird, but I did it. I wanted it, and I'm not a man that's easily discouraged when he wants something." His smile grew broad. "I wanted it and I found it. I want it and I'm going to have it." He drained his glass. "I traced it to the home of a Russian general—one Kemidov—in a Constantinople suburb. He didn't know a thing about it. It was nothing but a black enameled figure to him, but his natural contrariness kept him from selling it to me when I made him an offer. Perhaps in my eagerness I was a little unskillful, though not very. I don't know about that. But I did know I wanted it and I was afraid this stupid soldier might begin to investigate his property, might chip off some of the enamel. So I sent some—ah—agents to get it. Well, sir, they got it and I haven't got it." He stood up and carried his empty glass to the table. "But I'm going to get it. Your glass, sir."

"Then the bird doesn't belong to any of you," Spade asked, "but to a General Kemidov?"

"Belong?" the fat man said jovially. "Well, sir, you might say it belonged to the King of Spain, but I don't see how you can honestly grant anybody else clear title to it—except by right of possession. An article of that value that has passed from hand to hand by such means is clearly the property of whoever can get hold of it."

"Then it's Miss O'Shaughnessy's now?"

"No, sir, except as my agent."

Spade said, "Oh," ironically.

Gutman, looking thoughtfully at the stopper of the whiskey bottle in his hand, asked, "There's no doubt that she's got it?"

"Not much."

"Where?"

"I don't know exactly."

The fat man set the bottle on the table with a bang. "But you said you did," he protested.

Spade made a careless gesture with one hand. "I meant to say I know where to get it when the time comes."

Gutman's face arranged itself more happily. "When?"

"When I'm ready."

The fat man pursed his lips and, smiling with only slight uneasiness, asked, "Mr. Spade, where is Miss O'Shaughnessy now?"

"In my hands, safely tucked away."

Gutman smiled with approval. "Trust you for that, sir," he said. "Well now, sir, before we talk prices, answer me this: How soon can you—or will you—produce the falcon?"

"A couple of days."

The fat man nodded. "That is satisfactory. We— But I forget our nourishment." He turned to the table, poured whiskey, squirted charged water into it, set a glass at Spade's elbow, and held his own aloft. "Well, sir, here's to a fair bargain and profits large enough for both of us."

They drank. The fat man sat down. Spade asked, "What's your idea of a fair bargain?"

Gutman held his glass up to the light, looked affectionately at it, took another long drink, and said, "I have two proposals to make, sir. Take your choice. I will give you twenty-five thousand dollars when you deliver the falcon to me, and another twenty-five thousand as soon as I get to New York; or I will give you one quarter—twenty-five percent—of what I realize on the falcon. There you are, sir. An almost immediate fifty thousand dollars or a vastly greater sum within, say, a couple of months."

Spade drank and asked, "How much greater?"

"Vastly," the fat man repeated. "Who knows how much greater? Shall I say a hundred thousand, or a quarter of a million? Will you believe me if I name the sum that seems the probable minimum?"

"Why not?"

The fat man smacked his lips and lowered his voice to a purring murmur. "What would you say, sir, to half a million?"

Spade's yellow-gray eyes were faintly muddy. He said, "That's a hell of a lot of dough."

The fat man agreed. "That's a hell of a lot of dough." He leaned forward, patted Spade's knee, and said, "That is the absolute rock-bottom minimum—or Charilaos Konstantinides was a blithering idiot—and he wasn't."

Spade shut his eyes hard, opened them again. He said, "The—the minimum, huh? And the maximum?"

"The maximum?" Gutman held his empty hand out, palm up. "I refuse to guess. You'd think me crazy. I don't know. There's no telling how high it could go, sir, and that's the one and only truth about it."

Spade shook his head impatiently. A sharp frightened gleam awoke in his eyes—and was smothered by the deepening muddiness. He stood up, helping himself with his hands on the arms of his chair. He shook his head again and took an uncertain step forward. He laughed thickly and muttered, "Damn you."

Gutman jumped up and pushed his chair back.

Spade swung his head from side to side until his dull eyes were pointed at—if not focused on—the door. He took another step.

The fat man called sharply, "Wilmer!"

A door opened and the boy came in.

Spade took a third step. His face was gray now. His legs did not straighten again after his fourth step and his muddy eyes were almost covered by their lids. He took his fifth step.

The boy walked over and stood close to Spade, a little in front of him, but not directly between Spade and the door. The corners of his mouth twitched.

Spade essayed his sixth step.

The boy's leg darted out across Spade's leg, in front. Spade tripped over the interfering leg and crashed face down on the floor. The boy drew his right foot far back and kicked Spade's temple. The kick rolled Spade over on his side. Once more he tried to get up, could not, and went to sleep.

Chapter 6

SPADE, coming around the corner from the elevator at a few minutes past six in the morning, saw yellow light glowing through the frosted glass of his office door. He inserted the office key in the lock, clicked the door open, and went in.

Effie Perine sat sleeping with her head on her forearms, her forearms on her desk. She wore her coat and had one of Spade's overcoats wrapped cape-fashion around her.

Spade went over to the girl and put a hand on her shoulder.

She stirred, raised her head drowsily, and her eyelids fluttered. Suddenly she sat up straight, opening her eyes wide. She saw Spade, smiled, and rubbed her eyes with her fingers. "So you finally got back?" she said. "What time is it?"

"Six o'clock. What are you doing here?"

"You told me to stay till you got back or phoned."

"Oh, you're the sister of the boy who stood on the burning deck?"

She looked with dark excited eyes at his temple under the brim of his hat and exclaimed, "Oh, your head! What happened?"

His right temple was dark and swollen.

"I don't know whether I fell or was slugged. I don't think it amounts to much, but it hurts like hell." He barely touched it with his fingers, flinched, turned his grimace into a grim smile, and explained, "I went visiting, was fed knockout drops, and came to twelve hours later all spread out on a man's floor." He went to the washbowl in the corner of the office and ran cold water on a handkerchief.

"Did you find Miss O'Shaughnessy, Sam?"

"Not yet. Anything turn up after I left?"

"The district attorney's office phoned. He wants to see you."

"Bryan himself?"

"Yes, that's the way I understood it. And a boy came in with a message—that Mr. Gutman would be delighted to talk to you before five thirty."

"I got that," he said. "I met the boy downstairs, and talking to

Mr. Gutman got me this." He held the handkerchief to his temple.

"Is that the G. who phoned, Sam?"

"Yes."

"And what—"

Spade stared through the girl and spoke as if using speech to arrange his thoughts. "He wants something he thinks I can get. It was after I'd told him he'd have to wait a couple of days that he fed me the junk. It's not likely he thought I'd die. He'd know I'd be up and around in ten or twelve hours. So maybe the answer's that he figured he could get it without my help in that time if I was fixed so I couldn't butt in." He scowled. "I hope he was wrong." His stare became less distant. "You didn't get any word from the O'Shaughnessy?"

"No. Has this got anything to do with her?"

"Something."

"This thing he wants belongs to her?"

"Or to the King of Spain. Sweetheart, you've got an uncle who teaches history or something over at the university?"

"A cousin. Why?"

"If we brightened his life with an alleged historical secret four centuries old could we trust him to keep it dark awhile?"

"Oh, yes, Ted's good people."

"Fine. Get your pencil and book."

She got them and sat in her chair. Spade stood in front of her and dictated the story of the falcon as he had heard it from Gutman, from Charles V's grant to the Hospitallers up to—but no farther than—the enameled bird's arrival in Paris, repeating it with the accuracy of a trained interviewer.

When he had finished the girl shut her notebook and raised a smiling face to him. "Oh, isn't this thrilling?" she said. "It's—"

"Yes, or ridiculous. Now will you take it over and read it to your cousin and ask him what he thinks of it? And for God's sake make him keep it under his hat."

After a leisurely breakfast at the Palace, during which he read both morning papers, Spade went home, shaved, bathed, rubbed ice on his bruised temple, and put on fresh clothes.

He went to Brigid O'Shaughnessy's apartment at the Coronet. Nobody was in.

He went to the Alexandria Hotel. Gutman was not in. None of the other occupants of Gutman's suite were in. Spade learned that these other occupants were the fat man's secretary, Wilmer Cook, and his daughter Rhea, a brown-eyed fair-haired smallish girl of seventeen who the hotel staff said was beautiful. Spade was told that the Gutman party had arrived at the hotel, from New York, ten days before, and had not checked out.

Spade went to the Belvedere and found the hotel detective eating in the hotel café.

"Morning, Sam. Set down and bite an egg." The hotel detective stared at Spade's temple. "By God, somebody maced you plenty!"

"Thanks, I've had mine," Spade said as he sat down, and then, referring to his temple, "It looks worse than it is. How's my Cairo's conduct?"

"He went out not more than half an hour behind you yesterday and I ain't seen him since. He didn't sleep here again last night."

"How's chances of giving his room a casing while he's out?"

"Can do. You know I'm willing to go all the way with you all the time." Luke put his elbows on the table and screwed up his eyes at Spade. "Come on, we'll have that look-see."

They stopped at the desk long enough for Luke to "fix it so we'll get a ring if he comes in," and went up to Cairo's room. Cairo's bed was smooth and trim, but paper in wastebasket, unevenly drawn blinds, and a couple of rumpled towels in the bathroom showed that the chambermaid had not yet been in that morning.

Cairo's luggage consisted of a square trunk, a valise, and a Gladstone bag. Two suits and an overcoat hung in the closet over three pairs of carefully treed shoes.

The valise and bag were unlocked. Luke had the trunk unlocked by the time Spade had finished searching elsewhere.

"Blank so far," Spade said as they dug down into the trunk.

They found nothing interesting. Spade crossed the room and bent down over the wastebasket. "Well, this is our last shot."

He took a newspaper from the basket. His eyes brightened when he saw it was the previous day's *Call*. From the lower left-hand corner of the page that held shipping news a little more than two inches of the bottom of the second column had been torn out.

Immediately above the tear was a small caption ARRIVED TODAY followed by:

> 12:20 A.M.—*Capac* from Astoria.
> 5:05 A.M.—*Helen P. Drew* from Greenwood.
> 5:06 A.M.—*Albarado* from Bandon.

The tear passed through the next line, leaving only enough of its letters to make "from Sydney" inferable.

Spade put the *Call* down on the desk and looked into the waste-basket again. In the bottom of the basket he found a piece of newspaper rolled into a tiny ball.

He opened the ball carefully, smoothed it out on the desk, and fitted it into the torn part of the *Call*. The fit at the sides was exact, but between the top of the crumpled fragment and the inferable "from Sydney" half an inch was missing, sufficient space to have held announcement of six or seven boats' arrival.

Luke, leaning over his shoulder, asked, "What's this all about?"

"Looks like the gent's interested in a boat."

"Well, there's no law against that, or is there?" Luke said while Spade was folding the torn page and the crumpled fragment together and putting them into his coat pocket. "You all through here now?"

"Yes. Thanks a lot, Luke. Will you give me a ring as soon as he comes in?"

"Sure."

SPADE went to the business office of the *Call*, bought a copy of the previous day's issue, opened it to the shipping-news page, and compared it with the page taken from Cairo's wastebasket. The missing portion had read:

> 5:17 A.M.—*Tahiti* from Sydney and Papeete.
> 6:05 A.M.—*Admiral Peoples* from Astoria.
> 8:07 A.M.—*Caddopeak* from San Pedro.

8:17 A.M.—*Silverado* from San Pedro.
8:05 A.M.—*La Paloma* from Hong Kong.
9:03 A.M.—*Daisy Gray* from Seattle.

He read the list slowly and when he had finished he underscored Hong Kong with a fingernail and returned to his office.

He sat down at his desk, looked up a number in the telephone book, and used the telephone. "Kearny 1401, please. . . . Where is the *Paloma*, in from Hong Kong yesterday morning, docked?" He repeated the question. "Thanks."

He held the receiver hook down with his thumb for a moment, released it, and said, "Davenport 2020, please. . . . Detective bureau, please. . . . Is Sergeant Polhaus there? . . . Thanks. . . . Hello, Tom, this is Sam Spade. . . . Yes, I tried to get you yesterday afternoon. . . . Sure, suppose you go to lunch with me. . . . Right."

He kept the receiver to his ear while his thumb worked the hook again. "Davenport 0170, please. . . . Hello, this is Samuel Spade. My secretary got a phone message yesterday that Mr. Bryan wanted to see me. Will you ask him what time's the most convenient for him? . . . Yes, Spade, S-p-a-d-e." A long pause. "Two thirty? All right. Thanks."

EFFIE PERINE came in smiling, bright-eyed and rosy-faced. "Ted says it could be," she reported, "and he hopes it is. He's all excited over it."

"That's swell, as long as he doesn't get too enthusiastic to see through it if it's phony."

"Oh, he wouldn't—not Ted! He's too good at his stuff for that."

"Uh-huh, the whole damned Perine family's wonderful," Spade said, "including you and the smudge of soot on your nose."

She made a face at him while patting her nose with a powdered pink disc. "There was a boat on fire when I came back. They were towing it out from the pier and the smoke blew all over our ferryboat."

Spade put his hands on the arms of his chair. "Were you near enough to see the name of the boat?" he asked.

"Yes. *La Paloma.* Why?"

Spade smiled ruefully. "I'm damned if I know why, sister," he said.

Spade and Detective-sergeant Polhaus ate pickled pigs' feet at one of Big John's tables at the States Hof Brau.

Polhaus, balancing pale jelly on a fork halfway between plate and mouth, said, "Hey, listen, Sam! Forget about the other night. Dundy was dead wrong, but you know anybody's liable to lose their head if you ride them thataway. Ain't you ever going to grow up? What've you got to beef about? He didn't hurt you. You came out on top. What's the sense of making a grudge of it? You're just making a lot of grief for yourself."

Spade placed his knife and fork carefully together on his plate. His smile was faint and devoid of warmth. "With every bull in town working overtime trying to pile up grief for me, a little more won't hurt. I won't even know it's there."

Polhaus's ruddiness deepened. He said, "That's a swell thing to say to me."

They began to eat. Presently Spade asked, "See the boat on fire in the bay?"

"I saw the smoke. Be reasonable, Sam. Dundy was wrong and he knows it. Why don't you let it go at that?"

Spade said, "Phil Archer been in with any more hot tips?"

"Aw, hell! Dundy didn't think you shot Miles, but what else could he do except run the lead down? You'd've done the same thing in his place, and you know it."

"Yes?" Malice glittered in Spade's eyes. "What made him think I didn't do it? What makes you think I didn't? Or don't you?"

"Thursby shot Miles," Polhaus said.

"You think he did?"

"He did. That Webley was his, and the slug in Miles came out of it."

Spade nodded and said, "Then that leaves Thursby the only one I killed."

Polhaus squirmed in his chair. "Ain't you never going to forget that?" he complained earnestly. "That's out. You know it as well as I do."

Spade said, "All right. You know it's out and I know it's out. What does Dundy know?"

"He knows it's out."

"What woke him up?"

"Aw, Sam, he never really thought you'd—" Spade's smile checked Polhaus. He left the sentence incomplete and said, "We dug up a record on Thursby."

"Yes? Who was he?"

"Well, he was a St. Louis gunman the first we hear of him. He was picked up a lot of times back there for this and that, but he belonged to the Egan mob, so nothing much was ever done about any of it. A couple of years later he did a short hitch in Joliet for pistol-whipping a twist that had given him the needle, but after that he took up with Dixie Monahan and didn't have any trouble getting out whenever he happened to get in. This Thursby was Dixie's bodyguard and he took the runout with him when Dixie got in wrong with the rest of the boys over some debts he couldn't or wouldn't pay off. That was a couple of years back, and this is the first time Thursby's been seen since."

Spade asked, "Where'd you pick up all this news about Thursby?"

"Some of it's on the records. The rest—well—we got it here and there."

"From Cairo, for instance?"

Polhaus said, "Not a word of it. You poisoned that guy for us."

Spade laughed and looked at his watch. "I've got a date with the D.A. this afternoon."

"He send for you?"

"Yes."

Polhaus stood up. "You won't be doing me any favor," he said, "by telling him I've talked to you like this."

A LATHY youth ushered Spade into the district attorney's office. Spade went in smiling easily, saying easily, "Hello, Bryan!"

District Attorney Bryan stood up and held his hand out across his desk. He was a blond man of medium stature, perhaps forty-five years old, with aggressive blue eyes behind black-ribboned nose glasses, the overlarge mouth of an orator, and a wide dimpled chin. When he said, "How do you do, Spade?" his voice was resonant with latent power.

They shook hands and sat down.

The district attorney put his finger on one of the pearl buttons in a battery of four on his desk, said to the lathy youth who opened the door again, "Ask Mr. Thomas and Healy to come in," and then, rocking back in his chair, addressed Spade pleasantly. "You and the police haven't been hitting it off so well, have you?"

Spade made a negligent gesture with the fingers of his right hand. "Nothing serious," he said. "Dundy gets too enthusiastic."

The door opened to admit two men. The one to whom Spade said, "Hello, Thomas!" was the assistant district attorney, a sunburned stocky man of thirty in clothing and hair of a kindred unruliness.

He clapped Spade on the shoulder with a freckled hand, asked, "How's tricks?" and sat down beside him. The second man was younger and colorless. He took a seat a little apart from the others and balanced a stenographer's notebook on his knee, holding a green pencil over it.

Spade glanced his way, chuckled, and asked Bryan, "Anything I say will be used against me?"

Bryan smiled. "That always holds good." He took his glasses off, looked at them, and set them on his nose again. He looked through them at Spade and asked, "Who killed Thursby?"

Spade said, "I don't know."

Bryan rubbed his black eyeglass ribbon between thumb and fingers and said knowingly, "Perhaps you don't, but you certainly could make an excellent guess."

"Maybe, but I wouldn't."

The district attorney raised his eyebrows. "Why shouldn't you, if you've nothing to conceal?"

"Everybody," Spade said mildly, "has something to conceal."

"And you have—"

"My guesses, for one thing."

The district attorney looked down at his desk and then up at Spade. "I wish you wouldn't regard this as a formal inquiry at all. And please don't think I've any belief—much less confidence—in those theories the police seem to have formed."

Spade sighed and crossed his legs. "I'm glad of that." He felt in his pockets for tobacco and papers. "What's your theory?"

Bryan leaned forward in his chair and his eyes were hard and shiny as the lenses over them. "Tell me who Archer was shadowing Thursby for and I'll tell you who killed Thursby."

Spade's laugh was brief and scornful. "You're as wrong as Dundy," he said.

"Don't misunderstand me, Spade," Bryan said, knocking on the desk with his knuckles. "I don't say your client killed Thursby or had him killed, but I do say that, knowing who your client is, or was, I'll mighty soon know who killed Thursby."

Spade lighted his cigarette, removed it from his lips, emptied his lungs of smoke, and spoke as if puzzled. "I don't get that."

"You don't? Then suppose I put it this way: Where is Dixie Monahan?"

Spade's face retained its puzzled look. "Putting it that way doesn't help much," he said. "I still don't get it."

The district attorney took his glasses off and shook them for emphasis. He said, "We know Thursby was Monahan's bodyguard and went with him when Monahan found it wise to vanish from Chicago. We know Monahan welshed on something like two-hundred-thousand-dollars' worth of bets when he vanished. We don't know—not yet—who his creditors were." He put the glasses on again and smiled grimly. "But we all know what's likely to happen to a gambler who welshes, and to his bodyguard, when his creditors find him. It's happened before."

Spade ran his tongue over his lips and pulled his lips back over his teeth in an ugly grin. His voice was low and hoarse and passionate. "Well, what do you think? Did I kill him for his creditors? Or just find him and let them do their own killing?"

"No, no!" Bryan protested. "You misunderstand me."

"I hope I do," Spade said.

Bryan waved a hand. "I only mean that you might have been involved in it without knowing what it was. That could—"

"I see," Spade sneered. "You don't think I'm naughty. You just think I'm dumb."

"Nonsense." Bryan insisted, "Suppose someone came to you and engaged you to find Monahan, telling you they had reasons for thinking he was in the city. The someone might give you a completely false story. How could you tell what was behind it? How would you know it wasn't an ordinary piece of detective work? And under those circumstances you certainly couldn't be held responsible for your part in it unless"—his voice sank to a more impressive key and his words came out spaced and distinct—"you made yourself an accomplice by concealing your knowledge of the murderer's identity or information that would lead to his apprehension."

Anger was leaving Spade's face. No anger remained in his voice when he asked, "That's what you meant?"

"Precisely."

"All right. Then there's no hard feelings. But you're wrong. Nobody ever hired me to do anything about Dixie Monahan."

Bryan and Thomas exchanged glances. Bryan's eyes came back to Spade and he said, "But, by your own admission, somebody did hire you to do something about his bodyguard Thursby."

"Yes, about his ex-bodyguard Thursby."

"Ex?"

"Yes, ex."

"You know that Thursby was no longer associated with Monahan? You know that positively?"

Spade stretched out his hand and dropped the stub of his cigarette into an ashtray on the desk. He spoke carelessly. "I don't know anything positively except that my client wasn't interested in Monahan, had never been interested in Monahan. I heard that Thursby took Monahan out to the Orient and lost him."

Again the district attorney and his assistant exchanged glances.

"That opens up three new lines," Bryan said. He leaned back and stared at the ceiling for several seconds, then sat upright quickly. His orator's face was alight. "Number one: Thursby was killed by the gamblers Monahan had welshed on in Chicago. Number two: he was killed by friends of Monahan for ditching Monahan. Or number three: he sold Monahan out to his enemies and then fell out with them and they killed him."

Bryan smacked the back of his left hand down into the palm of his right. "In one of those three categories lies the solution. And you can give us the information that will enable us to determine the category."

Spade said, "Yes?" very lazily. "You wouldn't want the kind of information I could give you, Bryan. You couldn't use it."

Bryan sat up straight and squared his shoulders. His voice was stern without blustering. "You are not the judge of that. Right or wrong, I am nonetheless the district attorney."

Spade's lifted lip showed his eyetooth. "I thought this was an informal talk."

"I am a sworn officer of the law twenty-four hours a day," Bryan said, "and neither formality nor informality justifies your withholding from me evidence of crime, except of course"—he nodded meaningly—"on certain constitutional grounds."

"You mean if it might incriminate me?" Spade asked. His voice was placid, almost amused, but his face was not. "Well, I've got better grounds than that, or grounds that suit me better. My clients are entitled to a decent amount of secrecy. Maybe I can be made to talk to a grand jury or even a coroner's jury, but I haven't been called before either yet, and it's a cinch I'm not going to advertise my clients' business until I have to. Then again, you and the police have both accused me of being mixed up in the other night's murders. As far as I can see, my best chance of clearing myself of the trouble you're trying to make for me is by bringing in the murderers—all tied up. And my only chance of ever catching them and tying them up and bringing them in is by keeping away from you and the police, because neither of you shows any signs of knowing what in hell it's all about. Now if you want to go to the board and tell them I'm obstructing justice and ask them to revoke

97

my license, hop to it. You've tried it before and it didn't get you anything but a good laugh all around." He picked up his hat.

Bryan began, "But look here—"

Spade said, "And I don't want any more of these informal talks. I've got nothing to tell you or the police and I'm tired of being called things by every crackpot on the city payroll. If you want to see me, pinch me or subpoena me or something and I'll come down with my lawyer." He put his hat on his head, said, "See you at the inquest, maybe," and stalked out.

Chapter 7

SPADE went into the Hotel Sutter and telephoned the Alexandria. Gutman was not in. No member of Gutman's party was in. Spade telephoned the Belvedere. Cairo was not in, had not been in that day.

Spade went to his office.

Effie Perine's sunburned face was worried and questioning. "You haven't found her yet?" she asked.

He shook his head and went on stroking his bruised temple lightly in circles with his fingertips.

"You've got to find her, Sam. It's more than a day and she—"

He stirred and impatiently interrupted her, "I haven't got to do anything, but if you'll let me rest this damned head a minute or two I'll go out and find her."

She murmured, "Poor head," went around behind him, and stroked his temple in silence awhile. Then she asked, "You know where she is? Have you any idea?"

"I know where she went," he replied in a grudging tone.

"Where?" She was excited.

"Down to the boat you saw burning."

Her eyes opened until their brown was surrounded by white. "You went down there." It was not a question.

"I did not," Spade said.

"Sam," she cried angrily, "she may be—"

"She went down there," he said in a surly voice. "She wasn't taken. She went down there instead of to your house when she learned the boat was in. Well, what the hell?"

She glared at him between tightened lids. "Sam Spade," she said, "you're the most contemptible man God ever made when you want to be. Because she did something without confiding in you you'd sit here and do nothing when you know she's in danger, when you know she might be—"

Spade's face flushed. He said stubbornly, "She's pretty capable of taking care of herself and she knows where to come for help when she thinks she needs it, and when it suits her."

"That's spite," the girl cried, "and that's all it is! You're sore because she did something on her own hook, without telling you. Why shouldn't she? You haven't been so much on the level with her that she should trust you completely."

Spade said, "That's enough of that."

His tone brought a brief uneasy glint into her eyes, but she tossed her head and the glint vanished. She said, "If you don't go down there this very minute, Sam, I will and I'll take the police down there." Her voice trembled, broke, and was thin and wailing. "Oh, Sam, go!"

He stood up cursing her. Then he said, "Well, it'll be easier on my head than sitting here listening to you squawk." He looked at his watch. "You might as well lock up and go home."

She said, "I won't. I'm going to wait right here till you come back."

He said, "Do as you damned please," put his hat on, flinched, took it off, and went out carrying it in his hand.

An hour and a half later, at twenty minutes past five, Spade returned. He was cheerful. He came in asking, "What makes you so hard to get along with, sweetheart?"

"Me?"

"Yes, you." He put a finger on the tip of Effie Perine's nose and flattened it. "Anything doing while I was gone?"

"Luke—what's his name?—at the Belvedere called up to tell you Cairo has returned. That was about half an hour ago."

Spade snapped his mouth shut, turned with a long step, and started for the door.

"Did you find her?" the girl called.

"Tell you about it when I'm back," he replied without pausing and hurried out.

A TAXICAB brought Spade to the Belvedere within ten minutes of his departure from his office. He found Luke in the lobby. The hotel detective came grinning and shaking his head to meet Spade. "Fifteen minutes late," he said. "Your bird has fluttered."

Spade cursed his luck.

"Checked out—gone bag and baggage," Luke said. He took a battered memorandum book from a vest pocket, licked his thumb, thumbed pages, and held the book out open to Spade. "There's the number of the taxi that hauled him. I got that much for you."

"Thanks." Spade copied the number on the back of an envelope. "Any forwarding address?"

"No. He just come in carrying a big suitcase and went upstairs and packed and come down with his stuff and paid his bill and got a taxi and went without anybody being able to hear what he told the driver."

WHEN Spade got back to his office Effie Perine looked up at him inquisitively.

"Missed him," Spade grumbled and passed into his private room. She followed him in.

He sat in his chair and began to roll a cigarette. She sat on the desk in front of him and put her toes on a corner of his chair seat.

"What about Miss O'Shaughnessy?" she demanded.

"I missed her too," he replied, "but she had been there."

"On the *Paloma?*"

He set fire to his cigarette, pocketed his lighter, patted her shins, and said, "Yes, the *Paloma*. She got down there at a little after noon yesterday." He pulled his brows down. "That means she went straight there after leaving the cab at the Ferry Building. It's only a few piers away. The captain wasn't aboard. His name's

Jacobi and she asked for him by name. He was uptown on business. That would mean he didn't expect her, or not at that time anyway. She waited there till he came back at four o'clock. They spent the time from then till mealtime in his cabin and she ate with him."

He inhaled and exhaled smoke, turned his head aside to spit a yellow tobacco flake off his lip, and went on. "After the meal Captain Jacobi had three more visitors. One of them was Gutman and one was Cairo and one was the kid who delivered Gutman's message to you yesterday. Those three came together while Brigid was there and the five of them did a lot of talking in the captain's cabin. It's hard to get anything out of the crew, but there was a big row somewhere around eleven o'clock last night and the watchman beat it down there; but the captain met him outside and told him everything was all right."

He scowled and inhaled smoke again. "Well, they left around midnight—the captain and his four visitors all together. I got that from the watchman. The captain hasn't been back since. He didn't keep a date he had this noon with some shipping agents, and they haven't found him to tell him about the fire."

"And the fire?" she asked.

"I don't know. It was discovered in the hold late this morning. The chances are it got started sometime yesterday. They got it out all right, though it did damage enough. Nobody liked to talk about it much while the captain's away. It's the—"

The corridor door opened. Spade shut his mouth. Effie Perine jumped down from the desk, but a man opened the connecting door before she could reach it.

"Where's Spade?" the man asked.

His voice brought Spade up erect and alert in his chair. It was a voice harsh and rasping with agony and with the strain of keeping two words from being smothered by the liquid bubbling that ran under and behind them.

Effie Perine, frightened, stepped out of the man's way.

He stood in the doorway with his soft hat crushed between his head and the top of the doorframe: he was nearly seven feet tall.

A black overcoat cut long and straight and like a sheath, buttoned from throat to knees, exaggerated his leanness. His bony face—weather-coarsened, age-lined—was the color of wet sand and was wet with sweat on cheeks and chin. His eyes were dark and bloodshot and mad. Held tight against the left side of his chest by a black-sleeved arm that ended in a yellowish claw was a brown paper-wrapped parcel bound with thin rope—an ellipsoid somewhat larger than an American football.

The tall man stood in the doorway and there was nothing to show that he saw Spade. He said, "You know—" and then the liquid bubbling came up in his throat and submerged whatever else he said. Holding himself stiffly straight, not putting his hands out to break his fall, he fell forward as a tree falls.

Spade, wooden-faced and nimble, sprang from his chair and caught the falling man. When Spade caught him the man's mouth opened and a little blood spurted out, and the brown-wrapped parcel dropped from the man's hands and rolled across the floor until a foot of the desk stopped it. Spade lowered the man carefully until he lay on the floor on his left side. The man's eyes—dark and bloodshot, but not now mad—were wide open and still. His mouth was open as when blood had spurted from it, but no more blood came from it, and all his long body was as still as the floor it lay on.

Spade said, "Lock the door."

While Effie Perine, her teeth chattering, fumbled with the corridor door's lock Spade knelt beside the thin man, turned him over on his back, and ran a hand down inside his overcoat. When he withdrew the hand presently it came out smeared with blood. He took his lighter out of his pocket with his other hand, snapped on the flame, and held the flame close to first one and then the other of the thin man's eyes. The eyes—lids, balls, irises, and pupils—remained frozen, immobile. Spade rose and went to the washbowl in the outer office.

Effie Perine, wan and trembling and holding herself upright by means of a hand on the corridor door's knob and her back against its glass, whispered, "Is—is he—"

"Yes. Shot through the chest, maybe half a dozen times." Spade began to wash his hands.

"Oughtn't we—" she began, but he cut her short.

"It's too late for a doctor now and I've got to think before we do anything." He finished washing his hands and began to rinse the bowl. "He couldn't have come far with those in him. If he— Why in hell couldn't he have stood up long enough to say something?" He frowned at the girl and ran fingers through his hair. "We'll have a look at that bundle."

He went into the inner office again, stepped over the dead man's legs, and picked up the brown paper-wrapped parcel. He put it on his desk, turning it over so that the knotted part of the rope was uppermost. The knot was hard and tight. He took out his pocket-knife and cut the rope.

Spade's big fingers were busy with the inner husk of coarse gray paper, three sheets thick, that the brown paper's removal had revealed. His eyes were shining. When he had put the gray paper out of the way he had an egg-shaped mass of pale excelsior, wadded tight. His fingers tore the wad apart and then he had the foot-high figure of a bird, black as coal and shiny where its polish was not dulled by wood dust and fragments of excelsior.

Spade laughed. He put an arm around Effie Perine and crushed her body against his. "We've got the damned thing, angel," he said.

"Ouch!" she said, "you're hurting me."

The telephone bell rang.

He nodded at the girl. She turned to the desk and put the receiver to her ear. She said, "Hello. . . . Yes. . . . Who? . . . Oh, yes!" Her eyes became large. "Yes. . . . Yes. . . . Hold the line. . . ." Her mouth suddenly stretched wide and fearful. She cried, "Hello! Hello! Hello!" She rattled the prong up and down and cried, "Hello!" twice. Then she sobbed and spun around to face Spade, who was close beside her by now. "It was Miss O'Shaughnessy," she said wildly. "She wants you. She's at the Alexandria—in danger. Her voice was—oh, it was awful, Sam!—and something happened to her before she could finish. Go help her, Sam!"

Spade put the falcon down on the desk and scowled gloomily.

"I've got to take care of this fellow first," he said, pointing his thumb at the thin corpse on the floor.

She beat his chest with her fists, crying, "No, no—you've got to go to her. Don't you see, Sam? He had the thing that was hers and he came to you with it. Don't you see? He was helping her and they killed him and now she's— Oh, you've got to go!"

"All right." Spade pushed her away and bent over his desk, putting the black bird back into its nest of excelsior, bending the paper around it, working rapidly, making a larger and clumsy package. "As soon as I've gone phone the police. Tell them how it happened, but don't drag any names in. I got a phone call and I told you I had to go out, but I didn't say where. Tell it as it happened, but forget he had a bundle. And you don't know anything about this fellow and you can't talk about my business until you see me. Got it?"

"Yes, Sam. Who—do you know who he is?"

He grinned wolfishly. "Uh-uh," he said, "but I'd guess he was Captain Jacobi, master of *La Paloma.*" He picked up his hat and put it on. He looked thoughtfully at the dead man and then around the room.

"Hurry, Sam," the girl begged.

"Sure," he said, "I'll hurry. I'd keep the door locked till they come." He rubbed her cheek. "You're a damned good man, sister," he said and went out.

CARRYING the parcel lightly under his arm, Spade walked briskly from his office building to Kearny and Post streets, where he hailed a passing taxicab.

The taxicab carried him to the Pickwick bus terminal in Fifth Street. He checked the bird at the parcel room there, put the check into a stamped envelope, wrote "M. F. Holland" and a San Francisco post-office box number on the envelope, sealed it, and dropped it into a mailbox. From the bus terminal another taxicab carried him to the Alexandria Hotel.

Spade went up to suite 12 C and knocked on the door. The door was opened, when he had knocked a second time, by a small fair-haired girl in a shimmering yellow dressing gown—a small girl who clung desperately to the inner doorknob with both hands and gasped, "Mr. Spade?"

Spade said, "Yes," and caught her as she swayed.

Her body arched back over his arm and her head dropped straight back. Spade slid his supporting arm higher up her back and made her walk. He kicked the door shut, and he walked her up and down the green-carpeted room from wall to wall. They walked across and across the floor, the girl falteringly, with incoordinate steps, Spade surely on the balls of his feet with balance unaffected by her staggering.

He talked to her monotonously. "That's the stuff. Left, right, left, right. That's the stuff. One, two, three, four, one, two, three, now we turn." He shook her as they turned from the wall. "Now back again. One, two, three, four. Hold your head up." He shook her again. "That's the girl. Walk, walk, walk, walk." He shook her, more roughly, and increased their pace. "That's the trick. Left, right, left, right. . . ."

She shuddered and swallowed audibly. Spade began to chafe her arm and side and he put his mouth nearer her ear. "That's fine. You're doing fine. That's it. Step, step, step, step. Now we turn. Left, right, left, right. What'd they do—dope you?"

Her eyelids twitched up then for an instant over dulled golden-brown eyes and she managed to say all of "Yes" except the final consonant.

"That's fine," he said. "Keep them open. Open them wide—wide!" He shook her. "Keep walking," he ordered in a harsh voice, and then, "Who are you?"

Her "Rhea Gutman" was thick but intelligible.

"The daughter?"

"Yes." Now she was no farther from the final consonant than *sh*.

"Where's Brigid?"

She twisted convulsively around in his arms and caught at one of his hands with both of hers. He pulled his hand away quickly and looked at it. Across its back was a thin red scratch an inch and a half or more in length.

"What the hell?" he growled and examined her hands. Her left hand was empty. In her right hand, when he forced it open, lay a three-inch jade-headed steel bouquet pin. "What the hell?" he growled again and held the pin up in front of her eyes.

When she saw the pin she whimpered and opened her gown and showed him her body below her left breast—white flesh criss-crossed with red lines, dotted with tiny red dots, where the pin had scratched and punctured it. "To stay awake . . . walk . . . till you came. . . . She said you'd come . . . were so long." She swayed.

Brigid?" he demanded.

"Yes . . . took her . . . Bur-Burlingame . . . twenty-six Ancho . . . hurry . . . too late . . ." Her head fell over on her shoulder.

Spade pushed her head up. "Who took her there? Your father?"

"Yes . . . Wilmer . . . Cairo." She writhed and her eyelids twitched but did not open. ". . . kill her." Her head fell over again, and again he pushed it up.

He shook her brutally. "Stay awake till the doctor comes."

Fear opened her eyes and pushed for a moment the cloudiness from her face. "No, no," she cried thickly, "Father . . . kill me . . . swear you won't . . . he'd know . . . I did . . . for her . . . promise . . . won't . . . sleep . . . all right . . . morning . . ."

He shook her again. "You're sure you can sleep the stuff off all right?"

"Ye'." Her head fell down again.

"Where's your bed?"

She tried to raise a hand, but the effort had become too much for her. With the sigh of a tired child she let her whole body relax and crumple.

Spade caught her up in his arms and carried her into a bedroom. He turned back the bedclothes and laid the girl on the bed, fixed a pillow under her head, and put the covers up over her.

Then he opened the room's two windows and stood with his back to them staring at the sleeping girl. He stood there in the weakening light for perhaps five minutes. Finally he shook his thick sloping shoulders impatiently and went out, leaving the suite's outer door unlocked.

SPADE WENT TO A PHONE booth in Powell Street and called Davenport 2020. "Emergency Hospital, please. . . . Hello, there's a girl in suite twelve C at the Alexandria Hotel who has been drugged. . . . Yes, you'd better send somebody to take a look at her. . . . This is Mr. Hooper of the Alexandria."

He put the receiver on its prong and laughed. He called another number and said, "Hello, Frank. This is Sam Spade. . . . Can you let me have a car with a driver who'll keep his mouth shut? . . . To go down the peninsula right away. . . . Just a couple of hours. . . . Right. Have him pick me up at Joe's, Ellis Street, as soon as he can make it."

He went to Joe's Grill, asked the waiter to hurry his order of chops, baked potato, and sliced tomatoes, ate hurriedly, and was smoking a cigarette with his coffee when a thickset youngish man with a plaid cap set askew above pale eyes and a tough cheery face came into the grill and to his table.

"All set, Mr. Spade. She's full of gas and raring to go."

"Swell." Spade emptied his cup and went out with the driver. "Know where Ancho Avenue, or Road, is in Burlingame?"

"Nope, but if she's there we can find her."

"Let's do that," Spade said as he sat beside the chauffeur in the dark Cadillac sedan. "Twenty-six is the number we want, and the sooner the better, but we don't want to pull up at the front door."

"Correct."

AT A drugstore in Burlingame the chauffeur learned how to reach Ancho Avenue. Ten minutes later he stopped the sedan near a dark corner, turned off the lights, and waved his hand at the block ahead. "There she is," he said. "She ought to be on the other side, maybe the third or fourth house."

Spade said, "Right," and got out of the car. "Keep the engine going. We may have to leave in a hurry."

He crossed the street and went up the other side. In front of the second house from the corner Spade halted. On one of the gateposts that were massive out of all proportion to the fence flanking them a 2 and a 6 of pale metal caught what light there was. A square white card was nailed above them. Putting his face close to the card, Spade could see that it was a FOR SALE OR RENT sign. There was no gate between the posts.

Spade went up the cement walk to the door and listened. He could hear nothing. He tiptoed to a window and then to another. They were uncurtained except by inner darkness. He tried both windows. They were locked. He tried the door. It was locked.

Spade went back to the gatepost and, cupping the flame between his hands, held his lighter up to the FOR SALE OR RENT sign. It bore the printed name and address of a San Mateo real estate dealer and a line penciled in blue: *Key at 31.*

Number 31 was a square gray house across the street from, but a little farther up than 26. Lights glowed in its downstairs windows. Spade went up on the porch and rang the bell. A dark-haired girl of fourteen or fifteen opened the door. Spade, bowing and smiling, said, "I'd like to get the key to number twenty-six."

"I'll call Papa," she said and went back into the house calling, "Papa!"

A plump red-faced man, bald-headed and heavily mustached, appeared, carrying a newspaper.

Spade said, "I'd like to get the key to twenty-six."

The plump man looked doubtful. Spade showed him one of his business cards, put it back in his pocket, and said in a low voice, "We got a tip that there might be something hidden there."

The plump man's face and voice were eager. "Wait a minute," he said. "I'll go over with you."

A moment later he came back carrying a brass key attached to a black and red tag. Spade beckoned to the chauffeur as they passed the car and the chauffeur joined them. The plump man marched ahead with the key until they had gone up on the porch. Then he thrust the key into Spade's hand, mumbled, "Here you are," and stepped aside.

Spade unlocked the door and pushed it open. There was silence and darkness. Spade entered. The chauffeur came close behind him and then, at a little distance, the plump man followed them.

They searched the house from bottom to top, cautiously at first, then, finding nothing, boldly. The house was empty—unmistakably—and there was nothing to indicate that it had been visited in weeks.

SAYING, "Thanks, that's all," Spade left the sedan in front of the Alexandria. He went in to the desk, where a tall young man with a dark grave face said, "Good evening, Mr. Spade."

"Good evening." Spade drew the young man to one end of the desk. "These Gutmans—up in twelve C—are they in?"

The young man replied, "No," darting a quick glance at Spade. Then he looked away, hesitated, looked at Spade again, and murmured, "A funny thing happened in connection with them this evening, Mr. Spade. Somebody called the Emergency Hospital and told them there was a sick girl up there."

"And there wasn't?"

"Oh, no, there was nobody up there. They went out earlier in the evening."

Spade said, "Well, these practical jokers have to have their fun. Thanks."

He went to a telephone booth, called a number, and said, "Hello, Mrs. Perine? . . . Is Effie there? . . . Yes, please. . . . Hello, angel! What's the good word? . . . Fine, fine! Hold it. I'll be out in twenty minutes. . . . Right."

HALF an hour later Spade rang the doorbell of a two-story brick building in Ninth Avenue. Effie Perine opened the door. Her boyish face was tired and smiling. "Hello, boss," she said. "Enter." She said in a low voice, "If Ma says anything to you, Sam, be nice to her. She's all up in the air."

Spade grinned reassuringly and patted her shoulder.

She put her hands on his arm. "Miss O'Shaughnessy?"

"No," he growled. "I ran into a plant. Are you sure it was her voice?"

"Yes."

He made an unpleasant face. "Well, it was hooey."

She took him into a bright living room, sighed, and slumped down on one end of a sofa, smiling cheerfully up at him through her weariness.

He sat beside her and asked, "Everything went okay? Nothing said about the bundle?"

"Nothing. I told them what you told me to tell them, and they seemed to take it for granted that the phone call had something to do with it, and that you were out running it down."

"They took you down to the Hall?"

"Oh, yes, and they asked me loads of questions, but it was all— you know—routine."

He moved his shoulders. "Anybody you know, outside of the police, come around?"

"Yes." She sat up straight. "That boy—the one who brought the message from Gutman—was there. He didn't come in, but the police left the corridor door open while they were there and I saw him standing there. The next time I looked he was gone."

Spade grinned at her. "Damned lucky for you, sister, that the coppers got there first."

"Why?"

"He's a bad egg, that lad—poison. Was the dead man Jacobi?"

"Yes."

He pressed her hands and stood up. "I'm going to run along. You'd better hit the hay. You're all in. I want to sneak out before your mother catches me and gives me hell for dragging her lamb through gutters."

Chapter 8

Midnight was a few minutes away when Spade reached his home. He put his key into the street-door lock. Heels clicked rapidly on the sidewalk behind him. He let go the key and wheeled. Brigid O'Shaughnessy ran up the steps to him. She put her arms around him and hung on him, panting. "Oh, I thought you'd never come!" Her face was haggard, distraught, shaken by the tremors that shook her from head to foot.

With the hand not supporting her he felt for the key again, opened the door, and half lifted her inside. "You've been waiting?" he asked.

"Yes." Panting spaced her words. "In a—doorway—up the—street." They rode up to Spade's floor in the elevator and went around to his apartment. They went in. He shut the door and, with his arm around her again, took her back towards the living room. When they were within a step of the door the light in the living room went on. The girl cried out and clung to Spade.

Just inside the living-room door fat Gutman stood smiling benevolently at them. The boy Wilmer came out of the kitchen behind them. Black pistols were gigantic in his small hands. Cairo came from the bathroom. He too had a pistol.

Gutman said, "Well, sir, we're all here, as you can see for yourself. Now let's come in and sit down and be comfortable and talk."

Spade, with his arms around Brigid O'Shaughnessy, smiled meagerly over her head and said, "Sure, we'll talk."

Gutman stepped back from the door. Spade and the girl went in together. The boy and Cairo followed them in. Cairo stopped in the doorway. The boy put away one of his pistols and came up close behind Spade.

Spade turned his head far around to look down over his shoulder at the boy and said, "Get away. You're not going to frisk me."

The boy said, "Stand still. Shut up."

Spade's voice was level. "Get away. Put your paw on me and I'm going to make you use the gun. Ask your boss if he wants me shot up before we talk."

"Never mind, Wilmer," the fat man said. He frowned indulgently at Spade. "You are certainly a most headstrong individual. Well, let's be seated."

Spade said, "I told you I didn't like that punk," and took Brigid O'Shaughnessy to the sofa by the windows.

Gutman lowered himself into the padded rocking chair. Cairo chose the armchair by the table. The boy Wilmer did not sit down. He stood in the doorway where Cairo had stood, letting his one visible pistol hang down at his side, looking under curling lashes at Spade's body. Cairo put his pistol on the table beside him.

Spade took off his hat and tossed it to the other end of the sofa. He grinned at Gutman. "That daughter of yours has a nice body," he said, "too nice to be scratched up with pins."

Gutman's smile was affable if a bit oily. His voice was a suave purring. "Yes, sir, that was a shame, but you must admit that it served its purpose."

Spade's brows twitched together. "Anything would've," he said. "Naturally I wanted to see you as soon as I had the falcon. Cash customers—why not? I went to Burlingame expecting to run into this sort of a meeting. I didn't know you were blundering around trying to get me out of the way so you could find Jacobi again before he found me."

Gutman chuckled. "Well, sir," he said, "in any case, here we are having our little meeting, if that's what you wanted."

"That's what I wanted. How soon are you ready to make the first payment and take the falcon off my hands?"

Brigid O'Shaughnessy sat up straight and looked at Spade with surprised blue eyes. His eyes were steady on Gutman's. Gutman's twinkled merrily. He said, "Well, sir, as to that," and put a hand inside the breast of his coat and took a white envelope from his pocket. Turning the envelope over in his swollen hands, Gutman studied for a moment its blank white front and then its back, unsealed, with the flap tucked in. He raised his head, smiled amiably, and scaled the envelope into Spade's lap.

Spade picked it up deliberately and opened it deliberately. The contents of the envelope were thousand-dollar bills, smooth and stiff and new. He took them out and counted them. There were ten of them. Spade looked up smiling. He said mildly, "We were talking about more money than this."

"Yes, sir, we were," Gutman agreed, "but we were just talking then. This is actual money, genuine coin of the realm, sir. With a dollar of this you can buy more than with ten dollars of talk. There are more of us to be taken care of now." He moved his twinkling eyes and his fat head to indicate Cairo. "And—well, sir, in short— the situation has changed."

While Gutman talked Spade had tapped the edges of the ten bills into alignment and had returned them to their envelope. His reply to the fat man was careless. "Sure. You're together now, but I've got the falcon."

Joel Cairo spoke. Ugly hands grasping the arms of his chair, he leaned forward and said primly in his high-pitched thin voice, "I shouldn't think it would be necessary to remind you, Mr. Spade, that though you may have the falcon yet we certainly have you."

Spade grinned. "I'm trying not to let that worry me," he said. He put the envelope aside—on the sofa—and addressed Gutman. "We'll come back to the money later. There's another thing that's got to be taken care of first. We've got to have a fall guy."

The fat man frowned without comprehension, but before he could speak Spade was explaining. "The police have got to have a victim—somebody they can stick for those three murders. We—"

Now Gutman broke in with good-natured assurance. "Well, sir, from what we've seen and heard of you I don't think we'll have to bother ourselves about that. We can leave the handling of the police to you, all right."

"If that's what you think," Spade said, "you haven't seen or heard enough."

"Now come, Mr. Spade. You can't expect us to believe at this late date that you are the least bit afraid of the police, or that you are not quite able to handle—"

Spade interrupted Gutman irritably. "I'm not a damned bit afraid of them and I know how to handle them. That's what I'm trying to tell you. The way to handle them is to toss them a victim, somebody they can hang the works on."

"Well, sir, I grant you that's one way of doing it, but—"

" 'But' hell!" Spade said. "It's the only way. I know what I'm talking about. I've been through it all before and expect to go through it again. At one time or another I've had to tell everybody from the Supreme Court down to go to hell, and I've got away with it. I got away with it because I never let myself forget that a day of reckoning was coming. I never forget that when the day of reckoning comes I want to be all set to march into headquarters pushing a victim in front of me, saying, 'Here, you chumps, is your criminal.' The first time I can't do it my name's Mud. There hasn't been a first time yet. This isn't going to be it. That's flat."

Gutman's eyes flickered, but there was nothing of uneasiness in his voice. He said, "That's a system that's got a lot to recommend it, sir—by Gad, it has! And if it was any way practical this time I'd be the first to say, 'Stick to it by all means, sir.' But this just happens to be a case where it's not possible. Now maybe it will be a little more trouble to you than if you had your victim to hand over to the police, but"—he laughed and spread his hands—"you're not a man that's afraid of a little bit of trouble. You know how to do things and you know you'll land on your feet in the end, no matter what happens."

Spade's eyes had lost their warmth. "I know what I'm talking about," he said in a low, consciously patient tone. "This is my city and my game. I could manage to land on my feet—sure—this time, but the next time I tried to put over a fast one they'd stop me fast. Hell with that. You birds'll be in New York or Constantinople or someplace else. I'm in business here."

"But surely," Gutman began, "you can—"

"I can't," Spade said earnestly. "I won't. I mean it." He spoke rapidly in an agreeable, persuasive tone. "Listen to me, Gutman. I'm telling you what's best for all of us. If we don't give the police a fall guy it's ten to one they'll sooner or later stumble on information about the falcon. Then you'll have to duck for cover with it, and that's not going to help you make a fortune off it. Give them a fall guy and they'll stop right there."

"Well, sir, that's just the point," Gutman replied, and still only in his eyes was uneasiness faintly apparent. "Wouldn't you say they were stopped right now, and that the best thing for us to do is leave well enough alone?"

A forked vein began to swell in Spade's forehead. "They're not asleep, Gutman," he said in a restrained tone. "They're lying low, waiting. I'm in it up to my neck and they know it. That's all right as long as I do something when the time comes. But it won't be all right if I don't." His voice became persuasive again. "Listen,

Gutman, we've absolutely got to give them a victim. There's no way out of it. Let's give them the punk." He nodded pleasantly at the boy in the doorway. "He actually did shoot both of them—Thursby and Jacobi—didn't he? Anyway, he's made to order for the part. Let's pin the necessary evidence on him and turn him in."

The boy in the doorway tightened the corners of his mouth in what may have been a minute smile.

Gutman remained still and expressionless for a long moment. Then he decided to laugh. When he stopped laughing he said, "By Gad, sir, you're a character, that you are!" He took a white handkerchief from his pocket and wiped his eyes. "Yes, sir, there's never any telling what you'll do or say next, except that it's bound to be something astonishing."

"There's nothing funny about it."

"But, my dear man," Gutman objected, "can't you see? If I even for a moment thought of doing it— But that's ridiculous too. I feel towards Wilmer just exactly as if he were my own son. I really do. But if I even for a moment thought of doing what you propose, what do you think would keep Wilmer from telling the police every last detail about the falcon and all of us?"

Spade grinned with stiff lips. "If we had to," he said softly, "we could have him killed resisting arrest. But we won't have to go that far. Let him talk his head off. I promise you nobody'll do anything about it. That's easy enough to fix."

The fat man smiled genially, saying nothing for a moment, and then asked, "How are you going about fixing it so that Wilmer won't be able to do us any harm?"

"Bryan is like most district attorneys," Spade said. "He's more interested in how his record will look on paper than in anything else. He'd rather drop a doubtful case than try it and have it go against him. To be sure of convicting one man he'll let half a dozen equally guilty accomplices go free—if trying to convict them all might confuse his case.

"That's the choice we'll give him and he'll gobble it up. I can show him that if he starts fooling around trying to gather up everybody he's going to have a tangled case that no jury will be able to make heads or tails of, while if he sticks to the punk he can get a conviction standing on his head."

"Yes, but—" Gutman began, and stopped to look at the boy.

The boy advanced from the doorway, walking stiff-legged, with his legs apart, until he was almost in the center of the floor. The pistol in his hand still hung at his side, but his knuckles were white over its grip. His other hand was a small hard fist down at his other side. He said to Spade in a voice cramped by passion, "You bastard, get up on your feet and go for your heater!"

Spade smiled at the boy. His smile was not broad, but the amusement in it seemed genuine and unalloyed. He looked at Gutman and said, "Young Wild West." His voice matched his smile. "Maybe you ought to tell him that shooting me before you get your hands on the falcon would be bad for business."

Gutman's voice was too hoarse and gritty for the paternally admonishing tone it tried to achieve. "Now, now, Wilmer," he said, "we can't have any of that."

The boy, not taking his eyes from Spade, spoke in a choked voice out the side of his mouth. "Make him lay off me then. I'm going to fog him if he keeps it up and there won't be anything that'll stop me from doing it."

"Now, Wilmer," Gutman said and turned to Spade. His face and voice were under control now. "Your plan is, sir, as I said in the first place, not at all practical. Let's not say anything more about it."

Spade frowned at Gutman. "Let's get this straight. Am I wasting time talking to you? I thought this was your show. Should I do my talking to the punk? I know how to do that."

"No, sir," Gutman replied, "you're quite right in dealing with me."

Spade said, "All right. Now I've got another suggestion. It's not as good as the first, but it's better than nothing. Want to hear it?"

"Most assuredly."

"Give them Cairo."

Cairo hastily picked up his pistol from the table beside him. His black eyes darted their gaze from face to face. The opaqueness of his eyes made them seem flat, two-dimensional.

Gutman, looking as if he could not believe he had heard what he had heard, asked, "Do what?"

"Give the police Cairo."

Gutman seemed about to laugh, but he did not laugh. Finally he exclaimed, "Well, by Gad, sir!" in an uncertain tone.

"It's not as good as giving them the punk," Spade said. "Cairo's not a gunman and he carries a smaller gun than Thursby and Jacobi were shot with. We'll have to go to more trouble framing him, but that's better than not giving the police anybody."

Cairo cried in a voice shrill with indignation, "Suppose we give them you, Mr. Spade? How about that if you're so set on giving them somebody?"

Spade smiled at the Levantine and answered him evenly. "You people want the falcon. I've got it. A fall guy is part of the price I'm asking."

Cairo, his face and body twitching with excitement, exclaimed, "You seem to forget that you are not in a position to insist on anything."

Gutman said, in a voice that tried to make firmness ingratiating, "Come now, gentlemen, let's keep our discussion on a friendly basis; but there certainly is"—he was addressing Spade—"something in what Mr. Cairo says. You must take into consideration the—"

"Like hell I must." Spade flung his words out with a brutal sort of carelessness that gave them more weight than they could have gotten from dramatic emphasis or from loudness. "If you kill me, how are you going to get the bird? If I know you can't afford to kill me till you have it, how are you going to scare me into giving it to you?"

Gutman said fondly, "By Gad, sir, you are a character!"

Joel Cairo jumped up from his chair and went around behind the boy and behind Gutman's chair. He bent over the back of Gutman's chair and, screening his mouth and the fat man's ear with his empty hand, whispered. Gutman listened attentively, shutting his eyes.

Spade turned to the boy. "Two to one they're selling you out."

The boy did not say anything. A trembling in his knees began to shake the knees of his trousers.

Spade addressed Gutman. "I hope you're not letting yourself be influenced by the guns these pocket-edition desperadoes are waving."

Gutman opened his eyes. Cairo stopped whispering and stood erect behind the fat man's chair.

Spade said, "I've practiced taking them away from both of them, so there'll be no trouble there. The punk is—"

In a voice choked horribly by emotion the boy cried, "All right!" and jerked his pistol up in front of his chest.

Gutman flung a fat hand out at the boy's wrist, caught the wrist, and bore it and the gun down while Gutman's fat body was rising in haste from the rocking chair. Joel Cairo scurried around to the boy's other side and grasped his other arm. They wrestled with the boy, forcing his arms down, holding them down, while he struggled futilely against them. Words came out of the struggling group: fragments of the boy's incoherent speech—"right . . . go . . . bastard . . . smoke"; Gutman's "Now, now, Wilmer!" repeated many times; Cairo's "No, please, don't" and "Don't do that, Wilmer."

Wooden faced, dreamy eyed, Spade got up from the sofa and went over to the group. The boy, unable to cope with the weight against him, had stopped struggling. Cairo, still holding the boy's arm, stood partly in front of him, talking to him soothingly. Spade pushed Cairo aside gently and drove his left fist against the boy's chin. The boy's head snapped back as far as it could while his arms were held. Spade drove his right fist against the boy's chin.

Cairo sprang at Spade, clawing at his face with the curved stiff fingers of both hands. Spade blew his breath out and pushed the Levantine away. Cairo sprang at him again, tears in his eyes.

Spade laughed, "God, you're a pip!" and cuffed the side of

Cairo's face with an open hand, knocking him against the table.

Cairo cried, "Oh, you big coward!" and backed away from him.

Spade stooped to pick up Cairo's pistol from the floor, and then the boy's. He straightened up holding them in his left hand, dangling them upside down by their trigger guards from his forefinger.

Gutman had put the boy in the rocking chair and stood looking at him with troubled eyes in an uncertainly puckered face. Cairo went down on his knees beside the chair and began to chafe one of the boy's limp hands.

Spade felt the boy's chin with his fingers. "Nothing cracked," he said. "We'll spread him on the sofa." He put his right arm under the boy's arm and around his back, put his left forearm under the boy's knees, lifted him without apparent effort, and carried him to the sofa.

Brigid O'Shaughnessy got up quickly and Spade laid the boy there. With his right hand Spade patted the boy's clothes, found his second pistol, added it to the others in his left hand, and turned his back on the sofa. Cairo was already sitting beside the boy's head.

Spade clinked the pistols together in his hand and smiled cheerfully at Gutman. "Well," he said, "there's our fall guy."

Gutman's face was gray and his eyes were clouded. He looked at the floor and did not say anything.

Spade said, "Don't be a damned fool again. You let Cairo whisper to you and you held the kid while I pasted him. You can't laugh that off and you're likely to get yourself shot trying to."

Gutman moved his feet on the rug and said nothing.

Spade said, "And the other side of it is that you'll either say yes right now or I'll turn the falcon and the whole damned lot of you in."

Gutman raised his head and muttered through his teeth, "I don't like that, sir."

"You won't like it," Spade said. "Well?"

The fat man sighed and made a wry face and replied sadly, "You can have him."

Spade said, "That's swell."

Chapter 9

THE boy lay on his back on the sofa, a small figure that was—except for its breathing—altogether corpselike to the eye. Joel Cairo sat beside the boy, bending over him, rubbing his cheeks and wrists, smoothing his hair back from his forehead, whispering to him, and peering anxiously down at his white still face.

Gutman's face had lost its troubled cast and was becoming rosy again. He stood facing Spade, watching him without curiosity.

Spade, idly jingling his handful of pistols, nodded at Cairo's rounded back and asked Gutman, "It'll be all right with him?"

"I don't know," the fat man replied placidly. "That part will have to be strictly up to you, sir."

Spade said, "Cairo, let him rest. We're going to give him to the police. We ought to get the details fixed before he comes to."

Cairo left the sofa and went close to the fat man. "Please don't do this, Mr. Gutman," he begged. "You must realize that—"

Spade interrupted him. "That's settled. The question is, what are you going to do about it? Coming in? Or getting out?"

Though Gutman's smile was a bit sad, even wistful in its way, he nodded his head. "I don't like it either," he told the Levantine, "but we can't help ourselves now. We really can't."

Spade asked, "What are you doing, Cairo? In or out?"

Cairo wet his lips and turned slowly to face Spade. "Suppose," he said, and swallowed. "Have I—? Can I choose?"

"You can," Spade assured him seriously, "but you ought to know that if the answer is *out* we'll give you to the police with your boy friend."

"Oh, come, Mr. Spade," Gutman protested, "that is not—"

"Like hell we'll let him walk out on us," Spade said. "He'll either come in or he'll go in. We can't have a lot of loose ends hanging around." He directed a scowl at Cairo. "Well? Which?"

"You give me no choice." Cairo's narrow shoulders moved in a hopeless shrug. "I come in."

"Good," Spade said and looked at Gutman and at Brigid O'Shaughnessy. "Sit down."

The girl sat down gingerly on the end of the sofa by the unconscious boy's feet. Gutman returned to the padded rocking chair, and Cairo to the armchair. Spade put his handful of pistols on the table and sat on the table corner beside them. He looked at the watch on his wrist and said, "Two o'clock. I can't get the falcon till daylight, or maybe eight o'clock. We've got plenty of time to arrange everything."

Gutman looked at the sofa and at Spade again, sharply. "You have the envelope?"

Spade shook his head and said, "Miss O'Shaughnessy has it."

"Yes, I have it," she murmured, putting a hand inside her coat. "I picked it up. . . ."

"That's all right," Spade told her. "Hang on to it." He addressed Gutman. "We won't have to lose sight of each other. I can have the falcon brought here."

"That will be excellent," Gutman purred. "Then, sir, in exchange for the ten thousand dollars and Wilmer you will give us the falcon and an hour or two of grace—so we won't be in the city when you surrender him to the authorities."

Spade began to roll a cigarette. "Let's get the details fixed. Why did he shoot Thursby? And why and where and how did he shoot Jacobi?"

Gutman smiled indulgently, shaking his head. "Now come, sir, you can't expect that. We've given you the money and Wilmer. That is our part of the agreement."

"I do expect it," Spade said. He held his lighter to his cigarette. "A fall guy is what I asked for, and he's not a fall guy unless he's a cinch to take the fall. Well, to cinch that I've got to know what's what."

Gutman leaned forward and wagged a fat finger at the pistols on the table beside Spade's legs. "There's ample evidence of his guilt, sir. Both men were shot with those weapons. It's a very simple matter for the police-department experts to determine that the bullets that killed the men were fired from those weapons. And that, it seems to me, is ample proof of his guilt."

"Maybe," Spade agreed, "but the thing's more complicated than

THE MALTESE FALCON

that and I've got to know what happened so I can be sure the parts that won't fit in are covered up. Why did he kill Thursby?"

Gutman stopped rocking. "Thursby was a notorious killer and Miss O'Shaughnessy's ally. We knew that removing him in just that manner would make her stop and think that perhaps it would be best to patch up her differences with us after all, besides leaving her without so violent a protector. You see, sir, I am being candid with you?"

"Yes. Keep it up. You didn't think he might have the falcon?"

Gutman shook his head so that his round cheeks wobbled. "We didn't think that for a minute," he replied. He smiled benevolently. "We had the advantage of knowing Miss O'Shaughnessy far too well for that and, while we didn't know then that she had given the falcon to Captain Jacobi in Hong Kong to be brought over on the *Paloma* while they took a faster boat, still we didn't for a minute think that, if only one of them knew where it was, Thursby was the one."

Spade nodded thoughtfully and asked, "You didn't try to make a deal with him before you gave him the works?"

"Yes, sir, we certainly did. I talked to him myself that night. Wilmer had located him two days before and had been trying to follow him to wherever he was meeting Miss O'Shaughnessy, but Thursby was too crafty for that. So that night Wilmer went to his hotel, learned he wasn't in, and waited outside for him. I suppose Thursby returned immediately after killing your partner. Be that as it may, Wilmer brought him to see me. We could do nothing with him. He was quite determinedly loyal to Miss O'Shaughnessy. Well, sir, Wilmer followed him back to his hotel and did what he did."

Spade thought for a moment. "That sounds all right. Now Jacobi."

Gutman looked at Spade with grave eyes and said, "Captain Jacobi's death was entirely Miss O'Shaughnessy's fault."

The girl gasped, "Oh!" and put a hand to her mouth.

Spade's voice was heavy and even. "Never mind that now. Tell me what happened."

Gutman smiled. "Just as you say, sir," he said. "Well, Cairo, as you know, got in touch with me—I sent for him—after he left police headquarters the night—or morning—he was up here. We recognized the mutual advantage of pooling forces." He directed his smile at the Levantine. "Mr. Cairo is a man of nice judgment. The *Paloma* was his thought. He saw the notice of its arrival in the papers that morning and remembered that he had heard in Hong Kong that Jacobi and Miss O'Shaughnessy had been seen together. Well, sir, when he saw the notice of arrival in the paper he guessed just what had happened: she had given the bird to Jacobi to bring here for her. Jacobi did not know what it was, of course. Miss O'Shaughnessy is too discreet for that."

He beamed at the girl, rocked his chair twice, and went on. "Mr. Cairo and Wilmer and I went to call on Captain Jacobi and were fortunate enough to arrive while Miss O'Shaughnessy was there. In many ways it was a difficult conference, but finally, by midnight we had persuaded Miss O'Shaughnessy to come to terms, or so we thought. We then left the boat and set out for my hotel, where I was to pay Miss O'Shaughnessy and receive the bird. Well, sir, we mere men should have known better than to suppose ourselves capable of coping with her. En route she and Captain Jacobi and the falcon slipped completely through our fingers." He laughed merrily. "By Gad, sir, it was neatly done."

Spade looked at the girl. Her eyes, large and dark with pleading, met his. He asked Gutman, "You touched off the boat before you left?"

"Not intentionally, no, sir," the fat man replied, "though I daresay we—or Wilmer at least—were responsible for the fire. He had been out trying to find the falcon while the rest of us were talking in the cabin and no doubt was careless with matches."

"That's fine," Spade said. "If any slipup makes it necessary for us to try him for Jacobi's murder we can also hang an arson rap on him. All right. Now about the shooting."

"Well, sir, we dashed around town all day trying to find them and we found them late this afternoon. We'd found Miss O'Shaughnessy's apartment, and when we listened at the door we heard them moving around inside, so we were pretty confident we had them and rang the bell. When she asked us who we were and we told her—through the door—we heard a window going up.

"We knew what that meant, of course; so Wilmer hurried downstairs as fast as he could and around to the rear of the building to cover the fire escape. And when he turned into the alley he ran right plumb smack into Captain Jacobi running away with the falcon under his arm. Wilmer shot Jacobi—more than once—but Jacobi was too tough to either fall or drop the falcon, and he was too close for Wilmer to keep out of his way. He knocked Wilmer down and ran on. When Wilmer got up he could see a policeman coming up from the block below. So he had to give it up. He dodged into the open back door of the building next to the Coronet, through into the street, and then up to join us.

"Well, sir, there we were—stumped again. Miss O'Shaughnessy had opened the door for Mr. Cairo and me after she had shut the window behind Jacobi. We persuaded—that is the word, sir— her to tell us that she had told Jacobi to take the falcon to you. It seemed very unlikely that he'd live to go that far, even if the police didn't pick him up, but that was the only chance we had, sir. And so, once more, we persuaded Miss O'Shaughnessy to phone your office in an attempt to draw you away before Jacobi got there, and we sent Wilmer after him. Unfortunately it had taken us too long to decide and to persuade Miss O'Shaughnessy to—cooperate with us, and so you had the falcon before we could reach you."

The boy groaned, rolled over on his side, and put one foot on the floor. He raised himself on an elbow, opened his eyes wide, put the other foot down, stood up, and looked at Gutman.

Gutman smiled benignly at him and said, "Well, Wilmer, I'm sorry indeed to lose you, and I want you to know that I couldn't be any fonder of you if you were my own son; but—by Gad!—if you lose a son it's possible to get another—and there's only one Maltese falcon."

Spade laughed.

Cairo moved over and whispered in the boy's ear. The boy,

keeping his cold hazel eyes on Gutman's face, sat down on the sofa again. Cairo sat beside him.

Spade grinned at Gutman and addressed Brigid O'Shaughnessy. "I think it'd be swell if you'd see what you can find us to eat in the kitchen, with plenty of coffee. I don't like to leave my guests."

"Surely," she said and started towards the door.

Gutman stopped rocking. "Just a moment, my dear." He held up a thick hand. "Hadn't you better leave the envelope in here? You don't want to get grease spots on it."

The girl's eyes questioned Spade. He said in an indifferent tone, "It's still his."

She put her hand inside her coat, took out the envelope, and gave it to Spade. Spade tossed it into Gutman's lap, saying, "Sit on it if you're afraid of losing it."

"You misunderstand me," Gutman replied suavely. "It's not that at all, but business should be transacted in a businesslike manner." He opened the flap of the envelope, took out the thousand-dollar bills, counted them. "For instance, there are only nine bills here now." He spread them out on his fat knees and thighs. "There were ten when I handed it to you, as you very well know." His smile was broad and jovial and triumphant.

Spade looked at Brigid O'Shaughnessy and asked, "Well?"

She shook her head sidewise with emphasis. She did not say anything, though her lips moved slightly, as if she had tried to. Her face was frightened.

Spade held his hand out to Gutman and the fat man put the money into it. Spade counted the money—nine thousand-dollar bills—and returned it to Gutman. Then Spade stood up and his face was dull and placid. He spoke in a matter-of-fact voice. "I want to know about this. We"—he nodded at the girl, but without looking at her—"are going in the bathroom. The door will be open and I'll be facing it. Unless you want a three-story drop there's no way out of here except past the bathroom door. Don't try to make it. This trick upsets things. I've got to find the answer. It won't take long." He picked up the three pistols on the table and touched the girl's elbow. "Come on."

In the bathroom Brigid O'Shaughnessy found words. She put her hands up flat on Spade's chest and her face up close to his and whispered, "I did not take that bill, Sam."

"I don't think you did," he said, "but I've got to know. Take your clothes off."

"You won't take my word for it?"

"No. Take your clothes off."

"I won't."

"All right. We'll go back to the other room and I'll have them taken off."

She stepped back with a hand to her mouth. Her eyes were round and horrified. "You would?" she asked through her fingers.

"I will," he said. "I've got to know what happened to that bill and I'm not going to be held up by anybody's maidenly modesty."

"Oh, it isn't that." She came close to him and put her hands on his chest again. "I'm not ashamed to be naked before you, but—can't you see?—not like this."

He did not raise his voice. "I've got to know what happened to the bill," he said again. "Take them off."

She looked at his unblinking yellow-gray eyes and her face became pink and then white again. She drew herself up tall and began to undress. He sat on the side of the bathtub watching her and the open door. She removed her clothes swiftly, without fumbling, letting them fall down on the floor around her feet. When she was naked she stepped back from her clothing and stood looking at him. In her mien was pride without defiance or embarrassment.

He went down on one knee in front of her garments. He picked up each piece and examined it with fingers as well as eyes. He did not find the thousand-dollar bill. When he had finished he stood up holding her clothes out in his hands to her. "Thanks," he said. "Now I know."

She took the clothing from him. She did not say anything. He shut the bathroom door behind him and went into the living room.

Gutman smiled amiably at him from the rocking chair. "Find it?" he asked.

"No, I didn't find it. You palmed it."

The fat man chuckled. "I palmed it?"

"Yes," Spade said, jingling the pistols in his hand. "Do you want to say so or do you want to stand for a frisk?"

"Stand for—?"

"You're going to admit it," Spade said, "or I'm going to search you. There's no third way."

Gutman looked up at Spade's hard face and laughed outright. "By Gad, sir, I believe you would. I really do. You're a character, sir, if you don't mind my saying so."

"You palmed it," Spade said.

"Yes, sir, that I did." The fat man took a crumpled bill from his vest pocket, smoothed it on a wide thigh, took the envelope holding the nine bills from his coat pocket, and put the smoothed bill in with the others. "I must have my little joke every now and then, and I was curious to know what you'd do in a situation of that sort. I must say that you passed the test with flying colors, sir."

Brigid O'Shaughnessy, dressed again, came out of the bathroom, took a step towards the living room, turned around, went to the kitchen, and turned on the light.

Cairo edged closer to the boy on the sofa and began whispering in his ear again. The boy shrugged irritably.

Spade, looking at the pistols in his hand and then at Gutman, went out into the passageway, to the closet there. He opened the door, put the pistols inside on the top of a trunk, shut the door, locked it, put the key in his trouser pocket, and went to the kitchen door.

Brigid O'Shaughnessy was filling an aluminum percolator.

"Find everything?" Spade asked.

"Yes," she replied in a cool voice, not raising her head. Then she set the percolator aside and came to the door. She blushed and her eyes were large and moist and chiding. "You shouldn't have done that to me, Sam," she said softly.

"I had to find out, angel." He bent down, kissed her mouth lightly, and returned to the living room.

Gutman smiled at Spade and offered him the white envelope, saying, "This will soon be yours; you might as well take it now."

Spade did not take it. He sat in the armchair and said, "There's plenty of time for that. We haven't done enough talking about the money end. I ought to have more than ten thousand."

Gutman said, "Ten thousand dollars is a lot of money to be picked up in as few days and as easily as you're getting it."

"You think it's been so damned easy?" Spade asked, and shrugged. "Well, maybe, but that's my business."

"It certainly is," the fat man agreed. He moved his head to indicate the kitchen. "Are you sharing with her?"

Spade said, "That's my business too."

"It certainly is," the fat man agreed once more, "but"—he hesitated—"I'd like to give you a word of advice."

"Go ahead."

"If you don't—I daresay you'll give her some money in any event, but—if you don't give her as much as she thinks she ought to have, my word of advice is—be careful."

Spade's eyes held a mocking light. He asked, "Bad?"

"Bad," the fat man replied.

Spade grinned and began to roll a cigarette.

Cairo, still muttering, had put his arm around Wilmer's shoulders. Suddenly the boy pushed his arm away and turned on the sofa to face the Levantine. The boy's face held disgust and anger. He made a fist of one small hand and struck Cairo's mouth with it. Cairo cried out as a woman might have cried and drew back to the very end of the sofa. He took a silk handkerchief from his pocket and put it to his mouth. It came away daubed with blood. The boy snarled, "Keep away from me," and put his face between his hands.

Cairo's cry had brought Brigid O'Shaughnessy to the door. Spade, grinning, jerked a thumb at the sofa and told her, "The course of true love. How's the food coming along?"

"It's coming," she said, and went back to the kitchen.

Spade lighted his cigarette and addressed Gutman. "Let's talk about money."

"Willingly, sir, with all my heart," the fat man replied, "but I might as well tell you frankly right now that ten thousand is every cent I can raise. Of course, sir, you understand that is simply the first payment. Later—"

Spade laughed. "I know you'll give me millions later, but let's stick to this first payment now. Fifteen thousand?"

Gutman smiled and frowned and shook his head. "Mr. Spade, I've told you frankly and candidly and on my word of honor as a gentleman that ten thousand dollars is all the money I've got—every penny—and all I can raise."

Spade said gloomily, "That's not any too good, but if it's the best you can do—give it to me."

Gutman handed him the envelope. Spade counted the bills and was putting them in his pocket when Brigid O'Shaughnessy came in carrying a tray.

The boy would not eat. Cairo took a cup of coffee. The girl, Gutman, and Spade ate the scrambled eggs, bacon, toast, and marmalade she had prepared, and drank two cups of coffee apiece. Then they settled down to wait the rest of the night through.

Gutman smoked a cigar and read *Celebrated Criminal Cases of America*, now and then chuckling over or commenting on the parts of its contents that amused him. Cairo nursed his mouth and sulked on his end of the sofa. The boy lay down with his feet towards Cairo and went to sleep. Brigid O'Shaughnessy, in the armchair, dozed, listened to the fat man's comments, and carried on wide-spaced desultory conversations with Spade.

Spade rolled and smoked cigarettes and moved, without fidgeting or nervousness, around the room. He sat sometimes on an arm of the girl's chair, on the table corner, on the floor at her feet, on a straight-backed chair. He was wide-awake, cheerful, and full of vigor.

At half past five he went into the kitchen and made more coffee. Half an hour later the boy stirred, awakened, and sat up yawning. Gutman looked at his watch and questioned Spade, "Can you get it now?"

"Give me another hour."

Gutman nodded and went back to his book.

At seven o'clock Spade went to the telephone and called Effie Perine's number. "Hello, Mrs. Perine? . . . This is Mr. Spade. Will you let me talk to Effie, please? . . . Yes, it is. . . . Thanks." He whistled a tune softly. "Hello, angel. Sorry to get you up. Here's the plot: in our Holland box at the post office you'll find an envelope addressed in my scribble. There's a Pickwick bus parcel-room check in it—for the bundle we got yesterday. Will you get the bundle and bring it to me—pdq? . . . Yes, I'm home. . . . That's the girl—hustle. . . . By."

The street-door bell rang at ten minutes of eight. Spade went to the telephone box and pressed the button that released the lock. Gutman put down his book and rose smiling. "You don't mind if I go to the door with you?" he asked.

"Okay," Spade told him.

Gutman followed him to the corridor door. Spade opened it. Presently Effie Perine, carrying the brown-wrapped parcel, came from the elevator. After one glance she did not look at Gutman. She smiled at Spade and gave him the parcel.

He took it, saying, "Thanks a lot, lady. I'm sorry to spoil your day of rest, but this—"

"It's not the first one you've spoiled," she replied, laughing, and then, when it was apparent that he was not going to invite her in, asked, "Anything else?"

He shook his head. "No, thanks."

She said, "By-by," and went back to the elevator.

Spade shut the door and carried the parcel into the living room. Gutman's face was red and his cheeks quivered. Cairo and Brigid O'Shaughnessy came to the table as Spade put the parcel there. They were excited. The boy rose, pale and tense, but he remained by the sofa, staring at the others.

Spade stepped back from the table, saying, "There you are."

Gutman's fat fingers made short work of cord and paper and excelsior, and he had the black bird in his hands. "Ah," he said huskily, "now, after seventeen years!" His eyes were moist.

Cairo licked his red lips and worked his hands together. The girl's lower lip was between her teeth. She and Cairo, like Gutman, and like Spade and the boy, were breathing heavily.

Gutman set the bird down on the table again and fumbled at a pocket. "It's it," he said, "but we'll make sure." Sweat glistened on his round cheeks. His fingers twitched as he took out a gold pocket-knife and opened it.

Gutman turned the bird upside down and scraped an edge of its base with his knife. Black enamel came off in tiny curls, exposing blackened metal beneath. Gutman's knife blade bit into the metal, turning back a thin curved shaving. The inside of the shaving had the soft gray sheen of lead.

Gutman's breath hissed between his teeth. His face became turgid with hot blood. He twisted the bird around and hacked at its head. There too the edge of his knife bared lead. He let knife and bird bang down on the table while he wheeled to confront Spade. "It's a fake," he said hoarsely.

Spade's face had become somber. His nod was slow, but there was no slowness in his hand's going out to catch Brigid O'Shaughnessy's wrist. "All right," he growled, "you've had *your* little joke. Now tell us about it."

She cried, "No, Sam, no! That is the one I got from Kemidov. I swear—"

Joel Cairo thrust himself between Spade and Gutman and began to emit words in a shrill spluttering stream. "That's it! That's it! It was the Russian! I should have known! What a fool we thought him, and what fools he made of us!" Tears ran down the Levantine's cheeks and he danced up and down. "You bungled it!" he screamed at Gutman. "You and your stupid attempt to buy it from him! You fat fool! You let him know it was valuable and he found out how valuable and made a duplicate for us! No wonder we had so little trouble stealing it!"

Gutman's jaw sagged. He blinked vacant eyes. Then he shook himself and was again a jovial fat man. "Come, sir," he said good-naturedly, "there's no need of going on like that. Everybody errs at times and you may be sure this is every bit as severe a blow to me as to anyone else. Yes, that is the Russian's hand, there's no doubt of it. Well, sir, what do you suggest? Shall we stand here and shed tears and call each other names? Or shall we"—he paused and his smile was a cherub's—"go to Constantinople?"

Cairo took his hands from his face and his eyes bulged. He stammered, "You are—?" Amazement coming with full comprehension made him speechless.

Gutman patted his fat hands together. His eyes twinkled. His voice was a complacent throaty purring. "For seventeen years I have wanted that little item and have been trying to get it. If I must spend another year on the quest—well, sir—that will be an additional expenditure in time of only"—his lips moved silently as he calculated—"five and fifteen-seventeenths percent."

The Levantine giggled and cried, "I go with you!"

Spade suddenly released the girl's wrist and looked around the room. The boy was not there. Spade went into the passageway. The corridor door stood open. Spade made a dissatisfied mouth, shut the door, and returned to the living room. He looked at Gutman for a long time, sourly. Then he spoke, mimicking the fat man's throaty purr. "Well, sir, I must say you're a swell lot of thieves!"

Gutman chuckled. "We've little enough to boast about, and that's a fact, sir," he said. "But, well, we're none of us dead yet and there's not a bit of use thinking the world's come to an end just because we've run into a little setback." He brought his left hand from behind him and held it out towards Spade, pink smooth hilly palm up. "I'll have to ask you for that envelope, sir."

Spade did not move. His face was wooden. He said, "I held up my end. You got your dingus. It's your hard luck, not mine, that it wasn't what you wanted."

"Now come, sir," Gutman said persuasively, "we've all failed and there's no reason for expecting any one of us to bear the brunt of it, and . . ." He brought his right hand from behind him. In the hand was a small pistol, an ornately engraved and inlaid affair of silver and gold and mother-of-pearl. "In short, sir, I must ask you to return my ten thousand dollars."

Spade's face did not change. He shrugged and took the envelope from his pocket. He started to hold it out to Gutman, hesitated, opened the envelope, and took out one thousand-dollar bill. He put that bill into his trouser pocket. He tucked the envelope's flap in over the other bills and held it out to Gutman. "That'll take care of my time and expenses," he said.

Gutman, after a little pause, imitated Spade's shrug and accepted the envelope. He said, "Now, sir, we will say good-by to you, unless"—the fat puffs around his eyes crinkled—"you care to undertake the Constantinople expedition with us. You don't? Well, sir, frankly I'd like to have you along. You're a man to my liking, a man of many resources and nice judgment. Because we know you're a man of nice judgment we know we can say good-by with every assurance that you'll hold the details of our little enterprise in confidence. We know we can count on you to appreciate the fact that, as the situation now stands, any legal difficulties that come to us in connection with these last few days would likewise and equally come to you and the charming Miss O'Shaughnessy. You're too shrewd not to recognize that, sir, I'm sure."

"I understand that," Spade replied.

"I was sure you would. I'm also sure that, now there's no alternative, you'll somehow manage the police without a fall guy."

"I'll make out all right," Spade replied.

"I was sure you would. Well, sir, the shortest farewells are the best. Adieu." He made a portly bow. "And to you, Miss O'Shaughnessy, I leave the rara avis on the table as a little memento."

Chapter 10

For all of five minutes after the outer door had closed behind Casper Gutman and Joel Cairo, Spade, motionless, stood staring at the knob of the open living-room door. He had not looked at Brigid O'Shaughnessy, who stood by the table looking with uneasy eyes at him.

He picked up the telephone, called a number, and said, "Hello, is Sergeant Polhaus there? . . . Will you call him, please? This is Samuel Spade. . . ." He stared into space, waiting. "Hello, Tom, I've got something for you. . . . Yes, plenty. Here it is: Thursby and Jacobi were shot by a kid named Wilmer Cook." He described the boy minutely. "He's working for a man named Casper Gutman." He described Gutman. "That fellow Cairo you met here is in with them too. . . . Yes, that's it. . . . Gutman's staying at the Alexandria, suite twelve C, or was. They've just left here and they're blowing town, so you'll have to move fast, but I don't think they're expecting a pinch. . . . There's a girl in it too—Gutman's daughter." He described Rhea Gutman. "Watch yourself when you go up against the kid. He's supposed to be good with the gun. . . . That's right, Tom, and I've got some stuff here for you. I think I've got the guns he used. . . . That's right. Step on it—and luck to you!"

Spade slowly replaced receiver on prong. His eyes were glittering between straightened lids. He turned and took three long swift steps into the living room.

Brigid O'Shaughnessy, startled by the suddenness of his approach, let her breath out in a little laughing gasp.

Spade, face-to-face with her, very close to her, tall, big-boned and thick-muscled, coldly smiling, hard of jaw and eye, said, "They'll talk when they're nailed—about us. We're sitting on dynamite, and we've only got minutes to get set for the police. Give me all of it—fast. Gutman sent you and Cairo to Constantinople?"

"Y-yes, he sent me. I met Joe there and—and asked him to help me. Then we—"

"Wait. You asked Cairo to help you get it from Kemidov?"

"Yes."

"For Gutman?"

She hesitated again, squirmed under the hard angry glare of his eyes, swallowed, and said, "No, not then. We thought we would get it for ourselves."

"All right. Then?"

"Oh, then I began to be afraid that Joe wouldn't play fair with me, so—so I asked Floyd Thursby to help me."

"And he did. Well?"

"Well, we got it and went to Hong Kong."

"With Cairo? Or had you ditched him before that?"

"Yes. We left him in Constantinople, in jail—something about a check."

"Something you fixed up to hold him there?"

She looked shamefacedly at Spade and whispered, "Yes."

"Right. Now you and Thursby are in Hong Kong with the bird."

"Yes, and then—I didn't know him very well—I didn't know whether I could trust him. I thought it would be safer—anyway, I met Captain Jacobi and I knew his boat was coming here, so I asked him to bring a package for me—and that was the bird."

"All right. Then you and Thursby caught one of the fast boats over. Then what?"

"Then—then I was afraid of Gutman. I knew he had people—connections—everywhere, and he'd soon know what we had done. And I was afraid he'd have learned that we had left Hong Kong for San Francisco, but I had to wait here until Captain Jacobi's boat arrived. And I was afraid Gutman would find me—or find Floyd and buy him over. That's why I came to you and asked you to watch him for—"

"That's a lie," Spade said. "You had Thursby hooked and you knew it. He was a sucker for women. His record shows that—the only falls he took were over women. And once a chump, always a chump. You knew you had him safe."

She blushed and looked timidly at him.

He said, "You wanted to get him out of the way before Jacobi came with the loot. What was your scheme?"

"I—I knew he'd left the States with a gambler after some trouble. I didn't know what it was, but I thought that if it was anything serious and he saw a detective watching him he'd think it was on account of the old trouble, and would be frightened into going away."

"You told him he was being shadowed," Spade said confidently. "Miles hadn't many brains, but he wasn't clumsy enough to be spotted the first night."

"I told him, yes. When we went out for a walk that night I pretended to discover Mr. Archer following us and pointed him out to Floyd." She sobbed. "But please believe, Sam, that I wouldn't have done it if I had thought Floyd would kill him. I thought he'd be frightened into leaving the city."

Spade smiled wolfishly with his lips, but not at all with his eyes. He said, "Thursby didn't shoot him."

Incredulity joined astonishment in the girl's face.

Spade said, "Miles had too many years' experience as a detective to be caught like that by the man he was shadowing. Up a blind alley with his gun tucked away on his hip and his overcoat buttoned? Not a chance. He was as dumb as any man ought to be, but he wasn't quite that dumb."

He ran his tongue over the inside of his lips and smiled affectionately at the girl. He said, "But he'd've gone in there with you, angel, if he was sure nobody else was up there. You were his client, so he would have had no reason for not dropping the shadow on your say-so, and if you caught up with him and asked him to go in there he'd've gone. He was just dumb enough for that. He'd've looked you up and down and licked his lips and gone grinning from ear to ear—and then you could've stood as close to him as you liked in the dark and put a hole through him with the gun you had got from Thursby that evening."

Brigid O'Shaughnessy shrank back from him. She looked at him with terrified eyes and cried, "Don't—don't talk to me like that, Sam! You know I didn't! You know—"

"Stop it." He looked at the watch on his wrist. "The police will be blowing in any minute now and we're sitting on dynamite. Talk!"

She put the back of a hand on her forehead. "Oh, why do you accuse me of such a terrible—"

"Will you stop it?" he demanded in a low impatient voice. "This isn't the spot for the schoolgirl act. Listen to me. The pair of us are sitting under the gallows." He took hold of her wrists and made her stand up straight in front of him. "Talk!"

"I—I— How did you know he—he licked his lips and looked—"

Spade laughed harshly. "I knew Miles. But never mind that. Why did you shoot him?"

She twisted her wrists out of Spade's fingers and put her hands up around the back of his neck, pulling his head down until his mouth all but touched hers. Her voice was hushed, throbbing. "I didn't mean to, at first. I didn't, really. I meant what I told you, but when I saw Floyd couldn't be frightened I—"

Spade slapped her shoulder. He said, "That's a lie. You asked Miles and me to handle it ourselves. You wanted to be sure the shadower was somebody you knew and who knew you, so they'd go with you. You got the gun from Thursby that day—that night."

She swallowed with difficulty and her voice was humble. "Yes, that's a lie, Sam. I did intend to if Floyd— I—I can't look at you and tell you this, Sam." She pulled his head farther down until her cheek was against his cheek, her mouth by his ear, and whispered, "I knew Floyd wouldn't be easily frightened, but I thought that if he knew somebody was shadowing him either he'd— Oh, I can't say it, Sam!" She clung to him, sobbing.

Spade said, "You thought Floyd would tackle him and one or the other of them would go down. If Thursby was the one then you were rid of him. If Miles was, then you could see that Floyd was caught and you'd be rid of him. That it?"

"S-something like that."

"And when you found that Thursby didn't mean to tackle him you borrowed the gun and did it yourself. Right?"

"Yes—though not exactly."

"But exact enough. And you had that plan up your sleeve from the first. You thought Floyd would be nailed for the killing."

"I—I thought they'd hold him at least until after Captain Jacobi had arrived with the falcon and—"

"And you didn't know then that Gutman was here hunting for you. You didn't suspect that or you wouldn't have shaken your gunman. You knew Gutman was here as soon as you heard Thursby had been shot. Then you knew you needed another protector, so you came back to me. Right?"

"Yes, but—oh, sweetheart!—it wasn't only that. I would have come back to you sooner or later. From the first instant I saw you I knew—"

Spade said tenderly, "You angel! Well, if you get a good break you'll be out of San Quentin in twenty years and you can come back to me then."

She took her cheek away from his, drawing her head far back to stare up without comprehension at him.

He was pale. He said, "I hope they don't hang you, precious, by that sweet neck." He slid his hands up to caress her throat.

In an instant she was out of his arms, back against the table, crouching, both hands spread over her throat. Her dry mouth opened and closed. She said in a small parched voice, "You're not—" She could get no other words out.

Spade's face was yellow white now. His voice was soft, gentle. He said, "I'm going to send you over. The chances are you'll get off with life. That means you'll be out again in twenty years. You're an angel. I'll wait for you." He cleared his throat. "If they hang you I'll always remember you."

She dropped her hands and stood erect. Her face became smooth and untroubled except for the faintest of dubious glints in her eyes. She smiled back at him, gently. "Don't, Sam, don't say that even in fun. Oh, you frightened me for a moment! I really thought you— You know you do such wild and unpredictable things that—" She broke off.

Spade laughed. His yellow-white face was damp with sweat, and though he held his smile he could not hold softness in his voice. He croaked, "Don't be silly. You're taking the fall. One of us has got to take it, after the talking those birds will do. They'd hang me sure. You're likely to get a better break. Well?"

"But—but, Sam, you can't! Not after what we've been to each other. You can't—"

"Like hell I can't."

She took a long trembling breath. "You've been playing with me? Only pretending you cared—to trap me like this? You didn't care at all? You didn't—don't—l-love me?"

"I think I do," Spade said. "What of it?" The muscles holding his smile in place stood out like wales. "I'm not Thursby. I'm not Jacobi. I won't play the sap for you."

"That is not just," she cried. Tears came to her eyes. "It's unfair. It's contemptible of you. You know it was not that. You can't say that."

"Like hell I can't," Spade said. "You came into my bed to stop me asking questions. You led me out yesterday for Gutman with that phony call for help. Last night you came here with them and waited outside for me and came in with me. You were in my arms when the trap was sprung—I couldn't have gone for a gun if I'd had one on me and couldn't have made a fight of it if I had wanted to. And if they didn't take you with them it was only because Gutman's got too much sense to trust you except for short stretches when he has to and because he thought I'd play the sap for you and—not wanting to hurt you—wouldn't be able to hurt him."

Brigid O'Shaughnessy blinked her tears away. She took a step towards him and stood looking him in the eyes, straight and proud. "You called me a liar," she said. "Now you are lying. You're lying if you say you don't know down in your heart that, in spite of anything I've done, I love you."

Spade made a short abrupt bow. "Maybe I do," he said. "What of it? I should trust you? You who arranged that nice little trick for—for my predecessor, Thursby? You who knocked off Miles, a man you had nothing against, in cold blood, just like swatting a fly, for the sake of double-crossing Thursby? You who double-crossed Gutman, Cairo, Thursby—one, two, three? You who've never played square with me for half an hour at a stretch since I've known you? I should trust you? No, no, darling. I wouldn't do it even if I could. Why should I?"

Her eyes were steady under his and her hushed voice was steady when she replied. "Why should you? If you've been playing with me, if you do not love me, there is no answer to that. If you did, no answer would be needed."

Spade put a hand on her shoulder. The hand shook and jerked. "I don't care who loves who, I'm not going to play the sap for you. I won't walk in Thursby's and the others' footsteps. You killed Miles and you're going over for it."

"Don't say that, please." She took his hand from her shoulder and held it to her face. "Why must you do this to me, Sam? Surely Mr. Archer wasn't as much to you as—"

"Miles," Spade said hoarsely, "was a son of a bitch. I found that out the first week we were in business together and I meant to kick him out as soon as the year was up."

"Then what?"

Spade pulled his hand out of hers. He no longer either smiled or grimaced. He said, "Listen. When a man's partner is killed he's supposed to do something about it. It doesn't make any difference what you thought of him. He was your partner and you're supposed to do something about it. Then it happens we were in the detective business. Well, when one of your organization gets killed it's bad business to let the killer get away with it. It's bad all around—bad for that one organization, bad for every detective everywhere. Third, I'm a detective, and expecting me to run criminals down and then let them go free is like asking a dog to catch a rabbit and let it go. The only way I could have let you go was by letting Gutman and Cairo and the kid go. That's—"

"You're not serious," she said. "You don't expect me to think that these things you're saying are sufficient reason for sending me to the—"

"Wait till I'm through and then you can talk. Fourth, no matter what I wanted to do now it would be absolutely impossible for me to let you go without having myself dragged to the gallows with the others. Next, I've no reason in God's world to think I can trust you, and if I did this and got away with it you'd have something on me that you could use whenever you happened to want to. Now on the other side we've got what? All we've got is the fact that maybe you love me and maybe I love you."

"You know," she whispered, "whether you do or not."

"I don't. It's easy enough to be nuts about you." He looked hungrily from her hair to her feet and up to her eyes again. "But I don't know what that amounts to. Does anybody ever? Maybe next month I won't. Then what? Then I'll think I played the sap. Well, if I send you over I'll be sorry as hell—I'll have some rotten nights—but that'll pass."

She put her hands up to his cheeks and drew his face down again. "Look at me," she said, "and tell me the truth. Would you have done this to me if the falcon had been real and you had been paid your money?"

"What difference does that make now? Don't be too sure I'm as crooked as I'm supposed to be. That kind of reputation might be good business—bringing in high-priced jobs and making it easier to deal with the enemy."

She looked at him, saying nothing.

He moved his shoulders a little and said, "Well, a lot of money would have been at least one more item on the other side of the scales."

She put her face up to his face. Her mouth was slightly open with lips a little thrust out. She whispered, "If you loved me you'd need nothing more on that side."

She put her mouth to his, slowly, her arms around him, and came into his arms. She was in his arms when the doorbell rang.

SPADE, left arm around Brigid O'Shaughnessy, opened the corridor door. Lieutenant Dundy, Detective-sergeant Tom Polhaus, and two other detectives were there.

Spade said, "Hello, Tom. Get them?"

Polhaus said, "Got them."

"Swell. Come in. Here's another one for you." Spade pressed the girl forward. "She killed Miles. And I've got some exhibits—the boy's guns, one of Cairo's, a black statuette that all the hell was about, and a thousand-dollar bill that I was supposed to be bribed with." He looked at Dundy, drew his brows together, leaned forward to peer into the lieutenant's face, and burst out laughing. "What in hell's the matter with your little playmate, Tom? He looks heartbroken." He laughed again. "I bet when he heard Gutman's story he thought he had me at last."

"Cut it out, Sam," Tom grumbled. "We didn't think—"

"Like hell he didn't," Spade said merrily. "He came up here with his mouth watering, though you'd have sense enough to know I'd been stringing Gutman."

"Cut it out," Tom grumbled again, looking uneasily sidewise at his superior. "Anyways we got it from Cairo. Gutman's dead. The kid had just finished shooting him up when we got there."

Spade nodded. "He ought to have expected that," he said.

EFFIE PERINE put down her newspaper and jumped out of Spade's chair when he came into the office at a little after nine o'clock Monday morning.

He said, "Morning, angel."

"Is that—what the papers have—right?" she asked.

"Yes, ma'am." He dropped his hat on the desk and sat down. His face was pasty in color, but its lines were strong and cheerful and his eyes were clear.

The girl's brown eyes were peculiarly enlarged and there was a queer twist to her mouth. She stood beside him, staring down at him.

He raised his head, grinned, and said mockingly, "So much for your woman's intuition."

Her voice was queer as the expression on her face. "You did that, Sam, to her?"

He nodded. "Your Sam's a detective." He looked sharply at her. He put his arm around her waist, his hand on her hip. "She did kill Miles, angel," he said gently, "offhand, like that." He snapped the fingers of his other hand.

She escaped from his arm as if it had hurt her. "Don't, please, don't touch me," she said brokenly. "I know—I know you're right. You're right. But don't touch me now—not now."

Spade's face became pale as his collar.

The corridor door's knob rattled. Effie Perine turned quickly and went into the outer office, shutting the door behind her. When she came in again she shut it behind her.

She said in a small flat voice, "Iva is here."

Spade, looking down at his desk, nodded almost imperceptibly. "Yes," he said, and shivered. "Well, send her in."

The Franchise
Affair

The Franchise Affair

A CONDENSATION OF THE BOOK BY

Josephine Tey

ILLUSTRATED BY JOHN FALTER

Pretty Betty Kane had been missing
for a month when, at last, she turned up,
beaten and bruised, with a harrowing
story of being forcibly held by
two strange ladies in a crumbling old
mansion called The Franchise.
Her accusations play havoc with
a placid English market town and
with the gentlemanly bachelor routine of
lawyer Robert Blair, called on to defend
the two accused women against a
kidnapping charge and an outraged public.
   Josephine Tey has an international
reputation for finely wrought tales of
suspense, among them the well-loved
Brat Farrar and *Daughter of Time*.

1

IT WAS four o'clock of a spring evening; and Robert Blair was thinking of going home.

The office would not shut until five, of course. But when you are the only Blair, of Blair, Hayward, and Bennet, you go home when you think you will. And when your business is mostly wills, conveyancing, and investments your services are in small demand in the late afternoon. And when you live in Milford, where the last post goes out at 3:45, the day loses whatever momentum it ever had long before four o'clock.

It was not even likely that his telephone would ring. His golfing cronies would by now be somewhere between the fourteenth and the sixteenth hole. No one would ask him to dinner, because in Milford invitations to dinner are still written by hand and sent through the post. And Aunt Lin would not ring up and ask him to call for the fish on his way home, because this was her biweekly afternoon at the cinema.

So he sat there, in the lazy atmosphere of a spring evening in a little market town, staring at the last patch of sunlight on his brass-inlaid mahogany desk, and thought about going home. In the patch of sunlight was his tea tray. At 3:50 exactly on every working day Miss Tuff bore into his office a lacquer tray covered with a white cloth, bearing a cup of tea in blue-patterned china, and, on a plate to match, two biscuits.

It was when his eyes rested on the blue plate that Robert experienced an odd sensation in his chest. The sensation had to do with the placid certainty of the tea-and-biscuit routine. Until the last year or so he had found no fault with certainty or placidity. But once or twice lately an odd, unbidden thought had crossed his mind. As nearly as it could be put into words it was: This is all you are ever going to have. And with the thought would come that moment's heart-squeezing constriction in his chest.

This annoyed and puzzled Robert; he considered himself a happy and fortunate person. Certainly he had known since his schooldays that he would one day succeed his father at Blair, Hayward, and Bennet; and he had looked with good-natured pity on boys who had no niche in life ready-made for them; who had no Milford, full of friends and memories, waiting for them.

What, then, had his life lacked that a man might be supposed to miss? A wife? But he could have married if he had wanted to. Women showed no signs of disliking him.

A devoted mother? But what greater devotion could a mother have given him than Aunt Lin provided; dear doting Aunt Lin. Riches? What had he ever wanted that he could not buy?

An exciting life? But he had never wanted any greater excitement than a day's hunting or being all square at the sixteenth hole.

Then what? Why now, after forty, the "This is all you are ever going to have" thought?

Robert decided it was time to go. If he went now he could walk home down the High Street before the sunlight was off the east-side pavement. The street flowed south in a gentle slope—Georgian brick, Elizabethan timber and plaster, Victorian stone, Regency stucco—towards the Edwardian villas at the other end. Here and there, among the rose, white, and brown punctuated with pollarded lime trees, a front of black glass brazened it out, or the scarlet and gold of an American bazaar flaunted its bright promise. It was a fine, gay, busy little street, and Robert Blair loved it.

He had gathered his feet under him preparatory to getting up when his telephone rang.

"Is that Mr. Blair?" a woman's voice asked, a contralto voice that sounded breathless or hurried. "Oh, I am so glad to have caught you. My name is Sharpe, Marion Sharpe. I live with my mother at The Franchise. The house out on the Larborough road, you know."

"Yes, I know it," Blair said. He also knew Marion Sharpe by sight, as he knew everyone in the district. A tall, lean, dark woman of forty or so, much given to bright silk kerchiefs which accentuated her gypsy coloring. She drove a battered old car, from which she shopped in the mornings while her white-haired old mother sat in the back, upright and delicate. In profile old Mrs. Sharpe looked like Whistler's mother; when she turned full-face and you got the impact of her bright, pale, sea-gull's eyes she looked like a sibyl. An uncomfortable old person.

"You don't know me," the voice went on, "but I have seen you in Milford, and you look like such a kind person, and I need a lawyer. I mean, I need one now, this minute. I am in trouble and I thought that you would—"

"If it is your car—" Robert began. "In trouble" in Milford usually meant an offense against the traffic laws. He would pass her on to Carley, the bright lad at the other end of the street, who was popularly credited with the capacity to bail the devil out of hell.

"Car?" she said vaguely. "Oh, no. No, it isn't anything like that. It is something much more serious. It's Scotland Yard."

"Scotland Yard!"

To that sober country lawyer and gentleman, Robert Blair, Scotland Yard was as exotic as Xanadu or parachuting. The nearest he had ever come to it was to play golf with the local inspector, a good chap who played a very steady game.

"I haven't *murdered* anyone, if that is what you are thinking," the voice said hastily. "I'm supposed to have kidnapped someone. Or abducted them, or something. I can't explain over the telephone. And anyhow I need someone now, at once, and—"

"But, you know, I don't think it is me you need at all," Robert said. "My firm is not equipped to deal with a criminal case." This was clearly something for Ben Carley. He must edge her off onto Carley.

There was a moment's silence before Robert went on, "Benjamin Carley knows more about defending accused persons than anyone between here and—"

"What! That awful little man with the striped suits!" Her voice cracked, and there was another momentary silence. "I am sorry," she said presently. "That was silly. But you see, when I rang you up just now it was because I wanted someone I could trust to stand by me and see that I am not put upon. Mr. Blair, do please come. I need you *now*. There are people from Scotland Yard here in the house. And if you feel that it isn't something you want to be mixed up in you could always pass it on to someone else afterwards; couldn't you? If you would just come out here now and 'watch my interests,' or whatever you call it, for an hour, it may all pass over. I'm sure there is a mistake somewhere. Couldn't you please do that for me?"

On the whole Robert Blair thought that he could. He was too good-natured to refuse any reasonable appeal—and Marion Sharpe had given him a loophole if things grew difficult.

What could this "kidnapping" possibly be, he wondered as he walked round to the garage for his car? And who could she possibly be interested in kidnapping? A child? Some child with "expectations"? In spite of the large house out on the Larborough road the Sharpes gave the impression of having very little money. Or was it some child that they considered "ill used" by its natural guardians? That was possible.

Ah, well; they would no doubt be open to reason now that they had been startled by a visit from Scotland Yard. He was a little startled by Scotland Yard himself. Was the child so important that it was a matter for Headquarters?

Away beyond the horizon was Larborough—a city of a million human souls. Two miles out on the road to Larborough stood the house known as The Franchise, a flat white house built in the last days of the Regency, surrounded with a high brick wall with a

large double gate. It had no relation with anything in the countryside. No farm buildings in the background; no side gates into the
surrounding fields. The place was as irrelevant, as isolated, as a
child's toy dropped by the wayside. It had been occupied as long
as Robert could remember by an old man who had never been seen
in Milford. It was understood there that Marion Sharpe and her
mother had inherited The Franchise when the old man had died
three or four years ago.

The Sharpes had an odd air of being self-sufficient. Robert had
seen the daughter once or twice on the golf course. She drove a
long ball like a man and used her thin brown wrists like a professional. And that was all Robert knew about her.

As he brought the car to a stop in front of the tall iron gates, he
found that two other cars were already there. It needed only one
glance at the nearer to identify it as a police car. The further car,
he saw, belonged to Hallam, the local inspector who played such a
steady game of golf. There were three people in the police car: the
driver, and, in the back, a middle-aged woman, possibly a police
matron, and a young girl.

Robert pushed open one of the tall iron gates with frank curiosity. The iron lace of the original gates had been lined, in some
Victorian desire for privacy, with flat sheets of cast iron; and the
wall was so high that, except for a distant view of its roof and chimneys, he had never seen The Franchise.

His first feeling was disappointment. It was not the fallen-on-
evil-times look of the house—although that was evident; it was the
sheer ugliness of it. Everything was just a little wrong: the windows the wrong size, wrongly placed; the doorway the wrong
width, and the flight of steps the wrong height. The total result
was that instead of the bland contentment of its period the house
had a hard, antagonistic stare.

Before he could ring the bell the door was opened by Marion
Sharpe herself.

"I saw you coming," she said, putting out her hand. "I didn't
want you to ring because my mother lies down in the afternoons,
and I am hoping that we can get this business over before she

wakes up. Then she need never know anything about it. I am more grateful than I can say to you for coming."

Robert murmured something, and noticed, as she drew him into the hall, that her eyes, which he had expected to be a bright gypsy brown, were actually a gray hazel.

"The Law is in here," she said, pushing open a door and ushering him into a shabby drawing room.

Sitting on the edge of a beadwork chair was Hallam, looking sheepish. And by the window, entirely at his ease in a very nice piece of Hepplewhite, was Scotland Yard in the person of a youngish spare man in a well-tailored suit. As they got up, Hallam and Robert nodded to each other.

"You know Inspector Hallam, then?" Marion Sharpe said. "And this is Detective Inspector Grant, from Headquarters."

Grant shook hands and said: "I'm glad you've come, Mr. Blair. I couldn't very well proceed until Miss Sharpe had some kind of support; friendly if not legal, but if legal so much the better."

"I see. And what are you charging her with?"

"We are not charging her with anything—" Grant began, but Marion interrupted him.

"I am supposed to have kidnapped and beaten someone."

"*Beaten who?*" Robert said, staggered.

"A girl. Beaten her black and blue," she said, with a kind of relish in enormity. "She is waiting in a police car outside the gate."

"I think we had better begin at the beginning," Robert said, clutching after the normal.

"Perhaps I had better do the explaining," Grant said.

"Yes," said Miss Sharpe, "do. After all, it is your story."

Robert wondered a little at Marion Sharpe's cool mockery. She had not sounded cool over the telephone.

"Just before Easter," Grant began, "a girl called Elisabeth Kane, known as Betty Kane, who lived with her guardians near Aylesbury, went to spend a short holiday with a married aunt in Mainshill. Mainshill, as you know, is a suburb of Larborough. At the end of a week her guardians—Mr. and Mrs. Wynn—had a postcard from her saying that she was enjoying herself very much and was staying on. They took this to mean staying on for the duration of her school holiday, another three weeks. When Betty didn't turn up in time to go back to school, they took it for granted that she was playing truant and wrote to her aunt to send her back. The aunt, instead of getting on the telephone immediately, merely wrote back to the Wynns saying that her niece had left for Aylesbury a fortnight previously. The exchange of letters had taken the best part of another week, so that by the time the Wynns went to the police, Betty had been missing for four weeks. But before the police could really get going, the girl turned up at her home late one night, wearing only a dress and shoes and in a state of complete exhaustion."

"How old is the girl?" Robert asked.

"Fifteen. Nearly sixteen." He waited a moment to see if Robert had further questions, and then went on. "She said she had been 'kidnapped' in a car, but that was all the information anyone got from her before she lapsed into a semiconscious condition. When she recovered, two days later, the Wynns began to get her story from her. She said that while she was waiting for her return coach at the crossroads in Mainshill, a car pulled up at the curb with two women in it. The younger woman, who was driving, asked if they could give her a lift. The girl said that she was waiting for the Aylesbury coach, and they told her that it had already gone by. It was by then four o'clock, beginning to rain, and growing dark. The two women were very sympathetic and suggested that they should give her a lift to a place where she could get a different coach that would go through Aylesbury in half an hour's time. She accepted this gratefully and got in back beside the older woman."

Robert glanced at Marion Sharpe. Her face was calm. This was a story she had heard already. "It seemed to Betty," Grant continued, "that they had been traveling for a long time. It grew darker outside. She said something about how kind they were to take her so far out of their way, and the younger woman said that it was not out of their way, and that she would even have time to come in and have a cup of something hot with them before they took her on to catch the other coach. Eventually the younger woman got out, opened some gates, and then drove up to a house which it was too dark to see. She was taken into a large kitchen—"

"A kitchen?" Robert repeated.

"Yes, a kitchen. The older woman put some cold coffee on the stove to heat while the younger one cut sandwiches. While they ate and drank, the younger woman asked her if she would like to work as a maid for them for a little. She said that she wouldn't, that it was not at all the kind of job she would take.

As she talked, their faces began to grow blurred, and when they suggested that she might at least come upstairs and see what a nice bedroom she would have if she stayed she was too fuddled to do anything but follow them. That was all she remembered until she woke in daylight on a bed in a bare little attic. She was wearing only her slip, and there was no sign of the rest of her clothes. The door was locked, and the round window would not open. In any case—"

"*Round* window!" said Robert, uncomfortably.

But it was Marion who answered him. "Yes," she said, meaningfully. "A round window up in the roof."

Since his last thought as he came to her front door had been how badly placed was the round window in the roof, there seemed to Robert to be no adequate comment, and Grant went on.

"Presently the younger woman arrived with a bowl of porridge. The girl refused it and demanded her clothes and her release. The woman went away, leaving the porridge behind. Betty was alone till evening, when the same woman brought her cake and tea, and tried to talk her into giving the maid's job a trial. The girl again refused, and for days, she says, this alternate coaxing and bullying went on. Then she decided that if she could break the round window she might be able to get the attention of some passerby on the road. Unfortunately, she had managed only to crack the glass with a chair before the younger woman interrupted her. In a great passion, she snatched the chair from the girl and hit her with it until she was breathless. Then she went away, but in a few moments came back with what Betty thinks was a dog whip and beat her until she fainted.

"Next day the older woman appeared with an armful of bed linen and said that if Betty would not work she would at least sew. No sewing, no food. She was too stiff to sew and so had no food. The following day she was threatened with another beating if she did not sew. So she mended some of the linen and was given stew for supper. This arrangement lasted for some time, but whenever her sewing was unsatisfactory she was either beaten or deprived of food. Then one evening the older woman brought the usual bowl of stew and left, forgetting to lock the attic door. The girl ventured onto the landing. There was no sound, and she ran down the stairs to the first landing. Now she could hear the two women talking in the kitchen. She crept down to the front door. It was unlocked, and she ran out just as she was into the night."

"In her slip?" Robert asked.

"I forgot to say that the slip had been exchanged for her dress when she complained of the cold. There was no heat in the attic."

"If she ever was in an attic," Robert said.

"If, as you say, she ever was in an attic," the inspector agreed smoothly. "She does not remember much after that. She walked a great distance in the dark, she says. There was no traffic and she met no one. Then, on a main road, some time later, a truck driver saw her in his headlights and stopped to give her a lift. She was so tired that she fell straight asleep. She woke as the truck driver stopped to put her off at a familiar roadside in Aylesbury, less than two miles from her home. She heard a clock strike eleven. And shortly before midnight she arrived home."

2

THERE was a short silence.

"And this is the girl who is sitting in a car outside the gate of The Franchise at this moment?" said Robert.

"Yes."

"I take it that you have reasons for bringing her here?" Robert asked.

"Yes. When the girl had recovered sufficiently she was induced to tell her story to the police. It was taken down in shorthand as she told it. In that statement there were two things that helped the police a lot. One was that when she was driving with the two women they passed a bus that had MILFORD in a lighted sign on it. The other I will give you in her own words," Grant continued, taking out a notebook.

" 'From the window of the attic I could see a high brick wall with a big iron gate in the middle of it. There was a road on the further side of the wall, because I could see the telegraph posts. No, I couldn't see the traffic on it because the wall was too high. Just the tops of truckloads sometimes. You couldn't see through the gate because it had sheets of iron on the inside. Inside the gate the carriageway went straight for a little and then divided in two into a circle up to the door. No, it wasn't a garden, just grass.' "

Grant looked up.

"As far as we know—and the search has been thorough—there is no other house between Larborough and Milford which fulfills that description except The Franchise. Moreover," Grant went on, looking at his notes again, "the girl not only describes the house, she describes the two inhabitants—and describes them very accurately. 'A thin elderly woman with soft white hair, and a much younger woman, thin and tall and dark like a gypsy.' "

"Do you wonder that I wanted help in a hurry?" Marion Sharpe said, turning to Robert. "Can you imagine a more nightmarish piece of nonsense?"

"The girl's story is certainly the oddest mixture of the factual and the absurd," Robert said. "The idea that anyone would hope to enlist a servant by forcibly detaining her, to say nothing of beating and starving her, is incredible."

"No normal person would, of course," Grant agreed. "But believe me, in my first twelve months in the force I learned that there is no end to the extravagances of human conduct."

"I agree; but the extravagance is just as likely to be the girl's. After all, she is the one who had been missing for a month." He paused. "This girl—may we know something about her? Why guardians and not parents, for instance?"

"She is a war orphan. She was evacuated to the Aylesbury district as a small child during the war. She was an only child and was billeted with the Wynns, who had a boy four years older. About twelve months later both her parents were killed in an air raid and the Wynns, who had always wanted a daughter, were glad to keep her. She looks on them as her parents, since she can hardly remember the real ones."

"I see. And her record?"

"Excellent. A very quiet girl, by every account. Good at her schoolwork but not brilliant. Has never been in any kind of trouble. 'Transparently truthful' was the phrase one of her teachers used about her."

"When she eventually turned up at home, was there any evidence of the beatings she said she had been given?"

"Oh, yes. The Wynns' doctor saw her early next morning, and his statement is that she had been very extensively knocked about. Indeed, some of the bruises were still visible when she made her statement to us. And I should like to say that the Wynns are very sensible people. They have been greatly distressed but they have not tried to dramatize the affair, or allowed the girl to be an object of pity or interest."

The door opened noiselessly, and old Mrs. Sharpe appeared on the threshold. The short pieces of white hair round her face stood up on end, as her pillow had left them, and she looked more than ever like a sibyl. She pushed the door to behind her and surveyed the gathering with a malicious interest. "*Three* strange men!" she said, making a sound like the throaty squawk of a hen.

"Let me present them, Mother," Marion said, as the three got to their feet.

Far from being impressed or agitated by the presence of a lawyer and Scotland Yard in her drawing room, Mrs. Sharpe merely said to Grant in her dry voice, "You should not be sitting in that chair; you are much too heavy for it."

"Mother," Marion said, "the inspector wants us to see a young girl who is waiting in a car outside," and went on to give a brief account of Betty Kane's story.

"Remarkably interesting," said the old lady, seating herself with deliberation on an Empire sofa. "What did we beat her with?"

"A dog whip, I understand."

"Have we got a dog whip?"

"Have you any objections to meeting the girl, Mrs. Sharpe?" Grant asked.

"On the contrary, Inspector. I look forward to it with impatience. It is not every afternoon, I assure you, that I go to my rest a dull old woman and rise a potential monster."

As the inspector went out to the car Marion explained Blair's presence to her mother. "It was extraordinarily kind of him to come at such short notice," she added.

"You have my sympathy, Mr. Blair," the old lady said, unsympathetically.

"Why, Mrs. Sharpe?"

"I take it that criminal lunacy is a little out of your line."

"I find it extraordinarily stimulating," Robert said, refusing to be bullied.

This drew a flash of appreciation from her, something like the shadow of a smile. Robert had the odd feeling that she suddenly liked him. But she merely said tartly, "Yes, I expect the distractions of Milford are scarce and mild."

At this point Grant returned, holding the door open for a police matron and the girl.

Marion Sharpe stood up slowly, as if the better to face anything that might be coming to her, but her mother remained seated on the sofa as one giving an audience, her hands lying composedly in her lap. She was mistress of the situation.

Betty Kane was wearing her school coat, and low-heeled school shoes. She looked younger than Blair had anticipated. She was not very tall, and certainly not pretty. But she had—what was the word?—appeal. Her eyes, a darkish blue, were set wide apart in a heart-shaped face. Her hair was mouse-colored, but grew off her forehead in a good line. Below each cheekbone a slight hollow gave the face charm and pathos. Her lower lip was full, but the mouth was too small.

The girl's glance rested first on the old woman, and then went on to Marion. The glance held neither surprise nor triumph, and not much interest. "Yes, these are the women," she said.

"A remarkable liar," said old Mrs. Sharpe, in the tone in which one says: "A remarkable likeness."

"You say that we took you into the kitchen for coffee," Marion said. "Can you describe the kitchen?"

"I didn't pay much attention. It was a big one—with a stone floor, I think—and a row of bells."

"What kind of stove?"

"I didn't notice the stove, but the pan the old woman heated the coffee in was pale blue enamel with a lot of chips off round the bottom edge."

"I doubt if there is any kitchen in England that hasn't a pan exactly like that," Marion said. "We have three of them."

"Is the girl a virgin?" asked Mrs. Sharpe, in an interested tone.

In the startled pause that this produced, Robert was aware of Hallam's scandalized face. Grant said in cold reproof that the matter was irrelevant.

"You think so?" said the old lady. "If I had been missing for a month from my home it is the first thing that my mother would have wanted to know about me. However. Now that the girl has identified us, what do you propose to do? Arrest us?"

"Oh, no. Things are a long way from that at the moment. I want to take Miss Kane to the kitchen and the attic, so that her descriptions of them can be verified. If they are, my superior will decide what further steps to take."

"I see. A most admirable caution, Inspector." She rose to her feet and began to move towards the door and consequently towards Betty. For the first time the girl's eyes lit with expression, and a spasm of alarm crossed her features. When they were face-to-face, a yard or so apart, there was silence for a full five seconds while the old lady examined the girl with interest.

"For two people who are on beating terms, we are distressingly ill acquainted," Mrs. Sharpe said at last. "I hope to know you much better before this affair is finished, Miss Kane." She turned to

Robert and bowed. "Good-by, Mr. Blair. I hope you will continue to find us stimulating." And, ignoring the rest of the gathering, she walked out of the door that Hallam held open for her.

Robert paid her the tribute of a reluctant admiration. It was no small achievement to steal the interest from an outraged heroine.

"You have no objections to letting Miss Kane see the relevant parts of the house, Miss Sharpe?" Grant asked.

"Of course not. But before we go further I should like to say in Miss Kane's presence that I have never seen her before. I did not give her a lift anywhere, on any occasion. She was not brought into this house either by me or by my mother, nor was she kept here. I should like that to be clearly understood. And now, will you come and see the kitchen?"

AFTER the girl had identified the kitchen they ascended to the all-important attic. It was a square little box of a room, with the ceiling slanting abruptly down on three sides in conformity with the slate roof outside. It was lit only by the round window looking out to the front. The window was divided into four panes, one of which showed a badly starred crack.

The attic was completely bare of furnishing. Unnaturally bare, Robert thought, for so convenient and accessible a storeroom.

"There used to be furniture here when we first came," Marion said, as if answering his thoughts. "But when we found that we should be without help half the time we got rid of it."

Grant turned to Betty Kane with a questioning air.

"The bed was in that corner," she said, pointing to the corner away from the window. "And next it was the wooden commode. And in this corner behind the door there were three empty traveling cases—two suitcases and a trunk with a flat top. There was a chair, but she took it away after I tried to break the window." She referred to Marion without emotion, as if she were not present.

Grant crossed to the far corner and bent to examine the bare floor where the bed had stood, though even from where Robert was standing by the door he could see the marks of casters there.

"The bed was one of the things we got rid of," Marion said.

"What did you do with it?"

"Let me think. Oh, we gave it to the cowman's wife over at Staples Farm, four fields away over the rise."

"Where do you keep your spare luggage, Miss Sharpe?"

For the first time Marion hesitated. "We do have a large square trunk with a flat top, but my mother put a chintz cover on it and uses it to store things in her bedroom. My suitcases I keep in the cupboard on the first-floor landing."

"Miss Kane, do you remember what the cases looked like?"

"Oh, yes. One was brown leather with those sort of caps at the corners, and the other was one of those American-looking canvas-covered ones with stripes."

Well, that was definite enough. "May we see the suitcases in the cupboard?" Grant asked Marion.

"Certainly," Marion said, but she seemed unhappy.

On the lower landing she opened the cupboard door and stood back to let them look. Robert caught the unguarded flash of triumph on the girl's calm, childish face. It was a savage emotion, primitive, cruel, and very startling on the face of a schoolgirl.

The cupboard contained four suitcases; among them were a brown cowhide with protected corners, and a canvas-covered hatbox with a broad band of multicolored stripes down the middle.

"Are these the cases?" Grant asked.

"Yes," the girl said. "Those two."

"I am not going to disturb my mother again this afternoon," Marion said, with sudden anger. "I acknowledge that the trunk in her room is large and flat-topped. It has been there without interruption for the last three years."

"Very good, Miss Sharpe. And now the garage, if you please."

In the stables that had been converted long ago into a garage, the little group stood and surveyed the battered old gray car. Grant read out the girl's untechnical description of it as recorded in her statement. It fitted, but it would fit equally well at least a thousand cars on the roads of Britain today, Blair thought. " 'One of the wheels was painted a different shade from the others and didn't look as if it belonged,' " Grant finished reading.

In silence they looked at the darker gray of the near front wheel. There seemed nothing to say.

"Thank you very much, Miss Sharpe," Grant said at length. "You have been very helpful, and I am grateful. I shall be able to get you on the telephone any time in the next few days, I suppose?"

"Oh, yes, Inspector. We have no intention of going anywhere."

Grant escorted the girl back to the police car. Then he and Hallam took their leave, Hallam still with an air of apologizing for trespass.

Marion had gone out into the hall with them, leaving Robert in the drawing room. When she came back she was carrying a tray with sherry and glasses.

"I won't ask you to stay for dinner," she said, pouring the wine, "partly because our 'dinner' is not at all what you are used to. Did you know that your aunt's meals are famous in Milford? Even I have heard about them. And partly because—well, because, as my mother said, criminal lunacy is a little out of your line."

"About that," Robert said. "You do realize, don't you, that the girl has an enormous advantage over you. She is free to describe almost any object she likes as being part of your household. If it happens to be there, that is strong evidence for her. If it happens not to be there, the inference is merely that you have got rid of it. If the suitcases, for instance, had not been there, she could say that you had got rid of them because they had been in the attic and could be described."

"But she did describe them, without ever having seen them."

"She described two suitcases, you mean. Because you happened to have one of each of the common kinds her chances worked out at about even."

He picked up the glass of sherry that she had set down beside him, took a mouthful, and was astonished to find it admirable.

"But there was the odd wheel of the car," Marion said. "How did she know about that? How did she know about my mother and me, and what the house looked like? Our gates are never open. Even if she opened them and looked inside, she would not know about my mother and me."

"No chance of her having made friends with a maid? Or a gardener?"

"We have never had a gardener, and we have not had a maid for over a year. Just a girl from the farm who comes in once a week and does the rough cleaning."

Robert said sympathetically that it was a big house to have on her hands unaided.

"Yes, but two things help. I am not house-proud. And it is still so wonderful to have a home of our own that I am willing to put up with the disadvantages. Since my father died when I was very little, my mother and I had always lived in a Kensington boarding-house. We had just begun to feel settled down, and at home, when this happened."

For the first time since she had asked his help Robert felt the stirring of partisanship. "And all because a slip of a girl needs an alibi," he said. "We must find out more about Betty Kane."

"I can tell you one thing about her. She is oversexed."

"Is that just feminine intuition?"

"No. I am not very feminine and I have no intuition. But I have never known anyone—man or woman—with that color of eye who wasn't. That opaque dark blue, like a faded navy—it's infallible."

Robert smiled at her indulgently. She *was* very feminine after all.

"It is fascinating to speculate on what she really did during that month," Marion went on. "It affords me intense satisfaction that someone beat her black and blue. At least there is one person in this world who has arrived at a correct estimate of her. I hope I meet him someday, so that I may shake his hand."

"Him?"

"With those eyes it is bound to be a 'him.'"

"Well," Robert said, preparing to go, "I doubt very much whether Grant has a case that he will want to present in court. It would be the girl's word against yours. I don't think he could hope to get a verdict."

"If he *did* bring it to court," she said, coming to the door with him, "and *did* get a verdict, what would that mean for us?"

"I'm not sure whether it would be two years' imprisonment or seven years' penal servitude. But I'll look it up."

"Yes, do," she said. "There's quite a difference."

He decided that he liked her habit of mockery. And, remembering how nearly he had thrown her to Ben Carley, Robert blushed to himself as he walked to the gate.

"HAVE you had a busy day, dear?" Aunt Lin asked, opening her table napkin and arranging it across her plump lap.

This was a sentence that made sense but had no meaning. It was as much an overture to dinner as the spreading of Aunt Lin's napkin, and the exploratory movement of her right foot as she located the footstool which compensated for her short legs. Robert looked up the table at her with a more conscious benevolence than usual. After his visit to The Franchise the serenity of Aunt Lin's presence was very comforting, and he looked with a new awareness at the solid little figure with the short neck and the round pink face. The world for Aunt Lin began with Robert Blair and ended within a ten-mile radius of him.

"What kept you so late tonight, dear?" she asked, having finished her soup.

"I had to go out to The Franchise—that house on the Larborough road. They wanted some legal advice."

"Those odd people? I didn't know you knew them."

"I didn't. They just wanted my advice."

"I hope they pay you for it, dear. They have no money at all, you know. The father was in some kind of importing business—peanuts or something—and drank himself to death. Left them without a penny, poor things. Old Mrs. Sharpe ran a boardinghouse in London to make ends meet, and the daughter was a maid. They were just going to be turned into the street with their furniture, when the father's cousin at The Franchise died. So providential!"

"Aunt Lin! Where do you get those stories?"

"But it's true, dear. Perfectly true. I forget who told me—someone who had stayed in the same street in London—but it was first-hand, anyhow. Is it a nice house?"

"No, rather ugly. But they have some nice pieces of furniture."

"Not as well kept as ours, I'll be bound," she said, looking complacently at the polished sideboard and the gleaming chairs ranged against the wall. "By the way, I think Christina is going to be 'saved' again."

"Oh, poor Aunt Lin, what a bore for you! Is she changing her church again, then?"

"Yes. She has discovered that the Methodists are 'whited sepulchers,' so she is going to those Bethel people. She has been shouting hymns all morning. Once she begins on 'sword of the Lord' ones I know that it will be my turn to do the baking presently."

"Well, darling, you bake just as well as Christina."

"Oh, no, she doesn't," said Christina, coming in with the meat course. A big creature with untidy straight hair and a vague eye. "And if I'm not appreciated in this house, I'll go where I will be."

"Christina, my love!" Robert said, "you know very well that if you left I should follow you to the world's end. For your butter tarts, if for nothing else. Can we have butter tarts tomorrow, by the way?"

"Butter tarts are no food for unrepentant sinners. Besides, I don't think I have the butter."

Aunt Lin sighed gently as the door closed behind Christina. "Twenty years," she said meditatively. "You won't remember her when she first came from the orphanage. Fifteen, and so skinny, poor little brat." A tear glistened in Miss Bennet's blue eye.

"I hope she postpones the salvation until she has made those butter tarts," said Robert. "Did you enjoy your picture?"

"Well, dear, I couldn't forget that he had five wives."

"Who has?"

"*Had*, dear. One at a time. Gene Darrow. I must say, those little programs they give away are very informative but a little disillusioning. He was a student, you see. In the picture, I mean."

The gentle monologue went on, but Robert was not listening. He was back in the shabby drawing room at The Franchise, being gently mocked by Marion Sharpe. He came to the surface as they moved into the sitting room for coffee, and he heard his aunt asking, "Did those people at The Franchise have a maid, by the way? No? Well, I am not surprised. They starved the last one, you know. Gave her—"

"Oh, Aunt *Lin!*"

"I assure you. For breakfast she got crusts cut off the toast."

Robert was suddenly tired and depressed. If kind silly Aunt Lin saw no harm in repeating those absurd stories, what would the gossips of Milford achieve with the stuff of a real scandal?

3

IT WAS more than a week later that Mr. Heseltine, chief clerk at Blair, Hayward, and Bennet, put his gray head round Robert's door to say that Inspector Hallam was in the office and would like to see Mr. Blair for a moment.

When Mr. Heseltine had gone away to fetch the inspector, Robert noticed with surprise that he was apprehensive as he had not been since in the days of his youth he had approached a list of examination results. Was his life so placid that a stranger's dilemma should stir it to that extent? Or was it that the Sharpes had been so constantly in his thoughts for the last week that they had ceased to be strangers?

He braced himself for whatever Hallam was going to say; but all that emerged from Hallam's careful phrases was that Scotland Yard had decided that no proceedings would be taken on the present evidence. Blair noticed the "present evidence" and gauged its meaning accurately. They were not dropping the case, they were merely sitting quiet.

"I take it that they lacked corroborative evidence," Robert said.

"They couldn't trace the truck driver who gave Betty Kane the lift," Hallam answered. "They needed that truck driver," he added.

"Yes," Robert said, reflectively. "What did you make of Betty Kane?"

"I don't know. Nice kid. Just like any other girl of her age. Might have been one of my own."

This, Blair realized, was a very good sample of what they would be up against if it ever came to a case. The decent school coat, the mousy hair, the unmade-up young face with its appealing hollow below the cheekbone, the wide-set candid eyes—Betty was a prosecuting counsel's dream of a victim.

"Thank you for coming to see me," Robert said.

"The telephone in this town," Hallam said, "is about as private as the radio."

"Anyhow, thank you. I must let the Sharpes know at once."

As Hallam took his leave, Robert lifted the telephone receiver. He could not, as Hallam said, talk freely over the telephone, but he would call to say that he was coming out to see the Sharpes immediately and that the news was good. But with the bored and reluctant aid of the exchange he rang the number for a solid five minutes, without result. The Sharpes were not at home.

While he was still engaged with the exchange, young Nevil Bennet, the firm's very junior partner, strolled in, clad in his usual outrageous tweed, a pinkish shirt, and a purple tie. Robert, eyeing him over the receiver, wondered for the hundredth time what was going to become of Blair, Hayward, and Bennet when it slipped from his good Blair grasp into the hands of this young sprig. Nevil Bennet's chief interest in life was in writing poems of such originality that only Nevil himself could understand them. That the boy had brains Robert knew, but mere brains wouldn't take him far in Milford. Milford expected a man to stop being undergraduate when he reached graduate age. But there was no sign of Nevil's acceptance of the world outside his artistic coterie.

"Robert," Nevil said, as Robert finally laid down the receiver, "I thought I would run into Larborough this afternoon, if you haven't anything you want me to do."

"Can't you talk to her on the telephone?" Robert asked, Nevil being engaged, in the casual modern fashion, to the Bishop of Larborough's third daughter.

"Oh, it isn't Rosemary. She is in London for a week."

"A protest meeting at the Albert Hall, I suppose," said Robert. He was feeling disgruntled because of his failure to find the Sharpes at home.

"No, at the Guildhall," Nevil said.

"What is it this time?"

"The protest is against this country's refusal to give shelter to the patriot Kotovich."

"The said patriot is very badly wanted for murder in his own country, I understand."

"By his enemies, yes. But if I stay and explain the ramifications to you, I shall be late for the film."

"What film?"

"The French film I am going into Larborough to see."

Robert could scarcely protest against Nevil's activity, recalling that when he had first entered the firm he had spent many afternoons practicing mashie shots.

"Do you think you could pause long enough to drop a note into the letter box of The Franchise on your way to Larborough?" he asked.

"I might. I always wanted to see what was inside that wall. Who lives there now?"

"An old woman and her daughter."

"Daughter?" repeated Nevil, automatically pricking his ears.

"Middle-aged daughter."

"Oh. All right, I'll just get my coat."

Robert wrote merely that he had tried to talk to them, that he now had to go out on business, but that he would ring them up again when he was free, and that Scotland Yard had acknowledged that it had no case, as the case stood.

Nevil swept in with a dreadful raglan affair over his arm, snatched up the letter and disappeared with a "Tell Aunt Lin I may be late. She asked me over to dinner."

Robert donned his own sober gray hat and walked over to the Rose and Crown to meet his client—an old farmer. Old Mr. Wynyard was not yet there, and Robert, usually so lazily good-natured, was conscious of impatience. He sat down in the lounge and looked at the dog-eared journals lying on a coffee table. The only current magazine was *The Watchman*, a weekly review, and he picked it up reluctantly. It was the usual collection of protests, poems, and pedantry. He tried two poems, neither of which made sense to him, and flung the thing back on the table.

"England in the wrong again?" asked Ben Carley, pausing by Robert's chair and jerking his head at *The Watchman*.

"Hullo, Carley. How are you?"

"Not bad, thanks." Carley paused. "I saw your car outside The Franchise the other day."

"Yes," said Robert, and wondered a little. It was unlike Ben Carley to be blunt. And if he had seen Robert's car he had also seen the police cars.

"Is the rumor true about those two women?"

"What rumor?"

"*Are* they witches?"

"Are they supposed to be?" said Robert lightly.

"There's a strong support for the belief in the countryside, I understand," Carley said. Robert understood that the little man was offering him, tacitly, information that he thought ought to be useful to him.

"Ah well," Robert said, "since the cinema, God bless it, came to the country, an end has been put to witch-hunting."

"Don't you believe it. Give these Midland morons a good excuse and they'll witch-hunt with the best. Well, I'll be seeing you."

It was one of Robert's chief attractions that he was genuinely interested in people and in their troubles, and when old Mr. Wynyard arrived he listened to his rambling story with kindness; but as soon as their business was over he made straight for the hotel telephone.

It was Marion who answered, and her voice sounded warm. "You can't imagine what a relief your note was to us. What a charming nephew you have, by the way."

"Nephew?"

"The one who brought the note."

"He is not my nephew," Robert said coldly. Why was it so aging to be avuncular? "He is my first cousin once removed. But I am glad you liked him." This would not do; he would have to take the bull by the horns. "I should like to see you sometime to discuss

174

what we can do to straighten things out. To make things safer—"
He waited.

"Yes, of course. Perhaps we could look in at your office on Friday morning? That is our weekly shopping day. Or is Friday a busy day for you?"

"No, Friday would be quite convenient," Robert said, swallowing down his disappointment. "About noon?"

"Yes, that would do very well. Good-by, then, and thank you again for your support and help."

She rang off firmly and cleanly, without all the usual twitterings that Robert had come to expect from women.

He set off on his normal evening walk down the High Street, trying hard not to feel snubbed. After all, he told himself, he had not been anxious to go to The Franchise in the first instance, and had made his reluctance pretty plain; she was quite naturally avoiding a repetition of the circumstances.

Ah well, he thought, reaching home and flinging himself down in his favorite chair by the wood fire in the sitting room, when they came to the office on Friday he could do something to put the affair on a more personal basis. To wipe out the memory of that first unhappy refusal.

The quiet of the old house soothed him. Christina had been closeted in her room for two days, in prayer and meditation, and Aunt Lin was in the kitchen preparing dinner. There was a gay letter from Lettice, his only sister, who had driven a truck for several years of a bloody war, fallen in love with a tall silent Canadian, and was now raising five blond children in Saskatchewan. "Come out soon, Robin dear," she finished, "before the brats grow up and before the moss grows *right* round you. You know how *bad* Aunt Lin is for you!" Lettice and Aunt Lin had never seen eye to eye.

He was smiling, relaxed and reminiscent, when both his quiet and his peace were shattered by the sudden appearance of Nevil.

"Why didn't you *tell* me she was like that!" Nevil demanded.

"Who?"

"Marion Sharpe! Why didn't you tell me?"

"I didn't expect you would meet her," Robert said. "All you had to do was drop the letter through the door."

"There was nothing in the door to drop it through, so I rang, and *she* answered."

"And how did you know her name was Marion?" Robert asked.

"She told me. It does suit her, doesn't it? She couldn't be anything but Marion."

"You seem to have become remarkably intimate for a doorstep acquaintance."

"Oh, she gave me tea."

"Tea! I thought you were in a hurry to see a French film."

"I'm never in a hurry to do anything when a woman like Marion Sharpe invites me to tea. Have you noticed her eyes? That wonderful shading of gray into hazel. And the way her eyebrows lie above them, like the brushmark of a painter genius. I made a poem about them on the way home. Do you want to hear it?"

"No," Robert said firmly. "Did you enjoy your film?"

"Oh, I didn't go."

"You didn't *go!* What happened to your thirst for French cinema?"

"But Marion *is* French film. Even you must see that!" Robert winced at the "even you." "Reality. That is her great quality, isn't it? I've never met anyone as real as Marion is. She spoke very nicely of you, by the way."

"That was kind of her." Robert's tone was so dry that even Nevil caught the flavor of it.

"Don't you like her?" he asked in surprised disbelief.

Robert had ceased for the moment to be kind, lazy, and tolerant; he was just a tired man who hadn't yet had his dinner and was suffering from the memory of a snubbing.

"As far as I am concerned," he said, "Marion Sharpe is just a skinny woman of forty who lives with a rude old mother in an ugly old house, and needs legal advice on occasion like anyone else."

But even as the words came out he wanted to stop them, as if they were a betrayal of a friend.

"No, probably she *isn't* your cup of tea," Nevil said tolerantly.

"Nevil dear, do stop prancing about the hearthrug and put a log on the fire," Aunt Lin said, coming in flushed from her cooking and bearing the tray with the sherry. "Did you enjoy your French film, dear?"

"I didn't go. I had tea at The Franchise instead."

"With those strange people? What did you talk about?"

"Mountains—Maupassant—hens—"

"*Hens*, dear?"

"Yes, the concentrated evil of a hen's face in a close-up."

Aunt Lin looked vague. She turned to Robert, as to terra firma. "Had I better call on them, dear, if you are going to know them?" But household cares obliterated the question in her mind. "Don't dawdle too long over your sherry, or what I have in the oven will be spoiled. Thank goodness, Christina will be down again tomorrow." She paused. "I don't really think that I *will* call on those Franchise people, if it is all the same to you. Apart from being strangers and very odd, they quite frankly terrify me."

Yes, that was a sample of the reaction Robert might expect where the Sharpes were concerned. Ben Carley had gone out of his way today to let him know that, if there was police trouble at The Franchise, he wouldn't be able to count on an unprejudiced jury. He must take measures for the protection of the Sharpes. When he saw them on Friday he would suggest a private investigation by a paid agent.

But by Friday morning it was too late to take measures for the protection of the Sharpes. Robert had reckoned with the slow spread of whispers, but he had not reckoned with the *Ack-Emma*.

The *Ack-Emma* was Britain's latest tabloid newspaper. It was run on the principle that two thousand pounds for damages is a cheap price to pay for sales worth half a million. It had blacker headlines, more sensational pictures, and more indiscreet stories than any other British paper. And it was the *Ack-Emma* that blew the Franchise affair wide open.

Robert had driven out early into the country on that Friday morning to see an old woman who wanted to alter her will. He hummed to himself on the way back to his office through the spring countryside. He was looking forward to seeing Marion Sharpe in less than an hour. He had decided to forgive her for liking Nevil. After all, Nevil had never tried to palm her off on Carley. One must be fair.

He ran the car into the garage and strolled over to the office to pay his bill to Brough, who ran the office side of the garage. But it was Stanley Peters, ex-Royal Corps of Signals, who was there thumbing over dockets and invoices. "I just looked in to pay my bill," said Robert. "Bill usually has it ready."

"I expect it's somewhere around," Stanley said, still thumbing. "Have a look."

Robert picked up some loose papers and uncovered a newspaper picture of a girl's face. It reminded him of someone and he paused to look at it.

"Got it!" said Stanley in triumph, extracting Robert's bill from a clip. He swept the remaining loose papers on the desk into a pile and so laid bare to Robert's gaze the whole front page of that morning's *Ack-Emma*.

Cold with shock, Robert stared at it. Stanley noticed his absorption. "Nice little number, that," he said. "Reminds me of a bird I once had. Same far-apart eyes. Told the most original lies."

Robert went on staring.

THIS IS THE GIRL

said the paper in enormous black letters across the top of the page; and below it, occupying two-thirds of the page, was the girl's photograph. And then, in smaller but still obtrusive type, below:

IS THIS THE HOUSE?

and below it a photograph of The Franchise.

Across the bottom of the page was the legend:

THE GIRL SAYS YES: WHAT DO THE POLICE SAY?
See inside for the story.

Robert turned the page. Yes; it was all there, except for the Sharpes' name.

The girl's photograph appeared to be a studio portrait. Her hair had an arranged look, and she was wearing what looked like a party frock. Without her school coat she appeared feminine instead of merely female.

But it was still a pathetically young face, immature and appealing. The candid brow, the wide-set eyes, the bee-stung lip that gave her mouth the expression of a disappointed child—it made a formidable whole. Who would doubt a story told by that face?

"May I borrow this paper?" he asked Stanley.

"Take it," Stanley said. "There's nothing in it."

Robert was surprised. "Didn't you find this interesting?" he asked, indicating the front page.

Stanley cast a glance at the pictured face. "Not except that she reminded me of that bird I knew, lies and all."

"So you didn't believe the girl's story?"

"What do *you* think?" Stanley said, contemptuous.

"Where do you think she was, then, all that time?"

"I'd say very definitely—oh, but definitely—on the streets," Stanley said, and went out to attend to a customer.

Robert picked up the paper and went soberly away. At his own office he found that Inspector Hallam had been trying to get him by telephone. He reached for the receiver with one hand and laid the paper under old Mr. Heseltine's nose with the other.

"We are both in a spot, aren't we!" Hallam said, when they were connected, and raked his vocabulary for some epithets suitable to the *Ack-Emma.* "As if the police hadn't enough to do without having that rag on their tails!" he finished.

"Have you heard from the Yard?"

"Yes, but there's nothing they can do. Just grin and bear it. The police are always fair game."

Hallam said a few more things about the press, then asked, "Do the Sharpes know?"

"I shouldn't think so. But they are due here in about ten minutes, and I'll show it to them then."

"If it was ever possible for me to be sorry for that old battle-axe," Hallam said, "it would be at this minute."

"How did the *Ack-Emma* get the story? I thought the girl's guardians were against publicity."

"Grant says the girl's brother went off the deep end about the police taking no action and went to the *Ack-Emma* on his own. The paper is strong on the champion act. 'The *Ack-Emma* will see right done!'"

"A shocking story," Mr. Heseltine said when Robert had hung up. He had been looking at the newspaper with distaste. "And if I may say so, a quite shocking publication."

"That house," Robert said, "is The Franchise, where old Mrs. Sharpe and her daughter live, and where I went the other day, if you remember, to give them some legal advice."

"You mean that these people are our clients?"

"Yes."

"But, Mr. Robert, that is not at all in our line."

Robert winced at the dismay in his voice. "We are competent, I hope, to defend any client against a publication like the *Ack-Emma*," he said coldly.

Mr. Heseltine eyed the screaming rag on the table with displeasure.

"Do you believe the girl's story?" Robert asked.

"I don't see how she could have made it up," Mr. Heseltine said simply. "It is such a very circumstantial story, isn't it?"

"It is, indeed. But I saw the girl when she was brought to The Franchise to identify it last week and I don't believe a word she says." He paused a moment. "And you'll just have to trust my judgment about it, Timmy," he added, using his childhood name for the old clerk.

Whether it was the "Timmy" or the argument, it was apparent that Mr. Heseltine had no further protest to make.

"You'll be able to see the criminals for yourself," Robert said. "I hear their voices in the hall now. You might bring them in, will you?"

Mrs. Sharpe, moved by some instinct for convention, had donned a hat in honor of the occasion. It was a flattish affair of black satin, and the general effect was that of a doctor of learning. That the effect had not been wasted was obvious by the relieved look on Mr. Heseltine's face.

When they were alone Robert noticed that Marion had been waiting to say something.

"An odd thing happened this morning," she said. "We went to the Anne Boleyn place to have coffee as usual—and there were two vacant tables, but when Miss Truelove saw us coming she very hastily tilted the chairs against the tables and said they were reserved. You don't think she did that because rumor has begun to get busy already, do you?"

"No," Robert said sadly, "she did it because she has read this morning's *Ack-Emma*." He turned the newspaper front side up. "I am sorry to have bad news for you. For the moment, you'll just have to grit your teeth and take it, as small boys say."

"Oh, no!" Marion said in passionate protest, as her eye fell on the picture of The Franchise. And then there was unbroken silence while the two women absorbed the contents of the inner page.

"I take it," Mrs. Sharpe said at last, "that we have no redress against this sort of thing?"

"None," Robert said. "All the statements are perfectly true. And it is all statement and not comment."

"The whole thing is one huge implied comment that the police failed to do their duty," Marion said. "Do they think we bribed them?"

"I think the suggestion is that the humble victim has less pull with the police than the wicked rich."

"Rich," repeated Marion, her voice curdling with bitterness.

"Now," Robert continued, "if you are not too shocked to think, consider: We *know* that the girl was never at The Franchise, that she could not—"

But Marion interrupted him. "Do *you* know it?" she asked.

"Yes," Robert said.

Her eyes lost their challenge, and her glance dropped. "Thank you," she said quietly.

"If the girl was never there, how could she have seen the house and the two of you in or around it, walled about as it is," Robert said. "She did see it somehow. It is too unlikely for belief that she could be merely repeating a description that someone else gave her."

"You could see the house, I suppose, from the top deck of a bus," Marion said. "But there are no double-decker buses on the Milford route. Or from on top of a load of hay, but it is the wrong time of year for hay."

"It may be the wrong time for hay," croaked Mrs. Sharpe, "but there is no season for truckloads. I have seen trucks loaded with goods as high as any hay wagon."

"Yes," Marion said. "Suppose the lift the girl got was on a truck."

"There is only one thing against that. If a girl was given a lift on a truck, she would be in the cab. They wouldn't perch her up on top of the load. . . . No one ever came to The Franchise to ask the way, or to sell something, or to mend something—someone that the girl could have been with, even in the background?"

But no, they were both sure that no one had come within the time the girl had been missing.

"Then we take it for granted that what she learned about The Franchise she learned from being high enough on one occasion to see over the wall. We shall probably never know when or how. So our whole efforts will have to be devoted, not to proving that she wasn't at The Franchise, but that she *was* somewhere else!"

"And what chance is there of that?" Mrs. Sharpe asked.

"A better chance than before this was published," Robert said, indicating the front page of the *Ack-Emma*. "If we have any luck at all someone, somewhere, will observe that the story and the photograph do not fit, because they personally know her to have been elsewhere."

Marion's face lost a little of its bleak look, and even Mrs. Sharpe's thin back looked less rigid.

"But what can we do in the way of private investigation?" Mrs. Sharpe asked. "You realize, I expect, that we have very little money."

"To begin with I am going myself to see the various people involved," Robert said. "I want to find out what she was *likely* to do."

There was a few moments' silence.

"You are extraordinarily kind, Mr. Blair." In Mrs. Sharpe's manner there was a hint almost of surprise, as if kindness was not one of the things she had normally met with in life.

"When do you go?" Marion asked.

"Directly after lunch."

"Then we won't keep you," Mrs. Sharpe said, rising.

When Robert had seen them into their car, he called Nevil into his room and then picked up the phone to call Aunt Lin.

"I suppose you don't see the *Ack-Emma* ever?" he asked Nevil, as he waited for Aunt Lin to answer. "Have a look at this morning's. Hullo, Aunt Lin."

Peering over the telephone, Robert observed with satisfaction the naked shock on his cousin's bright young features.

"Be an angel, Aunt Lin, and pack a bag for me, will you? Just for overnight. . . ."

Nevil had torn the paper open and was now reading the story. "The blasted *swine!*" he said, falling back in his need on the vernacular. "Printing an obvious piece of sensationalism by an unbalanced adolescent!"

"And if I told you that the said adolescent is an ordinary, well-spoken-of schoolgirl who is anything but sensational?" Robert asked.

"Have you seen her?"

"Yes. That was why I first went to The Franchise last week, to be there when Scotland Yard brought the girl to confront the Sharpes."

"To be there on their behalf?" Nevil relaxed suddenly. "Oh, well; that's all right. For a moment I thought you were against them. Now we can join forces to put a spoke in the wheel of this—" he flicked the paper "—this moppet. What are you going to do about it, Robert?"

Robert told him, and added, "And you will hold the fort while I am gone."

4

THE WYNNS' home outside Aylesbury was in a countrified suburb, the kind of district where rows of semidetached houses creep along the edge of still unspoiled fields. The Wynns lived in one of a string of ramshackle red brick dwellings that set Robert's teeth on edge, so raw they were, so crude, so hangdog. But as he drove slowly up the road he was won over by the love that had gone into their decoration, for each garden was a small miracle of love-liness.

Number 39 Meadowside Lane had plain green grass bordered by a rockery. The windows were bare to the sun, the air, and the human gaze. This augured a nonconformity that Robert had not expected. He rang the bell.

Mrs. Wynn surprised him even more than her windows did. She was slight and young and still pretty, and had a pair of the most intelligent bright brown eyes Robert had ever seen.

When she saw a stranger she made an involuntary closing move-ment with the door, but a second glance at Robert seemed to reassure her. Robert explained his presence and added, "You are under no obligation to talk to me, but I hope very much that you won't refuse. I have told Inspector Grant at Scotland Yard that I was going to see you this afternoon, on my clients' behalf."

She stepped back to let him come past her. "I expect you have to do your best for those people if you are their lawyer. And we have nothing to hide. But if it is Betty you want to interview, I'm afraid you can't. We have sent her into the country to friends to avoid all the fuss. Leslie meant well, but it was a stupid thing to do."

"Leslie?"

"My son. Sit down, won't you?" She offered him one of the easy chairs in a pleasant, uncluttered sitting room. "He was too angry about the police to think clearly—angry about their failure to do anything. He has always been devoted to Betty. Indeed, until he got engaged they were inseparable."

Robert's ears pricked. "Engaged?" he asked.

"Yes. He got engaged just after the New Year to a very nice girl. We are all delighted."

"Was Betty delighted?"

"I expect she missed not coming first with him as she used to, but she was very nice about it," Mrs. Wynn said, looking at him with her intelligent eyes. "She *is* a nice girl, Mr. Blair. Believe me."

"Yes, I know. Everyone reports excellently of her. Is your son's fiancée a schoolfellow of hers?"

"No, her people have come recently to live near here, and he met her at a dance."

"So Betty had not met the fiancée?"

"None of us had. He rather sprang her on us. But we liked her so much we didn't mind."

"He must be very young to be settling down?"

"Oh, the whole thing is absurd, of course. He is twenty and she is eighteen. But they are very sweet together. And I was very young myself when I married, and I have been very happy. The only thing I lacked was a daughter, and Betty filled that gap."

"What does she want to do when she leaves school?"

"She doesn't know. I have a notion that she will marry early. Girls who have no particular bent fall easily into matrimony."

"When Betty failed to turn up in time to go back to school, you thought she was just playing truant?"

"Yes; she was growing bored with school. So we thought she was just 'taking advantage,' as they say."

"I see. Was she wearing school clothes on her holiday?"

For the first time Mrs. Wynn looked doubtfully at him, uncertain of his motive in asking. "No, she was wearing her weekend clothes. . . . You know that when she came back she was wearing only a frock and shoes?"

Robert nodded.

"I find it difficult to imagine women so depraved that they would treat a helpless child like that."

"If you could meet the women, Mrs. Wynn, you would find it still more difficult to imagine."

Robert then wanted to know about the bruises on the girl's body. Were they fresh bruises?

"Oh, quite fresh. Most of them had not begun to 'turn' even."

This surprised Robert a little.

"But there were older bruises as well, I take it."

"If there were, they had faded so much as to be unnoticeable."

"Mrs. Wynn," Robert went on, "has there never been any suspicion in your mind that Betty's story might not be true?"

"None. She has always been a truthful child. And how could she invent a long circumstantial story like that without being found out?"

"Did she tell her story to you all in a piece?"

"Oh, no; it was spread over a day or two. The outline, first. And then filling in the details as she remembered them."

"Her days of coma had not blurred her memory?"

"I don't think they would in any case. Betty has a photographic memory."

Has she indeed! thought Robert, both ears erect and wide open.

"Even as a small child she could look at the page of a book—a child's book, of course—and repeat most of the contents from the picture in her mind."

"I realize this is a subject that must be unpleasant for you," Robert said. "But perhaps you could tell me something about Betty's parents. What were they like?"

"Her parents? We never even saw them."

"But you had Betty for—what was it?—nine months?—before her parents were killed, hadn't you?"

"Yes, but her mother wrote shortly after Betty came to us and said that to come to see her would only upset the child, and that the best thing for everyone would be to leave her to us until such time as she could go back to London."

Robert's heart contracted with pity for this unknown dead woman who had been willing to tear her own heart out for her child.

"Did she settle down easily when she came? Or did she cry for her mother?"

"I don't remember her ever crying for her mother," Mrs. Wynn replied. "She fell in love with Leslie the first night—she was just a baby, you know—and I think her interest in him blotted out any grief she might have felt. And he, being four years older, was just the right age to feel protective. He still does—that is why we are in this mess today."

"How did this *Ack-Emma* affair happen? I know it was your son who went to the paper, but did you eventually come round to his—"

"Good heavens, no," Mrs. Wynn said indignantly. "My husband and I knew nothing about it until this morning, when Leslie laid an *Ack-Emma* under our noses. A little defiantly, I may add. He is not feeling too good about it now that it is done. If he had not been worked up—"

"I know. I know exactly how it happened. That tell-us-your-troubles-and-we'll-see-right-done of the *Ack-Emma*'s is insidious stuff." He rose. "You have been very kind indeed, Mrs. Wynn, and I am exceedingly grateful to you."

His tone was evidently more heartfelt than she had expected, and she looked doubtfully at him. What have I said to help you? she seemed to be asking, half dismayed.

He asked where Betty's parents had lived in London, and she told him. "There is nothing there now," she added. "Just open space. It is to be part of some new building scheme, but they have done nothing to it so far."

On the doorstep he said in parting, "Mrs. Wynn, if it ever occurs to you that anything in that story of Betty's does not ring true, I hope you won't decide that sleeping dogs are best left."

"Don't pin your faith to that hope, Mr. Blair. If I believed her at the beginning, I am not likely to doubt her later."

"One never knows. Someday it may occur to you that this or that does not fit. Something that has puzzled you deep down may refuse to be pushed down anymore."

She had walked to the gate with him, and as he spoke the last sentence he turned to take farewell of her. To his surprise something moved behind her eyes at that last remark of his.

So she wasn't certain after all.

And then, with what he always remembered afterwards as his only experience of telepathic communication, he paused and asked, "Had she anything in her pockets when she came home?"

There was the faintest tightening of the muscles round her mouth. "Just a lipstick," she said evenly.

"A lipstick! She is a little young for that, isn't she?"

"My dear Mr. Blair, they start experimenting with lipstick at the age of ten." She smiled and said good-by again and moved towards the house as he drove away.

So there was a lipstick. And its presence was something that puzzled Mrs. Wynn. Well, that was a straw that could be added to the little heap he had collected. To the fact that the girl had a photographic memory. To the fact that her adoring older brother had suddenly acquired a fiancée only a month or two ago. To the fact that she was bored with school.

To the fact—above all—that not even detached sensible Mrs. Wynn knew what went on in Betty Kane's mind. It was quite unbelievable that a girl of fifteen who had been the center of a young man's world could see herself supplanted overnight without reacting violently to the situation. But Betty had been "very nice about it."

To Robert it was proof that her candid young face was no guide at all to Betty Kane.

ROBERT had decided to kill a great many birds with one stone by spending the night in London.

To begin with, he wanted to have his hand held, and no one could do that to better purpose than his old school friend Kevin Macdermott. What Kevin did not know about crime was probably not so anyhow. And as a well-known defending counsel his knowledge of human nature was extensive and varied.

Robert and Kevin had first gravitated towards each other at school, and they had remained friends because they were complementary. To the Irish Kevin, Robert's equanimity was amusing, provocative, and restful. To Robert, Kevin's Celt flamboyance was exotic and fascinating.

Kevin had married happily, had a pleasant house near Weybridge and three hardy sons. For town purposes he kept a small apartment in St. Paul's Churchyard, and whenever Robert was in London they dined together, either at Kevin's apartment or at the latest place where Kevin had found good claret.

Kevin was to be at some Bar dinner tonight, so his secretary had said, but would Robert go along to the apartment after dinner and wait for him?

At the Fortescue, the old Edwardian hotel in Jermyn Street, they greeted him like a nephew, gave him "the room he had last time," and brought him up a tray on which reposed an ample tea.

Much refreshed, Robert went out into the evening to find the vacant space where that block of apartments had been, where both Betty Kane's parents had died in one shattering burst of high explosives. Across the street a row of small shops still stood as they had obviously stood for fifty years or more. He walked over to the tobacconist's to buy cigarettes. A tobacconist knows everything.

"Were you here when that happened?" Robert asked, inclining his head towards the vacant space across the street.

"Oh, the incident?" asked the rosy little man. "No, I was out on duty. Warden, I was."

"You would know the local people well, then. Do you remember a couple named Kane who lived in the block of apartments, by any chance?"

"The Kanes? Of course I do. They were the caretakers—in and out of this place all day. You knew them, sir?"

"No. But I met someone the other day who spoke of them."

The little man sucked his teeth with a derisive sound. "It was just her bad luck that the only evening in weeks that she was at home with her husband, a bomb had to come." He seemed to find a sardonic pleasure in the thought.

"Did she work somewhere in the evenings, then?" Robert asked.

"Work!" said the little man, with vast scorn. "Her! She was out having a good time. Out dancing with officers. Kane, he wanted her to go away to the country with that little girl of theirs, but would she? Not her! It's my opinion she was tickled to death to have the child off her hands."

"And her husband?"

"Ah, he was all right, Bert Kane was. Deserved better luck than that woman. Terribly fond of the little girl. Spoiled her, of course, but she was a nice kid, for all that. Demure."

Robert went out into the street both saddened and relieved. Sad for Bert Kane, who had deserved better; but relieved that Betty Kane's mother was not the loving woman he had pictured. And Betty on her part looked very like being her mother's daughter.

WHEN Robert arrived at Kevin's apartment, he found the "daily" woman waiting for him with her hat on. Mr. Macdermott's secretary had arranged for her to stay and let him in, she explained. There was whisky on the little table by the fire.

It was a pleasant little place, peaceful now that the roar of the city traffic was still. Robert poured himself a drink and then sat down and relaxed for the first time since he had gone out that morning. He was half asleep when he heard Kevin's key in the lock. "Well, what with Blair, Hayward, and Bennet," Kevin said cheerfully, "it can't be bankruptcy; so I suppose it's a woman."

Robert stood up. "Yes, but not the way you mean."

Kevin removed his jacket, poured himself a whisky, and sat down. "I needn't ask if you are up on business. I suppose you dash off again tomorrow after a ten a.m. interview with someone's solicitors."

"No," Robert said. "With Scotland Yard."

Kevin paused with his glass halfway to his mouth. "What has the Yard to do with your ivory tower?" he asked. The calm certainty of Blair, Hayward, and Bennet had always pricked Kevin into small gibes.

Robert took out his copy of Betty Kane's statement to the police. "This is a very short statement. I wish you would read it and tell me how it strikes you." He wanted the impact on Kevin, without preliminaries to dull the edge of it.

Kevin read the first paragraph swiftly and said, "This is the *Ack-Emma*'s protégée, I take it."

"I had no idea that you ever saw the *Ack-Emma*," Robert said, surprised.

"God love you, I feed on the *Ack-Emma*. No crime, no Kevin Macdermott." For four minutes his absorption was so complete that Robert felt alone in the room. "Humph!" Kevin said, coming out of it.

"Well?"

"I take it that your clients are the two women in the case, and not this girl?"

"Of course."

"Now you tell me your end," Kevin said, and listened while Robert gave him the whole story.

When Robert had finished, Kevin said, "So tonight the Yard is moving heaven and earth to find evidence that will back up the girl's story."

"I suppose so," said Robert, depressed. "But what I want to know is: Do you or do you not believe the girl's story?"

"I never believe anyone's story," Kevin pointed out with gentle malice. "What you really want to know is: Do I find the girl's version believable? And of course I do."

"But it's an absurd tale," Robert said, more hotly than he had intended, as he sat down again.

"There is nothing absurd about it. Women who live lonely lives do insane things—especially if they are poor gentlewomen. Only the other day an elderly woman was found to have kept her sister chained to a bed in a room no bigger than a good-sized cupboard. That is a much more unbelievable tale than this girl's."

Robert sank a little deeper into his depression.

"Here are two lonely women saddled with a big house in the country, one of them too old to do much household work and the other loathing it. What is the most likely form for their mild insanity to take? The capture of a girl to be servant to them, of course."

Damn Kevin and his counsel's mind!

"The girl they capture happens to be a blameless schoolgirl, conveniently far from home. Everyone is going to take her word against the women's. If I were the police I would have risked it." He shot an amused glance at Robert, sunk gloomily in his chair.

"Of course," Kevin continued, "they may have remembered a parallel case, where everyone believed the girl's heartrending story and were very thoroughly led up the garden."

"A parallel!" Robert said, sitting up. "When?"

"Seventeenth century. I forget the exact date."

"Oh," said Robert, dashed again.

"The nature of alibis has not changed much in two centuries," Macdermott said mildly. "If the seventeenth-century case is any guide, the girl's story is an alibi."

"Then you believe—I mean you find it believable—that the girl's story is all nonsense?"

"A complete invention from beginning to end."

"Kevin, you are maddening. You said you found it believable."

"So I do. I also find it believable that it is a tissue of lies. I can make a very good case for either side at the shortest notice."

He got up to help himself to more whisky, holding out his other hand for Robert's glass. But Robert shook his head without lifting his gaze from the fire. He was tired and beginning to be out of temper with Kevin.

"I wonder what she was doing all that month," Kevin said conversationally, taking a large gulp of whisky.

Robert's mouth opened to say, "Then you *do* believe the girl is a fake!" but he stopped himself in time. "If you drink so much whisky on top of claret, what *you* will be doing for a month is a cure, my lad," he said instead. And to his surprise Kevin sat down and laughed like a schoolboy.

"Oh, Rob, I love you," he said delightedly. "You are the very essence of England. You sit there so mild, so polite, and let people bait you, until they conclude that you are an old tabby, and then wham! out comes that businesslike paw." He picked up Robert's glass without a by-your-leave and rose to fill it. Robert let him. He was feeling better.

Detective Inspector Grant had been charming in his quiet reasonable way and had quite willingly agreed that Robert should be told about any letters that the *Ack-Emma* might provoke.

"Don't pin your hopes too firmly to that, will you?" he had said, in friendly warning. "For one helpful letter the Yard gets, it gets five thousand from the busybodies, the idle, the perverted, the cranks, the feel-it-my-duties. My God, how they write!"

"But there is a chance—"

"Oh, yes. There is a chance. And all these letters will have to be weeded out, however silly they are. Anything of importance will be passed on to you, I promise."

So Robert had come away pleased with the Yard and sorry for them. At least he, Robert, had a straight row to hoe. And moreover he had Kevin's approval of the row he had chosen.

Now Robert was speeding down the black shining Larborough road on his way to see Betty's aunt and uncle—the people she had stayed with on the memorable holiday. A Mr. and Mrs. Tilsit, they were, 93 Cherrill Street, Mainshill, Larborough. Mr. Tilsit was traveling agent for a firm of brush makers.

Cherrill Street was one long series of bay windows framed in dirty red brick. The sour soil on either side of each window that did duty for a garden grew only weedy wallflowers and moth-eaten forget-me-nots. What had Betty found in this rather dreary grimy street that made her so happy that she had wanted to stay on for the rest of her holidays?

Her aunt, Mrs. Tilsit, turned out to be one of those women whose minds are always on something else. They chat brightly with you, they agree with you, they offer advice, but their real attention is concentrated on anything except the subject in hand.

She seemed impressed with the appearance of Robert's car and asked him in to have a cup of tea. Robert felt that he could not drink with her without making plain his position. He did his best, but it was doubtful if she understood. Mention of her niece made none of the expected stir in her emotions.

"A most extraordinary thing that was, wasn't it?" she said. "Taking her away and beating her. What good did they think that was going to do them? Sit down, Mr. Blayne, come in and sit down."

While Mrs. Tilsit went into the kitchen Robert sat down and again considered the surroundings and wondered why Betty Kane had found them so good. Had she found a friend? A girl next door? A boy next door?

Mrs. Tilsit came back in what seemed like two minutes, bearing a tray with tea. At least, he thought, watching her pour, this woman explained one of the oddities in the affair: the fact that when the Wynns had written to have Betty sent home at once, her aunt had not flown to a telegraph office to break the news that Betty had left for home nearly a fortnight ago.

"I wasn't worried about her," Mrs. Tilsit said, as if in echo to his thoughts. "When they wrote from Aylesbury about her, I knew she would turn up all right, and she did. Well, nearly all right."

"She said she enjoyed her holiday here enormously."

"I suppose she did," she said vaguely.

"How did she pass her time? Did she make friends?"

"Oh, no, she was in Larborough most of the time."

"Larborough! How did she spend her time there?"

"Pictures, mostly. You can do that from morning till night in Larborough."

"Is that what Betty did?"

"Oh, no. She used to go in to the morning round because you get in cheaper before noon, and then she'd go bus riding."

"Bus riding. Where?"

"Oh, anywhere the fancy took her. She went to see the castle at Norton one day. Norton's the county town you know."

"Did she not come home to lunch, then?"

"No, she'd have coffee lunch somewhere. We always have our real meal at night anyhow, you see."

So the girl had been her own mistress for a good fortnight. Free to come and go without question. The cinema in the morning, or window gazing, a coffee lunch, a bus ride into the country in the afternoon. A blissful holiday for an adolescent—the first taste of unsupervised freedom.

But Betty Kane was no normal adolescent. She was the girl who had told that long and circumstantial story to the police without a tremor. The girl with four weeks of her life unaccounted for. The girl that someone had beaten unmercifully. How, then, had she spent her unsupervised freedom?

IT WAS with a feeling of escape that Robert drove into Larborough, where he sought out the main garage of the Larborough and District Motor Services. In the small office that guarded one side of the entrance a man in a bus inspector's uniform was going through papers on the desk.

Robert said that he wanted to see someone who would know about the Milford bus service.

"Timetable on the wall outside," the man said without looking up.

"I don't want to know about times. I want to know if you ever run a double-decker bus on the route to Milford."

"No," said the man.

"Never?" Robert asked.

This time there was no answer at all. "Listen," Robert said, "this is important. I am a partner in a firm of solicitors in Milford, and I—"

The man turned on him. "I don't care if you are the shah of Persia; there are *no double-decker buses on the Milford run!* And what do *you* want?" he added, noticing a mechanic who had been standing behind Robert in the doorway.

The mechanic hesitated, as if the business he had come on had been upset by a newer interest. "It's about those spares for Norton. Shall I—"

As Robert was edging past him out of the office, he felt a tug on his coat and realized that the mechanic wanted to talk to him outside. Robert went out and bent over his own car until the mechanic appeared at his elbow.

"You asking about double-decker buses to Milford? I couldn't contradict him straight out, you know; in the mood he's in now it'd be as much as my job's worth. Well, there are not supposed to be, but once or twice this year we've had to use a double-decker when one of the old single ones broke down unexpected."

"Would it be possible to find out exactly when a double-decker did run on that route?"

"Oh, certainly," the mechanic said, with a shade of bitterness. "In this firm it's recorded every time you spit. But the records are in there"—he tilted back his head to indicate the office—"and as long as *he's* there there's nothing doing."

Robert asked at what hour there would be something doing.

"Well—he goes off at the same time as me: six. But I could wait a few minutes and look up the schedules when he's gone, if it's very important to you. I'll meet you in the Bell, that's the pub at the end of the street, about a quarter past six. That do?"

That would do perfectly, Robert said. Perfectly.

5

"I suppose you know what you're doing, dear," Aunt Lin said, "but I can't help thinking it's very odd of you to defend people like that."

"I am not defending them," Robert said patiently, "I am representing them. And there is no evidence whatever that they are 'people like that.'"

Aunt Lin was standing in his doorway passing her prayer book from one hand to the other as she put on her white gloves. "Do you have to go out to their *house?* Surely they could come to the office tomorrow."

"If you stand there much longer you'll be late to church for the first time in ten years," Robert said.

"Oh, dear, the church bells have stopped, haven't they? I'll just have to slip into the Bracketts' pew. You won't stay to lunch at that place, will you, dear?"

"I don't suppose that I shall be invited."

But his welcome at The Franchise was so warm that he felt that he might very well be invited after all.

"I am sorry we refused to answer when you phoned last night,"

Marion apologized. "But after four or five heckling calls it seemed sensible to ignore the phone."

"Your telephone callers, were they male or female?"

"One male and four female, as far as I remember. When you rang this morning I thought they were beginning again, but perhaps such people don't get evil-minded before dark. We certainly provided the Saturday evening entertainment for a group of country youths."

"Good Lord!" Robert said. "Have you been harassed in other ways?"

"They congregated inside the gate and catcalled," she added. "Then Nevil found a bar of wood—"

"Nevil?"

"Yes, he came to pay what he called a visit of condolence. And he found a bar that could be wedged in the gateway to keep the thing shut; we have no key for it, you see. But of course that didn't stop them for long. They hoisted each other up on the wall and sat there in a row being offensive."

"Lack of education," old Mrs. Sharpe said thoughtfully, "is an extraordinary handicap when one is being offensive. They had no resource at all."

"We must see what police protection we can claim," said Robert. "Meanwhile I can tell you something pleasanter about that wall. I now know how the girl saw over it."

He told them about his talk with Mrs. Tilsit and his subsequent discovery that at the time Betty Kane was spending afternoons bus riding out of Larborough there were two occasions when a double-decker bus had to be substituted on the Milford run.

"But could anyone passing on top of a bus take in the house, the courtyard, we two, and the car, all together?" Marion asked.

"Have you ever traveled on the upper deck of a country bus? Even at a steady thirty-five, the pace seems funereal. You can see so much further, and you can see it so much longer. In addition, Betty Kane has a photographic memory." And he told them what Mrs. Wynn had said.

"Do we tell the police this?" Mrs. Sharpe asked.

"No. It doesn't prove anything; just solves the problem of how she knew about you. What she saw was the grass and the divided path, the car at the door with the odd wheel, two women—both individual—the round attic window in the roof. She had only to look at the picture in her mind and describe it. The day she used the picture for—the day she was supposed to have been kidnapped —was more than a month away and it was a thousand to one against your being able to say what you had done or where you had been on that day."

"It seems to me," Mrs. Sharpe said, "that the girl also took a great risk in choosing The Franchise, knowing nothing of its circumstances."

"Of course," Robert said. "But I don't think it was as big a gamble as you think. What you are saying is that for all the girl knew there might be a large household of young people and three maidservants at The Franchise."

"Yes."

"But I think she knew quite well that there were no such things."

"How could she?"

"Either she gossiped with the bus conductor, or—and I think this is the more likely—she overheard comment from her fellow passengers. You know the kind of thing: 'There are the Sharpes. Fancy living alone in a big house like that, just the two of them. And no maids willing to stay in a lonely place so far from shops and the pictures—' and so on. It is very much a local bus, and The Franchise is the only spot of human interest for miles."

"Yes, that makes sense."

"The girl says she was never in Milford and doesn't know where it is. But if a conductor remembered her, we could at least shake her story to that extent."

"I'm afraid, though," Mrs. Sharpe said, "that we will never really disprove her story unless we can say what she was doing in that month."

"Somehow I am far more hopeful of that today than I was on Friday morning," Robert said. "We know so much more about the girl now."

"What do you think she was really doing?" Mrs. Sharpe asked.

"I think she met someone in Larborough. We'll call him X. It's from that supposition that I think any inquiry of ours should start."

"And what do we do about engaging an agent?" asked Mrs. Sharpe.

"Well," Robert said, hesitating, "it had crossed my mind that you might let me pursue my own inquiries a little further before we engage a professional. Coming home in the car last night, I realized how much I should hate giving up the search to someone else."

"Mr. Blair," the old woman said, interrupting him, "you have been very kind in doing your best for us. But we cannot expect you to turn yourself into a private inquiry agent on our behalf."

"If Mr. Blair is willing to carry on a little longer," Marion said, "I think we should thank him heartily and accept. I know just how he feels. I wish I could go hunting myself."

"There will no doubt come a time when I shall have to turn it over to a proper inquiry agent," Robert said. "But as long as the search is on our doorsteps I do want to be the one to pursue it."

"How do you plan to go about it?" Marion asked.

"Well, I had thought of beginning with the coffee-lunch places in Larborough. There can't be so very many of them. Once she had met the hypothetical X, she may have lunched anywhere. But up till then she paid for her own lunches, and they were coffee ones. So I'll flourish the *Ack-Emma* at the waitresses and find out whether they have ever seen the girl in their place. Does that sound like sense to you?"

"Very good sense," Marion said.

Robert turned to Mrs. Sharpe. "But if you think you will be better served by a professional, then I shall bow out with—"

"I don't think we could be better served by anyone," Mrs. Sharpe said. "Marion, there is still some of the Amontillado, I think."

In the silence that succeeded Marion's departure to fetch the sherry, the quiet of the old house became apparent. Mrs. Sharpe and Robert were sitting in the drawing room, facing the window, looking out on the green square of the courtyard and faded pink of the brick wall. And as they looked the gate was pushed open and a group of seven or eight people appeared and stood gazing. Entirely at their ease they were, pointing out to each other facts of interest—the favorite being the round window in the roof.

Robert glanced at Mrs. Sharpe, but except for a tightening of her mouth she had not moved.

"Our public," she said at last, witheringly.

"Shall I go and move them on?" Robert said. "It's my fault for not putting back the wooden bar you left off for me."

"Let them be," she said. "They will go presently."

But the visitors showed no sign of going. Indeed, one group had moved round the house to inspect the outbuildings; and the rest were still there when Marion came back with the sherry. Robert was feeling small and inadequate. It went against the grain to stay there quietly and watch strangers prowling round as if they were contemplating buying the place. But what power had he to make them go? And how would he look in the Sharpes' eyes if he had to beat a retreat? While he hesitated, angry with himself and with those crude creatures outside, a tall young man in a regrettable tweed suit arrived.

"Nevil," breathed Marion, watching the scene.

Nevil surveyed the group with his most insufferable air of superiority, but they were evidently determined to stand their ground. He looked at them silently for a further few seconds, then fished in his inner pocket for something. At the first movement of his hand a strange difference came over the group. The outer members of it faded unobtrusively through the gate; the nearer ones lost their air of bravado. Finally there was a general exodus.

Nevil banged the gate to behind them, levered the wooden bar into place, and strolled up the path to the door, wiping his hands fastidiously on his handkerchief. And Marion ran out to the door to meet him.

"Nevil!" Robert heard her say. "How did you get rid of those creatures?"

"You've no idea how discreet people become if you take out a notebook and ask for their names and addresses," Nevil said.

"Hello, Robert. Good morning, Mrs. Sharpe. I'm actually on my way to Larborough to lunch with Rosemary and my prospective father-in-law, but I saw the gate open and these two cars outside, so I stopped to investigate. I didn't know Robert was here."

Nevil's quite innocent implication was that of course Robert was capable of dealing equally well with the situation. Robert could have brained him.

Nevil took his leave. "*Au revoir*, Mrs. Sharpe. Don't let Robert drink all the sherry."

When he had gone, Mrs. Sharpe asked, "Is the sherry too dry for you, Mr. Blair?"

"No, oh no, thank you, it is excellent." Was it possible that he had been looking sour? He stole a cautious glance at the old lady and thought that she was looking faintly amused. "I think I had better go before Miss Sharpe bars the gate behind Nevil," he said. "Otherwise she will have to come to the gate again with me."

"Won't you stay and have lunch with us?"

But Robert made his excuses. He didn't like the Robert Blair he was becoming. Petty and childish and inadequate. Nevil had gone by the time he reached the gate, and Marion was about to close it. She smiled at him. "I hoped you would stay for lunch, but in a way I'm rather relieved that you aren't."

"Are you indeed?"

"I made a blancmange, but it didn't stand up. I do faithfully what it says in the cookbook, but it hardly ever works out. So you will be better off with your Aunt Lin's apple tart."

"I'll let you know tomorrow night how I get on in Larborough," he said matter-of-factly. Since he was not on hens-and-Maupassant terms with her, he would keep the conversation to practicalities. "And I'll ring up Inspector Hallam and see if one of their men can give a look round The Franchise once or twice a day to discourage idlers."

"You are very kind, Mr. Blair," she said. "I can't imagine what it would be without you to lean on."

Well, if he couldn't be young and a poet, he could be a crutch. A dull thing, a thing resorted to only in emergencies, but useful.

At half past twelve on Monday, Robert staggered into the lounge of the Midland Hotel in Larborough, and called for strong waters. As far as he knew he had covered all the likely coffee shops in the center of the city and in not one of them had anyone remembered seeing Betty Kane. What was worse, everyone agreed that if she had been there they would have remembered her.

As Albert, the tubby little lounge waiter, set his drink in front of him, Robert asked, "I suppose you've never seen this girl in your place, Albert?"

Albert looked at the front page of the *Ack-Emma* and shook his head. "No sir. Looks a little young, sir, if I may say so, for the lounge of the Midland."

"She mightn't look so young with a hat on," Robert said, considering the photograph.

"A hat." Albert paused. "Now, wait a minute. A *hat*." Albert laid his little tray down and picked up the paper. "Yes, of course; that's the girl in the green hat!"

"You mean she came in here for coffee?"

"No, for tea. Fancy me not seeing that! Of course it's some time ago now. About six weeks or so, it must be. She always came early; just about three, when we start serving teas."

So that is what she did. Fool that he was not to have seen that! She had tea, not lunch, and after the cinema, not before.

"I noticed her because she always came alone. The first time she came I thought she was waiting for relations. That's the kind of kid she looked."

"Can you remember what she wore?"

"Oh, yes. She always wore the same things. A green hat and a frock to match it under a pale gray coat. Nice plain clothes and no airs. And then one day she picked up the man at the next table. You could have knocked me over with a feather."

"You mean he picked her up."

"Oh, no; it was the girl's doing. He hadn't even thought of her when he sat down there. And as neat a piece of business, let me tell you, sir, as if she had spent a lifetime at it." He gazed in wonder at the pictured face.

"What was the man like? Did you know him?"

"No, he wasn't one of our regulars. Dark. Youngish. Business gent, I should say."

"You wouldn't know him again, then."

"I might, sir, I might. But not to swear to. You—er—planning any swearing to, sir?"

Robert had known Albert for nearly twenty years and had always found him of an excellent discretion. "It's like this, Albert," he said. "These people are my clients." He tapped the photograph of The Franchise, and Albert gave vent to a low whistle.

"A tough spot for you, Mr. Blair."

"Yes, as you say, a tough spot. But mostly for them. You can imagine the lives these women are leading. They have had to ask the telephone exchange not to put through any more calls."

"Have the police dropped the case, then?"

"No, but they can't do anything to help *us*. What they are looking for is corroboration of the girl's story. They haven't found it yet, but you see the spot we are in. Unless we can find out where the girl was during the weeks she says she was at The Franchise, the Sharpes will be in the position of being permanently convicted of a thing they haven't even been accused of!"

He went in to have lunch, and then called Scotland Yard for a description of the clothes Betty was wearing when she was missing. And in less than seven minutes he had it. A green felt hat, a green wool frock to match, and a pale gray cloth coat with large gray buttons.

Well, at last he had found it, that starting point for inquiry. Jubilation filled him. He sat down in the lounge on his way out and wrote a note to tell Kevin Macdermott that the young woman from Aylesbury had a far less believable story than she had had on Friday night.

The hypothetical X had ceased to be hypothetical. He had become plain X. He, Robert, could go back to The Franchise in triumph. But how did one follow up a young dark business gent who had had tea in the lounge of the Midland about six weeks previously? Young dark business gents were the Midland's clientele; and as far as Robert could see all as like as two peas anyhow. He was very much afraid that this was where he bowed out and handed over to a professional bloodhound.

As HE neared the Sharpes' house, Robert grew anxious, wondering if Monday, too, had provided its quota of sightseers. But when he came within sight of it he found the long stretch of road deserted; and as he came nearer he saw why. At the gate of The Franchise was the solid, dark blue figure of a policeman.

Delighted that Hallam had been so generous with his scanty force, Robert stopped to exchange greetings, but the greeting died on his lips. Along the full length of the tall brick wall, in letters nearly six feet high, was splashed a slogan. FASCISTS! screamed the large white capitals. And again on the further side of the gate: FASCISTS!

"Move along, please," the policeman said, approaching Robert with polite menace. "No stopping here."

Robert got slowly out of the car.

"Oh, Mr. Blair. Didn't recognize you, sir. Sorry."

"Is it whitewash?"

"No, sir, best quality paint."

"Great heavens! I suppose you haven't got the culprits?"

"No, sir. I just came along on my evening beat to clear away the usual gapers and found it like that when I arrived. Two men in a car, if all reports are true."

"Do the Sharpes know about it?"

"Yes, I had to get in to telephone. We have a code now. I tie my handkerchief on the end of my nightstick and wave it over the top of the gate when I want to speak to them. Do you want to go in, sir?"

"No, no. I'll get the post office to let me through on the telephone. If this is going to continue they must get keys for the gate so that I can have a duplicate. Are you staying here?"

"The sergeant said when I telephoned that I was to stay till dark."

"No one overnight?"

"No, sir. No spare men for that. Anyhow, they'll be all right once it gets dark. The Larborough lot don't like the country once it gets dark."

Robert felt doubtful. Two women, alone in that big quiet house after dark, with hatred and violence just outside the wall—it was not a comfortable thought.

"Don't worry, sir," the policeman said, watching his face. "Nothing's going to happen to them. This is England, after all."

"So is the *Ack-Emma* England," Robert reminded him. But he got back into the car again. After all, it *was* England, famed for minding its own business. And it was no country hand that had splashed FASCISTS! on the wall. It was doubtful if the country had ever heard the term. The country, when it wanted insults, used older, Saxon words.

As ROBERT turned his car into the garage, Stanley, who was shrugging off his overalls, glanced at his face and asked, "Something the matter?"

"I've been trying to get someone to wipe a painted slogan off the walls of The Franchise, but everyone is extraordinarily busy all of a sudden."

"A slogan," Stanley said. "What kind of slogan?" And Bill, hearing the exchange, oozed himself through the narrow office door to listen.

Robert told them. "In best quality white paint, so the policeman on the beat assures me."

"When I was in the Signals," Stanley said, beginning to pull up his overalls again, "I was given a free tour of Italy. I escaped the malaria, and the Italians, and the partisans, but I got a phobia. I took a great dislike to slogans on walls."

"What'll we get it off with?" Bill asked.

"What's the good of owning the best equipped and most modern garage in Milford if we haven't something to take off a spot of paint?" Stanley said.

"Bless you," Robert said. "Bless you both. I have only one ambition tonight: to get that slogan off the wall before breakfast tomorrow. I'll get some work clothes on and come out after you."

"Look," Stanley said patiently, "we don't need any help for a little job like that. You haven't eaten yet and we have, and I've heard it said that Miss Bennet doesn't like her good meals spoiled."

The comfortable quiet of his home—so different from the dead silence of The Franchise—welcomed and soothed him. A faint smell of roasting apples escaped from the kitchen. Guilty at being the owner of this waiting peace, he picked up the telephone to talk to Marion.

"Oh, *you!* How nice," she said, when at last he had persuaded the post office that his intentions were honorable. "I'm so glad. I was wondering how we were going to talk to you, but I might have known that you would manage it. I suppose you've seen our wall decoration?"

Robert said yes, but that by the time the sun rose it would have gone. "The two men who own my garage have decided to obliterate it tonight."

"But—could 'seven maids with seven mops'—"

"If Stanley and Bill have set their minds on it, obliterated it will be. And I have more good news for you: I have established the fact that X exists. Betty Kane had tea with him one day. Picked him up at the Midland, in the lounge."

"Picked him up? But she is just a child, and so— Oh, well, she told that story, of course. After that anything is possible."

"You've had a bad day at The Franchise, haven't you?" he said, when he had finished the saga of the coffee-lunch shops.

"Yes, I feel dirty all over. The mail was the worst. We have decided that in future we shall burn all letters without opening them, unless we recognize the writing. One of the letters was from Nevil. Actually, it was a poem."

"Oh. Did you understand it?"

"No, but it is nice to have poems made to one's eyebrows," she said. "Though it is still nicer to have one's wall made clean. I do thank you for Bill and Stanley. If you want to be very kind, perhaps you would bring or send us some food tomorrow?"

"Food!" he said, horrified that he had not thought of that before. "Yes, of course. I forgot that you would not be able to shop."

She gave him a list of things, and then added, "I'm afraid we are taking up a great deal of your time."

"This has become a personal matter with me," he said.

"Personal?"

"The one ambition of my life is to discredit Betty Kane."

"Oh. Oh, I see." Her voice sounded half relieved, half—could it be?—disappointed. "Well, we shall look forward to seeing you to-morrow."

But she was to see him long before that.

He went to bed early, but about midnight he heard a car drive up, and presently through the open window he heard Bill's cautious call, "Mr. Blair! Hey, Mr. Blair!"

He was at the window almost at once. "What is it?"

"There's trouble at The Franchise. I've got to go for the police because the telephone wire is cut," Bill said.

"What kind of trouble?"

"Hooligans. I'll come in for you on my way back. In about four minutes."

"Is Stanley with the Sharpes?" Robert asked.

"Yes, Stan's having his head bound up. Back in a minute."

As Robert opened the front door, Bill was bringing his car to a standstill at the pavement.

"Now tell me," Robert said, as they moved away.

"Well, we finished getting the paint off by the light of the head lamps and began to put away our things. We'd just lit a cigarette and were going to push off when there was a crash of glass from the back of the house. We took our flashlights and went to have a look, one on each side. We heard more crashing of glass and realized they were making a night of it.

"When we caught up with them—I think there were seven—we switched off our lights before they could see that we were only two, and grabbed the nearest. Stan said, 'You take that one, Sergeant,' bluffing them we were police. Quite suddenly, it seemed, there was quiet and I realized that we were letting them get away, and I went after them with my flashlight on. The last of them was just being helped over the wall and I grabbed his legs. But he slipped from my hands and was over before I could grab him again. So I went back to find Stan. Someone had hit him a wallop over the head with a bottle and he was sitting on the ground, looking stunned. And then the lights went on in the house. Miss Sharpe came outside, and we got Stan in. I went to the phone, but Miss Sharpe said, 'That's no use. It's dead. We tried to call the police when they first arrived.' So I said I'd go fetch them and you, too. Miss Sharpe didn't want me to disturb you, but I thought you ought to be in on it."

"Quite right, Bill."

The gate was wide open as they drew up, the police car at the door, and the curtains waving gently in the night wind at the wrecked windows. In the living room Stanley was having a cut above his eyebrow attended to by Marion, a sergeant of police was taking notes, and his men were laying out exhibits, consisting of bricks, bottles, and pieces of paper with writing on them.

There were four messages. They read: "Get out!" "Get out or we'll make you!" "Foreign bitches!" and "This is only a sample!"

"Well, we've collected them all, I think," the sergeant said. "Now we'll search the garden for whatever other clues there may be." As he went out, Mrs. Sharpe came in with a steaming jug and cups.

"Ah, Mr. Blair," she said. "You still find us stimulating?"

Robert wondered what kind of occasion would find Mrs. Sharpe at a disadvantage.

Bill appeared with sticks from the kitchen and lighted a fire, Mrs. Sharpe poured hot coffee, and the color began to come back to Stan's face. By the time the policemen returned from the garden, the room had acquired a family-party air, in spite of the waving curtains and broken windows. Stanley and Bill, Robert noticed, seemed relaxed and at home. Perhaps it was because the Sharpes took them for granted, accepting this invasion of strangers as if it were an everyday occurrence.

"Do you plan to stay on here, ma'am?" the police sergeant asked.

"Certainly," Mrs. Sharpe said, pouring coffee for them.

"No," Robert said. "You mustn't, you really must not."

"It may not stop at broken windows," the sergeant said. "And you're a great responsibility to us as long as you are here, a responsibility we haven't really got the force to deal with."

"I'm truly sorry we are a nuisance to you, Sergeant. But this is our home, and here we are staying. And how much of our home would remain to come back to if it was left empty? If you are too short of men to guard human beings, you certainly have no men to guard empty property."

The sergeant looked slightly abashed. "Well, there is that, ma'am," he acknowledged, with reluctance.

When the police had taken their departure, Bill fetched a brush and shovel from the kitchen and swept up the broken glass in room after room.

"What you want is a lodger," said Stanley. "A lodger with a pistol. What d'you say I come and sleep here of nights? No meals, just sleeping night watchman."

It was evident by their expressions that both the Sharpes appreciated the fact that this was an open declaration of allegiance in what amounted to a local war.

"Haven't you got a wife?" Marion asked.

"Not of my own," Stanley said demurely.

"I imagine that if the customers at your garage found that you had become night watchman at The Franchise they would take their trade elsewhere," Mrs. Sharpe pointed out.

"Not them," Stanley said comfortably. "There's nowhere else to take it. Anyhow, I don't let my customers tell me what I do in my spare time."

And so it was settled. Robert was mightily relieved.

6

"I wonder if you would mind calling for the fish, Robert dear," Aunt Lin said on the telephone on Tuesday afternoon. "Nevil is coming to dinner."

Robert was feeling so pleased with himself that he was in a better humor than usual to support Nevil's society. He had arranged with a Larborough firm for the replacement of the Franchise windows; he had miraculously unearthed a key that fitted the Franchise gate; and he had personally taken out the groceries—together with an offering of the best flowers that Milford could supply.

He had got through his arrears of work with a mutely reproachful Mr. Heseltine, and Miss Tuff's tea tray was lying on his desk now, just as it had been a fortnight ago when he had lifted the receiver to hear Marion Sharpe's voice for the first time. Two short weeks ago. Today the tray held no reproach for him because he had stepped outside the routine it typified. He was on calling terms with Scotland Yard, he was agent for a pair of scandalous women, he had become an amateur sleuth, and he had been witness of mob violence. His whole world looked different.

He pushed the tea tray out of his way and went to work, and it was half past six before he looked at the clock again, and seven before he reached home.

The sitting-room door was ajar as usual, and he could hear Nevil's voice in the room beyond.

"On the contrary, I think you are being extremely silly," Nevil was saying.

With his coat half off, Robert paused to listen.

"You are interfering in something you know nothing whatever about; you can hardly claim that is an intelligent proceeding."

There was no answering voice, so Nevil must be talking to someone on the telephone.

"You are taking the part of an unbalanced adolescent in a case you know nothing about. You can tell your father for me that there is nothing Christian about it, just unwarranted interference. I'm not sure it isn't incitement to violence. . . . Yes, last night. . . . No, all their windows broken, and things painted on their walls. . . . If he is so interested in justice he might do something about that. But your lot are never interested in justice, are they? Only in injustice. . . . You make me sick. . . . Yes, I said you make me sick."

And the bang of the receiver on its rest indicated that the poet had said his say.

Robert hung up his coat in the closet and went in. Nevil with a face like thunder was pouring himself a stiff whisky.

"I'll have one, too," Robert said. "I couldn't help overhearing," he added. "That wasn't Rosemary, by any chance?"

"Who else? Is there anyone else in Britain capable of silliness like that?"

"Like what?"

"She has taken up the cause of the persecuted Betty Kane." Nevil gulped some whisky and glared at Robert as if Robert were responsible.

"Well, I don't suppose her stepping on the *Ack-Emma* bandwagon will have much effect one way or another."

"It isn't the *Ack-Emma*. It's *The Watchman*. That mental deficient she calls her father has written a letter about the poor abused child for Friday's issue. Yes, you may well look squeamish. As if we weren't coping with enough already!"

"Perhaps they won't print it," Robert said, less in hope than looking for comfort.

"You know very well they will print anything he chooses to send them. Whose money saved them just when they were going down for the third time? The bishop's, of course."

"His wife's, you mean." The bishop had married one of the two granddaughters of Cowan's Cranberry Sauce.

"All right, his wife's. And the bishop has *The Watchman* for a lay pulpit. And there isn't anything too silly for him to say in it, or too unlikely for them to print."

The telephone rang.

"If that's Rosemary, I'm in China," Nevil said.

But it was Kevin Macdermott.

"Well, sleuth," said Kevin. "My congratulations."

Robert sketched the happenings of last night for Kevin's benefit, and said, "I can't afford to be leisurely about it anymore. Something must be done as quickly as possible to clear them."

"You want me to give you the name of a private agent, is that it?"

"Yes, I suppose it has come to that. But I did wonder—"

"Wonder what?" Kevin asked, as he hesitated.

"Well, I did think of going to Grant at the Yard and telling him quite frankly what I had found out about the girl."

"So that they could do what?"

"So that they could investigate the girl's movements during that month instead of us."

"And you think they would?"

"Why not?"

"Because it wouldn't be worth their while. All they would do when they found out that she was not trustworthy would be to drop the case thankfully into oblivion. As you very well know. And the fact that she picked up a man at the Midland doesn't do anything to disprove her story that she was abducted by the Sharpes. In fact the only leg you have to stand on is Alec Ramsden, Five Spring Gardens, Fulham, South West. A very good private sleuth, take it from me. Tell him I gave you his name and he'll do you proud. If there's anything else I can do, just give me a ring."

Robert laid down the receiver, and at that moment Aunt Lin came in, pink and indignant. "Robert," she said, "did you know that you left the fish on the hall table and it has soaked through to the mahogany, and Christina was waiting for it. Really, I hardly know what's come over you in the past fortnight."

"I apologize, Aunt Lin, but it is not often I am saddled with a responsibility as serious as the Franchise affair, and you must forgive me if I am a little jaded."

"I don't think you are jaded at all. On the contrary, I have never seen you so pleased with yourself. I think you are positively *relishing* this sordid affair."

What was clearly a snort came from Nevil where he was sunk in an easy chair.

"Did you say something, Nevil, dear?"

The nursery tone clearly intimidated Nevil. "No, Aunt Lin," he said meekly.

But the snort had only too clearly been a snort. "I don't grudge you the drink, dear, but is that your *third* whisky? You mustn't get into bad habits if you are going to marry a bishop's daughter."

"I am not going to marry Rosemary."

Aunt Lin stared, aghast. "No!"

"I would as soon marry a radio set."

"But Nevil, dear, *why?*"

"She is a very silly creature. Almost as silly as *The Watchman*."

"Oh, come, dear; you've had a tiff; all engaged couples do. Don't take a small disagreement too seriously. You can ring her up before you go home tonight—"

"It is a quite fundamental disagreement," Nevil said coldly. "And there is no prospect whatever of my ringing her up."

"But Nevil, dear, what—"

The notes of the dinner gong floated through her protest and gave her pause. The drama of broken engagements gave place on the instant to more immediate concerns.

"That is the gong. I think you had better take your drink in with you, dear. Christina likes to serve the soup hot, and she is not in a very good mood tonight because of getting the fish so late."

WHEN Robert reached the office next morning, he found a long thin gray man propped against the door.

"Good morning," Robert said. "Did you want to see me?"

"No," said the gray man. "You wanted to see me."

"*I* did?"

"At least so your telegram said. I take it you're Mr. Blair?"

"Come in," said Robert, unlocking the door. "I am wonderfully relieved that you could come, Mr. Ramsden. And so quickly!"

"I had just finished a case. And Kevin Macdermott has done a lot for me."

"Perhaps the best way would be for you to read this statement," he said, handing Ramsden the copy of Betty Kane's statement to the police, "and then we can go on from there."

Ramsden took the typescript, sat down in the visitors' chair, and withdrew himself from Robert's presence.

"Yes, Mr. Blair?" he said presently, and Robert gave him the rest of the story, concluding with his unearthing of X.

"To find out more about X is your job, Mr. Ramsden. It would be great luck if he should be registered at the Midland for that period. Tell Albert, the lounge waiter, I sent you, by the way. I've known him a long time."

"Very good. I'll get over to Larborough now. I'll have a photograph of the girl by tomorrow, but perhaps you could lend me your *Ack-Emma* one for today."

"Certainly. How are you going to get a proper photograph of her?"

"Oh. Ways."

"There's just a chance that the conductor of one of those double-decker buses may remember her," Robert said as Ramsden was going.

At half past nine the staff arrived—one of the first being Nevil. Robert was astonished. Nevil was usually the last to arrive and the last to settle down. But today he went directly to his own room, shut the door firmly after him, and settled down to work.

By half past ten Robert realized that he was in need of more sustenance than an office cup of tea. He would go out and have a sandwich at the Rose and Crown.

It was still early for midmorning snacks, and the lounge was deserted except for Ben Carley, who was sitting by the window reading the *Ack-Emma*. In a small place like Milford the bond of their profession made them very nearly friends. So as a matter of course Robert sat down at Carley's table.

Carley lowered the *Ack-Emma* and regarded him with lively dark eyes. "The reaction seems to be dying down," he said. "Only one letter today."

"In the *Ack-Emma*, yes. But *The Watchman* is beginning a campaign of its own on Friday."

"*The Watchman!* Two sides of the same penny, when you come to think of it. Oh, well. That needn't worry you. The total circulation of *The Watchman* is about twenty thousand."

"Perhaps. But practically every one of those twenty thousand has a second cousin in the permanent civil service in this country. And when a string is pulled in the civil service a whole series of figures is yanked into action, willy-nilly."

Carley was silent a moment. "It's a pity," he said. "Just when the

Ack-Emma was losing way. Another two days and they would have dropped it for good. As it is, the response must have been terrific to warrant that amount of space."

"Yes," Robert agreed gloomily.

"By the way," Carley asked, "do you know the fat blonde who runs that sportswear shop next to the Anne Boleyn?"

"No. Why?"

"She lived at the same boardinghouse in London as the Sharpes, it seems; and she has a lovely story as to how Marion Sharpe once beat a dog half to death in a rage. Her clients loved that story. So did the Anne Boleyn customers. She goes there for her morning coffee." Carley paused. "Ah, well, it will blow over."

Robert looked surprised. "Blowing over won't help my clients at all," he said.

"What can you do?"

"Fight, of course. I propose to find out what the girl was really doing during those weeks."

Carley looked amused. "Just like that," he said, commenting on this tall order. His eyes went to the street beyond the leaded panes of the window, and the amusement in them faded to a fixed attention. He stared for a moment or two and then said softly, "Well! Of all the nerve!"

It was an admiring phrase, not an indignant one; and Robert turned to see what had occasioned it.

On the opposite side of the street was the Sharpes' battered old car, its odd front wheel well in evidence. And in the back, enthroned in her usual place, was Mrs. Sharpe. The car was outside the grocer's, and Marion was presumably inside shopping.

"What incredible folly!" Robert said angrily.

"Folly nothing," said Carley. "I wish they were clients of mine."

Robert fled from the room and reached the car just as Marion came out onto the pavement at the other side. "Mrs. Sharpe," he said sternly, "this is an extraordinarily silly thing to do."

"Oh, good morning, Mr. Blair," she said, in polite social tones. "Have you had your morning coffee, or would you like to accompany us to the Anne Boleyn?"

"Miss Sharpe!" he said, appealing to Marion, who was putting her packages down on the seat. "You must know that this is a silly thing to do."

"I honestly don't know whether it is or not," she said, "but it seems to be something that we must do. We found that neither of us could forget that snub at the Anne Boleyn. That condemnation without trial."

"We suffer from spiritual indigestion, Mr. Blair," said Mrs. Sharpe. "And we feel that at half past ten in the morning there must be a large number of free tables at the Anne Boleyn."

"But—"

"They will soon grow used to seeing monsters and take us for granted again," Marion said. "If you see a giraffe once a year it remains a spectacle; if you see it daily it becomes part of the scenery. We propose to become part of the Milford scenery once again."

"Very well, you plan to become part of the scenery. But do one thing for me just now." Already the curtains of first-floor windows were being drawn aside and faces were appearing. "Come have your coffee with me at the Rose and Crown instead. As a personal obligation to me as your agent, I ask you not to go into the Anne Boleyn today."

"*That* is blackmail," Mrs. Sharpe remarked.

"It is unanswerable, anyhow," Marion said, smiling faintly at him.

As they walked to the Rose and Crown, Robert had the exposed feeling of being out in an air raid. He was ashamed to see how relaxed and seemingly indifferent Marion swung along at his side, and hoped that his self-consciousness was not apparent.

Apart from a solitary waiter the lounge was deserted. As they seated themselves round a black oak table Marion said, "You heard that our windows are in again?"

"Yes," he replied. "I wish everything else was as easy."

He was unaware that there had been any change in his voice, but Marion searched his face and said, "Some new development?"

"I'm afraid there is. I was coming out this afternoon to tell you about it. It appears that just when the *Ack-Emma* is dropping the subject, *The Watchman* is going to take it up!"

"Have you spies in *The Watchman* office, Mr. Blair?" Mrs. Sharpe asked.

"No, it was Nevil who got wind of it. They are going to print a letter from his future father-in-law, the Bishop of Larborough."

"Hah!" said Mrs. Sharpe. "Toby Byrne."

"You know him?" asked Robert.

"He went to school with my nephew. Toby Byrne, indeed. He doesn't change."

"I gather that you didn't like him."

"I never knew him. He went home for the holidays once with my nephew and discovered that the stable lads got up at the crack of dawn. It was slavery, he said; and he went among the lads urging them to stand up for their rights. They used to mimic him for years afterwards; and he was not asked back."

"Yes, he doesn't change," agreed Robert. "He has been using the same technique ever since. The less he knows about a thing the more strongly he feels about it."

"How did Toby Byrne rise so high?" Mrs. Sharpe wondered.

"I assume that Cowan's Cranberry Sauce had no inconsiderable part in that."

"Ah, yes. His wife. I forgot. Sugar, Mr. Blair?"

"By the way, here are the two duplicate keys to the Franchise gate," Robert said. "I take it that I may keep one. The other you had better give to the police. I also have to inform you that you now have a private agent in your employ." And he told them about Alec Ramsden.

"No word of anyone recognizing the *Ack-Emma* photograph and writing to Scotland Yard?" Marion asked. "I had pinned my faith to that."

"Not so far. But between the good Lord and Alec Ramsden, we'll triumph in the end."

Marion looked at him soberly. "You really believe that, don't you," she said, as one noting a phenomenon.

"I do," he said.

"I should have a greater faith in a Lord who hadn't given Toby Byrne a bishopric," Mrs. Sharpe said. "When does Toby's letter appear, by the way?"

"On Friday morning."

"I can hardly wait," said Mrs. Sharpe.

7

THE BISHOP'S letter had run true to form. *The Watchman*, he said, was not, of course, condoning violence, but there were occasions when violence was but a symptom of a deep social unrest and resentment. The people to be blamed for the recent personal protests at The Franchise (a slight understatement, Robert thought) were the powers whose weakness, ineptitude, and lack of zeal had led to the injustice of a dropped case. It was part of the English heritage that justice should not only be done but that it should be shown to be done; and the place for that was in open court.

The "poor bruised body" of this young and blameless girl, his lordship said, was a crying indictment of a law that had failed to protect her and now failed to vindicate her. The whole conduct of this case was one that demanded the most searching scrutiny.

Robert deserted the office and took the copy of *The Watchman* out to The Franchise. It was a lovely day, the grass absurdly green and the dirty white front of the house glorified by the sun into a semblance of grace. They sat there in the shabby drawing room, the three of them, in great contentment. The *Ack-Emma* had ceased to mention the Sharpes; the bishop's letter was not after all as bad as it might have been; Alec Ramsden was busy on their behalf in Larborough; Stanley was proving himself "a great dear"; they had paid a second visit to Milford yesterday, and nothing untoward had happened to them beyond stares and black looks. Altogether, the feeling of the meeting was that it all might be worse.

Mrs. Sharpe broke a companionable pause. "I think that you should get in touch with our solicitors in London, who manage our affairs, so that you may know how much we have to come and go on, and can make corresponding arrangements for the spending of it in defense of our good name."

Robert took the address of the solicitors and went home to lunch with Aunt Lin, feeling happier than he had at any time since he had first caught sight of the *Ack-Emma*'s front page last Friday.

It was in this mood that he went back to the office. And it was in this mood that he picked up the receiver to answer Hallam's call.

"Mr. Blair?" Hallam said. "I'm at the Rose and Crown. I'm afraid I've got bad news for you. Inspector Grant's here."

"At the Rose and Crown?"

"Yes. And he's got a warrant to arrest the Sharpes."

"No! He *can't* have!"

"I expect it's a bit of a shock for you."

"You mean he has managed to get a witness—a corroborative witness?"

"He has two of them. The case is sewn up and tied with ribbon. Will you come over, or shall we go to you? I expect you'll want to come out with us."

"Out where? Oh, yes. Of course I shall. Where are you?"

"We're in Grant's bedroom. Number Five."

"All right. I'm coming straight over."

It was the dead period of the afternoon at the Rose and Crown and Robert reached the door of Number Five without meeting anyone. Grant, calm and polite as always, let him in. Hallam was leaning against the dressing table by the window.

"I understand that you hadn't expected this, Mr. Blair," Grant said.

"No, I hadn't. To be frank, it is a great shock to me."

"Sit down," Grant said. "I don't want to hurry you."

"You have new evidence, Inspector Hallam says."

"Yes, we have a man who saw Betty Kane being picked up by the car at the bus stop—"

"By *a* car," Robert said.

"Yes, if you like, by *a* car—but its description fits that of the Sharpes'."

"So do ten thousand others in Britain. And?"

"The girl from the farm, who went once a week to help clean The Franchise, will swear that she heard screams coming from the attic."

"*Went* once a week? Doesn't she go any longer?"

"Not since the Kane affair became common gossip."

"I see."

"Not very valuable pieces of evidence in themselves, but very valuable as proof of the girl's story. For instance, she really did miss that coach. Our witness says that it passed him about half a mile down the road. When he came in sight of the bus stop a few moments later, the girl was there waiting. It is a long straight road, the main London road through Mainshill—"

"I know. I know it."

"When he was still some way from the girl he saw the car stop by her, saw her get in, and saw her driven away."

"But not who drove the car?"

"No. It was too far away for that."

"And this girl from the farm—did she volunteer the information about the screaming?"

"Not to us. She spoke about it to her friends, and we acted on information, and found her quite willing to repeat the story on oath."

"Did she speak about it to her friends before the gossip about Betty Kane's abduction got round?"

"Yes."

That was unexpected, and Robert was rocked back on his heels. He got up and walked restlessly to the window and back.

"Thank you for being so frank," he said at last. "Now, I'm not minimizing the crime you are accusing these people of, but it *is* a misdemeanor and not a felony, so why a warrant for arrest? Surely a summons would meet the case perfectly?"

"In cases where the crime is aggravated—and my superiors take a grave view of the present one—a warrant may be issued," Grant said smoothly.

"But you could use your judgment," Robert said. "There is no question of these people not being there to answer the charge. When did you want them to appear, by the way?"

"I planned to bring them up at the police court on Monday."

"If The Franchise is left without occupants it will be a wreck in a week. It seems a pity to risk hooliganism just for the gesture of arrest. And I know Inspector Hallam has no men to spare for its protection."

The first change in Grant's face occurred at the mention of the possible wrecking of the house.

"There is something in what Mr. Blair says," Hallam said tentatively. "I doubt if the house would go untouched if it was empty. Especially if news of the arrest got about."

It took nearly half an hour to convince Grant, however. "Well," the inspector said at length, "you don't need me to serve a summons. I'll leave that to Hallam and get back to town. But I'll be in court on Monday. Can you be ready with your defense by Monday, do you think?"

"Inspector, with all the defense my clients have, we could be ready by teatime," Robert said bitterly.

So it was that Robert went out to The Franchise in Hallam's familiar car with a summons, sick with relief when he thought of the escape the Sharpes had had, and sick with apprehension when he thought of the fix they were in.

They pulled up at The Franchise and Robert opened the gate with his key. "I'll drive the car inside," Hallam said. "No need to advertise the fact that we're here."

As Robert got out of the car at the top of the circular drive, Marion came round the corner of the house, wearing gardening gloves and an old skirt. The wind had blown the heavy dark hair from her forehead into a soft smoke. The lighting of her whole face as she saw him thus unexpectedly made his heart turn over.

"How nice!" she said. "Mother is still resting, but she will be down soon and we can have some tea. I . . ." Her glance went to Hallam, and her voice died away. "Good afternoon, Inspector."

"Good afternoon, Miss Sharpe. I'm sorry to break into your mother's rest, but perhaps you would ask her to come down."

She paused a moment, and then led the way indoors. "Yes, certainly. Has there been some—some new development? Come in and sit down." She led them into the drawing room that Robert knew so well by now, and stood there, searching their faces.

"What is it?" she asked Robert.

"I think it would be easier if you fetched your mother and I told you both at the same time," Hallam said.

"Yes, of course," she agreed, but as she turned to go Mrs. Sharpe came into the room, her sea-gull's eyes bright and inquiring.

"Only two kinds of people," she said, "arrive in noiseless cars. Millionaires and the police."

"I'm afraid I'm even less welcome than usual, Mrs. Sharpe," Hallam said. "I've come to serve a summons on you and your daughter."

"A summons?" Marion said, puzzled.

"A summons to appear at the police court on Monday morning to answer a charge of abduction and assault." It was obvious that Hallam was not happy.

"I don't believe it," Marion said slowly. "I don't believe it. Why now?" She turned to Robert.

"The police think they have the corroborative evidence they needed," Robert said.

"What evidence?" Mrs. Sharpe asked, reacting for the first time.

"We can discuss the situation at greater length after Inspector Hallam has served you the summonses."

"You mean, we have to appear in court?" Marion asked.

"I'm afraid there is no alternative," Robert answered.

She seemed half intimidated by his shortness, half resentful at his lack of championship. And Hallam, as he handed the summons to her, seemed to be aware of this. "I think I ought to tell you, in case he doesn't, that but for Mr. Blair this wouldn't be a mere summons, it would be a warrant, and you would be sleeping to-night in a cell. Don't bother, Miss Sharpe; I'll let myself out."

After Hallam had left, Mrs. Sharpe asked, "Is that true?"

"Perfectly true," Robert said, and told them about Grant's arrival to arrest them.

"And what is this new evidence they think they have?"

"They have it all right," Robert said dryly. He told them about the girl being picked up on the London road through Mainshill. "But the other piece of evidence is much more serious. You told me once that you had a girl from the farm, who came in one day a week and cleaned for you."

"Rose Glyn, yes."

"I understand that since the gossip got round she doesn't come anymore."

"You mean the Betty Kane story? Oh, she was sacked before that ever came to light."

"*Sacked?*" Robert said sharply. "What did you sack her for?"

"Stealing," said old Mrs. Sharpe.

"She had always lifted a shilling or two from a purse if it was left around," supplemented Marion, "but because we needed help so badly we turned a blind eye. And then she took the watch I'd had for twenty years. I asked her about it, but of course she 'hadn't seen it.' That was too much. Next morning we walked over to the farm and said that we would not be needing her anymore."

"Was anyone else there at the time?"

"I don't think so. She doesn't belong to the farm—to Staples, I mean; they are delightful people. She is one of the laborer's daughters."

"How did she take it?"

"She grew beet red and bridled like a turkey-cock," Mrs. Sharpe said. "Why do you ask?"

"Because she will say on oath that when she was working here she heard screams coming from your attic."

"Will she indeed," said Mrs. Sharpe contemplatively.

"What is much worse, there is evidence that she mentioned the screams before there was any rumor of the Betty Kane trouble."

This produced a complete silence.

"That," said Marion at last, "is what is known as a facer."

"Yes. Definitely."

"A facer for you, too. You are faced with the possibility that we have been lying."

225

"Really, Marion!" he said impatiently, using her given name for the first time and not noticing that he had used it. "What I am faced with, if anything, is the choice between your word and the word of Rose Glyn's friends."

But she did not appear to be listening. "I wish," she said passionately, "oh, how I wish that we had one small, just one small piece of evidence on our side! We keep on saying 'It is not true,' but we have no way of *showing* that it is not true!"

"Sit down, Marion," her mother said. "A tantrum won't improve the situation."

"When I think what she has done to us I—"

"Think instead of the day when she is discredited in open court," Robert interrupted. "If I know anything of human nature, that will hurt Miss Kane a great deal worse than the beating someone gave her."

"You still believe that that is possible?" Marion said, incredulous.

"Yes. I don't quite know how we shall bring it about. But that we shall bring it about I do believe. All we have to show is that she did something else on the day she says you picked her up. Take away that first bit and her whole story collapses. And it is my ambition to take it away in public. Now I must go. I said that I would be at home after five o'clock if Ramsden wanted to ring up to report. And I want to ring Kevin Macdermott and get his help about counsel and things."

"I'm afraid that we—that I, rather—have been rather ungracious about this," Marion said. "You must forgive me if—"

"There is nothing to forgive. You have both taken it very well."

"How are you going to get back?" Mrs. Sharpe asked.

"The afternoon bus from Larborough will pick me up."

Marion walked to the gate with him. As they crossed the circle of grass enclosed by the branching driveway, he made difficult small talk, idle words to cover up a stark situation. What were the odds, he wondered, on Ramsden's turning up evidence in time for the court on Monday? In time to prevent the case being set for trial at the Assizes? Long odds against, wasn't it? And he had better grow used to the thought.

RAMSDEN'S REPORT WAS one of unqualified failure. He had failed to identify X as a resident at the Midland; he had therefore no information at all about him. And nowhere had he found even a trace of the girl. His men had made inquiries at the airports, the railway terminals, travel agencies, and the more likely hotels. No one claimed to have seen her.

After a good deal of effort Robert ran Kevin to earth at his home and broke the news that Scotland Yard had got its evidence. Kevin heard him out without comment.

"So you see, Kevin," Robert finished, "we're in a frightful jam."

"My advice to you is to 'give' them the police court, and concentrate on the Assizes," Kevin said.

"Kevin, couldn't you come down for the weekend, and let me talk to you about it? It's six years since you spent a night with us, so you're overdue anyhow."

"If I came, would you introduce me to your witches? And would Christina make me some butter tarts?"

"Assuredly."

"Well, I was looking forward to a Sunday riding on the downs. But a combination of witches and butter tarts is no small draw. I'll come," Kevin assured him, and hung up.

Robert wrote to The Franchise, via the faithful Stanley, to say that Kevin Macdermott was coming down for Saturday night, and could he bring him out to see them on Sunday afternoon?

"Do, please, come for lunch," Marion suggested by return.

"Do you think that Macdermott could be lured into defending them at Norton Assizes?" Nevil asked as he and Robert waited for Kevin to come down to dinner that Saturday night.

"I think he is much too busy for that, even if he were interested. But I'm hoping that one of his people will come."

"I really don't see why Marion should have to slave to provide Macdermott with lunch. Does he realize that she has to prepare and clear away and wash up every single thing?"

"It was Marion's own idea that he should come to lunch with them. I take it that she considers the extra trouble worthwhile."

"You simply don't know how to begin to appreciate a woman like Marion," said Nevil. "Do you know, I had a lovely time the other night. I found a book on torture, and I stayed awake till two o'clock choosing which one I would use on the Kane girl."

"I know what method I will choose," Robert said slowly. "I'm going to undress her in public. I'm going to strip her of every rag of pretense, so that everyone will see her for what she is."

Nevil looked curiously at him for a moment. "Amen," he said quietly. "I didn't know you felt like that about it, Robert." He was going to add something, but the door opened and Kevin Macdermott came in.

Eating solidly through Aunt Lin's superb dinner, Robert hoped that it was not going to be a mistake to take Kevin to Sunday lunch at The Franchise. He was desperately anxious that the Sharpes should make a success with Kevin; but was lunch at The Franchise likely to be an asset to their cause? A lunch cooked by Marion? For Kevin, who was a gourmet? He was glad that Marion had made the gesture, but misgiving was slowly growing in him.

At least Kevin seemed glad to be here, he thought, listening to Macdermott making open love to Aunt Lin. Dear Heaven, the Irish! Aunt Lin was like a girl, pink cheeked and radiant, absorbing flattery like a sponge and pouring it out again as charm. Listening to her talk, Robert was amused to find that the Sharpes had undergone a change in her mind. By the mere fact of being in danger of imprisonment, they had been promoted from "those odd people" to "poor things."

It was curious, Robert thought, looking round the table, that this family party—so gay, so warm, so secure—should be occasioned by the dire need of two helpless women in that dark and silent house. And in his heart he felt a chill anxiety and an ache. He lay long awake that night, and rose early. Just before eight o'clock a car stopped below his window and someone whistled a soft bugle call. Robert got up and put his head out of the window. Stanley was sitting in the car regarding him with tolerant benevolence.

"I have a message from Miss Sharpe. She says when you come out you're to take Betty Kane's statement with you, and that it's of the first importance. I'll say it's important! She's going round looking as if she had unearthed a million."

"Looking happy?" Robert asked, unbelieving. "Do you know what it is that Miss Sharpe is so happy about?"

"No. I did cast out a few feelers, but she's saving it up, it seems. Anyhow, don't forget the copy of the statement."

While Robert waited for breakfast he fished out the statement from among the papers in his briefcase, and read it through again with a new attention. He hoped passionately that Marion in her anxiety to obtain that "one small piece of evidence" was not exaggerating some trifling discrepancy into proof of dishonesty.

"WHAT has happened to young Bennet?" Kevin asked as they drove out to The Franchise.

"He wasn't asked to lunch," Robert said.

"I didn't mean that. What has happened to the strident suits and the superiority and the *Watchman* aggressiveness?"

"Oh, he has fallen out with *The Watchman* over this case. For the first time he has personal knowledge of a case *The Watchman* is pontificating about, and it has been a bit of a shock to him, I think."

"Is the reformation going to last?"

"Well, do you know, I shouldn't be a bit surprised if it did. He has grown up wonderfully in the last few days. I didn't know he even possessed a suit like the one he was wearing last night."

"I hope for your sake the change lasts. He has brains, the boy; and once he gets rid of his circus tricks he'll be an asset to the firm."

"Aunt Lin is distressed because he has split with Rosemary over the Franchise affair, and she is afraid he won't marry a bishop's daughter after all."

"Hooray! More power to him. I begin to like the boy. Is this the place?"

"Yes, this is The Franchise."

"A perfect mystery house."

"It wasn't a mystery house when it was built. The gates, as you can see, were scrollwork, so that the whole place was visible from the road. Backing the gate with the iron sheeting converted the house to something rather secret."

"A perfect house for Betty Kane's purpose anyhow."

Robert was to feel guilty afterwards that he had not had greater faith in Marion. The Sharpes had made no effort to provide a formal dining-room lunch. They had set a table in the window of the drawing room, where the sun fell on it. It was a cherrywood table, very pleasant in grain, and on it the wineglasses gleamed in a diamond brilliance.

"The dining room is an incredibly gloomy place," Mrs. Sharpe said. "Come and see it, Mr. Macdermott."

That too was typical. No sitting round with their sherry making small talk. Come and see our horrible dining room. And the visitor was part of the household before he knew it.

"Tell me," Robert said to Marion as they were left alone, "what is this about the—"

"No, I am not going to talk about it until after lunch. It is the 'small thing' that I was praying for to be evidence for *us*. Have you told Mr. Macdermott?"

"No, I thought it better—not to."

"Don't be afraid," she said reassuringly. "It will hold. Would you like to come to the kitchen and carry the tray of soup for me?"

Robert carried the tray with four flat bowls of soup, and Marion came after him with a large dish under a Sheffield plate cover. When they had drunk their soup, Marion put the large dish in front of her mother and a bottle of wine in front of Kevin. The dish was a *pot-au-feu* chicken with all its vegetables round it; and the wine was a Montrachet.

"A Montrachet!" Kevin said. "You wonderful woman."

"Robert told us you were a claret lover," Marion said, "but this white burgundy seemed to go with one of the Staples' fowls on a warm day."

Kevin said something about how seldom it was that women were interested in any wine that did not bubble.

"I was brought up to appreciate wine," Mrs. Sharpe said. "My husband had a fairly good cellar, though his palate was not as good as mine. But my brother at Lessways had a better cellar, and a fine palate to match."

"Lessways?" Kevin said, and looked at her as if searching for a resemblance. "You're not Charlie Meredith's sister, are you?"

"I am. Did you know Charles? But you couldn't. You are too young."

"The first pony I ever had of my own was bred by Charlie Meredith," Kevin said. "I had him for seven years and he never put a foot wrong."

And after that, of course, both of them ceased to take any further interest in the others, and not overmuch in the food.

"Your friend is a charmer, isn't he?" Marion said later, pouring the hot coffee in the kitchen. "A little Mephistophelian—one would be terribly afraid of him as opposing counsel—but a charmer."

"It's the Irish," Robert said gloomily. "It comes as natural to them as breathing. Us poor Saxons plod along our brutish way and wonder how they do it."

She had turned to give him the tray to carry and so was facing him with their hands almost touching. "The Saxons have the two qualities that I value most in this world. Kindness and dependability—or tolerance and responsibility, if you prefer the terms. Oh damn, I forgot the cream. Wait a moment. It's keeping cold in the washhouse."

As he carried the coffee to the drawing room Robert visualized the bone-chilling cold of those kitchen quarters in winter, now that a cook no longer lorded it over half a dozen servants and ordered coal for the range by the wagonload. He longed to take Marion away from the place.

As they drank their coffee he brought the conversation gently round to the possibility of their selling The Franchise and buying a cottage somewhere.

"No one would buy the place," Marion said. "It is a white elephant. Not big enough for a school, too remote for apartments, and too big for a family these days. It might make a good mad-house," she added thoughtfully, her eyes on the high brick wall

231

beyond the window. "It is a very peaceful place for tired nerves."

So she liked the silence, the stillness that had seemed to him so dead. The big quiet ugly house had been a haven.

"And now," Marion said, "you are invited to inspect the fatal attic."

"Yes," Kevin said, "I should be greatly interested to see the things that the girl professed to identify. All her statements seemed to me the result of logical guesses. Like the wooden commode—something that you would almost certainly find in a country house. Or the flat-topped trunk."

"Yes, it was rather terrifying at the time, the way she kept hitting on things we had. It was only afterwards I saw how little she really had identified. And she did make one complete bloomer, only no one thought of it until last night. Have you got the statement, Robert?"

"Yes." He took it out of his pocket.

They had climbed—she and Robert and Macdermott—the last flight of stairs, and she led them into the attic. "I came up here last night on my usual Saturday tour round the house with a mop."

Kevin was poking round the room and inspecting the view from the window. "So this is the view she described," he said.

"Yes," Marion said. "Robert, would you read the bit where she describes the view from the window?"

Robert looked up the relevant passage and began to read:

" 'From the window of the attic I could see a high brick wall with a big iron gate in the middle of it. There was a road on the further side of the wall, because I could see the telegraph posts. No, I couldn't see the traffic on it because the wall was too high. Just the tops of truckloads sometimes. You couldn't see through the gate because it had sheets of iron on the inside. Inside the gate the carriageway went straight for a little and then divided in two into a circle up to the door. No, it wasn't a garden, just—' "

"What?" yelled Kevin, straightening himself abruptly. "Read that last bit again, that bit about the carriageway."

" 'Inside the gate the carriageway went straight for a little and then divided in two into a circle up to the—' "

Kevin's shout of laughter stopped him.

"You see?" Marion said into the sudden silence.

"Yes," Kevin said softly, his pale bright eyes gloating on the view. "She arrived in darkness and fled in darkness, and she says she was locked in the room all the time, so she could have known nothing of that branching drive."

Robert moved over as Marion gave way to let him have her place, and so saw what they were talking about. The edge of the roof with its small parapet cut off the view of the courtyard before the carriageway branched at all. No one imprisoned in that room would know about the two half circles up to the doorway.

"My mother thinks that this is enough to discredit her," Marion said. She looked from Robert to Kevin, and back again, without much hope. "But you don't, do you?"

"No," Kevin said. "No. Not alone. With a clever counsel's help, she might say that she had deduced the circle from the swing of the car when she arrived. What she would normally have deduced, of course, would be the ordinary carriage sweep. No one would spontaneously think of anything as awkward as that circular drive. I think this tidbit should be kept for the Assizes."

"Yes, I thought you would say that," Marion said. "I'm not really disappointed. I was glad about it, not because I thought that it would free us of the charge but because it frees us of the doubt that must have—must have—" She stammered unexpectedly, avoiding Robert's eyes.

"Must have muddied our crystal minds," finished Kevin briskly, and cast a glance of pleased malice at Robert.

"So you still think that we had best bank everything on the Assizes?" Robert said.

"Yes. The Assizes at Norton will probably be less unpleasant than a police court in one's hometown, and the shorter the Sharpes' appearance tomorrow the better from their point of view."

This suited Robert well enough. He did not want a half decision, a dismissal. That would not be sufficient for his purpose where Betty Kane was concerned. He wanted the whole story of that month told in open court, in Betty Kane's presence. And by the

time the Assizes opened at Norton, he would, please God, have the story ready to tell.

"Who can we get to defend them?" he asked Kevin as they drove home to tea.

Kevin reached into a pocket and produced what was obviously an engagement book. "What is the date of the Assizes at Norton, do you know?" he asked.

Robert told him, and held his breath.

"It's just possible that I might be able to come down myself. Let me see."

Robert let him see in complete silence. One word, he felt, might ruin the magic.

"Yes," Kevin said. "I don't see why I shouldn't. I like your witches. It would give me great pleasure to defend them against that very nasty piece of work. How odd that Mrs. Sharpe should be old Charlie Meredith's sister. One of the best, the old boy was. I have never ceased to be grateful to him for that pony."

Robert listened, relaxed and amused. Clearly Kevin had given up any thought of the Sharpes' guilt long before he saw the view from the attic window. It was not possible that old Charlie Meredith's sister could have abducted anyone.

8

"I MUST say," Ben Carley remarked, eyeing the well-populated benches in the little court, "it's some time since the usual Monday morning gathering has had so much tone."

Robert was only too conscious that the audience in court was not the usual collection of loafers. The news had gone round that the Sharpes were to be charged. Grant had not appeared so far, but Hallam was there, talking to the sergeant who had come to The Franchise the night the hooligans wrecked the windows.

"How's your sleuth doing?" Carley asked.

"The sleuth's all right, but the problem is colossal," Robert said. "The proverbial needle just gives itself up by comparison."

"One girl against the world," mocked Ben. "I'm looking forward to seeing this floozie in the flesh. I suppose after all the fan mail she's had, and the offers of marriage, and the newspaper stories, she'll think a country police court too small an arena for her. Here we go."

Then Robert saw Grant come in quietly and sit in an observer's position at the back of the press bench, and he knew that the time had come.

The Sharpes came in together when their names were called and took their places in the horrid little pew as if they were merely taking their places in church. And then for the first time he was fully aware of what Marion must be suffering on her mother's behalf. Even if the Assizes saw them cleared of the charge, what would compensate them for what they had endured?

Old Mrs. Sharpe, he saw, was wearing her flat black satin hat and looked academic, respectable, but odd. Marion too was wearing a hat, possibly, he supposed, as some protection against the public gaze. It was a country felt, and its orthodoxy lessened to some extent her normal air of being a law unto herself.

And then he saw Betty Kane.

Robert had not seen her since she stood in the drawing room at The Franchise in her dark blue school coat, and he was surprised all over again by her youth and her candid innocence. She was wearing weekend clothes, a cloudy forget-me-not blue outfit that was calculated to bedevil the judgment of sober men. Her simple hat showed to advantage her charming brow and wide-set eyes.

When her name was called and she walked to the witness stand, Robert stole a glance at the faces in the courtroom. With the sole exception of Ben Carley, there was only one expression on the faces of the men: a sort of affectionate compassion. The women, he observed, had not surrendered so easily. The more motherly ones obviously responded to her youth and vulnerability, but the younger ones were merely curious.

Watching her as she was led through her story, Robert reminded himself of Albert's account of her: the cool expertness with which the "nicely brought-up girl" had pounced on the man she had chosen. She had a very pleasant voice, young and light and clear.

And she told her tale like a model witness, volunteering no extras, explicit in what she did say. The judge was obviously doting. The members of the police force were gently perspiring in sympathy. The body of the court was breathless and motionless.

She was apparently unaware of the effect she was having. She made no effort to make a point or to use a piece of information dramatically. And Robert found himself wondering whether she realized quite clearly how effective this was.

"And did you in fact mend the linen?"

"I was too stiff from the beating, that night. But I mended some later." Just as if she were saying: "I was too busy playing bridge." It gave an extraordinary air of truth to what she said.

"Do you want to examine, Mr. Blair?" the judge asked.

"No, sir. I have no questions."

This caused a slight stir of surprise and disappointment in the body of the court.

The girl was now followed by the corroborative witnesses.

The man who had seen her picked up by the car proved to be a post-office sorter called Piper. He was walking up the road through Mainshill when he noticed that a young girl was waiting at the stop for the London coaches. He noticed her because the London coach had overtaken him about half a minute previously, and he realized that she must just have missed it. While he was still some distance away, a car overtook him going at a good pace. He saw it slow down alongside the girl. She talked briefly to the driver, then got in and was driven away. He would not take an oath that the girl in question was Betty Kane, but he was certain in his own mind.

"Do you want to examine, Mr. Blair?"

"No, thank you, sir."

Then came Rose Glyn.

Robert's first impression was of the vulgar perfection of her teeth. There surely never had been any natural teeth as flashily perfect as Rose Glyn's. But her tale was lethal enough.

She had been in the habit of going to The Franchise every Monday to clean the house. On Monday, April 15, she was preparing to leave in the evening when she heard screaming coming from upstairs. When she ran to the foot of the stairs, Mrs. Sharpe came out of the drawing room and asked her what she was doing. When she said someone was screaming upstairs, Mrs. Sharpe said nonsense, that she was imagining things, and wasn't it time that she was going home. The screaming had stopped by then. While Mrs. Sharpe was talking Marion Sharpe came downstairs. She went with Mrs. Sharpe into the drawing room, and Mrs. Sharpe said something about "ought to be more careful." Rose was frightened, and went to the kitchen and took her money from where it was always left for her on the kitchen mantelpiece, and ran from the house. She decided that the following Monday she would give the Sharpes her week's notice; and in fact she had not worked for them since April 29.

Robert was faintly cheered by the bad impression she was patently making on everyone. From the expressions on the faces of her audience, no one would trust her with sixpence. But something far more damaging was needed to discount the evidence she had just given on oath.

Rose's friend Gladys Rees was small and pale. She was ill at ease and took the oath hesitatingly, but the gist of her evidence was clear. On the evening of Monday, April 15, she had gone walking with her friend Rose Glyn. And Rose had told her that she was scared of working at The Franchise because she had heard someone screaming in an upstairs room, and that when she went there next week she was going to give notice.

"I wonder what dear Rose has got on her," Carley said, as Gladys left the witness box.

"What makes you think she has anything?"

"The poor silly little rat was frightened stiff. She would never have come voluntarily. No, Rose Glyn has a lever of some sort."

"Do you happen to remember the number of your watch?" Robert asked Marion as he was driving the Sharpes back to The Franchise. "The one Rose Glyn stole."

"I didn't even know that watches had numbers," Marion said.

"Good ones do."

"Oh, mine was a good one, but I don't know anything about its number. It was very distinctive, though. It had a pale blue enamel face with gold figures."

"Roman figures?"

"Yes. Why do you ask? Even if I got it back I could never bear to wear it after that girl."

"It wasn't so much getting it back I thought of, as convicting her of having taken it."

"That would be nice."

"We have not yet thanked you for standing surety for our bail," Mrs. Sharpe said from the back of the car.

"If we began to thank him for all we owe him," Marion said, "there would be no end to it."

What *had* he been able to do for them? he thought sadly. They would go for trial at Norton little more than a fortnight hence, and they had no defense whatsoever.

THE NEWSPAPERS had a field day on Tuesday.

Now that the Franchise affair was a court case, it could no longer provide a crusade for either the *Ack-Emma* or *The Watchman*. Both, in their different ways, had used it for its momentary worth. But now the case was of national interest, reported by every kind of paper from Cornwall to Caithness, and showed signs of becoming a *cause célèbre*.

Meanwhile, Ramsden grew more and more monosyllabic on the telephone and less and less encouraging. For the first time Robert had a feeling of desperation.

Then one day when Robert turned up at The Franchise, Marion said, "I am glad you came, because something unexpected has happened. My watch has come back. Look!"

She produced a small, very dirty, white cardboard box, which contained her enamel-faced watch and the wrapping that had been round it. The wrapping was a square of pinkish tissue paper with a circular stamp reading SUN VALLEY, TRANSVAAL, and had evidently started life embracing an orange. On a torn piece

239

of paper was printed: I DON'T WANT NONE OF IT. The capital I was dotted like a small letter, after the fashion of illiterates.

"Why do you think she turned squeamish about it?" Marion wondered.

"I don't for a moment think she did," Robert said. "If Rose Glyn had wanted to be rid of it, she would have thrown it into a pond without a second thought. Someone else sent it back. Someone who was frightened. Someone with a rudimentary conscience, too. Now who would have a bad conscience about you just now? Gladys Rees?"

"You think perhaps she gave it to Gladys Rees?"

"That might explain how Rose got her to court to back up that 'screaming' story. If ever there was an unwilling witness it was Gladys on Monday. And if we could knock the prop of Gladys Rees from under Rose's story, it would undermine their whole case," Robert said. "It's their most valuable piece of evidence: that Rose had mentioned the screaming before there was any suggestion of a charge against you."

Robert drove back to Milford with the dirty white cardboard box in his pocket, and his mind full of this new possibility. In the office he found Mr. Ramsden waiting for him.

"Mr. Blair," he said, "we're wasting your money. And I don't like wasting your money."

"Do I understand that you are giving up?"

Mr. Ramsden stiffened noticeably. "You're throwing good money away on a long chance. It isn't even a good gamble."

"Well, I have something for your consideration that is definite enough to please you, I think." Robert fished the little cardboard box out of his pocket and told Ramsden the story of the watch. "The conclusion is inescapable," he said, "that it was Gladys who received the watch, and that was how Rose got her to back up her lies."

He paused to let Ramsden comment. Mr. Ramsden merely nodded, but it was an interested nod.

"Now we can't approach Gladys without being accused of intimidating a witness. All we can do is to concentrate on breaking her down at the Assizes. What I want to be able to say in court is that this printed scrap was written by Gladys Rees. With the evidence that it was Rose who stole the watch, we make the suggestion that Rose got rid of it by giving it to Gladys and then used pressure on her to testify to what is not true."

"So you want another specimen of Gladys Rees's printing."

"Yes. And coming along just now I was thinking it can't be very long since she left school. Perhaps her school could furnish one."

"Did she go to school here?" Ramsden asked.

"I understand she comes from the other side of the county."

"All right, I'll find out. About the search for the Kane girl—" Ramsden said slowly. "If you want my honest opinion, Mr. Blair, it is that we have missed her at one of the exits."

"Exits?"

"I think that she went out of the country, but looking so different that the schoolgirl photograph didn't convey her at all. The girl we're looking for didn't look a bit like that. When she *did* look like that, people recognized her at first glance. We traced her easily enough during her time in Larborough. But from then on it's a complete blank."

Robert sat doodling on Miss Tuff's nice fresh blotting paper. A herringbone pattern, very neat and decorative. "You see what this means, don't you? We are sunk."

"But you have this," Ramsden protested, indicating the printed scrap of paper that had come with the watch.

"That merely destroys the police case. It doesn't disprove Betty Kane's story. If the Sharpes are ever to be rid of this thing, the girl's story has to be shown to be nonsense, and our only chance of doing that is to find out where she was during those weeks."

"Yes. I see," said Ramsden. "But at least you've got insurance against the very worst happening—or will, when I get that printed evidence."

Robert flung down the pen he had been doodling with. "I'm not interested in insurance," he said with sudden heat. "I'm interested in justice. I have only one ambition at this moment. And that is to have Betty Kane's story disproved in open court. To have the full account of what she did during those weeks made public in her presence and duly backed up by irreproachable witnesses. What are our chances of that, do you think? And what—tell me—what have we left untried that could possibly help us?"

"I don't know," Mr. Ramsden said seriously. "Prayer, perhaps."

THIS, oddly enough, was also Aunt Lin's reaction.

Aunt Lin had become gradually reconciled to Robert's connection with the Franchise affair as it moved from the provincial-unsavory to the national-celebrated. It was, after all, no disgrace to be connected with a case that was reported in *The Times*. And of course it had never even remotely shadowed her mind that Robert would not win the case. She had taken that quite placidly for granted. The first hint of doubt came as a surprise to her. "But, Robert," she said, "you don't suppose for a moment that you are going to *lose* the case, do you?"

"On the contrary," Robert said, "I don't suppose for a moment that we shall win it. So far we have no case. And I don't think that the jury is going to like that at all."

"You are losing your sense of proportion, dear. After all, you have Kevin. I can't imagine Kevin traveling down to Norton to defend a case he is sure to lose." Aunt Lin eyed him over her soup spoon. "I don't think, you know, dear," she said, "that you have enough faith."

Robert refrained from saying that he had none at all where the Franchise affair was concerned.

"Now that I know you are worrying about the case, I shall most certainly put up some special prayers," Aunt Lin went on.

Her matter-of-fact tone restored Robert's good humor.

"Thank you, darling," he said in his normal good-natured voice.

She laid her spoon down, and a small teasing smile appeared on her round pink face. "I know that voice," she said. "It means that you're humoring me. But there's no need to, you know. It's I who am right about this, and you are wrong. Meanwhile I shall go along to St. Matthew's this evening and spend a little time praying that you will be given a piece of evidence tomorrow morning."

When Alec Ramsden walked into his room next morning with the piece of evidence, Robert's first thought was that nothing could prevent Aunt Lin taking credit for it.

Ramsden was both pleased with himself and amused. "You're a wonder, Mr. Blair. You had the right idea after all."

"You mean you've got what we wanted from her school!"

Ramsden laid a sheet of paper down on the desk in front of Robert. It appeared to be a freehand map of Canada, showing the principal divisions, towns, and rivers. It was inaccurate but very neat. Across the bottom was printed DOMINION OF CANADA. And in the righthand corner was the signature: Gladys Rees.

"I can hardly believe it," Robert said, feasting his eyes on Gladys Rees's handiwork.

"I'll take it up to town with me today, Mr. Blair, and have the handwriting expert's report before morning. Then I'll take it round to Mr. Macdermott tomorrow, if that's all right with you."

"Right?" said Robert. "It's perfect."

Kevin telephoned on the morrow, full of congratulations and jubilation. "You're a marvel, Rob. I'll make mincemeat of them."

Yes, it would be a lovely little exercise in cat-and-mouse play for Kevin; and the Sharpes would walk out of the court "free." Free to go back to their haunted house and their haunted existence, two half-mad witches who had once threatened and beaten a girl.

"You don't sound very gay, Rob. Is it getting you down?"

Robert said what he was thinking: that the Sharpes saved from prison would still be in a prison of Betty Kane's making.

"Perhaps not, perhaps not," Kevin said. "I'll do my best with the Kane girl over that howler about the divided path. Cheer up, Rob. At the very least her credit will be seriously shaken."

Kevin might successfully shake Betty Kane's credit with the Court, but on the present evidence he could do nothing to alter the strong feeling of partisanship that her case had aroused throughout the country. The Sharpes would stay condemned, and Betty Kane would "get away with it." The once easygoing Robert grew homicidal at the thought.

But it was not until the Assizes were only four days away that he confessed to Aunt Lin that the evidence did not suffice to defeat the charge.

"Don't you see, Aunt Lin, it isn't victory, it's defeat," he finished. "It isn't a verdict we're fighting for, it's justice. And we have no hope of getting it. Only a miracle can save us now."

"Then I shall pray for the miracle."

"You surely don't believe that an angel of the Lord is going to appear in my office with an account of what Betty Kane was doing for that month?" Robert said.

"The trouble with you, dear, is that you think of an angel of the Lord as a creature with wings, whereas he is probably a scruffy little man in a bowler hat. Anyhow, I shall pray very hard, and by tomorrow perhaps help will be sent."

THE ANGEL of the Lord was not a scruffy little man, as it turned out, and his hat was a continental affair of felt with a tightly rolled brim turned up all round. He arrived at Blair, Hayward, and Bennet's about half past eleven the following morning.

"Mr. Robert," Mr. Heseltine said, putting his head in at Robert's door, "there's a Mr. Lange in the office to see you."

Robert, who was not expecting angels of the Lord, said, "I'm busy. Find out tactfully what he wants, will you? Perhaps Nevil can deal with it."

"Yes, I'll find out, but his English is very thick."

"The man's a foreigner, you mean?"

"Yes. He comes from Copenhagen."

"Show him in, Timmy, show him in. Oh, merciful Heaven, do miracles really happen?"

Mr. Lange was round, solid, and dependable-looking.

"I keep a hotel in Copenhagen, Mr. Blair," he began, once the polite preliminaries were over with. "The Red Shoes Hotel it is called. But for a hobby I study the idiomatic English. So every day the newspapers that English visitors leave about are brought to me, and when I have leisure I pick one up and study it. Do I make myself clear, Mr. Blair?"

"Perfectly, perfectly, Mr. Lange," Robert said encouragingly.

"One day I take this paper from the pile, just as I might take any of the others." He took from his capacious pocket a folded copy of the *Ack-Emma* and spread it in front of Robert on the desk. It was the issue of Friday, May 10, with the photograph of Betty Kane occupying two-thirds of the page. "I look at this photograph. Then I look inside and read the story. Then I say to myself that this is most extraordinary. The paper say this is the photograph of Betty Kane. But it is also the photograph of Mrs. Chadwick, who stay at my hotel with her husband."

"What!"

Mr. Lange looked pleased. "You are interested? I so hoped you might be."

"Go on. Tell me."

"The fortnight that they stayed with me, while that poor girl was being beaten and starved in an English attic, Mrs. Chadwick was eating like a young wolf at my hotel and enjoying herself very much. Well, I said to myself, it is after all a photograph. And although the photo is just the way Mrs. Chadwick looked when she let down her hair to come to the costume ball—"

"How did she usually wear it?"

"She wore it brushed up, you see. But for her fancy dress she lets it hang down. Just like that there." He tapped the photograph. "So I say to myself, What has this girl in the paper to do, possibly, with little Mrs. Chadwick? So I am reasonable to myself. But I do not throw away the paper. When I am coming to England on business, I put it into my bag, and show it to my friend where I am staying. And my friend is instantly very excited and say, 'But it is now a police affair, and these women are about to be tried for what they are supposed to have done to this girl.' So my friend say, 'How sure are you, Einar, that that girl and your Mrs. Chadwick are one?' And I say, 'Very sure indeed I am.' So he say, 'Here in the paper is the name of the solicitor for the women. Tomorrow you will go down to this Milford and tell what you think to this Mr. Blair.' So here I am, Mr. Blair. And you are interested in what I say?"

Robert took out his handkerchief and mopped his forehead. "Do you believe in miracles, Mr. Lange?"

"But of course. Indeed, I have myself seen two."

"Well, you have just taken part in a third."

"So?" Mr. Lange beamed. "That makes me very content. You think, then, as I think, that they are one person, that girl and my guest at the Red Shoes?"

"I haven't a doubt of it. Have you the dates of her stay with you?"

"Oh, yes, indeed. Here they are. She and her husband arrived by air on Friday the twenty-ninth of March, and they left on the fifteenth of April, a Monday."

"Thank you. And her husband, what did he look like?"

"Young. Dark. Good-looking. A little—now, what is the word?"

"Flashy?"

"Ah, there it is. Flashy."

"Was he just on holiday?"

"No, oh, no. He was in Copenhagen on business."

"What kind of business?"

"That I do not know, I regret."

"What was his address in England?"

"London."

"Beautifully explicit. Will you forgive me a moment while I telephone? Do you smoke?" He opened the cigarette box and pushed it towards Mr. Lange. "Milford 195. You will do me the honor of having lunch with me, Mr. Lange, won't you? Aunt Lin? I have to go to London directly after lunch. . . . Will you be an angel and pack a small bag for me? And would it be all right if I brought someone back to take potluck for lunch today? . . . Oh, good. . . . Yes, I'll ask him." He covered the mouthpiece and said, "My aunt wants to know if you eat pastry?"

"Mr. Blair!" Mr. Lange said, with a wide smile and a wide gesture for his girth. "And you ask a Dane?"

"He loves it," Robert said into the telephone. "And I say, Aunt Lin. Were you doing anything important this afternoon? . . . Because what I think you ought to do is to go to St. Matthew's and give thanks. . . . Your angel of the Lord has arrived."

WHEN Robert went out to The Franchise three days later to drive the Sharpes over to Norton for the Assizes on the morrow, he found an almost bridal atmosphere in the place. Two absurd tubs of yellow wallflowers stood at the top of the steps, and the dark hall gleamed with flowers like a church decorated for a wedding.

"Nevil!" Marion said, with an explanatory wave of her hand to the massed glory. "He said the house should be *en fête*."

"I wish I had thought of it," Robert said.

"After the last few days, it surprises me that you can think at all. If it were not for you, we should not be rejoicing today."

"If it weren't for a man called Alexander Graham Bell, you mean. If it weren't for his invention, we should still be groping in the dark."

"I still don't see how you managed it all," Marion said.

"We each had our own phone. Kevin and his clerk at his chambers, me at his apartment in St. Paul's Churchyard, Alec Ramsden and three of his men at his office. First we had to make sure that none of the Chadwicks in the London telephone book had any connection with a Chadwick who had flown to Copenhagen on the twenty-ninth of March. Then we had to find out what kind of merchandise Britain sold to Denmark and what Denmark sold to us."

"To find out what company this man was traveling for?" Marion asked.

"Yes, that's right. The Danish tourist office poured information at us. From then on it was a tedious business of being put through to export and import managers and asking, 'Have you a man called Bernard Chadwick working for you?' The number of firms who *haven't* got a Bernard Chadwick working for them is unbelievable."

"I have no doubt of it!"

"I was so sick of the telephone that when it rang at my end I nearly didn't pick it up. I stared at it for quite a while before I realized that someone was trying to call me for a change."

"And it was Ramsden."

"Yes, it was Alec Ramsden. He said, 'We've got him. He buys porcelain for Brayne, Havard and Company.'"

"After that it was a rush to interview the people we needed and to obtain subpoenas and whatnot. But the whole lovely result will be waiting for us in the court at Norton tomorrow. Kevin can hardly wait."

"What had the girl intended to do?" Mrs. Sharpe asked. "Had she meant to go back to her people at all?"

"I don't think so," Robert said. "I think she was still filled with rage and resentment at ceasing to be the center of her brother's interest. An egotist like Betty Kane expects the world to adjust itself to her. The criminal always does, by the way."

"A charming creature," Mrs. Sharpe said.

"Yes. Even the Bishop of Larborough would find some difficulty in thinking up a case for her. His usual 'environment' hobbyhorse is no good this time. Betty Kane had everything that he recommends for the cure of the criminal: love, freedom to develop her talents, education, security. You should hear Nevil on the subject."

"Is Nevil's engagement definitely broken, then?" Marion asked.

"Definitely. Aunt Lin has hopes of the eldest Whittaker girl, a granddaughter of Karr's Krisps."

Marion laughed with him. "Is she nice, the Whittaker girl?"

"Yes. Fair, pretty, well brought up, musical but doesn't sing."

"I should like Nevil to get a nice wife. He needs a focus for his energies and emotions."

"At the moment the focus for both is The Franchise."

"I know. He has been a dear to us. Well, I suppose it is time that we were going. If anyone had told me last week that I should be leaving The Franchise to go to a triumph at Norton, I wouldn't have believed it. Poor Stanley can sleep in his own bed from now on."

"Isn't he sleeping here tonight?" Robert asked. "I don't like the idea of the house being left empty until the case is over."

"It is only for tonight. Tomorrow we shall be home again."

"All right, then, but I'll remind Hallam that the house will be empty tonight," Robert said, and left it there.

IT WAS LATE before Robert parted from Kevin and went to bed in one of the dark paneled rooms that made The Feathers in Norton famous. He fell asleep as soon as his head touched the pillow, and the telephone at his ear had been ringing for some moments before he became aware of it.

"Well?" he said, still half asleep.

It was Stanley. Could he come back to Milford? The Franchise was on fire. Robert was suddenly wide-awake.

"It's got a good hold," Stanley said, "but I think they can save it."

"I'll be over as soon as I can make it."

He made the twenty miles through the summer night in a time that the Robert Blair of a month ago would have considered inconceivable. As he tore through Milford and out into the country beyond, he saw the glow of the burning Franchise against the horizon, like the rising of a full moon.

The gates were wide open and the courtyard—bright in the flames—was crowded with the men and machines of the fire service. The first thing Robert saw, incongruous on the grass, was the beadwork chair from the drawing room, and a wave of hysteria rose in him. Someone had saved that, anyhow.

Stanley was almost unrecognizable. Sweat trickled down his blackened face so that his young skin looked seamed and old. "There's not enough water, but we've got quite a lot of the stuff out," he said.

Mattresses and bed linen were piled on the grass out of the way of the firemen. The furniture stood about, looking surprised and lost.

"Let's take the furniture further away," Stanley said. "It's not safe where it is."

So Robert found himself carting furniture through a fantastic scene, miserably identifying pieces that he had known in their proper sphere.

And then two things happened together. The first floor fell in with a crash. And as the new spout of flame lit the faces round him, he saw two youths whose countenances were alive with gloating. At the same moment he became aware that Stanley had seen them too. He saw Stanley's fist catch the further one under the chin with a crack that could be heard even over the noise of the flames, and the gloating face disappeared into the darkness of the trampled grass.

Robert had not hit anyone since he gave up boxing when he left school, and he had no intention of hitting anyone now. His right arm seemed to do all that was necessary of its own accord. And the second leering face went down into obscurity.

"Neat," remarked Stanley, sucking his skinned knuckles. And then, "Look!" he said.

The roof crumpled like a child's face when it is beginning to cry. The famous round window leaned a little and sank slowly inwards. A tongue of flame leaped up and fell again. Then the whole roof collapsed into the seething mass below, falling two floors to join the red wreck of the rest of the interior. The firemen moved back from the heat. The fire roared in triumph into the summer night.

When at last it died away Robert noticed with a vague surprise that the dawn had come. A calm gray dawn, full of promise. Quiet had come, too; the roar and the shoutings had faded to the soft hiss of water on the smoking skeleton.

"Well," said Stanley, "that seems to be that."

"How did it begin?" asked Bill, who had arrived too late to see anything but the wreck that was left.

"No one knows. It was well alight when the policeman arrived on his beat," Robert said. "What became of those two chaps, by the way?"

"The two we corrected?" Stanley said. "They went home."

"It's a pity that expression is no evidence."

"How are you going to tell them?" Stanley said, referring to the Sharpes.

"God knows," Robert said. "Am I to tell them first and let it spoil their triumph in court for them; or am I to let them have their triumph and face the awful comedown afterwards?"

"Let them have their triumph," Stanley said. "Nothing that happens afterwards can take that away from them."

"Perhaps you are right, Stan. I wish I knew. I had better book rooms at the Rose and Crown for them."

"They wouldn't like that," Stan said. "I've been thinking. My landlady would be glad to have them. She's always been on their side, and I'm sure they'd rather have her spare bedroom and sitting room than a hotel where they would be stared at."

"They would indeed, Stan. I should never have thought of it. You think your landlady would be willing?"

"They're her greatest interest in life at the moment. It would be like royalty coming to stay."

IT SEEMED to Robert that at least half Milford had managed to pack itself into the court at Norton.

It was very warm, and the packed court stirred uneasily throughout the preliminaries and through most of the prosecutor's account of the crime. His light dry voice was unemotional, his method matter-of-fact. And since the story he was telling was one which the spectators had all read about and discussed until it was threadbare, they withheld their attention from him and amused themselves by identifying friends in court.

Robert sat turning over and over in his pocket the little oblong of pasteboard that Christina had pressed into his hand on his departure yesterday, and rehearsing phrases for afterwards. The pasteboard bore in gold letters the words: NOT A SPARROW SHALL FALL. The sudden movement of a hundred bodies and the subsequent silence brought him back to the courtroom, and he realized that Betty Kane was taking the oath preparatory to giving evidence. Once again she gave her evidence in model fashion, her clear young voice audible to everyone in court. The girl's own account of her sufferings did what her counsel's had not done: roused the audience to an emotional reaction. The only difference this time was that the Bench was not doting. The Bench, indeed, if one was to judge by the expression on the face of Mr. Justice Saye, was very far from doting. At last Kevin rose to cross-examine.

"Miss Kane," he began in his gentlest drawl, "you say that it was dark when you arrived at The Franchise. Was it *really* so dark?"

This question, with its coaxing tone, made her think that he did not want it to be dark, and she reacted as he intended.

"Yes. Quite dark," she said.

"Too dark to see the outside of the house?"

"Yes, much too dark."

He appeared to give that up and try a new tack.

"Then the night you escaped. Perhaps that was not quite dark?"

"Oh, yes. That was even darker, if possible."

"So that you could not possibly have seen the outside of the house?"

"Never."

"Never. But when, in your statement to the police, you were describing what you could see from the window of your prison, you said that the carriageway from the gate to the door 'went straight for a little and then divided in two into a circle up to the door.'"

"Yes."

"How did you know it did that?"

"I could see it."

"From where?"

"From the window in the attic. It looked out on the courtyard in front of the house."

"But from the window in the attic it is possible to see only the straight part of the carriageway. The edge of the roof cuts off the rest. How did you know that the carriageway divided in two and made a circle up to the door?"

"I saw it! It is the way I described!"

"Certainly it is the way you described, but what you described was the view of the courtyard as seen by, let us say, someone looking over the wall, not by someone looking at it from the window in the attic."

"I take it," said the Court, "that you have a witness to the extent of the view from the window."

"Two, my lord."

The prosecutor, as Kevin had anticipated, rose to retrieve the situation as soon as Kevin had finished.

"Miss Kane," he said, "you arrived at The Franchise by car?"

"Yes."

"And that car, you say in your statement, was driven up to the door of the house. Now, if it was dark, the headlights must have been turned on and would illuminate not only the carriageway but most of the courtyard."

"Yes," she broke in, "yes, of course I must have seen the circle then. I knew I had seen it. I knew it." She glanced at Kevin for a moment as she stepped down.

She was succeeded in the witness box by Rose Glyn, who had bought both a new tomato-red frock and a new puce hat for her appearance. Again Robert was interested to note that even this emotional audience didn't like her. When Kevin suggested that Rose had in fact been dismissed and had not "given in her notice" at all, there was a So-that's-it! expression on every second face in court. But there was not much more that Kevin could do with her, and he let her go. He was waiting for Gladys Rees.

Gladys looked even less happy than she had in the police court at Milford. She had been scared stiff by the patient prosecutor, evidently regarding anything in a wig and gown as hostile. So Kevin became her wooer and protector. He asked about her school in soft reassuring syllables. The fright faded from her eyes and she answered quite calmly. Here, she quite obviously felt, was a friend.

"Now, Gladys, I am going to suggest to you that you did not want to come here today and give evidence against these two people at The Franchise."

"No, I didn't."

"But you came," he said, not accusing, just making the statement.

"Yes," she said, shamefaced.

"Why? Because you thought it was your duty?"

"No, oh no."

"Was it because someone forced you to come? Someone who held something over your head?" Kevin went on smoothly. "Someone who said, 'You say what I tell you to say or I'll tell about you'?"

She looked half hopeful, half bewildered. "I don't know," she said, falling back on the escape of the illiterate.

"Because if anyone made you tell lies by threatening you, they can be punished for it."

This was clearly a new idea to her.

"All these people have come here today to find out the truth about something. And his lordship would deal very sternly with anyone who had used threats to make you come here and say something that was not true. Do you understand that?"

"Yes," she said in a whisper.

"Now I am going to suggest to you what really happened, and you will tell me whether I am right. Someone you know took something from The Franchise—let us say a watch. She did not want the watch herself, perhaps, and so she handed it on to you. It may be that you did not want to take it, but you did not like to refuse her gift. So you took it. Now I suggest that presently that friend proposed to you that you should back up a story she was going to tell in court. You, being adverse to telling lies, said no. I further suggest that she then said to you, 'If you don't back me up I shall say that you took that watch from The Franchise yourself'—or some other threat of the sort."

He paused a moment, but Gladys merely looked bewildered.

"Now, I suggest that after you gave in and backed up your friend's untrue story, you were sorry and ashamed. So sorry and ashamed that the thought of keeping that watch any longer was unbearable to you. And that you then wrapped up the watch and sent it back to The Franchise by post with a note saying: 'I don't want none of it.'" He paused. "I suggest to you, Gladys, that this is what really happened."

But she had had time to take fright. "No," she said. "No, I never had that watch."

He picked up a paper and said, still mildly, "When you were at school, you were very good at drawing. So good that you had things put up for show at the school exhibition."

"Yes."

"I have here a map of Canada—a very neat map—which was one of your exhibits." It was taken across the court to her, while Kevin added to the jury, "It is a map of Canada which Gladys Rees made in her last year at school." And then to Gladys: "You made that map yourself and wrote your name in the corner?"

"Yes."

"And printed DOMINION OF CANADA across the bottom?"

"Yes."

"Good. Now, I have here the scrap of paper on which some-one printed the words: I DON'T WANT NONE OF IT. This scrap of paper was enclosed with the watch that was sent back to The Franchise. And I suggest that the printing of I DON'T WANT NONE is the same as the printing of DOMINION OF CANADA. That it was written by the same hand. And that that hand was yours."

"No," Gladys said, taking the scrap of paper and putting it hastily down on the ledge as though it might sting her. "I never. I never sent back no watch."

"Well, I shall bring evidence that these two printings are by the same hand. In the meantime the jury can inspect them at their leisure and arrive at their own conclusions. Thank you."

"My learned friend has suggested to you," said Miles Allison, the prosecutor, "that pressure was brought on you to come here. Is there any truth in that suggestion?"

She took some time to think this over. "No," she ventured at last. But the impression that was left with the jury was that she was an unwilling witness repeating a story that was someone else's invention.

Kevin went straight on with the matter of Gladys Rees, on the housewife principle of "getting his feet clear" before he began the real work of the day.

A handwriting expert gave evidence that the two samples of printing which had been put into court were by the same hand. Not only had he no doubt about it, but he had rarely been given an easier task because of the repetition of combinations of letters such as DO and AN and ON.

Now that he had established the fact that Gladys Rees had returned a watch stolen from The Franchise immediately after giving testimony against the Sharpes, Kevin was free to deal with Betty Kane's story. He could safely leave Rose Glyn to the police.

"Have you ever been abroad, Miss Kane?" he asked.

"Abroad?" she said, surprised. "No, never."

"You have not, for instance, been to Denmark lately? To Copenhagen, for instance?"

"No." There was no change in her expression.

"Do you know a man called Bernard Chadwick?"

She was suddenly wary. Robert was reminded of the subtle change in an animal that has been relaxed and becomes attentive. There is no alteration in pose, no actual physical change. There is only an added stillness, an awareness.

"No." The tone was colorless, uninterested.

"You did not stay with him at a hotel in Copenhagen?"

At this the audience gasped.

"No, as I told you, I have never been abroad at all."

"So that if I were to suggest that you spent those missing weeks in a hotel in Copenhagen and not in an attic at The Franchise, I should be mistaken."

"Quite mistaken."

"Thank you."

Kevin then called Bernard William Chadwick, and there was a craning forward and a murmur among the audience. This was a name that the newspaper readers did not recognize. What was he here to say?

He was here to say that he was a buyer of porcelain, fine china, and fancy goods of various kinds for a wholesale firm in London. That he was married and lived with his wife in a house in Ealing.

"You travel for your firm?" Kevin asked.

"Yes."

"In March of this year did you pay a visit to Larborough?"

"Yes."

"While you were in Larborough did you meet Betty Kane?"

"Yes."

"How did you meet her?"

"She picked me up."

There was an instant protest from the body of the courtroom. Whatever discrediting Rose Glyn and Gladys Rees had suffered,

Betty Kane, who looked so much like St. Bernadette, was still sacrosanct.

The judge rebuked the audience for the demonstration. He also rebuked the witness. He was not quite clear what "picking up" involved and would be grateful if the witness would confine himself to standard English in his replies.

"Will you tell the Court just how you did meet her," Kevin said.

"I had dropped into the Midland lounge for tea one day, and she—er—began to talk to me. She was having tea there."

"You did not speak to her first?"

"I didn't even notice her."

"How did she call attention to her presence then?"

"She smiled, and I smiled back and went on with my papers. Then she spoke to me. Asked what the papers were, and so on."

"So the acquaintance progressed."

"Yes. She said she was going to the flicks—to the pictures—and wouldn't I come, too? Well, I was finished for the day and she was a cute kid, so I said yes, if she liked. The result was that she met me next day and went out to the country in my car with me."

"On your business trips, you mean."

"Yes, she came for the ride, and we would have a meal somewhere in the country and tea before she went home to her aunt's place."

"Did she talk about her people to you?"

"Yes, she said how unhappy she was at home, where no one took any notice of her. She had a long string of complaints."

"And how long did this idyll in Larborough persist?"

"It turned out that we were leaving Larborough on the same day. She was going back to her people because her holiday was over—she had already extended it so that she could run about with me—and I was due to fly to Copenhagen on business. She then said she had no intention of going home and asked me to take her with me. I said nothing doing. I didn't think she was so much of an innocent child as she first seemed, but she was only sixteen, after all."

"She told you she was sixteen?"

"She had her sixteenth birthday in Larborough," Chadwick said with a wry twist of the mouth under the small dark mustache. "It cost me a gold lipstick."

Robert looked across at Mrs. Wynn and saw her cover her face with her hands. Leslie Wynn, sitting beside her, looked unbelieving and blank.

"You had no idea that actually she was still fifteen?"

"No. Not until the other day."

"Even so, you considered her an inexperienced child of sixteen. Why did you change your mind about her?"

"She—convinced me that she wasn't."

"Wasn't what?"

"Inexperienced."

"So after that you had no qualms about taking her with you on the trip abroad?"

"I had qualms in plenty, but by then I had learned—what fun she could be."

"So you took her abroad with you."

"Yes."

"As your wife?"

"Yes, as my wife."

"You had no qualms about any anxiety her people might suffer?"

"No. She said she still had a fortnight's holiday to come, and that her people would take it for granted that she was still with her aunt in Mainshill."

"Do you remember the date on which you left Larborough?"

"Yes, I picked her up at a coach stop in Mainshill on the afternoon of March the twenty-eighth. That was where she would normally have got her bus home."

Kevin left a pause after this piece of information, so that its full significance should have a chance. Robert, listening to the momentary quiet, thought that if the courtroom were empty the silence could not be more absolute.

"And you took her with you to Copenhagen. Where did you stay?"

"At the Red Shoes Hotel."

"For how long?"

"A fortnight."

There was a murmur of surprise at that.

"And then?"

"We came back to England together on the fifteenth of April. She had told me that she was due home on the sixteenth. But on the way over she told me that she had actually been due back on the eleventh and would now have been missing for four days."

"Did she say why she had misled you?"

"Yes. So that it would be impossible for her to go back. She said she was going to write to her people and say that she had a job and was quite happy and that they were not to look for her or worry about her."

"She had no compunction about the suffering that would cause parents who had been devoted to her?"

"No. She said her home bored her so much she could scream."

Against his will, Robert's eyes went to Mrs. Wynn, and came away again at once. It was crucifixion.

"What was your reaction to the new situation?"

"I was angry to begin with. It put me in a spot."

"Were you worried about the girl?"

"No, not particularly."

"Why?"

"By that time I had learned that she was very well able to take care of herself. Whoever was going to suffer in any situation she created, it wouldn't be Betty Kane."

The mention of her name suddenly reminded the audience that the girl they had just been hearing about was "their" Betty Kane. The one like Bernadette. And there was an uneasy movement, a taking of breath.

"Then what happened?" Kevin asked.

"After a lot of talk I decided the best thing to do would be to take her down to my bungalow on the river near Bourne End. We used it for weekends in the summer and for summer holidays, but only rarely for the rest of the year."

"When you say 'we,' you mean your wife and you."

"Yes. Betty agreed to that quite readily, and I drove her down."

"Did you stay there with her that night?"

"Yes."

"And on the following nights?"

"The following night I spent at home."

"And afterwards?"

"For a week after that I spent most nights at the bungalow."

"And then?"

"I went down one night and found that she had gone."

"What did you think had happened to her?"

"Well, she had been very bored for the last day or two—and there wasn't much to do there—so when I found she had gone I took it that she had found someone or something more exciting."

"You heard the girl Betty Kane give evidence today that she had been forcibly detained in a house near Milford?"

"Yes, I did."

"That is the girl who went with you to Copenhagen, stayed there for a fortnight with you, and subsequently lived with you in a bungalow near Bourne End?"

"Yes, that is the girl."

"That is all. Thank you."

There was a great sigh from the crowd as Kevin sat down and Bernard Chadwick waited for the prosecutor's questioning. Robert stole a look at Betty Kane, but for all the emotion her face showed just now she might have been listening to a reading of Stock Exchange prices. She appeared as calm as ever. The wide-set eyes and placid brow were still hiding, as they had all those years, the real Betty Kane.

"Mr. Chadwick," the prosecutor said, "this is a very *belated* story, isn't it?"

"Belated?"

"Yes. This case has been a matter for public comment for the past three weeks, or thereabouts. If, as you say, Betty Kane was with you during those weeks, why did you not go straight to the police and tell them so?"

"Because I didn't know anything about it."

"How was that?"

"Because I have been abroad again for my firm. I knew nothing about this case until a couple of days ago."

"I see. You have heard the girl's evidence as to her condition when she arrived home. Does anything in your story explain that?"

"No."

"It was not you who beat the girl?"

"No."

"You say you went down one night and looked for her, and found she had packed up and gone?"

"Yes."

"And yet she arrived home without belongings of any sort, and wearing only a dress and shoes."

"I didn't know that till much later."

"When you went down to the bungalow you found it tidy and deserted, with no sign of any hasty departure?"

"Yes. That's how I found it."

When Mary Frances Chadwick was summoned to give evidence, there was what amounted to a sensation in court. It was obvious that this was the wife; and this was fare that not even the most optimistic had anticipated.

Frances Chadwick was a tallish good-looking woman, a natural blonde with the clothes and figure of a girl who has modeled, but is growing a little plump now, and, if one was to judge from her good-natured face, not much caring.

She said that she was married to the previous witness, and lived with him in Ealing. They had no children. Yes, she remembered her husband's going to Larborough and his subsequent trip to Copenhagen. He arrived back from Copenhagen a day later than he had promised, and spent that night with her. During the following week she began to suspect that her husband had developed an interest elsewhere. The suspicion was confirmed when a friend told her that her husband had a guest at their river bungalow.

"Did you speak to your husband about it?" Kevin asked.

"No. That wouldn't have been any solution. He attracts them like flies."

"What did you do, then? Or plan to do?"

"What I always do with flies—I swat them."

"So you proceeded to the bungalow. And what did you find there?"

"I went late in the evening, hoping I would catch Barney there too."

"Is Barney your husband?"

"Yes. The door was unlocked so I walked straight in. A girl's voice called from the bedroom, 'Is that you, Barney? I've been so lonely for you.' I went in and found her lying on the bed in the kind of negligée you used to see in vamp films about ten years ago. She looked a mess, and I was a bit surprised at Barney. Well, we had the usual exchange—"

"The usual?"

"Yes. The what-are-you-doing-here stuff. The wronged wife and the light-of-love, you know. But for some reason or other there was something about this little tramp that turned my stomach."

"Please, Mrs. Chadwick!" the judge interposed.

"Well, I mean, I got to a stage when she riled me past bearing. I pulled her off the bed and gave her a smack on the side of the head. She looked so surprised it was funny. She said, 'You hit me!' and I said, 'A lot of people are going to hit you from now on, my poppet,' and gave her another smack. Well, from then on it was just a fight. I own that the odds were all on my side. I was bigger for one thing and in a flaming temper. Finally she tripped and went sprawling. When she didn't get up, I thought she had passed out. I mopped her face with a cold wet cloth, and then went into the kitchen to make some coffee. But when I got back to the bedroom, I found that the faint had been all an act. The girl had lit out. I took it for granted that she had dressed in a hurry and gone."

"And did you go, too?"

"I waited for an hour, thinking Barney might come. All the girl's things were lying about, so I slung them into her suitcase and put it in the cupboard under the stairs to the attic. And then when Barney didn't come I went away. I must have just missed him, because he did go down that night. But a couple of days later I told him what I had done."

"And what was his reaction?"

"He said it was a pity her mother hadn't done the same thing ten years ago."

"He was not worried as to what had become of her?"

"No. I was a bit, until he told me her home was only over at Aylesbury. She could quite easily cadge a lift that distance."

"So you dismissed the affair from your mind."

"Yes."

"But it must have come to your mind again when you read accounts of the Franchise affair?"

"No, it didn't. For one thing, I never knew the girl's name. And I just didn't connect a fifteen-year-old schoolgirl who was kidnapped and beaten somewhere in the Midlands with Barney's bit."

"If you had realized that the girls were identical, you would have told the police what you knew about her?"

"Certainly."

"You would not have hesitated owing to the fact that it was you who had administered the beating?"

"No. I would administer another tomorrow if I got the chance."

The prosecutor made no attempt to cross-examine. And Kevin moved to call his next witness. But the foreman of the jury was before him. The jury, the foreman said, would like his lordship to know that they had all the evidence they required.

"Who was this witness that you were about to call, Mr. Macdermott?" the judge asked.

"He is the owner of the hotel in Copenhagen, my lord. To speak to their having stayed there over the relevant period."

The judge turned inquiringly to the foreman, who consulted the other jurors. "No, my lord, we don't think it is necessary, subject to your lordship's correction, to hear the witness. We have reached our verdict already."

"In that case, any summing-up by me would be redundant. Do you want to retire?"

"No, my lord. We are unanimous."

10

"WE HAD better wait until the crowd thins out," Robert said. "Then they'll let us out the back way."

He was wondering why Marion looked so grave, so unrejoicing. Almost as if she were suffering from shock.

As if aware of his puzzlement, she said, "That woman. That poor woman. I can't think of anything else."

"Who?" Robert asked stupidly.

"Mrs. Wynn, the girl's guardian. Can you imagine anything more frightful? To have lost the roof over one's head is bad— Oh, yes, Robert my dear, you don't have to tell us—" She held out a late edition of the Larborough *Times*. "Yesterday that fire would have seemed to me an enormous tragedy. But compared with that woman's calvary it seems an incident. What *can* be more shattering than to find that the person you have loved all those years not only doesn't exist but has never existed? What is there *left* for someone like that?"

"Yes," Kevin said, "I couldn't bear to look at her. It was indecent, what she was suffering."

Out of the corner of his eye Robert saw that the police were converging in that polite casual way of theirs on the perjurers. He slipped an arm into Marion's and said, "Come; they'll let us go now, I think." And he told her of Stanley's arrangement with his landlady.

So it was to the little house on the outer rim of the "new" town that Marion and her mother came back; and it was in the front room at Miss Sim's that they sat down to celebrate, a sober little group: Marion, her mother, Robert, and Stanley. Kevin had had to go back to town. On the table there was a large bunch of garden flowers which had come with one of Aunt Lin's warm and gracious little notes.

"Will you golf with me tomorrow afternoon?" Robert asked Marion. "You have been cooped up too long."

"Yes, I should like that," she said.

THEY DROVE OUT to the golf course next day in high spirits, and Robert decided that he would ask her to marry him when they were having tea in the clubhouse afterwards. Or would there be too many people interrupting there, with their kind words on the result of the trial? Perhaps on the way home again?

Yes, he would ask her on the way home again.

This resolution lasted until he found that the thought of what was to come was spoiling his game. So on the ninth green he suddenly stopped waggling his putter at the ball, and said, "I want you to marry me, Marion."

"Do you, Robert?" She picked her own putter out of her bag, and dropped the bag at the edge of the green.

"You will, won't you?"

"No, Robert dear, I won't."

"But Marion! Why not?"

"Half a dozen reasons, any one of them good by themselves. For one, if a man is not married by the time he is forty, then marriage is not one of the things he wants out of life. Just something that has overtaken him, like rheumatism."

"Marion, for heaven's sake!"

"Then, you have Aunt Lin and I have my mother. I not only love my mother, I *like* her. I admire her and enjoy living with her. You, on the other hand, are used to being spoiled by Aunt Lin— oh, yes, you are!—and would miss, far more than you know, all the creature comforts that I wouldn't give you even if I knew how."

"Marion, it is *because* you don't cosset me that I want to marry you. Because you have an adult mind and a—"

"An adult mind is very nice to go to dinner with once a week, but after a lifetime with Aunt Lin you would find it a very poor exchange for good pastry in an uncritical atmosphere."

"There is one thing you haven't even mentioned," Robert said.

"What is that?"

"Don't you care for me at all?"

"Yes. I care for you a great deal. More than I have ever cared for anyone, I think. That is another reason why I won't marry you. And still another has to do with myself."

"With you?"

"You see, I am *not* a marrying *woman*. I don't want to have to put up with someone else's demands, someone else's colds in the head. Mother and I suit each other perfectly because we make no demands on each other. If one of us has a cold in the head she retires to her room without fuss until she is fit for human society again. But a husband would expect sympathy and attention and feeding. No, Robert. There are a hundred thousand women just panting to look after some man's cold; why pick on me?"

"Because I love you."

She looked slightly penitent. "I sound flippant, don't I? But what I say is good sound sense."

"But, Marion, it is a lonely life—and you will not have your mother forever."

"Knowing Mother as I do, I have no doubt that she will outlive me with perfect ease. You had better hole out; I see old Colonel Whittaker's foursome on the horizon."

Automatically he pushed his ball into the hole. "What have you and your mother thought of doing now that you have lost The Franchise?" he asked.

She delayed over her answer, as if it were difficult to say. Fussing with her bag, and keeping her back to him.

"We are going to Canada," she said.

He was aghast. "Why Canada?"

"I have a cousin who is a professor at McGill. He wrote some time ago to ask Mother if we would go out to keep house for him, but by that time we had inherited The Franchise and were very happy in England. So we said no. But the offer is still open. And we—we both will be glad to go now."

"I see."

"Don't look so downcast. You don't know what an escape you are having, my dear."

They finished the round in silence. But driving home, Robert smiled wryly to think that to all the new experiences that knowing the Sharpes had brought him was now added that of being a rejected suitor. The final, and perhaps the most surprising one.

Three days later, having sold their old car and what had been saved of their furniture, the Sharpes left Milford by the odd toy train that ran to the junction at Norton. Robert came to the junction with them to see them onto the fast train to London, where they would settle their affairs before going on to Canada.

"I always had a passion for traveling light," Marion said, referring to their scanty luggage, "but I never imagined it would be indulged to the extent of traveling with an overnight case to Canada."

But Robert could not think of small talk. He was filled with misery and desolation. The blossoms foamed along the line side, the fields were burnished with buttercups, but the world for him was gray ash and drizzle.

He watched the London train bear them away, and went home wondering how he could support Milford without the hope of seeing Marion's thin brown face at least once a day.

But on the whole he supported it very well. He took to golfing of an afternoon again; his form had not seriously deteriorated. He rejoiced Mr. Heseltine's heart by taking an interest in work. He suggested to Nevil that between them they might sort and catalogue the family records in the attic and perhaps make a book of them. By the time Marion's good-by letter from London came, three weeks later, the soft folds of life in Milford were already closing round him.

My very dear Robert,

This is a hasty au revoir note, just to let you know that we are both thinking of you. We leave on the morning plane to Montreal the day after tomorrow. Now that the moment is almost here we have discovered that what we both remember are the good and lovely things, and that the rest fades to comparative insignificance. This may be only nostalgia in advance. I don't know. I only know that it will always be happiness to remember you. And Nevil, and Stanley—and England.

Our united love to you, and our gratitude.

Marion Sharpe

He laid the letter down on his brass and mahogany desk.

Tomorrow at this time Marion would no longer be in England.

It was a desolating thought, but there was nothing to do but be sensible about it. What, indeed, was there to do about it?

And then three things happened at once.

Mr. Heseltine came in to say that Mrs. Lomax wanted to alter her will again and would he go out to the farm immediately.

Aunt Lin rang up and asked him to call for the fish on his way home. And Miss Tuff brought in his tea.

He looked for a long moment at the two biscuits on the plate. Then, with a gentle finality, he pushed the tray out of his way and reached for the telephone.

THE SUMMER rain beat on the airfield with a dreary persistence. Every now and then the wind would lift it and sweep the terminal buildings with it in one long brushstroke. The passengers bent their heads against the weather as they filed slowly to the Montreal plane. Robert, moving up at the tail of the queue, could see Mrs. Sharpe's flat black satin hat and the strands of her white hair being blown about. By the time he boarded the plane they were seated, and Mrs. Sharpe was already burrowing in her bag. As he walked up the aisle between the seats Marion looked up and saw him. Her face lighted with welcome and surprise.

"Robert!" she said. "Have you come to see us off?"

"No," Robert said. "I'm traveling by this plane. It's a public conveyance, you know."

"I know, but—you're going to Canada?"

"I am."

"What for?"

"To see my sister in Saskatchewan," Robert said demurely. "A much better pretext than a cousin at McGill."

She began to laugh, softly and consumedly.

"Oh, Robert, my dear," she said, "you can't imagine how revolting you are when you look smug!"

Red
Wind

Red Wind

A CONDENSATION OF
THE SHORT STORY BY

**Raymond
Chandler**

In Los Angeles anything can happen
when the hot, dry "Santa Ana" sweeps
in off the desert, and that night the
harsh red wind was blowing fiercely.
Still, Philip Marlowe, dropping in to a
neighborhood bar for a quiet drink, hardly expected
—all in one evening—to witness a murder,
hide a beautiful gun-toting fugitive and find
himself the target of a vengeful killer.

   This short story, with its taut atmosphere,
tough talk and complex plot, shows the art of
Raymond Chandler at its best.
Among his novels, *Farewell, My Lovely*,
The Big Sleep and *The Long Goodbye*
have been made into successful movies.

1

THERE was a desert wind blowing that night. It was one of those hot dry Santa Anas that come down through the mountain passes and curl your hair and make your nerves jump and your skin itch. On nights like that every booze party ends in a fight. Meek little wives feel the edge of the carving knife and study their husbands' necks. Anything can happen. You can even get a full glass of beer at a cocktail lounge.

I was getting one in a flossy new place across the street from the apartment house where I lived. It had been open about a week and it wasn't doing any business. The kid behind the bar was in his early twenties and looked as if he had never had a drink in his life.

There was only one other customer, a souse on a barstool, with his back to the door. He had a pile of dimes stacked in front of him, about two dollars' worth. He was drinking straight rye in small glasses, and he was all by himself in a world of his own.

I sat farther along the bar and got my glass of beer.

"Been in before, haven't you, mister?" the kid said.

"Uh-huh."

"Live around here?"

275

"In the Berglund Apartments across the street," I said. "And the name is Philip Marlowe."

"Mine's Lew Petrolle." He leaned close to me across the polished dark bar. "Know that guy?"

"No."

"I ought to call a taxi and send him home. He's doing his next week's drinking too soon."

"A night like this," I said. "Let him alone."

"Rye!" the drunk croaked, without looking up.

The kid looked at me and shrugged. "Should I?"

"Whose stomach is it? Not mine."

The kid poured him another rye. The drunk lifted coins off his pile with the care of a crack surgeon operating on a brain tumor.

The kid came back and put more beer in my glass. Every once in a while the wind blew the stained-glass door open a few inches. It was a heavy door.

"I don't like drunks in the first place, and in the second place I don't like them getting drunk in here, and in the third place I don't like them in the first place," the kid said.

"Warner Brothers could use that," I said.

"They did."

Just then a car squeaked to a stop outside, and a fellow came in who held the swinging door open and ranged the place quickly with flat, shiny dark eyes. He was well set up, dark, good-looking in a narrow-faced, tight-lipped way. He looked cool as well as under a tension of some sort. I guessed it was the hot wind.

The dark guy looked at the drunk's back, looked at me, then looked along the line of empty half booths at the other side of the place. He came on in—past where the drunk sat swaying and muttering to himself—and spoke to the bar kid.

"Seen a lady in here, buddy? Tall, pretty, brown hair, in a print bolero jacket over a white silk crepe dress. Wearing a wide-brimmed straw hat with a velvet band." He had a tight voice I didn't like.

"No, sir. Nobody like that's been in," the bar kid said.

"Thanks. Straight Scotch. Make it fast, will you?"

The kid gave it to him and the fellow paid and put the drink down in a gulp and started to go out. He took three or four steps and stopped. The drunk had turned on the barstool and was facing the dark guy now. The drunk was grinning. He swept a gun from somewhere so fast that it was just a blur coming out. He held it steady and he didn't look any drunker than I was. The dark guy stood quite still.

The drunk's gun was a .22 target automatic, with a large front sight. It made a couple of hard snaps, and a little smoke curled— very little. "So long, Waldo," the drunk said.

The dark guy took a week to fall down. He stumbled, caught himself, waved one arm, stumbled again. His hat fell off, and then he hit the floor with his face.

The drunk slid down off the stool and scooped his dimes into a pocket and moved towards the door. He turned sideways, holding the gun on the barman and me. The kid behind the bar didn't move or make the slightest sound. The drunk felt the door with his shoulder, keeping his eyes on us, then pushed through it backwards. When it was wide a hard gust of wind slammed in and lifted the hair of the dark guy on the floor. The drunk said, "Poor Waldo. I bet I made his nose bleed."

The door swung shut. I started to rush it. The car outside let out a roar. When I got onto the sidewalk it was disappearing around the corner. I got its license number the way I got my first million.

There were people and cars up and down the block as usual. Nobody acted as if a gun had gone off. The wind was making enough noise to make the hard rap of gunfire sound like a slammed door, even if anyone had heard it. I went back into the cocktail bar.

The kid was leaning over the bar and looking down at the dark guy's back. The dark guy hadn't moved. I bent down and felt his neck artery. He wouldn't move—ever.

I lit a cigarette and blew smoke at the ceiling and said shortly, "Get on the phone."

"I don't have one," the kid said. "I got enough expenses without that."

"You own this place?"

"I did till this happened."

He pulled his white coat off and came around the end of the bar. "I'll call from the phone booth across the street. Meanwhile, I'm locking this door," he said, taking keys out.

He went out, swung the door to and clicked the bolt into place. I bent down and rolled Waldo over. At first I couldn't even see where the shots went in. Then I saw a couple of tiny holes in his coat, over his heart, and a little blood on his shirt. The drunk was everything you could ask—as a killer.

I sat at the edge of one of the half booths and smoked cigarettes and watched Waldo's face get deader and deader. I wondered who the girl in the print jacket was, why Waldo had left his car running outside, why he was in a hurry, whether the drunk had been waiting for him or just happened to be there.

The prowl-car boys came in about eight minutes. The kid, Lew Petrolle, was back behind the bar by then, with his white coat on again, counting his money in the register and making notes in a little book. The prowl-car boys were the usual large size and one of them leaned down to feel Waldo's pulse.

"Seems to be dead," he said, and rolled him around a little more. "Oh yeah, I see where they went in. Nice clean work. You two see him get it?"

I said yes. The kid behind the bar said nothing. I told them about it, that the killer had left in Waldo's car.

The cop yanked Waldo's wallet out, went through it rapidly and whistled. "Plenty jack and no driver's license." He put the wallet away. "Okay, we didn't touch him, see? Just a chance we could find did he have a car and put it on the air."

The kid picked up a clean highball glass and began to polish it. He polished it all the rest of the time we were there.

A homicide fast-wagon sirened up outside and four men came in: two dicks, a photographer and a laboratory man.

One of the dicks was a short, dark, quiet, smiling man, with curly black hair and soft intelligent eyes. The other one was big, raw-boned, long-jawed, with a veined nose and glassy eyes. He looked tough, but as if he thought he was a little tougher than he was.

The short dick emptied Waldo's pockets and then his wallet and dumped everything into a large handkerchief. I saw a lot of currency, keys, cigarettes, another handkerchief. Then he got the kid up front.

The big dick pushed me back against the wall of the booth. "Give," he said. "I'm Copernik, detective lieutenant."

I put my wallet in front of him. He went through it, tossed it back, made a note in a book. "Philip Marlowe. A shamus, huh? You here on business?"

"Drinking business," I said. "I live just across the street."

"Know this kid up front?"

"I've been in here once since he opened up."

"See anything funny about him now?"

"No."

"Takes it too light for a young fellow, don't he? Never mind answering. Just tell the story."

I told it—three times. Once for him to get the outline, once for him to get the details and once for him to see if I had it too pat. At the end he said, "This dame interests me. And the killer called the guy Waldo, yet didn't seem to be anyways sure he would be in. I mean, if Waldo wasn't sure the dame would be here, how could the killer be sure Waldo would be here?"

"That's pretty deep," I said.

He studied me. "Sounds like a grudge job, don't it? Don't sound planned. No getaway except by accident. A guy don't leave his car unlocked—and the engine running—much in this town. And the killer works in front of two good witnesses. I don't like that."

"I don't like being a witness," I said. "The pay's too low."

He grinned. "Was the killer drunk, really?"

"With that shooting? No."

"Well, it's a simple job," he said. "The guy will have a record and he's left plenty prints. He had something on Waldo, but he wasn't meeting Waldo tonight. Waldo just dropped in to ask about a dame he had a date with and had missed connections on. But the killer sees Waldo and feeds him two in the right place and scrams and doesn't worry about you boys at all. It's that simple."

"Yeah," I said.

"It's so simple it stinks," Copernik said.

He took his felt hat off, tousled up his ratty blond hair and leaned his head on his hands. He had a long mean horseface.

"I was just thinking," I said. "This Waldo knew just how the girl was dressed. So he must already have been with her tonight."

"So what? Maybe he had to go to the can, and when he came back she had changed her mind about him."

"That's right," I said. But that wasn't what I was thinking. I was thinking that Waldo had described the girl's clothes in a way the ordinary man wouldn't know how to. Print bolero jacket over white silk crepe dress. I didn't even know what a bolero jacket was. And I might have said white dress or even white silk dress, but never white silk crepe dress.

After a while two men came with a basket. The kid, Lew Petrolle, was still talking to the short dark dick.

We all went down to headquarters.

Lew Petrolle was all right when they checked on him. His father had a grape ranch in Contra Costa County. He had given Lew a thousand dollars to go into business and the kid had opened the cocktail bar, neon sign and all, on eight hundred flat.

They let him go and told him to keep the bar closed until they were sure they didn't want to do any more printing. He shook hands all around and grinned and said he guessed the killing would be good for business after all, because people would come to him for the story and buy drinks while he was telling it.

"There's a guy won't ever do any worrying," Copernik said when he was gone. "Over anybody else."

"Poor Waldo," I said. "The killer's prints any good?"

"Kind of smudged," Copernik said sourly. "But we'll get a classification and teletype it to Washington sometime tonight. If it don't click, you'll be in for a day on the pictures downstairs."

I shook hands with him and his partner, whose name was Ybarra, and left. They didn't know who Waldo was yet either. Nothing in his pockets told.

2

I GOT back to my street about 9:00 p.m. The wind was still blowing, oven-hot, swirling dust and torn paper up against the walls.

I went into the lobby of the Berglund and rode the automatic elevator up to the fourth floor. When I stepped out, there was a tall girl standing there waiting for the car. She had brown wavy hair under a wide-brimmed straw hat with a velvet band. She wore a white dress that might have been silk crepe, and over it she wore what might have been a print bolero jacket.

I said, "Is that a bolero jacket?"

She gave me a distant glance with her wide blue eyes and made a motion as if to brush a cobweb out of the way.

"Yes. Would you mind—I'm rather in a hurry."

I didn't move. I blocked her off from the elevator. We stared at each other and she flushed very slowly.

"Better not go out on the street in those clothes," I said.

"Why, how dare you—"

Her voice had a soft light sound, like spring rain. The elevator clanked and started down again.

"You're in trouble," I said. "If the cops come here, you have just that much time to get out of the hall. First take off the hat and jacket—and snap it up!"

She didn't move. Her face seemed to whiten a little.

"Cops," I said, "are looking for you. In those clothes. Give me the chance and I'll tell you why."

She turned her head swiftly and looked back along the corridor. With her looks I didn't blame her for trying one more bluff.

"You're impertinent. I'm Mrs. Leroy in Apartment Thirty-one."

"Then you're on the wrong floor," I said. "This is the fourth." The elevator had stopped down in the lobby. The sound of doors being wrenched open came up the shaft.

"Off!" I rapped. "Now!"

She switched her hat off and slipped out of the bolero jacket. I grabbed them and wadded them under my arm. I took her elbow and turned with her down the hall.

281

"I live in Forty-two. The front one across from yours, just a floor up. Yours or mine; take your choice—and I'm not on the make."

She smoothed her hair with that quick gesture, like a bird preening itself. Ten thousand years of practice behind it.

"Mine," she said, and strode down the hall fast. The elevator stopped at the floor below. She stopped when it stopped. She turned and faced me.

"The stairs are back by the elevator shaft," I said gently.

"I don't have an apartment," she said.

"I didn't think you had."

"Are they searching for me?"

"Yes, on account of Waldo."

She stared at me. "Waldo?"

"Oh, you don't know Waldo?" I said.

The elevator started up in the shaft again. Panic flickered in her blue eyes.

"No," she said breathlessly, "but take me out of this hall."

We were almost at my door. I jammed the key in and heaved the door open, reaching in to switch lights on. She went in past me like a wave. Sandalwood floated on the air, very faint.

I shut the door and watched her stroll over to a card table on which I had a chess problem set out. Once inside, her panic had left her.

We both stood still then and listened to the distant clang of elevator doors and then steps—going the other way.

I grinned, but with strain, not pleasure. I went into the dressing room behind the wall bed and stuffed her hat and bolero jacket into a drawer. Then I went out to the kitchenette, dug out some extra-fine Scotch and made a couple of highballs.

When I went in with the drinks, she was sitting with a gun in her hand. It was a small automatic with a pearl grip. Her eyes were full of horror.

I stopped, with a glass in each hand, and said, "Maybe this hot wind has got you crazy too. I'm a private detective. I'll prove it if you let me."

She nodded slightly, and her face was white. I went over slowly and put a glass down beside her, then set mine down and got a card out that had no bent corners. I put the card down beside her drink and returned to mine.

"Never let a guy get that close to you," I said. "Not if you mean business. And your safety catch is on."

She shivered and put the gun back in her bag. She drank half the drink without stopping, put the glass down hard and picked the card up.

"I don't give many people that liquor," I said. "I can't afford to."

Her lips curled. "I supposed you would want money." Her hand was close to her bag again.

"Don't forget the safety catch," I said. Her hand stopped. I went on, "This fellow I called Waldo is quite tall, say five-eleven, slim, dark, brown eyes with a lot of glitter. Nose and mouth too thin. Dark suit, and in a hurry to find you. Am I getting anywhere?"

She took her glass again. "So that's Waldo," she said. "Well, what about him?"

"Well, there's a cocktail bar across the street— Say, where have you been all evening?"

"Sitting in my car," she said coldly, "most of the time."

"Didn't you see a fuss across the street up the block?"

Her eyes tried to say no and missed. Her lips said, "I saw policemen and searchlights. I supposed someone had been hurt."

"Someone was. Waldo. And he was looking for you before that. In the cocktail bar. He described you and your clothes."

Her mouth began to tremble and kept on trembling.

"I was in the bar," I said. "There was nobody in there but a drunk and the kid that runs it and myself. Then Waldo came in and asked about you, and the kid and I said no, we hadn't seen you, and he started to leave."

I sipped my drink while her eyes ate me.

"Just started to leave. Then this drunk that wasn't paying any attention to anyone called him Waldo and took a gun out. He shot him twice"—I snapped my fingers twice—"like that. Dead."

She fooled me. She laughed in my face. "So my husband hired

you to spy on me," she said. "I might have known the whole thing was an act. You and your Waldo."

I gawked at her.

"I never thought of him as jealous," she snapped. "Not of a man who had been our chauffeur anyhow. Not of Joseph Coates—"

I made motions in the air. "Lady, one of us has this book open at the wrong page. I don't know anybody named Joseph Coates. So help me, I didn't even know you had a chauffeur. People around here don't run to them."

She shook her head slowly and her hand stayed near her bag and her blue eyes had glitters in them. "Not good enough, Mr. Marlowe. I know you private detectives. You're all rotten. You tricked me into your apartment, if it is your apartment. Now you're trying to scare me. So you can blackmail me—as well as get money from my husband. All right," she said breathlessly, "how much do I have to pay?"

I put my empty glass aside and lit a cigarette. "Pardon me," I said. "My nerves are frayed."

She watched me without enough fear for any real guilt to be under it. "So Joseph Coates is his name," I said. "The guy that killed him called him Waldo."

She smiled tolerantly. "Don't stall. How much?"

"Why were you trying to meet this Joseph Coates?"

"I was going to buy back something he stole from me. Something that's valuable even in the ordinary way. Almost fifteen thousand dollars. The man I loved gave it to me. He's dead. There! He died in a burning plane. Now, go back and tell my husband that."

She grabbed her glass and finished what was left of her drink. "So he thinks I'm meeting Joseph. Well, I was. But I don't have to dig down that far if I want to play around. And don't bother about telling my husband. I'll tell him myself."

I grinned. "That's smart."

"Now I'm going," she said. "You just try and stop me." She snatched the pearl-handled gun out of her bag. I didn't move.

"Why, you nasty little string of nothing," she stormed. "How do

I know you're a private detective at all? You might be a crook. Your card means nothing. Anybody can have cards printed."

"Sure," I said. "And I suppose I'm smart enough to live here two years so I could blackmail you today for not meeting a man named Joseph Coates who was bumped off across the street under the name of Waldo. Have you got the money to buy this something that costs fifteen grand?"

"Oh! You think you'll hold me up, I suppose!"

"Oh!" I mimicked her. "I'm a stickup artist now, am I? Lady, will you please either put that gun away or take the safety catch off? It hurts my professional feelings to see a nice gun made a monkey of that way."

"Get out of my way," she said.

I didn't move. She didn't move. We were both sitting down—and not even close to each other.

"Let me in on one secret before you go," I pleaded. "What in hell were you doing in this building, if you didn't have an apartment here?"

"Stop being silly," she snapped. "I told you I lied about the apartment. It's Joseph Coates's apartment."

"Does my description of Waldo sound like Joseph Coates?"

She nodded sharply.

"All right. That's one fact learned at last. Don't you realize Waldo described your clothes before he was shot—that the description was passed on to the police—that the police don't know who Waldo is—and are looking for somebody in those clothes to help tell them? Don't you get that much?"

The gun suddenly started to shake in her hand. She looked down at it sort of vacantly, slowly put it back in her bag.

"I'm a fool," she whispered, "to be even talking to you." She stared at me for a long time, then pulled in a deep breath. "Joseph told me where he was staying. He was to meet me on the street near the bar, but I was late. It was full of police when I got there. So I went back and sat in my car for a while. Then I came up to Joseph's apartment and knocked. Then I went back to my car and waited again. I came up here three times in all. The last time,

I walked up a flight to take the elevator down again. I had already been seen twice on the third floor. I met you. That's all."

"You said something about a husband. Where is he?"

"He's at a meeting."

"Oh, a meeting," I said nastily.

"My husband's a very important man. He has lots of meetings. He's a hydroelectric engineer. He's been all over the world. I'd have you know—"

"Skip it," I said. "Whatever Joseph had on you is dead stock now. Like Joseph."

"He's really dead?" she whispered. "Really?"

"He's dead," I said.

She believed it at last. I hadn't thought she ever would.

The elevator stopped at my floor. I heard steps coming down the hall. We all have hunches. I put my finger to my lips. She didn't move now. Her face had a frozen look. The hot wind boomed against the shut windows. Windows have to be shut when a Santa Ana blows, heat or no heat.

The steps that came down the hall were the casual steps of one man. But they stopped outside my door, and somebody knocked. I pointed to the dressing room behind the wall bed. She stood up without a sound, her bag clenched against her side. I pointed again, to her glass. She lifted it swiftly, slid across the carpet and drew the door quietly shut after her.

I didn't know just what I was going to all this trouble for.

The knocking sounded again. My hands were wet. I creaked my chair and stood up and made a loud yawning sound. Then I went over and opened the door—without a gun. That was a mistake.

3

I DIDN'T know him at first. He'd had a hat on all the time over at the cocktail bar and he didn't have one on now. His hair ended completely and exactly where his hat would start. Above that line was hard white skin almost as glaring as scar tissue. He wasn't just twenty years older. He was a different man.

But I knew the gun he was holding, the .22 target automatic with the big front sight. And I knew his eyes. Bright, brittle, shallow eyes like the eyes of a lizard. He put the gun against my face very lightly and said between his teeth, "Yeah, me. Let's go on in."

I backed in just far enough so he could shut the door. I knew from his eyes that he would want me to do just that.

I wasn't scared. I was paralyzed.

When he had the door shut he backed me some more, slowly, until there was something against the back of my legs. "That's a card table," he said. "Some goon here plays chess. You?"

I swallowed. "I don't exactly play it. I just fool around."

"Chess takes two," he said with a hoarse softness, as if some cop had hit him across the windpipe with a blackjack once.

"It's a problem, not a game. I'm alone," I said, and my voice shook just enough.

"It don't make any difference," he said. "I'm washed up anyway. The bulls will be on me tomorrow, next week. What the hell? I just didn't like your map, pal. And that smug-faced kid in the bar coat that played left tackle for Fordham or something. To hell with guys like you guys."

His gun raked my cheek lightly, almost caressingly. He smiled. "It's kind of good business too. Just in case. An old con like me don't make good prints, all I got against me is two witnesses."

"What did Waldo do to you?" I tried to make it sound as if I wanted to know, instead of just not wanting to shake too hard.

"Stooled on a bank job in Michigan and got me four years. Four years in Michigan ain't no summer cruise."

"How'd you know he'd come in there?" I croaked.

"I didn't. I wanted to see him all right. I got a flash of him in this neighborhood night before last, but I lost him. Up to then I wasn't lookin' for him. Then I was. A cute guy, Waldo. How is he?"

"Dead," I said.

"I'm still good," he chuckled. "Drunk or sober. Well, that don't make no doughnuts for me now. They know me downtown yet?"

I didn't answer him quick enough. He jabbed the gun into my throat and I started to grab for it by instinct.

"Naw," he cautioned me softly. "Naw. You ain't that dumb."

I put my hands back down at my sides, open, the palms towards him. He would want them that way.

"They got your prints," I said. "I don't know how good."

"They'll be good enough—but not for Teletype work. Take 'em airmail time to Washington and back to check 'em right. Tell me why I came here, pal."

"You heard the kid and me talking in the bar. I told him my name, where I lived."

"That's how, pal. I said why." He smiled at me. It was a lousy smile to be the last one you might see.

"Skip it," I said. "The hangman won't ask you to guess why he's there."

"Say, you're tough at that. After you, I visit that kid, but I figure you're the guy to put the bee on first. I tailed him home from headquarters in the rented car Waldo had. Them funny dicks. You can sit in their laps and they don't know you. Start runnin' for a streetcar and they open up with machine guns and bump two pedestrians, a hacker asleep in his cab and an old scrubwoman."

He twisted the gun muzzle in my neck. His eyes looked madder than before. "I got time. Waldo's car don't get a report right away. And they won't make Waldo very soon. A smooth boy, Waldo."

"I'm going to vomit," I said, "if you don't take that gun out of my throat."

He smiled and moved the gun down to my heart. "This about right? Say when."

I must have spoken louder than I meant to. The door of the dressing room by the wall bed opened a crack. Then an inch. Then four inches. I stared hard into the bald-headed man's eyes. Very hard. I didn't want him to take his eyes off mine.

"Scared?" he asked softly.

I leaned against his gun and began to shake. I thought he would enjoy seeing me shake. The girl came through the door, her gun in her hand. I was sorry as hell for her. She'd try to make the door—or scream. Either way it would be curtains for both of us.

"Well, don't take all night about it," I bleated.

"I like this, pal," he smiled. "I'm like that."

The girl floated in the air, somewhere behind him. Nothing was ever more soundless than the way she moved. It wouldn't do her any good though. He wouldn't fool around with her at all.

"Suppose I yell," I said.

"Go ahead and yell," he said with his killer's smile.

She didn't go near the door. She was right behind him.

"Well—here's where I yell," I said.

As if that was the cue, she jabbed the gun hard into his ribs.

It was like a knee reflex. His mouth snapped open and his arms jumped out from his sides and he arched his back a little. His gun was pointing at my right eye, but it didn't go off. I sank and kneed him with all my strength in the groin. His chin came down and I hit it as if I was driving the last spike on the first transcontinental railroad. He writhed down gasping, his left side against the floor. I kicked his right shoulder—hard. The gun jumped away from him, skidded on the carpet, under a chair. I heard the chessmen tinkling onto the floor behind me somewhere.

The girl stood over him, looking down. Then her wide dark horrified eyes came up and fastened on mine.

"That buys me," I said. "Anything I have is yours—now and forever."

She didn't hear me. Her eyes were strained open so hard that the whites showed under the vivid blue irises. She backed quickly to the door with her little gun up, felt behind her for the knob and twisted it. She pulled the door open and slipped out.

She still had the safety catch set so that she couldn't fire it.

It was silent in the room now, in spite of the wind. Then I heard him gasping on the floor. His mouth looked like a black pit and his breath came in little waves, choked, stopped, came on again. His face had a greenish pallor. I pawed him for more guns and didn't find any. I got a pair of handcuffs out of my desk and snapped them on his wrists. His eyes measured me for a coffin, in spite of their suffering.

I went into the dressing room and opened the drawer of the chest. Her hat and jacket lay there on my shirts. I put them at the back and piled the shirts over them. Then I went out to the kitchenette and put down a stiff jolt of whiskey and stood a moment listening to the hot wind howl against the window glass.

The drink worked on me. I went back into the living room and opened a window. The guy on the floor hadn't noticed her sandalwood, but somebody else might.

I shut the window again and used the phone to dial headquarters. Copernik was still there. His smart-aleck voice said, "Yeah? Marlowe? Don't tell me. I bet you got an idea."

"Know who that killer is yet?"

"We're not saying, Marlowe."

"Okay. I don't care who he is. Just come and get him off the floor of my apartment."

"Damn!" Then his voice hushed and went down low. "Wait a minute, now." I seemed to hear a door shut. Then his voice again. "Shoot," he said softly.

"Handcuffed," I said. "All yours. I had to knee him, but he'll be all right. He came here to eliminate a witness."

Another pause. The voice was full of honey. "Now listen, boy, who else is in this with you?"

"Who else? Nobody. Just me."

"Keep it that way, boy. All quiet. Just sit tight. I'm practically there. Okay?"

"Yeah." I gave him the address again to save him time.

I got the .22 target gun from under the chair and sat holding it until Copernik's knuckles did a quiet tattoo on the door panel.

He was alone. He pushed me back into the room with a tight grin and stood with his back to the door, his hand under the left side of his coat—a big hard bony man with flat cruel eyes. He looked at the man on the floor. "Sure it's the guy?" His voice was hoarse.

"Positive. Where's Ybarra?"

"Oh, he was busy." Copernik didn't look at me when he said that. "Those your cuffs?"

"Yeah."

"Key." I tossed it to him. He went down swiftly on one knee beside the killer, took my cuffs off his wrists and tossed them to one side. He got his own off his hip, twisted the bald man's hands behind him and snapped the cuffs on.

"All right, you bastard," the killer said tonelessly.

Copernik grinned and balled his fist and hit the guy in the mouth a terrific blow. His head snapped back almost enough to break his neck. Blood dribbled from the lower corner of his mouth.

"Get a towel," Copernik ordered.

I got a hand towel. Copernik stuffed it between the handcuffed man's teeth, viciously, and stood up. "All right. Tell it," he said.

I told it—leaving the girl out completely. It sounded a little funny. Copernik watched me, said nothing. He rubbed the side of his veined nose.

I went over and gave him the .22. He looked at it casually, dropped it into his side pocket. His eyes had something in them and his face moved in a hard bright grin.

I bent down and began picking up my chessmen and dropping them into the box. Copernik watched me. I wanted him to think something out.

At last he came out with it. "This guy uses a twenty-two," he said, "because he's good enough to get by with that much gun. He knocks at your door, pokes that gat in your belly, says he's here to close your mouth for keeps—and yet you take him. You not having any gun. You take him alone. You're kind of good yourself, pal."

I twisted a chessman between my fingers.

"You got something on your mind, pal," Copernik said softly. "You wouldn't try to fool an old copper, would you, boy?"

The man on the floor made a vague sound behind the towel. His bald head glistened with sweat.

"What's the matter, pal? You been up to something?" Copernik almost whispered.

I looked at him quickly, looked away again. "All right," I said. "You know damn well I couldn't take him alone."

Copernik closed one eye and squinted at me amiably with the other. "Go on, pal. I kind of thought that too."

I shuffled around a little more, to make it look good. I said slowly, "There was a kid here who pulled a job over in Boyle Heights, a two-bit service-station stickup. I know his family. He's not really bad. He was here trying to beg train money off me. When the knock came, he sneaked in—there." I pointed at the wall bed and the door beside.

Copernik's head swiveled slowly, swiveled back. His eyes winked again. "And this kid had a gun," he said.

I nodded. "And he got behind him. That takes guts, Copernik. Give the kid a break. Let him stay out of it."

"Tag out for this kid?" Copernik asked softly.

"Not yet, he says. He's scared there will be."

"I'm a homicide man," he said. "I wouldn't know—or care."

I pointed down at the gagged and handcuffed man on the floor. "You took him, didn't you?" I said gently.

Copernik kept on smiling. A big whitish tongue came out and massaged his thick lower lip. "How'd I do it?" he whispered.

"You're a careful guy. You don't miss any angles. You dropped in on me to see whether I had any guns that matched the slugs out of Waldo."

Copernik went down on one knee again beside the killer. "Can you hear me, guy?" he asked. The man made some vague sound. Copernik stood up and yawned. "Who the hell cares what he says? Go on, pal."

"You wouldn't expect to find I had anything, but you wanted to look around my place. And while you were mousing around in there"—I pointed to the dressing room—"and me not saying anything, being a little sore, maybe, a knock came on the door. So handsome here came in with his twenty-two. So after a while you sneaked out and took him."

"Ah." Copernik grinned widely. "You're on, pal. I socked him and I kneed him and I took him. You didn't have no gun and the guy swiveled on me pretty sharp and I left-hooked him down the back stairs. Okay?"

"Okay," I said.

"You'll tell it like that downtown?"

"Yeah," I said.

"I'll protect you, pal. Treat me right and I'll always play ball. Forget about the kid that pulled the stickup. Let me know if he needs a break."

He held out his hand. I shook it. It was as clammy as a dead fish. Clammy hands and the people who own them make me sick.

"There's just one thing," I said. "This partner of yours—Ybarra. Won't he be a bit sore you didn't bring him along on this?"

"That guinea?" Copernik sneered. "To hell with him!" He came close to me and breathed in my face. "No mistakes, pal, about that story of ours."

His breath was bad. It would be.

4

THERE were just five of us in the chief of detectives' office when Copernik laid it before them: a stenographer, the chief, Copernik, myself, Ybarra. Ybarra sat on a chair tilted against the side wall. His hat was down over his eyes, but their softness loomed underneath, and the small still smile hung at the corners of his lips. He didn't look directly at Copernik. Copernik didn't look at him at all.

Outside in the corridor there had been photos of Copernik shaking hands with me, Copernik with his hat on straight and his gun in his hand and a stern, purposeful look on his face.

They said they knew who Waldo was, but they wouldn't tell me. I didn't believe they knew, because the chief of detectives had a morgue photo of Waldo on his desk. A beautiful job, his hair combed, his tie straight, the light hitting his eyes just right to make them glisten. Nobody would have known it was a photo of a dead man. He looked like a dance-hall sheik making up his mind whether to take the blonde or the redhead.

It was about midnight when I got home. The hot wind still burned and blustered. The outside door to the Berglund was locked, and while I was fumbling for my keys a low voice spoke to me out of the darkness.

All it said was, "Please!" but I knew it. I turned and looked at a dark Cadillac coupe parked just off the loading zone. Light from the street touched the brightness of the eyes of the woman sitting inside.

I went over there. "You're a darn fool," I said.

"Get in," she said.

I climbed in and she started the car and drove it a block and a half until she found a space to park. After she'd jockeyed us up to the curb she leaned back in the corner with her gloved hands on the wheel. She was all in black now, with a small foolish hat. I smelled the sandalwood in her perfume.

"I wasn't very nice to you, was I?" she said.

"All you did was save my life."

"What happened afterwards?"

"I called the law and fed a few lies to a cop I don't like and gave him all the credit for the pinch and that was that. The guy you took away from me was the man who killed Waldo."

"You mean . . . you didn't tell them about me?"

"Lady," I said again, "all you did was save my life. What else do you want done?"

She didn't say anything, or move.

"Nobody learned who you are from me," I went on. "Incidentally, I don't know myself."

"I'm Mrs. Frank C. Barsaly," she said. "Two twelve Fremont Place, Olympia two four five nine six. Is that what you wanted?"

"Thanks," I mumbled. "Why did you come back?" Then I snapped my fingers. "The hat and jacket. I'll go up and get them."

"It's more than that," she said. "I want my pearls."

I might have jumped a little. It seemed as if there had been enough without pearls.

A car tore by down the street, going twice as fast as it should. A thin bitter cloud of dust lifted in the streetlights and whirled and vanished. The girl ran the window up quickly against it.

"All right," I said. "Tell me about the pearls. We have had a murder and a mystery woman and a mad killer and a heroic rescue and a police detective framed into making a false report. Now we will have pearls."

"I was to buy them for five thousand dollars. From the man you call Waldo and I call Joseph Coates. He should have had them."

"No pearls," I said. "I saw what came out of his pockets. A lot of money, but no pearls."

"Could they be hidden in his apartment?"

"He could have had them hidden anywhere except in his pockets. How's Mr. Barsaly this hot night?"

"He's still at his meeting. Otherwise I couldn't have come."

"Well, you could have brought him," I said. "He could have sat in the rumble seat."

"Oh, I don't know," she said. "Frank weighs two hundred pounds and he's pretty solid. I don't think he would like to sit in the rumble seat."

"What the hell are we talking about anyway?"

She didn't answer. Her gloved hands tapped provokingly on the rim of the steering wheel. I turned a little and took hold of her.

When I let go she pulled as far away from me as she could and rubbed her glove against her mouth. I sat quite still.

We didn't speak for some time. Then she said very slowly, "I meant you to do that. But I wasn't always that way. It's only been since Stan Phillips was killed in his plane. If it hadn't been for that, I'd be Mrs. Phillips now. Stan gave me the pearls. They cost fifteen thousand dollars, Stan said once. Forty-one white pearls, the largest about a third of an inch across. I don't know how many grains. I never had them appraised, so I don't know those things. But I loved them on Stan's account. I loved Stan. The way you do just the one time. Can you understand?"

"What's your first name?" I asked.

"Lola."

"Go on talking, Lola." I got a cigarette out of my pocket and fumbled it between my fingers, just to give them something to do.

"They had a simple silver clasp in the shape of a two-bladed propeller. There was one small diamond where the boss would be.

I told Frank they were store pearls I had bought myself. You see—Frank is pretty jealous."

In the darkness she came closer to me and her side touched my side. But I didn't move this time. The wind howled and the trees shook. I kept on rolling the cigarette around in my fingers.

"I suppose you've read that story," she said. "About the wife and the real pearls and her telling her husband they were false?"

"I've read it," I said. "Maugham."

"I hired Joseph. My husband was in Argentina at the time. I was pretty lonely."

"*You* should be lonely," I said.

"Joseph and I went driving a good deal. Sometimes we had a drink or two together. But that's all. I don't go around—"

"You told him about the pearls," I said. "And when your two hundred pounds of beef came back from Argentina and kicked him out, Joseph took the pearls, because he knew they were real. And then offered them back to you for five grand."

"Yes," she said simply. "And of course I didn't want to go to the police."

"Poor Waldo," I said. "I feel kind of sorry for him. It was a hell of a time to run into an old friend that had a down on you."

I struck a match and lit the cigarette. "Hell with women—these fliers," I said. "And you're still in love with him, or think you are. Where did you keep the pearls?"

"In a box on my dressing table. With some other costume jewelry. I had to, if I ever wanted to wear them."

"And you think Joseph might have hidden them in his apartment. Thirty-one, wasn't it?"

"Yes," she said. "I guess it's a lot to ask."

I opened the door and got out of the car. "I've been paid," I said. "I'll go look. The doors in my building are not very obstinate. The cops will find out where Waldo lived when they publish his photo, but not tonight, I guess."

"It's awfully sweet of you," she said. "Shall I wait here?"

I didn't answer. I just stood there looking in at the shine of her eyes. Then I shut the car door and walked up the street. Even with the wind shriveling my face I could still smell the sandal-wood in her hair.

I unlocked the Berglund door and rode the elevator up to Three. Then I soft-footed along the silent corridor and peered down at the sill of Apartment 31. No light. I rapped—no answer. I took the piece of thick hard celluloid that pretended to be a cover for my driver's license and eased it between the lock and the jamb, leaning hard on the knob, pushing it towards the hinges. The lock snapped back with a small brittle sound, like an icicle breaking. The door yielded and I went in.

I shut the door and switched the light on. There was a queer smell in the air. I made it in a moment—the smell of dark-cured tobacco. I prowled over to a smoking stand and looked down at four brown butts—Mexican or South American cigarettes.

I only half searched the bathroom and the kitchenette. I knew there were no pearls in that apartment. I knew Waldo had been on his way out and that he was in a hurry and that something was riding him when he took two bullets from an old friend.

I went back to the living room and swung the wall bed and looked past its mirror side into the dressing room for signs of oc-cupancy. Swinging the bed farther, I was no longer looking for pearls. I was looking at a man.

He was small, middle-aged, iron gray at the temples, with a very dark skin, dressed in a fawn-colored suit with a wine-colored tie. His neat little brown hands hung limply by his sides. His small feet, in highly polished shoes, pointed almost at the floor. He was hanging by a belt around his neck from the metal top of the bed. His tongue stuck out farther than I thought it possible for a tongue to stick out.

He swung a little and I didn't like that, so I pulled the bed shut. I didn't have to touch him to know that he would be cold as ice.

I went around him into the dressing room and used my hand-kerchief on drawer knobs. The place was stripped clean except for the light litter of a man living alone.

I came out of there and began on the dead man. No wallet. Waldo would have taken that and ditched it. A flat box of cigarettes stamped in gold: LOUIS TAPIA Y CIA, MONTEVIDEO. Matches from the Spezzia Club. An underarm holster of dark-grained leather and in it a 9-millimeter Mauser—a gun you can blast through a wall with.

The Mauser made him a professional, so I didn't feel so badly. But not a very good professional, or bare hands would not have finished him.

I made a little sense of it, not much. Four of the brown cigarettes had been smoked, so there had been either waiting or discussion. Somewhere along the line Waldo had got the little man by the throat and held him in just the right way to make him pass out in a matter of seconds. Then Waldo had hung him up by the strap, probably dead already. That would account for haste, cleaning out the apartment, for Waldo's anxiety about the girl. It would account for the car left running outside the cocktail bar.

That is, it would account for these things if Waldo had killed him, if this was really Waldo's apartment—if I wasn't just being kidded.

I examined some more pockets. In the left trouser one I found a gold penknife, some silver. In the left hip pocket a handkerchief, folded, scented. In the right trouser pocket four or five tissue handkerchiefs. Under these there was a small new key case holding four new keys—car keys. Stamped in gold on the key case was: COMPLIMENTS OF R. K. VOGELSANG, INC.—THE PACKARD HOUSE.

I put everything as I had found it, swung the bed back, used my handkerchief on knobs and flat surfaces, killed the light and poked my nose out the door. The hall was empty. I went down to the street and around the corner.

The Cadillac hadn't moved. I opened the car door and leaned on it. She didn't seem to have moved, either. It was hard to see anything but her eyes and chin, but not hard to smell the sandalwood.

"That perfume," I said, "would drive a deacon nuts . . . no pearls."

"Well, thanks for trying," she said in a low, soft vibrant voice. "I guess I can stand it. Shall I . . . Do we . . . Or . . . ?"

"You go on home now," I said. "And whatever happens you never saw me before. Whatever happens. Just as you may never see me again."

"I'd hate that."

"Good luck, Lola." I shut the car door and stepped back.

The lights blazed on, the motor turned over. Against the wind at the corner the big coupe made a slow contemptuous turn and was gone.

I stood looking at the back of a brand-new Packard cabriolet, which was parked in front of the space left by Lola's car. It was dark, silent, with a blue dealer's sticker pasted to the corner of the shiny windshield. And in my mind I was looking at something else, a set of brand-new car keys in a key case stamped THE PACKARD HOUSE, upstairs in a dead man's pocket.

I went up to the front of the Packard and put a small pocket flash on the blue slip. It was the same dealer. Written in ink below his name and slogan was the owner's name and address—Eugénie Kolchenko, 5315 Arvieda Street, West Los Angeles.

It was crazy. I went back up to Apartment 31, jimmied the door as I had done before, stepped in behind the wall bed and took the key case from the trouser pocket of the neat brown corpse. I was back beside the Packard in five minutes.

5

IT WAS a small house—5315 Arvieda—with a circle of writhing eucalyptus trees in front of it. On the other side of the street one of those parties was going on where they come out and smash bottles on the sidewalk with a whoop like Yale making a touchdown against Princeton.

There was a wire fence at 5315 and some rose trees, and a flagged walk and a garage that was wide open and had no car in it. I rang the bell. There was a long wait, then the door opened rather suddenly.

I wasn't the man she had been expecting. I could see it in her glittering kohl-rimmed eyes. She just stood and looked at me, a long lean brunette, with rouged cheekbones, thick black hair parted in the middle, a mouth made for three-decker sandwiches, coral and gold pajamas, sandals—and gilded toenails.

She wasn't beautiful, she wasn't even pretty, but she looked as if things would happen where she was. Under her earlobes a couple of miniature temple bells gonged lightly in the breeze. She made a slow disdainful motion with a cigarette in a long holder.

"We-el, what ees it? You want sometheeng? You are lost from the party across the street?"

"Ha-ha," I said. "Quite a party, isn't it? No, I just brought your car home. Lost it, didn't you?"

"You have said what?" she got out at last.

"Your car." I pointed over my shoulder and kept my eyes on her. She was the type that uses a knife.

The long cigarette holder dropped very slowly to her side and the cigarette fell out of it. I stamped it out, and that put me in the hall. She backed away from me and I shut the door.

The hall was like the long hall of a railroad flat. Lamps glowed pinkly in iron brackets. There was a bead curtain at the end, a tiger skin on the floor. The place went with her.

"You're Miss Kolchenko?" I asked, not getting any more action.

"Ye-es. I am Mees Kolchenko. What the 'ell you want?"

She was looking at me now as if I had come to wash the windows but at an inconvenient time. I got a card out, held it out to her. "A detective?" she breathed.

"Yeah."

She said something in a spitting language. Then in English, "Come in out of thees damn wind."

"We're in," I said. "I just shut the door. Snap out of it, Nazimova. Who was he? The little guy?"

Beyond the bead curtain a man coughed. She tried to smile. It wasn't very successful. "A reward," she said softly. "You weel wait 'ere? Ten dollars it is fair to pay, no?"

"No," I said. I reached a finger towards her slowly. "He's dead." She jumped about three feet and let out a yell.

A chair creaked harshly. Feet pounded beyond the bead curtain, a large hand snatched it aside, and a big hard-looking blond man was with us. He had a purple robe over his pajamas, his right hand held something in his robe pocket. He stood quite still, his jaw out, his colorless eyes like gray ice. He looked like a man who would be hard to take out on an off-tackle play.

"What's the matter, honey?" He had a solid, burring voice, with just the right sappy tone to belong to a guy who would go for a woman with gilded toenails.

"I came about Miss Kolchenko's car," I said.

"Well, you could take your hat off. Just for a light workout."

I took it off and apologized.

"Okay." He kept his right hand shoved down hard in the purple pocket. "So you came about Miss Kolchenko's car. Take it from there."

I pushed past the woman and went closer to him. She shrank back against the wall. The big man said, "Just take it easy. I've got a gun in this pocket. Now about the car?"

"The man who borrowed it couldn't bring it," I said, and pushed the card I was still holding towards his face.

He barely glanced at it. "So what?" he said.

"Are you always this tough?" I asked. "Or only when you have your pajamas on?"

"So why couldn't he bring it himself?" he asked. "And skip the mushy talk."

The dark woman made a sound at my elbow.

"It's all right, honeybunch," the man said. "I'll handle this. Go on." She slid past both of us and flicked through the bead curtain.

I waited a little while. The big man didn't move a muscle. He didn't look any more bothered than a toad in the sun.

"He couldn't bring it because somebody bumped him off," I said. "Let's see you handle that."

"Yeah?" he said. "Did you bring him with you to prove it?"

"No," I said. "But if you put your tie and hat on, I'll take you down and show you."

"Who the hell did you say you were, now?"

"I didn't say. I thought maybe you could read." I held the card at him some more.

"Oh, that's right," he said. "'Philip Marlowe, Private Investigator.' Well, well. So I should go with you to look at who, why?"

"Maybe he stole the car," I said.

The big man nodded. "That's a thought. Maybe he did. Who?"

"The little brown guy who had the keys to it in his pocket and had it parked around the corner from the Berglund Apartments."

He thought that over without any apparent embarrassment. "You've got something there," he said. "Your card says private detective. Have you got some cops outside that were too shy to come in?"

"No, I'm alone."

He grinned. The grin showed white ridges in his tanned skin. "So you find somebody dead and take some keys and find a car and come riding out here—all alone. No cops. Am I right?"

"Correct."

He sighed. "Let's go inside." He yanked the bead curtain aside and made an opening for me to go through. "It might be you have an idea I ought to hear." As I went past him he turned, keeping his heavy pocket towards me.

We sat down in the living room and looked at each other across a dark floor, on which a few Navajo rugs made a decorating combination with some well-used overstuffed furniture, a small baby grand, and a tall Chinese lantern on a teakwood pedestal. The windows to the south were open. A fruit tree whipped about outside, adding its bit to the noise from across the street.

The big man eased back into a brocaded chair and put his slippered feet on a footstool. He kept his right hand where it had been since I met him—on his gun. The brunette hung around in the shadows and a bottle gurgled, and she poured half a glass of whiskey down her throat.

"It's all right, honeybunch," the man said. "It's all under control. Somebody bumped somebody off and this lad thinks we're interested. Just sit down and relax."

The girl sighed and curled up on a davenport. Her gilded toenails winked at me from the corner, where she kept herself quiet from then on.

I lit a cigarette and went into my story. It wasn't all true, but some of it was. I told them about the Berglund Apartments and that I had lived there and that Waldo was living there in Apartment 31 on the floor below mine and that I had been keeping an eye on him for business reasons.

"Waldo who?" the man put in. "And what business reasons?"

"It was an undercover job—from my angle," I said. "If you know what I mean." He reddened slightly.

I told him about the cocktail lounge across the street from the Berglund and what had happened there. I didn't tell him about the print bolero jacket or the girl who had worn it.

"I got back from the city hall without telling anybody I knew Waldo," I went on. "In due time, when I decided they couldn't find out where he lived tonight, I took the liberty of examining his apartment."

"Looking for what?" the big man said thickly.

"For some letters. I might mention in passing, there was nothing there at all—except a dead man. Strangled and hanging by a belt to the top of the wall bed—well out of sight. A small man, about forty-five, Mexican or South American, well-dressed in a fawn-colored—"

"That's enough," the big man said. "I'll bite, Marlowe. Was it a blackmail job you were on?"

"Yeah. The funny part was this little brown man had plenty of gun under his arm."

"He wouldn't have five hundred bucks in twenties in his pocket, of course?"

"He wouldn't. But Waldo had over seven hundred in currency when he was killed in the cocktail bar."

"Looks like I underrated this Waldo," the big man said calmly. "He took my guy and his payoff money, gun and all. Waldo have a gun?"

"Not on him."

"Get us a drink, honeybunch," the big man said. "Yes, I certainly did sell this Waldo person shorter than a bargain-counter shirt."

The brunette unwound her legs and made two drinks with soda and ice. She took herself another gill without trimmings, wound herself back on the davenport. Her big glittering black eyes watched me solemnly.

"Well, here's how," the big man said, lifting his glass in salute. "I haven't murdered anybody, but I've got a divorce suit on my hands from now on. You haven't murdered anybody, the way you tell it, but you laid an egg down at police headquarters. What the hell! I've still got honeybunch here. She's a White Russian I met in Shanghai. She's safe as a vault, and she looks as if she could cut your throat for a nickel. That's what I like about her. You get the glamour without the risk."

"You talk damn foolish," the girl spat at him.

"You look okay to me," the big man went on, ignoring her. "That is, for a keyhole peeper. Is there an out?"

"Yeah. But it will cost a little money."

"I expected that. How much?"

"Say another five hundred."

"Five hundred might do," the blond man said. "What do I get for it?"

"If I swing it, you get left out of the story. If I don't, you don't pay."

He thought it over. His face looked lined and tired now. "This second murder will make you talk," he grumbled. "And I still don't have what I was going to buy."

"Who was the little brown man?" I asked.

"Name's Leon Valesanos, a Uruguayan. Another of my importations. I'm in a business that takes me a lot of places. He was working in the Spezzia Club, on the strip of Sunset next to Beverly Hills. I gave him the five hundred to go down to this—this Waldo—and buy back some bills for stuff Miss Kolchenko charged to my account and had delivered here. That wasn't bright, was it? I had the bills in my briefcase and this Waldo got a chance to steal them. What's your hunch about what happened?"

I sipped my drink and looked at him down my nose. "Your

Uruguayan pal probably talked out, and Waldo didn't listen good. Then the little guy thought maybe that Mauser might help his argument—and Waldo was too quick for him. I wouldn't say Waldo was a killer—a blackmailer seldom is. Maybe he lost his temper and maybe he just held on to the little guy's neck too long. Then he had to take it on the lam. But he had another date, with more money coming up. And he worked the neighborhood, looking for the party. And accidentally he ran into a pal who was hostile enough and drunk enough to blow him down."

"There's a hell of a lot of coincidence in all this business," the big man said.

"It's the hot wind," I grinned. "Everybody's screwy tonight."

"For the five hundred you guarantee nothing? If I don't get my cover-up, you don't get your dough. Is that it?"

"That's it," I said, smiling at him.

He drained his highball. "I'm taking you up on it."

"There are just two things," I said softly, leaning forward in my chair. "Waldo had a getaway car parked outside the cocktail bar where he was killed, unlocked, with the motor running. The killer took it. There's always the chance of a kickback from that direction. You see, all Waldo's stuff must have been in that car."

"Including my bills and your letters."

"Yeah. But the police are reasonable about things like that, unless you're good for a lot of publicity. If you're not, I think I can eat some crow downtown and get by. If you are—that's the second thing. What did you say your name was?"

The answer was a long time coming. When it came I didn't get as much kick out of it as I thought I would. All at once it was too logical.

"Frank C. Barsaly," he said.

6

I WENT home in a taxi. When I unlocked the entrance door of the Berglund I smelled policeman. I looked at my wristwatch. It was nearly 3:00 a.m. In the dark corner of the lobby a man dozed in a chair with a newspaper over his face. Large feet stretched out before him.

I rode the elevator up to my floor, soft-footed along the hallway and unlocked my door. Light glared from a standing lamp by the easy chair, beyond the card table on which some of my chessmen were still scattered.

Copernik sat there with a stiff unpleasant grin on his face. The short dark man, Ybarra, sat across the room from him, silent, half smiling as usual. Copernik showed more of his big yellow horse teeth and said, "Hi. Long time no see. Been out with the girls?"

I shut the door and took my hat off and wiped the back of my neck slowly, over and over again.

"Take a seat, pal," Copernik drawled. "We got a powwow to make. Did you know you were low on hooch?"

"I could have guessed it," I said. I leaned against the wall.

Copernik kept on grinning. "I always did hate private dicks," he said, "but I never had a chance to twist one like I got tonight." He reached down lazily beside his chair and picked up the print bolero jacket, tossed it on the card table. He reached down again and put Lola's wide-brimmed hat beside it. "I bet you look cuter than all hell with these on," he said.

I took hold of a straight chair, twisted it around and straddled it, leaned my folded arms on the chair and looked at Copernik.

He got up with an elaborate slowness, walked across the room and stood in front of me. Then he lifted his open right hand and hit me across the face with it—hard. It stung, but I didn't move.

Ybarra looked at the wall, looked at the floor, looked at nothing.

"Shame on you, pal," Copernik said lazily. "The way you was taking care of this nice exclusive merchandise. Wadded down behind your old shirts."

He stood there over me for a moment. I didn't move or speak. He doubled a fist at his side, then shrugged and went back to the chair. "Okay," he said. "The rest will keep. Where did you get these things?"

"They belong to a lady."

"Do tell. Ain't you the lighthearted bastard! I'll tell you what lady they belong to. They belong to the lady a guy named Waldo asked about in a bar across the street, two minutes before he got shot dead."

I didn't say anything.

"You was curious about her yourself," Copernik sneered on. "But you were smart, pal. You fooled me."

"That wouldn't make me smart," I said.

His face twisted suddenly and he started to get up. Ybarra laughed softly, almost under his breath. Copernik's eyes swung on him, hung there.

"The guinea likes you," he said to me. "He thinks you're good."

The smile left Ybarra's face, but no expression took its place. No expression at all.

Copernik said, "You knew who the dame was all the time. You knew who Waldo was and where he lived. Right across the hall, a floor below you. You knew this Waldo person had bumped a guy off and started to lam, only he was anxious to meet up with this broad before he went away. Only he never got the chance. A heist guy from back East named Al Tessilore took care of that by taking care of Waldo. So you met the gal and hid her clothes and sent her on her way and kept your trap glued. That's the way guys like you make your beans. Am I right?"

"Yeah," I said. "Except that I only knew these things very recently. Who was Waldo?"

Ybarra, looking down at the floor, said very softly, "Waldo Ratigan. We got him from Washington by Teletype. He was a two-bit porch climber with a few small terms on him. He drove a car in a bank stickup job in Detroit. He turned the gang in later and got a nolle prosequi. One of the gang was this Al Tessilore. He hasn't talked a word, but we think the meeting across the street was purely accidental."

Ybarra spoke in the soft quiet voice of a man for whom sounds have a meaning.

I said, "Thanks, Ybarra. Can I smoke, or would Copernik kick it out of my mouth?"

Ybarra smiled suddenly. "You may smoke, sure," he said.

"The guinea likes you all right," Copernik jeered. "You never know what a guinea will like, do you?"

I lit a cigarette. Ybarra looked at Copernik and said very softly, "The word guinea—you overwork it. I don't like it so well applied to me."

"The hell with what you like, guinea."

Ybarra smiled a little more. "You are making a mistake," he said. He took a pocket nail file out and began to use it, looking down.

Copernik blared, "I smelled something rotten on you from the start, Marlowe. So when we make Waldo and Tessilore, Ybarra and me think we'll drift over and dabble a few more words with you. I bring one of Waldo's morgue photos, so on the way up, just as a matter of routine, we rout out the manager here and let him lamp it. And he knows the guy. He's here as A. B. Hummel, Apartment Thirty-one. So we go in there and find a stiff. Then we go round and round with that. Nobody knows him yet, but he's got some swell finger bruises under that strap and I hear they fit Waldo's fingers very nicely."

"That's something," I said. "I thought maybe I murdered him."

Copernik stared at me a long time. His face had stopped grinning and was just a hard brutal face now. "We got something else even," he said. "We got Waldo's getaway car—and what Waldo had in it to take with him."

I blew cigarette smoke jerkily. The wind pounded the windows. The air in the room was foul.

"Oh, we're bright boys," Copernik sneered. "We never figured you with that much guts. Take a look at this."

He plunged his bony hand into his coat pocket and drew something up slowly, drew it along the green top of the card table and left it there stretched out, gleaming. A string of white pearls with a clasp like a two-bladed propeller. Lola Barsaly's pearls. They shimmered softly in the thick smoky air.

After a long moment Copernik said almost gravely, "Nice, ain't they? Would you feel like telling us a story now, Mis-ter Marlowe?"

I stood up and walked across the room and stood looking down at the pearls. The largest was perhaps a third of an inch across.

They were pure white, iridescent, with a mellow softness. I lifted them slowly off the card table. They felt heavy, smooth, fine.

"Nice," I said. "A lot of the trouble was about these. Yeah, I'll talk now. They must be worth a lot of money."

Ybarra laughed behind me. It was a very gentle laugh. "About a hundred dollars," he said. "They're good phonies."

I lifted the pearls again. Copernik's glassy eyes gloated at me. "How do you tell?" I asked.

"I know pearls," Ybarra said. "These are good stuff, the kind women very often have made on purpose, as a kind of insurance. But they are slick like glass. Real pearls are gritty between the edges of the teeth. Try."

I put two or three of them between my teeth and moved my teeth back and forth, then sideways. Not quite biting them. They were hard and slick.

"Yes. They are very good," Ybarra said. "Several even have little waves and flat spots as real pearls might have."

"Would they cost fifteen grand—if they were real?" I asked.

"Probably. That's hard to say."

"This Waldo wasn't so bad," I said.

Copernik stood up quickly, but I didn't see him swing. His fist caught me on the side of the face, against the molars. I tasted blood at once. I staggered back and made it look worse than it was. "Sit down and talk, you bastard!" Copernik almost whispered.

I sat down and licked at the cut inside my mouth.

Ybarra filed at his nails.

"You found the beads in Waldo's car," I said, looking at Ybarra. "Find any papers?"

He shook his head without looking up.

"I believe you," I said. "Here it is. I never saw Waldo until he stepped into the cocktail bar tonight and asked about the girl. I knew nothing I didn't tell. When I got home and stepped out of the elevator, this girl in the print bolero jacket and the wide hat and the white silk crepe dress—all as he had described them—was waiting for the elevator, here on my floor. And she looked like a nice girl."

Copernik laughed jeeringly. It didn't make any difference to me. I had him cold. He was going to know it now, very soon.

"I knew what she was up against as a police witness," I said. "And I suspected there was something else to it. But I didn't suspect for a minute that there was anything wrong with her. She was just a nice girl in a jam, and she didn't even know she was in a jam. I got her in here. She pulled a gun on me. But she didn't mean to use it."

Copernik sat up very suddenly and began to lick his lips. His face had a look like wet gray stone.

"Waldo had been her chauffeur," I went on. "His name was then Joseph Coates. Her name is Mrs. Frank C. Barsaly. Her husband is a big hydroelectric engineer. Some guy gave her the pearls once and she told her husband they were just store pearls. Waldo got wise there was a romance behind them and when Barsaly came home from South America and fired him because he was too good-looking, he lifted the pearls."

Ybarra lifted his head suddenly and his teeth flashed. "You mean he didn't know they were phony?"

"I thought he fenced the real ones and had imitations fixed up. And he lifted something else," I said. "Some stuff from Barsaly's briefcase that showed he was keeping a woman . . . out on Arvieda. He was blackmailing wife and husband both, without either knowing about the other. Get it so far?"

"I get it," Copernik said harshly. "Get the hell on with it."

"Waldo wasn't afraid of them," I said. "He didn't conceal where he lived. The girl came down here tonight with five grand to buy back her pearls. When she didn't find Waldo she walked up a floor before she went back down. A woman's idea of being cagey. So I met her. So I brought her in here. So she was in that dressing room when Al Tessilore visited me to rub out a witness." I pointed to the dressing-room door. "So she came out with her little gun and stuck it in his back and saved my life."

Copernik didn't move. There was something horrible in his face now. Ybarra slipped his nail file into a small leather case and slowly tucked it into his pocket. "Is that all?" he said gently.

I nodded. "Except that she told me where Waldo's apartment was and I went in there and looked for the pearls. I found the dead man. In his pocket I found car keys in a case from a Packard agency. And down on the street I found the Packard and took it to where it came from. Barsaly's kept woman. Barsaly had sent a friend from the Spezzia Club down to buy something that linked him to his woman and the friend tried to buy it with his gun instead of Barsaly's money. Waldo beat him to the punch."

"Is that all?" Ybarra said softly.

"That's all," I said, licking the inside of my cheek.

Ybarra said slowly, "What do you want?"

Copernik's face convulsed and he slapped his long hard thigh. "This guy's good," he jeered. "He falls for a stray broad and breaks every law in the book and you ask him what does he want? I'll give him what he wants, guinea!"

Ybarra turned his head slowly and looked at him. "I don't think you will," he said. "I think you'll give him a clean bill of health and anything else he wants. He's giving you a lesson in police work."

Copernik didn't move or make a sound for a long minute. Then he leaned forward and his coat fell open. The butt of his service gun looked out of his underarm holster. "So what do you want?" he asked me.

"What's on the card table there. The jacket and hat and the phony pearls. And some names kept away from the papers. Is that too much?"

"Yeah, it's too much," Copernik said almost gently. He swayed sideways and his gun jumped neatly into his hand. He rested his forearm on his thigh and pointed the gun at my stomach.

"I like better that you get a slug in the guts resisting arrest," he said. "I like that better, because of a report I made out on Al Tessilore's arrest and how I made the pinch. Because of some photos of me that are in the morning sheets going out now. I like it better that you don't live long enough to laugh about that baby."

My mouth felt suddenly hot and dry. Far off I heard the wind booming. It seemed like the sound of guns.

Ybarra moved his feet on the floor and said coldly, "You've got a couple of cases all solved, Copernik. All you do for it is leave some woman's junk here and keep some names from the papers. Which means keeping them from the D.A. If he gets them anyway, too bad for you."

Copernik said, "I like the other way." The blue gun in his hand was like a rock. "And God help you if you don't back me up on it."

Ybarra said, "If the woman is brought out into the open you'll be a liar on a police report and a chiseler on your own partner. In a week they won't even speak your name at headquarters. The taste of it would make them sick."

The hammer clicked back on Copernik's gun and I watched his big finger slide in farther around the trigger.

Ybarra stood up. The gun jumped at him. He said, "We'll see how yellow a guinea is. I'm telling you to put that gun up, Sam."

Ybarra started to move. He moved four steps. Copernik was a man without a breath of movement, a stone man. Ybarra took one more step and quite suddenly the gun began to shake.

Ybarra spoke evenly. "Put it up, Sam. If you keep your head, everything lies the way it is. If you don't, you're gone."

He took one more step. Copernik's mouth opened wide and made a gasping sound, and then he sagged in the chair as if he had been hit on the head.

Ybarra jerked the gun out of his hand with a movement so quick it was no movement at all. "It's the hot wind, Sam. Let's forget it," he said in the same even, almost dainty, voice.

Copernik's shoulders sagged lower and he put his face in his hands. "Okay," he said between his fingers.

Ybarra went softly across the room and opened the door. He looked at me with lazy, half-closed eyes. "I'd do a lot for a woman who saved my life, too," he said. "I'm eating this dish, but as a cop you can't expect me to like it."

I said, "The little man in the wall bed is called Leon Valesanos. He was a croupier at the Spezzia Club."

"Thanks," Ybarra said. "Let's go, Sam."

Copernik got up heavily and walked across the room and out

of the open door and out of my sight. Ybarra stepped through the door after him and started to close it.

"Wait a minute," I said. He turned his head slowly, his hand on the door.

"I'm not in this for money. The Barsalys live at Two twelve Fremont Place. You can take the pearls to her. If Barsaly's name stays out of the paper I get five hundred dollars. It goes to the police fund. I'm not so damn smart as you think. It just happened that way—and you had a heel for a partner."

Ybarra looked across the room at the pearls on the card table. His eyes glistened. "You take them," he said. "The five hundred's okay. I think the fund has it coming."

He shut the door quietly.

7

I went out to the kitchenette and drank some Scotch and went back into the living room and called Lola Barsaly—late as it was. She answered the phone quickly, with no sleep in her voice.

"Marlowe," I said. "Okay your end?"

"Yes . . . yes," she said. "I'm alone."

"I found something," I said. "Or rather the police did. But your Joseph gypped you. I have a string of pearls. They're not real. He sold the real ones, I guess, and made you up a string of ringers, with your clasp."

She was silent for a long time. Then, a little faintly, "The police found them?"

"In Waldo's car. But they're not telling. We have a deal. Look at the papers in the morning and you'll be able to figure out why."

"Can I have the clasp?" she said.

"Yes. Can you meet me tomorrow at four in the Club Esquire bar?"

"You're really rather sweet," she said in a dragged-out voice. "I can. Frank is still at his meeting."

"Those meetings—they take it out of a guy," I said. We said good-by.

I called a West Los Angeles number. Barsaly was still there with the Russian girl.

"You can send me a check for five hundred in the morning," I told him. "Made out to the Police Relief Fund, if you want to. Because that's where it's going."

Copernik made the third page of the morning papers with two photos and a nice half column. The little brown man in Apartment 31 didn't make the paper at all. The Apartment House Association has a good lobby too.

I went out after breakfast and the wind was all gone. It was soft, cool, a little foggy. The sky was close and comfortable and gray. I rode down to the boulevard and picked out the best jewelry store and laid the string of pearls on a black velvet mat under a daylight-blue lamp. A man in a wing collar and striped trousers looked down at them languidly. "How good?" I asked.

"I'm sorry, sir. We don't make appraisals. I can give you the name of an appraiser."

"Don't kid me," I said. "They're Dutch."

He focused the light a little and leaned down and toyed with a few inches of the string.

"I want a string just like them, fitted to that clasp, and in a hurry."

He didn't look up. "They're not Dutch. They're Bohemian," he said.

"Okay, can you duplicate them?"

He shook his head and pushed the velvet pad away as if it soiled him. "In three months, perhaps. We don't blow glass like that in this country. If you wanted them matched—three months at least. And this house would not do that sort of thing at all."

I put a card under his black sleeve. "Give me a name that will—and not in three months—and maybe not exactly like them."

He shrugged, went away with the card, came back in five minutes and handed it back to me. There was something written on the back.

The old Levantine had a junk shop on Melrose. He wore a skullcap and two pairs of glasses and a full beard. He studied my pearls, shook his head sadly and said, "For twenty dollars I can make them almost so good. Not so good glass, you understand."

"How like will they look?"

He spread his firm strong hands. "I am telling you the truth," he said. "They would not fool a baby."

"Make them up," I said. "With this clasp. And I want the others back, too, of course."

"Yah. Two o'clock," he said.

Leon Valesanos made the afternoon papers. He had been found hanging in an unnamed apartment. The police were investigating.

At four o'clock I walked into the long cool bar of the Club Esquire and prowled along the row of booths until I found one where a woman sat alone. She wore a brown tailor-made suit with a severe mannish shirt and tie.

I sat down beside her and slipped a parcel containing her clothing along the seat. "You don't open that," I said. "In fact you can slip it into the incinerator as is, if you want to."

She looked at me with dark tired eyes. Her fingers twisted a thin glass that smelled of peppermint. "Thanks." Her face was very pale.

I ordered a highball. "Read the papers?"

"Yes."

"You understand now about this fellow Copernik who stole your act? That's why they won't change the story or bring you into it."

"It doesn't matter now," she said. "Thank you, all the same. Please—please show them to me."

I pulled the string of pearls out of my pocket and slid them across to her. The silver propeller clasp winked in the light of the wall bracket. The little diamond winked. The pearls were as dull as white soap. They didn't even match in size.

"You were right," she said tonelessly. "They are not my pearls."

The waiter came with my drink and she put her bag on them deftly. When he was gone she fingered them slowly once more, dropped them into the bag and gave me a dry mirthless smile. "I'll keep the clasp."

I said slowly, "You don't know anything about me. You saved

315

my life last night and we had a moment, but it was just a moment. There's a detective downtown named Ybarra, who was on the job when the pearls were found in Waldo's suitcase. In case you would like to make sure . . ."

She said, "Don't be silly. It's all finished. It was a memory. I'm too young to nurse memories. I loved Stan Phillips, but he's gone—long gone." She added quietly, "This morning my husband told me something I hadn't known. We are to separate. So I have very little to laugh about today."

"I'm sorry," I said lamely. "There's nothing to say. I may see you sometime. Maybe not. I don't move much in your circle. Good luck."

I stood up. We looked at each other for a moment. "You haven't touched your drink," she said.

"You drink it. That peppermint stuff will just make you sick."

I stood there a moment with a hand hard on the table.

"If anybody ever bothers you," I said, "let me know."

I went out of the bar without looking back at her, got into my car and drove west on Sunset and down all the way to the coast highway. Everywhere along the way gardens were full of withered and blackened leaves and flowers which the hot wind had burned.

But the ocean looked cool and languid and just the same as ever. I drove on almost to Malibu and then parked and went and sat on a big rock. It was about half tide and coming in. The air smelled of kelp. I watched the water for a while and then I pulled a string of Bohemian glass imitation pearls out of my pocket and cut the knot at one end and slipped the pearls off one by one.

When I had them all loose in my left hand I held them like that for a while and thought. There wasn't really anything to think about. I was sure.

"To the memory of Mr. Stan Phillips," I said aloud. "Just another four-flusher."

I flipped her pearls out into the water one by one at the floating sea gulls. They made little splashes and the sea gulls rose off the water and swooped at the splashes.

The Three Coffins

The Three Coffins

A CONDENSATION OF
THE BOOK BY

John Dickson Carr

ILLUSTRATED BY GUY DEEL

The back streets of London
were coated with freshly fallen snow—
yet although the killer struck twice,
he left no footprints.
Was he a diabolically clever man
of flesh and blood, or a ghost
risen vengefully from the grave?
Indeed, there were overtones
of the supernatural in these macabre murders,
and criminologist Dr. Gideon Fell,
who was also a dabbler in magic,
sifted through a maze of mystifying clues
to an astonishing conclusion.

    John Dickson Carr, who also writes
more conventional mysteries under
the name of Carter Dickson,
was born in Uniontown, Pennsylvania,
but has lived most of his life in England.
Among his best known books are
The Burning Court, Dark of the Moon
and *Papa Là-bas*.

I: The Threat

To the murder of Professor Grimaud, and later the equally incredible crime in Cagliostro Street, many fantastic terms could be applied—with reason. Those of Dr. Fell's friends who like impossible situations will not find in his casebook any puzzle more baffling or more terrifying. Thus: two murders were committed, in such fashion that the murderer must not only have been invisible, but lighter than air. According to the evidence, this person killed his first victim and literally disappeared. Again according to the evidence, he killed his second victim in the middle of an empty street, with watchers at either end; yet not a soul saw him, and no footprint appeared in the snow.

Naturally, Superintendent Hadley never for a moment believed in goblins or wizardry. And he was quite right. But several people began to wonder whether the figure which stalked through this case might not be a hollow shell. They began to wonder whether, if you took away the cap and the black coat and the child's false face, you might not reveal nothing inside.

The words "according to the evidence" have been used. We must be very careful about the evidence when it is not given at first hand. And in this case the reader must be told at the outset, to avoid useless confusion, on whose evidence he can absolutely rely. That is to say, it must be assumed that *somebody* is telling the truth—else there is no legitimate mystery.

Therefore it must be stated that Mr. Stuart Mills at Professor Grimaud's house was not lying, but was telling the whole business exactly as he saw it. Also it must be stated that the three independent witnesses of Cagliostro Street (Messieurs Short and Blackwin, and Police Constable Withers) were telling the truth.

Under these circumstances, one of the events which led up to the crime must be fully outlined. It is retold from Dr. Fell's notes, in essential details exactly as Stuart Mills later told it to Dr. Fell and Superintendent Hadley. It occurred on the night of Wednesday, February 6, three days before the murder, in the back parlor of the Warwick Tavern in Museum Street.

Dr. Charles Vernet Grimaud had lived in England for nearly thirty years, and spoke English without accent. Except for his habit of wearing an old-fashioned square-topped bowler hat and black string tie, he was even more British than his friends. Nobody knew much about his earlier years. He was of independent means, but he had chosen to be "occupied" and had been a teacher, a popular lecturer and writer. Of late he had held some vague unsalaried post at the British Museum. Low magic was his great interest: any form of picturesque supernatural devilry from vampirism to the Black Mass, over which he chuckled with childlike amusement.

A sound commonsense fellow, Grimaud, with a quizzical twinkle in his eye. He was of middle size, but he had a powerful chest and enormous physical stamina. Everybody in the neighborhood of the museum knew his closely trimmed black beard, his shells of eyeglasses, his upright walk. He lived just round the corner from the museum in a solid old house on the west side of Russell Square. The other occupants of the house were his daughter, Rosette, his housekeeper, Madame Dumont, his maid, Annie, his secretary, Stuart Mills, and a broken-down ex-teacher named Drayman, who looked after his books.

But his few real cronies were to be found at a sort of club they had instituted at the Warwick Tavern. They met several nights a week in the back room reserved for that purpose. The most regular attendants of the club were fussy bald-headed little Pettis, the authority on ghost stories, Mangan, the newspaperman, and Burnaby, the artist; but Dr. Grimaud was its undisputed ruler.

Nearly every night in the year (except Saturdays and Sundays, which he reserved for work) he would set out for the Warwick, accompanied by Stuart Mills. He would sit in his favorite armchair before a blazing fire, with a glass of hot rum and water, and hold forth autocratically. The discussions, Mills says, were often brilliant, although nobody except Pettis or Burnaby ever gave Grimaud serious battle. Despite his affability, he had a violent temper. He loved to tell stories of medieval sorcery and, at the end, abruptly explain all the puzzles in the fashion of a detective story. They were amusing evenings—until February 6, when the premonition of terror entered as suddenly as the wind blowing open a door.

The wind was blowing shrewdly that night, Mills says, with a threat of snow in the air. Besides himself and Grimaud, there were present at the fireside only Pettis and Mangan and Burnaby. Professor Grimaud had been speaking about the legend of vampirism.

"Frankly, what puzzles me," said Pettis, "is your attitude towards the whole business. Now, I study only fiction, only ghost stories that never happened. Yet in a way I believe in ghosts. You're an authority on attested happenings—things that we're forced to call facts unless we can refute 'em. You've made them the most important thing in your life, but you don't believe a word of them."

"Well, and why should I?" said Grimaud, drawing at his cigar. "It is not recorded that the temple priest was ever a very devout believer. However, that is beside the point. I am interested in the causes behind these superstitions. How did the superstition start? What gave it impetus, so that the gullible could believe? For example! We are speaking of the vampire legend. Now that is a belief which has existed since earliest times. But it got its firm grip on Europe when it swept in a blast out of Hungary between 1730 and 1735. Well, how did Hungary get its proof that dead men could leave their coffins, and float in the air in the form of straw or fluff until they took human shape for an attack?"

"Was there proof?" asked Burnaby.

Grimaud lifted his shoulders. "They exhumed bodies from churchyards. They found some in twisted positions, with blood on their faces and hands and shrouds. That was their proof. . . . But those were plague years. Think of all the poor devils who were buried alive though believed to be dead. Think how they struggled to get out. . . . You see? That's what I mean by the causes behind superstitions. That's what I am interested in."

"*I also,*" said a new voice, "*am interested in it.*"

Mills says they had not heard the man come in. Startled, they all turned round. The man, Mills says, stood back from the firelight, with the collar of his shabby black overcoat turned up and the brim of his shabby soft hat pulled down. His face was shaded by the gloved hand with which he was stroking his chin. Beyond the fact that he was tall and of gaunt build, Mills could tell nothing. But in his voice or bearing there was something vaguely familiar.

He spoke again. His voice was harsh, husky, and faintly foreign, with a sly triumph in it. "You must forgive me," he said, "for intruding. But I should like to ask Professor Grimaud a question."

Nobody thought of snubbing him, Mills says. Even Grimaud, who sat dark and solid, with his cigar halfway to his mouth, only barked, "Well?"

"You do not believe, then," the other went on, "that a man can get up out of his coffin, that he can move anywhere invisibly, and that he is as dangerous as anything out of hell?"

"I do not," Grimaud answered harshly. "Do you?"

"Yes. I have done it. But more! I have a brother who can do much more than I can, and is very dangerous to you. *I* don't want your life; he does. But if *he* calls on you . . ."

Young Mangan, an ex-footballer, jumped to his feet. Little Pettis peered round nervously. "Look here, Grimaud," said Pettis, "this fellow's stark mad. Shall I—" He made a gesture in the direction of the bell, but the stranger interposed.

"Look at Professor Grimaud," he said, "before you decide."

Grimaud was regarding him with a heavy contempt. "No, no, no! Let him alone. Let him talk about his brother and his coffins—"

"Three coffins," said the stranger.

"Three coffins," agreed Grimaud, "if you like. As many as you like, in God's name! Now perhaps you'll tell us who you are?"

The stranger's left hand came out of his pocket and laid a grubby card on the table. Somehow the sight of that prosaic visiting card seemed to restore sane values. Mills saw that the card read: PIERRE FLEY. ILLUSIONIST. In one corner was printed 2B CAGLIOSTRO STREET, W.C. 1, and over it was scribbled *Or % Academy Theatre.*

Grimaud laughed. "So," he remarked. "You are a conjurer. I don't suppose we might see one of your illusions?"

"With pleasure," said Fley unexpectedly. His movement was so quick that nobody anticipated it. It looked like an attack, and was nothing of the kind—in a physical sense. Grinning, he bent across the table towards Grimaud, his gloved hands twitching down the collar of his coat and twitching it back up again before anybody else could get a glimpse of him. Grimaud remained motionless.

"And now, before I go," said Fley curtly, "I have a last question for the famous professor. Someone will call on you one evening soon. I also am in danger when I associate with my brother, but I am prepared to run that risk. Someone, I repeat, will call on you. Would you rather I did—or shall I send my brother?"

"Send your brother," snarled Grimaud, "and be damned!"

The door had closed behind Fley before anybody moved or spoke. And the door also closes on the only clear view we have of the events leading up to the night of Saturday, February 9. The first deadly walking of the hollow man took place on that night, when the side streets of London were quiet with snow and the three coffins of the prophecy were filled at last.

THERE was roaring good humor that night round the fire in Dr. Fell's library at Number One Adelphi Terrace. The doctor sat enthroned in his largest, most comfortable, and decrepit chair, beaming with all his vastness behind his eyeglasses, and hammering his cane on the hearthrug as he chuckled. He was celebrating, and tonight there was double cause for revelry.

For one thing, his exuberant young friends, Ted and Dorothy Rampole, had arrived from America. For another, his friend Hadley—Superintendent Hadley of the Criminal Investigation Department—had just concluded a brilliant piece of work on the Bayswater forgery case, and was relaxing. Ted Rampole sat at one side of the hearth and Hadley at the other, with the doctor presiding between over a steaming bowl of punch. The Mesdames Fell, Hadley, and Rampole were upstairs conferring about something, and down here the Messieurs Fell and Hadley were engaged in violent argument about scientific criminology.

During one of his absentminded intervals of puttering about, Dr. Fell had started reading Gross, Jesserich, and Mitchell. He had been bitten. And now he claimed to have perfected Dr. Gross's method of deciphering the writing on burned paper.

Listening to Superintendent Hadley jeer at this, Ted Rampole let his mind drift drowsily. He could see the firelight moving on walls of books, and hear fine snow ticking the windowpanes behind drawn curtains. He grinned to himself in sheer amiability. He had nothing in the excellent world to irk him—or had he? Shifting, he stared at the fire. Little things popped up like a jack-in-the-box to jab you when you were most comfortable.

Criminal cases, Rampole mused. Of course there was nothing to it. It had been Mangan's eagerness to enrich a good story. All the same . . . "By the way," he said, "do the words 'three coffins' mean anything to you?"

There was an abrupt silence, and Hadley regarded him suspiciously. Dr. Fell blinked with a puzzled air. Then a twinkle appeared in his eye. "Heh," he said, and rubbed his hands. "Making peace between Hadley and me, hey? Or do you by any chance mean it? What coffins?"

"Well," said Rampole, "it's a queer business, unless Mangan was stretching things. I know Boyd Mangan quite well; he lived in America for a couple of years. He's a damned good fellow who's knocked about the world a lot and has a too-Celtic imagination." He paused, remembering Mangan's dark, rather slovenly good looks. "Anyhow, he's here in London working for the *Evening Ban-*

ner now. I ran into him this morning. He dragged me into a bar and poured out the whole story. Then," said Rampole, "when he learned I knew the great Dr. Fell—"

"Rats," said Hadley sharply. "Get down to cases."

"Shut up, Hadley," said Dr. Fell, highly delighted. "This sounds interesting, my boy. Well?"

"Well, it seems that he's a great admirer of a lecturer or writer named Grimaud. Also he has fallen hard for Grimaud's daughter. The old man and some of his friends have a habit of visiting a pub near the British Museum, and a few nights ago something happened which seems to have shaken Mangan up. While the old man was talking about corpses getting up out of their graves, or some such cheerful subject, in walked a tall queer-looking bird who began babbling some nonsense about himself and his brother really being able to leave their graves and float in the air like straw." Here Hadley made a disgusted noise and relaxed his attention, but Dr. Fell continued to look curiously at Rampole. "At the end this stranger made a threat that his brother would call on Professor Grimaud before long. The odd part was that, though Grimaud didn't turn a hair, Mangan swears he was scared green."

Hadley grunted. "What of it? Somebody with a scary old-womanish mind—"

"That's the point," growled Dr. Fell. "He isn't. I know Grimaud quite well. Go on, Rampole. How did it end?"

"Grimaud didn't say anything. In fact, after this stranger had gone, he dismissed it as a joke. But Mangan was still curious. This visitor, this Pierre Fley, had given Grimaud a card with the name of a theater on it. So the next day Mangan followed it up in the guise of getting a newspaper story. The theater turned out to be a disreputable music hall in the East End, staging nightly variety. Mangan didn't want to run into Fley. He got into talk with the stage-door keeper, who introduced him to an acrobat in the turn before Fley. This acrobat calls himself 'Pagliacci the Great,' although he's actually an Irishman named O'Rourke. He told Mangan what he knew.

"Fley is known at the theater as 'Loony.' They know nothing

about him; he speaks to nobody and ducks out after every show. But he is *good*. He does a sort of superconjuring, with a specialty in vanishing tricks. He works without an assistant, and all his props can go into a box the size of a coffin. If you know anything about magicians, you'll know what an incredible thing that is. In fact, the man seems hipped on the subject of coffins. Pagliacci the Great once asked him why, and Fley turned round with a grin and said, 'Three of us were once buried alive. Only one escaped.' Pagliacci said, 'And how did you escape?' To which Fley answered, 'I didn't, you see. I was one of the two who did not.'"

Hadley was tugging at the lobe of his ear. "Look here," he said uneasily. "The fellow's crazy, right enough. If he's got any imaginary grudge—if he tries to make trouble for the professor—"

"*Has* he tried to make trouble?" asked Dr. Fell.

Rampole shifted. "Some sort of letter has come for Professor Grimaud in every post since Wednesday. He has torn 'em up without saying anything, but somebody told his daughter about the affair at the pub, and she has begun to worry. Then yesterday Grimaud himself began to act queerly."

"How?" asked Dr. Fell. His eyes blinked sharply at Rampole.

"He phoned Mangan yesterday and said, 'I want you to be at the house Saturday evening. Somebody threatens to pay me a visit.' Naturally, Mangan advised warning the police, which Grimaud wouldn't hear of. Then Mangan said, 'But hang it, sir, this fellow's stark mad and he may be dangerous. Aren't you going to take *any* precautions to defend yourself?' To which the professor answered, 'Oh yes. I am going to buy a painting.'"

"A what?" demanded Hadley, sitting up.

"A painting to hang on the wall. No, I'm not joking. It seems he did buy it: it was a landscape of some sort, a weird business showing trees and gravestones. I haven't seen it, but I've heard that it was so huge it took two workmen to carry it upstairs. It was painted by an artist named Burnaby, who's a member of the club. . . . Anyhow, that's Grimaud's idea of defending himself."

"Have you got the address of the place, my boy?" Dr. Fell asked. . . . "Good. Better warm up your car, Hadley. When an alleged lunatic threatens a sane man, you may or may not be disturbed. But when a sane man begins to act exactly like the lunatic, then I know *I'm* jolly well disturbed." Wheezing, he hoisted himself up. "Come on, Hadley. We'll go look at the place, even if we only cruise past."

A sharp wind bit through the narrow streets round Dr. Fell's house; the snow had stopped. It lay white and unreal on the terrace. In the Strand, where it was theater hour, it was churned to dirty ruts. A clock said five minutes past ten as they turned up into Aldwych, and Dr. Fell roared for more speed. Finally the car shot into Russell Square.

Rampole saw the house—a plain, broad, three-storied stone front. Six steps led up to a big front door with a brass-edged letter slot and brass knob. Except for two windows glowing behind drawn blinds on the ground floor over the areaway, the place was dark. It seemed the most prosaic house in a prosaic neighborhood. But it did not remain so.

A blind was torn aside. One of the lighted windows went up with a bang just as they drove slowly past. A figure climbed on the sill, hesitated, and leaped. The leap carried him over the spiked area rails. He struck the pavement on one leg, slipped in the snow, and pitched out across the curb nearly under the wheels of the car.

Hadley jammed on his brakes. He was out of the car as it skidded against the curb, and had the man by the arm before he had gotten to his feet. But Rampole had caught a glimpse of the man's face in the headlights.

"Mangan!" he said. "What the devil—!"

Mangan was without a hat or overcoat. "Who's that?" he demanded hoarsely. "No, no, I'm all right! Let go, damn it!" He yanked loose from Hadley. "*Ted!* Listen. Get somebody. Hurry! There was a shot upstairs; we just heard it. He'd locked us in. . . ."

Looking behind him, Rampole could see a woman silhouetted against the window. Hadley cut through these incoherent words.

"Steady on. Who locked you in?"

"*He* did. Fley. He's still in there. Well, are you coming?"

He was already running for the front steps, with Hadley and

Rampole after him. The front door was unlocked; it swung open when Mangan wrenched the knob. The high hallway inside was dark except for a lamp burning far at the rear. Something seemed to be standing back there, looking at them, with a grotesque face; and then Rampole saw it was only a suit of Japanese armor decked out in its devil mask. Mangan hurried to a door at the right and turned the key that was in the lock. The door was opened from inside by the girl whose silhouette they had seen at the window. From upstairs they could hear a heavy banging noise.

"Boyd!" cried Rampole, feeling his heart rise in his throat. "This is Superintendent Hadley. Where is it? What is it?"

Mangan pointed at the staircase. "Carry on. I'll take care of Rosette. He's still upstairs. He can't get out. For God's sake be careful!"

Rampole hurried after Hadley up thick-carpeted stairs. The floor above was dark. But a light shone down from a niche in the staircase to the next floor, and the banging had changed to a series of thuds.

"Dr. Grimaud!" a voice was crying. "Answer me, will you?"

They went up the second staircase, under an open archway at its top, and into a broad hallway which ran the breadth of the house. It was paneled to the ceiling in oak, with three curtained windows in the long side opposite the staircase, and its thick black carpet deadened every footstep. There were two doors—facing each other from the narrow ends of the hall. The door far down at their left was open; the door at their right, about ten feet from the staircase, remained closed despite the man who was beating on it.

This man whirled round at their approach. Although there was no illumination in the hallway itself, a yellow light streamed through the arch from the niche on the staircase—from the stomach of a great brass Buddha in the niche—and they could see everything clearly. Full in the glow stood a breathless little man. He had a big goblinlike shock of hair on his big head, and peered terrified from behind big spectacles.

"Boyd?" he cried. "Drayman? I say, is that you? Who's there?"

"Police," said Hadley, and strode past him.

"You can't get in there," said the little man. "The door's locked on the inside. But we've got to get in. Somebody's in there with Grimaud. A gun went off— He won't answer. Where's Madame Dumont? That fellow's still in there, I tell you!"

Hadley turned round snappishly. "Stop dancing and find a pair of pliers. The key's in the lock; we'll turn it from the outside."

"I—I really don't know where—"

Hadley looked at Rampole. "Hop down to the toolbox in my car. It's under the back seat."

Rampole turned round to see Dr. Fell emerge through the arch, wheezing heavily. Then he went downstairs three at a time, and blundered for what seemed hours before he found the pliers. When he returned, Hadley, impassive, eased the pliers into the keyhole. His powerful hands clamped and began to turn.

"There's something moving in there—" said the little man.

"Got it," said Hadley. "Stand back!"

He braced himself and threw the door inward. It flapped back against the wall with a crash. Nothing came out, although something was trying to come out. Except for that, the bright room was empty. Something, on which Rampole saw a good deal of blood, was painfully trying to drag itself on hands and knees across the black carpet. It choked, rolled over on its side, and lay still.

II: The False Face

"STAY in the door, two of you," Hadley said curtly. "And if anybody's got weak nerves, don't look."

Dr. Fell lumbered in after him, and Rampole remained in the doorway with his arm extended across it. Professor Grimaud was heavy, but Hadley did not dare wrench. In that effort to crawl to the door there had been a hemorrhage which was not altogether internal, although Grimaud kept his teeth clenched against the blood. Hadley raised him up against one knee. His face had a bluish tinge under the mask of blackish gray stubble; his eyes were closed and sunken; and he was still trying to press a sodden handkerchief to the bullet hole in his chest. They heard his breath sink thinly. Despite a draft, there was still a sharp mist of powder smoke.

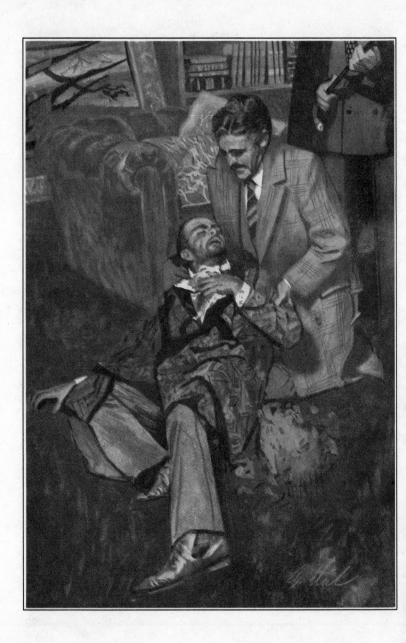

"Dead?" muttered Dr. Fell.

"Dying," said Hadley. "He got it through the lung." He whirled round towards the little man in the doorway. "Phone for an ambulance. Quick! There's not a chance, but he may be able to say something before—"

"Yes," said Dr. Fell somberly. "That's the thing we're most interested in, isn't it?"

"If it's the only thing we can do," Hadley answered coolly, "yes. Get me some sofa pillows from over there." When Grimaud's head lolled on one of the pillows, Hadley bent close. "Dr. Grimaud! Can you hear me?"

The waxy eyelids fluttered. Grimaud's eyes, half open, looked puzzled; he could not seem to understand what had happened. His barrel chest still rose and fell slightly.

"I am from the police, Dr. Grimaud. Who did this? Don't try to answer if you can't. Nod your head. Was it Pierre Fley?"

Grimaud distinctly shook his head.

"Who was it, then?"

Grimaud was eager; too eager, for it defeated him. He spoke for the first and last time. His lips stuttered in those words whose interpretation was so puzzling afterwards. Then he fainted.

The window in the left-hand wall was a few inches up, and a chill draft blew through. Rampole shivered. What had been a brilliant man lay inert on a couple of pillows, torn like a sack; with something rattling inside it to show that it lived, but no more. There was too much blood in the bright, quiet room. "My God!" Rampole said. "Isn't there anything we can *do*?"

Hadley was bitter. "Nothing, except get to work. 'Still in the house'? Fine lot of dummies!—oh, myself included." He pointed to the open window. "Of course the fellow was out of here before we were even inside the house."

Rampole looked round, seeing the place for the first time in focus. It was a room some fifteen feet square, with walls paneled in oak and thick black carpet on the floor. In the left-hand wall, as you stood at the door, was the window with its brown velvet draperies blowing. On either side of the window stretched high bookshelves with marble busts along the top. Just out from the window stood a great carved desk. A chair was pushed back from it; at the extreme left was a lamp of mosaic glass. The blotter was clean except for a tray of pens and a pile of note slips held down by a curious little figure—a buffalo carved in yellow jade.

Rampole looked across the room at the side opposite the window. In that wall was a large stone fireplace, flanked also by shelves and busts. Above the fireplace two fencing foils hung crossed behind a blazoned shield of arms. Only on that side of the room had furniture been disarranged. Just before the fire, a brown leather sofa had been knocked awry and a leather chair rolled back in a twisted-up hearthrug. There was blood on the sofa.

And finally, towards the rear wall of the room facing the door, Rampole saw the painting. Between the bookshelves in this wall there was a vast cleared space where cases had been removed; removed recently, for the marks of their bases were still indented in the carpet. The painting in its frame was fully seven feet broad by four feet high. It had been slashed across twice with a knife. Hadley propped it up behind the sofa.

"And that," he said, "is the painting he bought to defend himself with, is it? Look here, Fell, do you think Grimaud was just as mad as this fellow Fley?"

Dr. Fell pushed back his hat. "As Pierre Fley," he rumbled, "who *didn't* commit the crime. I say, Hadley, do you see any weapon?"

"I do not. First, there isn't any gun—a high-caliber automatic is what we want—and now there isn't any knife with which this thing was cut to blazes. It looks like an ordinary landscape to me."

It was not, Rampole thought, exactly ordinary. There was a sort of blowing power about it, as though the artist had painted in a fury and caught in oils the wind that whipped those crooked trees. You felt bleakness and terror. Low white mountains rose in the background, and in the foreground, through the branches of a crooked tree, you could see three headstones in rank grass. The headstones were toppling; in one way you looked at it, there was an illusion that the grave mounds had begun to heave and crack across. Even the slashes did not seem to disfigure it.

Rampole started a little as he heard a trampling of feet up the staircase in the hall. Boyd Mangan burst in. His black hair, which clung to his head in wirelike scrolls, looked rumpled. He took a quick look at the man on the floor.

"Mills told me," he said. "Is he—"

Hadley ignored this. "Did you get the ambulance?"

"Chaps with a stretcher—coming now. I remembered a hospital round the corner." He stood aside to admit two uniformed attendants, and behind them a little man with a bald head. "This is Dr. Peterson—er—the police. And that's your—patient."

Dr. Peterson hurried over. "Stretcher, boys," he said, after a brief look. "Take him easy." The stretcher was carried out.

"Any chance?" asked Hadley.

"He might last a couple of hours, probably less. If he hadn't the constitution of a bull he'd be dead already. Looks as though he's made a further lesion in the lung trying to exert himself." Dr. Peterson dived into his pocket. "You'll want to send your police surgeon round, won't you? Here's my card. I'll keep the bullet when I get it. What happened?"

"Murder," said Hadley. "Keep a nurse with him, and if he says anything have it taken down." As the doctor hurried out, Hadley scribbled on a leaf of his notebook and handed it to Mangan. "Go phone the Hunter Street police station with these instructions; they'll get in touch with the Yard. Dr. Watson is to go to this hospital, and the rest are to come here. Who's at the door?"

It was the small, thin, top-heavy youth who had been pounding at the door to begin with. In full light Rampole saw dull brown eyes magnified behind thick glasses, and a bony face sloping outwards to a large and loose mouth. His earlier terror had changed to inscrutable calm. He bowed, and said without expression, "I am Stuart Mills, Dr. Grimaud's secretary." His eyes moved round. "May I ask what has happened to the—culprit?" He had the appearance of addressing an audience, speaking in a singsong and raising and lowering his head as though from notes.

"Presumably," said Hadley, "he escaped through the window—"

"He must have been a very extraordinary man if he did that," the singsong voice interposed. "Have you examined the window?"

"He's right, Hadley," said Dr. Fell, wheezing. "Take a look! I tell you in all sincerity that, if our man didn't leave here by way of the door—"

"He did not," announced Mills. "I saw it all from start to finish."

"Then he must have been lighter than air. Open the window and look. H'mf, wait! We'd better search the room first."

There was nobody hidden in the room. Afterwards, growling, Hadley eased the window up. Unbroken snow—stretching flat up to the window frame itself—covered the sill outside.

Rampole bent out and looked round. There was a bright moon in the west, and every detail stood out sharp as a woodcut. It was fifty feet to the ground; the wall fell away in a smooth drop. Just below there was a backyard surrounded by a low wall. The snow lay unbroken in this courtyard, or any other as far as they could look, and along the tops of the walls. The only windows in the whole side of the house were on this top floor; and the nearest one to this room was in the hallway to the left, a good thirty feet away. To the right, the nearest window would have been in the adjoining house, an equal distance away. Finally, there stretched above this window a smooth upward run of stone for some fifteen feet to the roof—whose slope afforded neither hold for the fingers nor for the attaching of a rope.

But Hadley, craning his neck out, pointed malevolently. "All the same, that's it," he declared. "Look there! Suppose he first hitched a rope to a chimney or something, and had it dangling outside the window when he paid his visit. Then he kills Grimaud, swings out, climbs up to untie the rope from the chimney, and gets away. There will be plenty of tracks of *that*, right enough. So—"

"Yes," said Mills. "But I must tell you there aren't any. You see," he continued, "as soon as I perceived that the man in the false face had disappeared—"

"The *what?*" said Hadley.

"The false face. Do I make myself clear?"

"No. We must see whether we can't extract some sense presently, Mr. Mills. In the meantime, what is this business about the roof?"

"There are no tracks or marks of any nature on it, you see," the other answered, his eyes opened wide. "I repeat, gentlemen: when I saw that the man in the false face had evidently disappeared, I foresaw difficulties for myself—"

"Why?"

"Because I myself had this door under observation, and I was compelled to asseverate that the man had not come out. Very well. It was therefore deducible that he must have left (a) by way of a rope to the roof, or (b) by means of climbing up inside the chimney to the roof. This was a simple mathematical certainty.

"At the end of this hallway," pursued Mills, "I have my workroom. From there a door leads to the attic, and thence to a trapdoor opening out on the roof. By raising the trapdoor I could see clearly both sides of the roof over this room. The snow was not marked in any fashion."

"You didn't go out there?" demanded Hadley.

"No. I could not have kept my footing if I had."

Dr. Fell turned a radiant face. "And what then, my boy?" he inquired affably. "I mean, what did you think when your mathematical certainty was shot to blazes?"

Mills remained smiling. "Ah, that remains to be seen. I am a mathematician, sir. I never permit myself to think."

"Suppose you tell us exactly what did happen here tonight," urged Hadley, as he sat down at the desk and took out his notebook. "Easy, now! We'll lead up to it gradually. How long have you worked for Professor Grimaud?"

"For three years and eight months."

"What are your duties?"

"General secretarial duties. I have been assisting him in preparing his new work, *The Origin and History of Middle-European Superstitions, Together with*—"

"Quite so. How many people live in this house?"

"Besides Dr. Grimaud and myself, four. There is Rosette Grimaud, his daughter. Madame Dumont, who is housekeeper. An elderly friend of Dr. Grimaud, named Drayman. A maid whose last name I have not been told, but whose first name is Annie."

"How many were here tonight when this happened?"

Mills brought the toe of his shoe forward and studied it. "That I cannot say with certainty. I will tell you what I know." He rocked back and forth. "At the conclusion of dinner, at seven thirty, Dr. Grimaud came up here to work. This is his custom on Saturday evenings. He told me he did not wish to be disturbed until eleven o'clock; that is also the inviolable custom. He said, however, that he might have a visitor about half past nine."

"Did he say who this visitor might be?"

"He did not."

Hadley leaned forward. "Come, now, Mr. Mills! Haven't you heard of any threat to him? Didn't you hear what happened on Wednesday evening?"

"I—er—certainly. In fact, I was at the Warwick Tavern myself. I suppose Mangan told you?"

Uneasily, but with startling vividness, he sketched out the story. Meantime, Dr. Fell had stumped away and was going through an examination he made several times that night. He seemed most interested in the fireplace and then inspected the bloodstains splashing the top and right arm of the disarranged sofa. There were more bloodstains on the hearth, where a small coal fire had been nearly smothered under a drift of charred papers.

Dr. Fell was muttering to himself. He reared up to examine the escutcheon. To Rampole, no student of heraldry, this presented itself as a divided shield in red and blue and silver: a black eagle and crescent moon in the upper part, and in the lower a wedge of what looked like rooks on a chessboard. Dr. Fell did not speak until he began to examine the books on the shelves at the left of the fireplace, yanking them out and glancing at the title pages. Then he started to wave at the others excitedly.

"I say, Hadley, this is very rummy and revealing. *Yorick és Eliza levelei,* two volumes. *Shakspere Minden Munkái,* nine volumes. And here's a name. Ha. Do you know anything about these, Mr. Mills? They're the only books that haven't been dusted."

Mills was startled out of his recital. "I—I don't know. I believe they are from a batch that Dr. Grimaud meant for the attic. . . .

Where was I, Mr. Hadley? Ah yes! Well, when Dr. Grimaud told me that he might have a visitor tonight, I had no reason to assume it was the man of the Warwick Tavern. He did not say so."

"What, exactly, did he say?"

"I—you see, after dinner I was working in the big library downstairs. He suggested that I should come upstairs to my workroom at half past nine, sit with my door open, and—and 'keep an eye on' this room, in case—"

"In case?"

Mills cleared his throat. "He was not specific. So I simply carried out my orders exactly. I came up here at precisely half past nine—"

"Where were the others then?" asked Hadley.

"To the best of my knowledge, Miss Rosette Grimaud and Mangan were in the drawing room, playing cards. Drayman had told me that he was going out; I did not see him."

"And Madame Dumont?"

"I met her as I came up here. She was coming out with Dr. Grimaud's after-dinner coffee; that is to say, with the remnants of it. . . . I went to my workroom, left my door open, and drew out the typewriter desk so that I could face the hallway while I worked. At exactly"—he shut his eyes and opened them again— "at exactly fifteen minutes to ten I heard the front doorbell ring. The electric bell is on the second floor, and I heard it plainly.

"Two minutes later, Madame Dumont came up from the staircase. She was about to knock at the door when I was startled to see the—er—the tall man come upstairs directly after her. She turned round and saw him. She then exclaimed certain words which I am unable to repeat verbatim, but whose purport was to ask why he had not waited downstairs; and she seemed agitated. The—er—tall man made no reply. He walked to the door, and without haste turned down the collar of his coat and removed his cap, which he placed in his overcoat pocket. I think that he laughed, and that Madame Dumont cried out something, shrank back against the wall, and hurried to open the door. Dr. Grimaud appeared on the threshold in some evident annoyance; his exact

words were, 'What the devil is all this row about?' Then he stood
stock-still, looking up at the tall man; and his exact words were, 'In
God's name, who are *you?*'"

Mills's singsong voice was hurling the words faster; his smile
had become rather ghastly.

"Steady, Mr. Mills. Did you get a good look at this tall man?"

"A fairly good look. As he came up under the arch from the
staircase, he glanced in my direction. He was wearing a child's
false face, a species of mask in papier-mâché. I have an impression
that it was long, of a pinkish color, and had a wide-open mouth.
And, so far as my observation went, he did not remove it. I think
I am safe in asserting—"

"You are generally right, are you not?" asked a cold voice from
the doorway. "It was a false face. And, unfortunately, he did not
remove it."

III: The Impossible

SHE stood in the doorway, looking from one to the other of them.
Rampole received the impression of an extraordinary woman
with brilliant black eyes. She was short and of sturdy figure, with a
broad face and high cheekbones. Her dark brown hair was turned
under and she wore the plainest of dark dresses, yet she did not
look dowdy. Her dark eyes sought Hadley.

"I am Ernestine Dumont," she said. "I have come to help you
find the man who shot Charles." She spoke almost without accent,
but with a certain slur. "When I heard, I could not come up—at
first. Then I wished to go with him to the nursing home, but the
doctor would not let me. He said the police would wish to speak
with me."

Hadley rose and moved out a chair for her. "Please sit down,
madame. We should like to hear your statement in a moment. I
must ask you to listen to what Mr. Mills is saying, in case you
should be required to corroborate . . ."

She shivered in the cold from the open window, and Dr. Fell
lumbered over to close it. Then she glanced at the fireplace,

where the fire had nearly smoldered out under the mass of burned papers. Realizing Hadley's words over the gap, she nodded.

"Yes, of course. He is a nice poor fool boy, and he means well."

Mills showed no anger, if he felt any. He folded his arms. "If it gives the Pythoness any pleasure to think so," he sang imperturbably, "I have no objection. But—er—where was I?"

"Dr. Grimaud's words when he saw the visitor, you told us, were, 'In God's name, who are *you?*' Then?"

"Ah yes! He was not wearing his eyeglasses, which were hanging down by their cord; his sight is not good without them, and I am under the impression that he mistook the mask for a real face. But before he could raise the glasses, the stranger made a quick movement and darted in at the door. When he got inside—" Mills stopped, apparently puzzled. "I am under the impression that Madame Dumont, although she was shrinking back against the wall, closed the door after him. I recall that she had her hand on the knob."

Ernestine Dumont blazed. "What do you wish to be understood by that, little boy?" she asked. "That man kicked the door shut behind him. Then he turned the key in the lock."

"One moment, madame. . . . Is that true, Mr. Mills?"

"I wish it clearly understood," Mills sang, "that I am merely trying to give *every* fact and even every impression. I meant nothing. I accept the correction. He did, as the Pythoness says, turn the key in the lock. She began to call Dr. Grimaud's Christian name, and to shake the knob of the door. I heard voices inside, and then Dr. Grimaud called out to the Pythoness, rather angrily, 'Go away, you fool. I can handle this.'"

"I see. Did he seem—afraid, or anything of the sort?"

The secretary reflected. "On the contrary, I should have said that he sounded in a sense relieved."

"And you, madame: you obeyed and went away—"

"Yes."

"Even though," said Hadley suavely, "I presume it is not usual for jokers to call at the house in false faces? You knew, I suppose, of the threat to your employer?"

The word "employer" had stung her. "I have obeyed Charles Grimaud for over twenty years," said the woman very quietly. "And I have never known a situation which he could *not* handle. Obey! Of course I did; I would always obey."

Hadley turned back to the secretary. "Do you remember, Mr. Mills, the time at which this tall man went into the room?"

"It was at ten minutes to ten. There is a clock on my desk."

"And when did you hear the shot?"

"At exactly ten minutes past ten."

"You mean to say that you watched the door all that time?"

"I did, most assuredly." He cleared his throat. "I was the first to reach the door when the shot was fired. It was still locked on the inside, as you gentlemen saw—you yourselves arrived very shortly afterwards." Sweat broke out on his forehead as he met Hadley's cold eye. "Now I am aware, of course, that I am telling what must seem an absolutely incredible story." Quite suddenly his voice went high. "Yet, gentlemen, I *swear*—"

"That is all right, Stuart," the woman said. "I can confirm you."

Hadley was suavely grim. "That would be just as well, I think. One last question, Mr. Mills. Can you give an exact outward description of this caller?"

"I can state that he wore a long black overcoat and a brownish peaked cap. His trousers were darkish. His hair, when he took off the cap—" Mills stopped. "I do not wish to be fanciful, but his hair had a dark, painted, *shiny* look, almost as though it were made of papier-mâché. I believe he was wearing gloves, although he put his hands in his pockets. He was tall, three or four inches taller than Dr. Grimaud, and of a medium—er—anatomical structure."

"Did he look like the man Pierre Fley?"

"Well—yes—in a way, though I should have said this man was taller, and not so thin."

During this questioning the doctor had been lumbering about with annoyed digs of his cane at the carpet. He bent down to blink at things; looked at the painting, at the books, at the jade buffalo on the desk—and yet always he was watching Madame Dumont. She seemed to fascinate him. There was something rather terrible in that small bright eye, which would swing round the second he had finished looking at something. And the woman knew it. She tried to ignore him, but her glance would come round again.

"There are other questions, Mr. Mills," said Hadley, "particularly about this Warwick Tavern affair and that painting. But they can wait. Would you go ask Miss Grimaud and Mr. Mangan to come up here? Also Mr. Drayman, if he has returned? . . . Thanks. Stop a bit! Er—any questions, Fell?"

Dr. Fell shook his head with broad amiability. Rampole could see the woman's white knuckles tighten.

"*Must* your friend walk about in that way?" she cried abruptly. "It is maddening."

Hadley studied her. "I understand, madame. Unfortunately, that is his way."

"Who are you, then? You walk into my house—"

"I had better explain. I am the superintendent of the Criminal Investigation Department. This is Mr. Rampole. And the other man, of whom you may have heard, is Dr. Gideon Fell."

She nodded. "Well, well! Even so, must you forget your manners? Must you make the room freezing with your open windows? May we not at least have a fire to warm us?"

"I don't advise it," said Dr. Fell. "That is, until we see what papers have already been burned there."

Ernestine Dumont said wearily, "Oh, why must you be such fools? Why do you sit here? You know quite well who did this. It was the fellow Fley. Why don't you go after him?"

"Do you know Fley?" Hadley snapped.

"No, no, I never saw him! I mean, before this. But I know what Charles told me."

"Which was what?"

"Ah, *zut!* This Fley is a lunatic. Charles never knew him, but the man had some insane idea that Charles made fun of the occult. Well, Charles told me that he might call here tonight at half past nine. If he did, I was to admit him. But when I took down Charles's coffee tray at half past nine, Charles laughed and said that if the man had not arrived by then he would not come. He said, 'People with a grudge are prompt.'" She sat back, squaring her shoulders. "He was wrong. The doorbell rang at a quarter to ten. I answered it. There was a man on the step. He held out a visiting card and said, 'Will you take this to Professor Grimaud and ask if he will see me?'"

Hadley leaned against the edge of the sofa and studied her. "What about the false face, madame? Didn't you think that odd?"

"I did not *see* the false face! Have you noticed there is only one light in the downstairs hall? Well! There was a streetlamp behind him, and all I could see was his shape. He spoke so courteously, you understand, and handed in the card, that for a second I did not realize . . ." Tears brimmed over her eyes. "I am real, I am honest! If someone does you a hurt, good. You lie in wait for him and kill him. But you do not put on a painted mask, like old Drayman with the children on Guy Fawkes night; you do not hand in visiting cards and go upstairs and kill a man and then vanish out of a window!" Her cynical poise cracked in hysteria. "Oh, my God, Charles! My poor Charles!"

Hadley waited very quietly. She had herself in hand in a moment; the gust of emotion left her relieved. Then Hadley said, "Now at this time, we understand, Miss Grimaud and Mr. Mangan were in the drawing room near the front door?"

She looked at him. "Yes—yes, I suppose they were. I did not notice."

"Do you remember whether the drawing-room door was open or shut?"

"I should think it was shut, or I should have seen more light in the hall."

"Go on, please."

"Well, when the man gave me his visiting card, I wished to go up and get Charles to come down. So I said, 'Wait there and I will see.' And I slammed the door in his face, so that the spring lock caught. Then I went back to the lamp and looked at the card. And it was blank."

"Blank?"

"There was no writing or printing on it. I went up to show it to

Charles. But Mills has told you what happened. I was going to knock at the door, when I heard somebody come upstairs behind me. I looked round, and there he was. But I will swear, I will swear on the Cross, that I had locked that door downstairs. Well, I was not afraid! No! I asked him what he meant by coming upstairs. And still, you understand, I could not see the false face, because his back was to that bright light on the stairs. But he said, in French, 'Madame, you cannot keep me out like that,' and turned down his collar and put his cap in his pocket. I opened the door because I knew he would not dare face Charles, just as Charles opened it from inside. Then I saw the mask, which was a pinkish color like flesh. Before I could do anything he made a horrible jump inside, and kicked the door shut, and turned the key.

"I went away, as Charles ordered me to do. I went a little way down the stairs, where I could still see the door to this room, and I did not leave my post any more than poor Stuart did. It was—horrible. I was there when the shot was fired; I was there when Stuart ran to pound on the door; I was even there when you people began to come upstairs. But I could not stand it. I felt myself going faint, and I had just time to get to my room when I was—ill. But Stuart was right; nobody left that room. God help us both, we are telling the truth. However else that horror left the room, he did not leave by the door. . . . And now please, please, will you let me go to see Charles?"

PLAN OF TOP-FLOOR REAR

1. Where Grimaud's body was found.
2. Disarranged sofa, chair, and hearthrug.
3. Where painting was to have been hung.
4. Painting itself, against bookshelves.
5. Where Mills sat.
6. Where Madame Dumont stood.
7. Door leading to staircase communicating with trap in roof.

Dr. Fell answered. He was standing now with his back to the fireplace, a vast black-caped figure under the fencing foils and shield of arms. His eyeglasses were coming askew on his nose.

"Ma'am, we shall not detain you very long. And I don't in the least doubt your story, any more than I doubt Mills's. Before getting down to business, I will prove that I believe you. Ma'am, do you remember what time tonight it stopped snowing?"

She was looking at him with bright, defensive eyes. "I think it was about half past nine. Yes! When I came up to collect Charles's coffee tray, I looked out and I noticed that it had stopped. Does it matter?"

"Very much, ma'am. And you are right. It stopped about half past nine. Right, Hadley?"

The superintendent looked at Dr. Fell suspiciously. "Granting that it was half past nine, what then?"

"Not only had it stopped snowing forty minutes before the visitor escaped from this room," pursued the doctor with a meditative air, "but it had stopped fifteen minutes before the visitor even arrived at this house. That's true, ma'am? He rang the doorbell at quarter to ten? Good. . . . Now, Hadley, do you remember when *we* arrived? Did you notice that, before you and Rampole and young Mangan went charging in, *there wasn't a single footprint on the steps leading up to the front door, or even on the pavement leading to the steps?*"

"By God! That's right! The whole pavement was clean. It—" Hadley swung slowly round to Madame Dumont. "So this, you say, is your evidence of why you believe Madame's story? Fell, have you gone mad, too?"

Dr. Fell chuckled. "I say, son, why are you so flabbergasted? Apparently he sailed out of here without leaving a footprint. Why should it upset you to learn that he also sailed in?"

"I don't know," the other admitted. "But, hang it, it does! In my experience with locked-room murders, getting in and getting out are two very different things."

"Please listen. I say," Madame Dumont interposed, "that I am telling the absolute truth, so help me God!"

"And I believe you," said Dr. Fell. "You mustn't let Hadley overawe you. He will believe it, too, before I'm through with him. My point is this. I have shown you, haven't I, ma'am, that I have faith in what you have said? Very well. But I fancy I shall very strongly doubt what you are going to tell me in a moment."

"Please go on," the woman said stolidly.

"Thanks. Now, ma'am, how long have you been Grimaud's housekeeper? No, I'll change that. How long have you been with him?"

"For over twenty-five years," she answered. "I was more than his housekeeper—once."

She had been looking at her interlocked fingers, but now she lifted her head. Her eyes had a fierce, steady gaze. "I tell you that," she went on quietly, "in the hope that you will give me your word to keep silent. You will find it in your alien records at Bow Street, and you may make unnecessary trouble that has nothing to do with this matter. It is not for myself, you understand. Rosette Grimaud is my daughter. She was born here, and there had to be a record. But she does not know it—nobody knows it. Please, please, can I trust you to keep silent?"

"We shall certainly say nothing about it," said Dr. Fell. "As for the young lady, I'll bet she probably knows already. Children do. And she's trying to keep it from *you*. Humph. Let's forget it." He beamed. "What I wanted to ask you: where did you first meet Grimaud?"

She breathed hard. "In Paris."

"You are a Parisienne?"

"What? No, no, not by birth! I am of the provinces. But I worked there when I met him. I was a *costumière*—one of the women who made costumes for the opera and the ballet. We worked in the Opéra itself. You can find record of that! I was never married and my maiden name was Ernestine Dumont."

"And Grimaud?" Dr. Fell asked sharply. "Where was he from?"

"From the south of France, I think. But he studied at Paris. His family are all dead. He inherited their money."

There was an air of tension which these casual questions did not seem to warrant. Dr. Fell's next three questions were so extraordinary that Hadley stared up from his notebook and Ernestine Dumont shifted uneasily.

"What is your religious faith, ma'am?"

"I am a Unitarian. Why?"

"H'm. Did Grimaud ever visit the United States?"

"Never."

"Do the words 'seven towers' mean anything to you, ma'am?"

"No!" cried Ernestine Dumont, and went white.

Dr. Fell blinked at her. He lumbered out from the hearth and indicated the big painting with his cane, tracing out the line of the white mountains in the background of the picture.

"I won't ask you whether you know what this represents," he continued, "but I will ask you whether Grimaud told you why he bought it. What sort of charm was it supposed to contain, anyhow? What power did it have to ward off the bullet or the evil eye? What sort of influ—" He stopped, as though recalling something startling. Then he reached out, lifting the picture off the floor with one hand and turning it curiously from side to side. "Oh, my hat!" said Dr. Fell, with explosive absentmindedness. "Wow!"

"What is it?" demanded Hadley. "Do you see anything?"

"No, I don't see anything," said Dr. Fell. "That's just the point. Well, madame?"

"I think," said the woman in a shaky voice, "that you are the strangest man I ever met. No. I do not know what that thing is. Charles would not tell me. But it looks like a picture of a country that does not exist."

Dr. Fell nodded somberly. "I am afraid you are right, ma'am. I don't think it does exist. And if three people were buried there, it might be difficult to find them—mightn't it?"

"Will you stop talking this gibberish?" shouted Hadley; and then Hadley was taken aback by the fact that this gibberish had struck Ernestine Dumont like a blow.

"I am going," she said, getting to her feet. "You are crazy. You sit here raving while you let Pierre Fley escape. Why don't you go after him?"

"Because you see, ma'am . . . Grimaud himself said that Pierre Fley did not do this thing." While she was still staring at him, he let the painting fall back with a thump against the sofa.

Rampole was still looking at the painting when they heard footsteps on the stairs. It was heartening to see the prosaic, hatchet face of Sergeant Betts, with two cheerful plainclothesmen carrying the photographic and fingerprint apparatus. A uniformed policeman stood behind Mills, Boyd Mangan, and the girl who had been in the drawing room. The girl pushed through this group into the room.

"Boyd told me you wanted me," she said in an unsteady voice. "But I insisted on going over with the ambulance. You'd better get over there quickly, Aunt Ernestine. They say he's—going."

She tried to be efficient and peremptory, even in the way she drew off her gloves; but she could not manage it. Rampole saw that her hair was a honey blond color, bobbed and turned forward. Her face was firmly shaped, with a broad mouth, hazel eyes, and high cheekbones; not beautiful, but disturbing and vivid. She looked round quickly. She was not far from hysteria.

"Will you please hurry and tell me what you want?" she cried. "Don't you realize he's *dying?* Aunt Ernestine . . ."

"If these gentlemen are through with me," the woman said stolidly, "I will go." She was docile all of a sudden. But it was a heavy docility, with a half challenge in it—as though there were limits. Something bristled between these two women.

Hadley prolonged the silence, as though he were confronting two suspects with each other at Scotland Yard. Then he said briskly, "Mr. Mangan, will you take Miss Grimaud to Mr. Mills's room down the hall? Thank you. We shall be with you in a moment. . . . Betts!"

"Sir?"

"Did you bring ropes and a flashlight? . . . Good. I want you to go up on the roof and search for a footprint or a mark of any kind. Then go down to the yard, and both adjoining yards, and see if you can find any marks there. Mr. Mills will show you how to get to the roof. . . . Preston! Is Sergeant Preston here?"

A sharp-nosed young man bustled in from the hall.

"Go over this room for any secret entrance whatever, understand? And see if anybody could get up the chimney. . . . You fellows carry on with the prints and pictures. But don't disturb that burned paper in the fireplace. . . . Constable! Where the hell's that constable?"

"Here, sir."

"Did Bow Street phone the address of a man named Pierre Fley? . . . Right. Go to wherever he lives and bring him here. If he's not there, wait. Have they sent a man to the theater where he works? . . . All right. Hop to it, everybody."

He strode out into the hall, muttering. Dr. Fell, lumbering after him, was for the first time imbued with a ghoulish eagerness. He poked at the superintendent's arm.

"Look here, Hadley," he urged, "you go down and attend to the questioning, hey? I think I can be of much more service if I stay behind and assist those duffers with their photographs."

"No," said the other with heat. "I want to talk to you privately and plainly. What's all this mumbo jumbo about seven towers, and people buried in countries that never existed? I've seen you in these fits of mystification before, but never quite so bad."

He turned irascibly as Stuart Mills plucked at his arm. "Er—before I conduct the sergeant up to the roof," said Mills, "I think I had better tell you that in case you wish to see Mr. Drayman, he is here in the house."

"Drayman? Oh yes! When did he get back?"

Mills frowned. "So far as I am able to deduce, he never left. A short time ago I looked into his room. I discovered him asleep. It will be difficult to rouse him; I believe he has taken a sleeping tablet. Mr. Drayman is very fond of taking them."

"Rummiest household _I_ ever heard of," declared Hadley, after a pause, to nobody in particular. "Anything else?"

"Yes, sir. There is a friend of Dr. Grimaud's downstairs. He has just arrived. He is a member of the circle at the Warwick Tavern. His name is Pettis—Mr. Anthony Pettis."

"Pettis, eh?" repeated Dr. Fell, rubbing his chin. "I wonder if that's the Pettis who collects ghost stories and writes those excellent prefaces."

"Look here," said Hadley. "I can't see this fellow now. Get his address, will you? I'll call on him in the morning." He turned to Dr. Fell. "Now carry on about the seven towers and the country that never existed."

The doctor waited until Mills had led Sergeant Betts away, down the hall. Then he beckoned Hadley and Rampole towards the staircase.

"I'll lead up to the seven towers gradually," he said. "A few disjointed words—because they came from the victim—may be the most important clue of all. I mean those few mutterings from Grimaud just before he fainted. Remember, Hadley, you asked him whether Fley had shot him. He shook his head. Then you asked him who had done it. What did he say? I want to ask each of you what you thought you heard."

He looked at Rampole. The American hesitated. "The first thing he said sounded to me like *hover—*"

"Nonsense," interrupted Hadley. "I jotted it all down right away. The first thing he said was *bath* or *the bath*, though I'm hanged if I see—"

"Steady now. Your own gibberish," said Dr. Fell, "is a little worse than mine. Go on, Ted."

"Well, then I heard the words *not suicide*, and *he couldn't use rope*. Next there was some reference to a *roof* and to *snow* and to a *fox*. The last thing I heard sounded like *too much light*."

Hadley was indulgent. "You've got it all twisted. All the same, I'm bound to admit that my notes don't make much better sense. After the word *bath*, he said *salt* and *wine*. You're right about the rope, although I heard nothing about suicide. *Roof* and *snow* are correct; *too much light* came afterwards; then *got gun*. Finally, he did say something about a *fox*, and the last thing was something like *Don't blame poor—*"

Dr. Fell groaned. "This is terrible. Gents, I was going to explain what he said. But I am beaten by the staggering size of your respective ears. Wow!"

"Well, what's your version?" demanded Hadley.

The doctor stumped up and down. "I heard only the first few words. They make tolerably good sense—*if* I'm right. But the rest is a nightmare."

Hadley struck his notebook. "To put everything in order, Rampole, I'll write down what you heard for comparison."

"H'mf, yes. But let's just go back a bit. . . . First, my lad, what happened in that room after Grimaud was shot?"

"How the hell should I know?" roared Hadley. "If there's no secret entrance—"

"No, no, I don't mean how the vanishing trick was worked. You're obsessed with that business, Hadley; so obsessed that you don't stop to ask yourself what *else* happened. Let's get clear the obvious things for which we can find an explanation. Humph. Now, then, what clearly did happen in that room after the man was shot? First, all the marks centered round the fireplace—"

"You mean the fellow climbed up the chimney?"

"He absolutely didn't," said Dr. Fell testily. "That flue is wide, but not deep enough to get your fist through. Control yourself and think. First, a sofa was pushed away from in front of the fireplace; there was a good deal of blood on the top, as though Grimaud had slipped or leaned against it. The hearthrug was pulled away; there was blood on that; and a fireside chair was shoved away. Finally, I found spots of blood on the hearth and even in the fireplace. They led us to a huge mass of burned papers that had nearly smothered the fire.

"Now, consider the behavior of the faithful Madame Dumont. As soon as she came into that room, she was terribly concerned about that fireplace. She kept looking at it, and nearly grew hysterical when she saw I was doing so, too. She even made the foolish blunder of asking us to light a fire. Somebody, my boy, had tried to burn letters or documents there. She wanted to be certain they had been destroyed."

Hadley said heavily, "So she knew about it, then? And yet you said you believed her story?"

"Yes. I do believe her story—about the visitor and the crime.

What I don't believe is the information she gave us about herself and Grimaud. . . . Now think again what happened! The intruder shot Grimaud. Yet Grimaud, although he is still conscious, does not shout for help, or even open the door when Mills is pounding there. But he does do something. He does it with such a violent exertion that he tears wide open the wound in his lung—as you heard the doctor say.

"And I'll tell you what he did do. He knew he was a goner and that the police would be in. He had in his possession a mass of things that *must be* destroyed. It was more vital to destroy them than to catch the man who shot him. He lurched back and forth from that fireplace, burning this evidence. Hence the sofa knocked away, the stains of blood. . . . You understand now?"

There was a silence in the bright bleak hall.

"And the Dumont woman?" Hadley asked.

"She knew it, of course. It was their joint secret. And she happens to love him."

"If this is true, it must have been something pretty damned important that he destroyed," said Hadley. "What secret could they have had, anyway?"

Dr. Fell pressed his hands to his temples and ruffled his big mop of hair. "I may be able to tell you a little of it," he said, "although there are parts that puzzle me beyond hope. You see, neither Grimaud nor Dumont is French. They're both Magyar. To be precise: Grimaud came originally from Hungary. His real name is Károly, or Charles, Grimaud Horváth. He probably had a French mother. He came from the principality of Transylvania, formerly a part of the Hungarian kingdom but annexed by Rumania since the war. In the late nineties or early nineteen hundreds, Károly Grimaud Horváth and his two brothers were all sent to prison. Did I tell you he had two brothers? One we haven't seen, but the other now calls himself Pierre Fley.

"I don't know what crime the three brothers Horváth had committed, but they were sent to the prison of Siebenturmen, to work in the salt mines near Tradj in the Carpathian Mountains. Charles probably escaped. Now, the deadly secret in his life can't concern the fact that he was sent to prison or even that he escaped; the Hungarian kingdom is broken up, and its authority no longer exists. More probably he did some black devilry that concerned the other brothers; something horrible concerning those three coffins, and people buried alive, that would hang him even now if it were discovered. . . . That's all I can hazard at the moment."

IV: The Seven Towers

IN THE pause after this recital, Hadley eyed the doctor malevolently. "Are you joking?" he asked.

"Not about a thing like this. . . . Those three coffins!" muttered Dr. Fell. "I wish I could see a glimmer—something. . . ."

"You seem to have done pretty well. Have you been holding out information, or how do you know all that? Stop a bit!" He looked at his notebook. "*Hover. Bath. Salt. Wine.* In other words, you're trying to tell us that what Grimaud really said was *Horváth*, and *salt mine?*"

"He said it, Hadley. I heard him. You asked him for a name, didn't you? And he answered, Horváth."

"Which *you* say is his own name."

"Yes. Look here," said Dr. Fell. "It's like this. We hear from Ted Rampole about a queer customer who threatens Grimaud and talks about people buried alive. Grimaud takes this seriously; he has known that man before and knows what he is talking about, since for some reason he buys a picture depicting three graves. When you ask Grimaud who shot him, he answers with the name Horváth and says something about salt mines. Whether or not you think that's odd of a French professor, it is rather odd to find up over his mantelpiece the device of a shield graven thus: *coupé,* a demieagle issuant sable, in chief a moon argent. . . ."

"I think we may omit the heraldry," said Hadley. "What is it?"

"It's the arms of Transylvania. Dead since the war, of course, and hardly well known in England—or France—even before that. First a Slavic name, and then Slavic arms. Next, those books I showed you. They were English books translated into Magyar.

I couldn't pretend to read 'em, but I could at least recognize the complete works of Shakespeare, and Sterne's *Letters of Yorick to Eliza.* That was so startling that I examined 'em all."

"Why startling?" asked Rampole.

"Suppose a scholarly Frenchman wants to read a book by an English author. Well, he reads it in English, or he gets it translated into French. But he very seldom insists on getting its full flavor by first having it translated into Hungarian. No. Whoever owned those books, his native language was Hungarian. I went through all of 'em, hoping to find a name. When I found *Károly Grimaud Horváth, 1898,* faded out on one flyleaf, it seemed to put the tin hat on it.

"If Horváth was his real name, why had he kept up this pretense for so long? Think of the words *buried alive* and *salt mines* and there is a gleam. But, when you asked him who shot him, he said Horváth. He didn't mean himself, but somebody else named Horváth. While I was thinking of that, our excellent Mills was telling you about the man called Fley at the public house. Mills said that there seemed something very familiar about Fley, although he had never seen him before. Was it Grimaud he suggested? Brother, brother, brother! You see, there were three coffins, but Fley mentioned only two brothers. It sounded like a third.

"Then there entered the Slavic-looking Madame Dumont. If I could establish Grimaud as coming from Transylvania, it would narrow down our search when we tried to find out his history. But it had to be done delicately. Notice that carved figure of a buffalo on Grimaud's desk? What does that suggest to you?"

"It suggests the Wild West," the superintendent growled. "Buffalo Bill, Indians. Was that why you asked her whether Grimaud had ever been in the United States?"

Dr. Fell nodded. "You see, if he'd got that figure in an American curio shop . . . H'm. Hadley, I've been in Hungary. I went in my younger days, when I'd just read *Dracula.* They used buffaloes in Transylvania like oxen. Hungary was full of mixed religious beliefs; but Transylvania was Unitarian. I asked Madame Ernestine, and she qualified. Then I threw my hand grenade. If Grimaud had been innocently associated with salt mines, it wouldn't matter. But I named the only prison in Transylvania where convicts were used to work the salt mines. I named the Siebenturmen—or the Seven Towers—without even saying it was a prison. It almost finished her. Now perhaps you will understand my remark about the seven towers and the country that does not now exist."

"Yes," said Hadley, "so far as it goes, it seems reasonable enough. Your long shot about the prison worked. But the whole basis of your case, that there are three brothers, is pure surmise."

"Oh, admitted. But what then?"

"Only that it's the crucial point. Suppose Grimaud didn't mean that a person named Horváth had shot him, but was only referring to himself in some way? Then the murderer might be anybody. But if there are three brothers, and he did mean that, the thing is simple. Either Pierre Fley shot him, or Fley's brother did. We can put our hands on Fley at any time; as for the brother—"

"Are you sure you'd recognize the brother," said Dr. Fell reflectively, "if you met him? I was thinking of Grimaud. He spoke English perfectly, and also passed perfectly for a Frenchman. Then what about this third brother? Suppose he's right here somewhere in our midst, in some guise or other, and nobody knows him for what he really is?"

"Possibly. But we don't know anything about the brother."

"That's what bothers me, Hadley," said Dr. Fell. "We have two theoretical brothers who have taken French names: Charles and Pierre. For the sake of clearness and argument, let's call the third Henri. All we know about him is that Pierre appears to be using him as a threat. It is, 'I have a brother who can do much more than I can . . . who wants your life.' And so on. But no shape comes out of the smoke—neither man nor goblin. Son, it worries me. I think that ugly presence is behind the whole business, controlling it, using poor half-crazy Pierre for his own ends, and probably as dangerous to Pierre as to Charles. I can't help feeling that he's somewhere close at hand and watchful; that—" And Dr. Fell stared round curiously as though he expected to see something move or speak in the empty hall.

Hadley bit at the end of his clipped mustache. "Let's stick to the facts," he said. "I'll cable the Rumanian police tonight. But there may be few official records on Transylvania left. The Bolshies stormed through there just after the war, didn't they? Um. Anyhow, let's get after Mangan and Grimaud's daughter. I'm not entirely satisfied with *their* behavior. . . ."

"Eh? Why?"

"I mean, provided the Dumont woman is telling the truth," Hadley amended. "Wasn't Mangan here tonight at Grimaud's request, in case the visitor should drop in? Yes. Then he seems to have been rather a tame watchdog. He sits in the room near the front door with the door shut and only kicks up a row when he hears a shot and finds that the door has been locked. Is that logical?"

"Nothing is logical," said Dr. Fell. "Not even— But that can wait."

They went down the long hall, and Hadley assumed his most tactful and impassive manner when he opened the door. It was a room somewhat smaller than the other, lined with orderly books and filing cabinets. Under a green-shaded hanging lamp Mills's typewriter desk was drawn up facing the door. On one side of the machine neat manuscript sheets lay in a wire basket; on the other side stood a glass of milk, a dish of dried prunes, and a copy of Williamson's *Differential and Integral Calculus*.

Rosette Grimaud was sitting before a sickly fire. Hadley introduced the three of them. "Naturally, Miss Grimaud, I don't wish to distress you at this time—"

"Please don't say anything," she said. "I mean—about *that*. You see, I'm fond of him, but not so fond that it hurts terribly, unless somebody begins to talk about it."

She pressed her hands against her temples. She had her mother's intense personality shaped into blond Slavic beauty. She was restless, sleek, and puzzling. Behind her stood Mangan in gloomy helplessness.

"One thing, though," she went on, pounding her fist on the arm of the chair. "One thing before you start your third degree. Is it true what we hear about a man getting in—and out—and killing my father—without—without—"

"Harrumph!" Dr. Fell snorted. "Of course it's not true, Miss Grimaud. We know all about how the blighter worked his trick. Furthermore, there'll be no third degree, and your father has a fighting chance to pull through. Look here, Miss Grimaud, haven't I met you somewhere before?" He squinted. "H'm, yes. Got it! You're at London University, aren't you? Of course. And you're in a debating circle or something? It seems to me I officiated as chairman when your team debated Woman's Rights in the World."

"That's Rosette," assented Mangan gloomily. "She's a strong feminist."

"Heh-heh-heh," said Dr. Fell. "I remember now. She may be a feminist, my boy, but she has startling lapses. In fact, I remember—you were on the side for woman's rights, Miss Grimaud, and against the tyranny of man, were you not? Yes, yes. Then one lean female on your side carried on for twenty minutes about what woman needed for an ideal state of existence, and you seemed to get madder and madder. So when your turn came, you rose to proclaim that what woman needed for an ideal existence was less talking and more copulation."

"Good God!" said Mangan, and jumped.

"Well, you don't need to think—" said Rosette hotly.

"The effect of that terrible word was beyond description," said Dr. Fell. "I wonder whether you and Mr. Mangan often discuss these subjects. They must be enlightening talks. What was the argument about this evening, for instance?"

Both of them began to speak at once, chaotically. Dr. Fell beamed. "Yes." He nodded. "You understand now, don't you, that there's nothing to be afraid of in talking to the police? It'll be better, you know. Let's face the thing and clear it up sensibly now, among ourselves, hey?"

"Right," said Rosette. "Has somebody got a cigarette?"

Mangan fumbled to produce cigarettes. Then Dr. Fell pointed.

"Now, I want to know one thing," he continued. "Were you two kids so engrossed in each other that you didn't notice anything tonight until the rumpus started? As I understand it, Mangan, Professor Grimaud asked you here tonight to be on the lookout for possible trouble. Didn't you hear the doorbell?"

Mangan's face clouded. "I admit it's my fault. But at the time I never gave it a thought. Of course I heard the doorbell. In fact, we both spoke to the fellow—"

"You *what?*" interrupted Hadley, striding past Dr. Fell.

"Certainly. Otherwise you don't think I'd have let him get past me and upstairs, do you? But he said he was old Pettis—Anthony Pettis, you know."

"Pettis?" said Dr. Fell.

"Of course we know now that it wasn't Pettis," Mangan said. "Pettis must be all of five feet four inches tall. Besides, now I think back on it, it wasn't even an exact imitation of his voice. But he spoke in words Pettis always uses. . . ."

Dr. Fell scowled. "But didn't it strike you as queer that even a collector of ghost stories should walk about dressed up like a Fifth of November Guy? Is he addicted to pranks?"

Rosette Grimaud looked startled, and twitched round to look at Mangan. "Pranks?" Mangan repeated, and passed a hand nervously over his hair. "Lord, no! Pettis is as correct and fussy as they make 'em. But, you understand, we didn't see his face. We'd been sitting in that front room since after dinner—"

"Stop," interrupted Hadley. "Was the door to the hall open?"

"No. Hang it," said Mangan defensively. "But I knew we could hear the bell ring if it did ring. Besides—well, honestly, I didn't expect anything to happen. The professor gave us the impression at dinner that it was a hoax, that he had been inclined to get the wind up over nothing. . . ."

"You got that impression, too, Miss Grimaud?" Hadley asked.

"Yes, in a way. . . . But it's always hard to tell," she answered, "whether my father is annoyed or amused or just pretending both. He loves dramatic effects. But for the past three days, he's been acting so queerly that when Boyd told me about the man in that pub—"

"In what way was he acting queerly?"

"Well, muttering to himself, for instance. And suddenly roaring out over trifles, which he seldom does. But most of all it was those letters. He began to get them in every post, and he burned all of them." She hesitated. "I shouldn't have noticed at all, but my father is one of those people who can never get a letter in your presence without your instantly knowing what it's about or even who it's from. He'll explode, 'Damned swindler!' or, genially, 'Well, well, here's a letter from old So-and-so!' I don't know if you understand. . . ."

"We understand. Please go on."

"But when he got these notes he didn't say anything. Yesterday morning at breakfast, after he'd glanced at one, he got up, went over, and threw it in the fire. Just at that second Aunt Ernestine asked him if he'd have some more bacon. He whirled round and yelled, 'Go to hell!' It was so unexpected that before we had recovered our wits he'd stamped out of the room. That was the day he came back with that painting. He was good-humored again; he banged about, chuckling, and helped the cabman and somebody else cart it upstairs."

"Did he mention this man at the public house?" Hadley asked.

"Offhandedly, when I asked him. He said it was one of the quacks who often threatened him for jeering at—the history of magic. But I felt it wasn't merely that." She paused, looking at him unwinkingly. "I felt that this was the real thing. I've often wondered whether there was anything in my father's past life which might bring something like that on him."

It was a direct challenge. During the silence that followed she leaned back, regarding them with a faint smile. All the same, she was trembling.

Hadley appeared mildly surprised. "Bring something like that on him? I don't understand. Had you any reason to think so?"

"Oh, no reason! Just these fancies. Probably it's living with my father's hobby."

"Then let's get on with the story Mr. Mangan was telling," said Hadley. "Did Professor Grimaud tell you what time he expected a dangerous visitor?"

"Er—yes," said Mangan. He had taken out a handkerchief and was mopping his forehead. "That was another reason why I didn't tumble to who it might be. He was too early. The professor said ten o'clock, and this fellow arrived at a quarter to."

"I—see. Go on, Mr. Mangan."

"We had the radio on, and the music was loud. All the same, I heard the doorbell. I looked at the clock on the mantel, and it said a quarter to ten. I was getting up when I heard the front door open. Then I heard Mrs. Dumont's voice saying something like, 'Wait, I'll see,' and a sound as though the door slammed. I called out, 'Ahoy there! Who is it?' But the radio was making such a row that I naturally stepped over and shut it off. And just afterwards we heard Pettis—we both thought it was Pettis—call out, 'Hullo, children! It's Pettis. What's all this formality about seeing the governor? I'm going up and break in on him.'"

"Those were his exact words?"

"Yes. He always called Dr. Grimaud the governor; nobody else had the nerve to. . . . So we said, 'Righto,' and didn't bother any more about it. But I began to be watchful and jumpy, now that it was coming towards ten o'clock. . . ."

Hadley drew a design on the margin of his notebook.

"So the man who called himself Pettis," he mused, "spoke to you through the door without seeing you? How did he know you two were there?"

Mangan frowned. "He saw us through the window, I suppose, when he came up the front steps."

The superintendent was still drawing designs, meditatively. "Go on," he said. "You were waiting for ten o'clock—"

"And nothing happened," Mangan insisted. "But, a funny thing, every minute past ten I got more nervous instead of more relieved. I didn't really expect that there would be any trouble. But I kept picturing that dark hall, and the queer suit of armor with the mask. . . ." He shifted. "Anyway, it was nearly ten past ten when I felt I couldn't stand it any longer. I said to Rosette, 'Look here, let's get a drink—or do something.' So I went over to open the door, and it was locked on the outside. . . . I knew then that something was wrong. Just as I began yanking at the knob, we heard the shot, and Rosette screamed. 'That wasn't Pettis at all,' she said. 'He's got in.'"

"Can you fix the time of that?"

"Yes. It was just ten minutes past ten. Well, I tried to break the door down, but I couldn't. Then I thought about getting out through the window and in the front door, and I ran into you."

Hadley tapped the notebook with his pencil. "Was it customary for the front door to be unlocked, Mr. Mangan?"

"I don't know! But it was the only thing I could think of. Anyhow, it *was* unlocked."

"Yes. Have you anything to add to that, Miss Grimaud?"

Her eyelids drooped. "Not exactly. Boyd has told you everything just as it happened. But you people always want all kinds of queer things, don't you? Even if they don't seem to bear on the matter? Well, a little while before the doorbell rang, I was going over to get some cigarettes from a table between the windows and I heard from somewhere out in the street, or on the pavement in front of the door, a sound like—like a thud, as though a heavy object had fallen from a big height. I only pulled the blind back and peeped round the side of it, but I can swear the street was empty—" She stopped, and her lips fell open. "Oh, my *God!*"

"Yes, Miss Grimaud," said Hadley. "The blinds were all down, as you say. I especially noticed that, because Mr. Mangan got entangled with one when he jumped out. That was why I wondered how the visitor could have seen you through a window."

There was a silence, except for faint noises on the roof. Rampole glanced first at Dr. Fell, then at Hadley and at the girl.

"He thinks we're lying, Boyd," said Rosette Grimaud coolly.

Hadley smiled. "I don't think anything of the kind, Miss Grimaud, and I'm going to tell you why. Fell! I want you to listen to this," the superintendent pursued grimly. "I believe the story told by these two. And, in explaining why, I'll also explain the impossible situation—not all, but at least enough to narrow down the field of suspects, and to explain why there were no footprints in the snow."

"Oh, *that!*" said Dr. Fell contemptuously. "You know, for a second I hoped you had something. But that part is obvious."

Hadley kept his temper with a violent effort. "The man we want," he went on, "made no footprints on the pavement or up the steps—after the snow had stopped. He was in the house all the time. He had been in the house for some time. He was either (a) an inmate, or (b) somebody who had concealed himself there, using a key to the front door earlier in the evening. At the proper time he put on his fancy rig, stepped outside the front door on the swept doorstep, and rang the doorbell. This would explain how he knew Miss Grimaud and Mr. Mangan were in the front room when the blinds were drawn—he had seen them go in. It explains how, when the door was slammed in his face and he was told to wait outside, he could simply walk in—he had a key."

Dr. Fell was slowly shaking his head. Hadley squared his shoulders. "Now, then!" Hadley went on. "I've shown you two that I believe everything you say, because I want your help on the most important thing this tells us. . . . The man we want is no casual acquaintance. He knows this house inside out—the rooms, the habits of the occupants. He knows your phrases and nicknames. So I want to know all about everybody who's a frequent enough visitor to this house, everybody who is close enough to Dr. Grimaud, to answer the description."

Rosette moved uneasily. "You think—somebody like that . . . Oh, it's impossible! Of course, you haven't met everyone. You haven't met Annie—or Mr. Drayman, come to think of it. And outside of the people in this house my father has very few friends. There are only two who fit the qualifications, and neither of them could possibly be the man you want. They couldn't be, in the mere matter of their physical characteristics. One is Anthony Pettis; and he's no taller than I am. The other is Jerome Burnaby, the artist who did that queer picture. He has a deformity; a slight one, but it couldn't be disguised. Aunt Ernestine or Stuart would have known him instantly."

"All the same, what do you know about them?"

"Both are middle-aged, well-to-do, and putter about their hobbies. Pettis is bald-headed, fastidious, and clever." She glanced at Mangan. "And Jerome Burnaby—well, Jerome is fairly well known as an artist, though he'd rather be known as a criminologist. He likes to talk about crime. He's big and bluff and attractive in his way. He's a good bit older than I, but he's very fond of me, and Boyd is horribly jealous." She smiled.

"I don't like the fellow," said Mangan quietly. "But Rosette's right about one thing. He'd never do a thing like that."

Hadley scribbled again. "What is this deformity of his?"

"A clubfoot. You can see how he couldn't conceal it."

"Thank you. For the moment," said Hadley, shutting his notebook, "that will be all. I should suggest that you go along to the nursing home. Unless ... er ... any questions, Fell?"

The doctor stumped forward. He towered over the girl, peering down at her with his head on one side. "Just one last question," he said, adjusting his eyeglasses. "Now! Miss Grimaud, why are you so certain that the guilty person is this Mr. Drayman?"

V: The Bullet

HE NEVER received any answer to that question, although he received some illumination. "You *devil!*" cried Rosette Grimaud, and she flung herself past Dr. Fell and out into the hall, with Mangan after her. The door slammed.

Dr. Fell remained blinking at it. "She's her father's daughter, Hadley," he wheezed. "She goes just so far under emotional pressure; very quiet, powder packed into a cartridge; then some little thing jars the trigger, and—h'm. I wonder how much she knows?"

"It seems to me," said Hadley with asperity, "that you're always making a wild shot like a trick rifleman and knocking the cigarette out of somebody's mouth. What was that business about Drayman, anyhow?"

Dr. Fell folded his arms. "To begin with," he said, "I had stuck in my mind an odd remark made by Madame Dumont at the time she was most hysterical. She said, if you wish to kill somebody, 'you do not put on a painted mask, like old Drayman with

the children on Guy Fawkes night.' I filed away the suggestion of this Guy Fawkes specter, wondering what it meant. Then, unintentionally, I phrased a question about Pettis—when speaking to Rosette—with the words, 'dressed up like a Fifth of November Guy?' Did you notice her expression, Hadley? She was startled. My words had given her a hint. She didn't say anything at first, but she was thinking.

"Then she dragged in Drayman. 'You haven't met Annie—or Mr. Drayman, come to think of it.' The important news was in the postscript. . . ." Dr. Fell stumped round the typewriter desk. "We must rout him out. Who is this Drayman, this old friend who takes sleeping tablets and wears Fifth of November masks? What's his place in the household; what's he doing here, anyway?"

"You mean—blackmail?"

"No, but—" He paused as a rush of cold air blew his cloak.

A door across the room, evidently communicating with a staircase to the attic and the roof, opened, and Stuart Mills popped in. His mouth was bluish and a large wool muffler was wound round his neck; but he looked warm with satisfaction. He chattered: "I have been watching your detective, gentlemen, from the top of the trapdoor. He has caused a few landslides, but . . ."

"And what did Betts discover up there?" Hadley asked.

Betts, entering, answered for himself. He looked as though he had taken a header in a ski jump as he stamped and slapped the snow from his clothes.

"Sir," he announced, "you can take my word for it that not even a bird's lit on that roof. I've covered every foot of it." He stripped off his gloves. "I had myself tied on a rope to each of the chimneys, so I could get down and crawl along the gutters. There's no mark of any kind, nothing round the edges or the chimneys, nothing anywhere. If anybody got up on that roof tonight, he must have been lighter than air. Now I'll have a look at the back garden."

"But—" cried Hadley.

"Quite so," said Dr. Fell. "Look here, we'd better go see what your bloodhounds are doing in the other room."

Sergeant Preston, fuming a little, pulled open the hall door as though he had been summoned. He looked at Hadley. "It's taken time, sir," he reported, "because we had to pull out all those bookcases. But there's no secret entrance of any kind. Chimney's solid and flue's broad but only about two or three inches deep."

"Fingerprints?"

"Plenty of prints, except— You raised and lowered that window yourself, didn't you, sir? I recognized your prints. And there's nothing else on the glass or the woodwork, not even a smudge. If anybody went out there, he must have stood back and dived out head first without touching anything."

"That's enough, thanks," said Hadley. "Wait downstairs. Get after that back garden, Betts." He wheeled round. "Mr. Mills, what do you know about this man Drayman?"

Mills's singsong voice took on a guarded quality. "It is true, sir, that he offers a subject for curiosity. But I know very little. He has been here some years, I am informed, and he was forced to give up his academic work because he had gone almost blind. He is still almost blind, in spite of treatment. He appealed to Dr. Grimaud for help."

"Had he some sort of claim on Dr. Grimaud?"

The secretary frowned. "I cannot say. I have heard it mentioned that Dr. Grimaud knew him at Paris, where he studied. And once when Dr. Grimaud had, let us say, imbibed a convivial glass, I heard him state that Mr. Drayman had once saved his life."

Dr. Fell, looking at him curiously, said, "And why is he so interested in Guy Fawkes night?"

"Guy Faw— Ah!" Mills uttered a bleat of laughter. "I see! I did not follow. You see, he is very fond of children. He had two of his own, who were killed—by the falling of a roof, I believe, some years ago. After that his wife did not survive long. Then he began to lose his sight. . . . He likes to help children in their games, and his favorite occasion seems to be the Fifth of November. He saves up throughout the year to buy illuminations and trappings, and builds a Guy for a procession to—"

A sharp knocking at the door was followed by the appearance of Sergeant Preston. "A chap from the hospital just brought this over for you, sir," he reported. He handed over an envelope and a cardboard box like a jeweler's box.

Hadley ripped open the letter, glanced at it, and swore. "He's gone," he snapped, "and not a word. . . . Here, read this!"

Rampole looked over Dr. Fell's shoulder as the latter read.

For Superintendent Hadley:

Grimaud died at 11:30. I am sending you the bullet, a thirty-eight. He was conscious just before the end. He said certain things which can be attested by two of my nurses and myself; but he might have been wandering. I knew him pretty well, but I certainly never knew he had a brother. He spoke exactly as follows:

"It was my brother who did it. I never thought he would shoot. God knows how he got out of that room. One second he was there, and the next he wasn't. Get a pencil and paper, quick! I want to tell you who my brother is, so that you won't think I'm raving."

His shouting brought on the final hemorrhage, and he died without saying anything else.

E. H. Peterson, M.D.

They all looked at each other. After a pause the superintendent spoke in a heavy voice. "'God knows,'" he repeated, "'how he got out of that room.'"

Dr. Fell walked over aimlessly, sighed, and settled himself down in the largest chair.

"Damn," said Hadley in a flat voice. "'It was my brother.' Well, which brother? And why haven't I had any message from that constable? Where's the man who was to pick up brother Pierre at that theater? Have the whole blasted lot of them gone to sleep and—"

"We mustn't get the wind up about this thing," interposed Fell, as Hadley began to stamp and declaim rather wildly. He turned to Mills. "Go wake up Mr. Drayman and fetch him up here, son," he said.

When the door had closed, Hadley sat down and stared at the floor. "Have you got any concrete suggestions, Fell?" he asked.

"Yes. Later, if you'll permit it, I am going to apply Gross's test."

"Apply what?"

"Gross's test. Don't you remember? We were talking about it tonight. I'm going to collect all burned and half-burned paper in that fireplace, to see whether Gross's test will bring out the writing. Perhaps a line here and there might give me a hint about what was more important to Grimaud than saving his own life."

"And how do you work this trick?"

"You'll see. . . . Yes, Sergeant, what is it?"

Sergeant Betts was not quite so plastered with snow this time. "I've been all over that back garden, sir," he reported. "And the two adjoining ones, and the tops of all the walls. There's no footprint or any kind of mark. But I believe we've caught a fish, Preston and I. As I was coming back through the house, down the stairs comes running a tallish old bloke, plunging away with his hand on the banister rail. He ran over to a clothes closet and banged about as though he wasn't familiar with the place, until he got on his overcoat and hat, and then made for the door. He says his name's Drayman. . . ."

"I've heard his sight isn't too good," said Dr. Fell. "Send him in."

The man who entered was, in his own way, impressive. His long, quiet face was hollowed at the temples; his gray hair grew far back on the skull, giving him a great height of forehead. His bright blue eyes looked gentle and puzzled. Despite his stoop he was still tall. There was nothing of humor in the face, but a great deal of apologetic good nature. He wore a dark overcoat buttoned up to the chin, and he held a hat pressed against his chest.

"I am sorry, gentlemen," he said in a deep voice. "I know I should have come to see you before going over there. But young Mr. Mangan woke me up to tell me what had happened. I felt I had to go and see Grimaud. . . ."

Rampole had a feeling that Drayman was still dull-witted and uncertain from sleep or sleeping drugs. He did not sit down until Hadley asked him to do so.

"Dr. Grimaud is dead," said Hadley.

Drayman shut his eyes and opened them again. "God rest his soul," he said very quietly. "Charles Grimaud was a good friend."

Hadley studied him. "Then you will understand that to tell everything, *everything* you might happen to know, will be the only way to help us catch the murderer of your friend?"

"I— Yes, of course."

"We wish to know something of his past life, Mr. Drayman. You knew him well. Where did you first know him?"

Drayman's long face looked muddled. "In Paris. He took his doctorate at the university in 1905, the same year I . . . the same year I knew him." He shaded his eyes with his hand. "Grimaud was very brilliant. He obtained an associate professorship at Dijon the year afterwards. But a relative died, or something of the sort, and left him well provided for. He—he gave up his work and came to England. Or so I understand. I did not see him again until years afterwards."

"Did you ever know him before 1905?"

"No."

Hadley leaned forward. "Where did you save his life?"

"Save his life? I don't understand."

"You saved his life," Hadley stated, "near the prison of Siebenturmen, in the Carpathian Mountains, when he was escaping. *Didn't you?*"

The other sat upright, his hands clenched. "Did I?" he asked.

"There's no use going on with this. We know everything—even to dates, now that you've supplied them. It would have taken Károly Horváth four years at least to get his doctorate at Paris. We can narrow down the time of his conviction and escape to three years. With that information," said Hadley, "I can cable Bucharest and get full details within twelve hours. You had better tell the truth, you see. I want to know all you know of Károly Horváth— and his two brothers. One of those two brothers killed him. Finally, I'll remind you that withholding information of this kind is a serious offense. Well?"

Drayman remained for a time with his hand shading his eyes. Then he looked up, staring across the room. "Sir, I am perfectly willing to give you any information you wish, if it will help Charles Grimaud. But I don't see the sense of raking up old scandal."

"Not even to find the brother who killed him?"

Drayman made a slight gesture, frowning. "Look here, I can honestly tell you to forget such an idea. He did have two brothers. And they were imprisoned for a political offense. I imagine half the young fire-eaters of the time must have been. . . . Forget the two brothers. They have both been dead a good many years."

It was so quiet in the room that Rampole heard the wheezing breaths of Dr. Fell.

"How do you know that?" Hadley said to Drayman.

"Grimaud told me," said the other. "Besides, all the newspapers from Budapest to Brassó were shouting about it at the time. They died of bubonic plague."

Hadley was suave. "If, of course, you could prove this . . ."

"I can only tell you what I saw myself." He reflected—rather uneasily, Rampole thought. "It was a horrible business. Grimaud and I never spoke of it afterwards. That was agreed. But I haven't forgotten it—any detail of it."

He was silent, tapping his fingers at his temple. Then he went on. "It was in August or September of 1900 . . . or was it 1901? Anyhow, I might begin in the style of a French romance. I might begin, 'Towards dusk of a cool September day in the year 19—, a solitary horseman might have been seen hurrying along a road'— and what a devil of a road!—'in a rugged valley below the Carpathian Mountains.' I was the horseman; it was coming on to rain, and I was trying to reach Tradj before dark." He smiled. "There was a sort of fairy-tale wildness and darkness about those cold forests and gorges. And I myself was at the romantic Byronic age; I even carried a pistol. Anyhow, there I was going along a snaky road in the bleakest part, with a storm blowing up, and I had good cause for having the creeps. Plague had broken out in the whole area, and in the last village I had passed through they had told me it was raging at the salt mines ahead. But I was hoping to meet an English friend of mine, also a tourist, at Tradj. Also I wanted a look at the prison, which got its name after seven white hills, like a low range of mountains, just behind. So I had gone on.

"I knew I must be getting near the prison, for I could see the white hills ahead. But, just as it was getting dark, I came down into a hollow past three graves. They had been freshly dug, but no living person was in sight."

Hadley broke in. "A place," he said, "just like the one in the painting Dr. Grimaud bought from Mr. Burnaby."

"I—I don't know," answered Drayman, startled. "Is it?"

"Didn't you see the picture?"

"Not very well. A general outline—trees, ordinary landscape—"

"And three headstones . . . ?"

"Then I don't know where Burnaby got his inspiration," the other said dully. "God knows *I* never told him. Also there were no headstones over these graves; there were simply three crosses made of sticks.

"But I was telling you. I sat there on my horse, looking at those graves. They looked wild enough, with the greenish black landscape and the white hills beyond. And the next thing I knew my horse reared and nearly threw me. I slued round and, when I looked back, I saw what was wrong with the horse. The mound of one grave was upheaving. There was a cracking noise; something began to twist and wriggle; and a dark-colored thing came groping up out of the mound. It was only a hand moving the fingers—but I don't think I have ever seen anything more horrible. By that time," Drayman went on, "I was thinking of vampires and all the legends of hell. Frankly, the thing scared me silly. I tried to curb the horse with one hand while I got out my revolver. When I looked back again, the thing had climbed clear out of the grave and was coming towards me.

"That, gentlemen, was how I met one of my best friends. The man reached down and seized a spade, which somebody who dug the grave must have forgotten. Still he came on. I yelled in English, 'What do you want?' The man stopped. After a second he answered in English, with an outlandish accent. 'Help,' he said, 'help, milord; don't be afraid,' or something of the sort. The man was not tall, but very powerful; his face was dark and swollen, with little scaly spots which gave it a pinkish look in the twilight. And down came the rain while he was still standing there.

"He stood in the rain, crying out to me, and he said something like, 'Look, milord, I am not dead of plague like those two poor devils,' and pointed at the graves. 'I am not infected at all. See how the rain washes it off. It is my own blood which I have pricked out of my skin.' Then he went on to say that he was not a criminal, but a political offender, escaping from the prison.

"Help him? Naturally I did. I was fired by the idea. He explained to me that he was one of three brothers, students at the University of Klausenburg, who had been arrested in an insurrection for an independent Transylvania. The three of them were in the same cell, and two had died of the pestilence. With the help of the prison doctor, also a convict, he had faked the same symptoms—and feigned death. It wasn't likely that anybody would go close to test the doctor's judgment; the whole prison was mad with fear. They would bury the bodies at some distance from the prison. Most of all, they would do a quick job of nailing the lids. The doctor had smuggled in a pair of nail cutters, which my resurrected friend showed me. A powerful man, if he kept his nerve and didn't use up too much air, could force up the lid with his head enough to wedge the nail cutters into the loose space. Afterwards he could dig up through loose ground.

"His mother, he said, had been French, and he spoke the language perfectly. We decided that he had better make for France, where he could set up a new identity. He had a little money hidden, and there was a girl in his native town—"

"I think we know who the girl was," Hadley said. "For the moment, we can leave Madame Dumont out of this. What then?"

"She could be trusted to bring the money and follow him to Paris," Drayman continued. "It wasn't likely that there would be a hue and cry—in fact, there wasn't any. Even though Grimaud was so frightened that he tore away from that neighborhood before he would even shave or put on a suit of my clothes, we excited no suspicion. There were no compulsory passports for aliens in those days, and he posed on the way out of Hungary as the English friend I had expected to meet at Tradj. Once into France . . . you know the rest. Now, gentlemen!" Drayman drew a shuddering breath, stiffened, and faced them. "You can verify everything—"

"Just one question, Mr Drayman," interjected Dr. Fell. "That prison, now ... was it well or badly managed?"

The question was so quiet, and yet so startling, that Hadley whirled round.

Drayman was puzzled. "I do not know, sir. But I do know it was under fire from a number of officials; they were bitter against the prison authorities for letting the disease get started. By the way, the dead men's names were published; I saw them. And I ask you again, what's the good of raking up old scandals? It's not any particular discredit to Grimaud, but—"

"Yes, that's the point," rumbled Dr. Fell, peering at him curiously. "It's not discreditable at all. Is it anything to make a man bury all traces of his past life?"

"But it might become a discredit to Ernestine Dumont," said Drayman, raising his voice. "And what about Grimaud's daughter? All this digging into the mess rests on some wild guess that one or both of his brothers might be alive. They're dead, and the dead don't get out of their graves. May I ask where you got such a notion as that one of Grimaud's brothers killed him?"

"From Grimaud himself," said Hadley. "He said that the murderer was his brother."

For a second Rampole thought Drayman had not understood. Then the man shakily got up from his chair, and as though he could not breathe he fumbled to open his coat.

"But I tell you it's fantastic! Are you implying that this mountebank who threatened him was one of his brothers? I don't understand." Drayman lifted his shoulders. "Was there anything else you wished to ask me?"

"How did you spend the evening?"

"I was asleep. I— You see, there are pains. Behind my eyeballs. I had them so badly at dinner that instead of going out—I was to go to a concert—I took a sleeping tablet and lay down. Unfortunately, I don't remember anything after about half past seven."

Hadley was studying his open overcoat, keeping very quiet, but with a dangerous expression like a man about to pounce.

"I see. Did you undress when you went to bed, Mr. Drayman?"

"I beg your— Undress? No. I took off my shoes. Why?"

"Did you leave your room at any time?"

"No."

"Then how did you get that blood on your jacket? . . . Yes, that's it. Get up! Now take off your overcoat."

Standing uncertainly and pulling off the overcoat, Drayman moved his hand slowly across his own chest. He was wearing a light gray suit, against which the stain splashed vividly. It ran from the left side of the jacket, over the chest, and down across the right pocket. His fingers found it and stopped.

"I don't know what it is," he muttered. "But it can't be blood!"

"We shall have to see," Hadley said. "Take off the jacket, please. I'm afraid I must ask you to leave it with us." He watched while Drayman with unsteady fingers took off the jacket and handed it to him.

"Betts! Preston!" Hadley called. "Betts, get this jacket to the pathologist for analysis of this stain. Preston, go with Mr. Drayman and have a look round his room. . . . Mr. Drayman, I'm going to ask you to come down to the Yard in the morning. That's all."

Drayman blundered out, trailing the overcoat behind him.

The bleak room was quiet. Hadley shook his head. "It's got me, Fell," he admitted. "I don't know whether I'm coming or going."

"When I gather up those papers from the fireplace," grunted Dr. Fell, "I'm going home to think. Because what I think now—"

"Yes?"

"Is plain horrible." With a gust of energy Dr. Fell surged up out of the chair and jammed his shovel hat down over his eyes. "You'll have to cable for the real truth. Ha! Yes. But it's the story about the three coffins I don't believe—although Drayman may believe it, God knows! Unless our whole theory is blown to blazes, we've got to assume that the two Horváth brothers aren't dead. Hey?"

"The question being . . ."

"What happened to them. Yes. What I think might have happened is based on the assumption that Drayman believes he's telling the truth. First point! I don't believe for a second that those brothers were sent to prison for a political offense. Grimaud, with his 'little money hidden,' escapes from prison. He lies low for five years and then suddenly 'inherits' a substantial fortune under an entirely different name. He slides out of France to enjoy it without comment. Second point, supporting! Where's the dangerous secret in Grimaud's life, if all this is true? Most people would consider that Monte Cristo escape as merely romantic."

"You mean—"

"I mean," said Dr. Fell in a quiet voice, "Grimaud was alive when he was nailed up in his coffin. Suppose the other two were alive, too? Suppose all three deaths were faked as Grimaud's was faked? Suppose there were two living people in those other coffins? But they couldn't come out . . . because Grimaud had the nail cutters. Once he got out, it would have been easy for him to let the others out, as they had arranged. But he decided to let them lie buried, because then there would be nobody to share the money that all three had stolen. A brilliant crime, you see. Brilliant."

Hadley muttered something, his face rather wild as he got up.

"Oh, I know it's a black business!" rumbled Dr. Fell. "But it's the only thing that will explain this case, and why a man *would* be hounded if those brothers ever climbed out of their graves. Why was Grimaud so anxious to rush Drayman away from that spot without even getting out of his convict garb? Well, those graves were shallow. If, as time went on, the brothers found themselves choking to death . . . and still nobody had let them out . . . they might begin to shriek and pound in their coffins."

Hadley got out a handkerchief and mopped his face.

"Would any swine . . ." he said in an incredulous voice. "No, Fell. It's all imagination. Besides, in that case they wouldn't have climbed up out of their graves. They'd be dead."

"Would they?" said Dr. Fell. "Don't forget the spade that some poor devil left behind when he'd dug the grave. Prisons don't permit *that* sort of negligence. They would send back after it. Man, I can see it in every detail, even if I haven't proof to support it! Back come a couple of warders looking for that spade. They see or hear what Grimaud was afraid Drayman would see or hear. They dig up the coffins; and the two brothers are rolled out, fainting and bloody, but alive."

"And no hue and cry after Grimaud? Why, they'd have torn Hungary apart looking for the man who had escaped and—"

"Yes. I thought of that, too, and asked about it. The prison authorities would have done just that . . . if they weren't being so bitterly attacked that their heads were in danger at the time. What do you think the attackers would have said if it became known that, through carelessness, they allowed a thing like that to happen? Much better to shove those two brothers into close confinement and keep quiet about the third."

"It's all theory," said Hadley, after a pause. "But, if it's true, I could come close to believing in evil spirits. God knows Grimaud got what he deserved. And we've got to go on trying to find his murderer just the same."

"You talk of evil spirits," said Dr. Fell. "And I tell you that in some way I can't fathom there's a worse evil spirit than Grimaud; and that's X, that's the hollow man, that's brother Henri." He pointed with his stick. "Why? Why does Pierre Fley admit he fears him? It would be reasonable for Grimaud to fear his enemy; but why does Fley even fear his brother and his ally against the common antagonist?"

Hadley buttoned up his coat. "*You* go home if you like," he said. "We've finished here. But I'm going after Fley. Whoever the other brother is, Fley knows. And he's going to lead us to the murderer. Ready?"

They did not learn it until the next morning; but Fley, in fact, was already dead, shot down with the same pistol that had killed Grimaud. And the murderer was invisible before the eyes of witnesses, and still he had left no footprint in the snow.

VI: The Murder by Magic

WHEN Dr. Fell hammered on the door at nine o'clock next morning, both his guests were drowsy. Rampole had gotten very little sleep the night before. When he and the doctor returned at half past one, Dorothy had been eager to hear all the details, and her husband was not at all unwilling to tell them. They equipped themselves with cigarettes and beer and retired to their room, where they had talked for hours.

Rampole struggled out of bed when Dr. Fell knocked; he dressed hastily and stumbled downstairs. In the library a roaring fire had been lighted, and breakfast was set out in the embrasure of the bay window. It was a leaden day, the sky already moving with snow. Dr. Fell, fully dressed, sat at the table and stared at a newspaper.

"Brother Henri . . ." he rumbled, and struck the paper. "Oh, yes. He's at it again. Hadley just phoned and he'll be here any minute. If we thought we had a hard problem on our hands last night— look at *this* one! It's crowded Grimaud's murder clean off the front page. Fortunately, they haven't spotted the connection be- tween 'em, or else Hadley's given 'em the word to keep off. Here!"

Rampole, as coffee was poured, saw the headlines. MAGICIAN MURDERED BY MAGIC! said one. RIDDLE OF CAGLIOSTRO STREET.

"Cagliostro Street?" the American said. "Where in the name of sanity is Cagliostro Street?"

"You'd never hear of it ordinarily," grunted Dr. Fell. "It's one of those streets hidden behind streets, and not more than three min- utes' walk from Grimaud's house—a little cul-de-sac on the other side of Russell Square. It has some tradesmen's shops overflow- ing from Lamb's Conduit Street, and the rest lodging houses. . . . Brother Henri left Grimaud's place after the shooting, walked over there, hung about, and then completed the work."

Rampole ran his eye down the story.

The body of the man found murdered last night in Cagliostro Street, W.C. 1, has been identified as that of Pierre Fley, a French conjurer and illusionist. Although he had been performing for some months at a music hall in Commercial Road, E.C., he took lodgings two weeks ago in Cagliostro Street. About half past ten last night, he was found shot to death under circumstances which seem to indicate that a magician was murdered by magic. Nothing was

seen and no trace left, three witnesses testify, although they all distinctly heard a voice say, "The second bullet is for you."

Cagliostro Street is two hundred yards long and ends in a blank brick wall. A few night-lights were burning. At the beginning of the street there are a few shops, closed at that time, and the pavements were swept in front of them. But, beginning some twenty yards on, there was unbroken snow on the pavement and the street.

Mr. Jesse Short and Mr. R. G. Blackwin, Birmingham visitors to London, were on their way to visit a friend with lodgings near the end of the street. They were walking on the right-hand pavement, and had their backs to the mouth of the street. Mr. Blackwin, who was turning round to make sure of the numbers on the doors, noticed a man walking some distance behind them. This man, who was tall and wore a slouch hat, was walking slowly and rather nervously in the middle of the street, looking round him. At the same time, Police Constable Henry Withers—whose beat was along Lamb's Conduit Street—reached the entrance to Cagliostro Street. And in the space of three or four seconds the thing happened.

Mr. Short and Mr. Blackwin heard a scream behind them. They then heard someone distinctly say, "The second bullet is for you," and a laugh followed by a muffled pistol shot. As they whirled round, the man behind staggered, screamed again, and pitched forward on his face.

The street, they could see, was absolutely empty from end to end. Moreover, the man was walking in the middle of it, and both state that there were no footprints in the snow but his own. This is confirmed by P. C. Withers, who came running from the mouth of the street. In the light from a jeweler's window, they could see the victim lying face downward, his arms spread out, and blood jetting from a bullet hole under his left shoulder blade. The weapon—a long-barreled .38 Colt revolver, of a pattern thirty years out of date—had been thrown away some ten feet behind.

The witnesses saw that the man was still breathing, and carried him to the office of Dr. M. R. Jenkins near the end of the street, while the constable made certain there were no footprints. The victim died, without speaking, not long afterwards.

Then occurred the most startling disclosures. The man's overcoat round the wound was burned and singed black, showing that the weapon must have been pressed against his back or held only a few inches away. But Dr. Jenkins gave it as his opinion—later confirmed by the police—that suicide was not possible. No man, he stated, could have held any pistol in such a way as to shoot himself through the back at that angle, and more especially with the long-barreled weapon which was used. It was murder, but an incredible murder. If the man had been shot from some distance away, from a window or door, the absence of a murderer and even the absence of footprints would mean nothing. But he was shot by someone who stood beside him, spoke to him, and vanished.

No papers or marks of identification could be found in the man's clothes. After some delay he was sent to the mortuary. . . .

"But what about the officer Hadley sent round to pick Fley up?" Rampole asked.

"The whole hullabaloo was over by the time he got there. He ran into the policeman, Hadley says, when Withers was still making inquiries from door to door. Then he put two and two together. Meantime, the man Hadley had sent to the music hall also in quest of Fley had phoned through that Fley wasn't there. Fley had told the theater manager he had no intention of doing his turn that night, and had walked out. . . . Well, to identify the body at the mortuary they got hold of Fley's landlord in Cagliostro Street, and also somebody from the music hall, an Irishman with an Italian name. Harrumph, yes. It was Fley, and he's dead. Bah!"

"And this story," cried Rampole, "is actually true?"

He was answered by Hadley, who stamped in belligerently. "It's true, right enough," he said. "I let the papers splash it out so we could broadcast an appeal for information from anybody who knew Pierre Fley or his damned brother Henri. Fell, that nickname you gave him sticks in my head! At least we soon ought to know what his real name is. I've cabled Bucharest."

"For God's sake go easy!" urged Dr. Fell. "I suppose you've been at it all night? Sit down and console the inner man."

Hadley said he wanted nothing to eat. But, after he had finished two helpings of bacon and eggs and drunk several cups of coffee, he mellowed into a more normal mood. "Now, then! Let's begin," he said, as he took papers from his briefcase, "by checking over this newspaper account point by point. First, as to these chaps Black-win and Short. We wired Birmingham and found that they're prosperous, sound people, good witnesses in a thing like this. The constable, Withers, is thoroughly reliable. I also had a brief look at the street. It's no Piccadilly Circus for illumination, but at least it's not dark enough for any man in his five wits to be mis-taken about what he saw. As to footprints, if Withers swears there weren't any, I'll take his word for it.

"Now, about the weapon. Fley was shot with a bullet from that Colt .38, and so was Grimaud. There were two exploded cartridge cases in the magazine. The gun is so old that we haven't a ghost of a chance of being able to trace it."

Dr. Fell grunted. "Well. Did you trace Fley's movements?"

"Yes," said Hadley. "My officer talked to both the theater mana-ger and an acrobat named O'Rourke, who was friendly with Fley and identified the body later.

"Saturday, naturally, is the big night down Limehouse way. Fley's first night turn was to begin at eight fifteen. About five min-utes before then, O'Rourke—who had broken his wrist and couldn't go on—sneaked down into the cellar for a smoke. They have a coal furnace there."

Hadley unfolded a closely written sheet of paper. "Here is what O'Rourke said, just as Somers took it down."

The minute I got downstairs, I heard a noise like somebody smashing kindling wood. Then I did get a jump. The furnace door was open, and there was old Loony with a hatchet, busting hell out of the few properties he owned and shoving them in the fire. I said, "For cat's sake, Loony, what are you doing?" He said, in that queer way of his, "I am destroying my equipment, Signor Pagliacci. My work is finished; I shall not need them any longer"—and, zingo! In went his faked ropes and the hollow bamboo rods for his cabinet. I said, "Loony, pull yourself together. You go on in a few minutes, and you're not even dressed." He said, "Didn't I tell you? I am going to see my brother. He will do something that will settle an old affair for both of us."

Well, he walked over to the stairs and then turned round. His face had a queer creepy look. He said, "In case anything happens to me after he has done the business, you will find my brother in the same street where I myself live. That is not where he really resides, but he has taken a room there." Then he lifts his hat courteously and says, "Good night, signor. I am going back to my grave." And up the stairs this lunatic walks without another word.

Hadley folded up the sheet and replaced it in his briefcase.

"Yes, he was a good showman," said Dr. Fell. "What then?"

"The question occurred to me," Hadley went on, "where was Fley *going* when he was shot? Not to his own room. He lived at the beginning of the street, and had gone past his lodging. When he was shot he was a little over halfway down the street. I've sent Somers to turn out every house past the middle, looking for *any* new or suspicious or otherwise noticeable lodger."

Dr. Fell, who had been slouched far down in the big chair, hoisted himself up. "It's *wrong*! I tell you it's all wrong!" he roared. "It's no matter of hocus-pocus within four walls. There's a street. There's a man walking along it in the snow. Scream, words, bang! Witnesses turn, and murderer gone. Where? Did the pistol come flying through the air like a thrown knife, explode against Fley's back, and spin away?"

"Rubbish!"

"I know it's rubbish. But I still ask the question." Dr. Fell nodded. He removed his eyeglasses and pressed a hand over his eyes. "I say, how does this new development affect the Russell Square group? I mean, can't we now eliminate a few of those? Even if they were telling us lies, they still weren't out hurling Colt revolvers in the middle of Cagliostro Street."

"We could eliminate one or two—if the Cagliostro Street business had occurred a little later, or even a little earlier. It didn't. Fley was shot at ten twenty-five—about fifteen minutes after Grimaud. Brother Henri took no chances; he moved quickly. You know, Fell, I'm learning new wrinkles in crime. If you want to commit a couple of shrewd murders, don't commit one and then hang about waiting for the dramatic moment to pull off the other. Hit once—

and then hit again instantly, while the watchers are still so muddled by the first that nobody, including the police, can definitely remember who was where at a given time. Can we?"

"Now, now," growled Dr. Fell, to conceal the fact that he couldn't. "It ought to be easy to work out a timetable. We arrived at Grimaud's . . . when?"

Hadley was jotting on a slip of paper. "Just as Mangan jumped out the window; say two minutes after the shot, or ten twelve. We ran upstairs, found the door locked, got pliers, and opened the door. Three minutes more. Then Mangan phoned and the ambulance was round very quickly—probably in five minutes. That's ten twenty. And what about the next five minutes, the time just before the second murder? Rosette Grimaud, alone, rode over in the ambulance with her father. Mangan, alone, was downstairs doing some telephoning for me. Nobody saw Drayman all this time and for a long while afterwards. As to Mills and the Dumont woman—h'm. Well, yes; it does clear them. Mills was talking to us until at least ten thirty, and Madame Dumont joined him very shortly; they both stayed with us for a while. That tears it."

Dr. Fell chuckled. "In fact," he said reflectively, "we know exactly what we did before. The only people it clears are the ones we were sure were innocent, who had to be telling the truth. By the way, Hadley, did you get anything last night out of searching Drayman's room? And what about that blood?"

"Oh, it's human blood, right enough, but there was nothing in Drayman's room that gave a clue to it—or to anything else. There were some pasteboard masks, yes. But they were elaborate affairs with whiskers and goggle eyes; nothing in plain pink—"

He was interrupted by a maidservant. "There's a gentleman downstairs, sir," she said to Dr. Fell, "who wants to see either you or the superintendent. A Mr. Anthony Pettis, sir."

DR. FELL, rumbling and chuckling and spilling ashes from his pipe, surged up cordially to greet the visitor. Mr. Pettis bowed to each of them.

"You must excuse me, gentlemen, for intruding," he said. "But I understand you were looking for me last night, so I thought I'd better hunt you out. They gave me this address at Scotland Yard."

Dr. Fell was already stripping off his guest's overcoat and showing him into a chair. Mr. Pettis grinned. He was a small, neat, starched man with shrewd prominent eyes, a shiny bald head, and a booming voice. When he spoke he had a trick of sitting forward in his chair and clasping his hands.

"It's a bad business about Grimaud," he said, and hestitated. "Naturally, I wish to do everything I can to help."

Dr. Fell introduced everybody. "I've been wanting to meet you for some time; we've written a few things on the same lines. What'll you drink? Whisky? Brandy and soda?"

"It's rather early," said Pettis. "Still, if you insist—thanks! I'm familiar with your book on the supernatural in English fiction, but I don't agree with you that a ghost in a story should always be malignant. . . ."

"Of course it should always be malignant. The more malignant," thundered Dr. Fell, "the better. Sir, I say now—"

"Easy on, will you?" demanded Hadley. "It's Mr. Pettis who wants to do the talking." When he saw Dr. Fell's puffings subside into a grin, he went on smoothly. "First, Mr. Pettis, I must ask you to give an account of your movements last night. Especially between, say, nine thirty and ten thirty?"

Pettis put down his glass. "Then you mean, Mr. Hadley—after all, I *am* under suspicion?"

"Grimaud's caller said he was you. Didn't you know that?"

"Said he was me?" cried Pettis. "What do you mean?" He stared as Hadley explained.

"Therefore, if you'll disprove it by giving an account of your movements last night . . ." Hadley took out his notebook.

"I went to the theater," said Pettis, troubled. "To His Majesty's Theatre. I hope I can establish that; I went alone."

"And after the theater? What time did you get out?"

"Near enough to eleven. I was restless. I thought I might drop in on Grimaud and have a drink with him. Well, Mills told me what had happened. I asked to see you, or whoever was in charge. I waited a long time, and then I was informed that Superintendent Hadley would see me in the morning. So I went to the hospital to see how Grimaud was getting on. I got there just as he died. Now, Mr. Hadley, I know this is a terrible business, but I will swear to you—"

"Just a minute! Before we go on, I understand that whoever imitated you used all your tricks of address, and so on, correctly? Good! Then who would you suspect of being able to do that?"

"Or wanting to do it," the other said sharply. Putting his fingertips together, he stared out of the long windows. "Don't think I'm trying to evade your question, Mr. Hadley," he went on. "Frankly, I can't think of anybody. But this puzzle bothers me apart from the danger, in a way, to myself. For instance, let's suppose, for the sake of argument, that I am the murderer."

He looked mockingly at Hadley, who had straightened up.

"Hold on! I am not the murderer, but let's suppose it. I go to kill Grimaud in some outlandish disguise. Then is it likely that I would blatantly sing out my real name to those young people? That's the first view. But the very shrewd investigator would answer, 'Yes, a clever murderer might do just that. It would be the most effective way of bamboozling all the people who had jumped to the first conclusion. He changed his voice a very little, just enough so that people would remember it afterwards. He spoke as Pettis because he wanted people to think it *wasn't* Pettis.' Had you thought of that?"

"Oh yes," said Dr. Fell. "It was the first thing I did think of."

Pettis nodded. "Then you will have thought of the answer to that, which clears me either way. If I were to do a thing like that, it isn't my voice I should have altered slightly. If the hearers accepted it to begin with, they might not later have the doubts I wanted them to have. But," he said, "I should have made one slip in my speech. I should have said something obviously not like myself, which later they would have remembered. And this the visitor didn't do. His imitation was too thorough, which seems to excuse me. Whether you take the forthright view or the subtle one, I can plead not guilty."

Hadley laughed, and his gaze traveled from Pettis to Dr. Fell. "You two are birds of a feather," he said. "I like these gyrations. But I'll tell you from practical experience, Mr. Pettis, that a criminal who tried anything like that would find himself in the soup. The police would take the forthright view—and hang him."

"As you would hang me," said Pettis, "if you could find contributory evidence?"

"Exactly."

"Well—er—that's frank, anyhow," said Pettis. "Er—shall I go on?"

"Go on, certainly," urged the superintendent affably. "We can get ideas even from a clever man."

Whether or not that was a deliberate sting, it had a result nobody expected. Pettis smiled.

"Yes, I think you can," he agreed. "Even ideas you should have had yourselves. Let me take one instance. You—or somebody—got himself quoted at some length in all the papers this morning, about Grimaud's murder. You showed how the murderer was careful to ensure unbroken snow for his vanishing trick. He could be sure that it would snow last night, lay all his plans accordingly, and gamble on waiting until the snow stopped for the working of his scheme. Is that correct?"

"I said something of the sort, yes. What of it?"

"Then I think you should have remembered," Pettis answered, "yesterday's weather forecast said there would be no snow at all."

"Well done!" boomed Dr. Fell. He blinked at Pettis. "I never thought of it. Hadley, this changes things altogether! This—"

"Yes," said Hadley. "It does seem to alter matters. Blast it! Any more ideas, Pettis?"

"That's all, I'm afraid. . . . As to why someone imitated my voice, the only reason I can think of is that I'm the only one of the group who has no definite orbit on Saturday night and might not be able to prove an alibi. . . . Any good mimic could have pulled it off; still, who knew just how I addressed those people?"

"What about the circle at the Warwick Tavern? There were others besides the ones we've heard about, weren't there?"

"Oh, yes. There were two other irregulars. But I can't see either as a candidate. There's old Mornington, who has a post at the museum; he's got a cracked tenor that would never pass for me. There's Swayle, but I believe he was speaking on the wireless last night, about ant life or something. . . ."

"Speaking at what time?"

"Nine forty-five, I believe. Besides, neither of them ever visited Grimaud's house. Burnaby and I were his only close friends. But I didn't do it, and Burnaby was playing cards."

"I suppose Mr. Burnaby really was playing cards?"

"I'll give you odds he was. A man would have to be an outstanding fathead to commit a murder on the one night when his absence from a certain group would surely be noticed."

This impressed the superintendent more than anything Pettis had yet said. "You know," he said, scowling, "that Burnaby painted the picture which Dr. Grimaud bought to defend himself?"

"To defend himself? How? From what?"

"We don't know. I was hoping you might be able to explain it." Hadley studied him. "Do you know how Burnaby came to paint that picture, or when he did it?"

"I think he did it a year or two ago. I remember asking him what it was intended to represent. He said, 'An imaginative conception of something I never saw.' The thing had been lying about the studio, collecting dust, for so long that I was surprised when Grimaud came charging in on Friday and asked for it."

Hadley leaned forward. "You were there, then?"

"At the studio? Yes. I'd dropped in for some reason or other—I forget what. Grimaud came stumping in and said, with that machine-gun snap of his, 'Burnaby, where's your salt-mountain picture? I want it. What's your price?' Burnaby said, 'The thing's yours, man, if you want it; take it.' Grimaud said, 'No, I have a use for it and I insist on buying it.' Well, when Burnaby named some fool price like ten shillings, Grimaud quite solemnly wrote a check for ten shillings. He took the picture downstairs, and I got him a cab to take it away in."

"Was it wrapped up?" asked Dr. Fell sharply.

Pettis regarded him curiously. "I wonder why you ask that?"

390

he said. "I was just going to mention the fuss Grimaud made about wrapping it. He insisted on going downstairs and getting yards of brown paper from somebody's shop."

"You don't know whether Grimaud went straight home?"

"No. He may have gone to have it framed."

Dr. Fell sat back with a grunt and let the subject go without more questions. Hadley kept on for some time, but nothing of importance was elicited, so far as Rampole could see. At last Pettis rose to go just as Big Ben was striking ten. "By the way, gentlemen," he said, "I wonder if you'd all have lunch with me on a dreary Sunday? I have rooms at the Imperial, just the other side of Russell Square. You're investigating in that neighborhood; besides, if Dr. Fell feels inclined to discuss ghost stories—"

He smiled. The doctor cut in to accept before Hadley could refuse, and Pettis left. Afterwards they all looked at each other.

"Well?" growled Hadley. "Straightforward enough, it seemed to me. Of course we'll check it up. The point is, why should *any* of them commit a crime on the one night when absence would be bound to be noticed?"

"And the weather forecast said it wouldn't snow," said Dr. Fell. "Hadley, that shoots everything to blazes! I don't see . . . Cagliostro Street! Let's go on to Cagliostro Street. Anywhere is better than this darkness."

Fuming, he stumped over after his cloak and shovel hat.

VII: The Secret Flat

TOWARDS the Guilford Street end of Lamb's Conduit Street on the west side, the entrance to Cagliostro Street is tucked between a stationer's and a butcher's. It looks so much like an alley that you would miss it if you were not watching for the sign. Past these two buildings, it suddenly widens to an unexpected breadth and runs straight for two hundred yards to a blank brick wall at the end.

On this gray winter Sunday the street was deserted to the point of ghostliness. It was with an eerie feeling that Rampole stood with Hadley and Dr. Fell at the entrance, staring down it. An overflow of shops from Lamb's Conduit Street stretched only a little way on either side. They were all shuttered, or had their windows covered with a steel fretwork. Beyond, there were two rows of flat four-story houses in dark red brick, with window frames in white or yellow. The snow had melted to patches of gray slush, despite a sharp wind that was swooping through the entrance.

"Cheerful," grunted Dr. Fell. He lumbered forward. "Now, before we attract attention, show me where Fley was when he was hit. And where did he live, by the way?"

Hadley pointed at a tobacconist's. "Up over that place; just at the beginning of the street. We'll go up presently. Now, come along and get roughly the middle point of the street. . . ." He went ahead, pacing. "The swept pavements and the marked street ended somewhere about here; say, more or less, a hundred and fifty feet. Then unmarked snow. A distance beyond that, nearer to another hundred and fifty . . . *here.*" He stopped and turned round. "Halfway up, center of the roadway. You can see how broad the road is; walking there, he was thirty feet from any house on *either* side. If he'd been walking on the pavement, we might have constructed some wild theory of a person leaning out a window, with the gun fastened to a pole—"

"Nonsense!"

"All right, nonsense," said Hadley with violence. "But if there was no hanky-panky like that, what *was* there? Now, stay where you are and keep facing the same direction." He paced again to a point farther on and then moved over to the right-hand pavement. "Here's where Blackwin and Short were when they heard the scream. You're walking along there in the middle of the street. I'm ahead of you. I whirl round—so. How far am I from you now?"

Rampole, who had drawn off from both of them, saw Dr. Fell standing big and alone in the middle of an empty rectangle.

"Why, those two chaps," said the doctor, pushing back his shovel hat, "were not much more than thirty feet ahead! Hadley, he was in the middle of a snow desert. Yet they whirl round when they hear the shot . . . h'm . . . h'mf. . . ."

"Exactly. Next, as to lights. You're taking the part of Fley. On your right—a little ahead and just beyond the door of Number Eighteen—you see a streetlamp. Some distance behind, also on the right, you see that jeweler's window? Right. There was a light burning in that, in the show window. Now, can you explain to me how two people, standing here, could possibly be mistaken about whether they saw anybody near Fley?"

Dr. Fell's voice rose and echoed. His cloak flapped, and his eyes danced wildly. "Jeweler's—" he repeated. "Jeweler's! And a light in it. . . ." He went over to look owlishly into the window. Inside were displayed trays of cheap rings and watches, and in the middle a big round-hooded German clock, with moving eyes in its sun of a face, which began to tinkle eleven. Dr. Fell stared at the moving eyes, which had an unpleasant effect of seeming to watch with idiot amusement the place where a man had been killed. It lent a touch of the horrible to Cagliostro Street. Then Dr. Fell stumped back to the middle of the street.

"But that," he said—obstinately, as though he were continuing an argument—"that is on the right-hand side of the street. And Fley was shot through the back from the *left* side. If we assume that . . . I don't know! Even granting that the murderer could walk on snow without leaving a footprint, can we at least decide where he came from?"

"He came from here," said a voice.

The rising of the wind seemed to whirl the words about them, and for one second in that gusty half-light Rampole had a mad vision of flying things, of hearing words from an invisible man. Then he turned and, with a drop of anticlimax, saw the explanation. A thickset young man with a reddish face and a bowler pulled down on his forehead was coming down the steps from the door of Number 18. He grinned as he saluted Hadley.

"I'm Somers, sir. Remember, you asked me to find out where the dead one, the Frenchie, was going when he was killed? And to find out what landlady had any sort of rum lodger that might be the man we're looking for? . . . Well, I've found out about the rum lodger. He came from *here*."

Hadley's eyes traveled up to the doorway, where another figure stood hesitating. Somers followed the glance.

"That's Mr. O'Rourke, sir," he said. "Chap from the music hall, you know, who identified the Frenchie last night. He's been giving me a bit of help this morning."

The figure detached itself from the gloom and came down the steps. He looked thin despite his heavy overcoat; thin and powerful. In looks he was swarthily reminiscent of the Italian, an effect that was heightened by a luxuriant black mustache with waxed ends. Beneath this a large curved pipe hung from one corner of his mouth. "O'Rourke's the name, yes," he said. "I hope you don't mind my butting in, gents. You see, I knew old Loony. . . . If I'd had any sense, I'd have followed him last night—"

"Yes. If you'll come along, sir," Somers said to Hadley, "I've got something important to show you. The landlady'll tell you about the lodger. But first I'd like you to see his rooms."

"What's in his rooms?"

"Well, sir, blood, for one thing," replied Somers. "And also a queer sort of rope. . . ." He assumed an expression of satisfaction as he saw Hadley's face. "You'll be interested in that rope, and in other things. The fellow's a burglar of some sort, by the look of his outfit. Miss Hake—that's the landlady—says he's had the rooms for some time, but he's only used them one or two times since—"

"Come *on*," said Hadley.

Somers led them into a gloomy hallway and up three flights of stairs. The house was narrow, and had one furnished flat on each floor. The door of the top floor—close up near a ladder which led to the roof—stood open. Somers took them through it into a darkish passage with three doors.

"In here first, sir," he said. "It's the bathroom. I had to put a shilling in the electric meter to get light."

He pressed a switch. The bathroom was a dingy converted storeroom, with glazed paper on the wall in imitation of tile, worn oilcloth on the floor, a top-heavy hot-water heater, and a wavy mirror hung over a washstand with bowl and pitcher. "Effort made to clean the place up, you see, sir," Somers went on. "But you'll still see reddish traces in the bath; that was where he washed his hands. And over behind this clothes hamper"—he swung the hamper to one side and produced a still-damp face-cloth with patches of dull pink—"he sponged his clothes with that."

"Well done," said Hadley softly. "The other rooms, now."

Somebody's personality permeated those rooms like the sickly yellow of the electric lights. Heavy curtains were drawn across the windows in the front room. Under a light on a broad table lay an assortment of little steel tools with rounded heads and curved ends (Hadley said, "Lockpicks, eh?"), an assortment of detached locks, and a sheaf of notes. There were a microscope, a box fitted with glass slides, a bench of chemicals with labeled test tubes in a rack, a wall of books, and in one corner a small iron safe.

"If he's a burglar," said the superintendent, "he's the most modern and scientific burglar I've seen. I didn't know this trick was known in England. Recognize it, Fell?"

"There's a big hole cut right out of the iron in the top, sir," put in Somers. "If he used a blowpipe, it's the neatest job I ever saw."

"It's easier than that," said Hadley. "This is the Krupp preparation. I'm not strong on chemistry, but I think this is powdered aluminum and ferrous oxide. You mix the powder on top of the safe, you add—what is it?—powdered magnesium, and set a match to it. It doesn't explode. It simply generates heat and melts a hole straight through the metal. . . . See that metal tube on the table? It's a detectascope, or what they call a fisheye lens. You can put it to a hole in the wall and see everything that's going on in the next room. What do you think of this, Fell?"

"Yes, yes," said the doctor, with a vacant stare. "But where's that rope? I'm interested in that rope."

"Other room, sir. Back room," said Somers. "It's got up in rather grand style, like an Eastern . . . you know."

Presumably he meant harem. There was a spurious Turkish floridity about the rich-colored couches, hangings, tassels, and gimcracks. Hadley flung back the curtains. Winter daylight intruded, making sickly the illusion. They looked out on the backs of the houses along Guilford Street and on an alley winding up towards the back of the Children's Hospital. But Hadley did not consider that for long. He pounced on the coil of rope that lay across a divan.

It was thin but very strong, knotted at intervals of one foot, and with a curious device hooked to one end. This looked like a black rubber cup, something larger than a coffee cup.

"Wow!" said Dr. Fell. "Look here, is that—"

Hadley nodded. "I've heard of them, but I never saw one before. See here! It's a suction cup."

"You mean," said Rampole, "a burglar could force that thing against a wall, and its pressure would hold him on the rope?"

Hadley hesitated. "That's how they *say* it works. Of course—"

O'Rourke, who had been eyeing the rope, cleared his throat for attention. "Look, gents," he said, "I don't want to butt in, but I think that's all bunk."

Hadley swung round. "How so?"

"I'll make you a little bet," said the other, "that this thing belonged to Loony Fley. Give it to me for a second and I'll see."

He took the rope and ran his fingers gently along it until he reached the middle. Then he nodded with satisfaction. He twirled his fingers and suddenly held his hands apart with the air of a conjurer. The rope came in two pieces.

"Uh-huh. See this? The rope's tapped. It's fitted with a screw in one side and a thread in the other, and you can twist it together like a screw in wood. You can't see the joint; you can examine the rope all you like, and yet it won't come apart under any pressure. Get the idea? Members of the audience tie the illusionist up tight in his cabinet. This joint of the rope goes across his hands. The watchers outside can hold the ends of the rope tight to make sure he don't try to get out of it. See? But he unscrews the thing with his teeth, holds the rope taut with his knees, and all kinds of hell start to pop inside the cabinet. Wonder! Mystification! Greatest show on earth!" O'Rourke regarded them amiably. "Yes. That was one of Loony's ropes."

"I don't doubt that," said Hadley. "But what about the suction cup?"

"You've heard of the Indian rope trick? Fakir throws a rope up in the air; boy climbs up it—whoosh! He disappears. Loony was trying to dope out a means of doing it. I think that suction cup was to catch the rope somewhere when it was thrown up."

"And somebody was to climb up," said Hadley in a heavy voice. "Climb up, and disappear?"

"We-el, a kid— But that thing won't support a man's weight. Look, gents! I'd try it for you, and swing out the window, only I don't want to break my neck; and besides, my wrist is out of kilter."

"I think we've still got enough evidence," said Hadley. "You say this fellow's bolted, Somers? Any description of him?"

Somers nodded. "We shouldn't have difficulty pulling him in, sir. He goes under the name of Jerome Burnaby; he's got a pretty distinctive appearance—and he has a clubfoot."

THE next sound was the vast, dust-shaking noise of Dr. Fell's mirth. Sitting down on a red-and-yellow divan, which sagged alarmingly, he chortled and pounded his stick on the floor.

"Stung!" said Dr. Fell. "Stung, me bonny boys! Heh-heh-heh. Bang goes the ghost. Bang goes the evidence. Oh, my eye!"

"What do you mean, stung?" demanded Hadley. "Doesn't this pretty well convince you that Burnaby's guilty?"

"It convinces me absolutely that he's innocent," said Dr. Fell. "I was afraid we should find just this sort of thing when we saw the other room. It was a little too good to be true."

"If you would mind explaining . . . ?"

"Not at all," said the doctor affably. "Hadley, did you ever know of any burglar, any criminal at all, who ever had his hideaway arranged with such atmospheric effect? With the lockpicks on the table, the brooding microscope, the sinister chemicals, and so on? The real criminal takes care to have his haunt looking more respectable than a churchwarden's. This display doesn't even remind me of somebody playing at being a burglar. But if you'll think for a second, you'll see what it does remind you of, out of a hundred stories and films. It's like somebody playing detective."

Hadley rubbed his chin thoughtfully and peered round.

"When you were a kid," pursued Dr. Fell, "didn't you ever play the Great Detective, and wish for a secret lair in some secret street where you could pursue your deadly studies? Didn't somebody say Burnaby was a fierce amateur criminologist? Maybe he's writing a book. Anyhow, he has done, in a sophisticated way, just what a lot of other grown-up children have wished to do. He's created an alter ego."

"Stop a bit," said Hadley. "I admit there's an unconvincing look about the place, yes. I admit it has a movieish appearance. But this rope is Fley's, remember. And what about the blood?"

Dr. Fell nodded. "Hm'f, yes. Don't misunderstand. I don't say these rooms mightn't play a part in the business; I'm only warning you not to believe too much in Burnaby's evil double life."

"We'll soon find out about that," growled Hadley. "Somers! Go over to Mr. Jerome Burnaby's other flat. Thirteen A Bloomsbury Square. Bring him here; but don't ask or answer any questions. And when you go downstairs, send up that landlady."

He stalked about the room, kicking at the furniture, as Somers hurried out. O'Rourke, who had sat down, waved his pipe.

"Well, gents," he said, "I like to see the bloodhounds on the trail. Is there anything else you'd like to ask *me?*"

Hadley went through the papers in the briefcase. "This is your statement—right?" He read it briefly. "Are you positive he said his brother had taken lodgings in this street?"

"Yes, sir; he said he'd seen him hanging around here."

Hadley glanced up sharply. "That's not the same thing. Which did he say?"

O'Rourke thought this a quibble. "Oh, well, he said, 'He's got a room there; I've seen him hanging around.' Or something."

"That's not very definite, is it? Think again!"

"Well, hell's bells, I *am* thinking!" protested O'Rourke. "Somebody reels off a lot of stuff like that; and then afterwards they ask you questions about it and seem to think you're lying if you can't repeat every word. Sorry, partner, but that's the best I can do."

Hadley reflected, and then decided on a course. "I suppose you've seen the newspapers?" he said.

"Yes." O'Rourke's eyes narrowed. "Why ask me about that?"

"Some sort of illusion, or stage trick, must have been used to kill both those men. You say you've known magicians. Can you think of any trick that would explain how it was done?"

O'Rourke laughed. "Look, I'll tell you straight. When I offered to swing out the window on that rope, I was afraid you were getting ideas. I mean about me." He chuckled. "Forget it! It'd take a miracle man to work any stunt like that with a rope, even if he had a rope and could walk without leaving any tracks. But as for the other business . . . well!" Frowning, O'Rourke brushed up his mustache with the stem of his pipe. "Here, I'll give you an example of a whopping big vanishing trick. You can even work it outdoors. Out rides the illusionist, in a grand blue uniform, on a grand white horse. Out come his gang of attendants, in white uniforms, with the usual hoopla. They go round in a circle once, and then two attendants whisk up a great big fan which—just for a moment, see?—hides the man on the horse. Down comes the fan, which is tossed out in the audience to show it's okay; but the man on the horse has vanished—vanished straight from the middle of a ten-acre field. Heigh-ho!"

"And how do you get out of that one?" demanded Dr. Fell.

"Easy! The man's never left the field. But you don't see him. You don't see him because that grand blue uniform is made of paper—*over* a real white one. As soon as the fan goes up, he tears off the blue one and stuffs it under the white. He jumps off the horse and joins the gang of white-uniformed attendants. Point is, nobody ever takes the trouble to *count* them attendants beforehand, and they all exit without anybody ever seeing. That's the basis of most tricks. You're looking at something you don't see, or you'll swear you've seen something that's not there. And most tricks, here's another point, can only be worked if the illusionist has a confederate. An attendant, or several attendants, like those white-uniformed fellows."

The stuffy, gaudily colored room was quiet. Wind rattled at the windows. Distantly there was a noise of church bells, and the honking of a taxi that passed and died. Hadley shook his notebook.

"We're getting off the track," he said. "It's clever enough, yes; but how does it apply to this problem?"

"It don't," admitted O'Rourke. "I'm telling you—well, because you asked. I don't want to discourage you—"

Dr. Fell interrupted. "Clear the decks for action, Hadley. We're about to have visitors. Look out the window. But keep back!"

Below them, where the alley curved out between houses, two figures shouldered against the wind. One Rampole recognized as Rosette Grimaud. The other was a tall man with a cane, whose right boot was of abnormal thickness.

"Get the lights out in those other rooms," said Hadley swiftly. He turned to O'Rourke. "I'll ask you a favor. Get downstairs and stop that landlady from coming up. Pull the door shut after you!"

Hadley was already out into the passage, snapping off the lights. He drew the curtains so that only a pencil of light slanted into the room. "We'll sit here quietly," he said. "If they've got anything on their minds, they may blurt it out as soon as they get inside the flat. What do you think of O'Rourke, by the way?"

"I think," stated Dr. Fell with energy, "that O'Rourke is the most enlightening witness we have heard so far in this nightmare. He is, in fact, almost as enlightening as the church bells."

Hadley turned. "Church bells? What church bells?"

"Any church bells," said Dr. Fell. "I tell you that to me in my heathen blindness the thought of those bells has brought light and balm. It may save me from making an awful mistake. . . . Light, Hadley! Light at last, and glorious messages in the belfry."

"Are you sure it's not something else in the belfry? For God's sake, will you tell me what you mean? I suppose the church bells tell you how the vanishing trick was worked?"

"No," said Dr. Fell. "They tell me the name of the murderer."

There was a palpable stillness in the room, as of breath restrained to bursting. Downstairs a door closed. Faintly through the quiet house they heard footsteps coming up the staircase. At last a key scraped in the lock of the outer door, which opened and closed again. There was another click as the light in the hallway was snapped on.

"So you've lost the key I gave you," a man's harsh voice spoke. "And you say you didn't come here last night, after all?"

"Not last night," said Rosette Grimaud's voice, "or any other night." She laughed. "I never had any intention of coming. Did you have a pleasant time waiting for me?"

The man's voice rose. "You little devil," he said. "I'm going to tell *you* something. I wasn't here either. If you think all you have to do is crack the whip to send people through hoops—well, you can go through the hoops yourself. I wasn't here."

"That's a lie, Jerome," said Rosette calmly.

"You think so, eh? Why?"

Two figures appeared against the light of the partly opened door. Hadley reached out and drew back the curtains. "We also would like to know the answer to that, Mr. Burnaby," he said.

The flood of murky daylight in their faces caught them off guard. Rosette Grimaud cried out; Jerome Burnaby stood motionless, his chest rising and falling. He had a strong, furrowed face, and eyes which seemed to have lost their color with anger. Taking off his hat and overcoat, he tossed them on a divan with a swashbuckling air. "Well?" he said. "Is this a holdup, or what?"

The girl laid her fur coat aside. "Jerome," she said, "they're the police."

Burnaby went on with ironical jocularity. "Oh! The police, eh? I'm honored. Breaking and entering?"

"You are the tenant of this flat," said Hadley, with equal suavity, "not the owner. If suspicious behavior is seen . . ."

"Damn you," Burnaby said, and half raised the cane, "what do you want here?"

"First of all, before we forget it, Miss Grimaud was saying that you were in this flat last night. Were you?"

"I was not."

"You were not. . . . Was he, Miss Grimaud?"

She spoke in a breathless way, evidently angry but determined to show no emotion. "Since you overheard," she answered, "it's no good my denying it, is there? I don't see why you're interested. It can't have anything to do with—my father's death. Whatever else Jerome is, he's not a murderer. But since for some reason you *are* interested, I've a good mind to have the whole thing thrashed out now. Some version of this, I can see, is going to get back to Boyd. It might as well be the true one.... I'll begin by saying, yes, Jerome was in this flat last night."

"How do you know that, Miss Grimaud? Were you here?"

"No. But I saw a light in this room at half past ten."

Burnaby, rubbing his chin, looked at her blankly. Rampole could have sworn that the man was genuinely startled. "I say, Rosette," he observed, "are you sure you know what you're talking about?"

"Yes. Quite sure."

Hadley cut in. "At half past ten? How did you happen to see this light when you were at your own home with us?"

"No, I wasn't—if you remember. Not at that time. I was at the hospital, where my father was dying. The back of the hospital faces the back of this house and I happened to be near a window. I noticed there was a light in this room; and, I think, the bathroom, too...."

"How do you know the rooms," said Hadley sharply, "if you've never been here before?"

"I took jolly good care to observe when we came in just now," she answered. "I *didn't* know the rooms last night; I only knew he had this flat."

Burnaby was contemplating her with curiosity. "Are you sure you weren't mistaken about the rooms, Rosette?"

"Positive, my dear. This is the house on the left-hand side at the corner of the alley, and you have the top floor."

"And you say you saw *me?*"

"No, I say I saw a light. But you and I are the only ones who know about this flat. And, since you'd invited me here, and said you'd be here..."

"By God!" said Burnaby. "I'm interested to see how far you'll go." He sat down heavily in a chair and continued to study her out of his pale eyes. "Please go on!"

Rosette whirled round, but her resolution seemed to crack. "I—

I said we'd have this out," she appealed to Hadley, "but now I don't know whether I want to. If I could decide about him, whether he's really sympathetic, and just a nice bluff old—old—"

"For Lord's sake don't say friend of the family," snapped Burnaby. "Personally, I wish I could decide about you—whether you think you're telling the truth, or whether you're a lying little vixen."

She went on steadily, "Or whether he's a sort of polite blackmailer. Oh, not for money!" She blazed again. "Vixen? Yes, if you like. I admit it. I've been that—but why? Because you've poisoned everything with all the hints you've dropped. . . ."

"Hints about what?" Hadley intervened.

"Oh, about my father's past life." She clenched her hands. "About my birth. But that doesn't bother me. It's this business about some horrible thing—about my father—I don't know! Then, last night, Jerome asked me to come over here—why, why? I thought, Well, is it because that's the night Boyd always sees me, and it will tickle Jerome's vanity no end to choose just that night? But I didn't—please understand me!—want to think Jerome was trying a little blackmail. I like him; and that's what makes it so awful."

"We might clear it up, then," said Hadley. "Were you hinting, Mr. Burnaby?" There was a long silence while Burnaby examined his hands. Something in the posture of his bent head, in his heavy breathing, as though he were trying to make up his mind, kept Hadley from prompting him until he raised his head.

"I never thought—" Burnaby said. "Hinting. Yes, in strict accuracy, I suppose I was. But never intentionally. I never thought—" He stared at Rosette. "Maybe you mean only what you think is a subtle question. . . ." He shrugged his shoulders despairingly. "To me it was an interesting deductive game, that's all. I didn't even think of it as prying. Rosette, if that's the only reason for your interest in me—thinking I was a blackmailer, and afraid of me—then I'm sorry." He looked slowly round the room. "Take a look at this place, gentlemen. The front room especially. . . . Then you'll know the answer. The Great Detective. The poor ass with the deformed foot, dreaming."

For a second Hadley hesitated. "And did the Great Detective find out anything about Dr. Grimaud's past?"

"No. . . . If I had, do you think I'd be apt to tell you?"

"We'll see if we can't persuade you. Do you know that there are bloodstains in that bathroom of yours, where Miss Grimaud says she saw a light last night? Do you know that Pierre Fley was murdered outside your door not long before half past ten?"

Rosette Grimaud cried out, and Burnaby jerked up his head.

"Fley mur— Bloodstains! No! Where?"

"Fley had a room in this street. We think he was coming here when he died. Anyhow, he was shot in the street outside here by the same man who killed Dr. Grimaud. Can you prove who you are, Mr. Burnaby? Can you prove, for instance, that you are not actually Grimaud's and Fley's brother?"

The other stared at him. He hoisted himself up shakily from the chair. "Good God, man! Are you mad?" he asked. "Brother! . . . No, I'm not his brother. Do you think if I were his brother I should be interested in . . ." He checked himself, glancing at Rosette. "Certainly I can prove it. I have a birth certificate somewhere. I—I can produce people who've known me all my life!"

Hadley held up the coil of rope. "What about this rope? Is it a part of your Great Detective scheme, too?"

"That? I never saw it before."

Rampole glanced at Rosette Grimaud. Her face was set, but the tears brimmed over her eyes.

"And can you prove," Hadley continued, "that you were not in this flat last night?"

Relief lightened Burnaby's face. "Yes, fortunately I can. I was at my club from eight o'clock—or thereabouts—until past eleven. Ask the three people I played poker with the whole of that time. I wasn't here. I didn't leave any bloodstains. I didn't kill Fley, Grimaud, or anybody else." His heavy jaw came out. "Now, then, what do you think of *that?*"

Hadley had turned to Rosette. "You still insist that you saw a light here?"

"Yes! . . . But, Jerome, truly, I never meant—"

"Even though, when my man arrived here this morning, the electric meter was cut off and the lights would not work?"

"I— Yes, it's still true! But what I wanted to say—"

"Let's suppose Mr. Burnaby is telling the truth about last night. You say he invited you here. Is it likely that he invited you here when he intended to be at his club?"

Burnaby lurched forward and put a hand on Hadley's arm. "Steady! Let's get this straightened out, Inspector. That's what I did. It was a swine's trick, but—I did it. Look here, have I *got* to explain?"

"Now, now!" Dr. Fell took out a red bandanna and blew his nose with a loud honking, to attract attention. Then he blinked at them. "Hadley, let me put in a soothing word. Mr. Burnaby did that, as he expressed it himself, to make her jump through a hoop. Now, about the question of the light not working, that's not nearly so ominous as it sounds. It's a shilling meter, d'ye see. Somebody was here and left the lights burning; so the meter used up a bob's worth of electricity, and then the lights went out. Blast it, Hadley, we've got ample proof there *was* somebody here last night. The question is, who?" He looked at the others. "H'm. You two say nobody else knew of this place. But—assuming your story to be straight, Mr. Burnaby—somebody else must have known of it."

"I can only tell you I didn't speak of it," insisted Burnaby. "Unless somebody noticed me coming here ... unless—"

"Unless, in other words, I told somebody about it?" Rosette flared. "But I didn't."

"But you have a key to the place?" asked Dr. Fell.

"I had a key to the place. I lost it."

"When?"

"Oh, how should I know?" She walked round the room. "I kept it in my bag, and I only noticed this morning that it was gone. But one thing I insist on knowing." She stopped, facing Burnaby. "If it was only a nasty little fondness for detective work and you didn't really mean anything, then speak up. What do you know about my father? Tell me! I don't mind. They're the police, and they'll find out anyway. Now, don't act!"

"That's good advice, Mr. Burnaby. You painted a picture," said Hadley, "that I was going to ask about. What did you know about Dr. Grimaud?"

Burnaby's pale gray eyes gleamed sardonically. He said, "Very well, Rosette! I'll tell you in a few words what I'd have told you long ago, if I had known it worried you. Your father was once imprisoned at the salt mines in Hungary, and he escaped. Not very terrible, is it?"

"In prison! What for?"

"For trying to start a revolution, I was told. My own guess is for theft. You see, I'm being frank."

Hadley cut in quickly. "Where did you learn that?".

Burnaby stiffened. "I'd better tell you, if only to prove I'm no busybody. You talk about that picture. It was an accident—though I had a bad time persuading Grimaud of that. It was all on account of a damned magic-lantern lecture."

"A what?"

"A magic-lantern lecture. I ducked into the thing to get out of the rain one night; it was out in North London, a parish hall, about eighteen months ago." Wryly Burnaby twiddled his thumbs. "Chap was lecturing on Hungary: lantern slides and ghostly atmosphere to thrill the churchgoers. But, by George, it caught my imagination!" His eyes gleamed. "There was one slide—something like what I painted—three lonely graves in an unhallowed place. It gave me an idea, and I came home and worked like fury on it. The lecturer implied that they were vampires' graves, you see? Well, I told everybody it was an imaginative conception of something I never saw. But when Grimaud saw it, it gave him a hell of a turn! And then, in my sinister innocence, out I came with the remark, 'You'll notice how the earth is cracking on one grave. He's just getting out.' My mind was still running on vampires, of course. But he didn't know that. For a second I thought he was coming at me with a palette knife."

It was a straightforward story Burnaby told. Grimaud, he said, had questioned him about that picture; questioned him, watched him, too, until even a less imaginative man would have been suspicious. The tension of being under surveillance had set him to solve the puzzle in self-defense. A few pieces of handwriting in books in Grimaud's library; the shield of arms over the mantel-piece; a casual word dropped . . . Then, he continued, about three months before the murder Grimaud had collared him and, under an oath of secrecy, told him the truth—exactly the story Drayman had told last night: the plague, the two dead brothers, the escape.

"That's *all?*" Rosette cried. "That's all there is to it?"

"That's all, my dear," Burnaby answered, folding his arms. "But I didn't want to tell it to the police."

"Supposing all this to be true, Mr. Burnaby," said Hadley, "you were at the Warwick Tavern the night Fley came in?"

"Yes."

"Knowing what you did, didn't you connect Fley with that business in the past?"

Burnaby hesitated. "Frankly, yes. I walked home with Grimaud on that night. We sat down in his study, and he took an extra large whisky. I thought he was going to tell me something. He seemed to be looking very hard at the fireplace—"

"By the way," Dr. Fell put in, so casually that Rampole jumped, "where did he keep his personal papers? Do you know?"

The other glanced sharply at him. "I think he kept them in a locked drawer in that big desk."

"Go on."

"There was one of those uncomfortable silences; and then, well, I took the plunge and said, 'Who was it?' Grimaud shifted in the chair, and finally he said, 'I don't know. It's been a long time. It may have been the doctor.'"

"Doctor? You mean the one who certified him as dead of plague at the prison?" asked Hadley.

"Yes. Look here, must I go on with this? . . . All right, all right! 'Back for a little blackmail,' he said. I said, 'Yes, but what can he do?'—trying to draw him out. I thought it must be more serious than a political offense, or it wouldn't carry weight after so long. He said, 'Oh, *he* won't do anything. He never had the nerve.' Then

Grimaud said, with that barking directness of his, 'You want to marry Rosette, don't you?' I admitted it. He said, 'Very well; you shall.' I laughed and said something about Rosette's having another preference. He said, 'Bah! The young one! I'll fix that.'"

Rosette was looking at Burnaby with a hard, luminous stare. "So you had it all arranged, did you?" she said.

"Oh Lord, don't fly off the handle! I was asked what happened." He turned back to the others. "Well, gentlemen, that's all I can tell you. When he came in on Friday to get that picture, I was puzzled. But I let him have it."

Hadley, who had been writing in his notebook, went on without speaking. Then he looked at Rosette. "I want to know," he said, "why, if you always refused to come over here with Mr. Burnaby, you suddenly decided on coming this morning?"

"To have it out with him. And—and then things were so unpleasant, you see, when we found that coat with the blood on it—"

"When you found *what?*" said Hadley.

"The coat with blood inside it. I—I didn't mention it, did I? Well, you didn't give me any chance! The minute we walked in here, you leaped out at us. . . . The coat was hanging in the closet in the hall. Jerome found it."

"Whose coat?"

"That's the odd part! I never saw it before. It's new. It wouldn't have fitted anybody at our house. It was too big for father—and it's a flashy tweed of the kind he'd have shuddered at, anyway; it would have swallowed Stuart Mills, and yet it isn't big enough for old Drayman."

"*I see,*" said Dr. Fell, and puffed out his cheeks.

"You see what?" snapped Hadley.

"I see where Drayman got the blood on him last night."

"You mean he wore the coat?"

"No, no! Remember what your sergeant said. He said that Drayman, half blind, came downstairs and blundered round in the closet getting his coat. Hadley, he brushed close up against that coat when the blood was fresh. No wonder he couldn't understand afterwards how it got there. Doesn't that clear up a good deal?"

"No, I'm damned if it does! We're going over there now."

Dr. Fell shook his head. "You go along, Hadley. Just let Rampole come with me. There's something I must see now. Something that changes the whole twist of the case."

"What?"

"Pierre Fley's lodgings," said Dr. Fell, and shouldered out with his cape whirling behind him.

VIII: The Chameleon Overcoat

"But what do you expect to find there?" remonstrated Hadley, following Dr. Fell. "Somers has already been through the place!"

"I don't expect to find anything," grumbled the doctor, whose spirits appeared to have sunk to a depth of gloom. "I can only say I hope to find traces of brother Henri. His trademark, so to speak. His ... oh, my hat, brother Henri, damn you!"

Before leaving Burnaby's lodging house, the doctor held up everybody for some time with a searching examination of Miss Hake, the landlady. The questioning of Miss Hake, Dr. Fell admitted, was not productive. A faded, agreeable spinster with wandering wits, she could give little information. She had been at the moving pictures last night from eight until eleven, and at a friend's house in Gray's Inn Road until nearly midnight. She had not even known of the murder until that morning. As to her other lodgers, a veterinary surgeon and an American student and his wife, all three had been out on the night before.

Somers, who had now returned from his futile errand to Burnaby's other flat, was sent to check on this story; Hadley set out for Grimaud's house with Rosette and Burnaby; and Dr. Fell, with Rampole in tow, went on to Pierre Fley's lodgings to tackle the landlord.

The tobacconist's shop at Number 2 was bleak and dark-painted. Energy at a clanking bell finally brought James Dolberman, a small, tight-lipped old man with large knuckles and a shiny black muslin coat. His view of the whole matter was that it was no business of his.

Staring past them, he bit off a few grudging answers. Yes, he had a lodger, a man named Fley. He occupied a bed-sitting-room on the top floor. He had been there two weeks. No, the landlord didn't know anything about him. The landlord hardly ever saw him. There were no other lodgers.

Did he know Fley was dead? Yes, he did; there had been a policeman here asking fool questions already. What about the shooting last night? He had been belowstairs with the radio on; he knew nothing about it.

Had Fley had any visitors? No. Were there any suspicious-looking strangers, any people associated with Fley, hereabouts?

This had an unexpected result: the landlord grew almost voluble. Yes, there was something the police ought to see to, instead of wasting taxpayers' money! He had seen somebody dodging round this place, watching it, once even speaking to Fley. No, he couldn't give any description—that was the police's business.

"But isn't there anything," said Dr. Fell, "you can give as description? Any clothes, anything of that sort? Hey?"

"He *might*," Dolberman conceded, "have been wearing a kind of fancy overcoat. Of a light yellow tweed. You wish to go upstairs? Here is the key. The door is outside."

Dr. Fell puffed as he and Rampole stamped up a narrow stairway through a house surprisingly sound despite its flimsy appearance. On the top floor a grimy skylight admitted a faint glow on the landing. There was only one door. It opened on a low cave of a room whose window had evidently not been opened in some time. After fumbling in the gloom Dr. Fell found a gas mantle. The ragged light showed a neat but very grimy room with blue cabbages on the wallpaper and a white iron bed. On the bureau lay a folded note under a bottle of ink. Only one touch remained of Pierre Fley's weird and twisted brain: it was as though they saw Fley himself, in his rusty evening clothes and top hat, standing by the bureau for a performance. Over the mirror hung framed an old-fashioned motto in curly script of gilt and black and red. The spidery scrollwork read, *Vengeance is mine; I will repay, saith the Lord.*

Wheezing in the quiet, Dr. Fell lumbered over to the bureau and picked up the folded note. The message, Rampole saw, had almost the air of a proclamation.

James Dolberman, Esq.
I am leaving you my few belongings, such as they are, in lieu of a week's notice. I shall not need them again. I am going back to my grave.

Pierre Fley

"Why," said Rampole, "this insistent harping on 'I am going back to my grave'? What does it mean?"

Dr. Fell did not answer. His mood sank lower and lower as he inspected the tattered gray carpet. "Not a trace," he groaned. "Not a bus ticket or anything. His possessions? No, I don't want to see his possessions. I suppose Somers had a look through those. Come on; we'll go back and join Hadley."

They walked gloomily to Russell Square under the overcast sky. As they went up the steps, Hadley saw them through the drawing-room window and came to open the front door. "That overcoat—" Hadley was in a state of wrath. "Come in and listen, Fell. Maybe it'll make sense to you. We're faced with what you would probably call the Mystery of the Chameleon Overcoat."

Inside the drawing room tension was thick in the air. It was a room furnished in heavy old-fashioned luxury, with bronze groups holding lights, and curtains stiff with lace. Burnaby lounged on a sofa. Rosette was walking about with quick, angry steps. In one corner stood Ernestine Dumont, her hands on her hips. Finally, Boyd Mangan stood with his back to the fire.

"I know the damn overcoat fits me!" Mangan was saying, with an air of fierce repetition. "But it's not my coat. In the first place, I always wear a waterproof—"

Hadley figuratively rapped for attention. The entrance of Dr. Fell and Rampole seemed to soothe Mangan. "Look here, Ted, I'll put it up to you." He took Rampole's arm and pulled him over in front of the fire. "When I got here for dinner last night, I went to hang up my coat—my waterproof—in the closet in the hall. I switched on the light because I was carrying books I wanted to put on the shelf. And I saw an overcoat, an extra coat, hanging on a hook in the corner. It was about the same size as that yellow tweed one; just the same, I should have said, only it was black."

"An extra coat," repeated Dr. Fell. He looked curiously at Mangan. "Why do you say an extra coat, my boy? If you see a line of coats in somebody's house, does the idea of an extra one ever enter your head? Eh?"

"I knew the coats people have here. *And*," replied Mangan, "I particularly noticed this one, because I thought it must be Burnaby's, and I wondered if he was here. . . ."

"Mangan," Burnaby said with an indulgent air, "is very observant, Dr. Fell. Especially where I am concerned."

"Got any objections?" asked Mangan. He turned angrily back to Dr. Fell. "Anyway, I noticed the coat. Then, when Burnaby came here this morning and found that coat with the blood inside it . . . well, the yellow one was hanging where the black one had been. Of course, the only explanation is that there were two overcoats. But what kind of crazy business is it? I'll swear that coat last night didn't belong to anybody here. You can see for yourself that the tweed one doesn't. Did the murderer wear one, or both, or neither? Besides, that black coat had a queer look about it—"

"Queer?" interrupted Dr. Fell. "How do you mean, queer?"

Ernestine Dumont came forward. She looked more withered this morning; her eyelids were puffed; yet her black eyes still glittered. "Bah!" she said. "Why go on with all this foolishness?" She looked at Mangan. "No, no, I think you are trying to tell the truth, you understand. But I think you have mixed it up a little. . . . The yellow coat was there last night, yes. Early, before dinner. It was hanging on the hook where he says he saw the black one. I saw it myself."

"But—" cried Mangan.

"Now, now," boomed Dr. Fell soothingly. "Let's see if we can't straighten this out. If you saw the coat there, ma'am, didn't it strike you as unusual?"

"No, not at all." She nodded towards Mangan. "I did not see him arrive. I supposed it was his."

"Who did let you in, by the way?" Dr. Fell asked Mangan.

"Annie. But I hung up my things myself. I'll swear—"

"Better have Annie up, if she's here, Hadley," said Dr. Fell. "This problem of the chameleon overcoat intrigues me."

"I've already spoken to Annie," Hadley said, as Rosette Grimaud strode past him and rang a bell. "She tells a straight story. She was out last night. But I haven't asked her about this."

Everybody was quiet when Annie answered the bell. Annie was a long-nosed serious-minded girl. She looked capable; she also looked hard-worked. Standing at the doorway, her cap precise on her head, she regarded Hadley with level brown eyes. She was upset, but not nervous.

"One thing I neglected to ask you about last night," said the superintendent. "You let Mr. Mangan in, did you?"

"Yes, sir."

"About what time was that?"

"Couldn't say exactly, sir." She seemed puzzled. "Might have been half an hour before dinner."

"Did you see him hang up his hat and coat?"

"Yes, sir! He never gives them to me, or I'd—"

"But did you look into the clothes closet?"

"Oh, I see. . . . Yes, sir, I did! I went back through the front hall, going to the kitchen, a few minutes later. And I noticed he'd left the light on in the closet, so I turned it out. . . ."

Hadley leaned forward. "Now be careful! You know about the yellow tweed overcoat that was found in that closet this morning? Good! Do you remember the hook it was hanging from?"

"Yes, sir, I do. I was in the front hall this morning when Mr. Burnaby found the coat."

"Then the question, Annie, is about the color of that coat. When you looked into that closet last night, was it yellow or black?"

She stared at him. "Yellow or black, sir? Sir, *at that time there was no coat hanging from that hook at all.*"

A babble of voices crossed and clashed: Mangan furious, Rosette almost hysterically mocking, Burnaby amused. Only Ernestine Dumont remained wearily silent. For a full minute Hadley studied Annie's set, earnest face. Then Dr. Fell chuckled. "Well, cheer up," he urged. "At least it hasn't turned another color on us. And I must insist it's a very revealing fact. H'mf. Yes. Come along, Hadley. Lunch is what we want. Lunch!"

THE coffee was on the table, the cigars were lighted. Hadley, Pettis, Rampole, and Dr. Fell sat round the glow of a red-shaded table lamp in the vast, dusky dining room at Pettis's hotel. Dr. Fell was gesturing expansively with his cigar and giving his companions an amiable lecture on detective fiction when Mangan appeared in the dining room.

He was pale. He hurried towards them and stood by the table, drawing his breath in gasps. "Not something else?" asked Hadley, pushing back his chair.

"No," said Mangan. "But you'd better get back to the house. Drayman has had an apoplectic stroke, or something like that. He's not dead. But he's in a bad way. He was trying to get in touch with you when he had the stroke. . . . He keeps talking wildly about somebody in his room, and fireworks, and chimneys."

They went quickly to Russell Square. Again there were three people—three people strained and with frayed nerves—waiting in the drawing room. Stuart Mills, who stood with his back to the fireplace, kept clearing his throat. Rosette looked half frantic. Ernestine Dumont sat quietly. Burnaby had gone.

"You cannot see him," said Madame Dumont. "The doctor is with him now. Probably he is mad."

"Suppose you tell us exactly what happened to Mr. Drayman," Hadley said. "Is he in any grave danger?"

Madame Dumont shrugged. "He collapsed. He is unconscious now. We have no idea what caused it. His heart?"

Again Mills cleared his throat. "If, sir, you have any idea of—um—foul play, you may dismiss it," he said. "Strangely enough, the same people were together this afternoon who were together last night. The Pythoness and I"—he bowed towards Ernestine

Dumont—"were upstairs in my workroom. I understand that Miss Grimaud and our friend Mangan were down here—"

Rosette jerked her head. "You had better hear it from the beginning. Did Boyd tell you about Drayman coming down here first?"

"No, I didn't tell 'em anything," Mangan answered. He swung round. "It was about half an hour ago. Rosette and I were here alone. I'd had a row with Burnaby—the usual thing. Everybody was fighting about that overcoat, and we'd all separated. Burnaby had gone. Anyhow, Drayman walked in here and asked me how he could get in touch with you. He acted as though he might have discovered something. So we said, 'What is it?' He doddered a little and said, 'I've found something missing from my room, and it makes me remember something I'd forgotten about last night.' It was all about some hallucination that, while he was lying down last night after he'd taken the sleeping tablet, somebody had come into his room."

"Before the—crime?"

"Yes. And when we asked him who it was, he simply tapped his head and said, 'I really can't say.' We both got annoyed. . . ." Mangan appeared uncomfortable. "Only, damn it all, if I hadn't said what I did—"

"Said what?" asked Hadley.

"I said, 'Well, if you've discovered so much, why don't you go up to the scene of the 'orrid murder and see if you can't discover some more?' And he took me seriously. He said, 'Yes, I believe I will. I had better make sure.' And with that, out he went! Maybe twenty minutes later we heard him blundering downstairs. Then we heard a choking sound and a thud. I opened the door, and there he was lying doubled up with his face all congested. Of course, we sent for the doctor. He hasn't said anything except to rave about chimneys and fireworks."

Mills took a little hopping step forward. "If you will allow me to take up the story," he said. "With the Pythoness's permission."

"Ah, bah!" the woman cried. Her eyes blazed. "The Pythoness this, the Pythoness that. God! What do you know of human men or sympathy or— Drayman may be a little mad. He may be full of drugs. But he is a good man, and if he dies I shall pray for his soul."

"Shall I—er—go on?" observed Mills imperturbably.

"Yes, you shall go on," the woman mimicked, and was silent.

"The Pythoness and I were in my workroom on the top floor—opposite the study, as you know. And again the door was open. I was shifting some papers, and I noticed Mr. Drayman come up and go into the study. He closed the door, and after some time he came out, in what I can only describe as a panting and unsteady condition. I received an impression that he had been indulging in violent exercise. And—er—I might add something. When he was picked up after the stroke, I observed that his hands and sleeves were covered with soot."

"The chimney," Pettis murmured, and Hadley turned round towards Dr. Fell. It gave Rampole a shock to see that the doctor was no longer in the room. A person of his girth can, as a rule, make small success of an effort to fade mysteriously away; but he was gone, and Rampole thought he knew where.

"Follow him up there," Hadley said to Rampole. "See that he doesn't work any of his blasted mystification. Now, Mr. Mills—"

Rampole went out into the somber hall. The house was so quiet that, as he mounted the stairs, the sudden shrilling of the telephone bell in the lower hall made him jump. No lights burned on the top floor; again such a stillness that he could hear Annie's voice answering the telephone far below.

The study was dusky. Standing motionless in his black cloak before the window, Dr. Fell leaned on his cane and stared out into the sunset. The creaking of the door did not rouse him. Rampole said, "Did you find anything?"

"Well, I think I know the truth," Dr. Fell answered reflectively, "and tonight I shall probably be able to prove it. H'mf. Yes. D'ye see, I've been standing here wondering what to do about it. It's the old problem, son, and it becomes more difficult each year I live. . . . What is justice? I've asked it at the end of nearly every case I ever handled. I see faces rise, and sick souls and bad dreams. . . . No matter. Shall we go downstairs?"

"But what about the fireplace?" insisted Rampole. He peered

at it. A little soot had been scattered on the hearth. "Is there a secret passage, after all?"

"Oh no. Nobody got up there."

"But," said Rampole desperately, "if this brother Henri—"

"Yes," said a heavy voice from the doorway, "brother Henri."

It was Hadley. He stood in the doorway, a sheet of paper crumpled in his hand; and in the dull quietness of his tone of voice Rampole recognized despair. Closing the door softly behind him, Hadley went on. "It was our own fault, I know, for being hypnotized by a theory. It ran away with us—and now we've got to start the whole case afresh. Damn the rotten, impossible . . . !" He stared at the sheet of paper. "A phone call just came through from the Yard. They've heard from Bucharest."

Dr. Fell nodded. "You're going to say that brother Henri—"

"*There is no brother Henri,*" said Hadley. "*The third of the three Horváth brothers died over thirty years ago.*"

IN THE cold, quiet, darkening study Hadley walked over to the broad desk and spread out the crumpled sheet so that the others could read.

"There's no possibility of a mistake," he went on. "The case is very well known, it seems. The whole cablegram they sent was very long, but I've copied the important parts from what they read over the phone. Take a look."

No difficulty about information desired. Two men now in my personal service were at Siebenturmen as warders in 1900, and confirm record. Facts: Károly Grimaud Horváth, Pierre Fley Horváth, and Nicholas Revéi Horváth were sons of Professor Károly Horváth (of Klausenburg University) and Cécile Fley Horváth (French), his wife. For robbery of Kunar Bank at Brassó, November 1898, the three brothers were sentenced, January 1899, to twenty years' penal servitude. Bank watchman died of injuries inflicted, and loot never recovered; believed to have been hidden. All three, with aid of prison doctor during plague scare of August 1900, made daring attempt at escape by being certified as dead, and buried in plague ground. J. Lahner and R. Görgei, warders, returning to graves an hour later to retrieve a spade, noticed disturbance had taken place on earth at grave of Károly Horváth. Investigation showed coffin open and empty. Digging into other two graves, warders found Pierre Horváth bloody and insensible, but still alive. Nicholas Horváth had already suffocated to death. Nicholas reburied after absolute certainty made the man was dead; Pierre returned to prison. Scandal hushed up, no chase of fugitive, and story never discovered until end of war. Pierre Fley Horváth never mentally responsible afterwards. Released January 1919, having served full term. Assure you no doubt whatever third brother dead.

Alexander Cuza, Police Director, Bucharest

"Oh yes," said Hadley, when they had finished reading. "It confirms the reconstruction right enough, except for the little point that we've been chasing a ghost as the murderer. Brother Henri— or brother Nicholas, to be exact—never did leave his grave. He's there yet. And the whole case—"

Dr. Fell rapped his knuckles on the paper. "It's my fault, Hadley," he admitted. "I was hypnotized by brother Henri."

"Well, it won't do us any good just to admit the mistake. How the devil are we going to explain all those crazy remarks of Fley's now? Private vendetta! Vengeance! Now that that's swept away, what is there left?"

Dr. Fell pointed rather malevolently with his stick. "Don't you see what's left?" he roared. "Don't you see the connecting thread? There might be any number of motives, plain or obscure, why a person would kill Grimaud. Mills or Dumont or Burnaby or—yes, anybody *might* have killed Grimaud. Also, anybody might have killed Fley; but not, I must point out, anybody in the same circle or group of people. Why should Fley be killed by a member of Grimaud's group, none of whom had presumably ever seen him before? If these murders are the work of one person, where is the connecting link? A respected professor in Bloomsbury and a tramp actor with a prison record. Where's the human motive that ties those two together in the murderer's mind, unless it is a link that goes back into the past?"

419

"I can think of one person who is associated with both from the past," Hadley pointed out.

"Who? You mean the Dumont woman?"

"Yes."

"No, my lad. Dumont is an impossible suspect. As the double killer, anyway, she is absolutely o-u-t. Why? Because at the time of Fley's death, sworn to by three good men and true, she was here in this room, talking to us."

Hadley studied Dr. Fell. "I know this mood. I know it very well," he asserted. "It's the beginning of some more blasted mystification. What are you trying to show me, anyhow?"

"First," said Dr. Fell, "that Mills told the truth. And, second, that I know the real murderer."

"Who is somebody we've seen and talked to?"

"Oh yes, very much so."

"And have we got a chance of . . . ?"

Dr. Fell, an absent, fierce, almost pitying expression on his face, stared at the desk. "Yes, Lord help us all," he said, "I suppose you've got to. In the meantime, I'm going home."

"Home?"

"To apply Gross's test," said Dr. Fell.

He turned away, but he did not immediately go. As the sunset light outside deepened to purple, and dust-colored shadows swallowed up the room, he remained for a long time staring at the slashed picture, which caught the last glow with its turbulent power. The three coffins were filled at last.

IX: The Hollow Man

THAT night Dr. Fell shut himself up in the small cubbyhole off the library which was reserved for what he called his scientific experiments and what Mrs. Fell called "that horrible messing about." The tireless Hadley had already gone off to check alibis, and Mrs. Fell was at church.

Rampole and Dorothy sat on opposite sides of the library fireplace, looking at each other. "Ever since last night," he commented,

"I've been hearing about Gross's method for reading burned letters. But nobody seems to know what it is."

"I know what it is," she told him, with an air of triumph. "I looked it up while you people were dashing about this afternoon. Gross says that the writing on charred fragments stands out quite clearly, usually white or gray against a black background, but sometimes with the colors reversed. Did you ever notice that?"

"Can't say I have. Is it true?"

She frowned. "It works with cardboard boxes that have printing on them, boxes of soap flakes or things like that. But regular writing . . . Anyway, you're supposed to get a lot of transparent tracing paper and pin it to a board. As you pick up each of the charred pieces of paper, you cover a place on the tracing paper with mucilage, press the charred paper down—"

"When it's crumpled up like that? It'll break, won't it?"

"Aha! That's the trick, Gross says. You have to soften the fragments. You arrange a frame two or three inches high, with all the bits under it, and then you stretch a damp cloth across it. That puts the papers in a damp atmosphere, and they straighten out. When they're all flattened out, you cut out the tracing paper round each fragment. Then you reconstruct them on a sheet of glass. Like a jigsaw puzzle. Afterwards you press a second sheet of glass over the first and bind the edges, and look through both against the light. It sounds simple. But I'll bet you anything it won't work!"

"The important thing is whether you could get enough words out of a letter to make sense of it," Rampole declared. "But what does Dr. Fell expect to find?"

This was the subject of an argument which was carried on far into the night, while outside the night wind whirled by, and behind the closed door they could hear Dr. Fell blundering round his cubbyhole.

RAMPOLE slept until past ten the next morning. When he went downstairs to breakfast, the maid was indignant as she set out bacon and eggs. "The doctor's just gone up to have a wash, sir," she informed him. "He was up all night on them scientific things. I don't know what Mrs. Fell will say, indeed I don't. Superintendent Hadley's just got here. He's in the library."

Rampole found Hadley impatiently knocking his heels against the fender. "Any news?" he asked.

"Yes, and important news," Hadley said. "Both Pettis and Burnaby have cast-iron alibis. I saw Burnaby's three card-playing friends last night. Burnaby was playing poker on Saturday night from eight o'clock to nearly half past eleven. And this morning Betts has been to the theater where Pettis said he saw the play that night. Well, he did. One of the bar attendants at the theater knows him by sight. It seems that the second act ends at five past ten. A few minutes afterwards, during the interval, this attendant is willing to swear he served Pettis with a whisky and soda."

He stopped as they heard from the hall the familiar lumbering step. Dr. Fell pushed open the door.

"Well?" prompted Hadley. "Did you find out what you wanted to know from those papers?"

Dr. Fell fumbled after, found, and lit his black pipe before he answered. Then he chuckled wryly.

"Yes, I found out what I wanted to know. Hadley, twice in my theories on Saturday night I unintentionally led you wrong. Still, mine wasn't the only blunder. Chance and circumstance made an even worse blunder, and they've combined to make a terrifying puzzle out of what is really only a commonplace, ugly murder case. Oh, there was shrewdness to the murderer; I admit that. But—yes, I've found out what I wanted to know."

"Well? What was the writing on those papers?"

"Nothing," said Dr. Fell.

There was something eerie in the heavy way he spoke the word. "You mean," cried Hadley, "the experiment didn't work?"

"No, I mean that the experiment did work. I mean that there was *nothing* on those papers," boomed Dr. Fell. "Not a single line or scrap of handwriting. Except—well, yes. There were a few bits of thick cardboard with one or two printed letters."

"But why burn letters unless—"

"Because they weren't letters. That's where we went wrong. Don't you see even yet what they were? . . . Well, Hadley, we'd better finish the whole mess up. You want to meet the Invisible Murderer? You want to meet the damned ghoul and hollow man? Very well. Got your car? Then come. *I'm going to see if I can't extract a confession* from somebody at Grimaud's house."

Rampole saw the end looming and was afraid of it, without an idea as to what it might be. In Hadley's car they were quiet. And the quietest of all was Dr. Fell.

All the blinds were drawn on the house in Russell Square. Dr. Fell pressed the bell. After a long interval Annie answered it.

"We should like to see Madame Dumont," said Dr. Fell.

"She is in with the—in there," the girl answered, pointing towards the drawing room. "I'll call—" She swallowed.

Dr. Fell shook his head. He moved over with surprising quietness and softly opened the drawing-room door.

The thick lace curtains muffled what little light filtered through. The room looked vaster, and its furniture was lost in shadow except for one piece of furniture of gleaming black metal lined with satin. It was an open coffin. Thin candles were burning round it. It seemed to Rampole that those candles, or else the faint thickness of flowers and incense in the air, moved the scene weirdly from dun London to some place of crags and blasts among the Hungarian mountains—where the gold cross loomed guard against devils, and garlic wreaths kept off the prowling vampire.

Yet this was not the thing they first noticed. Ernestine Dumont knelt beside the coffin, one hand gripping its edge. Her eyes were sunken and smeared. Her breast heaved jerkily. Yet round her shoulders she had wound a gay, heavy, long-fringed shawl, with red brocade and bead embroidery that burned with a shifting glitter in the candlelight. It was the last touch of the barbaric.

And then she saw them. Both hands suddenly gripped the edge of the coffin, as though she would shield the dead.

"It will do you good, madame, to confess," said Dr. Fell very gently. "Believe me, it will do you good."

For a second Rampole thought she had stopped breathing. She

made a sound as though she were half coughing. "Confess?" she said as she turned to face them. "So that is what you think, you fools? Well, I do not care. Confess! Confess to murder?"

"No," said Dr. Fell. His voice, in that one quiet monosyllable, had a heavy note. And now she stared at him with fright as he moved towards her. "No," said Dr. Fell. "You are not the murderer. Let me tell you what you are." He towered over her, black against the candlelight, but he still spoke gently.

"Yesterday, you see, a man named O'Rourke told us several things. Among them was the fact that certain illusions can only be worked with the aid of a confederate. This was no exception. You were the confederate of the illusionist and murderer."

"The hollow man," said Ernestine Dumont, and began to laugh hysterically.

"The hollow man," said Dr. Fell, and turned to Hadley, "in a real sense. The hollow man whose naming was a terrible, ironic jest, even if we did not know it, because it was the exact truth. Do you want to see the murderer you have been hunting all through this case? The murderer lies *there*," said Dr. Fell, "but God forbid that we should judge him now."

And with a slow gesture he pointed to the white, dead, tight-lipped face of Dr. Charles Grimaud.

DR. FELL continued to look at the woman, who had again shrunk against the side of the coffin as though to defend it.

"Ma'am," he went on, "the man you loved is dead. He is beyond the reach of the law now, and whatever he has done, he has paid for it. Our immediate problem, yours and mine, is to hush this thing up so that the living may not be hurt. But, you see, you are implicated, even though you took no actual hand in the murder. Believe me, ma'am, if I could explain the whole thing without bringing you into it at all, I should do so. I know you have suffered. But you will see for yourself that such a course is impossible."

Something in his voice seemed to touch her as gently as sleep after tears. Her hysteria had gone. "Do you know?" she asked him, almost eagerly. "Do not fool me! Do you really know?"

"Yes, I really know."

"Go upstairs. Go to *his* room," she said, "and I will join you. I cannot face you just now. I must think, and— But please do not speak to anybody until I come. I will not run away."

Dr. Fell's fierce gesture silenced Hadley as they went out. Still in silence they tramped up the gloomy stairs to the top floor. Once more they came into the study, where it was so dark that Hadley switched on the mosaic lamp at the desk. After he had made sure the door was closed, Hadley turned round. "Are you trying to tell me that Grimaud killed Fley?" he demanded.

"Yes."

"While he was lying unconscious and dying under the eyes of witnesses in a hospital, he went to Cagliostro Street and—"

"Not then," said Dr. Fell quietly. "You see, Fley was killed before Grimaud. And, worst of all, Grimaud was trying to tell us the truth when he knew he was dying. Sit down, and I'll see if I can explain it. Once you have grasped three essential points, the thing will explain itself."

He lowered himself, wheezing, into the chair behind the desk. Then he went on. "The three essential points, then, are these. One, there is no brother Henri; there are only two brothers. Two, both these brothers were speaking the truth. Three, a question of time has turned the case wrong way round.

"Now remember yesterday morning! I already had some occasion to believe there was something queer about that business in Cagliostro Street. The shooting there, we were told by three witnesses who agreed precisely, took place at just ten twenty-five. I wondered, idly, why they corroborated each other with such startling exactitude. In the usual street accident, witnesses don't generally agree about the time with such precision. There must have been some reason for their exactitude.

"Of course there was a reason. Some distance behind where the murdered man fell there was a lighted show window—the only lighted window thereabouts—of a jeweler's shop. It was the first place to which the constable rushed in search of the murderer; it quite naturally focused their attention. And, facing them from that window, there was an enormous clock of unusual design. It was inevitable that the constable should look to it for the time, and natural that the others should also. Hence their agreement.

"But one thing bothered me a little. After Grimaud was shot, Hadley summoned his men to this house and instantly dispatched one of them to pick up Fley as a suspect. Now, then, those men arrived here . . . about what time?"

"About ten forty," said Rampole, calculating roughly.

"And," said Dr. Fell, "a man went immediately to get Fley. This man must have arrived in Cagliostro Street . . . when? Between fifteen and twenty minutes after Fley was presumed to have been killed. But in the space of that brief time what has happened? An incredible number of things! Fley has been carried to the doctor's house, he has died, an examination has been made, an effort undertaken to identify Fley; and then, 'after some delay,' in the words of the newspaper account, the van is sent for and Fley removed to the mortuary. All this! For, when Hadley's detective arrived in Cagliostro Street to pick up Fley, he found the whole business finished—and the constable back making inquiries from door to door. Unfortunately, I was so dense that I didn't see the significance of this even yesterday when I saw the clock in the jeweler's window.

"Think back once more. Yesterday we had breakfast at my house; Pettis dropped in, and we talked to him until . . . when?"

"Until ten o'clock," Hadley answered. "Yes! I remember; Big Ben was striking as Pettis got up to go."

"Quite right. He left us, and afterwards we put on our hats and coats and drove *straight* to Cagliostro Street. Now, allow any reasonable margin of time you like for our putting on our hats, going downstairs, driving a short distance on deserted roads Sunday morning—a drive that took us only ten minutes when there was Saturday-night traffic. The whole process can hardly have taken twenty minutes in all. But in Cagliostro Street you showed me the jeweler's shop, and that fancy clock was just striking *eleven*.

"Even then in my musing density it never occurred to me to look at that clock and wonder, just as in their excitement it never

occurred to the three witnesses last night. Just afterwards, you recall, Somers and O'Rourke summoned us up to Burnaby's flat. We
made a long investigation, and then had a talk with O'Rourke.
And while O'Rourke was speaking, I heard church bells.

"Well, what time *do* church bells begin to ring? Not after eleven
o'clock; the service has begun. Usually before eleven, for a preparatory bell. But, if I accepted the evidence of that German
clock, it must then be a very long time past eleven o'clock. Then
my dull mind woke up. I remembered Big Ben and our drive to
Cagliostro Street. The combination of those bells and Big Ben—
against—hem!—a trumpery foreign clock! In other words, *the
clock in that jeweler's window was more than forty minutes fast.
Hence the shooting in Cagliostro Street the night before could not
have taken place at twenty-five minutes past ten. Actually it must
have taken place a short time previous to a quarter to ten. Say,
roughly, at nine forty—some minutes before the man in the false
face rang the bell of this house at nine forty-five.*"

"But I still don't see," protested Hadley. "If Grimaud, as you
say, shot Fley in Cagliostro Street just before nine forty-five—"

"I didn't say that," said Dr. Fell.

"*What?*"

"You'll understand if you follow my patient elucidation from
the beginning. On Wednesday night of last week—when Fley first
appeared out of the past, apparently out of his grave, to confront
his brother at the Warwick Tavern—Grimaud resolved to kill him.
In the whole case, you see, Grimaud was the only person with a
motive for killing Fley. And, my God! Hadley, but he did have a
motive! He was rich, he was respected; the past was buried. And
then, all of a sudden, a door blows open to admit this grinning
stranger, who is his brother Pierre. Grimaud, in escaping from
prison, had murdered one of his brothers by leaving him buried
alive; he would have murdered the other except for an accident.
He could still be extradited and hanged—and Pierre Fley had
traced him.

"Now, bear in mind exactly what Fley said when he confronted
Grimaud at the tavern. Study *why* he said certain things. Why, if

he were intent merely on private vengeance, did he choose to confront Grimaud in the presence of friends and speak in just the innuendos he used? He used his *dead* brother as a threat; and it was the only time he did speak of that *dead* brother. Why did he say, 'I have a brother who can do much more than I can'? Because the dead brother could hang Grimaud! Why did he say, '*I* don't want your life; he does'? Why did he say, 'Someone will call on you. Would you rather I did—or shall I send my brother?' And why did he hand Grimaud his card on which his own address was written? The giving of that card, combined with his words and later actions, is significant. What Fley really meant, veiled so that he could throw a scare into Grimaud before witnesses, was this: You, my brother, are fat and rich on the proceeds of a robbery we both committed when we were young. I am poor—and I hate my work. Now will you come and call on me, so that we can arrange this matter, or shall I set the police on you?"

"Blackmail," said Hadley softly.

"Yes. Mark how Fley twisted round his meaning in his last threatening words to Grimaud. 'I *also* am in danger when I associate with my brother, but I am prepared to run that risk.' And in that case, as always afterwards, he was referring in strict truth to *Grimaud.* You, my brother, might also kill me as you killed the other, but I will risk it. So shall I call on you amiably, or will my other dead brother come to hang you?

"Think of his behavior afterwards, on the night of his murder. Remember the glee he had smashing up his illusion properties? And the words he used to O'Rourke: 'My work is finished; I shall not need them any longer. . . . Didn't I tell you? I am going to see my brother. He will do something that will settle an old affair for both of us.'

"Meaning, of course, that Grimaud had agreed to come to terms. Fley meant that he was leaving his old life for good; going back to his grave as a dead man with plenty of money. Still, he knew that his brother was tricky. He couldn't leave a specific warning with O'Rourke, in case Grimaud really meant to pay; but he threw out a hint:

"In case anything happens to me . . . you will find my brother in the same street where I myself live. That is not where he really resides, but he has taken a room there.

"I'll explain that last statement in just a moment. But go back to Grimaud. Now, Grimaud never had any intention of coming to terms with Fley. That wily mind of Grimaud's was determined not to suffer any nonsense from this inconvenient brother. Fley must die—but this was difficult.

"If Fley had come to him in private, without anybody ever being able to associate Fley's name with his, it would have been simple. But Fley had been too shrewd for that. He had blazoned forth his own name and address before a group of Grimaud's friends. Awkward! Now if Fley is found murdered, somebody is likely to say, 'Hullo! Isn't that the same chap who . . .' And then presently there may be dangerous inquiries; because Lord knows what Fley may have told *other* people about Grimaud. The only thing he isn't likely to have confided to somebody else is his last deadly hold over Grimaud; and that is the thing about which he must be silenced. However Fley dies, there are likely to be inquiries concerning Grimaud. The only thing to do is frankly to pretend that Fley is after his life; to send himself threatening letters—not too obviously; to stir up the household; finally, to inform everybody that Fley has threatened to call on him on the night he himself plans to call on Fley.

"The effect he intended to produce was this: The murderous Fley should be seen calling on him on Saturday night. There should be witnesses to this. The two should be together alone when Fley goes into his study. A row is heard, the sound of a fight, a shot, and a fall. The door being opened, Grimaud should be found alone—a nasty-looking but superficial wound from a bullet scratched along his side. No weapon is there. Out of the window hangs a rope belonging to Fley, by which Fley is assumed to have escaped. Remember, it had been predicted that there would be *no* snow that night, so it would have been impossible to trace footprints. Grimaud would say, 'He thought he killed me; I pretended to be dead; and he escaped. No, don't set the police on him, poor devil. I'm not hurt.' And the next morning Fley would have been found dead in his own room. He would have been found, a suicide, having pressed his own gun against his chest and pulled the trigger. The gun is beside him. A suicide note lies on the table. In despair at thinking he has killed Grimaud, he has shot himself. . . . That, gentlemen, was the illusion Grimaud intended to produce."

"But how did he do it?" demanded Hadley. "And, anyway, it didn't turn out like that!"

"No. You see, the plan miscarried. The latter part of the illusion of Fley calling on him in his study, when actually Fley would already have been dead in the Cagliostro Street house—I'll deal with in its proper place. Grimaud, with the aid of Madame Dumont, had already made certain preparations.

"He had told Fley to meet him at Fley's room on the top floor over the tobacconist's at nine o'clock on the Saturday night, for a cash settlement. You recall that Fley, gleefully throwing up his job, left the theater in Limehouse at about eight fifteen.

"Grimaud had chosen Saturday night because that night, by inviolable custom, he remained alone all evening in his study without anyone being allowed to disturb him. He chose that night because he needed to use the areaway door, and go and come by way of the basement; and Saturday night was the night out for Annie, who had her quarters there. You'll remember that, after he went up to his study at seven thirty, nobody *did* see him until, according .to the evidence, he opened the study door to admit the visitor at nine fifty. Madame Dumont claimed to have spoken to him in the study at nine thirty, when she gathered up the coffee things. I'll tell you shortly why I disbelieved that statement—the fact is, he was not in the study at all; he was in Cagliostro Street.

"Madame Dumont had been told to lurk round the study door at nine thirty and to come out for some excuse. Why? Because Grimaud had ordered Mills to come upstairs at nine thirty and watch the study door from the room down the hall. Mills was to be the dupe of the illusion Grimaud meant to work. But if—as he

431

came upstairs near the study door—Mills had for any reason taken it into his head to try to speak with Grimaud, or see him, Dumont was there to head him off. Dumont was to wait in the archway and keep Mills away from that door if he showed any curiosity.

"Mills was chosen as the dupe of the illusion. Why? Because although he was so conscientious that he would carry out his instructions to the tick, he would be so afraid of 'Fley' that he would not interfere when the hollow man came stalking up those stairs. It was not only that he must not attack the man in the false face before the man got into the study—as, for instance, Mangan or even Drayman might have done—but also that he must not even venture out of his room. He had been told to stay in that room, and he would. Finally, he had been chosen because he was a very short man, a fact which will presently become clear.

"Now, he was told to go upstairs and watch at nine thirty. This was because the hollow man was timed to make his appearance only a little afterwards; although, in fact, the hollow man was late. Mark one discrepancy. Mills was told nine thirty—but Mangan was told ten o'clock! The reason is obvious. There was to be somebody downstairs to testify that a visitor had really arrived by the front door, confirming Dumont. But Mangan might be inclined towards curiosity about this visitor; he might be inclined to challenge the hollow man . . . unless he had first been jokingly told by Grimaud that the visitor would probably not arrive at all, or, if he did arrive, it could not possibly be before ten o'clock. All that was necessary was to throw his mind off, and make him hesitate long enough for the hollow man to get upstairs past that dangerous door. And, if worse came to worst, Mangan and Rosette could be locked in.

"For everybody else: Annie was out, Drayman had been supplied with a ticket to a concert, Burnaby was unquestionably playing cards, and Pettis was at the theater. The field was clear.

"Grimaud slipped out of the house—probably about ten minutes before nine o'clock—using the area door up to the street. Trouble had already started. It had been snowing heavily for some time, contrary to rules. But Grimaud did not regard it as serious trouble. He believed he could do the business and return by half past nine, and that it would still be snowing heavily enough to gloss over any footprints that he would make, and cause no comment on the absence of any footprints the visitor later *should* have made when the visitor would be supposed to have swung down from his window. In any case, his plans had been carried too far for him to back out.

"When he left the house, he was carrying an old untraceable Colt revolver, loaded with just two bullets. The sort of hat he wore I don't know, but his overcoat was a light yellow, glaring tweed several sizes too large. He bought it because it was the kind of coat he had never been known to wear and because nobody would recognize him in it if he were to be seen. He—"

Hadley intervened. "Stop a bit! What about that business of the overcoats changing color?"

"Again I've got to ask you to wait until we get to the last illusion he worked; that's a part of it. Well, Grimaud's purpose was to call on Fley. There he would speak with Fley amiably for a time. He would say something like, 'You must leave this hovel, brother! You will be comfortably off now; so why not leave these useless possessions behind and come to my house? Let your landlord have the damned things in place of notice!' Any sort of speech, you see, the purpose being to make Fley write one of his ambiguous notes for the landlord. 'I am leaving for good. I am going back to my grave.' Anything *that could be understood as a suicide note when Fley was found dead with a gun in his hand.*"

Dr. Fell leaned forward. "And then Grimaud would take out his Colt, jam it against Fley's chest, and pull the trigger.

"It was the top floor of an otherwise empty house. As you have seen, the walls are astonishingly thick and solid. The landlord lived far down in the basement. No shot, especially a muffled one, could have been heard. It might be some time before the body was discovered; it would certainly not be before morning. And in the meantime, after killing Fley, Grimaud would turn the same gun on himself to give himself a slight wound. He had, as we know from that little episode of the three coffins years before, the constitution of an ox and the nerve of hell. Then he would leave the gun lying beside Fley. He would quite coolly clap a handkerchief or cotton wool across his own wound, which must be *inside* the coat; bind it with adhesive tape until the time came to rip it open—and go back home to work his illusion, which should prove that Fley came to see him. That Fley shot him, and then returned to Cagliostro Street and used the same gun for suicide, no coroner's jury would afterwards doubt.

"That, as I say, was what Grimaud *intended* to do. It would have been an ingenious murder; I doubt whether we should ever have questioned Fley's suicide.

"Now, there was only one difficulty about accomplishing this plan. If anybody were seen visiting Fley's house, the fat would be in the fire. It might not appear so easily as suicide. There was only one entrance from the street—the door beside the tobacconist's. And he was wearing a conspicuous coat, in which he had reconnoitered the ground before—Dolberman, the tobacconist, had seen him hanging about. He found the solution of his difficulty in Burnaby's secret flat.

"You see, of course, that Grimaud was likeliest to have known of Burnaby's flat in Cagliostro Street? Burnaby himself told us that when Grimaud suspected him of having an ulterior motive in painting that picture, Grimaud had not only questioned him—he had *watched* him. He knew of the flat. He knew from spying that Rosette had a key. And so, when the time came, he stole it.

"The house in which Burnaby had his flat was on the same side of the street as the house where Fley lived. All those houses are built side by side, with flat roofs; so that you have only to step over a low wall to walk on the roofs from one end of the street to the other. Both men, remember, lived on the top floor. You recall what we saw when we went up to look at Burnaby's flat—just beside the door to the flat?"

Hadley nodded. "A ladder going to a trapdoor in the roof."

"Exactly. And on the landing outside Fley's room there is a low skylight also communicating with the roof. Grimaud had only to go to Cagliostro Street by the back way, never appearing in the street itself, but going up the alley which we saw from Burnaby's window. He came in the back door and went up to the roof. Then he followed the roofs to Fley's lodgings, descended through the skylight, and could both enter and leave the place without a soul seeing him. Moreover, he knew that that night Burnaby would be playing cards elsewhere.

"He must have got to Fley's lodgings before Fley arrived there himself; it wouldn't do to make Fley suspicious by being seen coming from the roof. And then everything went wrong. We know that Fley had some suspicions already. This may have been caused by Grimaud's request for Fley to bring along one of his long conjuring ropes. . . . Grimaud wanted that rope as evidence to use later against Fley. Or it may have been caused by Fley's knowledge that Grimaud had been hanging about in Cagliostro Street, thereby making Fley believe he had taken a room in the street.

"The brothers met in that gaslit room at nine. What they talked about we don't know. But evidently Grimaud lulled Fley's suspicions; they became pleasant and amiable; and Grimaud jocularly persuaded him to write that note for the landlord. Then—"

"I'm not disputing all this," said Hadley quietly, "but how do you happen to know it?"

"Grimaud told us," said Dr. Fell, and Hadley stared.

"Oh yes. Once I had tumbled to that terrible mistake in times, I could understand. You'll see. But to continue.

"Fley had written his note. He had got into his hat and coat for departure—because Grimaud wished it to be assumed that he had killed himself just after having returned from a journey *outdoors:* his return from the phantom visit to Grimaud, in other words. They were all ready to go. And then Grimaud leaped.

"Whether Fley was subconsciously on his guard; whether he ran for the door, since he was no match for the powerful Grimaud; this we do not know. But Grimaud, with the gun against Fley's coat as Fley wrenched round, made a hellish mistake. He fired. And he put the bullet in the wrong place. Instead of getting his victim through the heart, he got him under the left shoulder blade. It was a fatal wound, but far from instantly fatal.

"Of course Fley went down. It was the wisest course, or Grimaud might have finished him. But Grimaud, for a second, must have lost his nerve. This might have wrecked his whole plan. *Could* a man shoot himself in that spot? If not, God help the murderer. And worse—Fley had screamed out before the bullet went home, and Grimaud thought he heard pursuers.

"He had sense enough, even in that hellish moment, to keep his head. He jammed the pistol into the hand of the motionless Fley, lying on his face. He picked up the rope. Somehow the plan must go on. But he couldn't risk the noise of another shot to be heard by people possibly listening. He darted out of the room and up to the roof. He heard imaginary pursuers everywhere; maybe some grisly recollection came back to him of three graves in a storm below the Hungarian mountains. He dashed for the trapdoor at Burnaby's and down into the dark of Burnaby's flat.

"And, meantime, what has happened? Pierre Fley is fatally hurt. But he still has the ribs of that iron frame which once enabled him to survive being buried alive. The murderer has gone. And Fley will *not* give in. He must get help. He must get to ...

"*To a doctor*, Hadley. You asked yesterday why Fley was walking towards the other end of the street, towards the end of a blind alley. Because a doctor lived there: the doctor to whose office he later was carried. He gets up, still in his hat and overcoat. The gun has been put into his hand; he rams it in his pocket. Down he goes, as steadily as he can, to a silent street where no alarm has been raised. He walks on. . . .

"Have you asked yourself why he was walking in the middle of the street, looking sharply round? Because he knew the murderer to be lurking somewhere, and he expected another attack. . . .

"But what has happened to Grimaud? Although Grimaud has heard no pursuit, he is half insane with wondering. But stop a moment! If there has been any discovery, he will be able to know by looking for a second out into the street. He can go down to the front door and peer out, can't he? No danger in that, since the house where Burnaby lives is deserted that night.

"He goes downstairs. He opens the door softly, having unbuttoned his coat to wind the rope round him inside that overcoat. He opens the door—full in the glow of a streetlamp just beyond the door—and facing him, walking slowly in the middle of the street, is the man he left for dead in the other house less than ten minutes ago.

"And for the last time those brothers come face-to-face.

"Grimaud's shirt is a target under that streetlamp. And Fley, mad with pain, does not hesitate. He screams. *He* cries the words, 'The second bullet is for *you!*'—just before he whips up the same pistol and fires.

"That last effort is too much. The hemorrhage has got him, and he knows it. He screams again, lets go of the gun as he tries to throw it—now empty—at Grimaud; and then he pitches forward on his face. That, my lads, is the shot which the three witnesses heard in Cagliostro Street. It was the shot which struck Grimaud in the chest just before he had time to close the door."

X: The Unraveling

"AND then?" prompted Hadley, as Dr. Fell paused and lowered his head.

"The three witnesses did not see Grimaud, of course," went on Dr. Fell, "because he was never outside the door; never within twenty feet of the man who *seemed* to have been murdered in the middle of a snow desert. Of course Fley already had the wound, which jetted blood from the last convulsion. Of course any deduction from the direction of the wound was useless. Of course there were no fingerprints on the gun, since it landed in snow and in a literal sense had been washed clean."

"By God!" said Hadley. "It fulfills every condition of the facts, and yet I never thought of it. . . . But go on. Grimaud?"

"Grimaud is inside the door. He knows he's got it in his chest; but he doesn't think it's serious. After all, he's only got what he was going to give himself—a wound. But his plan has crashed to hell! How is he to know, by the way, that the clock at the jeweler's will be fast? He doesn't even know that Fley is dead. All he is sure of is that Fley will never now be found a suicide, in his room. He assumes that Fley—dangerously wounded, yes, but still able to talk—is out in that street with a policeman running towards him. Grimaud is undone.

"He can't stay in that hall. He'd better have a look at his wound, though, and make sure he doesn't leave a trail of blood. Where? Up he goes to Burnaby's flat and switches on the lights. Here's the rope wound round him . . . no use for *that* now; he can't pretend Fley called on him, when Fley may now be talking with the police. He flings the rope off and leaves it.

"A look at the wound next. There's blood all over the inside of that light tweed overcoat, and blood on his inner clothes. But the wound is of small consequence. He's got his handkerchief and adhesive tape, and he can plug himself up. Károly Horváth, whom nothing can kill, feels as steady and fresh as ever. But he patches himself up—hence the blood in Burnaby's bathroom—and tries to collect his wits. What time is it? Good God! It's nearly a quarter to ten. Got to get out and hurry home before they catch him. . . .

"And he leaves the lights on. They burned up a shilling's worth and went out later in the night. They were on three-quarters of an hour afterwards, anyhow, when Rosette saw them.

"I think his sanity returns as he hurries home. *Is* he caught? It seems inevitable. Yet is there any loophole, any ghost of a chance? There *is* one chance, so thin that it's almost useless; but the only one. That's to carry through his original scheme and pretend that Fley has called on him and given him that wound *in his own house*. Fley still has the gun. It will be Grimaud's word, and his witnesses' word, that he never left the house all evening! Whereas they can swear that Fley did come to see him—and then let the damned police try to prove anything! Grimaud has thrown away the rope Fley was supposed to have used. But it's a toss-up, a last daring of the devil, the only course in an extremity. . . .

"Fley shot him at about twenty minutes to ten. He gets back here at a quarter to ten or a little after. Getting into the house without leaving a footprint in the snow? Easy, for a man with a constitution like an ox, and only slightly wounded! By the way, I believe he was really wounded only slightly, and that he'd live now to hang, if he hadn't done certain things; you'll see. He'll return by way of the steps down to the areaway, and the area door, as arranged. How? Well, there is snow on the areaway steps, of course. But the entrance to the areaway steps is beside the next house, isn't it? And, at the foot of the area steps, the basement door is protected from snow by a projection: the projection of the main front steps overhanging. So that there is no snow exactly in front of the area door. If he can get down there without leaving a mark—

"He can. He can approach from the other direction, as though he were going to the house next door, and then simply jump down the area steps to the cleared patch below. . . . Don't I seem to remember a thud, which Rosette Grimaud heard just before the front doorbell rang?"

"But didn't he ring the front doorbell?"

"Oh yes—but from inside. After he'd gone into the house by the area door, and up to where Ernestine Dumont was waiting for him. Then they were ready to perform their illusion."

"Yes," said Hadley. "Now we come to the illusion. How was it done, and how do you know how it was done?"

Dr. Fell sat back and tapped his fingertips together. "How do I know? Well, I think my first suggestion was the weight of that picture." He pointed at the big slashed canvas leaning against the wall. "Yes. But that wasn't very helpful, until I remembered something else. . . ."

"Weight of the picture? Yes, the picture," growled Hadley. "How does *it* figure in the blasted business, anyhow? It doesn't weigh very much. You yourself picked it up with one hand."

Dr. Fell sat up with excitement. "Exactly. You've hit it. I picked it up with one hand. . . . Then why should it take two husky men, the cabman and one extra, to carry it upstairs? It did, you know. That was twice pointed out to us. Grimaud, when he took it from Burnaby's studio, easily carried it downstairs. Yet, when he returned here with that same painting late in the afternoon, two people had a job carting it up. Where had it picked up so much weight? He didn't have glass put in it. And why did Grimaud insist on having the picture wrapped up? It wasn't a very farfetched deduction to think that he used that picture as a blind to hide something that the men were carrying up, unintentionally, along with it, in the same parcel. Something very big . . . seven feet by four . . . h'm. . . ."

"But there couldn't have been anything," objected Hadley, "or we'd have found it in this room, wouldn't we? In any case the thing must have been almost absolutely flat, or it would have been noticed in the wrappings of the picture. What sort of object is as big as seven feet by four, yet thin enough not to be noticed inside the wrappings of a picture; and which can be spirited out of sight when you wish?"

"A mirror," said Dr. Fell. He went on. "And it can be spirited out of sight, as you put it, merely by being pushed up the very shallow flue of that very broad chimney—and propped up on the ledge inside where the chimney turns. You don't need magic. You only need to be damnably strong in the arms. Now, look round this room. What do you see in the wall directly opposite the door?"

"Nothing," said Hadley. "I mean, there's only blank paneled wall where the bookcases have been cleared away."

"So if you were out in that hall looking in, you would see only black carpet, no furniture, and to the rear an expanse of blank oak-paneled wall?"

"Yes."

"Now, Ted, open the door and look out into the hall," said Dr. Fell. "What about the walls and carpet out there?"

Rampole made a feint of looking, although he knew. "They're just the same," he said. "The floor is one solid carpet running to the baseboards, like this one, and the paneling is the same."

"Right! By the way, Hadley," pursued Dr. Fell, "you might drag out that mirror from behind the bookcase over there. It's been behind the bookcase since yesterday afternoon, when Drayman found it in the chimney. It was lifting it down that brought on his stroke. We'll try a little experiment. I want you to take that mirror, Hadley, and set it up just inside the door, so that when you open the door—it opens inwards and to the right, you see, as you come in from the hall—the edge of the door at its outermost swing is a few inches away from the mirror."

Hadley trundled out the object he found behind the bookcase. It was higher and wider than the door. Its base rested flat on the carpet, and it was supported upright by a heavy swing base on the right-hand side as you faced it. Hadley regarded it curiously.

"Set it up inside the door?"

"Yes. The door will only swing open a short distance; you'll see an aperture only a couple of feet wide at the most. . . . Try it!"

"I know, but if you do that . . . well, somebody sitting in the room down at the end of the hall, where Mills was, would see his own reflection smack in the middle of the mirror."

"Not at all. Not at the angle—a slight angle—to which I'm going to tilt it. You'll see. The two of you go down there where Mills was while I adjust it. Keep your eyes off until I sing out."

Hadley, muttering, but still highly interested, tramped down after Rampole. They kept their eyes off until they heard the doctor's hail, and then turned round.

The hallway was gloomy and its black-carpeted length ran down to a closed door. Dr. Fell stood outside that door, a little to the right of it and well back from it against the wall. His hand stretched out across to the knob.

"Here she goes!" He grunted, and quickly opened the door—hesitated—and closed it. "Well? What did you see?"

DIAGRAM TO ILLUSTRATE ILLUSION

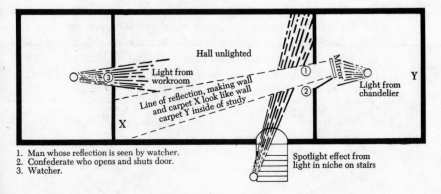

1. Man whose reflection is seen by watcher.
2. Confederate who opens and shuts door.
3. Watcher.

"I saw the room inside," returned Hadley. "Or at least I thought I did. I saw the carpet and the rear wall. It seemed a very big room."

"You didn't see that," said Dr. Fell. "As a matter of fact, you saw the reflection of the paneled wall immediately to the right of the door where you're standing, and the carpet going up to it. That's why it seemed so big a room: you were looking at a double length of reflection. This mirror is bigger than the door, you know. And you didn't see a reflection of the door itself because it opens inwards to the right. If you looked carefully, you might have seen a line of what looks like shadow just along the top edge of the door. That's where the top edge of the mirror inevitably reflects, being taller, an inch or so of the *inner* top edge of the door. But your attention would be concentrated on any figures you saw. . . . Did you see me, by the way?"

"No; you were too far over. You had your arm across the door to the knob, and kept back."

"Yes. As Dumont was standing. Now try a last experiment before I explain how the whole mechanism worked. Ted, you sit down in the chair behind that desk—where Mills was sitting. You're much taller than he is, but it will illustrate the idea. I'm going to stand outside, with this door open, and look at myself in the mirror. Just tell me what you see."

In the ghostly light, with the door partly open, a figure of Dr. Fell stood inside the door, looking at another figure of Dr. Fell standing on the threshold and confronting himself—fixed and motionless, with a startled look. The effect was rather eerie.

"I don't touch the door, you see," a voice boomed at them. By the illusion of the moving lips Rampole would have sworn that the Dr. Fell inside the door was speaking. The mirror threw the voice back like a sounding board. "Somebody obligingly opens and closes the door for me—somebody standing at my right. I don't touch the door, or my reflection would have to do likewise. Quick, what do you notice?"

"Why—one of you is very much taller," said Rampole.

"Which one?"

"You yourself: the figure in the hall."

"Exactly. First because you're seeing it at a distance, but the most important thing is that you're sitting down. To a man the size of Mills I should look like a giant. Hey? H'mf. Hah. Yes. Now if I make a quick move to dodge in at that door, and at the same time my confederate at the right makes a quick confusing move with me and slams the door, in the muddled illusion the figure inside seems to be—"

"Jumping in front of you to keep you out."

"Yes. Now come and read the evidence, if Hadley has it."

When they were again in the room, Dr. Fell sank into a chair, sighing. "I'm sorry, gents. I should have realized the truth long before, from the careful, methodical, exact Mr. Mills's evidence. Let me see if I can repeat from memory his exact words. Check me up, Hadley. H'm." He rapped his knuckles against his head and scowled. "Like this:

"She [Dumont] was about to knock at the door when I was startled to see the tall man come upstairs directly after her. She turned round and saw him. She exclaimed certain words. . . . The tall man made no reply. He walked to the door, and without haste turned down the collar of his coat and removed his cap, which he placed in his overcoat pocket. . . .

"You see, gents? He had to do that, because the reflection couldn't show a cap and couldn't show a collar turned up when the figure inside must appear to be wearing a dressing gown. But I wondered *why* he was so methodical about that, since apparently he didn't remove the mask—"

"Yes, what about that mask? Mills says he didn't—"

"Mills didn't see him take it off; I'll show you why as soon as we go on with Mills:

"Madame Dumont cried out something, shrank back against the wall, and hurried to open the door. Dr. Grimaud appeared on the threshold. . . .

"Appeared! That's precisely what he did do. Our methodical witness is uncomfortably exact. But Dumont? There was the first flaw. A frightened woman, looking up at a terrifying figure while she's standing before the door of a room in which there's a man who will protect her, doesn't *shrink back*. She rushes towards the door to get protection. Anyhow, follow Mills's testimony. He says, Grimaud was not wearing his eyeglasses—they wouldn't have fitted behind that mask. But the natural movement of a man inside, I thought, would have been to raise his glasses. Grimaud—according to Mills—stands *stock-still* the whole time; like the stranger, with his hands in his pockets. Now for the damning part. Mills says, 'I am under the impression that Madame Dumont, although she was shrinking back against the wall, closed the door after him. I recall that she had her hand on the knob.' Not a natural action for her, either! She contradicted him—but Mills was right.

"Now here was my difficulty: if Grimaud was alone in that room, if he simply walked in on his own reflection, what became of his clothes? What about that long black overcoat, the brown peaked cap, even the false face? They weren't in the room. Then I remembered that Ernestine Dumont's profession had been the making of costumes for the opera and ballet; I remembered a story O'Rourke had told us; and I knew—"

"Well?"

"That Grimaud had burned them," said Dr. Fell. "He had burned them because they were made of paper, like the uniform of the vanishing horseman described by O'Rourke. He couldn't risk the long, dangerous business of burning real clothes in that fire; he had to work too fast. They had to be torn up and burned. And bundles of loose, blank sheets of writing paper—perfectly blank!—had to be burned on top of them to hide the fact that some of it was colored paper. Dangerous letters! Oh my God, I could murder myself for thinking such a thing!" He shook his fist. "When there was no blood trail, no bloodstain at all, going to the drawer in his desk where he did keep his important papers! And there was another reason for burning papers. . . . They had to conceal the fragments of the shot."

"Shot?"

"Don't forget that a pistol was supposed to have been fired in that room. Of course, what the witnesses really heard was a heavy firecracker—pinched from the hoard Drayman always keeps, as you know, for Guy Fawkes night. Drayman discovered the missing thunderbolt; I think that's how he tumbled to the scheme, and why he kept muttering about fireworks. Well, the fragments of an exploding firecracker fly wide. They're heavy cardboard, hard to burn, and they had to be destroyed in the fire or hidden in that drift of papers. I found some of them. Of course we should have realized no bullet had really been fired. Modern cartridges—such as you informed me were used in that Colt revolver—have smokeless powder. You can smell it, but you can't see it. And yet there was a *haze* in this room, left by the firecracker.

"Ah, well, let's recapitulate! Grimaud's heavy crepe-paper uniform consisted of a black coat—black and long like a dressing gown, and having at the front shiny lapels which would show like a dressing gown when you turned down the collar to face your own image. It consisted of a paper cap, to which the false face was attached—so that in sweeping off the cap you simply folded both together and shoved 'em into your pocket. The real dressing gown, by the way, was already in this room while Grimaud was out. And the black uniform, early last evening, had been incautiously hung up in the closet downstairs.

"Mangan, unfortunately, spotted it. The watchful Dumont knew that he spotted it and whisked it out of that cupboard to a safer place as soon as he went away. She, naturally, never saw a yellow tweed coat hanging there at all. Grimaud had it upstairs here with him, ready for his expedition. But it was found in the closet yesterday afternoon, and she had to pretend it had been there all the time. Hence the chameleon overcoat.

"You can now make a reconstruction of just what happened when Grimaud, after killing Fley and getting a bullet himself, returned to the house on Saturday night. Right at the start of the illusion, he and his confederate were in dangerous trouble. You see, Grimaud was late. He'd expected to be back by nine thirty—and he didn't get here until a quarter to ten. The longer he delayed, the nearer it got to the time he had told *Mangan* to expect a visitor, and now Mangan would be expecting the visitor he had been told to watch. It was touch and go, and I rather imagine the cool Grimaud was fairly close to insane. He got up through the basement entrance, where his confederate was waiting. The tweed coat, with the blood inside it, went into the hall closet to be disposed of presently—and it never was, because he died. Dumont eased open the door, rang the bell by putting her hand out, and then went to 'answer' it while Grimaud was getting ready with his uniform.

"But they delayed too long. Mangan called out, and Grimaud, growing panicky, made a blunder to ward off immediate detection. He said that he was Pettis, and locked them in. You notice that Pettis is the only one with a voice of the same bass quality as Grimaud's? Yes, it was a spur-of-the-moment error, but his only wish was to writhe like a footballer down a field and *somehow* escape those hands for the moment.

"The illusion at the door of his study was performed; he was alone in his room. His jacket, probably with blood on it, had been taken in charge by Dumont; he wore the uniform over his shirt sleeves, open shirt, and bandaged wound. He had only to lock the door behind him, put on his real dressing gown, destroy the paper uniform, and get that mirror up into the chimney. . . .

"That, I say again, was the finish. The blood had begun to flow again, you see. No ordinary man, wounded, could have stood the strain under which he had already been. He wasn't killed by Fley's bullet. He ripped his own lung like a rotted piece of rubber when he tried to—and superhumanly did—lift that mirror into its hiding place. Then was when he began to bleed from the mouth like a slashed artery; when he staggered against the couch, knocked away the chair, and reeled forward in his last successful effort to ignite the firecracker. After all the hates and dodgings and plans, the world was slowly going black. He tried to scream out and he could not, for the blood was welling in his throat. And at that moment Charles Grimaud suddenly knew what he would never have believed possible, the breaking of the last and most shattering mirror illusion in his bitter life. . . ."

"Well?"

"He knew that he was dying," said Dr. Fell. "And, stranger than any of his dreams, he was glad."

The heavy leaden light had begun to darken again with snow. Dr. Fell's voice sounded weirdly in the chill room. Then they saw that the door was opening and that in it stood the figure of a woman with a damned face. A damned face and a black dress, but round her shoulders was still drawn a red brocade shawl for love of the dead.

"You see, he confessed," Dr. Fell said in the same low, monotonous tone. "He tried to tell us the truth about his killing of Fley, and Fley's killing of him. Only we did not choose to understand, and I didn't understand until I knew from the clock what must have happened in Cagliostro Street. Man, man, don't you see? Take first the statement made just before he died:

"It was my brother who did it. I never thought he would shoot. God knows how he got out of that room. . . ."

"You mean Fley's room in Cagliostro Street, after Fley had been left for dead?" demanded Hadley.

"Yes. And the horrible shock of coming on him suddenly, as Grimaud opened the door under the streetlight. You see:

"One second he was there, and the next he wasn't. . . . I want to tell you who my brother is, so you won't think I'm raving.

"For, of course he did not think anybody knew about Fley. Now, in the light of that, examine the muddled, half-choked words with which he tried to explain the whole puzzle to us.

"First he tried to tell us about the Horváths and the salt mine. But he went on to the killing of Fley, and what Fley had done to him. 'Not suicide.' When he'd seen Fley in the street, he couldn't make Fley's death the suicide he pretended. 'He couldn't use rope.' Fley couldn't, after that, be supposed to use the rope that Grimaud had discarded as useless. 'Roof.' Grimaud did not mean this roof, but the other roof which he crossed when he left Fley's room. 'Snow.' The snow had stopped and wrecked his plans. 'Too *much light.'* There's the crux, Hadley! When he looked out into the street, there was too much light from the streetlamp; Fley recognized him, and fired. *'Got gun.'* Naturally, Fley had got the gun then. *'Fox.'* The mask, the Guy Fawkes charade he tried to work. But finally, *'Don't blame poor—'* Not Drayman; he didn't mean Drayman. But it was a last apology for the one thing, I think, of which he was ashamed; the one piece of imposture he would never have done. 'Don't blame poor Pettis; I didn't mean to implicate him.'"

For a long time nobody spoke.

"Yes," Hadley agreed dully. "Yes. All except one thing. What about the slashing of that picture, and where did the knife go?"

"The slashing of the picture, I think, was an extra touch of the picturesque to help the illusion. Grimaud did it—or so I imagine. As for the knife, I frankly don't know. Grimaud probably had it here, and put it up the chimney beside the mirror so that the invisible man should seem to be doubly armed. But it isn't on the chimney ledge now. I should suppose that Drayman found it yesterday and took it away—"

"That is the one point," said a voice, "on which you are wrong."

Ernestine Dumont remained in the doorway, her hands folded across the shawl at her breast. But she was smiling.

"I have heard everything you said," she went on. "Perhaps you can hang me, or perhaps not. That is not important. I do know that after so many years it is not quite worthwhile going on without Charles. I took the knife, my friend. I had another use for it."

She was still smiling, and there was a blaze of pride in her eyes. Rampole saw what her hands were hiding. He saw her totter suddenly, but he was too late to catch her when she pitched forward on her face. Dr. Fell lumbered out of his chair and remained staring at her with a face as white as her own.

"I have committed another crime, Hadley," he said. "I have guessed the truth again."

The Death of
Don Juan

The Death of
Don Juan

A CONDENSATION OF
THE SHORT STORY BY

**Ellery
Queen**

Ellery Queen was having a much
deserved vacation when impresario
Scutney Bluefield invited him to see his
small-town production of the play
The Death of Don Juan. It was far from
the mind of the famous criminal investigator
that this innocent invitation would involve
him in a backstage murder.

One of the best known names in
American detective fiction, Ellery Queen
is the pseudonym of Frederic Dannay and
the late Manfred B. Lee. Their stories have been
frequently dramatized both in film and on television,
and some of Queen's most famous adventures are
told in *The Roman Hat Mystery,*
The Chinese Orange Mystery
and *Calamity Town.*

ACT I

Scene 1

An EARLY account of the death of Don Juan Tenorio, fourteenth-century Spanish libertine—who, according to his valet, enjoyed the embraces of no fewer than 2954 mistresses during his lifetime—relates that the great lover was murdered in a monastery by Franciscan monks enraged by his virility. For four hundred years poets and dramatists have passed up this ending to Don Juan's mighty career as too unimaginative.

No such charge can be brought against *their* versions, and the tale counts among its affectionate adapters Molière, Mozart's librettist Da Ponte, Dumas *père*, Balzac, and Shaw. Now to the roster must be added the modest name of Ellery Queen, who has fathered his own. According to Ellery, Don Juan was really murdered in a New England town named Wrightsville, and this is how it came about.

Wrightsville's dramatic appetite was catered to by the Bijou Theater in High Village, owned and operated by Scutney Bluefield. Scutney Bluefield was a rare specimen in the Wrightsville zoo. Where the young of the first families grew up to work with their money, Scutney played with it. As he often said, his vocation was hobbies. He collected such unexpected things as chastity belts,

Minié balls, and shrunken heads. The old Bluefield mansion on the hill was usually infested with freeloaders no one in Wrightsville had ever laid eyes on—"my people collection," he called them. He flitted from Yoga to Zen to voodoo, and then came back to the Congregational church.

Scutney Bluefield looked like a rabbit about to drop its first litter, but there was a sweet, stubborn innocence in the portly little bachelor that some found appealing.

He bought the Bijou because he discovered The Theater. To prepare himself, he lived for two years in New York studying drama, then hurried home to organize an amateur company.

"My plan," he told the Wrightsville *Record* reporter, "is to establish a permanent repertory theater, a year-round project to be staffed by local talent."

Scutney's secret weapon was Joan Truslow. Joanie was what the boys at the Lions luncheons called "real stacked," with natural ash-blond hair and enormous spring-violet eyes. She was the first to answer Scutney's call, and her audition awed him.

"*Wonderful*," he had confided to Roger Fowler. "That girl will make us all *proud*."

Rodge was not comforted. A chemical engineer, he had used his cut of Great-Uncle Fowler's pie to buy one of the blackened brick plants standing idle along the Willow River in Low Village and to convert it to Fowler Chemicals, Inc. His interest in Scutney Bluefield's Playhouse was Joan Truslow, whom he had been chasing since puberty. To keep an eye on her, young Fowler had offered his services to Scutney as a technician-in-charge, responsible for carpentry, props, lights, and other dreary indispensables.

Scutney did the Bijou over, inside and out, and renamed it the Playhouse. It cost him a fortune, and it was a resounding flop, Joanie Truslow notwithstanding. Scutney tried Shaw, Kaufman and Hart, Tennessee Williams; comedy, farce, melodrama, and tragedy. They continued to play to dwindling houses.

"Of course, we're not very *good* yet," Scutney reflected aloud after a lethal week.

"Joan's colossal, and you know it," Rodge Fowler said in spite of himself. "But look, Scutney, how much more of your ancestral dough are you prepared to drop into this cultural outhouse we call home?"

Scutney said in his precise, immovable way, "I am *not* giving up yet, Roger." Still, the empty seats kept spreading like a rash; so Scutney Bluefield flung himself into the Viking throne in his catch-all study, and he thought and thought.

All at once the name Archer Dullman flew into his head.

Ten minutes later Wrightsville's patron of the performing arts was driving lickety-hop for the airport and the next plane connection to New York.

Scene 2

ELLERY checked in at the Hollis, showered and changed, cased the lobby, toured the square, and returned to the hotel without having seen a single familiar face.

He was waiting for the maître d' in a queue of strangers at the entrance to the main dining room when a voice behind him said, "Mr. Queen, I presume?"

"Roger!" Ellery wrung young Fowler's hand like Dr. Livingstone at Ujiji. The truth was, he had met Rodge Fowler less than half a dozen times during his visits to Wrightsville. "How are you? What's happened to this town?"

"I'm fine, and it's still here with certain modifications," Roger said. "What brings you thisaway?"

"I'm bound for the Mahoganies—vacation. I hear you're Wrightsville's latest outbreak of industrial genius."

"That's what they tell me, but who told you?"

"I'm a *Record* mail subscriber from way back. How come you've joined a drama group, Rodge? I thought you got your kicks in a chem lab."

"Love," Roger said hollowly. "Or whatever they're calling it these days."

"Of course. Joan Truslow. But isn't the company folding? That ought to drop Joanie back into your lap."

Roger looked glum. *"The Death of Don Juan."*

"That old stand of corn? Even Wrightsville—"

"You're not getting the message, man. Starring Mark Manson. Complete with doublet, hose, and codpiece. We open tomorrow night."

"Manson." Ellery stared. "Who dug him up?"

"Scutney Bluefield, via some Times Square undertaker named Archer Dullman. Manson's a pretty lively corpse though. We're sold out for the run."

"The Death of Don Juan," Ellery said admiringly. "This I've got to see."

"There's Scutney at that corner table now, with Manson and Dullman. I'm meeting them for supper. Why not join us?"

Ellery had forgotten how much like a happy rabbit Scutney Bluefield looked. "I'm *delighted* you're here for the opening," Scutney cried when they came up. "You will be, Ellery, won't you?"

"If I have to hang from a rafter. I haven't had the pleasure of attending one of Mr. Manson's performances in—" Ellery had been about to say "in a great many years," but he changed it to "in some time."

"How are things at the Embassy, Mr. Green?" Manson asked sadly, tilting his cocktail glass, finding it empty, running his forefinger around the inside of the glass, and licking the finger. The wavering finger then pushed the empty glass into alignment with nine others, whereupon Manson smiled at Ellery and fell asleep.

Scutney looked peevish. "I do hope—"

"Don't worry, Bluefield. He never misses a curtain."

Ellery turned, surprised. The speaker was the man introduced to him as Archer Dullman. Dullman was not large and not small, neither fat nor thin, ruddy nor pale. Hair, eyes, voice were neutral.

"Are you Mr. Manson's manager, Mr. Dullman?"

"It's a buck."

Ellery buttered a roll. "By the way, isn't it an Actors Equity rule that members may not perform with amateurs?"

It was Scutney who answered; in rather a hurry, Ellery thought.

"Oh, but you can almost always get Equity's permission in special cases. Ah, the soup!" He greeted the arrival of their waitress with relief. "Best chowder in town. Right, Minnie?"

Ellery wondered what was bugging the little man.

"They've been calling us the Haunted Playhouse and laughing their heads off." Scutney was chortling. "Who's laughing now?"

"Not me," Rodge Fowler growled. "That scene on the couch between Manson and Joan in the first act is an absolute disgrace."

"How would you expect Don Juan to act on a couch?" Dullman asked with a smile.

"You didn't have to direct it that way, Dullman!"

"Oh, you're directing?" Ellery murmured. But nobody heard him.

Manson chose that moment to wake up. He peered around the crowded dining room and staggered to his feet. His hairpiece had come loose and slipped to one side, exposing a hemisphere of dead-white scalp. "My dear, dear friends." He stood there like some aged Caesar in his cups, bowing to his people; and then, with simple confidence, he slid into Dullman's arms.

Scutney and Roger were half out of their chairs. But Ellery was already supporting the actor's other side. Between them they dragged Manson, graciously smiling, from the dining room. The lobby seethed with people attending a Ladies Aid ball; a great many were waiting for the elevators.

"We can't maneuver him through that mob, Dullman. What floor is he on?"

"Second."

"Then let's walk him up. Manson, lift your feet. That's it. You're doing nobly."

Ellery and Dullman hustled him up the staircase toward the mezzanine. Scutney and Roger came running up behind them.

"How is he?" Scutney panted.

"Beginning to feel pain, I think," Ellery said. "How about it, Manson?"

"My dear sir," the actor said indulgently. "Anyone would think I am intoxicated. Really, this is undignified and unnecessary."

He achieved the mezzanine landing and paused there to re-cuperate. Ellery glanced at Dullman, and Dullman nodded. They released him. It was a mistake.

Ellery grabbed in vain. "*Catch him!*" But both Scutney and Roger stood there, stunned. Manson, still smiling, toppled back-ward between them.

Fascinated, they watched the star of *The Death of Don Juan* bounce his way step after step down the long marble staircase until he landed on the lobby floor and lay still.

Scene 3

THEY went straight from the hospital to Dullman's room at the Hollis. Dullman sat down at the telephone.

"Long distance? New York City. Phil Stone, theatrical agent, West Forty-fourth Street."

"Stone." Scutney was hopping about the room. "I don't know him, Archer."

"So you don't know him," the New Yorker grunted. "Phil? Arch Dullman."

"So what do you want?" Ellery could hear Stone's bass rasp distinctly.

"Phil, I'm in a spot up here—"

"Up where?"

"Wrightsville. New England."

"Never heard. Can't be a show town. What are you, in a new racket?"

"There's a stock company here just getting started. I made a deal for Mark Manson with this producer to do *The Death of Don Juan.*"

"What producer?"

"Scutney Bluefield."

"Whatney Bluefield?"

"Never mind! Opening's tomorrow night. Tonight Manson falls down a staircase in the hotel and breaks the wrist and a couple fingers of his right hand, besides cracking two ribs. They've taped his ribs and put a cast on his forearm and hand. He won't be able to work for weeks." A drop of perspiration coursed down Dullman's nose. "Phil—how about Foster Benedict?"

Stone's guffaw rattled the telephone.

"Foster Benedict?" Scutney Bluefield looked astounded. He leaped to Dullman's free ear. "You get him, Archer!"

But Ellery was watching Rodge Fowler. At the sound of Benedict's name Roger had gripped the arms of his chair as if a nerve had been jabbed.

Scutney snatched the phone from Dullman, who remained nearby. "Scutney Bluefield here," he said nervously. "Do I understand, Mr. Stone, that Foster Benedict is available for a two-week engagement in *The Death of Don Juan*, to start tomorrow night?"

"Mr. Benedict's resting between engagements. I don't know if I could talk him into going right back to work."

"How well does he know the part?"

"Foster's done that turkey so many times he quacks. That's another reason it might not interest him. He's sick of it."

"How much," Scutney asked, not without humor, "will it take to cure him?"

Stone said carelessly, "Fifteen hundred a week might do it."

"Give me that phone!" Dullman said. "Who do you think you're dealing with, Phil? Benedict's washed up in Hollywood, dead on Broadway, and TV's had a bellyful of him. I wouldn't let Mr. Bluefield touch him with a skunk pole if Manson's accident hadn't left us over this barrel. Seven-fifty, Phil, take it or leave it."

After ten seconds the agent said, "I'll call you back." Dullman gave him the Hollis phone number and hung up.

Scutney began to hop around the room again.

"You're asking for it," Roger Fowler said tightly. "Benedict's a bad actor, Scutney. And I'm not referring to his professional competence."

"*Please*, Roger," the little man said testily. "Don't I have enough on my mind?"

Twelve minutes later the telephone rang.

Scutney snatched it up. "Yes?"

"We're taking," Stone said. "But you understand, Mr. Bluefield, you got to clear this deal with Equity yourself."

"Yes, yes. First thing in the morning."

"Hold it," Dullman said.

"Hold it," Scutney said.

Dullman whispered something into Scutney's ear, then wearily lay down on the bed.

Scutney pursed his lips. "According to my information, Mr. Stone, Benedict might start out tomorrow for Wrightsville and wind up in a Montreal hotel room with some girl he picked up en route. Can you guarantee delivery?"

"I'll put him on the plane. That's the best I can do."

Scutney glanced anxiously at Dullman. Dullman shrugged. "Well, all right, but try to get Benedict here."

"Up in his lines," Dullman said.

"Up in his lines," Scutney said, and he hung up. "Archer, that was an inspiration!" Dullman grunted.

"You're dead set on going ahead with this?" Roger said grimly.

"Now, Rodge," Scutney said.

Dullman began to snore.

Ellery thought the whole performance extraordinary.

Scene 4

It HAD been an exasperating day for Scutney Bluefield. The little man had been on the long-distance phone to Equity since early morning. By the time the details were straightened out to Equity's satisfaction and Foster Benedict was airborne to Boston, where he had to change planes, he was on a schedule so tight that he could not hope to set down in Wrightsville before 7:55 p.m. This would give the actor barely enough time to make up, get into costume, and dash onstage for the 8:30 curtain.

Ellery made his way around the square and into Lower Main under a filthy sky. A short time later he walked into the lobby of the Bijou, pushed through one of the new black-patent Leatherette doors, and entered Scutney Bluefield's Playhouse.

The elegantly done-over interior lay under a heavy hush as Ellery slipped down the last aisle on his right and through the stage door. He found himself in a cramped triangle of space, the stage to his left. To his right a single door displayed a painted star and a placard hastily lettered MR. BENEDICT. A narrow iron ladder led to a tiny railed landing above and another dressing room.

Curious, Ellery opened the starred door and looked in. Scutney had outdone himself here. Brilliant lighting switched on in the windowless room at the opening of the door. Air conditioning hummed softly. Costumes lay thrown about and the handsome tri-mirrored dressing table was a clutter of wigs, hand props, and pots of theatrical makeup, evidently as Manson had left them before his accident.

Impressed, Ellery backed out. He edged around an open metal chest marked TOOLS and made his way behind the upstage flat to the other side of the theater. Here a spiral of iron steps led up to half a dozen additional dressing rooms. Beneath them, at stage level, a door announced MR. BLUEFIELD. KEEP OUT.

Ellery knocked.

Scutney's voice screamed, "I said *nobody!*"

"It's Ellery Queen."

"Oh. Come in."

The office was a little symphony in stainless steel. Scutney sat at his desk, eyes fixed on a telephone.

Arch Dullman stood at the one window, chewing on a dead cigar. He did not turn around.

Ellery dropped into a chair. "Storm trouble?"

The bunny nose twitched. "Benedict phoned from the airport in Boston. All planes grounded."

The window lit up as if an atom bomb had gone off. Dullman jumped back and Scutney shot to his feet. A crash followed. Immediately the heavens opened and the alley below the window became a river.

"This whole damn production is jinxed," Dullman said, glancing at his watch. "They'll be starting to come in soon, Bluefield. We'll have to postpone."

"And give them another chance to laugh at me?" The little Blue-field jaw enlarged. "We're holding that curtain, Archer. Boston should clear any minute. It's only a half-hour flight."

Dullman went out. Ellery heard him order the houselights switched on and the curtain closed.

The phone came to life at 8:25. Scutney pounced on it. "What did I tell you? He's on his way!"

FOSTER BENEDICT got to the Playhouse at 9:18 p.m. The rain had stopped, but the alley leading to the stage entrance was dotted with puddles, and the actor had to hop and sidestep to avoid them. From his scowl, he took the puddles as a personal affront. Scutney and Dullman hopped and sidestepped along with him, both talking at once.

The company waiting expectantly in the stage entrance pressed back as Benedict approached. He strode past them without a glance, leaving an aroma of whiskey and eau de cologne behind him. If he was drunk, Ellery could detect no evidence of it.

Rodge Fowler was stern-jawed. And pretty, blond Joan Truslow, Ellery noticed, looked as if she had just been slapped.

Foster Benedict glanced about. "You—Mr. Bluefish, is it? Where's my dressing room?"

"At the other side of the stage, Mr. Benedict," Scutney puffed. "But there's no time—"

"They've been sitting out there for over an hour," Dullman said. The booing and stamping of the audience had been audible in the alley.

"Ah." The actor seated himself in the stage doorman's chair. "The voice of Wrightsburg."

"Wrights*ville*," Scutney said. "Mr. Benedict, really—"

"And these, I gather," Benedict said, inspecting the silent cast, "are the so-called actors in this misbegotten exercise in theatrical folly?"

"Mr. Benedict," Scutney said again, "*please!*"

Ellery had not seen Benedict for a long time. The face that had once been called the handsomest in the American theater looked

462

like overhandled dough. Sacs bulged under the malicious eyes. The once taut throat was beginning to string. Only the rich and supple voice was the same.

"The little lady there," the actor said, his stare settling on Joan. "An orchid in the cabbage patch. What does she play, Dullman? The heroine, I hope."

"Yes, yes," Dullman said. "But there's no time for introductions or anything, Benedict. You'll have to go on as you are for the first act—"

"My makeup box, Phil." Benedict extended his arm and snapped his fingers, his eyes still on Joan. Her face was chalky. Ellery glanced at Roger's hands. They were fists.

"Phil Stone isn't here," Dullman said. "Remember? And there's no time to make up, either! Manson's stuff is still in the star dressing room and you can use his when you dress between acts. Look, are you going on or aren't you?"

"Mr. Benedict." Scutney was trembling. "I give you precisely thirty seconds to get out on that stage and take your position for the curtain. Or I prefer charges to Equity."

The actor rose, smiling. "If I recall the stage business, dear heart, and believe me I do," he said to Joan, "we'll have an enchanting opportunity to become better acquainted during the first act. Then perhaps a little champagne supper after the performance? All *right*, Bluefish!" he said crossly. "Just as I am, eh?" He shrugged. "Well, I've played the idiotic role every other way. It may be amusing at that."

He stalked onstage.

"Places!" Dullman bellowed. The cast scurried. "Fowler. Fowler?"

Roger came to life.

"Where's that lights man of yours? Get with it, will you?" As Roger walked away, Dullman froze. "Is that Benedict out there making a *speech?*"

"In the too, too solid flesh," Ellery said, peeping from the wings. Benedict had stepped out on the apron and was explaining with comical gestures why "this distinguished Wrongsville audience" was about to see the great Foster Benedict perform Act One of *The Death of Don Juan*—"the biggest egg ever laid by a turkey"—in street clothes and *sans* makeup. The audience was beginning to titter and clap.

Ellery turned at a gurgle behind him. Scutney's nose was twitching again.

"What is he *doing*? Who does he think he *is*?"

They could only watch helplessly while Benedict played the buffoon. His exit was a triumph of extemporization. He bowed gravely, assumed a ballet stance, and then, like Nijinsky, he took off in a mighty leap for the wings.

Scene 5

ELLERY and Scutney Bluefield watched the first act from the rear of the theater in total disbelief.

Benedict deliberately paraphrased speech after speech. The bewildered amateurs waiting for their cues forgot their lines. Then he capered, struck attitudes, addressed broad asides to the rocking audience. He transformed the old melodrama into a slapstick farce.

Ellery glanced at Scutney. What he saw made him murmur hastily, "He's doing far more damage to himself than to you."

But Scutney said in pink-eyed fury, "It's me they're howling at," and he groped his way through the lobby doors and disappeared.

The seduction scene was an interminable embarrassment. Once during the scene, in sheer self-defense, Joan did something that made Benedict yelp. But he immediately tossed an ad lib to the audience, and in the ensuing shriek of laughter returned to the attack. At the scene's conclusion Joan stumbled off the stage like a sleepwalker.

The curtain came down at last. Ushers opened the fire-exit doors at both sides of the theater. People, wiping their eyes, pushed into the alleys. Ellery wriggled through the lobby to the street and lit a bitter-tasting cigarette. Long after the warning buzzer sounded, he lingered on the sidewalk.

Finally, he went in.

The houselights were still on. Surprised, Ellery glanced at his watch. Probably Benedict needed extra time to get into costume and make up for the second act. Or perhaps—the thought pleased him—Roger had punched him in the nose.

The houselights remained on. The audience began to shuffle, murmur, cough.

Ellery walked to the extreme left aisle and made for the stage door. It was deathly quiet backstage.

Scutney Bluefield's door was open, and Arch Dullman was stamping up and down the office. He seized Ellery.

"Seen Bluefield anywhere?"

"No," Ellery said. "What's wrong?"

"Benedict won't answer his call," Dullman said. "I don't give a damn who he thinks he is. Even a sucker like Bluefield deserves a better shake. Queen, do me a favor and get him out of there."

Ellery's built-in alarm was jangling for all it was worth. "You'd better come with me."

They hurried behind the upstage flat to the other side of the theater. Ellery rapped on the starred door. He rapped again. "Mr. Benedict?"

There was no answer.

"Mr. Benedict, you're holding up the curtain."

Silence. Ellery opened the door.

Foster Benedict, his back to the door, was in the chair at the dressing table, half lying among the wigs and makeup boxes.

He was partly dressed in a Don Juan costume. The shirt was of flowing white silk, and just below the left shoulder blade, from the apex of a wet red ragged stain, the handle of a knife protruded.

ACT II
Scene 1

"DON'T touch him," Ellery said.

Dullman glared at him. "You're kidding." His mouth opened and his cigar fell out. He stooped and fumbled for it.

Ellery leaned over the dressing table, keeping his hands to himself. The skin was a mud-yellow and the lips were already cyanotic. Benedict's eyes were open. As Ellery's face came within their focus they fluttered and rolled.

He saw now that the stain was spreading.

"Bluefield," Dullman said. "My God, where's Bluefield? I've got to find Bluefield."

"Never mind Bluefield. I saw a doctor I know in the audience, Dr. Conklin Farnham. Hurry, Dullman."

Dullman turned blindly to the doorway. It was blocked by the cast and the stagehands. Joan Truslow had her hand to her mouth, looking at the blood and the knife. As Dullman broke through, he collided with Roger Fowler, coming fast.

"What's going on? Where's Joan?"

"Out of my way, damn you." Dullman stumbled toward the stage.

Ellery shut the door and went quickly back to the dressing table. "Benedict, can you talk?"

The lips trembled a little. The jaws opened and closed and opened again, and a thick sound came out. It was just a sound, meaningless.

"Who knifed you?"

The jaws moved again. This time not even the thick sound came out.

"Benedict, do you hear me? If you understand what I'm saying, blink."

The eyelids came down and went up.

"Rest a moment. You're going to be all right." You're going to be dead, Ellery thought. The door burst open. Dr. Farnham hurried in. Dullman ran in after him, shut the door, and leaned against it.

"Hello, Conk," Ellery said. "All I want from him is a name."

Dr. Farnham glanced at the knife wound and his mouth thinned out. He took Benedict's dangling arm without raising it and placed his fingertips on the artery. Then he felt the artery in the temple, examined the staring eyes.

"Call an ambulance."

"And the police," Ellery said.

Arch Dullman opened the door, said something to someone, and shut the door again.

Ellery saw that the bloodstain was no longer spreading. "I've got to talk to him, Conk. Is it all right?"

The doctor nodded. His lips formed the words, Any minute now.

"Benedict," Ellery said. "Use the eye signal again. Do you still hear me?"

Benedict blinked.

"Listen. You were sitting here making up. Someone opened your door and crossed the room. You could see who it was in the mirror. Who was it came at you with the knife?"

The bluing lips parted. The tongue fluttered. Finally a grudging gurgle emerged. Dr. Farnham was feeling for the pulse again.

"He's going, Ellery." This time he said the words aloud.

"You're dying, man," Ellery cried. "Who knifed you?"

The struggle was an admirable thing. The dying man was really trying to communicate. Without warning he raised his head a full inch from the dressing table and held it there quite steadily.

But from his mouth now, in a whisper, came two words.

Then the head fell back to the table with a noise like wood. The actor seemed to clear his throat. His body stiffened, his breath emptied long and gently, and then he was altogether empty.

"He's dead," Dr. Farnham said after a moment.

Dullman said in a queer voice, "What did he say?"

"You heard him, Conk," Ellery said.

"Yes," the doctor said. " 'The heroine.' "

"The heroine?" Dullman laughed incredulously.

"He didn't know her name," Ellery said, as if this explained something important.

"I don't understand," Dr. Farnham said.

"Benedict arrived so late tonight there wasn't time for introductions. He could only identify her by her role in the play. The heroine."

Someone rapped on the door. Dullman opened it.

"I'm told something's happened to Mr. Benedict—"

"Well, look who's here," Dullman said. "Come on in, Bluefield."

Scene 2

SCUTNEY BLUEFIELD's shoes and the cuffs of his trousers were soaked.

"I've been walking and walking. You see, I couldn't stand what he was doing to the play. I felt that if I stayed one minute longer—"

"Scutney," Ellery said.

"And how dreadful," Scutney went on, still looking at the occupied chair. "I mean, he doesn't look human anymore, does he? I've never seen this kind of death."

"Scutney—"

"But he brought it on himself, wouldn't you say? You can't go about humiliating people that way. People who've never done you any harm. Who killed him?"

Ellery swung the little man around. "You'll have to talk to your audience, Scutney. I think you'd better use the word accident. And tell your ushers privately not to allow anyone to leave the theater until the police get here."

"Who killed him?"

"Will you do that?"

"Yes, of course," Scutney said. He squished out, leaving a damp trail.

Ellery wandered back to the dressing table. All at once he stooped for a closer look at the knife handle. Then he dug out of his pocket a small leather case which contained a powerful little lens. Through it Ellery examined the handle of the knife on both sides. The heavy haft had been recently wound in black plastic friction tape. An eighth of an inch from the edge, the tape showed a straight line of thin, irregular indentations some five-eighths of an inch long. In a corresponding position on the underside there was a line of indentations similar in character and length.

Ellery stowed away his lens. "By the way, Dullman, have you seen this knife before?"

"It's not mine. I don't know whose it is."

"But you have seen it before." When Dullman did not answer,

Ellery added, "Believe me, I know how sincerely you wish you were out of this." The way Dullman's glance shifted made Ellery smile faintly. "Where have you seen this knife before?"

Dullman said reluctantly, "I don't know if it's the same one."

"Granted. But where did you see one like it?"

"In that metal tool chest just outside. It was a big-bladed knife with a black-taped handle. From the look of this one I'd say they're the same, but I can't swear to it."

"When did you see it last?"

"I didn't see it 'last,' I saw it once. It was after the first-act curtain. Benedict had weakened one of the legs of the set couch with his damn-fool gymnastics during that scene with the Truslow girl. So I decided to fix the leg myself. I went for tools, and the knife was lying in the top tray of the chest in plain sight."

"Did you notice any peculiar-looking indentations in the tape?"

"Indentations?"

"Impressions. Come here, Dullman. But don't touch it."

Dullman looked and shook his head. "I didn't see anything like that. I'm sure I'd have noticed. I remember thinking how shiny and new-looking the tape was."

"How soon after the curtain came down was this?"

"Right after. Benedict was just coming offstage. He went into the dressing room here while I was poking around in the tools."

"He was alone?"

"He was alone."

"Did you talk to him?"

Dullman examined the pulpy end of his cigar. "You might say he talked to me."

"What did he say?"

"Why, he explained—with one of those famous stage leers of his —exactly what his plans were for after the performance. Spelled it out," Dullman said, jamming the cigar back in his mouth, "in four-letter words."

"And you said to him?"

"Nothing. Look, Queen, you and the doctor here say you heard who Benedict put the finger on. So what the hell."

"Who occupies the dressing room just above this one?"

"Joan Truslow."

Ellery went out.

The lid of the chest marked Tools was open, as he had seen it on his backstage tour early in the evening. There was no knife in the tray, or anywhere else in the chest. If Dullman was telling the truth, the knife in Foster Benedict's back almost certainly had come from this tool chest.

Ellery heard two sirens coming on fast outside.

He glanced up at the narrow landing. The upper dressing-room door was halfway open.

He sprang to the iron ladder.

Scene 3

ELLERY knocked and stepped into Joan Truslow's tiny dressing room at once, shutting the door behind him.

Joan and Roger jumped apart. Tears had left a clownish design in the girl's makeup.

Ellery set his back against the door.

"Do you make a habit of barging into ladies' dressing rooms?" Roger said truculently.

But Joan put her hand on Roger's arm. "How is he, Mr. Queen?"

"Benedict? Oh, he died."

He studied her reaction carefully. It told nothing.

"I'm sorry," she said. "Even though he was beastly."

"I saw his lips moving during your speeches in that couch scene. What was he saying to you, Joan?"

"Vile things. I can't repeat them."

"The police just got here."

She betrayed herself by the overly natural manner in which she turned away and sat down at her dressing table to begin repairing her makeup.

"Anyway, what are people supposed to do, go into mourning?" Roger said. "He was a smutty old man. If ever anyone asked for it, he did."

Ellery kept watching Joan's reflection in the mirror. "You know, Rodge, that remark rather surprises me. Granted Benedict's outrageous behavior tonight, it was hardly sufficient reason to stick a knife in his back. Wouldn't you say?" The lipstick in Joan's fingers kept flying. "Or—on second thought—does either of you know of a sufficient reason? On the part of anyone?"

"How could we know a thing like that?"

"Speak for yourself, Rodge." Ellery smiled. "How about you, Joan?"

She murmured, "Me?" and shook her head.

"Well." Ellery pushed away from the door. "Oh, Roger, last night in Arch Dullman's room, when Benedict was first mentioned as a substitute for Manson, I got the impression you knew Benedict from somewhere. Was I imagining things?"

"I can't help your impressions."

"Then you never met him before tonight?"

Roger glared. "Are you accusing me of Benedict's murder?"

"Are you afraid I may have cause to?"

"You'd better get out of here!"

"Unfortunately, you won't be able to take that attitude with the police."

"Get out!"

Ellery shrugged as part of his own act. He had baited Roger to catch Joan off guard. And he had caught her. She had continued her elaborate toilet at the mirror as if they were discussing the weather. His hostile exchange with Roger should have made her show some sign of alarm, or anxiety, or at least interest.

He left gloomily.

HE WAS not prepared for the police officer he found in charge below, despite a forewarning of long standing. On the retirement of Wrightsville's perennial chief of police, Dakin, the old Yankee had written Ellery about his successor.

"Selectmen brought in this Anselm Newby from Connhaven," Dakin had written, "where he was a police captain with a mighty good record. Newby's young and he's tough and far as I know he's honest and he does know modern police methods. But he's maybe not as smart as he thinks."

Ellery had visualized Chief of Police Newby as a large man with muscles, a jaw, and a Marine sergeant's voice. Instead, the man in the chief's cap who turned to look him over when he was admitted to the dressing room was short and slight, almost delicately built.

"I was just going to send a man looking for you, Mr. Queen." Chief Newby's quiet voice was another surprise. "Where've you been?"

The quiet voice covered a sting, and the eyes were of an inorganic blue, unfeeling as mineral.

"Talking to members of the company."

"Like Joan Truslow?"

Ellery thought very quickly. "Joan was one of them, Chief. I didn't mention Benedict's talking before he died, of course. But as long as we had to wait for you—"

"Mr. Queen," Newby said. "Let's understand each other right off. In Wrightsville a police investigation is run by one man. Me."

"To my knowledge it's never been run any other way. However, I've known and liked this town and its people for a long time. You can't stop me from keeping my eyes open and reaching my own conclusions. And broadcasting them, if necessary."

Anselm Newby stared at him. Ellery stared back.

"I've already talked to Dr. Farnham and Mr. Dullman," Newby said suddenly, and Ellery knew he had won a small victory. "You tell me your version."

Ellery gave him an unembroidered account. The police chief listened without comment, interrupting only to acknowledge the arrival of the coroner and issue orders to uniformed men coming in to report. Throughout Ellery's recital Newby kept an eye on a young police technician who had been going over the room for fingerprints and was now taking photographs. Times had certainly changed in Wrightsville.

"Those words Benedict said, you heard them yourself?" the chief asked when Ellery stopped. "This wasn't something Farnham heard and repeated to you?"

"We both heard them. I'm positive Dullman did, too, although he pretended he hadn't."

"Why would he do that?"

"Because to admit he heard Benedict's accusation would mean becoming an important witness in a sensational murder case. Dullman can't stand the publicity."

"I thought show people live on publicity."

"Not Dullman. For an Actors Equity member like Benedict or Manson to work in an amateur company, it has to be a legitimately amateur operation from start to finish. Arch Dullman is an operator. He makes an undercover deal with someone like Scutney Bluefield —desperate to run a successful amateur playhouse. Dullman delivers a name actor—one who's passé in the big time and who'll do anything for eating money—in return for taking over behind the scenes, with Bluefield fronting for him."

"What's Dullman get out of it?"

"He pockets most—or all—of the box-office take," Ellery said. "If this deal with Bluefield became a matter of public record, Dullman might never represent a professional actor again."

"I see." Newby was watching his technician. The knife had been removed from Benedict's back and it was lying on the table. It was a long, hefty hunting knife, honed to a wicked edge.

The coroner grunted, "I'm through for now," and opened the door. Two ambulance men came in at his nod and took the body out. "I'll do the post first thing in the morning."

"Could a woman have sunk the knife to the hilt?" Newby asked.

"Far's I can tell without an autopsy, it went into the heart without striking bone. If that's so, a kid could have done it." The coroner left.

Newby walked over to the table. The technician was packing his gear. "Find any prints on the knife?"

"No, sir. It was either handled with a handkerchief or gloves or wiped off afterward."

"What about prints elsewhere?"

"Some of Benedict's on the dressing table and on the makeup stuff, and a lot of someone else's, a man's."

473

"Those would be Manson's. He used this room all week. No woman's prints, Bill?"

"No, sir. But about this knife. There are some queer marks on the handle."

"Marks?" Newby picked up the knife by the tip of the blade and scrutinized the haft. He seemed puzzled.

"There's some on the other side, too."

The chief turned the knife over. "Any notion what made these?"

"Well, no, sir."

Newby studied the marks again. Without looking around he said, "Mr. Queen, did you happen to notice these marks?"

"Yes," Ellery said.

The chief waited, as if for Ellery to go on. But Ellery did not go on. Newby's ears slowly reddened. "Bill, suppose we try to identify these marks? Right?"

"Yes, sir."

Newby stalked out to the stage. Meekly, Ellery followed.

The little police chief's interrogation of the company was surgical. In short order he established that between the lowering of the curtain and the discovery of the dying man, every member of the cast except Joan Truslow had either been in view of someone else or could otherwise prove an alibi. With equal economy he disposed of the stagehands.

He had long since released the audience. Now he sent the cast and the crew home. On the emptying of the theater the curtain had been raised and the houselights turned off. Scutney Bluefield and Archer Dullman sat in gloom and silence on the set couch. For the first time Ellery sensed an impatience, almost an eagerness, in Newby.

"Well, gentlemen, it's getting late—"

"Chief," Scutney asked, "are you intending to close me down?"

"No call for that, Mr. Bluefield. We'll just seal off that dressing room."

"Then I can go ahead with rehearsals?"

"Better figure on day after tomorrow. The prosecutor's office will be all over the place till then."

Scutney struggled off the couch.

"Oh, one thing before you go, Mr. Bluefield. Did you see or hear anything tonight that might help us out?"

Scutney said, "I wasn't here," and trudged off the stage.

"You, Mr. Dullman?"

"I told you all I know, Chief." Dullman shifted the remains of his cigar to the other side of his mouth. "Is it all right with you if I go see my client before somebody does a carving job on him?"

"Sure. Just don't leave town."

When Dullman was gone, Newby made for the stage steps.

"Chief," Ellery said.

Newby paused.

"You don't have much of a case, you know."

The policeman trotted down into the orchestra. He selected the aisle seat in the third row center and settled himself. Like a critic, Ellery thought. A critic who's already made up his mind.

"Gotch," Chief Newby called.

"Yes, sir."

"Get Miss Truslow."

Scene 4

JOAN sailed out of the wings chin up, braced. But all she saw was Ellery straddling a chair far upstage, and she began to look around uncertainly.

Roger yelled, "You down there—Newby!" and ran over to the footlights. "What's the idea keeping Miss Truslow a prisoner in her dressing room all this time?"

"Roger," Joan said.

"Sit down, Miss Truslow," Newby's soft voice said from below. "You, too, Fowler."

Joan sat down immediately.

Whatever it was that Roger glimpsed in her violet eyes, it silenced him. He joined her on the couch.

Newby said, "Miss Truslow, when did you make your last stage exit?"

"At the end of my scene with Foster Benedict on the couch."

"How long before the act ended was that?"

"About ten minutes."

"Did you go right to your dressing room?"

"Yes."

"In doing that, you had to pass by the tool chest. Was it open?"

"The chest? I can't say. I didn't notice much of anything." Joan caught her hands in the act of twisting in her lap, and she stilled them. "I was badly upset. They must have told you what he—the way he carried on during our big scene."

"Yes. I hear he gave you a rough time." The little chief sounded sympathetic. "But you did notice the tool chest later, Miss Truslow, didn't you?"

She looked up. "Later?"

"In the intermission. After Benedict got to his dressing room."

Joan blinked into the lights. "But you don't understand, Chief Newby. I went straight to my dressing room and I stayed there. I was . . . frozen, I suppose is the word. I just sat asking myself how I was going to get through the rest of the play."

"While you were up there, did you hear anything going on in the room below? Benedict's dressing room?"

"I don't remember hearing anything."

"When *did* you first leave your dressing room, Miss Truslow?"

"When I heard all the commotion downstairs. After he was found."

"Fowler," Newby said suddenly, "Queen found you with this girl. How come?"

"How come?" Roger snapped. "I hauled her out of the crowd around Benedict's doorway and up to her dressing room so I could put my arms around her in privacy when she broke down, which she promptly did. Wasn't that sneaky of me?"

"Then that was the first time you saw her after she left the stage?"

"I couldn't get to her before, though God knows I wanted to. I was too tied up backstage—" Roger halted. "What are you trying to prove, anyway, Newby?"

"Miss Truslow, how well did you know Foster Benedict?"
Ellery saw Joan go stiff. "Know him?"

"Were you two acquainted? Ever see him before tonight?"
She said something.

"What? I couldn't hear that."

Joan cleared her throat. "No."

"Logan." A police officer jumped off the apron and darted to his
chief. Newby said something behind his hand. The man hurried
up the aisle and out of the theater.

"Miss Truslow, a witness says that when Benedict went into
his dressing room the tool chest was open and a big knife with
a taped handle was lying in the tray. I'll ask you again. Did you
leave your dressing room, climb down, go to the chest—"

"I didn't," Joan cried.

"—go to the chest, pick up the knife—"

"Hold it." Roger was on his feet. "You really want to know
about that knife, Newby? It's mine."

"Oh?" Newby sat waiting.

"If you'll strip the tape off you'll find my initials machine-
stamped into the haft," Roger said quickly. "I've used it on hunting trips for years. I brought it to the theater just today. We'd
bought some new guy rope yesterday and I needed a sharp knife—"

"I know all about the ownership of the knife." Newby smiled.
"The question isn't who owned the knife, or even who put it in the
tool chest. It's who took it out of the chest and used it on Benedict.
Miss Truslow—"

"Excuse me," Ellery said. The chief was startled into silence.
"Roger, when did you tape the handle?"

"Tonight, after the play started. I'd used it in replacing a frayed
guy rope and I hadn't been able to keep a good grip on it because
my hands were sweaty from the heat backstage. So I wound elec-
trician's tape around the haft in case I had to use it again in an
emergency during the performance."

"When did you drop it into the chest?"

"Near the end of the act."

Newby was quiet. Then he said, "Now I want to be sure I have this right, Miss Truslow. You claim you went from the stage straight to your dressing room, you stayed there all the time Benedict was being knifed in the room right under yours, you didn't hear a sound, you didn't come down till after Benedict was found dying, and at no time did you touch the knife. Is that it?"

"That's it." Joan jumped up and walked over to the footlights. "Now let me ask you a question, Chief Newby. Why are you treating me as if you've decided I killed Foster Benedict?"

"Didn't you?" Newby asked.

"I did not kill him!"

"Somebody said you did."

Joan peered and blinked through the glare in her eyes. "But that's not possible. It isn't true. I can't imagine anyone making up a story like that about me. Who said it?"

"Benedict, in the presence of witnesses, a few seconds before he died."

Joan said something unintelligible. Newby and Ellery sprang to their feet. But Roger was closest, and he caught her just as her legs gave way.

ACT III
Scene 1

ELLERY awoke at noon. He leaped for the door and took in the *Record*. For the first time in years its front page ran a two-line banner:

MURDER HITS WRIGHTSVILLE
FAMOUS STAGE STAR SLAIN!

The account of the crime was wordy and inaccurate. There were publicity photos of Benedict and the cast. Chief Anselm Newby's contribution was boxed but uninformative. There was a story on Mark Manson under a photograph showing him at a bar, uninjured arm holding aloft a cocktail glass: "Mr. Manson was found at the Hollis bar at a late hour last night on his discharge from Wrightsville General Hospital, in company of his manager, Archer Dullman. Asked to comment on the tragedy, Mr. Manson said, 'Words truly fail me, sir, which is why you discover me saying it with martinis.'"

The sole reference in print to Joan was a cryptic "Miss Joan Truslow and Mr. Roger Fowler of the Playhouse staff could not be located for a statement as we went to press."

Of Foster Benedict's dying words no mention was made.

Ellery ordered breakfast and hurried for his shower.

He was finishing his second cup of coffee when the telephone rang. It was Roger.

"Where the devil did you hide Joan last night?"

"In my Aunt Carrie's house." Roger sounded harassed. "She's in Europe, left me a key. Joan was in no condition to face reporters. Her father knows where we are, but that's all."

"Didn't you tell Newby?"

"Tell Newby? It's Newby who smuggled us over to Aunt Carrie's. Considerate guy, Newby. He has a cop staked out in the backyard and another in plain clothes parked across the street in an unmarked car."

Ellery said nothing.

"Far as I know, Newby has no direct evidence against Joan," Roger said grimly. "Just those last words of a dying man whose mind was already in outer space. Just the same, I'll feel better with a lawyer around. Before I call one in, though . . ." Roger hesitated. "What I mean is, I'm sorry I blew my stack last night. Would you come over here right away?"

"Where is it?" Ellery chuckled.

Roger gave him an address on State Street, in the oldest residential quarter of town.

It was an immaculately preserved eighteenth-century mansion under the protection of the great elms that were the pride of State Street. The black shades were drawn, and from the street the clapboard house looked shut down. Ellery strolled around to the rear and knocked on the back door, pretending not to notice the policeman lurking inside a latticed summerhouse. Roger admitted him, then led the way through a huge kitchen and along a cool hall to a stately parlor whose furniture was under dust covers.

Joan was waiting in an armchair. She looked tired and withdrawn. "This is all Roger's idea," she said, managing a smile. "From the way he's been carrying on—"

"Do you want my help, Joan?"

"Well, if Roger's right—"

"I'm afraid he is."

"But it's so stupid, Mr. Queen. Why would Foster Benedict accuse me? I didn't go near him . . . I've always hated knives," she cried. "I couldn't use a knife on a trout."

"It isn't a trout that was knifed. Joan, look at me."

She raised her head.

"Did you kill Benedict?"

"No! How many times do I have to say it?"

He lit a cigarette while he weighed her anger, for he knew she was an actress of talent and resource. "All right, Rodge," Ellery said suddenly. "Speak your piece."

"It's not mine. It's Joan's."

"I'm all ears, Joan."

Her chest rose. "I lied to Chief Newby when I said I'd never known Foster Benedict before last night. I met Foster six years ago here in Wrightsville. I was still in high school. Roger was home from college for the summer."

"In *Wrightsville?*"

"I know, he acted as if he'd never heard of Wrightsville. But then I realized it wasn't an act at all. He'd simply forgotten, Mr. Queen. He was one of Scutney Bluefield's houseguests for a few weeks that summer."

"He didn't even remember Scutney," Roger said bitterly.

"Benedict practiced houseguesting as a form of unemployment insurance," Ellery remarked. "Dullman claims he averaged fourteen, fifteen hosts a year. Go on, Joan."

"I was sixteen, and Foster Benedict had been my secret crush for years," Joan said in a low voice. "When I read in the *Record* that he was staying at Mr. Bluefield's, I phoned him."

She flushed. "You can imagine the conversation—how much I admired his work, my stage ambitions . . . He must have been having a dull time because he said he'd like to meet me. I was in heaven. He began to take me out. Drives up to the lake. Moonlight readings . . . I certainly asked for it."

She sat forward nervously. "Would you believe that when he promised me a part in his next play I actually fell for it?" Joan laughed. "And then he went away, and I wrote him some desperate love letters he didn't bother to answer, and I didn't see or hear from him again until last night.

"And then when he made his royal entrance into the Playhouse, he not only didn't remember Wrightsville, or Mr. Bluefield, he'd forgotten me, too." She was staring into the mirror of the time-polished floor. "I'd meant so little to him not even my features had registered, let alone my name."

"I warned you six years ago Benedict was poison," Roger said, "but would you listen? Ellery, if you knew how many times I've begged her to get off this acting kick and marry me—"

"Let's get to you, Rodge. I take it your evasions last night covered up a prior acquaintance with Benedict, too?"

"How could I explain without dragging Joan into it?"

"Then you met him at the same time."

"I knew she was dating him—a high school kid!—and I'd read of his weakness for the young ones. I was fit to be tied. I collared him one night after he took Joan home and I warned him to lay off. I said I'd kill him, or some such juvenile big talk. He laughed in my face and I knocked him cold."

"Did the brawl get into the *Record*?"

Roger shrugged. "It was a one-day wonder."

"And was Joan named in the story?"

"Well, yes. Some oaf at headquarters shot his mouth off. Dakin—that was when he was chief—Dakin fired him."

Ellery shook his head. "You two are beyond belief. How did you expect to keep a thing like that from Newby? Last night when you denied having known Benedict, Joan, didn't you notice Newby send one of his men on an errand? He's a city-trained policeman—

he wouldn't take your word. He'd check the *Record* morgue and his own headquarters files. So Newby either knows already, or he'll very soon learn, that you lied to him on a crucial question, and exactly what happened six years ago. Don't you see what you've handed him on a silver platter?"

Joan was mute.

"From Newby's viewpoint there's a strong circumstantial case against you, Joan. Situated in the only other dressing room on that side of the theater, you had the best opportunity to kill Benedict without being seen. The weapon? You wouldn't have had to move a step out of your way en route to Benedict's dressing room to take the knife from the tool chest. What's been holding Newby up is motive."

Joan's lips moved, but nothing came out.

"With the background of that romance between you six years ago in this very town, Joan, and your lie about it, Benedict's humiliation of you in public last night takes on an entirely different meaning. It becomes a motive that would convince anybody.

"Add to opportunity, weapon, and motive Benedict's dying declaration, and you see how near you are to being formally charged with the murder."

"You're a help," Roger stormed. "I thought you'd be on Joan's side."

"And on yours, Roger?"

"Mine?"

"Don't you know you're Newby's ace in the hole? You threatened six years ago to kill Benedict—"

"Are you serious? That was just talk!"

"—and you beat him up. You've admitted the knife that killed Benedict is yours, and you brought it to the theater the day of the murder. If not for Benedict's statement, Newby would have a stronger case against you than against Joan. As it is, Rodge, you may be facing an accessory charge."

For once Roger found nothing to say. Joan's hand stole into his.

"However," Ellery said briskly. "Joan, do you still maintain you didn't kill Benedict?"

"Of course. Because I didn't."

"Would you be willing to take a test that might prove you didn't?"

"You mean a lie-detector test?"

"Something far more direct. On the other hand, I've got to point out that if you did kill Benedict, this test might constitute evidence against you as damning as a fingerprint."

Joan rose. "What do I do, Mr. Queen?"

"Rodge, ask the police officer in the car parked across the street to drive Joan and you to Newby's office. I'll meet you there."

"Can't you go with us?" Roger asked.

"I have something to pick up first," Ellery said, "at a hardware store."

Scene 2

ELLERY walked into Anselm Newby's office with a small package under his arm to find Joan and Roger seated close together under Newby's mineral eye. A tall, thin man in a business suit turned from the window as he entered.

"Fowler's been telling me about some test or other you want to make, Queen," the little police chief said acidly. "I thought we'd agreed you were to keep your nose out of this case."

"That was a unilateral agreement, you'll recall," Ellery said, smiling. "However, I'm sure you wouldn't want to make a false arrest, and the prosecutor of Wright County wouldn't want to try a hopeless case. Isn't that so, Mr. Odham?" he asked the man at the window.

"So you know who I am." The tall man came forward with a grin and pumped Ellery's hand.

"Mr. Odham," Ellery said, "you *were* about to charge Joan Truslow with the Benedict murder, weren't you? I haven't dared ask the chief."

Newby glared and Prosecutor Odham chuckled. But there was no humor in his frosty gray eyes.

"What have you got, Mr. Queen?"

Ellery said to the police chief, "May I see the knife?"

Newby opened the safe behind his desk and brought out a shallow box padded with surgical cotton. The bloodstained knife lay on the cotton.

"This thin, short line of indentations in the tape of the handle." Ellery made no attempt to touch the knife. "Have you determined yet what made them, Chief?"

"Why?"

"Because they may either blow up your case against Joan or nail it down. Have you decided what kind of marks these are?"

"I suppose you know!"

"Anse," Odham said. "No, Mr. Queen, we haven't. I take it you have?"

"Yes."

"Well?" Newby said. "What are they marks of?"

"Teeth."

"Teeth?" The prosecutor looked startled. So did Joan and Roger.

"Maybe they're teeth marks and maybe they're not," Newby said slowly, "though I admit we didn't think of teeth. But even if they are. Only two could be involved—"

"Four," Ellery said. "Two upper and two lower—there are corresponding impressions on the other side of the haft. What's more, I'm positive they're the front teeth."

"Suppose they are. These could only be edge impressions, and they're certainly not distinctive enough for a positive identification."

"You may be right," Ellery said soberly. "They may not prove to be positive evidence. But they may well prove to be negative evidence."

"What's that supposed to mean?"

"Suppose I can demonstrate that Joan Truslow's teeth couldn't possibly have left these marks? Mind you, I don't know whether they demonstrate any such thing, but I've explained to her the risk she's running. Nevertheless, she's agreed to the test."

"Is that so, Miss Truslow?" the prosecutor demanded.

Joan nodded. She had a death grip on the sides of her chair seat.

Odham said, "Then, Mr. Queen, you go right ahead."

Ellery's package remained intact. "Before I do, let's be sure we agree on the significance of the teeth marks. Last night Roger told us he didn't put the freshly taped knife in the tool chest until the act was nearly over. Rodge, were those marks in the tape when you dropped the knife in the chest?"

"You've forgotten," Roger said shortly. "I've never seen them."

"My error. Take a look."

Roger rose and took a look. "I don't see how they could have been. The knife wasn't out of my possession until I put it in the chest, and I'm certainly not in the habit of gnawing on knife handles." He went back to Joan's side and sat down.

"What would you expect Fowler to say?" Newby said.

Joan's hand checked Roger just in time.

"Well, if you won't accept Roger's testimony," Ellery said, "consider Arch Dullman's. Dullman last night said he saw the knife in the tool chest directly after the curtain came down—as Benedict came offstage, in fact—and he was positive there were no indentations in the tape at that time. Didn't Dullman tell you that, Chief?"

Newby chewed his lip.

"By the testimony, then, someone bit into the tape after Benedict entered his dressing room and before we found him. In other words, during the murder period." Ellery began to unwrap his package. "The one person who we know beyond dispute handled the knife during the murder period was the murderer. It's a reasonable conclusion that the impressions were made by the murderer's teeth."

Chief Newby was grimly silent. But Odham said, "Go on, Mr. Queen, go on."

Out of the wrappings Ellery took a roll of new black plastic friction tape and a large hunting knife. He handed roll and knife to Roger. "You taped the original knife, Rodge. Do a repeat on this one." Roger set to work. "Meanwhile, Joan, I'd like you to take a close look at the original."

Joan got up and walked over to Newby. She seemed calmer than the chief.

"Notice the exact position of the marks relative to the edge of the handle," Ellery said.

"About an eighth of an inch from the edge."

Ellery took the test knife from Roger and gave it to Joan. "I want you to take two bites. First with your front teeth about an eighth of an inch from the edge, as in the other one." He looked at her. "Go ahead, Joan."

But Joan stood painfully still.

"The moment of truth, Joan?" Ellery said with a smile. "Do it."

Joan breathed in, placed the haft to her mouth, and bit into it firmly. Ellery took it from her at once and examined the marks. "Good! Now I want you to take a second bite—well clear of the first, Joan, so the two don't overlap. This time, though, make it a full bite."

When she returned the knife Ellery ran to the window. "May I have the other one, Chief?" He was already studying the test impressions through his lens. Newby, quite pale, brought the murder weapon, Odham at his heels.

Joan and Roger remained where they were, in a dreadful quiet.

"See for yourselves."

The police chief peered, squinted, compared. He went back to his desk for a transparent ruler. He made a great many deliberate measurements. When he was through examining the upper surfaces of the hafts he turned the knives over and did it all again.

Finally he looked up. "I guess, Mr. Odham," he said in a rather hollow voice, "you'd best check these yourself."

The prosecutor seized knives and lens. Afterward, there was a glint of anger in his eyes. "No impressions of any two adjoining teeth, either in the matching bite or the full set, are identical with the impressions on the murder knife. Same sort of marks, all right, but entirely different in detail—not as wide, not the same spacing—there can't be any doubt about it. You have a lot to thank Mr. Queen for, Miss Truslow. And so do we, Anse. I'll be talking to you later."

Not until Odham was gone did Joan's defenses crumble. She sank into Roger's arms, sobbing.

Ellery turned to the window, waiting for Newby's explosion. To his surprise nothing happened, and he turned back. There was the slender little chief, slumped on his tail, feet on desk, looking human.

"I sure had it coming, Queen," he said ruefully. "What gripes me most is having put all my eggs in one basket. Boom."

Ellery grinned. "I've laid my quota of omelets. Do you know anyone in this business who hasn't?"

Newby got to his feet. "Well, now what? Between Benedict's putting the finger on this girl and your removing it, I'm worse off than when I started. Can you make any sense out of this, Queen?"

"To a certain point."

"What point's that?"

Ellery tucked his lens away. "I know now who did the job on Benedict and why, if that's any help."

"Thanks, buddy."

"No, I mean it."

"I wish I could appreciate the rib"—Newby sighed—"but somehow I'm not in the mood."

"But it's not a rib, Chief. The only thing is, I haven't a particle of proof." Ellery rubbed his nose as Newby gaped. "Though there *is* a notion stirring . . . and if it should work . . ."

Scene 3

THE following morning's *Record* shouted:

LOCAL GIRL CLEARED IN KILLING!

The lead story was marked EXCLUSIVE and began:

Joan Truslow of the Wrightsville Playhouse company was proved innocent yesterday of the Foster Benedict murder by Ellery Queen, the *Record* learned last night from an unusually reliable source.

Chief Anselm Newby would neither affirm nor deny the *Record's* information.

"I will say that Miss Truslow is not a suspect," Newby told

the *Record*. "However, we are not satisfied with some of her testimony. She will be questioned further soon." Chief Newby admitted that Miss Truslow is believed to be withholding testimony vital to the solution of the murder.

By press time last night Miss Truslow had not been located by newsmen. She is said to be hiding out somewhere in town.

The *Record* story's EXCLUSIVE tag was an understandable brag. Wire service and metropolitan newspaper reporters had invaded Wrightsville at the first flash of Foster Benedict's slaying, and the war for news raged through the town.

Scutney Bluefield had sent out a call for his entire company. They converged on the Playhouse the morning the *Record* story broke to find the forces of the press drawn up in battle array. In a moment the surrounded locals were under full-scale attack; and Scutney, purple from shouting, sent to police headquarters for reinforcements.

A wild fifteen minutes later Chief Newby laid down the terms of a truce.

"You people have one hour out here for interviews with Mr. Bluefield's company," the chief snapped. "Nobody gets into the theater after that without a signed pass from me."

As it turned out, the newsmen retired from the field in less than half their allotted time. One of their two chief objectives was not present: Ellery had slipped out of the Hollis early in the morning and disappeared. Their other target, Joan, who showed up at the Playhouse with Roger, had refused to parley. To every question fired at her about the "testimony vital to the solution" she was reported to be withholding, Joan looked more frightened and shook her head violently. "I have nothing to say, nothing," she kept repeating. Nor would she reveal where she was staying.

After the press had gone Chief Newby stationed police at the stage entrance, fire exits, and in the lobby. So it was with slightly hysterical laughter that the company greeted Scutney Bluefield's opening words: "Alone at last." They were assembled onstage under the working lights. Scutney had hopped up on a set chair.

"You'll all be happy to hear that we're going right ahead with *The Death of Don Juan.*" He raised his little paw for silence. "With due respect to the late Foster Benedict, he saw fit to make a farcical joke out of our production. We're going to do it *properly.*"

Someone called out, "But, Mr. Bluefield, we don't have a Don Juan."

Scutney showed his teeth. "Ah, but we will have, and a good one, too. I shan't disclose his name because I haven't completed the business arrangements. He should be joining us the day after tomorrow.

"I spent most of yesterday making cuts and line changes and revising some of the business, especially in Act One, where I think we've been in danger of wrong audience reactions. Today and tomorrow we'll go over the changes, so we ought to be in good shape when our new Don Juan gets here. Meanwhile, as a favor to me, Mr. Manson has kindly consented to walk through the part for us. Does anyone need a pencil?"

They plunged into the work with relief.

The day passed quickly, and it was almost 10:00 p.m. when Scutney called a halt. The company began to disperse.

"Not you, Miss Truslow!"

Joan stopped in her tracks. It was Chief Newby.

"I haven't wanted to interfere with Mr. Bluefield's working day. But now, Miss Truslow, you and I are going to have a real old-fashioned heart-to-heart talk. Whether it takes five minutes or all night is up to you. I think you know what I'm talking about."

Joan groped for one of the set chairs. "I have nothing to tell you! Why won't you let me alone?"

"She's out on her feet, Chief," Roger protested. "Can't this wait?"

"Not anymore," Newby said quietly. "You stay where you are, Miss Truslow, while I get rid of the newspapermen hanging around outside. I don't want the papers in on this."

The theater emptied. Lights began winking out. One harsh spotlight remained onstage. Joan cowered in its glare.

"Roger, what am I going to do? I don't know what to do."

"You know what to do, Joanie," Roger said gently.

"He won't let go of me till . . ."

"Till you tell him what you're hiding?" Roger pushed a curl of damp blond hair back from her forehead. "I know you've been hiding something, darling. I've known it longer than Newby. What is it? Can't you tell even me?"

Joan's hands quivered in her lap.

"He's bound to get it out of you tonight."

"Rodge—I'm afraid."

"That's why I want you to share it with me. Look, Joan, I love you. What good would I be if I didn't share your troubles?"

"Rodge . . ."

"Tell me."

She swallowed twice, hard, looking around nervously. The deep silence of the theater seemed to reassure her.

"All right. All right, Rodge. . . . The other night—during the intermission—when I was in my dressing room feeling so hurt by Foster's not remembering me . . ."

"Yes?"

"I decided to go down to his dressing room and—and . . . Oh, Rodge, I don't know why I wanted to! Maybe to tell him what I thought of him. . . . I was about to step onto the ladder from the landing when I heard Foster's dressing-room door open below, and . . . *I saw him.*"

"The murderer?" Roger cried.

Joan nodded, shuddering. "I saw him sneak out . . . and away."

"Did you recognize him?"

"Yes."

"But my God, Joan, why didn't you tell Newby?"

"Because he'd accuse me of making it up. At that time the chief was sure I'd done it."

"But now he knows you didn't!"

"Now I'm just plain scared, Roger."

"That Benedict's killer will come after you? He's not getting the chance!" Roger cupped her chin fiercely. "You're ending this nightmare right now, young lady. Let me get out of these work clothes, and then you're going outside to tell Newby who murdered Benedict—and the more reporters that hear it the better. Don't move from here, Joanie. I'm only going as far as the prop room—I'll be right back!"

The darkness swallowed him. His rapid footsteps died away.

Joan found herself alone on the stage.

She was perched stiff-backed on the edge of the big Spanish chair at the base of the light cone formed by the spot. The dark surrounded and held her fast, like walls.

The dark and the silence made her uneasy.

Joan began to move her head, small, jerky movements, furtive glances over her shoulder, toward the invisible wings, out into the blackness crouching beyond the dead footlights.

"Rodge?" she called.

The quaver of her own voice only brought the silence closer.

"*Roger?*"

Joan curled up in the chair suddenly and shut her eyes tight. Then in the next moment a bulky blob of something detached itself from the murky formlessness upstage and crept toward the light.

It began to take stealthy shape.

The shape of a man.

Of a man with something gripped at chest level.

A knife.

"*Now!*" Ellery's roar dropped from the catwalk far over the stage like a bomb.

Quick as Chief Newby and his men were, Roger was quicker. He hurtled out of the wings and launched himself at the man with the knife like a swimmer at the start of a race. He hit the man at the knees and the man went over with a crash that rattled the stage. The knife went skittering off somewhere. The man kicked out viciously. Roger fell on him and there was a sickening *crack!* and the man screamed, once. Then he was still.

As soon as he could, Chief Newby hurried to the set chair. "That was as good an act as Broadway ever saw! And it took real guts, Miss Truslow." He bent over the chair, puzzled. "Miss Truslow?"

But Miss Truslow was no longer acting. Miss Truslow had peacefully passed out.

Scene 4

ONE of the waitresses in the Hollis private dining room was clearing the table as the other poured their coffee. Under the cloth Joan's fingers were interwoven with Roger's.

"Queen, where's the dessert you promised?" Chief Newby asked. "I've got a lot to do at headquarters."

"No dessert for me," Joan said dreamily.

"Likewise," Roger said likewise.

"You don't eat this dessert," the chief explained, "you listen to it. Anyway, *I'm* listening."

"Well, it goes like this," Ellery began. "I kept urging Benedict, as he was dying, to tell me who stabbed him. When he was able to get some words out, seconds before he died, Conk Farnham and I were sure we heard him say, 'The heroine,' an unmistakable accusation of you, Joan. You were heroine of the play, and Benedict didn't know—or, as it turned out, didn't remember—your name.

"But then the tooth-mark test proved Joan's innocence. So Benedict couldn't have meant the heroine of the play. He must have meant a word that sounded like heroine but meant something else. There's only one word that sounds like heroine-with-an-e, and that's heroin-without-an-e.

"The fact was," Ellery continued, "Benedict wasn't answering my who-did-it question at all. His dying mind had rambled off to another element of the crime. Heroin. The narcotic."

He emptied his coffee cup, and Chief Newby hastily refilled it.

"But no dope was found," Joan protested. "Where could dope have come into it?"

"Just what I asked myself. To answer it called for reconstructing the situation.

"When the act ended, Benedict entered the star dressing room for the first time. He had forgotten to bring along his makeup kit and Arch Dullman had told him to use the makeup in the dressing room. In view of Benedict's dying statement, it was now clear that he must have opened one of the boxes, perhaps labeled makeup powder, and instead of finding powder in it he found heroin."

"Benedict's finding of the dope just pointed to the killer," Newby objected. "You claimed to be dead certain."

"I was. I had another line to him that tied him to the killing hand and foot," Ellery said. "Thusly:

"The killer obviously didn't get to the dressing room until Benedict was already there—if he'd been able to beat Benedict to the room no murder would have been necessary. He'd simply have taken the heroin and walked out.

"So now I had him standing outside the dressing room, with Benedict inside exploring the unfamiliar makeup materials, one box of which contained the heroin.

"Let's take a good look at this killer. He's in a panic. He has to shut Benedict's mouth about the dope before Benedict can open it. And there's the tool chest a step or two from the door, the tape-handled knife lying temptingly in the tray.

"Killer therefore grabs knife.

"Now he has the knife clutched in one hot little hand. All he has to do is open the dressing-room door with the other—"

"Which he can't do!" Newby exclaimed.

"Exactly. The haft of the knife showed his teeth marks—he had held the knife in his mouth. A man with two normal hands who must grip a knife in one and open a door with the other has no need to put the knife in his mouth. Plainly, then, he didn't have the use of both hands. One must have been incapacitated.

"And that could mean only Mark Manson, one of whose hands was in a cast that extended to the elbow."

Joan made a face. "Really, Roger, was it necessary to break his wrist all over again last night?"

"I didn't like where he'd aimed that kick." Roger grinned.

"You sure make it sound easy, Queen!" Newby said.

Ellery sighed. "Well, the rest followed easily, at any rate. The night before, the hospital said they would keep Manson under observation for twenty-four hours. So he must have been discharged too late on opening night to get to the theater before the play started. He must have arrived during intermission.

"With the audience in the alleys and the fire-exit doors open, all Manson had to do was drape his jacket over his injured arm to conceal the cast, stroll into the theater, and make his way to the backstage door on the side where the star dressing room is. He simply wasn't noticed then or afterward, when he slipped out and parked in the Hollis bar—where Dullman and the *Record* reporter found him."

"But Mark Manson and *dope*," Joan said.

Ellery shrugged. "Manson's an old man, Joan, with no theatrical future except an actors' home and his scrapbooks. But he's still traveling in stock, hitting small towns and big-city suburbs. It's made the perfect cover for a narcotics distributor. No glory, but loot galore."

"He did a keen Wrightsville business before he took that tumble. We've already picked up the two local pushers he supplied." Chief Newby folded his napkin grimly. "Middlemen in the dope racket are usually too scared to talk, but Manson got real chatty last night. Maybe he figures it'll help when he comes up on the murder rap. The Feds are pulling in the big fish now."

Ellery pushed his chair back. "And that, dear hearts, is my cue to leave. That vacation is still waiting for me in the Mahoganies."

"And for yours truly it's back to work," Newby said, following suit.

"Wait! Please?" Joan was tugging at Roger's sleeve. "Rodge . . . haven't you always said—"

"Yes?" Roger said alertly.

"I mean, who wants to be an actress?"

That was how it came about that young Roger Fowler was seen streaking across the square that afternoon with young Joan Truslow in breathless tow, taking the shortcut to the town clerk's office, while far behind puffed the chief of police and the visiting Mr. Queen, their two witnesses required by law.

The League of
Frightened Men

The League of
Frightened Men

A CONDENSATION OF
THE BOOK BY

Rex Stout

ILLUSTRATED BY GILBERT STONE

When Judge Harrison fell—or was pushed—
from a rocky seaside cliff, a cryptic warning
was mailed to thirty-four of his friends.
One by one, they too were to die.
Art dealer Eugene Dreyer took—
or was given—poison, and again written
threats were received. Then Andy Hibbard
disappeared, and a third malevolent
warning was written.

Banded together by fear, the survivors
engage the services of Nero Wolfe.
This legendary private eye uncovers a truth
far stranger than fiction—but not
before another man is murdered.

Rex Stout, creator of Nero Wolfe, is the
author of many thrillers, including
Black Orchids, Some Buried Caesar and
Death of a Doxy. He was for many years
president of the Mystery Writers of America,
and lives now with his family
in Brewster, New York.

I

WOLFE and I sat in the office Friday afternoon. As it turned out, the name of Paul Chapin, and his slick and thrifty notions about getting vengeance at wholesale without paying for it, would have come to our notice pretty soon in any event; but that Friday afternoon the combination of an early November rain and a lack of profitable business that had lasted so long it was beginning to be painful, brought us an opening scene—a prologue, not a part of the main action—of the show that was about ready to begin.

Wolfe was drinking beer and looking at pictures of snowflakes in a book someone had sent him from Czechoslovakia. I was reading the morning paper, thinking to find an item or two that would tickle the brain which seemed about ready to dry up on me. I had already gone through the paper twice and was only hanging onto it as an excuse to keep my eyes open. Wolfe seemed absorbed in the snowflakes. Looking at him, I thought to myself, He's fighting his way through a raging blizzard. I said aloud, "You mustn't go to sleep, sir, you'll freeze to death."

Wolfe turned a page, paying no attention to me. I said, "Horstmann says the shipment from Caracas was twelve bulbs short."

Still no result. Wolfe turned another page. I stared at him a while and then said, "Did you see the piece in the paper about the woman who has a pet monkey which sleeps at the head of her bed and wraps its tail around her wrist? Did you see the one about the man on the witness stand in a case about an obscene book, and the lawyer asked him what was his purpose in writing the book, and he said because he had committed a murder and all murderers had to talk about their crimes and that was his way of talking about it? Not that I get the idea, about his purpose. If a book's dirty it's dirty, and what's the difference how it got that way? You might as well say—"

I stopped. There was no stirring of his massive frame; but I saw his right forefinger wiggle faintly, and I knew I had him. He said, "Archie. Shut up."

I grinned. "Shall I go to a movie?"

"By all means. At once."

"I'm not trying to pick a quarrel, sir. I'm just breaking under the strain of trying to figure out a third way of crossing my legs. I've been at it over a week now." I swerved. "I stick to it, if a book's dirty it's dirty, no matter if the author had a string of purposes as long as a rainy day. That guy on the witness stand yesterday said he wrote the book as a means of confessing without putting himself in jeopardy, and any obscenity in it was only incidental. So the judge soaked him fifty bucks for contempt of court and chased him off the stand."

Wolfe put a marker in the book and laid it on the desk, and leaned himself back, gently ponderous, in his specially constructed enormous chair. "Well?"

"Nothing maybe. I guess he's a nut. His name is Paul Chapin and he's written several books. The title of this one is *Devil Take the Hindmost*. He's a cripple; it mentions here about his getting up to the stand with his crippled leg."

Wolfe sighed, and rose from his chair. The clock on the wall said one minute till four—time for him to go up to the plant rooms. He moved across to the door. At the threshold he paused. "Archie. Phone Murger's to send over at once a copy of *Devil Take the Hindmost*."

"Maybe they won't. It's suppressed pending the court decision."

"Nonsense. Speak to Murger. What good is an obscenity trial except to popularize literature?"

AFTER breakfast the next morning, Saturday, I was in the office trying to pretend there might be something to do if I looked for it. Wolfe, of course, wouldn't be down until eleven o'clock. The roof of the old brownstone house on West Thirty-fifth Street was glassed in and partitioned into rooms where varying conditions of temperature and humidity were maintained—by the vigilance of Theodore Horstmann—for the ten thousand orchids that lined the benches and shelves. Wolfe once said that the orchids were his concubines: expensive, parasitic, and temperamental. In all weathers and under any circumstances, his four hours a day on the roof with Horstmann—from nine to eleven in the morning and from four to six in the afternoon—were inviolable.

At eleven Wolfe came in and said good morning. The mail didn't take long. I tapped off a few short letters and went out with them to the mailbox. When I got back Wolfe was starting on a second bottle of beer, and I thought I saw a look in his half-closed eyes. He said, "Archie. You will remember that last month you were away for ten days, and that during your absence two young men were here to perform your duties."

I grinned. One man had been from the Metropolitan Agency as Wolfe's bodyguard, and the other had been a stenographer from Miller's. "Sure," I said. "Two could handle it on a sprint."

"Just so. On one of those days a man came here and asked me to intercept his destiny. It proved not feasible to accept his commission. . . ."

I had opened a drawer of my desk and taken out a loose-leaf binder and flipped through the sheets in it to the page I wanted. "I've got it, sir. I've read it twice."

"The man's name was Hibbard."

I nodded, glancing over the typewritten pages. "Andrew Hibbard. Instructor in psychology at Columbia University. It was on October twentieth, a Saturday, that's two weeks ago today."

Wolfe emptied his glass, leaned back in his chair, and laced his fingers in front of his belly. "Suppose you read it."

"Okay. First there's a description of Mr. Hibbard. 'Small gentleman, around fifty, pointed nose, dark eyes—'"

"Enough. For that I can plunder my memory."

"Yes, sir." I read from the typewritten sheets: "'How do you do, sir, my name is—'"

"Pass the amenities."

I glanced down the page. "'Mr. Hibbard: My card has told you I am in the psychology department at Columbia. Since you are an expert, you probably observe on my face the stigmata of fright bordering on panic.'

"'Mr. Wolfe: I observe that you are upset.'

"'Mr. Hibbard: I am under an intolerable strain. My life is in danger. . . . Mr. Wolfe, I am going to be killed.'

"'Mr. Wolfe: When? How?'"

Wolfe put in, "Archie. You may delete the misters."

"Okay. Well. Next we have—'Hibbard: That I can't tell you, since I don't know. There are things about this I do know, also, which I must keep to myself. I can tell you . . . well . . . twenty-five years ago I inflicted a lasting injury on a boy. I was not alone, there were others in it, but chance made me chiefly responsible. It was a boyish prank . . . with a tragic outcome. I have never forgiven myself. Neither have the others, and all through these years some of us have had the idea of making up for it, of carrying the burden. We have acted on the idea—sometimes. You know how it is; we are busy men, most of us. But we have never denied the burden. That was difficult, for pawn—that is, as the boy advanced into manhood he became increasingly peculiar. Certainly in college he possessed brilliance. Later the brilliance perhaps remained, but became distorted. At a certain point—'"

Wolfe interrupted me. "A moment. Go back a few sentences. Beginning 'that was difficult, for pawn'—did you say pawn?"

I found it. "That's it. Pawn. I don't get it."

"Neither did the stenographer. Proceed."

"'At a certain point, some five years ago, his brilliance seemed

505

to find itself in maturity. He . . . he did things which aroused admiration and interest. Convinced though I was that he was psychopathic, I felt less concern for him than I had before. The awakening came in a startling manner. There was a reunion—a gathering—and one of us was killed—died—we thought by accident. But he—that is, the man we had injured—was there; and a few days later each of us received through the mail a communication from him saying that he had killed one of us and that the rest would follow; that he had embarked on a ship of vengeance.'

"'Wolfe: Indeed. Did you then inform the police?'

"'Hibbard: We had no evidence. The communications were typewritten, unsigned, and were expressed in ambiguous terms which rendered them worthless as evidence. He had even disguised his style, very cleverly, but it was plain enough to us. Each of us got one; not only those who had been present at the gathering, but all members of the league. Of course—'

"'Wolfe: The league?'

"'Hibbard: Many years ago, when some of us were discussing this, someone suggested that we should call ourselves the League of Atonement. The phrase hung on. . . . I was going to say that a few of us who live in New York made a sort of an investigation. We had a talk with him, and he denied sending the warnings. He seemed amused, in his dark soul, and unconcerned.'

"'Wolfe: Just so. And?'

"'Hibbard: Nothing happened for three months. Then another of us was found dead. The police said suicide. But two days later a second warning was mailed to each of us, obviously from the same source.'

"'Wolfe: This time, naturally, you went to the police.'

"'Hibbard: The others did. I was against it, but they did go—'

"'Wolfe: Why were you against it?'

"'Hibbard: We were still without evidence. Also . . . well . . . I could not bring myself to join in a demand for retribution from the man we had injured . . . you understand . . .'

"'Wolfe: Quite. First, the police could find no proof. Second, they might.'

"'Hibbard: I was not engaged in an essay on logic. In any case, the police got nowhere. He made total asses of them. He described to me their questioning—'

"'Wolfe: You still saw him?'

"'Hibbard: Of course. We were friends. After the police questioned him, questioned all of us, and came out empty-handed, some of the group got private detectives. That was twelve days ago. The detectives are having the same success as the police.'

"'Wolfe: Indeed. What agencies?'

"'Hibbard: That is irrelevant. The point is that something happened, and the plain fact is that I'm too scared to go on. I want to hire you to protect my life.'

"'Wolfe: What happened?'

"'Hibbard: He came to me and said something, that's all. It would be of no advantage to repeat it. My shameful admission is that I'm afraid to go to bed and I'm afraid to get up. I'm afraid to eat. I want whatever measure of security you can sell me. After all my scientific exploration of the human psyche, I am reduced to this single primitive concern: I am terribly afraid of being killed. The friend who suggested my coming here said that you have only one weakness. She did not call it cupidity—I forget her phrasing—but I have ample private means besides my salary, and I am in no state of mind for haggling.'

"'Wolfe: I always need money. That is of course my affair. I will undertake to disembark this gentleman from his ship of vengeance for the sum of ten thousand dollars.'

"'Hibbard: I have failed to make myself clear. I have not told you his name. I shall not. I wish your services as a safeguard for myself, not as an agency for his destruction. I would not be a party to that, even in the face of death.'

"'Wolfe: Do I understand that you wish to engage me to protect your life without taking any steps whatever to expose and restrain this man?'

"'Hibbard: Precisely. And I have been told that once your talents are committed to an enterprise—'

"'Wolfe: I have no talents. I have genius or nothing. In this

case, nothing. No, Mr. Hibbard; what you need, should you persist in your quixotic attitude, is first, if you have dependents,
generous life insurance; and second, a patient acceptance of the
fact that your death is only a matter of time. If he has decided to
kill you, and if he possesses half the brilliance you grant him—you
will die. There are so many methods available for killing a fellow
being! But you may not, after all, be his next victim, or even the
next or the next; and it is quite possible that he may run into bad
luck, or that one of your league members, less romantic than you,
may engage my services. That would save you.'

"'Hibbard: But . . . you wouldn't refuse. You can't refuse a thing
like this. My God! You are my only hope.'

"'Wolfe: I do refuse. I can undertake to render this man harmless, to remove the threat—'

"'Hibbard: No. No!'"

Wolfe stopped me. "That will do, Archie."

I looked up. "There's only a little more."

"There is nothing further except Mr. Hibbard's confused protes-
tations and my admirable steadfastness."

"I'm surprised you let him go. After all—"

Wolfe reached to the desk to ring for Fritz. "To tell you the
truth, Archie, I entertained a notion, but nothing came of it. It is
odd that you should have innocently been the cause of its revival."

"I don't get you."

Fritz came with beer. Wolfe poured a glass, gulped, and leaned
back again. He resumed. "By annoying me about the man on the
witness stand. I resigned myself to your tantrum because it was
nearly four o'clock. As you know, the book came. I read it last
night, and this will amuse you. Paul Chapin, the man on the witness stand, the author of *Devil Take the Hindmost*, is the villain
of Andrew Hibbard's tale."

"The hell he is." I gave Wolfe a look. "How do you know?"

"Pedestrian mental processes. Mr. Hibbard employed the unusual phrase, 'embark on a ship of vengeance,' and that phrase occurs twice in *Devil Take the Hindmost*. Mr. Hibbard did not say,
as the stenographer has it, 'that was difficult, for pawn' which is

of course meaningless; he said, 'that was difficult, for Paul,' and caught himself up pronouncing the name. Mr. Hibbard said things indicating that the man was a writer, for instance speaking of his disguising his style in the warnings. Mr. Hibbard said that five years ago the man 'did things which aroused admiration.' I telephoned two or three people this morning. In 1929 Paul Chapin's first successful book was published, and in 1930 his second. Also, Chapin is a cripple through an injury which he suffered twenty-five years ago in a hazing accident at Harvard."

"I see. All right. Now that you know who the guy is, everything is cozy. But who are you going to send a bill to?"

Wolfe smiled slightly. "Get Mr. Andrew Hibbard on the phone. At Columbia, or at his home. I will speak to him. You keep your wire and take it down as usual."

I got the number from the book and called it, monkeying around with four or five people at the university. But no one seemed to know where Hibbard was. He wasn't at his home either.

"It is two minutes to one," Wolfe said. "Try again after lunch."

I got up and stretched. It was at that moment the telephone rang. I sat down again, and got it. It was a woman's voice, and she asked to speak to Nero Wolfe. I asked if I might have her name, and she said "Evelyn Hibbard." It was a coincidence. She must have been trying to get our number while I was talking. I told her to hold the line and put my hand over the transmitter.

I grinned at Wolfe. "It's a Hibbard. A female Hibbard named Evelyn. Voice young, maybe a daughter. Take it."

He took his receiver off and I put mine back to my ear and got my pad and pencil ready.

"I have a note of introduction to you from a friend, Mr. Wolfe," Evelyn Hibbard began. "Could I see you at once? I could be there in fifteen minutes."

"I'm sorry, Miss Hibbard, I am engaged. Could you come at a quarter past two?"

"Oh." A little gasp floated after that. "I had hopes . . . I just decided ten minutes ago. Mr. Wolfe, it is very urgent. If you could possibly . . ."

"If you would describe the urgency."

"I'd rather not, on the telephone—but that's silly. It's my uncle, Andrew Hibbard. He went to see you two weeks ago, you may remember. He has disappeared." Her voice caught.

"Indeed. When?"

"Tuesday evening. Four days ago."

"You have had no word of him?"

"Nothing at all."

I saw Wolfe's eyes shift to take in the clock and shift again towards the door, where Fritz stood on the threshold waiting to announce lunch. "Since ninety hours have passed, another one may be risked. Will a quarter past two be convenient?"

"If you can't . . . All right. I'll be there."

Two receivers were returned simultaneously to their racks. Fritz spoke as usual, "Luncheon, sir."

II

THIS Evelyn Hibbard was little and dark and smart. Her nose was too pointed and she took too much advantage of her eyelashes, but nobody that knew merchandise would have put her on a bargain counter. I was at my desk, of course, with my pad, and she sat straight in the chair, keeping her handsome dark eyes level on Wolfe. She had brought with her a package wrapped in brown paper and held it on her lap.

She said that she lived with her uncle in an apartment on 113th Street. Her mother had died when she was young. Her father had remarried and lived in California. Her uncle was single. He, Uncle Andrew, had gone out alone Tuesday evening around nine o'clock, remarking that he would get some air. He had not returned.

"He has never stayed away like this before?" Wolfe asked. "You have no idea where he may be?"

"No. But I have an idea . . . I think . . . he has been killed."

Wolfe opened his eyes a little. "On the telephone you mentioned his visit to me. Do you know what its purpose was?"

"I know all about it." She stopped a moment. "I think my uncle has been murdered, and the man who killed him is Paul Chapin, the writer. I came here to tell you that."

Wolfe said, "Thank you for coming, but it might be more to the point to engage the attention of the police."

She nodded. "The police have been engaged since Wednesday noon. They have been willing so far, at the request of the university, to keep the matter quiet. But you don't know—" Her voice tightened. "Paul Chapin has the cunning and subtlety of all the things he mentioned in his first warning, the one he sent after he killed Judge Harrison. He is genuinely evil ... dangerous...."

"There, Miss Hibbard. There now." Wolfe sighed. "You mentioned the first warning. Do you have a copy of it?"

She nodded. "I have." She indicated the package on her lap. "I have all the warnings, including—" she swallowed "—the last one. Dr. Burton gave me his."

"The one after the apparent suicide?"

"No. The one ... Another one came this morning. I suppose to all of them."

"I see. What else have you in that package?"

"I have letters which Paul Chapin has written to my uncle, and a book of records showing sums advanced to him from 1919 to 1928 by my uncle and others, and a list of the names and addresses of the members—that is, of the men who were present in 1909 when the accident happened."

"You have all that? Why not give it to the police?"

Evelyn Hibbard shook her head. "The police would get no help from them, but you might."

I glanced up and saw Wolfe's lips pushing out a little. He said, "If the package could perhaps be opened? I am especially interested in that first warning."

She began to untie the string. I got up to help. She handed me the package and I put it on Wolfe's desk and got the paper off. Inside it was a large cardboard letter file, old and faded but intact. I passed it to Wolfe, and he opened it.

Evelyn Hibbard said, "Under *I*. My uncle did not call them warnings. He called them intimations."

Wolfe nodded. "Of destiny, I suppose." He removed papers from the file. "Your uncle is indeed a romantic. Oh yes, I say *is*. It is wise to reject all suppositions until surmise can stand on the legs of fact. Here it is. Ah! 'Ye should have killed me.' May I read it?"

She nodded. He read:

> "Ye should have killed me, watched the last mean sigh
> Sneak through my nostril like a fugitive slave.
> Ye killed the man, but not
> The snake, the fox, the mouse that nibbles his hole,
> The patient cat, the hawk, the ape that grins,
> The wolf, the crocodile, the worm that works his way
> Up through the slime and down again to hide.
> Ah! All these ye left in me,
> And killed the man.
> Ye should have killed me!

> "Long ago I said, trust time. Time will take its toll.
> I said to the snake, the ape, the cat, the worm:
> Trust time, for all your aptitudes together
> Are not as sure and deadly. But now they said:
> Time is too slow; let us, Master.
> I felt them in me. I saw the night, the sea,
> The rocks, the neutral stars, the ready cliff.
> I heard ye all about, and I heard them:
> Master, let us. Master, count for us!
> I saw one there, secure at the edge of death;
> I counted: One!
> I shall count two I know, and three and four . . .
> Not waiting for time's toll.
> Ye should have killed me."

Wolfe glanced from the paper to Miss Hibbard. "It would seem likely that Mr. Chapin pushed the judge over the edge of a cliff. There was a cliff handy?"

"Yes. It was in Massachusetts, up near Marblehead. Last June. A crowd was there at Fillmore Collard's place. Judge Harrison had come east from Indiana for his son's graduation from Harvard.

They missed him that night, and the next morning they found his body at the foot of the cliff, beaten among the rocks by the surf."

"Mr. Chapin was among them?"

She nodded. "He was there."

"Don't tell me the gathering was for purposes of atonement? Was it a meeting of this incredible league?"

"Oh no. The crowd was just a crowd, mostly from the class of 1912. Seven or eight of the—well, league—were there."

Wolfe nodded. "And this quasi-poetic warning came to each of them after they had returned to their homes?"

"Yes, a few days later."

"I see. You know, of course, that many of the most effective warnings in history were in verse. As for the merits of Mr. Chapin's execution, I suspect him of plagiarism. It has been many years since I have read Spenser, but in a crack of my memory there is a catalogue of beasts— Archie. If you wouldn't mind, bring me that Spenser? The third shelf, at the right of the door."

I took the book over and handed it to him, and he opened it and began skimming. "*The Shepheardes Calender,* I am certain, and I think *September*. Even if I find it, a petty triumph. You will forgive me, Miss Hibbard? *Bulls that bene bate . . . Cocke on his dunghill. . . .* No, certainly not that. I shall forgo the triumph. It isn't here." He handed the book to Miss Hibbard. "A fine example of bookmaking, worth a glance from you."

She summoned enough politeness to look at it, turn it over in her hand, and glance inside. Wolfe was back at the papers he had taken from the file. He was saying, "Doubtless I have tried your patience, Miss Hibbard. I am sorry. May I ask two questions?"

"Certainly."

"First, do you know whether your uncle recently took out a large amount of life insurance?"

"I think so. Yes. But, Mr. Wolfe, that has nothing to do with—"

"Were you the beneficiary?"

"I don't know. He told me you spoke to him of insurance, and then he had rushed it through and they had distributed it among four companies. I suppose I was the beneficiary."

"Not Paul Chapin?"

She said, "That hadn't occurred to me. Perhaps."

Wolfe nodded. "Yes, your uncle might do that. Now, the second question. Why did you come to see me?"

She gave him her eyes straight. "I want you to find proof of Paul Chapin's guilt, and see that he pays the penalty. You told my uncle ten thousand dollars. I can pay that."

"Do you have a personal hostility for Mr. Chapin?"

She frowned. "I hate Paul Chapin, because I loved my uncle and Paul Chapin was ruining his life. Ruined his life . . ."

"There, Miss Hibbard. Please. You did not intend to engage me to find your uncle?"

"I think I have no hope . . . I think I dare not. But then—even if you find him, there will still be Paul Chapin."

"Just so." Wolfe sighed, and turned his eyes to me. "Archie. Please wrap up Miss Hibbard's file for her."

She was protesting, "But you will need that—"

"I'm sorry, Miss Hibbard. I can't undertake your commission."

She stared at him. He said, "The affair is in the hands of the police and the district attorney. I would be hopelessly handicapped. I shall have to bid you good day."

She exploded. "Mr. Wolfe, it's outrageous! I've told you all about it . . . the reason you give is no reason at all!"

"Please, Miss Hibbard. I have said no, and I have given you my reason. That is sufficient." He got up from his chair.

She, on her feet too, had taken the package from me and was mad as hell. Before turning to go she said, "But what can I do?"

"I can make one suggestion. If you still wish my services, and the police have made no progress, come see me next Wednesday."

"But that's four whole days—"

"I'm sorry. Good day, Miss Hibbard."

I went to open the door for her. When I got back to the office Wolfe was seated again, making little circles with the tip of his finger on the arm of his chair. I said, "That girl's mad. I would say, on a guess, about one-fifth as mad as I am. A trick is okay, and a deep trick is the staff of life for some people, but . . ."

"Archie." He stirred a little. "It was desirable to get rid of Miss Hibbard without delay, for there is a great deal to be done. Take a telegram."

I sat down. I wasn't within a hundred miles of it, and that always irritated me. Wolfe dictated:

"Regarding recent developments and third Chapin warning you are requested to attend meeting this address nine o'clock Monday evening November fifth. Sign it Nero Wolfe and address."

"Sure. Just send it to anybody I happen to think of?"

Wolfe had lifted up the edge of his desk blotter and taken a sheet of paper from underneath. He said, "Here are the names. Include those in Boston, Philadelphia, and Washington; those farther away can be informed later by letter. Also, make copies of the list."

I had taken the paper from him and a glance showed me what it was. I said, "So that's why you had me get the Spenser, so she would have something to look at. Why did you steal it? She would have let you have it."

"Probably not. I didn't care to risk it. You must realize that I couldn't very well accept her as a client and then propose to others, especially to a group—" Wolfe sighed. "It appears this will be an expensive business, and there is no reason why Miss Hibbard should bear the burden alone. Now take a letter to Miss Hibbard and mail it this evening by special delivery: 'I find that the enclosed paper did not get back into your file this afternoon. If you are still of a mind to see me next Wednesday, do not hesitate to call upon me.'"

"Yes, sir. And send her the list?"

"Naturally. I believe you know the home address of Mr. Higgam of the Metropolitan Trust Company?"

I nodded.

"Find him tomorrow and give him a copy of the list. Ask him to procure first thing Monday morning a financial report on the men listed. We want the information by six o'clock Monday. Get in touch with Saul Panzer and tell him to report here Monday evening at eight thirty. Fred Durkin likewise. Find out if Gore,

Orrie Cather and two others—your selection—will be available for Tuesday morning."

I grinned. "How about the Sixty-first Regiment?"

"They will be our reserve. As soon as you have sent the telegrams, phone Miss Hibbard at her home. Employ your charm. Make an appointment to call on her this evening. If you get to see her, tell her that you have my leave to offer your assistance if she wishes it. It will afford you an opportunity to amass a collection of facts from her."

Wolfe was getting up from his chair. Before he got started for the door, I asked, "What was the idea asking her about the life insurance?"

"That? Merely the possibility that Chapin was the beneficiary. Miss Hibbard was sure he would kill her uncle, would evade discovery, and would collect a huge fortune for his pains. So she killed her uncle herself, and disposed of the body so that it could not be found. You might go into that with her this evening."

I said, "You think I won't? I'll get her alibi."

THERE was plenty doing Saturday evening and Sunday. I saw Evelyn Hibbard and had three hours with her, and got hold of the bank guy, and got Saul and Fred and the other boys lined up. There were five or six phone calls from members of the league who had got the telegrams. Some were scared, some sore, and one was just curious. As the phone calls came I checked them off on a copy of the list and made notes. Hibbard's original list had a date at the top, February 16, 1931, and was typewritten. Some of the addresses had been changed later with a pen, so evidently it had been kept up-to-date. The list was like this:

> Andrew Hibbard, psychologist
> Ferdinand Bowen, stockbroker
> Loring A. Burton, doctor
> Eugene Dreyer, art dealer
> Alexander Drummond, florist
> George R. Pratt, politician
> Nicholas Cabot, lawyer

Augustus Farrell, architect
Wm. R. Harrison, judge
Fillmore Collard, textile-mill owner
Edwin Robert Byron, magazine editor
L. M. Irving, social worker
Lewis Palmer, Federal Housing Administration
Julius Adler, lawyer
Theodore Gaines, banker
Pitney Scott, taxi driver
Michael Ayers, newspaperman
Arthur Kommers, sales manager
Wallace McKenna, congressman from Illinois
Sidney Lang, real estate
Roland Erskine, actor
Leopold Elkus, surgeon
F. L. Ingalls, travel bureau
Archibald Mollison, professor
Richard M. Tuttle, boys' school
T. R. Donovan
Phillip Leonard
Allan W. Gardner
Hans Weber

But the real fun Sunday came in the middle of the afternoon. Someone had leaked Hibbard's disappearance and the Sunday papers had it, though they didn't give it a heavy play. When the doorbell rang around three o'clock and I saw two huskies standing there, I surmised at first glance it was a couple of bureau dicks. Then I recognized one of them and threw the door wide with a grin. "Hello, hello. You late from church?"

"Nero Wolfe in?"

I nodded. "You want to see him? Leap the doorsill, gentlemen." I asked them to wait in the hall and went to the office and told Wolfe that Del Bascom of the Bascom Detective Agency was there with one of his men and wanted to see him.

Wolfe nodded, and I went out and brought them in. While I shoved up a chair for his man, Bascom went across to the desk to shake hands, saying, "It's been nearly two years since I've seen you, Mr. Wolfe. Remember? The hay fever case. Remember the clerk that didn't see the guy lifting the emeralds because he was sneezing?"

"I do indeed, Mr. Bascom. That young man had invention, to employ so common an affliction for so unusual a purpose."

"Yeah. I'd have been left scratching my ear for a bite if it hadn't been for you. I'll never forget that." Bascom crossed his legs and cleared his throat. "You taken on anything new lately?"

"No."

The other dick squeaked all of a sudden, "I heard different."

"Well, who opened your valve?" Bascom glared at him. "Did I request you to clamp your trap when we came in here?"

Wolfe said, "You were saying, Mr. Bascom?"

"I might as well come to the point. I'm on a tough case. I've got five men on it. I'm pulling down close to a thousand dollars a week, four weeks now. When I wind it up I'll get a fee that will keep me off of relief all winter."

"That's fine."

"And what I'm here for is to ask you to lay off."

Wolfe's brows went up a shade. "Lay off?"

Bascom slid forward in his chair and got earnest. "Look here, Mr. Wolfe. It's the Chapin case. I've been on it for four weeks. Pratt and Cabot and Dr. Burton are paying me. Pratt phoned me last night and said if I wanted to hang my own price tag on Paul Chapin I'd better get a move on because Nero Wolfe was about to begin. That was how I found out about the telegrams you sent." Bascom laid a fist on the desk for emphasis. "Mr. Wolfe. As you know, it is improper for a lawyer to solicit a client away from another lawyer. No lawyer with any decency would ever try it. And don't you think our profession is as dignified as the law?"

Bascom waited for an answer, his eyes on Wolfe's face. Wolfe finally said, "You mean, keep out of the Chapin case? I am sorry to have to refuse your request."

"Yeah. I thought you would." Bascom took his fist off the desk and relaxed a little. "My brother claimed you regarded yourself as a gentleman but you wasn't a sap."

"Neither, I fear."

"Well, now that that's out of the way, maybe we can talk business. I'm ready to offer you a bargain. In these four weeks we've dug up a lot of dope, and it's cost us a lot of money to get it. It's confidential naturally, but you can have all the dope and I'll confer with you on it anytime . . . for one thousand dollars."

Wolfe shook his head gently. "But, Mr. Bascom, all of your reports will be available to me."

"Sure, but you'd really get some dope if I let you question my men. I'd throw that in."

"I will pay one hundred dollars for what you offer. I will not haggle. And do not think me discourteous if I say that I am busy." Wolfe's finger moved to indicate the books before him on the desk. "There are the five novels written by Paul Chapin. I am reading them. I agree with you that this is a difficult case. It is possible, though extremely unlikely, that I shall have it solved by midnight."

I swallowed a grin. Wolfe liked bravado; it was one of his best tricks.

Bascom stared at him. After a moment he pushed his chair back and got up, and the dick next to me lifted himself with a grunt. Bascom said, "Don't let me keep you."

"Do you wish the hundred dollars?"

Bascom, turning, nodded. "I'll take it."

I went across to open the door, and they followed.

III

I HADN'T looked for the line to start forming until around nine on Monday evening, but it lacked twenty minutes of that when I heard Fritz going down the hall and the front door opening. Then Fritz ushered in the first victim. He almost needed a shave, his pants were baggy, and his hair wasn't combed. His pale blue eyes darted around and landed on me.

"Hell," he said, "you aren't Nero Wolfe."

I admitted it. I exposed my identity. He said, "I'm Mike Ayers. I'm in the city room at the *Tribune*. I told the editor I had to have

THE LEAGUE OF FRIGHTENED MEN

the evening off to get my life saved. Any chance of a drink around here?"

I said, "Gin or gin?"

He grinned. "I'd like a Scotch. Straight."

I went over to the table Fritz and I had fixed up in the alcove, and poured it. I had to pour him another drink before the next customers arrived.

This time it was a pair, Ferdinand Bowen, the stockbroker, and Dr. Loring A. Burton. Burton was a big, fine-looking guy with dark hair and black eyes and a tired mouth. Bowen was medium-sized, and he was tired all over. He was trim in black and white, and had little feet in neat pumps, and neat little lady-hands in neat little gray gloves.

I took Burton and Bowen to the office and explained that Wolfe would be down soon and showed them Mike Ayers. He called Bowen Ferdie and Burton Lorelei and offered them a drink. Then he poured another for himself. Fritz brought in Alexander Drummond, the florist, a neat little duck with a thin mustache. After that they came more or less all together: Pratt, the Tammany assemblyman, Adler and Cabot, lawyers, Kommers, sales manager from Philadelphia, Edwin Robert Byron, magazine editor, Augustus Farrell, architect, and a bird named Lee Mitchell, from Boston, who said he represented both Collard and Gaines. He had a letter from Gaines.

That made twelve accounted for, figuring both Collard and Gaines in, at ten minutes past nine. I went to Wolfe's desk and gave Fritz's button three short pokes. In a couple of minutes I heard the faint hum of the elevator.

The door of the office opened and everybody turned their heads. Wolfe came in, waddled halfway to his desk, turned, and said, "Good evening, gentlemen." He went to his chair, got his grip on the arms, and lowered himself.

I handed Wolfe a list showing those who were present, and he glanced over it. He looked up and spoke. "I am glad to see that Mr. Cabot and Mr. Adler are here. Both, I believe, attorneys. Their knowledge and their trained minds will restrain us from vulgar errors. I note also the presence of Mr. Michael Ayers, a journalist, so I merely remark that the risk of publicity—"

Mike Ayers growled, "I'm not a journalist, I'm a newshound."

"How drunk are you?"

"Hell, how do I know?"

Julius Adler, the lawyer, looking like a necktie clerk, put in, "My name is Adler. We realize that Mr. Ayers is lit, Mr. Wolfe, but after all we don't suppose that you invited us here to censor our private habits. You have something to say to us?"

"Mr. Adler. Your remark illustrates what I knew would be the chief hindrance in my conversation with you gentlemen. I was aware that you would be antagonistic at the outset. You are all badly frightened, and a frightened man is hostile almost by reflex."

"Nonsense." It was Cabot, the other lawyer. "We are not frightened. If you have anything to say to us, say it."

Wolfe nodded. "If you aren't frightened, there is nothing to discuss. You might as well go home." Wolfe let his eyes move slowly across the eleven faces. "You see, gentlemen, I invited you here this evening only after making a number of assumptions. The first is that Mr. Paul Chapin has murdered two, possibly three, of your friends. The second, that you are apprehensive that he will murder you. The third, that my abilities are equal to the task of removing your apprehension; and the fourth, that you will be willing to pay well for that service. Well?"

They glanced at one another. Nicholas Cabot said, "We are convinced that Paul Chapin is a dangerous enemy of society. That naturally concerns us. As to your abilities . . ."

Wolfe wiggled a finger at him. "If it amuses you to maintain the fiction that you came here this evening to protect society, the question still is, how much is it worth to you?"

A new voice broke in, smooth and easy. It was Edwin Robert Byron, the magazine editor. "I'd just as soon say I'm scared, but the point is, what does Mr. Wolfe propose to do about it?"

Mike Ayers got up and started for the table in the alcove. Halfway there he turned and blurted at them, "You're damned tootin' we're scared. You've heard of our little organization, Wolfe, you old faker? The League of Atonement? We're changing it to the Craven Club, or maybe the League of the White Feather." He filled his glass and lifted it. "Fellow members! To the League of the White Feather!" He downed the drink in one swallow.

Lee Mitchell of Boston got to his feet. "If I may remark, gentlemen." He coughed. "I am authorized to say that both Mr. Collard and Mr. Gaines have satisfied themselves of the standing of Mr. Wolfe, and they are ready to entertain his suggestions."

"Good." Wolfe's tone cut short the buzz of comment. "Archie. If you will just pass out those slips."

I had them in the top drawer of my desk, and I took them and handed them around. Wolfe had rung for beer and was filling his glass. After he had half emptied it he said, "That, as you see, is merely a list of your names with a sum of money noted after each. I can explain it most easily by reading to you a memorandum which I have here. For the sake of brevity I have referred to you—those absent as well as those present—as 'the league.' The memorandum provides:

"1. I undertake to remove from the league all apprehension and expectation of injury from
  (a) Paul Chapin.
  (b) The person or persons who sent the warnings.
  (c) The person or persons responsible for the deaths of Wm. R. Harrison and Eugene Dreyer, and for the disappearance of Andrew Hibbard.
"2. Decision as to my satisfactory performance shall be made by a majority vote of the members of the league.
"3. Expenses shall be borne by me, and in the event of my failure the league shall be under no obligation to pay them.
"4. Upon decision that the undertaking has been satisfactorily performed, the members of the league will pay me, each the amount set after his name on the attached list.

"I believe that covers it."

"It's preposterous," Nicholas Cabot retorted. "I won't even discuss it." Julius Adler said with a smile, "I think we should thank

Mr. Wolfe's secretary for adding it up and saving us the shock. Fifty-six thousand, nine hundred and fifteen dollars. Well!" His brows went up and stayed up. Kommers, who had come up from Philadelphia, made his maiden speech. "I don't know much about your abilities, Mr. Wolfe, but I've learned something new about nerve." Others began to join in the chorus.

Wolfe waited, and in about a minute put up his hand. "Please, gentlemen. If you think the price exorbitant you are under no compulsion to buy. However, I may observe that on Saturday Miss Evelyn Hibbard offered to pay me ten thousand dollars for the service proposed. There is no single item on that list as high as ten thousand dollars; and Miss Hibbard is not herself in jeopardy."

George Pratt said, "Yeah, and you turned her down so you could soak us."

"Anyhow, this is preposterous," Nicholas Cabot said. He had gone to Wolfe's desk and was standing there looking at the memorandum. "What's all this hocus-pocus about person or persons responsible? What we want is Paul Chapin put where he belongs."

Wolfe sighed. "I could not undertake specifically to get Mr. Chapin convicted of murder, because if investigation proved him innocent two difficulties would present themselves. First, I would have to frame him in order to collect my money, and second, the real perpetrator of these indiscretions would remain free to continue his career, and—"

"Rubbish." Cabot pushed the memorandum impatiently away. "We know it is Chapin."

Wolfe nodded. "I too am convinced that it is Chapin you should fear. But in preparing this memorandum I thought it well to cover all contingencies. After all, what is really known? Very little. For instance, what if Hibbard, tormented by remorse, was driven to undertake vengeance on behalf of the man you all had injured? What if, after killing two of you, he found he couldn't stomach it, and went off somewhere and ended his own life? Or what if another of you, or even an outsider, proceeded to balance some personal accounts, and took advantage of the Chapin stew to lay a false scent? You say rubbish, but why not cover the contingencies?"

Cabot pulled the memorandum back beneath his eyes. Julius Adler got up and went to the desk and joined in the inspection. There was some murmuring among the others.

Wolfe said, "I will mention two little points I did not include in the memorandum. I shall of course expect that you should cooperate with me. I can do little without your help."

Three or four heads nodded. George Pratt, with the group at the desk, said, "Good here."

"The second point, about the money. In my opinion, the sums I have listed are adequate but not extortionate. If I fail to satisfy you I get nothing, so it comes to this: Would Mr. Gaines be willing at this moment to pay me eight thousand dollars, and Dr. Burton seven thousand, and Mr. Michael Ayers one hundred and eighty, in return for freedom from the fear which has fastened itself upon them? I take it that you agree that it is proper to grade the amounts in accordance with ability to pay."

Again heads nodded. I grinned to myself.

Cabot said, "You can cross Elkus out. He's as sentimental as Andy Hibbard was. He'd sooner see us all killed than help catch Paul Chapin."

"Indeed. We shall see. Gentlemen. My understanding is that you are all convinced that Paul Chapin is a murderer, that he has threatened you with murder, and that he should be caught, discovered, convicted, and executed. I am going to ask Mr. Goodwin to call off your names. If my understanding is correct, you will please respond with yes."

I took up the list on which I had checked those present. Before I could call one, Lee Mitchell said, "On that I can answer for Mr. Collard and Mr. Gaines. Their response is yes."

Cabot now spoke up again. "Before we go on with the vote, I would like to put in a word in favor of Mr. Wolfe's proposal. What else can we do? The police are helpless; they are equipped to frustrate many kinds of men, but not Paul Chapin—I grant him his quality. Three of us hired detectives a month ago, and they spent days looking for the typewriter on which the warnings were written and never even found it."

There was a stir, but no one spoke. I began with the list. "Ferdinand Bowen."

The broker said, husky but firm, "Yes."

"Dr. Loring A. Burton."

Burton looked around, swallowed, and said explosively, "Yes, of course! Yes!"

Farrell said to him, "I should hope so. The wonder is you weren't first."

I called the others, Farrell, Drummond, Cabot, Pratt, Byron, Adler, Kommers; they all said yes. I called, "Michael Ayers." He was sprawled in his chair and bawled out, "Yes!"

I turned to Wolfe. "That's all, sir."

I usually heard Fritz when he went down the front hall to answer the doorbell, but that time I didn't. So I was surprised when I saw the door of the office opening.

Fritz came in three steps. "A gentleman to see you, sir. He told me to say, Mr. Paul Chapin."

"Indeed." Wolfe didn't move. "Show him in."

PAUL CHAPIN limped in with his walking stick and stopped a few paces from the door. He looked at the group, tossed his head up twice, and said, "Hello, fellows," then limped forward again, far enough into the room so he could see Wolfe. He was dressed for evening, a dark suit. He wasn't a big guy at all; you couldn't call him skinny, but you could see the bone structure of his face—flat cheeks, an ordinary nose, and light-colored eyes. When he turned his back to me so as to face Wolfe I saw that his coat didn't hang straight down over his right hip pocket, and I uncrossed my legs and brought my feet back to position, just in case.

Wolfe had his fingers intertwined on his belly. "I am Nero Wolfe. You are Mr. Chapin?"

Paul Chapin nodded. "I was at the theater. They've done a book of mine into a play. Then I thought I'd drop in here."

"Which book? I've read all of them."

"You have? I wouldn't suppose . . . *The Iron Heel.*"

"Oh yes. That one. Accept my congratulations."

"Thank you. I hope you don't mind my dropping in. I knew of this gathering, of course. I learned of it from Lorrie Burton and Alex Drummond."

Chapin kept his eyes on Wolfe, ignoring the others. They were regarding him with varying reactions on their faces: Mitchell of Boston with curiosity, Bowen with a sour poker face, Cabot with uncomfortable indignation.

Of a sudden Dr. Burton left his chair, strode over to Chapin, and grabbed him by the arm. "Paul, for God's sake," he said, "get out of here!"

Drummond, the florist, put in a ferocious squeal. "This is the limit, Paul! You dirty murdering rat!"

Others, breaking their tension, found their tongues. Wolfe stopped them. He said sharply, "Gentlemen! Mr. Chapin is my guest!" He looked at Chapin, leaning on his stick. "You should sit down. Take a chair."

"No, thanks. I'll be going in a moment." Chapin sent a smile around; it would have been a pleasant one but for his unsmiling light-colored eyes. "I've been standing on one foot for twenty-five years. Of course all of you know that; I don't need to tell you. I'm sorry if I've annoyed you by coming here; really, I wouldn't disconcert you fellows for anything. You've all been too kind to me." He turned to Wolfe. "But I didn't come here to say that, I came to see you. I just wanted to say that my friends have wasted a lot of time and money pursuing a mirage. I tell you straight, Mr. Wolfe, it's been a shock to me. That they should suspect *me*, knowing as they do how grateful I am for all their kindness! Really, incredible."

"Perhaps then you have a theory regarding the incidents that have disturbed your friends? It might help us," Wolfe said.

"I'm afraid not." Chapin shook his head regretfully. "Of course, it appears more than likely that it's a practical joke—"

"Death is not a joke, Mr. Chapin."

"Oh, no? Would you dare to assert that my death would not be a joke, a howling anticlimax, considering what has preceded it?"

"So you adhere to the joke theory," Wolfe said.

"It seems likely. So far as I am concerned, Mr. Wolfe, the only point is this: I suffer from the delusion of my friends that I am a source of peril to them. Actually, they are afraid of me. Of *me!* I am myself afraid! Afraid of all sorts of things. For instance, on account of my physical inadequacy, I go in constant fear of violent attack, and I habitually am armed. See—"

Paul Chapin had us going all right. As his right hand started under the edge of his jacket, there were two or three cries of warning from the group, and I took it on the jump. I damn near toppled him over, but I had a grip on his wrist and saved him from a tumble. With my left hand I jerked the gun from his hip pocket.

"Archie!" Wolfe snapped at me. "Release Mr. Chapin."

I let go his wrist. "Give him back his—article," Wolfe ordered.

The gun was a thirty-two, an old veteran, and a glance showed me it wasn't loaded. Paul Chapin held out his hand and I put the gun in it.

Wolfe said, "Confound you, Archie. You have deprived Mr. Chapin of the opportunity for a dramatic and effective gesture. I am sorry. May I see the gun, Mr. Chapin?"

Chapin handed it to him. Wolfe threw the cylinder out and back, cocked it, and snapped the trigger. He said, "An ugly weapon. Guns terrify me. May I show it to Mr. Goodwin?"

Chapin shrugged his shoulders, and Wolfe handed the gun to me. I cocked it, saw what Wolfe had seen, and grinned. Then I looked up and saw Paul Chapin's eyes on me and stopped grinning. Behind them was something I wouldn't have cared to bring into plain sight. I handed him the gun, and he stuck it back into his hip pocket. He said in an easy tone, "That's it, you see. The effect is psychological. I learned a good deal about psychology from my friend Andy Hibbard."

George Pratt stepped to Chapin. His hands were working at his sides as he stammered, "You—you snake! If you weren't a damned cripple I'd knock you so far—"

Chapin showed no alarm. "Yes, George. And what made me a damned cripple?"

Pratt didn't retreat. "I helped to, once. Sure I did. That was an accident. Can't you ever forget it? Is there no man in you at all?"

"Man? No." Chapin smiled at him with his mouth. He looked around at the others. "You fellows are all men though. Aren't you? Everyone. God bless you." He turned to Wolfe. "Good evening, sir. Thank you for your courtesy."

He inclined his head to Wolfe and to me, and turned to go. His stick had thumped three times on the rug when he was halted by Wolfe's voice. "Mr. Chapin. May I ask you for a few minutes more? Just a small—"

Nicholas Cabot broke in. "For God's sake, Wolfe, let him go—"

"Please, Mr. Cabot. Just a small favor, Mr. Chapin. Since you are innocent of any ill intent, I trust you will help me in a little test. Would you help me out?"

I thought Chapin looked careful. He said, "Perhaps. What is it?"

"Would you be good enough to sit at Mr. Goodwin's desk and type something at my dictation?"

"Why should I?" He hesitated, looked around, and saw twelve pairs of eyes at him; then he smiled and said easily, "But for that matter, why shouldn't I?" He limped back towards my desk. He leaned his stick up against the desk and got himself into the chair, shoving his bum leg under with his hand. Then he looked around at Wolfe and said, "Shall I double-space it?"

"Single spacing will most nearly resemble the original. Are you ready?" Wolfe suddenly put volume and depth into his voice: "*'Ye should have killed me'*—comma—*'watched the last mean sigh—'*"

There was complete silence. Then Chapin's fingers got through the first three words, but they stopped at the *l* in killed, stopped completely. There was silence again. You could have heard a feather falling. Then Paul Chapin got himself onto his feet, took his stick, and thumped past me. Before he got to the door he stopped and turned.

He said, "I would have been glad to help in any authentic test, Mr. Wolfe, but I wouldn't care to be the victim of a vulgar and obvious trick."

Wolfe murmured, "Archie," and I went out to help him on with his coat and open the door for him.

IV

WHEN I got back to the office Cabot, the lawyer, was saying, "I have an idea you'll collect your fees, Mr. Wolfe."

Wolfe sighed. "For my part, I have an idea that if I collect my fees I shall have earned them. Your friend Mr. Chapin is a man of quality."

Cabot nodded. "Paul Chapin is a distorted genius."

"All genius is distorted. Including my own. How did Paul Chapin acquire his special distortion? I mean the famous accident. I understand it was at college, a hazing affair."

"Yes. It was pretty terrible." Cabot sat on the edge of the desk. "I suppose Paul was distorted from the beginning. He was a freshman, the rest of us were sophomores and on up. Do you know the Yard at Harvard?"

"I have never been there."

"Well. There were dormitories—Thayer Hall. We were having a beer night downstairs when a fellow came in and said he couldn't get in his room; he had left his key inside. We all began to clap."

"That was a masterpiece, to forget one's key?"

"Oh no. We were clapping the opportunity. By getting out another window you could make your way along a narrow ledge to the window of any locked room and get in that way. Whenever an upperclassman forgot his key it was the custom to conscript a freshman for that service. Well, when this fellow—it was Andy Hibbard—when he announced he had locked himself out, of course we looked around for a victim. Somebody looked out in the hall and saw Chapin going by, and called to him to come in.

"Paul had a personality, a force in him, already at that age. Anyhow, we had been inclined to let him alone. Now, here he was delivered to us by chance. Somebody told him what was expected of him. He was quite cool about it. He asked what floor Andy's room was on, and we told him the fourth. He said he was sorry, in that case he couldn't do it. Bill Harrison asked him if he had vertigo. He said no. We marched him upstairs, thirty-five of us. We didn't touch him. He went, because he knew what would happen if he didn't."

"What would happen?"

"Oh, whatever might occur to us. You know college kids."

"As few as possible."

"I'll never forget Paul's face as he was getting out of the hall window, backwards. It was white as a sheet. He got onto the ledge all right, and moved along a little, his hand stretched out as far as he could, trying to reach the next window. Then all of a sudden he began to tremble, and down he went."

Cabot reached in his pocket for a cigarette. "That's all. That's what happened."

Wolfe grunted. "You say there were thirty-five of you?"

"Yes. We chipped in, of course, and did all we could. He was in the hospital two months and had three operations. The day he left the hospital he sent all of us copies of a poem he had written. Thanking us. There was only one of us smart enough to see what kind of thanks it was. Pitney Scott."

"Pitney Scott is a taxi driver."

Cabot raised his brows. "You should write our class history, Mr. Wolfe. Pit took to drink in 1930, one of the depression casualties. I see you have him down for five dollars. I'll pay it."

Wolfe reached out and pressed the button for Fritz. Fritz appeared, and Wolfe nodded for beer. "Mr. Cabot, what does Mr. Chapin mean when he says that you killed the man in him? Is it merely poetry, or is it also technical information?"

"I don't know." Cabot's eyes fell. "I couldn't say—you'd have to ask his doctor."

"Or his wife," Alex Drummond horned in.

Wolfe snapped at him, "Whose wife?"

"Why, Paul's."

Wolfe, astonished, looked at Cabot and demanded, "What is this nonsense?"

Cabot nodded. "Sure, Paul has a wife."

Wolfe poured a glass of beer, and gulped half of it. "Tell me about her," he said.

"Well . . ." Cabot looked for words. "Paul Chapin is full of distortions, let us say, and his wife is one of them. Her name was Dora Ritter. He married her three years ago, and they live in an apartment on Perry Street."

"What is she like and who was she?"

Cabot hesitated again. This time he was looking for a way out. He finally said, "You'd better get it from Burton himself." He turned and called, "Lorrie! Come over here a minute."

Dr. Burton looked around, and crossed to Wolfe's desk. Cabot said to him, "Mr. Wolfe has just asked me who Paul's wife was. I'd rather you'd tell him."

"Why not you, or anybody? Everybody knows it." Burton sounded irritated.

Cabot smiled. "Maybe I'm being overdelicate."

"I think you are." Burton turned to Wolfe. "Dora Ritter was a maid in my wife's employ. She is around fifty, extremely homely, disconcertingly competent, and stubborn as a wet boot. Paul Chapin married her in 1931."

"What did he marry her for and how long had he known her?" Wolfe wagged a finger. "I must ask you to bear with me, Dr. Burton. I have read all of Paul Chapin's novels, and so naturally supposed I had a fairly complete understanding of his character. I thought him incapable of following any of the emotional or practical channels leading to matrimony. I need to have disclosed everything about her that is discoverable."

"Oh. You do." Burton looked at him, sizing him up, with sour steadiness. "Then I might as well disclose it myself. I presume you don't know that of all this group I was the only one who knew Paul Chapin before the college days. We came from the same town—I more or less grew up with him. He was in love with a girl, and finally, through persistence, reached an understanding with her before he went away to college. Then the accident occurred, and he was crippled, and it was all off. In my opinion it would have been off anyway, sooner or later. I didn't go home for my vacations; I spent my summers working. It wasn't until after I was through with medical school that I went back for a visit, and discovered that this girl had become . . . that is . . . I married her, and we came to New York. I was lucky in my profession. I made a lot of money. I think it was in 1923 that my wife engaged Dora Ritter as a personal maid—she was with us eight years. One day Paul came to me and said he was going to marry Dora. He made a nasty scene out of it."

"So he married her," Wolf said. "Do you ever see her?"

Burton hesitated, then went on. "She comes once or twice a week to dress my wife's hair, and occasionally to sew. I am usually not at home."

Wolfe took some beer. "Thank you, Doctor. Mr. Chapin's romance no longer upsets me, since it fits my presumptions. By the way, this probably clears up another little point. Archie, would you ask Mr. Farrell to join us?"

I went and got Farrell, who was at the table pouring a drink.

"Mr. Farrell," Wolfe said. "Earlier this evening you remarked to Dr. Burton that it was a wonder he was not the first. I supposed that you meant the first victim of Mr. Chapin's campaign. Did that remark mean anything in particular?"

Farrell looked uncomfortable. "Did I say that?"

Wolfe said patiently, "Dr. Burton has just been telling me of Chapin's marriage and the former occupation of his wife."

"Then what are you asking me for?"

"Don't be testy, Mr. Farrell," said Wolfe. "That was the basis of your remark?"

"Of course. But what the devil have Lorrie Burton's private affairs got to do with it? I thought what we are going to pay you for is to stop—"

He broke off. His face got red and he finished in a completely different tone. "Forgive me. I forgot for a moment."

"Forgot what?" said Wolfe.

"Only that I'm out of it. On your list you've got me down for ten dollars. Your sources of information are up-to-date. Have you any idea what architects have been up against the past four years? You're not thinking of doing any building, Mr. Wolfe? A telephone stand or a dog kennel or anything? I'd be glad to submit designs— Oh, the devil— Come on, Lorrie, come and finish your drink." He took Burton's arm.

George Pratt said to Cabot, "Let's have a little refreshment, Nick," and they followed Farrell and Burton.

Alex Drummond was left alone at the corner of Wolfe's desk. He looked at Wolfe with his bright little eyes, stepped closer to him, and made his voice low. "Uh—Mr. Wolfe. I imagine your sources of information are pretty good."

Wolfe said without looking at him, "They are superlative."

"Uh—I was wondering why you have Gaines down for eight thousand and Burton for seven thousand and so on, and Ferd Bowen for only twelve hundred? He's something in Wall Street— I mean really something. The firm of Galbraith and Bowen . . ." Drummond made his voice a little lower. "Frankly, it's more than curiosity . . . he handles a few little investments for me . . ."

Wolfe looked at him and looked away again. I thought for a minute he wasn't going to reply at all, but he did. "Don't bother to disparage your investments. It can have no effect on the amount of your payment to me, for that has already been calculated and recorded. As for your question, my sources of information may be superlative, but they are not infallible."

"But if you could just tell me in confidence—"

"If you will excuse me." Wolfe raised his voice a little. "Gentlemen. Gentlemen? Could I have a word with you?"

They approached his desk. Two or three still in chairs stayed there. Drummond trotted around to the far side of the desk. Ayers flopped into a chair, yawning. Wolfe was handing it to them in his handsome manner. "The hour is getting late, and I would not wish to detain you. I take it that we are in agreement—"

Arthur Kommers interrupted. "I ought to leave in a minute to catch the midnight back to Philadelphia. Do you want my initials on that thing?"

"Not at present," Wolfe replied. "I shall ask Mr. Cabot to prepare copies in his office tomorrow and send them to me for distribution." He glanced at the lawyer, and Cabot nodded. "Thank you. . . . In that connection," Wolfe continued, "Mr. Farrell, I wish to make a proposal to you. To be broke is not a disgrace, it is only a catastrophe. You can help me by sending copies of the memorandum to those members of the league not present this evening, and arranging for their cooperation. I will pay you twenty dollars a day. There will be other little jobs for you."

The architect was staring at him. "You're quite a guy, Mr. Wolfe. But I'm not a detective."

"I shall keep my demands modest."

"All right." Farrell laughed. "I can use the money."

"Good. Report here tomorrow at eleven. Dr. Burton, could you dine with me tomorrow evening?"

Without hesitation, Burton shook his head. "I'm sorry, Mr. Wolfe, I can't come." He hesitated, and went on. "More frankly, I won't. I answered yes to the question you put this evening, and I'll pay my share, but that's as far as I'll go. I'll not confer on ways and means of getting Paul Chapin convicted and electrocuted. Oh, don't misunderstand me. It's only a temperamental prejudice. I wouldn't move a finger to protect Paul. In fact, I am ready to defeat him by a violence equal to his own."

"You are ready?" Wolfe had opened his eyes on him. "You mean you are prepared?"

"Not specially." Burton looked irritated. "I only meant . . . well, for years I've kept an automatic pistol in the drawer of my study table. One evening last week Paul came to see me. On account of recent events I told the maid to keep him in the reception hall; and before joining him I took the pistol from the drawer and stuck it in my pocket. That was all I meant by ready."

Wolfe sighed. "Very well, sir. By all means cling to the tattered shreds of humanity that are left you. I would like to ask, gentlemen: which of you were most intimate with Mr. Hibbard?"

They looked at each other. George Pratt said, "We all saw Andy off and on."

Wolfe gazed at him a moment, then glanced at the clock. "Well, gentlemen," he said, "so far as our business is concerned I need not further detain you."

Cabot picked up the memorandum and put it in his pocket.

"I'll send you the copies in the morning. Good night, Mr. Wolfe."

The others got moving. They drifted to the hall, and I went out and stood around while they got their hats and coats on.

After I had shut the door and bolted it I went back to the office and sat down at my desk. I said, "This bird Chapin is a lunatic, and it's long past midnight. I'm good and sleepy."

Wolfe closed his eyes and murmured, "A page in your notebook." I opened a drawer and took out a book and pencil.

"Phone Mr. Cabot's office at nine o'clock and make sure that the memorandums will be here by eleven, ready for Mr. Farrell. Ask where the reports from the Bascom agency are and arrange to get them. The men will be here at eight?"

"Yes, sir."

"Send one of them to get the reports. Put three of them on Paul Chapin, first thing. We want a complete record of his movements. Tell them to phone anything of significance. Saul Panzer is to get his nose onto Andrew Hibbard's last discoverable footstep. Tell him to phone me at eleven thirty."

"Yes, sir."

"Put Cather onto Chapin's past, outside the circle of our clients, especially the past two years. He might succeed in striking an harmonious chord with Dora Chapin."

"Maybe I could do that myself. She's probably a lulu."

"Your special province will be the deaths of Harrison and Dreyer. First read the Bascom reports, then proceed. Wherever original investigation is indicated and seems still feasible after the lapse of time, undertake it. Do not call upon any of our clients until Mr. Farrell has seen them. That's all. It's late."

Wolfe opened his eyes, blinked, and closed them again. But I noticed that the tip of his finger was doing a little circle on the arm of the chair. I said, "Maybe you're troubled by the same thing I am. Why is this Mr. Chapin giving hip room to a Civil War gat that's about as murderous as a beanshooter?"

"I'm not troubled, Archie." But his finger didn't stop. "I'm wondering whether another bottle of beer before going to bed would be judicious."

"You've had six since dinner. Speaking of Chapin's cannon—is it possible he was carrying it to take attention from another gun, the real thing? I mean, psychologically . . ."

Wolfe pushed back his chair with determination. "Archie. As a man of action you are tolerable, you are even competent. But I will not for one moment put up with you as a psychologist. I am going to bed."

V

I WOULD like to say right here that I know when I'm out of my class. Paul Chapin hadn't been in Nero Wolfe's office more than three minutes Monday night when I saw he was all Greek to me. When people begin to get deep and complicated they mix me up. But reports never do. With reports, no matter how many puzzles they've got that don't seem to fit at first, I'm there forty ways from Sunday. I spent six hours Tuesday with the accounts of Judge Wm. R. Harrison's death—reading the Bascom reports, talking with six people, including thirty minutes on long distance with Fillmore Collard—and I decided three things: first, that if it was murder it was impromptu; second, that if anybody killed him it was Paul Chapin; and third, that there was as much chance of proving it as of proving that honesty was the best policy.

It had happened nearly five months back. Paul Chapin had driven up to Harvard with Leopold Elkus, the surgeon, who had gone because he had a son graduating. Judge Harrison had come on from Indianapolis for the same reason. Drummond, Elkus told me, went back every June. Cabot and Sidney Lang and Bowen had been in Boston on business. Fillmore Collard had invited his old classmates for the weekend to his place near Marblehead.

Saturday evening after dinner a group had strolled through the grounds to the edge of a hundred-foot cliff. Four, among them Cabot and Elkus, had stayed in the house playing bridge. Paul Chapin had hobbled along with the strollers. They had separated, some going to the stables with Collard to see a sick horse, some back to the house. It was an hour or so later that they missed Harrison, but not until midnight did they become really concerned. Daylight came before the tide was out enough for them to find his body at the foot of the cliff, wedged among the rocks.

A tragic accident and a ruined party. It had had no significance beyond that until the Wednesday following, when the typewritten poem came to each member of the league. Those who could, got together, and considered, and tried to remember everything about the incident. After the interval of four days there was a good deal of disagreement. Two of them were positive that Chapin had limped along after the group strolling to the house; Sidney Lang had seen him reading a book soon after the group returned, and was of the opinion that he had not stirred from his seat for an hour or more.

All the league was in on it now, for they had all got warnings. Two or three were inclined to laugh it off. Some were in favor of turning it over to the police, but they were talked down, chiefly by Hibbard and Burton and Elkus. In the end they delegated a committee composed of Burton, Cabot, and Lang to call on Chapin.

At their insistence he described his Saturday evening movements; he had caught up with the group at the cliff and had left with those who returned to the house; he had not noticed Harrison sitting on the cliff's edge. At the house he had stayed in a chair with a book until aroused by the hubbub over Harrison's absence—approaching midnight. That was his smiling story. He had been not angry, but delicately hurt, that his best friends could think him capable of wishing injury to one of them. As for the warnings they had received, he said, his sorrow that they should suspect him was lost in his indignation that he should be accused of so miserable a piece of versifying.

Who had sent the warnings, if he hadn't? He had no idea. Of course it could have been done by anyone knowing of that ancient accident. The postmark might furnish a hint, or the envelopes and paper, or the typewriting itself. As he had offered his helpful suggestions he had got up and limped over to his typewriter, patted it, and smiled at them. "I'm sure that stuff wasn't written on this, unless one of you fellows used it when I wasn't looking."

Nicholas Cabot had been tough enough to go over and type a few lines on it. A later examination had shown that Chapin was quite correct.

The committee had made its report, but weeks had gone by and the thing had petered out. Most of the league, convinced that the warning was a practical joke, made a point of continuing their friendly relations with Chapin.

I reported all this to Wolfe Tuesday evening. His comment was, "Then the death of this Judge Harrison was extempore. Let us forget it; it might clutter up our minds. If Mr. Chapin had been content with that man's death, he might have considered himself safely avenged. But his vanity undid him; he wrote that threat and sent it broadcast. That was dangerous."

"How sure are you that he sent the threat?"

"Did I not say he did? But so much for Judge Harrison. I would tell you about Mr. Hibbard, though there is nothing to tell. His niece, Miss Evelyn Hibbard, called on me this morning, having received a report of last evening's gathering."

"Did she spill anything new?"

"She has made another thorough search of the apartment, and can find nothing whatever missing. Saul Panzer, after a full day, had only one little morsel to offer. A news vendor at 116th Street and Broadway saw Mr. Hibbard enter the subway between nine and ten o'clock last Tuesday evening."

"That was the only bite Saul got?"

Wolfe nodded. "The police had got that too, and no more, though it has been a full week since Mr. Hibbard disappeared. As for Mr. Chapin, it would be useless to question him. He has told both Bascom and the police that he spent last Tuesday evening in his apartment, and his wife sustains him."

Wolfe poured a glass of beer. "But on the most critical front, at the moment, we have met success. Mr. Farrell has gained the adherence of twenty individuals to the memorandum—all but Dr. Elkus in the city, and all but one without, over the telephone.

Mr. Pitney Scott, the taxi driver, is excluded from these statistics; there would be no profit in hounding him, but you might find occasion to give him a glance; he arouses my curiosity, faintly, in another direction. Mr. Farrell is also collecting the warnings, all copies except those in the possession of the police."

The telephone rang. I heard a few words, and nodded at Wolfe. "Here's Farrell now." Wolfe pulled his phone over, and I kept my receiver to my ear.

After we had hung up, I said, "What? Farrell taking Mr. Somebody to lunch at the Harvard Club? You're spending money like a drunken sailor."

Wolfe rubbed his nose. "I requested Mr. Farrell to arrange for an interview with Mr. Oglethorpe. I did not contemplate feeding him. It is now beyond remedy. Mr. Oglethorpe is a member of the firm which publishes Mr. Chapin's books, and Mr. Farrell is slightly acquainted with him."

I grinned. "Well, you're stuck."

Wolfe said, "Upstairs this morning I spent twenty minutes considering where Paul Chapin might elect to type something which he would not wish to be traced to him. One possibility was that Mr. Chapin would call at the office of his publisher and request the use of a typewriter. If Mr. Farrell discovers that he did, he may be able to get Mr. Oglethorpe's permission to let him have a sample from the machine that Chapin used. Incidentally, we have an additional contributor, Miss Evelyn Hibbard. I arranged it with her this morning. The amount is three thousand dollars." He sighed. "I made a large reduction from the ten thousand she offered, on account of the altered circumstances."

I had been waiting for that. "You understand, sir, I wouldn't accuse you of trying to put anything over. I know you just forgot that Miss Hibbard is *my* client. I went to see her Saturday at your suggestion. Remember, sir? So of course any arrangement she might make could only be with my advice and consent."

Wolfe murmured, "Preposterous. Puerile trickery."

I sighed. "Of course you understand the ethics of it, I don't have to explain—"

He cut me off. "How much would you advise your client to pay?"

"One thousand bucks."

"Absurd. In view of her original offer—"

"All right. I won't haggle. I'll split the difference with you. Two thousand."

Wolfe shut his eyes. "Done, confound you. Enter it in the cashbook. Now take your notebook. Tomorrow morning . . ."

WEDNESDAY morning pretty early I was sitting in the kitchen when Fritz returned from a trip to the front door to say that Fred Durkin wanted to see me. When I got to the office Fred was sitting there impatiently. "Can I see Wolfe?"

"You know damn well you can't. Up to eleven o'clock Mr. Nero Wolfe is a horticulturist."

"This is special."

"Not special enough for that. Spill it to the chief of staff. Why aren't you on Chapin's tail?"

"I don't start until nine. I'll be there." He grunted with disgust. "Listen here, Archie. It's a washout."

"What's the matter with it?"

"Well, you put three of us on this to cover Chapin twenty-four hours a day, and it's a washout. Chapin lives in an apartment house at 203 Perry Street. He's on the fifth floor. The house has a big court in the back. The idea is that there's another house on the court, facing on Eleventh Street, built by the same landlord. Anybody that wants to can go out of the Perry Street house the back way, cross the court, and go through a passage and come out on Eleventh Street. So, parked in a cigar store on Perry Street, I feel about as useful as if I was watching Yankee Stadium for a woman in a dark hat. I just wanted to tell Wolfe what he's paying me money for."

"Okay. So we need three more men, for Eleventh Street."

"Wait a minute." Fred waved a hand at me. "That's not all of it. The other trouble is that the traffic cop at the corner is going to run us in. For blocking the street. There's too many of us now. There's a feller from the Homicide Squad, and a little guy with a brown cap and a pink necktie that must be one of Bascom's men. Yesterday afternoon a taxi drives up and stops in front of 203, and Chapin hobbles out and gets in the taxi. The hustle around there was like Fifth Avenue in front of St. Patrick's at one o'clock Sunday, but we all three got taxis and followed. He went to the Harvard Club and stayed there a couple of hours. Honest, Archie. Three of us, but I was in front."

"Yeah. It sounds swell."

"My idea was this, why couldn't we pal up? Bascom and the town dicks could cover Eleventh Street and let us on Perry Street have a little peace. How's that for an idea?"

"Rotten. Wolfe's not using any secondhand tailing. I'll get three men from the Metropolitan Agency and we'll cover Eleventh Street. Get back on the job and don't lose Chapin. I'll get in touch with Bascom and maybe he'll call his dog off. Run along now."

Durkin shrugged, then beat it.

I got the agency on the telephone and gave them the dope. Then I sat for a minute and wondered who was keeping Bascom on the job, before I went to the garage for the roadster.

I had collected a few facts about the Dreyer business in my wanderings the day before. Eugene Dreyer, art dealer, had been found dead on the morning of Thursday, September 20, in the office of his gallery on Madison Avenue. He had been dead about twelve hours, and the cause had been nitroglycerin poisoning. After an investigation the police had pronounced it suicide. But on the Monday following, the second warnings arrived. They read like this:

> Two.
> Ye should have killed me.
> Two;
> And with no ready cliff, rocks waiting below,
> I let the snake and fox collaborate.
> They found the deadly oil, sweet-burning, cunningly
> Devised in tablets easily dissolved.

And I, their Master, I,
I found the time, the safe way to his throat,
And counted: two.
I am unhurried but sure.
Three and four and five and six and seven. . . .
Ye should have killed me.

Wolfe said it was better than the first one because it was shorter.

This time the League of Atonement forgot all about practical jokes and yelled to the cops and the DA's office to come on back and nab Chapin; suicide was out. The only ones that hadn't seemed to develop an acute case of tremors were Dr. Burton and Leopold Elkus, the surgeon. Elkus, of course, had been in on Dreyer's death, but I'm coming to that.

My date with Elkus that Wednesday morning was for nine thirty, but I made an early start because I wanted to stop off at Fifty-sixth Street for a look at the Dreyer gallery. It wasn't a gallery anymore, but a bookstore. A middle-aged woman said of course I could look around. Everything had been changed. But the little room on the right, where the body had been found, was still an office, with a desk and a typewriter and so on. I called the woman over and pointed at a door in the back wall. "I wonder if you could tell me. Is that the closet where Mr. Eugene Dreyer kept the materials for mixing his drinks?"

She looked hazy. "Mr. Dreyer . . . oh . . . that's the man . . ."

"The man that committed suicide in this room, yes, ma'am."

She seemed startled. "I hadn't realized it was right in this room. . . ."

I said, "Thank you, ma'am," and went back to the street and got in the roadster. People who quit living a year ago Christmas and haven't found out about it yet give me a pain.

Leopold Elkus hadn't quit living, I discovered when I got to him in his private room, but he was a sad guy. He was medium-sized, with a big head, and strong black eyes that kept floating away from you. He invited me to sit down and said in a friendly soft voice, "Understand, Mr. Goodwin, I am seeing you only as a courtesy to my friends. I have explained to Mr. Farrell that I will not support the enterprise of your employer."

"Okay." I grinned at him. "I just want to ask some questions about September nineteenth, when Eugene Dreyer died."

"I have already answered any question you could possibly put. To the police several times, and to that incredible detective . . ."

"Right. But just as a matter of courtesy to your friends, there's no reason why you shouldn't answer them once more, is there? I understand the other witness, the art expert, has gone back to Italy."

He nodded. "Mr. Santini sailed some time ago."

"Then you're my only source of firsthand information. There's no sense in my trying to ask you a lot of trick questions. Why don't you just tell me about it?"

He smiled a sad smile. "Here is the story, Mr. Goodwin. You know, of course, that Eugene Dreyer was an old friend of mine, a classmate in college. He was pretty successful with his art gallery before the depression. I bought things from him occasionally. Six years ago I gave Dreyer a tentative order for three Mantegnas—two small ones and a larger one. The paintings were in France. Paul Chapin happened to be in Europe at that time, and I wrote to ask him to look at them. After I received his report I ordered them. You know, I suppose, that for ten years Paul Chapin tried to be a painter. His work was interesting, but not good.

"The paintings arrived at a time when I had no leisure for a proper examination. I accepted them and paid one hundred and sixty thousand dollars for them. I did not at first suspect them of imposture, but a few remarks made by experts finally aroused my suspicion. In September, nearly two months ago now, Enrico Santini, who knows Mantegna as I know the human viscera, visited this country. I asked him to look at my Mantegnas, and he pronounced them frauds. He further said that it was not possible that any reputable dealer had handled them in good faith.

"I told Eugene that I wished to return the pictures and receive my money back without delay. He said he had not the money. I insisted that he must find it or suffer the consequences. He demanded an interview with Mr. Santini.

"It was arranged that I should call at five o'clock Wednesday afternoon with Mr. Santini and Paul Chapin. Paul was included on account of the inspection he had given the pictures in France. We arrived—"

I interrupted. "Just a minute, Doctor. Did Paul Chapin get to the gallery before you did?"

"No. We arrived together. I called for him at the Harvard Club. At the gallery Eugene mixed highballs for us. I was embarrassed and therefore brusque. I asked Mr. Santini to make a statement and he did so. Dreyer contradicted him and called on Paul for his views, in obvious expectation of support. Paul smiled around at us, and said that a month after the pictures had been shipped to New York he had learned that they had been painted by Vasseult, the greatest forger of this century. Paul also said that he had kept silent about it because his affection for both Eugene and myself was so great that he could take no step that would injure either of us.

"I feared Eugene would collapse. He was plainly as astonished as he was hurt. I was of course embarrassed into silence. Mr. Santini and Paul and I left the gallery together. It was noon the following day when I learned that Eugene had committed suicide by drinking nitroglycerin—apparently within a few minutes after we left."

I looked at him awhile, then straightened up in my chair and asked, "What made *you* think it was suicide?"

"Now, Mr. Goodwin." He smiled at me, sadder than ever. "You know perfectly well why I thought it was suicide. The police thought so, and the circumstances indicated it."

"My mistake." I grinned. "Did Paul Chapin have any opportunity to put the nitroglycerin tablets in Dreyer's highball? The cops seem to have the impression that you think he didn't."

Dr. Elkus nodded. "I labored to produce that impression, and Mr. Santini agreed with me. He went to the gallery with us, and we all entered the office together. Paul sat at least six feet away from Eugene. He touched no glass but his own. Eugene prepared the drinks and handed them around; we had only one. Departing, Paul preceded me through the door. Mr. Santini was ahead."

"Yeah. But in a fracas like that, so much excitement, there must have been some moving around, walking back and forth . . ."

"Not at all. We were not excited, except Eugene. He was the only one who left his chair."

"Did he change his coat, or put it on or anything, after you got there?"

"No. He wore a morning coat. He did not remove it. The bottle with what was left of the nitroglycerin was found in the pocket of his coat."

I sat back and looked at him again. I said, "Will you have lunch with Mr. Nero Wolfe tomorrow at one o'clock?"

He shook his head. "No. Not any day. And give up your hope, too, to demonstrate the guilt of Paul Chapin in the death of Eugene Dreyer. It is not feasible. I know it isn't; I was there."

I got up from my chair and thanked him. But before I started for the door I said, "By the way, you know that second warning Paul Chapin wrote—anyhow, somebody wrote it. Is nitroglycerin oily and sweet-burning?"

He smiled. "Nitroglycerin is unquestionably oily. It is said to have a sweet, burning taste."

I thanked him again and went out, and down to the street. I got in the roadster, stepped on the starter, and headed for home. The best bet I could think of at the moment was a try at Santini. The police had only questioned him once on account of his sailing for Italy. There was a smart guy in Rome who had turned in a good one on a previous case. We could cable him and set him on Santini. I'd have to persuade Wolfe it was worth about ninety-nine dollars in transatlantic words.

It took me five minutes to dig out the address of the Roman snoop. Wolfe came down right at eleven. I was impatient, but I knew I'd have to wait until he had glanced through the mail, fixed the orchids in the vase, and rung for beer. After that was all over he murmured, "Had you thought of venturing forth?"

"I tiptoed out at eight thirty and just got back."

Fritz brought his beer and he poured a glass. I told him all about Elkus. Then I handed him my own notion about the Roman. Right away, as I expected, he got restive. He blinked, and drank some more beer. He said, "You can cable four thousand miles for a fact or an object, but not for a subtlety like this."

I tried an argument on him, but I was stopped in the middle of it by the sound of Fritz going down the hall to answer the doorbell. I waited to see who it was.

Fritz stepped in and closed the door behind him. He said there was a lady there to see Wolfe.

"Show her in, Fritz."

She came in and stood looking straight at Wolfe. She wasn't really ugly, I mean she wasn't hideous. Wolfe said it right the next day: to look at her made you despair of ever seeing a pretty woman again. She had on a dark gray woolen coat with a hat to match, and an enormous gray fur piece was fastened around her neck. She sat down on the chair I pulled up for her and said in a strong voice, "I had a hard time getting here. I think I'm going to faint."

Wolfe said, "I hope not. A little brandy?"

"No, thank you." She put her hand up under the fur piece. "I've been wounded. Back there. You'd better look at it."

Wolfe shot me a glance, and I went. She got the thing unfastened, and I lifted it off. I gave a gasp. The back of the fur piece, inside, was soaked. The collar of her coat was soaked too. Blood was still oozing out from gashes across the back of her neck. I dropped the fur piece on the floor and said to her, "For God's sake, keep still. Don't move your head." I looked at Wolfe and said, "Somebody's tried to cut her head off. I can't tell how far they got."

She spoke to Wolfe. "My husband. He wanted to kill me."

Wolfe's eyes on her were half closed. "Then you're Dora Ritter."

She shook her head and said, "I am Dora Chapin. I have been married three years."

VI

Wolfe sat looking at Dora Chapin, his lips pushing out and in.

She said, "He got into a fit. One of his cold fits."

Wolfe said politely, "I didn't know Mr. Chapin had fits. Feel her pulse, Archie."

I reached out and got her wrist. While I was counting she began to talk. "He doesn't have fits exactly. It's a look that comes into his eyes. When I see that look I am terrified, but he has never done anything to me before."

She jerked her hand away to pull something wrapped in newspaper out of her bag, a big leather one. She unrolled the newspaper and held up a kitchen knife that had blood on it. "He must have been getting ready for me when he was out in the kitchen."

I took the knife from her and laid it on the desk, on top of the newspaper, and said to Wolfe, "Her pulse is okay."

Wolfe got to his feet. He said, "Please do not move, Mrs. Chapin," and walked around behind her and took a look at her neck. I hadn't seen him so active for a month or more. Peering at the gashes, he said, "Please tilt your head forward, just a little, and back again." She did so, and the blood spurted out.

Wolfe straightened up. "Get a doctor, Archie."

"I don't need a doctor. I just wanted to show you—"

"If you please, madam. For the moment my judgment must prevail . . ."

When I phoned Dr. Vollmer someone told me he was just leaving. As I hopped down the stoop to catch him, I noticed a taxi there at the curb: our visitor's, of course. A couple of hundred feet east Dr. Vollmer's blue coupe was standing, and he was just getting in.

I let out a yell and sprinted up to tell him about the casualty that had dropped in on us. As we turned in at our stoop I took another look at the taxi standing there, and I nearly lost my aplomb for a second when the driver looked straight at me and tipped me a wink.

Fritz was in the hall and told me that Wolfe had gone to the kitchen and would return when the doctor had finished. I took Vollmer into the office and introduced him to Dora Chapin. He poked around a little and said she might have to be sewed up and he could tell better if he could wash her off. I showed him where the bathroom was and the bandages and iodine and so on.

"I'll call Fritz in to help you," I said. "I've got an errand out front. If you need me, I'll be there."

The taxi was still there. The driver just looked at me. I said, "Greetings."

He said, "I very seldom talk enough to say greetings."

"I don't blame you. May I glance inside?" I asked.

I pulled the door open and stuck my head in far enough to get a good look at the framed card fastened to the panel, showing the driver's picture and name. I backed out again and grinned at him. "So your name is Pitney Scott. I've got you down on a list I made up for a contribution of five dollars."

"I heard about that list. You can cross me off. Last week I made eighteen dollars and twenty cents."

"You know what it's for."

He nodded. "You want to save my life. Listen, my dear fellow, to charge five dollars for saving my life would be outrageous. Rank profiteering." He laughed. "Have you got a drink in your house?"

"How about two dollars? Make it two."

"You're still way high."

Though it was cold for November he had no gloves and his hands were red and rough. He got his stiff fingers into a pocket, came out with some chicken feed, and pushed a nickel at me. "Now that I don't owe you anything, have you got a drink?"

"What flavor do you want?"

He leaned towards me and a look came into his eyes. His voice got harsh and not friendly at all. "Can't you take a joke? I don't drink when I'm driving. Is that woman hurt much?"

"I don't think so. The doctor'll fix her up. Do you take her places often? Or her husband?"

He was still harsh. "I take her when she calls me. Paul Chapin too. They give me their trade when they can, for old time's sake." He laughed, and the harshness went.

"Did you know," I said, "there's a reward of five thousand dollars for finding Andrew Hibbard? Alive or dead."

It looked to me as if I had hit something. His face changed; he looked surprised. "Well, he's a valuable man; that's not too much to offer for him. Who offered the reward?"

"His niece. It'll be in the papers tomorrow."

"Good for her. God bless her." He laughed. "I want a cigarette."

I got a packet out and lit us both up. His fingers weren't steady at all, and I began to feel sorry for him. So I said, "Hibbard's home is up at University Heights. If you drove downtown somewhere—say around Perry Street—and from there to 116th, ordinarily what would you get for it? Let's see—that'd be around a dollar and a half. But if going uptown you happened to have your old classmate Andrew Hibbard with you—or just his corpse—instead of a dollar fifty you'd get five grand. As you see, it all depends on your cargo." I blew cigarette smoke out of the corner of my mouth.

"Listen, you." His voice went harsh again. "Beat it. Go back in the house or you'll catch cold."

I prodded at him a little, then went back into the house. Wolfe was still in the kitchen in the wooden chair where he always sat to direct Fritz. I said, "Pitney Scott's out front. The taxi driver. He brought Dora Chapin. He paid me a nickel for his share, and says that's all it's worth. He knows something about Andrew Hibbard."

"What does he know?"

"Search me. I told him about the reward Miss Hibbard is offering, and he looked like get thee behind me, Satan. I was thinking of suggesting that you go out and look at him."

"Out?" Wolfe raised his head at me. "Out and down the stoop?"

"Yeah, just on the sidewalk. He's right there."

Wolfe shut his eyes. "Just dismiss the notion entirely, Archie.

It is not feasible. And did you say he actually gave you a nickel?"

"Yes, and where's it going to get you to act eccentric with a dipsomaniac taxi driver?"

"That will do. Go and see if Mrs. Chapin has been made presentable."

I found that Dr. Vollmer had finished with his patient in the bathroom and had her back in a chair in the office, with her neck bandaged. I took the doc to the kitchen. Wolfe opened his eyes at him.

"Quite a novel method of attack, Mr. Wolfe," Vollmer said, "hacking at her from behind like that. He got into one of the posterior externals; I had to shave off some of her hair."

"You will want her name and address for your record."

The doctor nodded. "She should be all right in a few days. I took fourteen stitches. Her husband must be a remarkable and unconventional man. She is remarkable too: the Spartan type. She didn't even clench her hands while I was sewing her."

Vollmer went. Wolfe got to his feet, and preceded me to the office. Then he was back in his chair and she was sitting facing him. He was saying to her, "I am glad it was no worse, Mrs. Chapin. Mr. Goodwin tells me your cab is waiting. We need not detain you longer."

She had her eyes fixed on him again. "Don't you want me to tell you about it?"

Wolfe's head went left and right. "It isn't necessary, Mrs. Chapin. You should go home and rest. I can understand your reluctance to notify the police; after all, one's own husband . . . I'll attend to that for you."

"I don't want the police." That woman could certainly fix her stare on you. "Do you think I want my husband arrested? With his standing and position . . . That's why I came to you. . . ."

Wolfe wagged a finger at her. "Unfortunately for you, you came to the one man in the world who would at once understand what really happened. It was unavoidable, I suppose, since it was precisely that man, myself, whom you wished to delude. The devil of it is that I have a deep aversion to being deluded. Let's just call it quits. You really do need rest and quiet now. Go on home."

For a minute I thought she was going to get up and go. She started to. Then she said, "You're trying to talk so I won't understand you, but I do."

"Good. Then there is no need—"

She snapped at him suddenly and violently. "You're a fat fool!"

Wolfe shook his head. "Fat visibly, a fool only in the broader sense, as a common characteristic of the race. That was not magnanimous of you, Mrs. Chapin, since I had refrained from demonstrating your own foolishness. I'll do that now." He moved a finger to indicate the knife which still lay on the newspaper on the desk. "Archie, will you please clean that homely weapon."

I picked up the knife and stood there with it, looking from her to him. "Wash off the evidence?"

"If you please." After I came back from cleaning the knife, Wolfe instructed me, "Now grip the handle firmly in your right hand. Come towards the desk, so Mrs. Chapin can see you better; turn your back. So. Elevate your arm and pull the knife across your neck; kindly be sure to use the back of the blade. You noted the length and the position of the cuts on Mrs. Chapin? Duplicate them on yourself. . . . Yes, good. A little higher for that one. That will do. . . . You see, Mrs. Chapin? He did it quite neatly, don't you think? You are too intelligent to expect us to think that wounds on the back of the neck could not have been self-inflicted." He stopped, because he had no one to talk to except me. Without a word, Dora Chapin just got up and went; Wolfe went on with his speech until she was through the office door. I noticed she was leaving her knife, but thought we might as well have it in our collection of odds and ends.

Wolfe was now glancing at a letter that had come in the morning mail. He said, "The things a woman will think of are beyond belief. I knew a woman once in Hungary . . ."

He was just trying to keep me from annoying him about business. I cut in. "It's time for me to brush up a little on this case we've got. You can give me a shove by explaining how you knew Dora Chapin did her own manicuring."

Wolfe shook his head. "I remind you merely: I have read all of Paul Chapin's novels. In two of them Dora Chapin is a character. The woman who married Dr. Burton, Paul Chapin's unattainable, seems to be in four out of five. Read the books, and I shall be more inclined to discuss the conclusions they have led me to. But even then, of course, God made you and me, in certain respects, quite unequal, and I would not attempt to place plain to your eyes the sights my own have discerned."

Fritz came to the door and said lunch was ready.

THAT Wednesday afternoon, after lunch, I was sore. Wolfe went indifferent on me; he even went contrary. He wouldn't cable the guy in Rome to talk with Santini; he said it was futile and expected me to take his word for it. He wouldn't help me drag Leopold Elkus into the office; according to him, that was futile too. He kept trying to read while I was after him. He said there were only two men in the case whom he felt any inclination to talk to: Andrew Hibbard and Paul Chapin; and he wasn't ready yet for Chapin and he didn't know where Hibbard was, or whether he was alive or dead.

A little after two Fred Durkin phoned. He said that Paul Chapin had been to the barber and a drugstore, and that the town dick and the guy in the brown cap and pink necktie were still on deck, and he was thinking of forming a club.

Wolfe went on reading. About a quarter to three Orrie Cather called up and said he had got hold of something he wanted to show us and could he come on up with it. I told him yes. Then, just before Orrie arrived, a call came that made Wolfe put down his book. It was from Farrell, the architect. He said he had had a nice lunch at the Harvard Club and he was phoning from Mr. Oglethorpe's office. Paul Chapin had on several occasions found it convenient to make use of a typewriter there, but there was some disagreement as to which one, so he was going to take samples from a dozen of them.

I said, "Okay, that one's turning brown. But you've just started. What the hell are we waiting for? It's all right for you, you can keep occupied, you've got a book to read— What the devil is it, anyhow?"

I got up to take a squint at it: *The Chasm of the Mind* by Andrew Hibbard. I grunted. "Huh, maybe that's where he is, maybe he fell in."

"Long ago." Wolfe sighed. "Poor Hibbard, he couldn't exclude his poetic tendencies even from his title. Any more than Chapin can exclude his savagery from his plots."

I dropped back into my chair. "Listen, boss, all I'm asking for is just a little halfway cooperation! One lousy little cablegram to Rome! . . . Now, what the hell do *you* want?"

The last was for Fritz. He had appeared in the door. Then I saw someone standing behind him and said, "Come on in, Orrie."

Orrie Cather had a bundle about the size of a small suitcase, wrapped in brown paper and tied with heavy string. He set it down on the desk, and I shoved up a chair for him.

"What is it?" I asked.

"Search me. I brought it here to open it."

Wolfe said to Orrie, "Go on."

Orrie grinned. "Well, it may be a lot of nothing at all, but . . ."

"Let us arrive at the package," Wolfe said.

"Right. This morning I dropped in at the Greenwich Bookshop. I got talking with the guy, and I said I might like to get one of Paul Chapin's books, and he handed me one, and I looked it over—"

I snorted and stopped him. Orrie looked surprised, and Wolfe moved his eyes at me.

"Then I said Chapin must be an interesting guy and had he ever seen him, and he said sure, Chapin lived in that neighborhood and came in pretty often. He showed me a photograph of Chapin, autographed, on the wall with some others. A woman in the back of the shop called out to the guy that that reminded her, Mr. Chapin never had come for the package he had left there a couple of weeks ago, and with Christmas stuff coming in the package was in the way, and hadn't he better phone Mr.

Chapin to send for it. I got my book and went down the street to a lunch counter to think."

Wolfe nodded sympathetically.

Orrie went on. "I figured it this way. What if Chapin had something in his place he didn't want the cops to see? He might take it to his friends at the bookshop and ask them to keep it for him. It would be about as safe there as anywhere. Anyhow, I decided to do Chapin the favor of taking a look at his package for him. I got an envelope and a piece of paper from a stationery store and went to a real estate office and bummed the use of a typewriter and wrote a nice note to the bookshop, doing a pretty good imitation of Chapin's signature on the autographed photograph. I waited awhile and then I got a boy and sent him to the bookshop with the note. I'm telling you it worked and they gave it to him." Orrie nodded his head at the desk. "That's it."

I started to untie the string around the package. Orrie wiped his hand across his forehead and said, "By God, if it's just fishing tackle or light bulbs, you'll have to give me a drink." I took off the paper, several thicknesses. Inside was an oblong box made out of light tan calfskin, beautifully made, with fine lines of tooling around the edges. "It's locked," I said.

I went to the safe and got a couple of my bunches of keys, and in a few minutes I had it. Orrie stood up and looked in with me. We didn't say anything for a second, then we stared at each other. I never saw him look so disgusted.

Wolfe said, "Empty?"

"No, sir. It's not his, it's hers. I mean Dora Chapin's. Gloves and stockings and other dainties."

"Indeed." To my surprise Wolfe showed interest. His lips pushed out and in. He was even going to get up.

"Indeed. I suspect—yes, it must be. Archie. Kindly remove them and spread them on the desk. . . . Ha, more intimate still! But mostly stockings and gloves. What we are displaying on this desk top is the soul of a man. Do you notice that the gloves, varying as they do in color and material, are all of a size? Could you ask more of loyalty and fidelity? *O, that I were a glove upon that hand* . . . But let us not be carried away. We cannot afford to forget that these articles are expensive, that they must have cost Dr. Burton something around three hundred dollars, and that he therefore had a right to expect that they should get more wear. Some of them, indeed, are practically new."

I cut him off. "Where does Burton come in?"

Wolfe held up a stocking to look through it at the light.

"Where does Burton come in?" I repeated.

"He paid for these, his wife wore them, Dora Ritter—later Chapin—appropriated them, and Paul Chapin treasured them."

"How do you know all that?"

"How could I help but know it? Here are these worn things, kept by Paul Chapin in an elegant and locked receptacle. You saw the size of Dora Chapin's hands, you see these gloves; they are not hers. You heard Monday evening the story of Chapin's infatuation with the woman who is now Dr. Burton's wife. You know that for years Dora Chapin was Mrs. Burton's personal maid, and that she still attends her at least once a week. Knowing these things—"

"Okay! But maybe Chapin took them himself."

"Most unlikely. Surely he did not strip the stockings from her legs. The faithful Dora—"

"Faithful to who? Mrs. Burton, swiping her duds?"

"Archie. Having seen Dora, can you not grant her rarity? Faithfulness to an employer is one of the dullest and most vulgar of loyalties. Having seen Dora, I suspect that it was sympathy for the bitter torment in the romantic cripple's heart that accounts for her faithfulness. It may even account for her continuing to visit Mrs. Burton when her marriage freed her from the practical necessity. What a stroke of luck for Chapin! The beloved odor, the intimate textile from the skin of his adored, is delivered to him as it may be required. Archie. Repack the box, with feeling, lock it, and find a place for it in the cabinet. Orrie, you may go. You have not brought us the solution of our case, but you have lifted the curtain to another room of the edifice we are exploring."

Orrie went down the hall whistling.

VII

I HAD a nice new piece of leather of my own. Sitting at my desk around five o'clock that Wednesday afternoon, I took it out of my inside breast pocket and looked at it. It was brown ostrich skin, and tooled in gold all over the outside. On one side were orchids; the other side was covered with Colt automatics, fifty-two perfect little gold pistols all aiming at the center. Inside was stamped in gold: *A. G. from N. W.* Wolfe had given it to me on October 23, and I didn't even know he knew when my birthday was. I might have traded it for New York City if you had thrown in a couple of good suburbs.

When Fritz came and said Inspector Cramer was there I put it back in my pocket.

I let Cramer get eased into a chair and said, "Mr. Wolfe can't come down. He's upstairs in the plant rooms."

"I didn't expect him to. I've known Nero Wolfe longer than you have, sonny. Did he tell you what I told him on the phone?"

I patted my notebook. "I've got it down."

"Okay. What went on here night before last? Is it true that Wolfe nicked George Pratt for four thousand dollars?"

"He didn't nick anybody. He offered something for sale, and they gave him the order."

"You know Pratt? Pratt thinks it's funny that he has to shell out to a private dick when the city maintains such a magnificent force of brave, intelligent men to cope with such problems."

"Indeed." I bit my lip. "Maybe he was referring to the Department of Health."

Cramer grunted. He sat back and pulled at his pipe. Then he said, "I had a funny experience this afternoon. A woman called up and said she wanted Nero Wolfe arrested because he had tried to cut her throat."

I said, "I wonder who it could have been."

"I'll bet you're puzzled. Then a couple of hours later a guy came to see me. By invitation. He was a taxi driver. He said he didn't care to take the rap for perjury, and that he saw blood on her when she got in his cab on Perry Street." He went on, more forceful and rugged. "Look here, Goodwin. What the hell's the idea? I've tried that Chapin woman three times, and I couldn't get her to break down enough to tell me what her name was. Wolfe gets in the case late Monday night, and here already, Wednesday morning, she's chasing up to his office to show him her operation. What the hell gets them coming like that?"

I grinned. "It's his sympathetic nature, Inspector."

"Yeah. Who carved her neck?"

I shook my head. "If I know that secret, it's buried here." I tapped my chest.

"Now listen to me. I've been after Chapin ever since Dreyer was croaked, and what I've got on him is exactly nothing. Maybe he killed Harrison, and I'm damn sure he killed Dreyer, and it looks like he got Hibbard, and he's got me feeling like a Staten Island flatfoot. He's as slick as a wet pavement."

I nodded. "He's slick."

"Well, I've tried this and that. For one thing, I've got it figured that his wife hates him and probably knows enough about it so she might spill it. When I heard she'd dashed up here to see Wolfe, I naturally surmised that he had learned things."

"But, Inspector. Wait a minute. If you think she came here friendly, how do you account for her calling up to get Wolfe arrested? Why she phoned you—she's psychopathic. So's her husband psychopathic. That's Park Avenue for batty."

Cramer nodded. "I've heard the word."

"You say you're sure he killed Dreyer?"

He nodded again. "I think Dreyer was murdered by Paul Chapin and Leopold Elkus."

"You don't say!" I looked at him. "Elkus, huh?"

"Yeah. You and Wolfe won't talk. Do you want me to talk?"

"I'd love it."

He filled his pipe. "Do you know that Dreyer bought the nitroglycerin tablets the day after Elkus phoned him that the pictures were phony? Maybe he had ideas about suicide and maybe he didn't; I think he didn't; there's several things people take nitro-glycerin for in small doses."

He took a drag at the pipe. "Dreyer had had the tablets for a week, and Chapin could have got them when he was at the gallery a couple of hours Monday afternoon, probably for a talk about Elkus's pictures, and then saved them for an opening. The opening came Wednesday afternoon. I know what Elkus and Santini said when they were questioned that Thursday morning. But since then I've sent a request to Italy, and they had a good long talk with Santini. He says he forgot to mention that after they all left the of-fice Elkus went back for something and was in the office alone for maybe half a minute. What if Dreyer's glass was there half full, and Elkus, having got the tablets from Chapin, fixed it up for him?"

"What for? Just for a prank?"

"We're working on that now. Suppose the pictures Dreyer sold Elkus were the real thing—it was six years ago—and Elkus put them away and substituted phonies for them, and then demanded his money back? We're looking into that."

I grinned. "Why don't you just decide to believe it was suicide after all, and let it go at that?"

"Even if I wanted to, George Pratt and that bunch wouldn't let me. They got those warnings. I don't blame them. Those things sound like business to me." He stuck his paw in his breast pocket and pulled out some papers and began looking through them. He said, "Listen to this one, the one he sent last Friday, three days after Hibbard disappeared:

> "One. Two. Three.
> Ye cannot see what I see:
> His bloody head, his misery, his eyes
> Dead but for terror and the wretched hope
> That this last blow, this finis, will not fall.

> "One. Two. Three.
> Ye cannot hear what I hear:
> His moan for pity, now his desperate breath
> To suck the air in through the bubbling blood.

> *"And I hear, too, in me the happy rhythm,*
> *The happy boastful strutting of my soul.*
> *Yes! Hear! It boasts:*
> *One. Two. Three.*
> *Ye should have killed me.*

"I ask you, does that sound like business?" Cramer folded it up again. "I'll say it does. That's why, as far as Andrew Hibbard is concerned, all I'm interested in is stiffs."

"If you get Elkus wrong you may gum it," I said.

"Uh-huh." Cramer pulled at his pipe. "I hope not to gum it. I suppose you know Elkus has got a shadow on Paul Chapin? What's he suspicious about?"

I lifted my brows a little. "No. I didn't know that." I remembered that I never had got hold of Del Bascom to ask him about the dick in the brown cap and pink necktie. "I thought that runt keeping the boys company down there was one of Bascom's experts."

"Bascom's been off the case since yesterday morning. Try having a talk with the runt. I did, last night, for two hours. He says he's got a right to keep his mouth shut. But I'm going to find out who he's reporting to."

"I thought you said Elkus."

"Who else could it be? Do you know?"

I shook my head. "Hope to die."

"I'm not exactly a boob. I know Wolfe expects to open up this Chapin and get well paid for it, and therefore if I expected him to pass me any cards out of his hand I *would* be a boob. But you might tell me this, and I swear you won't regret it. When Dora Chapin was here this morning did she tell Wolfe she saw nitro-glycerin tablets in her husband's pocket anytime between September eleventh and September nineteenth?"

I grinned at him. "She wasn't asked about it, and she said nothing about it. She just came here to get her throat cut."

"Uh-huh." Cramer got up from his chair. "Well, so long. I'll say much obliged some other day."

Since he was an inspector, I went to the hall, opened the door for him, and let him out. Then I went back to the office. It looked dismal and gloomy. Wolfe was still upstairs monkeying with the plants. I decided to go out and find a stone somewhere and turn it up to see what was under it.

I DIDN'T know Perry Street much, and was surprised when I walked up in front of number 203. It was quite a joint, stucco to look Spanish. On both sides were old brick houses. On my side of the street was a string of dingy stores: stationery, laundry, delicatessen, cigar store. I moved along and looked in. At the delicatessen I stopped and went inside. There were two or three customers, and Fred Durkin was leaning against the end of the counter with a cheese sandwich and a bottle of beer. I turned around and went out, and walked back down to where the roadster was and got inside. In a couple of minutes Fred came along and climbed in beside me. I asked him, "Where's the other club members?"

He grinned. "Oh, they're around. The city feller is probably in the laundry, I think he likes the smell. I suppose Pinkie is down at the next corner, in the Coffee Pot."

"You call him Pinkie?"

"Oh, that's for his necktie. What do you want me to call him?"

I looked at him. "You chinned any with this Pinkie?"

"No. He hides somewhere and thinks."

"Okay. Go on back to your pickle emporium."

Fred climbed out and went. In a minute I got out too, and walked down to the Coffee Pot. There were three little tables along the wall and half a dozen customers at the counter. Pinkie was alone at one of the little tables, working on a bowl of soup. I went over alongside him and said, keeping my voice low, "Oh, here you are. The boss wants to see you right away. Make it snappy."

He stared at me a couple of seconds, and then squeaked so that I nearly jumped. "You're a filthy liar."

The little runt! I could have jerked his gold teeth out. I slid the other chair back with my toe and sat down and put my elbows on the table and looked at him. "I said the boss wants to see you."

"Oh, yeah?" He sneered at me with his mouth open, showing his gilded incisors. "Who was I talking to a while ago on the damn telephone?"

I grinned. "Listen here a minute. I can see you're tough. Do you want a good job?"

"Yeah. That's why I've got one. If you'd just move away from my table . . ."

"All right, I will. Go on and eat your soup, and don't try to scare me with your bad manners."

He dropped his spoon in the soup bowl. "What the hell do you want, anyway?"

"Well," I said, "a certain guy has got the idea that you're selling him out, and I thought the quickest way to find out was to ask you. How many people are you working for?"

"Of all the goddam curiosity!" He got up from his chair and picked up the soup bowl and carried it to the table at the end. I got up and went and sat down across from him. I reached in my pocket and got out my roll and peeled off a pair of twenties.

"Look here," I said, "here's forty bucks. Half now if you tell me who's paying you, and the other half as soon as I check it. I'll find out, anyhow, this'll just save time."

I'll be damned if he didn't get up and pick up his soup again and start back for the first table. A couple of the customers began to laugh, and the counterman called out, "Hey, let the guy eat his soup, maybe he just don't like you."

I tossed a coin on the counter and said, "Give him some more soup and put poison in it." Then I left.

I walked the block back to the roadster, not in a hurry. I couldn't figure the runt at all. Was it possible that a dick that looked like that was as honest as that? The inspector's idea didn't seem to make sense, even if Leopold Elkus had helped out that day with Dreyer's highball. Why would he put a shadow on Chapin? If it wasn't Elkus, who was it? It might have been any one of the bunch who thought he needed his own reports of Chapin's activities, but why all the mystery?

It was nearly dinnertime when I got home. Wolfe was in the office, leaning over a piece of paper, inspecting it with a magnifying glass. There was a little pile of similar papers under a weight. The typewriting on the paper began, *Ye should have killed me, watched the last mean sigh.* It was the first warning.

Pretty soon he looked up and blinked. I asked, "Are these Farrell's samples?"

"Yes. Mr. Farrell brought them ten minutes ago. He decided to get a specimen from each machine in Mr. Oglethorpe's office. I have examined two, and discarded them—those marked with red pencil." He sighed. "You haven't washed for dinner. There are two pheasants which should not be kept waiting."

After dinner we worked together at Farrell's samples; there were sixteen of them. We did a thorough job of it, not finally eliminating one until we had both examined it. Wolfe loved that kind of work; when he had gone through a sample and made sure that the *a* wasn't off the line and the *n* wasn't cockeyed, he grunted with satisfaction. But as we neared the bottom of the pile with the red pencil unanimous, I wasn't getting any gayer.

Around ten o'clock I got up and handed the last one across to him, and then went to the kitchen and got a pitcher of milk. When I came back to the office Wolfe had fastened the sheets together with a clip and put the originals in their envelope.

I said, "Well. This has been a fine pregnant evening."

Wolfe leaned back and got his fingers twined. "We have established a fact: that Chapin did not type the warnings in his publisher's office. But he did type them, so the machine exists and can be found. I have already another suggestion for Mr. Farrell—"

"Maybe I could offer one. Tell him to get samples from the machines in Leopold Elkus's office."

Wolfe's brows went up. "Why particularly Elkus?"

"Inspector Cramer got the idea of having someone in Italy get in touch with Mr. Santini. Dumb idea, of course, but he got it. Santini remembered that after they all left the office that day Elkus went back for something and was in there alone for maybe half a minute. Plenty of time to drop some tablets into a highball."

"But hardly enough to filch the bottle from Mr. Dreyer's pocket and return it again."

"Chapin did that himself some time previously and gave them to Elkus."

"Indeed. This was in the newsreels?"

"It's in Cramer's bean. But it may also be in his bag one of these days. Another item is that Elkus has got a shadow on Chapin."

"That likewise is in Mr. Cramer's bean?"

"Yeah, likewise. But one of those dicks—"

"Archie." Wolfe wiggled a finger at me. "Consider what we have engaged to do: free our clients from fear of Paul Chapin's designs. Even if it were possible to prove that Dr. Elkus poisoned Mr. Dreyer's drink—which I strongly doubt—to what purpose should we attempt it?"

"How are you going to prove Chapin guilty of Dreyer's murder unless you also prove how Elkus did his part?"

Wolfe nodded. "I haven't the slightest expectation of proving Chapin guilty of Dreyer's murder."

"Then what the devil—" I got that much out before I realized exactly what he had said.

He went on. "Paul Chapin is possessed of a demon. He is also an extraordinarily astute man. But emotionally he is infantile—as witness his taking Dora Ritter to proxy for her mistress."

I drank milk. Wolfe continued. "Since Mr. Chapin has an aversion to factual proof and has the intellectual equipment to preclude it, let us attack him where he is weak. His emotions. Proof will not be needed in this case, facts will do for us. I need two more of them, possibly three, before I can feel confident of persuading Mr. Chapin to confess his guilt."

I said, "Confess, huh? What are the facts?"

"First, to find Mr. Hibbard. Second, to find the typewriter on which Chapin wrote the menacing verses. Third—the possibility—to learn if he has ever kissed his wife. That may not be needed. Given the first two, I probably should not wait for it."

I looked at him. Sometimes I thought I could tell how much he was being fanciful. "Then I might as well phone Fred and Bill and Orrie and the others to check out."

"By no means. Mr. Chapin himself might lead us to the typewriter or to Mr. Hibbard."

"All this sounds like your delicate way of telling me that on the Dreyer thing you've decided I'm a washout and you think I might try something else. Okay. What else?"

Wolfe's cheeks unfolded a little. "It would be gratifying if you should discover Mr. Hibbard."

"Fifteen thousand cops have been looking for Hibbard for eight days. Where shall I bring him when I find him?"

"If alive, here. If dead, he will care as little as I."

VIII

THE next morning, Thursday, I was in the office by eight o'clock, taking another good look at the photograph of her uncle which Evelyn Hibbard had given to us. Saul Panzer had phoned and I told him to meet me in the McAlpin lobby at 8:30. After I had soaked in the photograph I made a phone call to Inspector Cramer. Cramer was friendly. He said if a body of a man was washed up on Montauk Point, or found in a coal mine at Scranton, he would know about it in ten minutes. That satisfied me that there was no sense in my wasting time looking for a dead Hibbard; I'd better concentrate on the possibility of a live one.

I went to the McAlpin and talked it over with Saul Panzer. It was obvious from the instructions Saul had been following that Wolfe thought Chapin's third warning was a fake and that Hibbard was still alive. Saul had been digging up every connection Hibbard had had in and around the city for the past five years.

For my part, I believed the third warning. But I couldn't see that there was anything better to be done than to smell around places where Hibbard had once been alive. I left the general list—neighbors, friends, pupils—to Saul, and chose for myself the members of the league.

The *Tribune* office was only seven blocks away, so I called there first, but Mike Ayers wasn't in. Next I went up on Park Avenue, to Drummond's florist shop. He was all ready for a talk and wanted to know many things, but he had nothing to offer in exchange. From there I went back down to Thirty-ninth Street to see Edwin Robert Byron, the editor. For over half an hour about all he found time for was "Excuse me" as he was reaching for the telephone.

Leaving Byron a little before eleven, I decided to roll over to the house for any new instructions, since it was only a couple of blocks out of my way to the next call.

Wolfe was in the office. Out of one of the envelopes that had come in the morning mail he took some pieces of paper that looked familiar. He looked up at me and handed me one of the sheets, a different size from the others. I read it:

Here are two more samples which I failed to deliver with the others. I found them in another pocket. I am called suddenly to Philadelphia on a chance at a commission, and am mailing them to you so you will have them first thing in the morning.   Augustus Farrell

Wolfe was already inspecting one of the samples with his magnifying glass. I felt my blood coming up to my head, which meant a hunch. After a little, Wolfe pushed the sheet aside and reached for the other one. He moved the glass along, intent, but a little too rapidly for me not to suspect that he had had a hunch too. At length he looked up at me, and sighed. "No."

I demanded, "You mean it's not it? Let me see the damn things."

He pushed them across and I got the glass and gave them a look. Wolfe was saying, "It is a pity Mr. Farrell has deserted us. He does not, by the way, mention his return." He picked up the note from Farrell and looked at it. "I believe, Archie, that you had best abandon the Hibbard search temporarily—" He stopped himself, and said in a different tone, "Mr. Goodwin. Hand me the glass."

I gave it to him. His using my formal handle when we were alone meant that he was excited almost beyond control. Then I saw what he wanted the glass for. He was looking through it at the note from Farrell! I stared at him. Finally Wolfe said, "Indeed."

He gave me the note and the glass. I saw it at a glance, that *a* off the line and a little to the left, and the *n* cockeyed, and all the other signs. I laid it on the table and grinned at Wolfe. "Old Eagle Eye. Damn me for missing it."

He said, "Archie. Whom can we telephone in Philadelphia to learn where an architect in pursuit of a commission might possibly be found?"

"Why don't you phone Farrell's friends here and see if you can get a line on him?" I said. "I'll take the train down to Philly and call you up as soon as I arrive."

I caught the noon train to Philadelphia, had lunch on the diner, and phoned Wolfe from the Broad Street station at two o'clock.

He had no dope, except the names of a few friends of Farrell's. I telephoned all I could get hold of, and chased around all afternoon to the Fine Arts Club, an architectural magazine, and the newspapers to see if they knew who intended to build something. I was beginning to wonder if Farrell hadn't come to Philadelphia at all.

But around six o'clock I got him. I had taken to phoning architects, and one of them told me that a Mr. Allenby who had got rich was going to build a library for his Missouri birthplace. I phoned Allenby, and was told that Mr. Farrell was expected at his home for dinner. I snatched a pair of sandwiches and went out there, and then had to wait until he had finished his meal.

Farrell came to me in Mr. Allenby's library, and I allowed him ten seconds for surprise. Then I asked him. "Last night you wrote a note to Nero Wolfe. Where's the typewriter you wrote it on?"

He said, "I suppose it's where I left it. I didn't take it away."

"Well, where was it? The machine you wrote that note on is the one Paul Chapin used for his poems."

"No!" He stared at me, and laughed. "By God, that's good. After working so hard to get all those samples—I'll be damned. I used a typewriter at the Harvard Club."

"Oh. You did. Where do they keep this typewriter?"

"It's in a sort of an alcove off the smoking room. A great many of the members use it, off and on."

I sat down. "Well, this is nice. Thousands of them use it."

"Hardly thousands, but quite a few—"

"Have you ever seen Paul Chapin use it?"

"I'm pretty sure I have— Yes, in that little chair with his game leg pushed under—"

"Do many of your other friends belong to the club?"

"Oh, yes, nearly all. Mike Ayers doesn't, and I believe Leo Elkus resigned a few years ago. . . ."

"All right." I got up and thanked him for nothing. Then I went out to seek the air and a train to New York.

FRIDAY morning I was sitting in the office at 8:30 when the inside phone buzzed. It was Wolfe from his bedroom.

I told him about the typewriter at the Harvard Club. "The good thing about this is that it rules out all Yale men. You can see Chapin wanted to make it as simple as possible."

Wolfe's low murmur was in my ear: "Excellent."

"Yeah. Swell."

"No, Archie. I mean it. Please find someone willing to favor us who is a member of the Harvard Club—not one of our present clients. Perhaps Albert Wright would do. Ask him to go to the club this morning and take you as a guest. After that, purchase a new typewriter and take it with you to the club. Bring away the one that is there and leave the new one; manage it as you please. Then, bring it here."

"A good new typewriter costs one hundred dollars."

"I know that. It is not necessary to speak of it."

That was how it happened that at ten o'clock that Friday morning I sat in the smoking room of the Harvard Club with Albert Wright, a vice-president of Eastern Electric, a typewriter under a rubberized cover on the floor at my feet. Wright had been very nice, as he should have been, since about all he owed to Wolfe was his wife and family. That was one of the neatest blackmailing cases . . . but let it rest. I was saying, "This is it. It's that typewriter in the alcove that I showed you the number of. Mr. Wolfe wants it." Wright raised his brows.

I went on. "Of course you don't care why, but if you do maybe he'll tell you someday. I've got a brand-new Underwood." I touched it with my toe. "I take it in there and leave it, and bring away the junk, that's all. It's just a playful lark; the club gets what it needs and Mr. Wolfe gets what he wants."

Wright sat a minute and looked at me, and then smiled. "Go on with your lark. I'll wait downstairs."

There was nothing to it. I walked into the alcove, pulled the junk aside and transferred the shiny cover to the old machine, put the new one in its place, picked up the junk and walked out.

At the street entrance Wright shook hands with me. He said, "Tell Wolfe my regards will still be warm even if I get kicked out of the Harvard Club for helping to steal a typewriter."

I grinned. "Steal, my eye, it nearly broke my heart to leave that new Underwood there."

When I got to the house it wasn't eleven yet. I carried the type-writer into the office. But I didn't get more than six feet inside the door before I stopped. Sitting there turning over the pages of a book was Paul Chapin.

Something I don't often do, I went tongue-tied. I suppose it was because I had under my arm the typewriter he had written his poems on. I stood and stared at him. He glanced up and informed me politely, "I'm waiting for Mr. Wolfe."

He turned another page in the book, and I saw it was *Devil Take the Hindmost*, the one Wolfe had marked things in. I said, "Does he know you're here?"

"Oh yes. His man told him some time ago. I've been here"—he glanced at his wrist—"half an hour."

There hadn't been any sign of his noticing what I was carrying. I put it down on my desk and went to Wolfe's desk and glanced through the morning mail.

When Wolfe entered the office he stopped inside the door and said, "Good morning, Archie." Then he turned to Chapin, bowed slightly with a sort of mammoth elegance, and said, "Good morning, sir." He proceeded to his desk and looked through the mail. He rang for Fritz, and when Fritz came, nodded for beer. Then he looked at me. "You saw Mr. Wright? Your errand was successful?"

"Yes, sir. In the bag."

"Good. If you would please move a chair up for Mr. Chapin. If you would come closer, sir?" He opened a bottle of beer.

Chapin hobbled over to the desk. He paid no attention to the chair I placed for him, but stood there leaning on his stick. He said, "I've come for my box."

"Ah! Of course. I might have known." Wolfe had turned on his gracious tone. "If you wouldn't mind, Mr. Chapin, may I ask how you knew I had it?"

Chapin smiled. "I inquired for my package where I had left it, Mr. Wolfe, and learned of the ruse by which it had been stolen. It was obvious that the likeliest thief was you."

Wolfe leaned back and got comfortable. "I am considering the scantiness of all vocabularies. Take, for example, the procedure by which you acquired the contents of that box, and I got box and all; both of us are by definition thieves; a word implying condemnation and contempt, and yet neither of us would concede that he has earned it. So much for words—"

"You said contents. You haven't opened the box?"

"My dear sir! Who could resist such a temptation?"

"You broke the lock."

"No. It surrendered easily."

"You probably . . ." Chapin stopped and stood silent, his face displaying no feeling at all. Then he continued. "In that case I don't want it. . . . But that's preposterous—I must have it."

Wolfe looked at him with half-closed eyes and said nothing. "Damn you," Chapin demanded, suddenly hoarse, "where is it?"

Wolfe wagged a finger at him. "Mr. Chapin. Sit down."

Still there was no change on Chapin's face. His light-colored eyes glanced aside at the chair I had placed for him. He limped three steps and sat down. He looked at Wolfe and said, "For twenty years I lived on pity. I despised it, but I lived on it, because a hungry man takes what he can get. Then I found something else to sustain me. I got a measure of pride in achievement, I ate bread that I earned, I threw away the stick that I needed to walk with, one that had been given me, and bought one of my own. I was done with pity. But today, Mr. Wolfe, I ask for it. I discovered an hour ago that you had got my box. I plead with you. The box is mine by purchase. The contents are mine by . . . by sacrifice. I ask you to give it back to me."

"Well. What plea have you to offer?"

"The plea of my need, and your indifference."

"You are wrong there, Mr. Chapin. I need it too."

"It is valueless to you."

"But, my dear sir." Wolfe wiggled a finger. "If I permit you to be the judge of your own needs you must grant me the same privilege. I need your box here in order to be sure that you will come to see me whenever I am ready for you. When the time comes, it will not be merely my possession of it that will persuade you to give me what I intend to get. I shall leave that, for the moment, as cryptic as it sounds. Archie. In order that Mr. Chapin may not suspect us of gullery, bring the box, please."

I went and unlocked the cabinet and got the box from the shelf and put it down on Wolfe's desk.

Chapin's hands were grasping the arms of his chair, as if to lift himself up. He said, "May I open it?"

"No. I'm sorry, Mr. Chapin. You won't touch it."

The cripple leaned forward there, looking Wolfe in the eyes. All of a sudden he began to laugh. It was a hell of a laugh, I thought it was going to choke him. Then it petered out and he turned around, got hold of his stick, and stood up.

Wolfe said, "The next time you come here, Mr. Chapin, you may take the box with you."

Chapin shook his head. His tone was new, sharper. "I think not. You're making a mistake. You're forgetting that I've had twenty years' practice at renunciation."

Wolfe said, "On the contrary, that's what I'm counting on. The only question will be, which of two sacrifices you will select. If I know you, and I think I do, I know where your choice will lie."

"I'll make it now." I stared at Chapin's incredible smile. He put his left hand on the desk to steady himself, and with his right hand he lifted his stick up and gently let its tip come to rest on the surface of the desk. He slid the tip along until it was against the side of the box, and then pushed, steadily. The box moved, approached the edge, and tumbled to the floor.

Chapin didn't look at the box; he directed his smile at Wolfe. "I told you, sir, I had learned to live on pity. I am learning now to live without it." He hobbled to the door and on out. We heard him in the hall, shuffling to keep his balance as he got into his coat. Then the outer door opened and closed.

Wolfe sighed. "Pick it up, Archie. Put it away. It is astonishing, the effect a little literary and financial success will produce on a spiritual ailment."

He rang for beer.

IX

AFTER lunch I got in the roadster to hunt for Hibbard. I had about as much hope of finding him as of getting a mash note from Greta Garbo, but I went on poking around.

Among other weak stabs I made that Friday afternoon was a visit to the office of Ferdinand Bowen, the stockbroker, since Hibbard had an account with Galbraith & Bowen that had been fairly active. Entering the office on the twentieth floor of one of the Wall Street buildings, I told myself I'd better advise Wolfe to boost Bowen's contribution to the pot, no matter what the bank report said. Galbraith & Bowen had one of those layouts that give you the feeling that a girl would have to be at least a duchess to get a job there as a stenographer.

I was taken into Bowen's own room. It was as big as a dance hall. Bowen sat behind a beautiful dark brown desk with nothing on it but the *Wall Street Journal* and an ashtray. One of his little hands held a long fat cigarette. He thought he was being decent when he grunted at me to sit down.

I asked him about the last time he had seen Andrew Hibbard. He had to think. Finally he decided the last time had been more than a week before Hibbard disappeared, around the twentieth of

October, at the theater. Nothing of any significance had been said, Bowen declared, nothing with any bearing on the present situation.

I said, "Hibbard had a trading account with your firm?"

He nodded. "For a long while, over ten years. It wasn't very active, mostly back and forth in bonds."

"You see, one thing that might help would be any evidence that when Hibbard left his apartment that Tuesday evening he had an idea that he might not be back again. For instance, during the few days preceding his disappearance, did he make any unusual arrangements regarding his account here?"

Bowen shook his head. "No. I would have been told . . . but I'll make sure." There had been no transaction on Andy's account for over two weeks, and there were no instructions from him.

That was a good sample of the steady progress I made with the other six members of the league I called on, so I was all elated when I breezed in home around dinnertime. I didn't even feel like listening to the charming gusto of Wolfe's conversation.

After dinner I started to tell Wolfe about all the runs I had scored that afternoon, but he asked me to bring him the atlas and began to look at maps. There were all sorts of toys he was apt to begin playing with when he should have had his mind on business, but the worst of all was the atlas. Without bothering to say good night to him, for I knew he wouldn't answer, I picked up his copy of *Devil Take the Hindmost* and went upstairs to my room, stopping in the kitchen for a pitcher of milk.

After I had got into pajamas and slippers I deposited myself in my most comfortable chair and took a crack at Paul Chapin's book. I saw there were quite a few places Wolfe had marked. I decided to concentrate on those, and I took them at random:

She said, "That's why I admire you. . . . I don't like a man too squeamish to butcher his own meat."

The trouble with war is that we are not men enough for it; it properly requires for its sublime sacrifices the blood and bones and flesh of heroes . . .

There was a lot of that. It got monotonous, and I skipped around. Near the middle of the book he had marked a whole chapter which told about a guy croaking two other guys by manicuring them with an axe. Later I came across things like this, for instance:

. . . for what counted was not the worship of violence, but the practice of it. Not the turbulent and complex emotion, but the act.

At eleven o'clock I gave up. I thought I detected a hint that the author of that book was reasonably bloodthirsty, but I had some faint suspicions on that score already. I dropped the book, stretched for a good yawn, and hopped for the hay.

Saturday morning I started out again. I called on Elkus, Lang, Mike Ayers, Adler, Cabot, and Pratt. I phoned Wolfe at a quarter to one, expecting to be invited home to lunch, and instead he asked me to grab a bite somewhere and run out to Mineola for him. Ditson had phoned to say that he had a dozen bulbs of a new Miltonia just arrived from England.

I got back to Thirty-fifth Street around 3:30, and took the bulbs in the office to show them to Wolfe. He looked them over carefully, and asked me to take them upstairs to Horstmann. I went up, and came back down to the office, intending to stop only a minute to enter the bulbs in the record book. But Wolfe, from his chair, said, "Archie."

I knew from the tone it was the start of a speech, so I settled back. He went on. "I should consider myself an inferior workman if I ignored a fact which the event proved actually to have significance. That is why I wish to make this apology to myself in your hearing."

I nodded. "I'm hanging on. Apology for what?"

"For bad workmanship. You may remember that on Wednesday evening, sixty-five hours ago, you were describing for me the contents of Inspector Cramer's bean."

I grinned. "Yeah."

"You told me that it was his belief that Dr. Elkus was having

Mr. Chapin shadowed. And then you started a sentence; I think you said; 'But one of those dicks—' I was impatient, and I stopped you. I should have let you finish. Pray do so now."

I nodded. "But since you've dumped the Dreyer thing into the ash can, what does it matter whether Elkus—"

"Archie. Confound it, I care nothing about Elkus; what I want is your sentence about a dick. What dick? Where is he?"

"Didn't I say? Tailing Paul Chapin."

"One of Mr. Cramer's men?"

I shook my head. "Cramer has a man there, but this bird's an extra. Cramer wondered who was paying him and had him in for a conference, but he never says anything but cuss words. I thought maybe he was Bascom's, but no."

"Have you seen him?"

"Yeah, I went down there."

"Describe him."

"Well . . . he weighs a hundred and thirty-five, five feet seven. Brown cap and pink necktie. A cat scratched him on the cheek and he didn't clean it up very well. Brown eyes, pointed nose, wide thin mouth, pale healthy skin."

"Hair?"

"He kept his cap on."

Wolfe sighed. The tip of his finger was doing a little circle on the arm of his chair. He said, "Sixty-five hours. Get him and bring him here at once. By persuasion if possible, but bring him."

I DROVE to Perry Street and parked fifty feet down from the Coffee Pot. I walked to the little café and glanced in. Pinkie wasn't there; it was nearly two hours till his soup time. I went to the next corner without a sign of Pinkie, Fred Durkin, or anything that looked like a city detective. Not so good, I thought, for of course it meant that the beasts of prey were out trailing their quarry, and the quarry might stay out till midnight.

I drove around the block to get the roadster into a better position, and sat in it and waited. It was getting dark. A little before six a taxi came along and stopped in front of 203. Chapin got out, paid, and hobbled inside the building. Pretty soon I saw Fred Durkin walking up from the corner. I moved over to make room for him beside me.

Durkin grinned. "This whole layout's a joke."

"Where's Pinkie?"

"He's around. He was behind me on the ride just now—there he goes, look, the Coffee Pot. It's time for his chow."

I had seen him going in. I said, "All right. Now listen. Do they sell beer at that joint on the corner?" He nodded yes. "Okay. Take the town dick there—" I pointed to Cramer's man standing on the corner "—and keep him there until my car's gone from in front of the Coffee Pot. I'm going to take Pinkie for a ride. Now beat it."

Pinkie was there, at the same table as before, with what looked like the same bowl of soup. I walked over to him and stopped at his elbow. He looked up and said, "Well, goddam it."

I said, "Come on, Inspector Cramer wants to see you," and took bracelets out of one pocket and my automatic out of another.

There must have been something in my eyes that made him suspicious. He said, "I don't believe it. Show me your goddam badge."

I couldn't afford an argument. I grabbed his collar and lifted him up out of his chair and set him on his feet. Then I snapped the handcuffs on him and told him, "Get going." I heard one or two mutters from the other customers, but didn't bother to look.

Pinkie went nice. Instead of trying to hide the bracelets, like most of them do, he held his hands stuck out in front. The only danger was that a flatfoot might happen along outside and offer to help me, and the roadster wasn't a police car. But all I saw was curious citizens. I shoved him in the car, and climbed in after him. I had left the engine running, just in case of a hurry. I rolled off, got to Seventh Avenue, and turned north.

I said, "Now listen. I've got two pieces of information. First, to ease your mind, I'm taking you to Thirty-fifth Street to call on Mr. Nero Wolfe. Second, if you open your trap to advertise anything—"

"I have no desire whatsoever to call—"

"Shut up." But I was grinning inside, for his voice was different; he was already jumping his character.

WOLFE WAS SITTING in the office with an empty beer glass. He looked at Pinkie, nodded faintly, then spoke suddenly to me. "Archie. Take Mr. Hibbard's cap, remove the handcuffs, and place a chair for him."

I did those things. This gentleman represented the second fact Wolfe had demanded, and I was glad to wait on him. He held his hands out for me to take the bracelets off, but it seemed to be an effort for him, and a glance at his eyes showed me that he wasn't feeling any too prime. I eased the chair up back of his knees, and all of a sudden he slumped into it and buried his face in his hands.

Wolfe tipped me a nod, and I went to the liquor cabinet and poured a stiff one and brought it over. I said, "Here, try this."

Finally he looked up. "What is it?"

"It's a goddam drink of rye whiskey."

He downed half of it, spluttered a little, and swallowed the rest. Then he cleared his throat twice, and said conversationally, "The truth of the matter is, I am not an adventurous man. I have been under a terrible strain for eleven days." He looked at me. "Could I have a little more whiskey?"

I got it for him. He said, "This is a relief. The whiskey is, of course, but I was referring particularly to this opportunity to become articulate again. I have a confession to make, Mr. Wolfe. I have learned more in these eleven days masquerading as a roughneck than in all the previous forty-three years of my existence. You don't mind if I talk? God, how I want to talk!"

Wolfe murmured, "This room is hardened to it." He rang for beer.

"Thank you. In these eleven days I have learned that psychology, as a formal science, is pure hocus-pocus. I have fed a half-starved child with my own hands. I have seen two men batter each other with their fists until the blood ran. I have seen a tough boy of the street pick up a wilted flower from the gutter. It is utterly amazing, I tell you, how people do things they happen to feel like doing. And I have been an instructor in psychology for seventeen years! Could I have a little more whiskey?"

I saw no warning from Wolfe, so I went and filled the

glass again. This time I brought some White Rock for a chaser.

Wolfe said, "Mr. Hibbard. I wonder if I could interpose a question or two. First I must observe that before your eleven days' education began you had learned enough to preserve your disguise, though the entire police force—and one or two other people—were looking for you. Really an achievement."

"Oh well. That sort of thing is rule of thumb," Hibbard said. "The first rule, of course, is, nothing that looks like disguise. My best items were the necktie and the scratch on my cheek. My profanity, I fear, was not well done. But my great mistake was the teeth; it was the very devil to get the gold leaf cemented on, and I was forced to confine my diet almost exclusively to milk and soup. But the clothing I am proud of."

"Yes, the clothing." Wolfe looked him over. "Excellent. Where did you get it?"

"A secondhand store on Grand Street. I changed in a subway toilet, and so was properly dressed when I went to rent a room on the lower West Side."

"What did you hope to accomplish?"

Hibbard had to consider. He finally said, "So help me, I don't know. When I left home, all that I felt moving me was fear. Fear had me, and all I was aware of was a desire to get near Paul Chapin and keep him under my eye. I knew if I told anyone, there would be danger of his getting on to me. But the last few days I have begun to suspect that in some gully of my mind, far below consciousness, was a desire to kill him. I believe I have been working up to it, and I still am."

Wolfe emptied his glass. "Naturally you do not know that Mr. Chapin has mailed verses to your friends stating explicitly that he killed you by clubbing you over the head."

"Oh yes. I know that."

"Who told you?"

"Pit. Pitney Scott."

"Then you did keep a bridge open," Wolfe said.

"No. The third day I was around there I met him face-to-face by bad luck, and of course he recognized me." Hibbard suddenly stopped, and turned a little pale. "There goes another illusion—I thought Pit . . ."

"Keep your illusion, Mr. Hibbard. Mr. Scott has told us nothing; it was Mr. Goodwin's acuteness of observation and my feeling for phenomena that uncovered you. But to resume: if you knew that Mr. Chapin had sent those verses, falsely boasting of murdering you, it is hard to see how you could keep your respect for him as an assassin."

Hibbard nodded. "You make a logical point, certainly. But logic has nothing to do with it. It was on the day that Pit Scott showed me those verses about me sucking air in through my blood that I discovered that I wanted to kill Paul."

Wolfe sighed. "Mr. Hibbard. Three weeks ago you were horrified at the thought that Mr. Chapin should account legally for his crimes; today you are determined to kill him yourself. You do intend to kill him?"

"I think so."

"You are armed?"

"No. I . . . no. He is physically a weakling."

"Indeed." The shadows on Wolfe's face altered; his cheeks were unfolding. "You will rip him apart with your bare hands."

"I might," Hibbard snapped. "Now I would like you to let me go. There is no reason—"

"Mr. Hibbard. Wait, please. Do you know of an arrangement I have entered into with your friends?"

"Yes. Pit Scott told me."

"Further, do you know that there, on Mr. Goodwin's desk, is the typewriter on which Mr. Chapin wrote his verses? Yes, it was at the Harvard Club; we negotiated a trade. Do you know that I am ready for a complete penetration of Mr. Chapin's defenses, in spite of his pathetic bravado? Do you know that within forty-eight hours I shall be prepared to submit to you and your friends a confession from Mr. Chapin of his guilt, and to remove satisfactorily all your apprehensions?"

Hibbard emptied his whiskey glass, put it on the desk, and stared at Wolfe. "I don't believe it."

"Of course you do. You merely don't want to." Wolfe stopped to look at Fritz, who had appeared on the threshold, then glanced at the clock; it was 7:25. He said, "I'm sorry, Fritz. Three of us will dine, at eight o'clock. Will that be possible?"

"Yes, sir."

"Good. Mr. Hibbard, I shall need your cooperation. I mentioned forty-eight hours. I would like to have you remain here as my guest for that period. Will you?"

Hibbard shook his head. "I don't believe you. You may have the typewriter, but you don't know Paul Chapin as I do. I don't believe you'll get him to confess, ever in God's world."

"I assure you, I will. If you will agree to stay under this roof incommunicado until Monday evening, and I have not closed the Chapin account forever, you will be free to resume your whimsical adventure without fear of any betrayal from us."

"And if I refused?" Hibbard said. "If I got up now to walk out, what would you do?"

"Well . . . you see, Mr. Hibbard, it is important to my plans that your discovery should remain unknown until the proper moment. There are various ways of keeping a desired guest. The most amiable is to persuade him to accept an invitation; another would be to lock him up."

Hibbard nodded. "What did I tell you? You see how people go ahead and do things they feel like doing? Miraculous!"

"It is indeed. Archie, if you would show Mr. Hibbard the south room, the one above mine. Fritz has aired it and the heat is on."

"Oh." I grinned. "You had it prepared."

"Certainly."

I started out with Hibbard, but Wolfe's voice came again and we turned. "You understand the arrangement, sir; you are to communicate with no one whatever. The desire to reassure your niece will be next to irresistible."

"I'll resist it."

The door of the south room stood open. I looked around. Orchids were in a bowl on the table; fresh towels were in the bathroom. Not bad for a strictly male household. As I started out the door again, I was stopped by Hibbard. "Say, do you happen to have a dark brown necktie?"

I grinned and went to my room and picked out a genteel solid color, and took it up to him.

DOWN in the office Wolfe sat with his eyes shut. "Archie," he said. "There are still eighteen minutes before dinner, and we might as well make use of them. I am suffering from my habitual impatience when nothing remains but the finishing touches. Take your notebook."

I got it out, and a pencil.

"Make three copies of this, the original on the good bond. Date it tomorrow, November eleventh—ha, Armistice Day! Most appropriate. It will have a heading in caps as follows: CONFESSION OF PAUL CHAPIN REGARDING THE DEATHS OF WILLIAM R. HARRISON AND EUGENE DREYER AND THE WRITING AND DISPATCHING OF CERTAIN INFORMATIVE AND THREATENING VERSES. It is a concession to him to call them verses, but we should be magnanimous somewhere. . . ."

The telephone rang.

I put my notebook down and reached for it. I barely got a sound out before I was stopped by an excited whisper in my ear: "Archie, listen. Quick, I may be pulled off. Get up here as fast as you can—Doc Burton's, Ninetieth Street. Burton's croaked. Chapin got him with a gat, pumped him full. The cops have got him clean—"

There were noises, but no more words. I hung up and turned to Wolfe. I said, "That was Fred Durkin. Paul Chapin has just shot Dr. Burton and killed him. At his apartment on Ninetieth Street. They caught him red-handed. Fred invites me up to see the show."

Wolfe sighed. He murmured, "Nonsense."

"Nonsense hell. Fred's not a genius, but I never saw him mistake a pinochle game for a murder. It looks like tailing Chapin wasn't such a bad idea after all—"

"Archie. Shut up." Wolfe's lips were pushing out and in as fast as I had ever seen them. After ten seconds he said, "Consider this, please. Durkin's conversation was interrupted?"

"Yeah, he was pulled off."

"By the police, of course. The police take Chapin for murdering Burton; he is convicted and executed, and where are we? What of our engagements? We are lost."

I stared at him. "Damn that cripple—"

"Don't damn him. Save him. Save him for us. Go there at once, fast. I need the facts. I need enough of them to save Paul Chapin. Go and get them."

I jumped.

X

I KEPT on the west side as far as Eighty-sixth Street and then shot crosstown and through Central Park. The case had cracked wide open and I was on my way, and that was all sweetness and light, but on the other hand Fred's story of the event decorated by Wolfe's comments looked like nothing but bad weather.

I pulled up short of the Burton number on Ninetieth Street, and jumped to the sidewalk. I was nearly to the entrance when a big car came along and stopped quick, and two men got out. I took a look, then called, "Inspector Cramer! This is luck." I started to walk along in with him.

He stopped. "Oh! You. Nothing doing. Beat it."

I fell back. People were gathering, there was already quite a crowd, and a cop was there herding them. In the confusion I was pretty sure he hadn't heard the little passage between Cramer and me. I faded away, and went to where I had parked the roadster. I opened up the back and got out a black bag I kept packed for emergencies. I went back to the entrance and pushed through the line while the cop was busy on the other side. Inside was the doorman and another cop. I stepped up to them and said, "Medical Examiner. What apartment is it?" The cop looked me over and took me to the elevator and said, "Take this gent to the fifth floor."

The door of the Burton apartment was open. I breezed in. There was a mob in the big reception hall, mostly flatfeet and dicks standing around looking bored. Inspector Cramer was by the table listening to one of them. I walked over to him and said his name.

He looked around, surprised, "Well, in the name of—"

"Listen, Inspector. Just a second. I'm not going to steal the prisoner or the evidence or anything else. I've got a right to curiosity and that's all I expect to satisfy."

"What have you got in that bag?"

"Shirts and socks. I used it to bring me up."

He grunted. "Leave it here on the table, and if you get in the way . . ."

Being careful not to bump anyone, I got back against the wall. I took a look. It was a room seventeen feet by twenty, on a guess, nearly square. One end was mostly windows, curtained. At the other end was the entrance door. One long wall, the one I was standing against, had pictures and a couple of stands with vases of flowers. In the other wall, nearly to the corner, was a double door, closed, leading of course to the apartment proper. The rest of that wall, about ten feet of it, had curtains to match those at the end. I figured it was closets for wraps. The light was from the ceiling, indirect, with switches at the double door and the entrance door. There was a good-sized table in the middle of the room. Near where I stood was a stand with a telephone and a chair.

In a chair at the end of the table, Paul Chapin was sitting. I couldn't see his face, he was turned wrong. Doc Burton was on the floor, at the other end of the table. He just looked dead and fairly comfortable. From where I was I couldn't see much blood. The dicks and a medical guy buzzed around. Inspector Cramer had left the room by the double door, to see Mrs. Burton I supposed. A young woman came in from outside and made a scene; it appeared that it was her father that had been croaked. She had been out somewhere, and she took it hard.

I moseyed around to get a slant at Chapin. He looked at me, but there wasn't any sign of his being aware he had ever seen me before. He had on a brown overcoat, unbuttoned, and tan gloves. He was slouched over; his hands were resting on his good knee, fastened with handcuffs. There was nothing in his face, just nothing.

I thought to myself that this was the first piece of real hundred-percent bad luck I had ever known Nero Wolfe to have. Then I remembered what I was there for, and that I had gone around for two days pretending to hunt Andrew Hibbard knowing all the time it was hopeless, and that Hibbard was at that moment eating scallops and arguing psychology with Wolfe. And until Wolfe himself said finish, hopeless was out.

I got against the wall again and surveyed the field. The medical guy was done. When Cramer returned from questioning the members of the household, there would probably be no delay in removing the body and the prisoner, and then there would be nothing to keep anybody else here, except a dick out in the hall maybe, to keep annoyance away from the family.

I went over and got my bag from the table, carelessly. Then I wandered back to the wall where the curtains were. I stood with my back to them. Keeping my eyes on the array of dicks scattered around, I felt behind me with my foot and found that the floor continued flush. If it was a closet back of the curtains it was built into the wall. I kept my eyes busy; I had to pick an instant when every dick there had his face turned. Luck came that time—the phone rang on the stand by the other wall. They all turned involuntarily. I had my hand behind me ready to pull the curtain aside, and back I went, and let the curtain fall again.

The closet was all of three feet deep and I had plenty of room. I eased the black bag onto the floor in a corner and got behind what felt like a woman's fur coat. One thing there had been no help for: Chapin had seen me. His light-colored eyes had been right on me as I backed in.

I stood there in the dark, and after a while wished I had remembered to bring an oxygen tank. It was all of half an hour before Cramer returned to the reception hall. I heard the double door opening, and then Cramer handing out orders. A dick with a hoarse voice told another one to carry Chapin's stick and he'd help him walk; they were taking him away. There were directions from Cramer about removing Burton's body, and in a couple of minutes the tramp of heavy feet as they carried it out. It sounded like there were only two dicks left; I began to be afraid Cramer had ordered them to stay for some reason or other, but pretty soon I heard them going away too.

I waited five minutes. Then I pulled the edge of the curtain a little and took a slant. Empty. All gone. I went over and turned the knob of the double doors, and walked through. I was in a room about five times the size of the reception hall, dimly lighted, furnished up to the hilt. There was a door at the far end and a wide open arch halfway down one side. I heard voices from somewhere. I went on in a ways and called, "Hello! Mrs. Burton!"

The voices stopped. A guy appeared in the arch, trying to look important. He was just a kid, around twenty-two, handsome, and dressed up. He said, "We thought you had all gone."

"Yeah. All but me. I have to see Mrs. Burton."

"But he said . . . the inspector said she wouldn't be bothered."

"I'm sorry, I have to see her. Just a few questions."

He opened his mouth and shut it, then turned and beat it. In a minute he came back and nodded me along.

We went through a room and a sort of a hall and into another room. A woman was sitting on a couch, another woman in a chair, and the daughter I had seen in the reception hall was standing behind the couch. I suppose Mrs. Loring A. Burton wasn't at her best that evening, but a glance was enough to show you she was quite a person. She had a straight thin nose, a warm mouth, fine dark eyes. Her hair was piled in braids at the back, pulled back to show her temples and brow, which made the most of the effect.

I told her I had a few confidential questions to ask and I'd like to see her alone. The daughter stared at me with red eyes. Mrs. Burton asked, "Confidential to whom?"

"To Paul Chapin. I'd rather not . . ." I looked around.

She looked around too. I saw that the kid wasn't the son and heir after all, it was the daughter he was interested in. Mrs. Burton said, "What does it matter? Go to my room—you don't mind, Alice?"

The woman in the chair said she didn't, and got up. The kid took hold of the daughter's arm to steer her.

After they went out, Mrs. Burton said, "Well?"

I said, "Do you know who Nero Wolfe is?"

"Nero Wolfe? Yes."

"Dr. Burton and his friends entered into an agreement—"

She interrupted me. "I know all about it. My husband . . ." She stopped. The way she suddenly clasped her fingers tight showed that a bust-up was nearer to coming than I had supposed. But she soon got it shoved under again. "My husband told me all about it."

I nodded. "That saves time. I work for Nero Wolfe, my name's Goodwin. I've got some questions to ask, and I can't be polite and wait for a week, I've got to ask them now. Just tell me this: Did you see Paul Chapin shoot your husband?"

"No. But I've already—"

"Did anybody see him?"

"No."

I took a breath. At least, then, we weren't floating with our bellies up. I said, "All right. Then it's a question of how you feel. How you feel about this, for instance, that Paul Chapin didn't shoot your husband at all."

She stared at me. "What do you mean—"

"Here's what I'm getting at, Mrs. Burton. I know your husband didn't hate Paul Chapin. How about you, did you hate him? Disregard what happened tonight, how much did you hate him?"

For a second I thought I'd carried her along; then I saw a change coming in her eyes. She was going to ritz me out. I rushed in ahead of it. "Listen, Mrs. Burton, right now, in a cabinet down in Nero Wolfe's office, there is a leather box. It's beautiful tan leather, with fine gold tooling on it, and it's full nearly to the top with your gloves and stockings. Now wait a minute, give me a chance. It belongs to Paul Chapin. Dora Ritter hooked them and gave them to him. It's his treasure. Nero Wolfe says Chapin's soul is in that box. The reason I want to know whether you hate Paul Chapin is this: what if he didn't kill your husband? Would you like to see them hang it on him anyway?"

She said, "I don't know what you're driving at."

"I'm interested in seeing that Paul Chapin gets no more than is coming to him."

She unclasped her hands and said, "You may sit down."

"Okay. Now tell me how it happened. Who was here?"

"My husband and I, and the cook and the maid."

"What about the woman you called Alice?"

"That is my oldest friend. She came just a little while ago."

"And?"

"I was in my room dressing. We were dining out. My daughter was out somewhere. My husband came to my room for a cigarette. The maid came and said Paul Chapin was there. My husband left to go to the foyer to see him, but he didn't go direct; he went back through his room and his study. The last time Paul had come my husband had gone to his study and got a revolver out of the drawer. I thought it was childish. This time I stood and listened to see if he did it again, and he did—I heard the drawer opening. Then he called to me, and I answered, 'What is it?' and he called back, 'Nothing, never mind.' That was the last . . . those were his last words I heard. I heard him walking through the apartment— I listened, I suppose, because I was wondering what Paul could want. Then I heard noises—not loud, the foyer is so far away from my room—then shots. I ran. The maid came out of the dining room and followed me. We ran to the foyer. It was dark, and we couldn't see. I heard a noise, someone falling, and Paul's voice saying my name. I turned on the light switch, and saw Paul on his knee, trying to get up. He said he was trying to hop to the switch. Then I saw Lorrie, on the floor at the end of the table. I ran to him and called to the maid to go for a doctor. I don't know what Paul did then, the first I knew some men came—"

"All right, hold it."

She stopped. I looked at her a minute. She had clasped her hands again. I took out a pad and pencil, and said, "Now wait a minute. Let's go back to the beginning. On his way to see Paul Chapin, your husband called to you from the study, and then said never mind. Have you any idea what he was going to say?"

"No, how could I—"

"Okay. The way you told it, he called to you after he opened the drawer. Was that the way it was?"

She nodded. "I'm sure it was after I heard the drawer open. I was listening."

"Yeah. Then you heard him walking to the foyer, and then you heard noises. What kind of noises?"

"I don't know. Just movements. The noises were faint."

"Did you hear your husband closing the foyer door after he got there?"

"No. I wouldn't hear that unless it banged."

"Then we'll try this. Since you were listening, there was a moment when you figured that he had reached the foyer. You know what I mean, the feeling that he was there. When I say 'Now,' that will mean that he has just reached the foyer, and you begin feeling the passing of time. Feel it as near the same as you can, and when it's time for the first shot to go off, you say 'Now.' Get it? . . . *Now.*"

I looked at the second hand of my watch; it went crawling up from the 30. She said, "*Now.*"

I stared at her. "My God, that was only six seconds."

She nodded. "It was as short as that, I'm sure it was."

"In that case . . . all right. Then you ran to the foyer, and there was no light there. You switched it on and saw Chapin kneeling, trying to get up. Did he have a gun in his hand?"

"No. He had his coat and gloves on. I didn't see a gun . . . anywhere."

"Did Inspector Cramer tell you about the gun?"

She nodded. "It was my husband's. He shot . . . it had been fired four times. They found it on the floor."

"When you turned on the light Chapin was saying something."

"He was saying 'Anne, my dear Anne, I was trying to hop to the switch.' He had fallen."

I finished scratching on the pad, and looked up at her. I said, "Now to go back again. Were you at home all afternoon?"

"No. I was at a gallery looking at prints, and then at a tea. I got home around six."

"Was your husband here when you got here?"

"Yes, he was in his study with Ferdinand Bowen."

"So Mr. Bowen was here. Do you know what for?"

"No. That is . . . no."

"Now come, Mrs. Burton. What was Bowen here for?"

"He was asking a financial favor. That's all I know."

"Did he get it?"

"No. But this has no connection . . . no more of this."

"Okay. When did Bowen leave?"

"Soon after I arrived, I should say a quarter past six. Perhaps twenty after; it was about ten minutes before Dora came, and she was punctual at six thirty."

I looked at her. "You mean Dora Chapin?"

"Yes. She came to do my hair."

"I'll be damned. And when did she leave?"

"About a quarter past seven." She paused to calculate. "Yes, that would be right. A few minutes later, perhaps."

"So Dora Chapin left here at seven twenty and Paul Chapin arrived at half past. That's interesting; they almost collided. Who else was here after six o'clock?"

"No one. My daughter left around half past six, a little before Dora came. Of course I don't understand— Oh, it's absurd to try to talk about this—absurd . . ."

I said, "Maybe it's absurd not to."

She shook her head. "I saw farther inside myself this evening than I have ever seen before. It wasn't when I saw my husband dead, it wasn't when I stood alone in my room trying to realize he was dead. It was sitting here with that police inspector, with him telling me that I would have to testify in court so that Paul Chapin can be convicted and punished. I don't want him punished. My husband is dead, isn't that enough? And if I don't want Paul punished, what is it I want to hold onto? Is it pity? I have never pitied him. I have been pretty insolent with life, but not insolent enough to pity Paul Chapin."

She got up, abruptly, and lit a cigarette. "I have always disliked Paul Chapin. Once, when I was eighteen years old, I promised to marry him. When I learned of his accident I was delighted, because I wouldn't have to keep my promise. I didn't know that then but I realized it later. At no time have I pitied him. I dislike him intensely. I have had occasion to analyze this; it is his deformity that is intolerable. Not his physical deformity. The deformity of his nervous system, of his brain. Women have been fascinated by it, but the two or three who surrendered to it got only contempt for a reward."

"He married Dora Ritter. She's a woman."

"Yes, but she is consecrated to a denial of her womanhood. I am fond of her, I understand her. She knows what beauty is, and she sees herself. That forced her, long ago, to the denial, and her strength of will has maintained it. Paul understood her too. He married her to show his contempt for me; he told me so. And as for Dora—she hates him, but she would die for him. Fiercely and secretly she longed for the dignity of marriage, and it was a miracle of luck that Paul offered it under the only circumstances that could make it acceptable to her. Oh, they understand each other!"

I said, "I'm surprised she was here today. I understood she had a bad accident Wednesday. She seems to have some character."

"It could be called that. Her character comes from her indifference to everything except Paul Chapin."

"You say Dora hates Chapin. She left here at seven twenty. Chapin arrived at seven thirty, ten minutes later. What if she waited in the hall outside and came back in with him? She could have snatched the gun from your husband's pocket and done the shooting and beat it before you could get there. That might explain the light being out; she might have flipped the switch before she opened the outer door. Maybe Chapin had no idea what she was up to—"

She was shaking her head. "I don't believe that. As far as Dora could like any man, she liked Lorrie. She wouldn't do that."

"Not even to make a reservation for Chapin in the electric chair?"

Mrs. Burton looked at me, and a little shudder ran over her. She said, "That's horrible."

"Of course it's horrible. Whatever we pull out of this bag, it won't be a pleasant surprise for anyone, except maybe Chapin. Anyone at all might have done it—anyone who could get into that foyer and who knew Chapin was there and that Dr. Burton would come. Now, what about the maid? Could I see her?"

She got up and pushed a button. I noticed that with her back turned you could have taken her for twenty. She turned and came back to the couch as the inner door opened and the whole outfit appeared: cook, maid, friend Alice, daughter, and boy friend. The cook was carrying a tray. Mrs. Burton said, "Thank you, Henny, not now. I really couldn't. And the rest of you . . . if you don't mind . . . we wish to see Rose a few minutes. Just Rose."

"But, mother, really—"

"No, dear. Please, just a few minutes. Come here, Rose."

They faded back through the door. The maid came and stood in front of us and tried some swallowing which didn't seem to work. Mrs. Burton told her I wanted to ask her some questions, and she looked at me as if I was going to sell her down the river.

I said, "Rose, did you go to the door when Dora Chapin came this evening?"

"Yes, sir."

"When she left did you let her out?"

"No, sir. I never do. She just went."

"Where were you when she went?"

"I was in the dining room. I was dusting the glasses in there."

"Then I suppose you didn't let Mr. Bowen out either."

"No, I didn't let him out, but that was a long time before."

"You answered the door when Mr. Chapin came."

"Yes, sir."

"Now see if you can remember this. What did Mr. Chapin say to you?"

She looked down at the floor. I said, "Come on, Rose. You know, Mr. Chapin came in, and you took his hat and coat—"

She looked up. "I didn't take his hat and coat. He kept his coat on, and his gloves. He said to tell Dr. Burton he was there."

"Did he stand by the door or walk to a chair to sit down?"

"I don't know. I came back in to tell Dr. Burton."

"Was the light turned on in the foyer?"

"Yes, sir. Of course."

"After you told Dr. Burton, where did you go?"

"I went back to the dining room."

"Did Dr. Burton go to the foyer right away?"

She nodded. "Well . . . maybe not right away. He went pretty soon."

"Okay." I got up from my chair. "Now I'm going to ask you to do something. You go to the dining room and start taking down the glasses. I'll walk from the study past the dining-room door and on to the foyer. You hear me go by, and you decide when enough time has passed for the first shot to go off. Then you yell 'Now' loud enough for me to hear you in the foyer. Do you understand?"

"The shots all came together," Rose said.

"All right. You yell when the time comes. First you'd better tell the people inside or they'll be running out here—"

Mrs. Burton interposed, "I'll tell them. Rose, take Mr. Goodwin to the study and show him how to go."

Rose apparently avoided the bedrooms by taking me around by a side hall, for we entered the study direct from that. She showed me how to go, by another door, and left me there. I looked around; books, leather chairs, and a flat-top desk by a window, where the gun had been kept. Then I went out by the other door, got my eye on the watch, and followed directions. I struck a medium pace, past the dining-room door, across the central hall, and through the drawing room; opened the door into the foyer, went in and closed it—

It was a good thing the folks had been warned, for Rose yelling *Now* sounded even to me like the last scream of doom. I went back in faster than I had come, for fear she might try it again. She had beat it back to the room where Mrs. Burton was. When I entered she was standing by the couch with her face white as a sheet. Mrs. Burton was reaching up to pat her arm. I went over and sat down.

I said, "Two seconds at the most. Of course she rushed it, but it shows it must have been quick. Okay, Rose. You're a good brave girl. Just a couple more questions. When you heard the shots you ran to the foyer with Mrs. Burton. Is that right?"

"Yes, sir."

"What did you see when you got there?"

"I didn't see anything. It was dark."

"What did you hear?"

"I heard something on the floor and then I heard Mr. Chapin saying Mrs. Burton's name and the light went on and I saw him."

"What was he doing?"

"He was trying to get up."

"Did he have a gun in his hand?"

"No, sir. He had his hands on the floor getting up."

"And then you saw Dr. Burton."

"Yes, sir." She swallowed.

"What did you do then?"

"Well . . . I stood there, I guess . . . then Mrs. Burton told me to go for a doctor and I ran out and ran downstairs—"

"Okay, hold it."

I looked back over my notes. There was another point that I thought ought to be attended to. I looked at Mrs. Burton. "That's all for Rose. It's all for me too, except—"

She looked up at the maid and nodded at her. "You'd better go to bed, Rose. Good night. Go and get some sleep."

The maid gave me a look, and turned and went. As soon as the door had closed behind her I got up from my chair.

I said, "I'm going, but I've got to ask a favor of you. You'll have to take my word for it that Nero Wolfe's interest in this business is the same as yours. You don't want Paul Chapin to burn in the electric chair for killing your husband, and neither does he. But he'll need some kind of standing, for instance, if he wants to ask Inspector Cramer to let him see the gun. I can't quite see Paul Chapin engaging him, but how about you? Of course there wouldn't be any fee, even if we did something you wanted done."

I looked at her. Her head was still up, but the signs of a flop were in her eyes and at the corners of her mouth.

I said to her, "Just say yes or no. What about it?"

She shook her head. I thought she was saying no to me, but then she spoke: "My husband would disapprove of what I am doing now—I think he would. He would say, let Fate do her job. He is dead . . . Oh yes, he is dead . . . but I will say what I always said, I will not keep my hand from any job if I think it's mine. He would not want me to make any concessions to him, dead." She rose to her feet abruptly and added, "Even if he wanted me to I doubt if I could. Good night, Mr. Goodwin." She held out her hand.

I took it. I said, "Maybe I get you, but I like plain words. Nero Wolfe can say he is acting in your behalf, is that it?"

She nodded. I turned and left the room.

XI

At two o'clock that night—Sunday morning—I sat at my desk in the office and yawned. Wolfe, behind his own desk, was looking at a schedule I had typed out for him. Hibbard had long since gone to bed. The schedule looked like this:

6:05 Mrs. Burton arrives home. Present in apartment: Burton, daughter, Bowen, maid, cook.
6:20 Bowen leaves.
6:25 Daughter leaves.
6:30 Dora Chapin arrives.
7:20 Dora Chapin leaves.
7:30 Paul Chapin arrives.
7:33 Burton is shot.
7:50 Fred Durkin phones.

I looked at my carbon and yawned again. Finally Wolfe said, "You understand, Archie. I think it would be possible for us to go ahead without assuming the drudgery of discovering the murderer of Dr. Burton. Our weak spot is that we are committed to refer our success to the vote of our group of clients. We must not only make things happen, we must make our clients vote that they have happened. That arrangement makes it necessary for us to learn who killed Dr. Burton, so that if the vote cannot be sufficiently swayed by reason it can be bullied by melodrama."

I said, "I'm sleepy."

Wolfe nodded. "Yes, I know. Now, the worst aspect of this Burton development, from our standpoint, is that Mr. Chapin cannot come here to get his box—or for anything else. It will be necessary to make arrangements to see him. What jail will they keep him in?"

"The Tombs is the most likely."

Wolfe sighed. "It's more than two miles, nearer three, I suppose. The last time I left this house was early in September, for the privilege of dining at the same table with Albert Einstein. Ah well, there is no escaping an expedition to the Tombs. Not, however, until we know who killed Dr. Burton."

"And not forgetting that before the night's out Chapin may confess for Cramer."

"Archie." Wolfe wagged a finger at me. "Have I not made it clear to you? That Mr. Chapin killed Dr. Burton is not possible. It is past two o'clock, time for bed. Good night, sleep well."

Sunday morning I slept late. I had been given three chores for that day, and by the time I called down to Fritz that I was out of the bathtub he had lined a casserole with butter, put in it six tablespoons of cream, three fresh eggs, four sausages, salt, pepper, paprika, and chives, and conveyed it to the oven.

Andrew Hibbard was in the office with the morning paper. He said that he had had breakfast, and that he wished he had some of his own clothes. I told him that Wolfe was up on the top floor with the orchids and that he would be welcome up there if he cared to see them. He decided to go. I went to the kitchen and took my time with the casserole. Then I went to the garage and got the roadster and moseyed downtown.

Cramer was in his office when I got there. He was smoking a big cigar and looked contented. He whirled his chair around to face me and asked me what I wanted.

I told him, "I want lots of things. But what I'd really like is to have a little talk with Chapin."

Cramer grinned. He said, "I wouldn't mind having a talk with Chapin myself. I spent four hours on him last night, and he wouldn't even tell me how old he is or what lawyer he wants. He won't talk to anyone except his wife. You know, I've had a little experience greasing tongues, but he tops them all."

"Did you try pinching him?"

"Haven't touched him. But I had an idea you'd be wanting to see him. And I've decided nothing doing. Considering how we got him, I don't see why you're interested anyhow."

"Okay. It just means Wolfe will have to arrange it at the DA's office."

"Let him. If he does, I won't butt in. Listen, now that you've asked me a favor and I've turned you down, how about doing one for me? Tell me what you want to see him for?"

I grinned. "I have to ask him what he wants us to do with what's left of Andrew Hibbard until he gets a chance to tend to it."

Cramer stared at me. "You wouldn't kid me."

"I wouldn't dream of it. Look here, Inspector, there must be some human quality in you somewhere. Today's my birthday. Let me see him."

"Not a chance."

I told him much obliged for all his many kindnesses, and left.

I got in the roadster and headed north. At Fourteenth Street I went to a cigar store and phoned Wolfe. I told him, "Cramer wouldn't let me see him."

Wolfe said, "Excellent. Proceed to Mrs. Burton."

I went back to the roadster and rolled on uptown.

The maid let me into the apartment, and I was taken to Mrs. Burton, who sat in her room in a chair by the window. She looked pale. I told her I only had a few questions Nero Wolfe had given me. I read the first one from my pad:

"Did Paul Chapin say anything whatever to you last night besides what you have already told me?"

She said, "No, nothing."

"Inspector Cramer showed you the gun that your husband was shot with. How sure are you that it was your husband's?"

She said, "Quite sure. His initials were on it."

"During the fifty minutes that Dora Chapin was in the apartment last evening, was there any time when she went to the study, and if so was there anyone else in the study at that time?"

She said, "No." Then a frown came into her eyes. "But wait—yes, there was. Soon after she came I sent her to the study for a book. I suppose there was no one there. My husband was in his room dressing."

"This next one is the last. Do you know if Mr. Bowen was at any time alone in the study?"

She said, "Yes, he was. My husband came to my room to ask me a question."

I put the pad in my pocket, and said to her, "You might tell me what the question was. It could be important."

Her eyes frowned again. "Very well. He asked me if I cared enough for Estelle Bowen—Mr. Bowen's wife—to make a considerable sacrifice for her. I said no."

"Did he tell you what he meant?"

"No."

"All right. That's all. You haven't slept any."

"No."

I told her thank you, and I beat it. On my way downtown I phoned Wolfe again. I told him what I had gathered from Mrs. Burton, and he told me that he and Andrew Hibbard were playing cribbage.

It was twenty minutes past noon when I got to Perry Street. There was a taxi parked in front of the entrance at 203. I let the roadster slide to the curb opposite, and got out. I stepped across to the sidewalk and went alongside; the driver's head was tilted over against the frame and his eyes were closed. I leaned in and said, "Good morning, Mr. Scott."

He came to with a start and looked at me. He blinked. "Oh," he said, "it's little Nero Wolfe. When was it I saw you, Wednesday? Only four days ago. You keeping busy?"

"I'm managing, and the name is Archie Goodwin." I leaned in a little farther. "Look here, Pitney Scott. When Nero Wolfe heard how you recognized Andrew Hibbard over a week ago, but didn't claim the five-grand reward when it was offered, he said you have an admirable sense of humor. It just occurred to me that you ought to know that your friend Hibbard is at present a guest up at our house. He'd like to stay undercover for another couple of days, till we get this whole thing straightened out. If you should happen to turn mercenary, you won't lose anything by keeping your sense of humor."

He grunted. "So. You got Andy. And you only need a couple of days to straighten it all out. I thought *all* detectives were dumb."

"We are. I'm so dumb I don't even know whether it was you that took Dora Chapin up to Ninetieth Street last evening and brought her back again."

He looked at me. "I didn't drive Mrs. Chapin to Burton's last night because she went in her own car."

"Oh. She drives herself."

"Sure. I don't know why she's using me today, unless it's because she doesn't want to park her car in front of the Tombs— there she comes now."

I went back a step. Dora Chapin had come out of the 203 entrance and was headed for the taxi. She had on another coat and another fur piece, but the face was the same. She didn't seem to have noticed me, let alone recognized me; then she stopped and turned her eyes straight at me, and for the first time I saw an expression in them that I could give a name to, and it wasn't fondness. I said, "Mrs. Chapin. Could I ride with you? I'd like to tell you—"

She climbed inside and slammed the door. Pitney Scott stepped on the starter, put the gear in, and started to roll. I stood and watched the taxi go, not very jubilant, because it was her I had come down there to see.

I walked to the corner and bought a *Times* and went to the roadster and made myself comfortable. Unless she had some kind of pull, they wouldn't let her stay very long at the Tombs.

It was nearly two o'clock when I looked up for the eightieth time at the sound of a car and saw the taxi slowing down. Pitney

Scott and Dora Chapin both got out and went in the building. I decided not to do any more waiting. I entered 203 and went to the elevator and said fifth floor. The man looked at me with the usual weary suspicion but didn't bother with questions.

I can't very well pretend to be proud of what happened that afternoon at Paul Chapin's apartment, but I can't agree that it was quite as dumb as one or two subsequent remarks of Wolfe's made it out to be. Anyway, this is how it happened:

Dora Chapin came to the door and opened it, and I got my foot inside the threshold. She asked me what I wanted, and I said I had something to ask Pitney Scott. She said he would be down in half an hour and I could wait downstairs.

I said, "Listen, Mrs. Chapin. I want to ask you something too. You think I'm against your husband, but I'm not, I'm for him. He hasn't got many friends left, and I've got something to say. Let me in."

She threw the door wide open and said, "Come in."

Maybe that shift in her welcome should have made me suspicious, but it didn't. I went in and followed her across the hall, through a big sitting room and dining room, and into the kitchen. In the kitchen at an enamel-top table was Pitney Scott, consuming a hunk of fried chicken. There was a platter of it with four or five pieces left. I said to Dora Chapin, "Maybe we can go in front and leave Mr. Scott to enjoy himself."

She nodded at a chair and pointed to the chicken. "There's plenty." She turned to Scott. "I'll fix you a drink."

He shook his head, and chewed and swallowed. "I've been off it for ten days now, Mrs. Chapin. When the coffee's ready I'd appreciate that." He nodded towards the platter. "Come on and help me," he said to me.

I got into the chair and Scott passed the platter. Dora Chapin had gone to the stove to turn the fire down under the percolator. There was still a lot of bandage at the back of her neck, and it looked unattractive where her hair had been shaved off. She went into the dining room, and after a while came back with coffee cups and a bowl of sugar.

Of course it was in the coffee, she probably put it right in the pot. It tasted all right, but she must have put in all the sleeping tablets she could get hold of, for God knows it was potent. I began to feel it when I was reaching to hand Scott a cigarette, and at the same time I saw the look on his face. He tried to get up out of his chair, but couldn't make it. That was the last I remember, him trying to get out of his chair, but I must have done one or two things after that, because when I came out of it I was in the dining room.

It was dark. For a while that was all I knew, because I couldn't move and I was fighting to get my eyes open. I could see, off to my right, two large oblongs of dim light, and I concentrated on deciding what they were. It came with a burst that they were windows, and the street was lit.

I rolled over on the floor and my hand landed on something metal, sharp. I pulled myself to my knees and began to crawl. I bumped into a table and a chair or two, and finally into the wall. I crawled around the wall with my shoulder against it, detouring for furniture, and at last I felt a door. Feeling above me, I found the switch and pushed the light on. I crawled over to where there was some stuff on the floor and saw that the metal thing that had startled me was my ring of keys. My wallet was there too, and my pad and pencil, handkerchief—things from my pockets.

I looked around for a telephone, but there wasn't any, so I crawled to the sitting room and found the light switch by the door and turned it on. The phone was on a stand by the farther wall. It looked so far away that I just wanted to lie down and give it up. But I finally got to the stand and sat down on the floor against it, then reached up for the receiver and shoved it against my ear, and heard a man's voice, very faint. I said Wolfe's phone number and heard him say he couldn't hear me, so I yelled it. After a while I heard another voice and I yelled, "I want Nero Wolfe!"

The other voice mumbled and I asked who it was, and got it into my bean that it was Fritz. I told him to get Wolfe on, and he said Wolfe wasn't there. He mumbled a lot of stuff and I told him to say it again louder and slower.

"I said, Archie, Mr. Wolfe went to look for you. Somebody came to get him, and he told me he was going for you. Archie, where are you? Mr. Wolfe said—"

I was having a hard time holding the phone, and it dropped to the floor, and my head fell into my hands with my eyes closed, and I suppose what I was doing you would call crying.

I HAVEN'T the slightest idea how long I sat there on the floor trying to force myself to pick up the telephone again. Finally I heard a noise. At last it seeped into me that someone seemed to be trying to knock the door down. I grabbed the top of the telephone stand and pulled myself up, and decided I could keep to my feet if I didn't let go of the wall, so I followed it around into the hall to the entrance door where the noise was. I got my hands on the knob, and the door flew open and down I went. The two guys that came in stood and looked at me, and I heard remarks about full to the gills and leaving the receiver off the hook.

By that time I could talk better. I said enough so that one of them beat it for a doctor, and the other one helped me get up and steered me to the kitchen. Pitney Scott was curled up on the floor. He was dead to the world.

By working the wall again, I got back to the dining room and sat on the floor and began collecting my things. I got worried because I couldn't figure out what was missing. Then I realized it was the leather case Wolfe had given me, with pistols on one side and orchids on the other, that I carried my police and fire cards in. And, by God, I started to cry again. I was doing that when the other guy came back with the doctor.

The doctor insisted that before he could give me anything he'd have to know just what I had inside of me, and he went to the bathroom to investigate bottles and boxes. I was beginning to have thoughts and they were starting to bust in my head. Why had Dora Chapin knocked me out and then taken nothing but that leather case? Then I suddenly remembered that there had been something peculiar about Scott curled up on the floor, and I turned around and started for the kitchen. I looked at Scott and saw what it was: he was in his shirt sleeves. His gray taxi driver's jacket was gone. I was trying to decide why that was important when the doctor came in with a glass of brown stuff in his hand. He watched me drink it, and then went over and knelt down by Scott.

I put the empty glass on the table and got hold of the guy who had gone for the doctor—by this time I recognized him as the elevator man—and told him to go downstairs and see if Scott's taxi was at the curb. Then I made it to the telephone stand. I got the operator, and gave her Wolfe's number. Fritz answered. I said, "This is Archie. What was it you told me a while ago?"

"Why . . . Mr. Wolfe is gone." I could tell he was trying not to let his voice shake. "He told me he was going to get you."

"Wait a minute, Fritz. Talk slow. What time is it? My watch says a quarter to seven."

"Yes. That's right. Mr. Wolfe has been gone nearly four hours. Archie, where are you?"

"To hell with where I am. Did someone come for him?"

"Yes. I went to the door, and a man handed me an envelope."

"Was it a taxi driver?"

"Yes, I think so. I took the envelope to Mr. Wolfe, and pretty soon he came to the kitchen and told me he was going. Mr. Hibbard helped him into his coat—"

"Did you see the taxi?"

"Yes, I went out with Mr. Wolfe and opened the door of the cab for him. Archie, for God's sake, tell me what I can do—"

"You can't do anything. Hold the fort, Fritz, and sit tight. I'll call again as soon as I have anything to say."

I hung up. My head was pounding like the hammers of hell. The elevator man had come back and was standing there. I looked at him and he said Scott's taxi was gone.

I called Cramer's office but they couldn't find him. Then I tried his home. I didn't know a cop's voice could ever sound so welcome to me. I told him where I was and what had happened. "That crazy Chapin woman has stolen a taxi and she's got Nero Wolfe in it taking him somewhere. She got him four hours ago and she's had time to get to Albany or anywhere else. Listen, Inspector, for

God's sake. Send out a general alarm for a brown taxi, license plate MO 29-6342. Got it down? Will you put the radios on it? Listen, the dope I was cooking up was that it was her that croaked Doc Burton. By God, if I ever get my hands on her. . . . I'm not excited. Okay, Inspector, thanks."

I got up and went to open a window and damn near fell out. The way I felt I was sure of two things: first, that if my head went on like that much longer it would blow up, and second, that Wolfe was dead. It seemed obvious that after that woman once got him into the taxi there was nothing for her to do with him but kill him. I stood holding onto the window jamb and leaned out enough so I could see below. There was the roadster. I had an idea that if I could get down there and get it started I could drive it all right.

I let go of the window jamb and started across the room, and just as I got to the hall the telephone rang. I could walk a little better. I went back to the telephone stand and picked up the receiver and said hello. A voice said, "Chelsea two, three nine two four? Please give me Mr. Chapin's apartment."

I nearly dropped the receiver. I said, "Who is this?"

The voice said, "This is someone who wishes to be connected with Mr. Chapin's apartment. Didn't I make that clear?"

I let the phone down and pressed it against one of my ribs for a moment, not wanting to make a fool of myself. Then I put it up to my mouth again. "Excuse me for asking who it is. It sounded like Nero Wolfe. Where are you?"

"Ah! Archie. After what Mrs. Chapin has told me, I scarcely expected to find you operating an apartment-house switchboard. I am much relieved. How are you feeling?"

"Swell. Wonderful. How are you?"

"Fairly comfortable. The jolting of that infernal taxicab . . . ah well. Archie. I would dislike very much to enter that taxicab again. If it is practical, get the sedan and come for me. I am at the Bronx River Inn, near the Woodlawn railroad station. You know where that is?"

"I know. I'll be there."

"No great hurry. I am fairly comfortable."

The click of his ringing off was in my ear.

I was damn good and sore. Certainly not at Wolfe, not even at myself, just sore. Sore because I had phoned Cramer an SOS, sore because Wolfe was to hell and gone faraway, and sore because it was up to me to get there and there was no doubt at all about the shape I was in. I picked up the phone and called Steve at the garage on Tenth Avenue and told him to fill the sedan with gas and put it at the curb. Then I got my hat and made it to the hall, and on out to the elevator.

I DON'T believe yet that I drove the roadster from Perry Street to the garage but I got there, stopped out in front, and blew my horn. Steve came out. I told him he had to get in the sedan and drive me to the Bronx. He went inside, and I transferred to the sedan at the curb. Pretty soon he came back and we shoved off. I told him where to go and let my head fall back against the cushion, but I didn't dare to let my eyes shut. My window was down and the cold air slapped me, and it seemed we were going a million miles a minute in a swift sweeping circle.

After a while Steve said, "Here we are, mister."

We had stopped. I grunted and lifted my head. I had a feeling the Bronx River Inn had come to us instead of us to it. Steve asked, "Can you navigate?"

"Sure." I set my jaw, and opened the door and climbed out.

In the main room a few customers were scattered at tables here and there. The customer I was looking for was in the far corner. Dora Chapin was facing him, with her back to me. I could see the bandages on her neck as I walked over there.

Wolfe nodded at me. "Good evening, Archie. You have met Mrs. Chapin. Sit down. You don't look as if standing was very enjoyable." He lifted his glass of beer and took a couple of swallows. I sat down. He asked me if I wanted some milk and I shook my head. He said, "By putting me in touch with Mrs. Chapin, you have brought us to the solution of our problem. Mrs. Chapin has been kind enough—"

That was the last I heard. The only other thing I remembered was that a tight wire which had been stretched between my temples, holding them together, suddenly parted with a twang.

XII

MONDAY morning when I woke up I saw Doc Vollmer standing there beside me.

He grinned. "I just stopped in to see how it went with what I pumped into you last night."

It struck me that the room seemed full of light. "What time is it?"

"Quarter to twelve."

"No!" I twisted to see the clock. "Holy murder!" I jerked myself upright, and someone jabbed a thousand ice picks into my skull. I put my hands up to it and tried moving it slowly. I said to Vollmer, "What's this I've got here, my head?"

He laughed. "It'll be all right."

"And it's noon." I slid to my feet and started for the bathroom. "Look out, I might run into you."

He laughed again and beat it.

I made it as snappy as I could with my dizziness, and went downstairs hanging onto the banister.

Wolfe, in his chair, looked up and said, "But, Archie. Should you be up?"

"Yeah. Not only should I be up, I should have been up. You know how it is, I'm a man of action."

His cheeks unfolded. "And I, of course, am supersedentary. A comical interchange of roles, that you rode home last evening with your head on my lap all the way. But we can pursue these amenities another time. Now there is business. Could you take some notes, and break your fast with our lunch? . . . Good. I spoke on the telephone this morning with the district attorney himself. It has been arranged that I shall see Mr. Chapin at the Tombs at two thirty this afternoon. You will remember that on Saturday evening I was beginning to dictate to you the confession of Paul Chapin, when we were interrupted by news from Fred Durkin.

If you will turn to that page we can go on. I'll have to have it by two o'clock."

So as it turned out I didn't eat lunch with Wolfe and Hibbard. The dictating wasn't done until nearly one, and I had the typing to do. I wanted this typed just right, this document that Paul Chapin was to sign, and with my head I had to take my time and concentrate.

When Wolfe came into the office at a quarter to two I was getting the three copies clipped into brown folders. He took them and started on the instructions for my afternoon. He explained that he had asked for a driver from the garage because I would be busy with other things. He also explained that on account of the possibility of visitors he had procured from Hibbard a promise that he would stay in his room until dinnertime.

Fritz came to the door and said the car was there. Wolfe told him he would be ready in a few minutes.

What gave me a new idea of the dimensions of Wolfe's nerve was the disclosure that a good part of the arrangements had been completed for a meeting of the league, in the office that evening at nine o'clock. Before he had seen Chapin at all! Wolfe had gone ahead and telephoned Boston and Philadelphia and Washington, and six or eight of them in New York, and the meeting was on. My job was to get in touch with the others and ensure as full an attendance as we could get. Just before he left he told me to go see Mrs. Burton and dictated two questions to ask her. Fritz was standing there holding his coat. Wolfe said, "And I was almost forgetting that our guests will be thirsty. Fritz, put the coat down and come here, and we shall see what we need. Archie, if you don't mind you had better start, you should be back by three. . . . Let us see, Fritz. I noticed last week that Mr. Cabot prefers Aylmer's soda—"

I walked to the garage for the roadster, and the sharp air glistened in my lungs. After I got the car out into the light I looked it over and couldn't find a scratch on it. Then I got back in and headed toward Ninetieth Street.

Wolfe had said that both of the questions I was to ask Mrs.

Burton were quite important. The first was simple: Did Dr. Burton telephone Paul Chapin between 6:50 and 7:00 Saturday evening and ask him to come to see him?

The second was more complicated: At 6:30 Saturday evening a pair of gray gloves was lying on the table in the Burton foyer. Were the gloves removed between then and 7:20 by anyone in the apartment?

I got a break. Everybody was home. Rose had me wait in the drawing room and Mrs. Burton came to me there. The first question took about nine seconds; the answer was no, definitely. Dr. Burton had done no telephoning after 6:30 Saturday evening. The second question required more time. Mrs. Burton herself had not been in the foyer between the time she returned home, around six, and 7:33, when the sound of the shots had taken her there on the run. She said she had left no gloves on that table, and certainly had removed none. She sent for Rose, and I asked her if she had removed a pair of gloves from the foyer table between 6:30 and 7:20 Saturday evening.

Rose looked at Mrs. Burton instead of me. "No, ma'am, I didn't take the gloves. But Mrs. Chapin—" She hesitated.

I said, "You saw some gloves there. When?"

"When I went to let Mrs. Chapin in."

"Did Mrs. Chapin take them?"

"No, sir. That's when I noticed them, when she picked them up. She picked them up and then put them down again."

"You didn't go back later and get them?"

"No, sir, I didn't."

That settled that.

It was after three when I got back to the office, and I got busy on the phone. There were eight names left for me that Wolfe hadn't been able to get. He had told me the line to take, that we were prepared to mail our bills to our clients, the signers of the memorandum, but that before doing so we would like to explain our position to them in a body and receive their approval. Which again spoke fairly well for Wolfe's nerve, inasmuch as our clients knew damn well that it was the cops who had grabbed Chapin for Burton's murder and that we had had about as much to do with it as the lions in front of the New York Public Library.

While I was on the trail of Roland Erskine, the actor, the phone rang. I answered, and it was Wolfe. "Archie? What luck at Mrs. Burton's?"

"Burton didn't phone, and nobody took any gloves."

"But perhaps the maid saw them?"

"Oh. You knew that too. She did. She saw Mrs. Chapin pick them up and put them down again."

"Excellent. I am telephoning because I have just made a promise and I wish to redeem it without delay. Take Mr. Chapin's box from the cabinet, wrap it carefully, and convey it to his apartment and deliver it to Mrs. Chapin."

"Okay. Did you get the confession signed?"

"I did. But I forgot to say, before you wrap Mr. Chapin's box take out a pair of gloves, gray leather, and keep them."

I hung up. The fat devil had put it over again.

Wolfe had said without delay, so I wrapped the box up and drove down to Perry Street with it, removing a pair of gloves first in accordance with instructions. At 203 I went to the elevator man and said to him, "Take this package up to Mrs. Chapin on the fifth floor. Then come back and I'll give you a quarter."

So I kept Wolfe's promise for him and got the package delivered without running any unnecessary risk of being invited in for tea. Then I beat it back home to resume at the telephone. I only got two of the remaining three members, but a telegram had come from Boston saying that Collard and Gaines would be there, and Mollison was coming down from New Haven.

When Wolfe appeared around 6:30 he was lugging a stack of books and I saw they were Paul Chapin's novels. He put them on his desk and sat down and rang for beer.

He gave me some instructions for the evening, and then I observed that it was about time I got acquainted with the mystery of the pair of gloves on the foyer table. To my surprise he agreed with me.

610

He said, "That was the contribution of Mrs. Chapin. She arrived at the Burton apartment, as you know, at six thirty. The maid called Rose let her in. As she passed through the foyer she saw a pair of gloves on the table, and she stopped to pick them up. She says she intended to take them in to Mrs. Burton, but it would not be uncharitable to surmise that she had in mind starting a new treasure box for her husband. She gives two reasons for returning the gloves to the table: that the maid was looking at her, and that the gloves seemed heavier than any she had known Mrs. Burton to wear. At any rate, she left them there. And when she went through the foyer, alone, on the way out, the gloves were gone."

"I see. And that proves she didn't croak Burton."

"It does. And it identifies the murderer. If factual corroboration is needed of Mrs. Chapin's innocence, which seems unlikely, it can be established that at half past seven she was receiving a summons from a policeman at Park Avenue and Fiftieth Street for passing a red light."

"I suppose you got her confidence by promising her orchids."

"I got her confidence by telling her the truth, that the conviction of her husband for murder would cost me many thousands of dollars. She had been convinced, as was Chapin himself, that I was responsible for framing him, and that you did the killing of Dr. Burton, I merely devised it. Mrs. Chapin, believing that, seized an opportunity. With you and Pitney Scott fast asleep, she went through your pockets, took his cap and jacket, and drove the taxicab here. She handed an envelope to Fritz at the door and returned to the cab. She had written a note that was brief and quite clear: 'Archie Goodwin will be dead in two hours unless you get in my taxi and go where I drive you.' And it was signed with her name, Dora Chapin. What persuaded me was the presence in the envelope of the leather case you had seemed to like."

He paused for a glass of beer, and resumed. "The only distressing aspect of the episode came from Mrs. Chapin's romantic idea of what constitutes a remote and secluded spot. I lowered the glass between us and shouted at the back of her ear that if she did not stop within three minutes I would call for help at every visible human being. I convinced her. She turned into a byroad and soon stopped under a clump of trees.

"This will amuse you. She had a weapon. A kitchen knife! By the way, that carving she exhibited to us last Wednesday was done on her own initiative; her husband disapproved. At that time the game was still one of establishing Mr. Chapin in the minds of his friends as a dangerous and murderous fellow, without involving him in any demonstrable guilt. At all events, her purpose was to force me to reveal the skulduggery by which her husband had been entrapped."

"Yeah. And?"

He drank beer. "Nothing much. After I had explained the situation to her, we discussed it. It seemed pointless to continue our conference in that cold, forbidding spot, and besides, when I learned what had happened to you I thought it best to reach a telephone with as little delay as possible. . . . Ah! Mr. Hibbard, I trust the long afternoon has been fairly tolerable."

Hibbard walked in, looking a little groggy, still wearing my brown necktie. Behind him came Fritz, to announce dinner.

XIII

THEY piled in early. By nine o'clock ten of them had arrived. Four of them I hadn't seen before: Collard and Gaines from Boston, Irving from Philadelphia, and Professor Mollison of Yale. Mike Ayers, stony sober on arrival, helped me get drinks around. At nine sharp Leopold Elkus joined the throng; I had no idea what Wolfe had told him to get him there. More came, among them Augustus Farrell, who had phoned on Saturday that he was back from Philadelphia and had landed the commission for Mr. Allenby's library.

There were fifteen of them present at a quarter past nine, which was the time Wolfe had told me he would make his entrance.

It was a good entrance all right. He came three paces in and stood there, until they had all turned to look at him and the talking had stopped. He said, "Good evening, gentlemen." Then he faced the door and nodded at Fritz. Fritz moved aside, and Andrew Hibbard walked in.

That started the first uproar. Pratt and Mike Ayers were the quickest to react. They both yelled "Andy!" and jumped for him. Others followed. They encircled him, shouted at him, grabbed his hands, and pounded him on the back.

Wolfe had eluded the stampede. He had got to his desk and lowered himself into his chair, and Fritz had brought him beer. I looked at him, and was glad I did, for it wasn't often he felt like winking at me and I wouldn't have wanted to miss it. The commotion went on a while longer. Then Cabot and Farrell began shooing them into chairs, and they subsided.

Wolfe started the ball rolling. He sat pretty straight, his chin down, his eyes open on them.

"Gentlemen. Thank you for being here this evening. Even if we should later come to disagreement, we are all glad that Mr. Hibbard is with us. Mr. Goodwin and I are gratified that we were able to play the Stanley to his Livingstone."

Wolfe took some papers from his drawer. "I have here, gentlemen, a copy of the memorandum of our agreement. One of my undertakings was to remove from you all apprehension of the person or persons responsible for the disappearance of Andrew Hibbard. I take it that that has been accomplished? You have no fear of Mr. Hibbard himself? Good. Then that much is done." He paused to look them over, face by face, and went on. "For the rest, it will be necessary to read you a document." He put the memorandum down and picked up another paper, sheets clipped to a brown paper jacket.

"This, gentlemen, is dated today and signed with the name of Paul Chapin. At the top it is headed, CONFESSION OF PAUL CHAPIN REGARDING THE DEATHS OF WILLIAM R. HARRISON AND EUGENE DREYER AND THE WRITING AND DISPATCHING OF CERTAIN INFORMATIVE AND THREATENING VERSES. It reads as follows—"

Cabot, the lawyer, butted in. "Mr. Wolfe. Of course this is interesting, but in view of what has happened is it necessary?"

"Quite." Wolfe didn't look up. "If you will permit me:

. "I, Paul Chapin, of 203 Perry Street, New York City, hereby confess that I was in no way concerned in the death of Judge William R. Harrison. To the best of my knowledge and belief his death was accidental.

"I further confess that I was in no way concerned in the death of Eugene Dreyer. To the best of my knowledge and belief he committed suicide.

"I further confess—"

Julius Adler's mild sarcastic voice took the air. "This is drivel. Chapin has maintained throughout—"

Wolfe stopped him, and all of them. "Gentlemen! Please. If you will withhold comments until the end."

Drummond squeaked, "Let him finish," and Wolfe continued:

"I further confess that the verses received by certain persons on three separate occasions were composed, typed, and mailed by me. They were intended to convey the information that I had killed Harrison, Dreyer, and Hibbard, and that it was my purpose to kill others. That ends my confession. The rest is explanation, which I offer at Nero Wolfe's request.

"The idea of the verses, which came to me after Harrison's death, was at first only one of the fantasies which occupy a mind accustomed to invention. I composed them. They were good, at least for one purpose, and they worked beyond my expectations.

"Three months later the death of Dreyer offered another opportunity, which of course was irresistible. The second verses were even more successful than the first ones. I need not try to describe the satisfaction it gave me to fill with terror the insolent breasts which for so many years had bulged their pity at me.

"I supplemented the effect of the verses verbally, with certain of my friends, whenever a safe opportunity offered, and this was more fertile with Andrew Hibbard than with anyone else. It ended by his becoming so terrified that he ran away. As soon as I learned of his disappearance I decided to take advantage of it. I sent the third verses. The result was nothing short of magnificent, indeed it proved to be too magnificent. I had never heard of Nero Wolfe. I went to his office that evening for the pleasure of seeing my friends, and to look at Wolfe. I saw that he was acute and intuitive, and that my diversion was probably at an end. An attempt was made by my wife to impress Wolfe, but it failed.

"There are other points that might be touched upon, but I believe none of them require explanation.

"I will only add that I am not responsible for the literary quality of this document. It was written by Nero Wolfe.

Paul Chapin."

Wolfe finished, dropped the confession to the table, and leaned back. "Now, gentlemen. If you wish to comment."

There were mumblings. Ferdinand Bowen, the stockbroker, spoke up: "It seems to me Adler has commented for all of us. Drivel."

Wolfe nodded. "I can understand that viewpoint. But my position is that I have met my obligations under the memorandum and that the payments are due."

"My dear sir!" It was Nicholas Cabot. "Preposterous."

"I think not. What I undertook to do was to remove your fear of Paul Chapin. Andrew Hibbard is here. As for the deaths of Harrison and Dreyer, it should have been obvious to all of you that Chapin had nothing to do with them. You had known him all his mature life. Have you read his books? Why are they so concerned with murder? Why does every page have its hymn to violence? The truth is that Paul Chapin has murdered all of you, and will doubtless do so again, in his books. Let him, gentlemen, and go on breathing.

"Consult the memorandum. There remains only the matter of the warnings. Chapin admits he sent them, and tells you how and why and where. There will be no sequels, and even if there were I should not suppose they would alarm you."

Wolfe drank beer, and wiped his lips. He resumed: "I offer you the security I undertook to get for you, but you are no longer interested in it because you already have something just as good: namely, that Chapin is in the Tombs charged with the murder of Dr. Burton and can no longer threaten you. . . . Mr. Cabot, I ask you as a lawyer, is that exposition of the situation correct?"

"I think . . ." Cabot pursed his lips, and after a moment went on, "I think it is remarkably ingenious rubbish."

Wolfe nodded. "I take it, gentlemen, that Mr. Cabot's opinion is approximately unanimous. Yes? . . . So it becomes necessary for me to introduce a new consideration. This: that Chapin did not kill Dr. Burton, that I can establish his innocence, and that if tried he will be acquitted."

That started the second uproar. Leopold Elkus jumped out of his chair and grabbed Wolfe's hand and began pumping it. He was yelling something about justice and gratitude and how great and grand Wolfe was. The others, busy with their own remarks, didn't pay any attention to him.

Wolfe lifted his hand at them. "Gentlemen! If you please. I seem to have startled you. You of course expect me to support my statement with evidence. I offer these items. First, at a few minutes before seven on Saturday evening Paul Chapin received a telephone call from Dr. Burton, who asked Chapin to come to see him immediately. A little later Chapin left to go to Ninetieth Street, arriving there at seven thirty. But there was something wrong with that telephone call, namely, that his wife says that Dr. Burton never made it. It seems likely, therefore, that there was somewhere a third person who was taking upon himself the functions of fate. Yet Mr. Chapin told his wife of the telephone call, and she told me; and there is the switchboard operator at the Chapin apartment house, who relayed the call.

"Item two. Consider the details of what is supposed to have happened in the Burton foyer. Dr. Burton took the pistol from his desk and went to the foyer. Chapin, there waiting for him, took the pistol from him, shot him four times, turned out the light, threw the pistol on the floor, and then got down on his hands and knees to look for it in the dark. What a picture! According to the story of Mrs. Burton and of the maid, Dr. Burton had been in the foyer not more than six seconds, possibly less, when the shots were fired. Burton was a good-sized man, and powerful. Chapin is small and cannot even walk without support. Well . . . I am now going

to count six seconds for you. One . . . two . . . three . . . four . . .
five . . . six. That was six seconds. In that space of time the crippled
Chapin is supposed to have got the gun from Burton, shot him,
dropped the gun, hobbled to the switch to turn off the light, and
hobbled back to the table to fall to the floor. In your juridical
capacity, gentlemen, what do you think of that?"

Leopold Elkus stood up and glared at the group, then said
loudly and clearly, "Anyone who ever believed that is no better
than a cretin." He looked at Wolfe. "I shall have apologies for you,
sir, when this kindergarten is over." He sat down.

"Thank you, Dr. Elkus. Item three, for what conceivable reason
did Chapin turn out the light? The actions even of a murderer
should be in some degree explicable, and to believe that Chapin
shot Burton and then hobbled to the wall to turn out the light is
to believe nonsense."

George Pratt spoke up. "I'll tell you what I believe, Wolfe. I believe we hired you to get Paul Chapin into trouble, not out of it."

Nicholas Cabot demanded, "What does Chapin have to say?
Did he shoot or didn't he?"

Wolfe shook his head and his cheeks unfolded a little. "Oh no,
Mr. Cabot. It is possible that Mr. Chapin will have to tell his story
on the witness stand in his own defense. You can hardly expect
me to disclose it in advance to those who may consider themselves
his enemies."

"What the hell, no one would believe him anyway." It was
Ferdinand Bowen now. "He'd cook up a tale, of course."

Wolfe turned his eyes on Bowen and sighed. "Well, gentlemen,
I have presented my case. I could offer further points for your
consideration: for instance, the likelihood that if Chapin intended
to kill Dr. Burton he would have gone provided with a weapon.
Also, Chapin's constitutional incapacity for any form of violent
action, which I discovered through his novels. Surely I have offered
enough to show you the purely literary nature of Chapin's attempt
at vengeance. The question is this, have I satisfactorily performed
my undertaking? I think I have. But it is you who are to decide it,
by vote. Archie. If you will please call the names."

They began to talk. Bowen muttered to his neighbor, Gaines, the banker from Boston, "Pretty slick, but he's a damn fool if he thinks we'll fall for it."

Cabot said to Wolfe, "I shall vote no. In case Chapin does get an acquittal, and evidence is presented—"

Wolfe nodded at me, and I started the roll call. On the list I was using they were alphabetical.

"Julius Adler."

"No. I would like to say—"

Wolfe cut him off. "The no is sufficient. Proceed, Archie."

"Michael Ayers."

"Yes!" He made it emphatic.

"Ferdinand Bowen."

"No."

When it was even, seven for and seven against, and just one more to go, I knew what it would be before I called it. It was George Pratt, the Tammany bird who had tried to get Inspector Cramer worried about his four grand. I said it:

"George R. Pratt."

"No."

I counted them over to make sure, and turned to Wolfe. "Seven yeses and eight noes."

They all began talking. Wolfe leaned back and shut his eyes. Two or three of them directed questions at him, but he kept his eyes closed and paid no attention. Finally he picked up a paper-weight and rapped on the desk. They looked around and began to quiet down.

He spoke. "Gentlemen. I must again ask your indulgence—"

But Cabot was feeling his oats. He broke in, snappy: "We have voted. According to the memorandum, that settles it."

Wolfe got snappy too. "It settles that vote, sir. It does not settle the destiny of the human race. If you wish to leave us, of course you may, but we would still have a quorum without you. Please heed me. I have a specific reason to hope that one of you will decide to change your vote. Well, gentlemen? I shall give you one minute."

They shook their heads. One or two spoke, but mostly they were silent, gazing at Wolfe. He had taken out his watch and kept his eyes on it. At the end of the minute he returned it to his pocket and looked up.

He sighed. "Then I must proceed to my second appeal. This time, Mr. Bowen, it is to you alone. I ask you to change your vote to yes. You of course know why. Will you vote yes?"

They all looked at the stockbroker. Including me. He damn near stuttered, shooting it back at Wolfe. "Certainly not. Why should I?" His mouth stayed open; he thought he would talk some more, and then he thought he wouldn't.

Wolfe sighed again. "Mr. Bowen, you are a simpleton. Gentlemen, I would like to explain briefly why I have not done sooner what I am going to do now. There were two reasons: because I am not fond of interfering in affairs that are not my concern, and because it would be expensive for me. To be exact, it will cost me twelve hundred dollars, the amount of Mr. Bowen's payment under the memorandum. Besides that, as I have said, it was none of my business. I will hunt anyone down if you pay me enough. But no one has offered to pay me for discovering the murderer of Dr. Burton. By exposing him and delivering him to justice I shall lose twelve hundred dollars, but I shall ensure the collection of a larger sum. Now. Mr. Farrell, would you mind moving to another chair? And you, Archie, take the seat Mr. Farrell is vacating, next to Mr. Bowen."

I moved. My eyes hadn't left Bowen since Wolfe had asked him to vote yes, and now all eyes were on him. Wolfe had him plenty perplexed.

Wolfe was now on the phone. Nobody on the chairs moved a hair while he was talking.

"Inspector Cramer? This is Nero Wolfe. Good evening, sir. Inspector, I would like you to do me a favor. Will you send a man to my office—perhaps two would be better—for the murderer of Dr. Loring A. Burton? I have him here. . . . Of course, proof; what good is certainty without proof? . . . By all means, if you wish to come yourself. Certainly."

He pushed the phone back, and Bowen jumped up. His knees were trembling, and so were his little lady-hands. I took advantage of his being up to feel his rear for a gun, and my hands startled him. He forgot what he was going to say to Wolfe and turned on me, and by God he hauled off and kicked me on the shin. I got up and grabbed him and pushed him back into his chair and observed to him, "You try another friendly gesture like that and I'll paste you one."

Drummond, who had been sitting next to Bowen, on the other side, moved away. Several others got up.

Wolfe said, "Sit down, gentlemen. Archie, kindly bring Mr. Bowen closer. If it is necessary to prod him, you may do so."

I stood up and told the stockbroker to find his feet. He didn't move and he didn't look up; his hands were in his lap twisting in a knot and there were various colors distributed over his face and neck. I said, "Get a move on or I'll move you." I grabbed his collar and jerked him up. I admit he was pitiful.

He looked around at them, and tried to keep the quaver out of his voice. "Fellows. You understand why . . . if I don't say anything now to . . . to this ridiculous . . ."

He couldn't finish it anyhow, so I pulled a chair up and sat him in it, then I perched on the edge of Wolfe's desk. Wolfe turned to face him.

"Mr. Bowen. Just now you used the word ridiculous; may I borrow it from you? You are the most ridiculous murderer I have ever met. You planned the most hazardous of all crimes as if you were devising a harmless parlor game.

"You stole a large sum from Dr. Burton through his account with your firm. You found that he had discovered the theft, and on Saturday you went to his apartment to appeal to him. Burton left you in his study, to ask his wife if she cared enough for Estelle Bowen to make a big sacrifice for her, and his wife said no. During his absence you anticipated his answer, got his automatic pistol from the drawer of his desk, and put it in your pocket. You knew that he kept a gun there because he said so in this room a week ago tonight. Would you like a drink?"

Bowen made no reply or movement.

Wolfe was going on: "Soon you left, at twenty minutes past six. You went alone to the foyer and the Burtons thought you had gone. You went to the telephone to call Paul Chapin. You had your gloves in your hand, and you laid them on the table. But before your call had gone through you were interrupted by the sound of someone approaching in the drawing room. Alarmed, you ran for the curtained closet next to the light switch and the double doors. You got behind the curtain before Miss Burton, the daughter of the house, came through, leaving the apartment.

"You realized that you had left your gloves lying on the table. You would need them to keep fingerprints from the gun—and, by the way, did it not occur to you that the phone would show prints? But you did not at once dash out for your gloves, because almost at once you heard the maid going to open the entrance door. She was letting in Dora Chapin, who had arrived to do Mrs. Burton's hair.

"Mr. Paul Chapin was out Saturday afternoon. This morning the switchboard operator at 203 Perry Street told me that there was a phone call for Mr. Chapin fifteen or twenty minutes before he arrived home. So it seems likely that about six forty you emerged from your hiding place, got the gloves, and tried the phone again, but there was no answer from the Chapin apartment. You returned to the closet, and fifteen minutes later you tried again. Of course you did not know that this phone call of yours, at about five minutes to seven, happened to coincide with Mr. Chapin's entrance into the hall of 203 Perry Street; the switchboard operator called to him, and he answered at the switchboard itself, so the operator heard it. Apparently you imitated Dr. Burton's voice with some success, for Mr. Chapin was deceived. He went upstairs to his apartment for a few minutes, and then came down to take a cab to Ninetieth Street.

"After phoning Chapin you returned again to the closet. In about thirty-five minutes Chapin arrived and was admitted by the maid. You kept your ears keen and heard him sit down in a chair that would turn his back to you; you had your gloves on, and the gun in your right hand ready for action. You heard Dr. Burton's steps crossing the drawing room, and the instant the sound came of his hand on the doorknob, you moved. Your left fingers found the light switch at the edge of the curtain, and the foyer was in darkness except for the dim light that wandered through the door from the drawing room that Dr. Burton had opened. You jumped from the closet, shoved Chapin off his chair onto the floor—not difficult with a cripple, was it, Mr. Bowen? By that time Dr. Burton had approached and was quite close when you shot him, and there was enough light from the drawing-room door for you to tell where his middle was. You pulled the trigger and held it for four shots, then threw the gun to the floor—and made your exit, after closing the double door. In the hall you ran to the stairs, and ran down five flights to the basement, and out the service entrance. You calculated that the guilt of Paul Chapin would be so obvious that no questions would be asked of anyone who might have seen you in the building.

"Now, Mr. Bowen, you made many mistakes, but none so idiotic as your sole reliance on Chapin's obvious guilt, for that one was the father of all the others. Why in the name of heaven didn't you turn on the light again as you went out? And why didn't you wait until Chapin and Burton had talked a minute or two before you acted? Another inexcusable thing was your carelessness in leaving the gloves on the table. I know; you were so sure that they would be sure of Chapin that you thought nothing else mattered. I tell you this, sir, your exposure is a credit to no one, least of all to me."

Wolfe stopped abruptly and turned to ring Fritz for beer. Bowen was just sitting in his chair, shaking all over.

Leopold Elkus came up and stood three feet from Bowen, staring at him. Mike Ayers appeared with a drink; he held it out to me and I took it and drank it. Andrew Hibbard came up to me and said, "I hope now I will be permitted to telephone my niece. May I make the call upstairs?"

I said, "By all means."

Nicholas Cabot went up to Wolfe and said, "I'm going, Mr.

Wolfe. I want to say there's no reason why you shouldn't get that twelve hundred dollars from Bowen. It's a legal obligation. If you'd like me to handle the collection, I'd be glad to do it and expect no fee. Let me know."

XIV

THREE days later I was sitting at my desk bending my thoughts towards a little relaxation in the shape of an afternoon movie. Wolfe was in his chair, leaning back with his eyes shut. Fritz came to the door and said, "A man to see you, sir. Mr. Paul Chapin." Wolfe opened his eyes to a slit, and nodded. Chapin hobbled in and the strong light from the windows gave me a better look at him than I had ever had. He gave me only half a glance as he thumped across to Wolfe's desk. I moved a chair around for him.

"Good morning, Mr. Chapin." Wolfe nearly opened his eyes. "You won't be seated? I beg you . . . thanks. It gives me genuine discomfort to see people stand. Allow me to congratulate you on your appearance. If I had spent three days in the Tombs prison, as you did, I would be nothing but a wraith, a tattered remnant."

Chapin perched on the edge of the chair with his stick upright in front. He said, "I sit for a moment only, to relieve you of discomfort. I came for the pair of gloves which you removed from my box."

"A disappointment." Wolfe sighed. "I was thinking you had taken the trouble to call to convey your gratitude for my saving you from the electric chair."

Chapin's lips twisted. "I am as grateful as you would expect me to be. So we needn't waste time on that. May I have the gloves?"

"You may. Archie, if you please."

I got the gloves from a drawer of my desk and handed them across to Wolfe. He leaned back and sighed again.

"You know, Mr. Chapin, I never got to use them. I retained them, from your box, to demonstrate a point Monday evening by showing how nearly they fitted Mr. Bowen, thus explaining how

623

your wife could mistake Mr. Bowen's gloves for a pair of Mrs. Burton's; but since he wilted like a dendrobium with root rot there was no occasion for it. Now"—Wolfe wiggled a finger—"I don't expect you to believe this, but it is nevertheless true that I kept them because I wanted to see you."

Paul Chapin, saying nothing, reached out for the gloves. Wolfe pulled them back a little. "Just a morsel of patience, Mr. Chapin. I wanted to see you because I had an apology to make."

"I came for my gloves. You may keep the apology."

"But, my dear sir!" Wolfe wiggled a finger again. "Permit me at least to apologize for forging your name."

Chapin lifted his brows. Wolfe turned to me. "A copy of the confession, Archie."

Chapin read the confession twice. He first glanced at it, ran through it rapidly, then took a squint at Wolfe, and read the confession all over again, not nearly so fast. Then he tossed it over to the desk. "Fantastic," he declared. "Set down that way, prosaically, baldly, it sounds fantastic. Doesn't it?"

Wolfe nodded. "It struck me, Mr. Chapin, that you went to a great deal of trouble for a pitifully meager result. Of course, you understand that I required this document for the impression it would make on your friends, and knowing the impossibility of persuading you to sign it for me, I was compelled to write your name myself. That is what I wish to apologize for. Here are your gloves, sir. I take it that my apology is accepted."

The cripple took the gloves, felt them, put them in his inside breast pocket, grabbed the arms of his chair, and raised himself. He stood leaning on his stick.

"You knew I wouldn't sign such a document? How did you know that?"

"Because I had read your books. I had seen you. I was acquainted with your—let us say, your indomitable spirit."

"You have another name for it?"

"Many. Your appalling infantile contumacy. It got you a crippled leg. It got you a wife. It very nearly got you two thousand volts of electricity."

Chapin smiled. "So you read my books. Read the next one. I'm putting you in it—a leading character."

"Naturally." Wolfe opened his eyes. "And of course I die violently. I warn you, Mr. Chapin, I resent that. I actively resent it. . . ." He was talking to no one; or at least, merely to the back of a cripple who was hobbling to the door.

At the threshold Chapin turned for a moment, long enough for us to see him smile and hear him say, "You will die, sir, in the most abhorrent manner conceivable to an appalling infantile imagination. I promise you."

He went.

Later I could permit myself a grin at the thought of the awful fate in store for Nero Wolfe, but for the moment I had my mind back on Monday afternoon. I remembered that when I had left to call on Mrs. Burton, Wolfe had been there discussing soda water with Fritz, and when I returned he had gone, and so had the sedan. But not to the Tombs to see Paul Chapin. He had never left the house. The sedan had gone back to the garage, and Wolfe to his room, with his coat and hat and stick and gloves, to drink beer in his easy chair. And at a quarter to four it was from his room that he had telephoned me to take the box to Mrs. Chapin, to give him a chance to fake a return. Of course Fritz had been in on it, so he had fooled me too. And Hibbard shooed off to the third floor for the afternoon . . .

They had made a monkey of *me* all right.

I said to Wolfe, "I had intended to go to a movie after lunch, but now I can't. I've got work ahead. I've got to figure out certain suggestions to make to Paul Chapin for his next book. My head is full of ideas."

"Indeed." Wolfe's bulk came forward to permit him to ring for beer. "Archie." He nodded at me gravely. "Your head full of ideas? Even my death by violence is not too high a price for so rare and happy a phenomenon as that."

The Third Man

The Third Man

BY

Graham Greene

ILLUSTRATED BY CECIL VIEWEG

This haunting crime-and-suspense mystery
is set in Vienna, smashed and bombed
out at the close of war and under
four-power occupation. Into this bleak scene
comes Rollo Martins, at the invitation of his
old friend Harry Lime. But instead,
he finds himself at Harry's funeral,
and apart from his shock at this, he senses something
faintly false about it: *Is* Harry actually dead?
His search for the truth leads Martins into danger
and a desperate chase through the most
hidden recesses of the stricken city.

   Graham Greene has a distinguished
reputation not only for suspense stories
but as the author of highly regarded serious
novels such as *The Power and the Glory* and
Brighton Rock. The Third Man was made
into a classic motion picture,
directed by Carol Reed.

1

ONE never knows when the blow may fall. When I saw Rollo Martins first I made this note on him for my security police files: "In normal circumstances a cheerful fool. Drinks too much and may cause a little trouble. Whenever a woman passes raises his eyes and makes some comment, but I get the impression that really he'd rather not be bothered. Has never really grown up and perhaps that accounts for the way he worshipped Lime." I wrote there that phrase "in normal circumstances" because I met him first at Harry Lime's funeral. It was February, and the gravediggers had been forced to use electric drills to open the frozen ground in Vienna's Central Cemetery. It was as if even nature were doing its best to reject Lime, but we got him in at last and laid the earth back on him like bricks. He was vaulted in, and Rollo Martins walked quickly away as though his long gangly legs wanted to break into a run, and the tears of a boy ran down his thirty-five-year-old cheeks. Rollo Martins believed in friendship, and that was why what happend later was a worse shock to him than it would have been to you or me (you because you would have put it down to an illusion and me because at once a rational explanation—however wrongly—would have come to my mind).

If only he had come to tell me then, what a lot of trouble would have been saved.

If you are to understand this strange rather sad story you must have an impression at least of the background—the smashed dreary city of Vienna divided up in zones among the four powers; the Russian, the British, the American, the French zones, regions marked only by notice boards, and in the center of the city, surrounded by the Ring with its heavy public buildings and its prancing statuary, the Innere Stadt under the control of all four powers. In this once fashionable Innere Stadt each power in turn, for a month at a time, takes, as we call it, "the chair," and becomes responsible for security; at night, if you were fool enough to waste your Austrian schillings on a nightclub, you would be fairly certain to see the International Patrol at work—four military police, one from each power, communicating with each other, if they communicated at all, in the common language of their enemy. I never knew Vienna between the wars, and I am too young to remember the old Vienna with its Strauss music and its bogus easy charm; to me it is simply a city of undignified ruins which turned that February into great glaciers of snow and ice. The Danube was a gray flat muddy river a long way off across the second bezirk, the Russian zone, where the Prater lay smashed and desolate and full of weeds, only the Great Wheel revolving slowly over the foundations of merry-go-rounds like abandoned millstones, the rusting iron of smashed tanks which nobody had cleared away, the frost-nipped weeds where the snow was thin. I haven't enough imagination to picture it as it had once been, any more than I can picture Sacher's Hotel as other than a transit hotel for English officers or see the Kärntnerstrasse as a fashionable shopping street instead of a street which exists, most of it, only at eye level, repaired up to the first story. A Russian soldier in a fur cap goes by with a rifle over his shoulder, and men in overcoats sip ersatz coffee in the windows of the Old Vienna. This was roughly the Vienna to which Rollo Martins came on February seventh last year. I have reconstructed the affair as best I can from my own files and from what Martins told me. It is as accurate as I can make it—I haven't invented a line of dialogue, though I can't vouch for Martins' memory; an ugly story if you leave out the girl: grim and sad and unrelieved if it were not for that absurd episode of the British Cultural Relations Society lecturer.

2

A BRITISH subject can still travel if he is content to take with him only five English pounds which he is forbidden to spend abroad, but if Rollo Martins had not received an invitation from Lime he would not have been allowed to enter Austria, which counts still as occupied territory. Lime had suggested that Martins might write up the business of looking after the international refugees, and although it wasn't Martins' usual line, he had consented. It would give him a holiday, and he badly needed a holiday after the incident in Dublin and the other incident in Amsterdam; he always tried to dismiss women as "incidents," things that simply happen to him without any will of his own, acts of God in the eyes of insurance agents. He had a haggard look when he arrived in Vienna and a habit of looking over his shoulder that for a time made me suspicious of him until I realized that he went in fear that one of, say, six people might turn up unexpectedly. He told me vaguely that he had been mixing his drinks—that was another way of putting it.

Rollo Martins' usual line was the writing of cheap paper-covered Westerns under the name of Buck Dexter. His public was large but unremunerative. He couldn't have afforded Vienna if Lime had not offered to pay his expenses when he got there out of some vaguely described propaganda fund. Lime could also, he said, keep him supplied with paper bafs—the only currency in use from a penny upwards in British hotels and clubs. So it was with exactly five unusable pound notes that Martins arrived in Vienna.

An odd incident had occurred at Frankfurt, where the plane from London grounded for an hour. Martins was eating a hamburger in the American canteen (a kindly airline supplied the passengers with a voucher for sixty-five cents' worth of food) when a man he could recognize from twenty feet away as a journalist approached his table.

"You Mr. Dexter?" he asked.

"Yes," Martins said, taken off his guard.

"You look younger than your photographs," the man said. "Like to make a statement? I represent the local forces paper here. We'd like to know what you think of Frankfurt."

"I only touched down ten minutes ago."

"Fair enough," the man said. "What about views on the American novel?"

"I don't read them," Martins said.

"The well-known acid humor," the journalist said. He pointed at a small gray-haired man with two protruding teeth, nibbling a bit of bread. "Happen to know if that's Carey?"

"No. What Carey?"

"J. G. Carey of course."

"I've never heard of him."

"You novelists live out of the world. He's my real assignment," and Martins watched him make across the room for the great Carey, who greeted him with a false headline smile, laying down his crust. Dexter wasn't the man's assignment, but Martins couldn't help feeling a certain pride—nobody had ever before referred to him as a novelist; and that sense of pride and importance carried him over the disappointment when Lime was not there to meet him at the airport. We never get accustomed to being less important to other people than they are to us—Martins felt the little jab of dispensability, standing by the bus door, watching the snow come sifting down, so thinly and softly that the great drifts among the ruined buildings had an air of permanence, as though they were not the result of this meager fall, but lay, forever, above the line of perpetual snow.

There was no Lime to meet him at the Hotel Astoria where the bus landed him, and no message—only a cryptic one for Mr. Dexter from someone he had never heard of called Crabbin. "We expected you on tomorrow's plane. Please stay where you are. On the way round. Hotel room booked," but Rollo Martins wasn't the kind of man who stayed around. If you stayed around in a hotel lounge sooner or later incidents occurred; one mixed one's drinks. I can hear Rollo Martins saying to me now, "I've done with incidents. No more incidents," before he plunged head first into the most serious incident of all. There was always a conflict in Rollo Martins—between the absurd Christian name and the sturdy Dutch (four generations back) surname. Rollo looked at every woman that passed, and Martins renounced them forever. I don't know which of them wrote the Westerns.

Martins had been given Lime's address and he felt no curiosity about the man called Crabbin; it was too obvious that a mistake had been made, though he didn't yet connect it with the conversation at Frankfurt. Lime had written that he could put Martins up in his own flat, a large apartment on the edge of Vienna that had been requisitioned from a Nazi owner. Lime could pay for the taxi when he arrived, so Martins drove straight away to the building lying in the third (British) zone. He kept the taxi waiting while he mounted to the third floor.

How quickly one becomes aware of silence even in so silent a city as Vienna with the snow steadily settling. Martins hadn't reached the second floor before he was convinced that he would not find Lime there, but the silence was deeper than just absence —it was as if he would not find Harry Lime anywhere in Vienna, and, as he reached the third floor and saw the big black bow over the door handle, anywhere in the world at all. Of course it might have been a cook who had died, a housekeeper, anybody but Harry Lime, but he knew—he felt he had known twenty stairs down—that Lime, the Lime he had hero-worshipped now for twenty years, since the first meeting in a grim school corridor with a cracked bell ringing for prayers, was gone. Martins wasn't wrong, not entirely wrong. After he had rung the bell half a dozen times a small man with a sullen expression put his head out from another flat and told him in a tone of vexation, "It's no use ringing like that. There's nobody there. He's dead."

"Herr Lime?"

"Herr Lime of course."

Martins said to me later, "At first it didn't mean a thing. It was just a bit of information, like those paragraphs in *The Times* they call 'News in Brief.' I said to him, 'When did it happen? How?' "

"He was run over by a car," the man said. "Last Thursday." He added sullenly, as if really this were none of his business, "They are burying him this afternoon. You've only just missed them."

"Them?"

"Oh, a couple of friends and the coffin."

"Wasn't he in hospital?"

"There was no sense in taking him to hospital. He was killed here on his own doorstep—instantaneously. The right-hand mud-guard struck him on his shoulder and bowled him over in front like a rabbit."

It was only then, Martins told me, when the man used the word "rabbit," that the dead Harry Lime came alive, became the boy with the gun which he had shown Martins the means of "borrowing"; a boy starting up among the long sandy barrows of Brickworth Common saying, "Shoot, you fool, shoot! There," and the rabbit limped to cover, wounded by Martins' shot.

"Where are they burying him?" he asked the stranger on the landing.

"In the Central Cemetery. They'll have a hard time of it in this frost."

He had no idea how to pay for his taxi, or indeed where in Vienna he could find a room in which he could live for five English pounds, but that problem had to be postponed until he had seen the last of Harry Lime. He drove straight out of town into the suburb (British zone) where the Central Cemetery lay. One passed through the Russian zone to reach it, and took a shortcut through the American zone, which you couldn't mistake because of the ice-cream parlors in every street. The trams ran along the high wall of the Central Cemetery, and for a mile on the other side of the rails stretched the monumental masons and the market gardeners—an apparently endless chain of gravestones waiting for owners and wreaths waiting for mourners.

Martins had not realized the size of this huge snowbound park where he was making his last rendezvous with Lime. It was as if Harry had left a message to him, "Meet me in Hyde Park," without specifying a spot between the Achilles statue and Lancaster Gate; the avenues of graves, each avenue numbered and lettered, stretched out like the spokes of an enormous wheel; they drove for a half mile towards the west, then turned and drove a half mile north, turned south. . . . The snow gave the great pompous family headstones an air of grotesque comedy; a toupee of snow slipped sideways over an angelic face, a saint wore a heavy white mustache, and a shako of snow tipped at a drunken angle over the bust of a superior civil servant called Wolfgang Gottman. Even this cemetery was zoned between the powers: the Russian zone was marked by huge statues of armed men, the French by rows of anonymous wooden crosses and a torn tired tricolor flag. Then Martins remembered that Lime was a Catholic and was unlikely to be buried in the British one for which they had been vainly searching. So back they drove through the heart of a forest where the graves lay like wolves under the trees, winking white eyes under the gloom of the evergreens. Once from under the trees emerged a group of three men in strange eighteenth-century black and silver uniforms with three-cornered hats, pushing a kind of barrow: they crossed a ride in the forest of graves and disappeared again.

It was just chance that they found the funeral in time—one patch in the enormous park where the snow had been shoveled aside and a tiny group was gathered, apparently bent on some very private business. A priest was speaking, his words coming secretively through the thin patient snow, and a coffin was on the point of being lowered into the ground. Two men in lounge suits stood at the graveside; one carried a wreath that he obviously had forgotten to drop onto the coffin, for his companion nudged his elbow so that he came to with a start and dropped the flowers. A girl stood a little way away with her hands over her face, and I stood twenty yards away by another grave, watching with relief the last of Lime and noticing carefully who was there—just a man in a mackintosh I was to Martins. He came up to me and said, "Could you tell me who they are burying?"

"A fellow called Lime," I said, and was astonished to see the tears start to this stranger's eyes: he didn't look like a man who wept, nor was Lime the kind of man whom I thought likely to have mourners—genuine mourners with genuine tears. There was the girl of course, but one excepts women from all such generalizations.

Martins stood there, till the end, close beside me. He said to me later that as an old friend he didn't want to intrude on these newer ones—Lime's death belonged to them, let them have it. He was under the sentimental illusion that Lime's life—twenty years of it anyway—belonged to him. As soon as the affair was over—I am not a religious man and always feel a little impatient with the fuss that surrounds death—Martins strode away on his long gangly legs that always seemed likely to get entangled together, back to his taxi. He made no attempt to speak to anyone, and the tears now were really running, at any rate the few meager drops that any of us can squeeze out at our age.

One's file, you know, is never quite complete; a case is never really closed, even after a century, when all the participants are dead. So I followed Martins: I knew the other three: I wanted to know the stranger. I caught him up by his taxi and said, "I haven't any transport. Would you give me a lift into town?"

"Of course," he said. I knew the driver of my jeep would spot me as we came out and follow us unobtrusively. As we drove away I noticed he never looked behind—it's nearly always the fake mourners and the fake lovers who take that last look, who wait waving on platforms, instead of clearing quickly out, not looking back. Is it perhaps that they love themselves so much and want to keep themselves in the sight of others, even of the dead?

I said, "My name's Calloway."

"Martins," he said.

"You were a friend of Lime?"

"Yes." Most people in the last week would have hesitated before they admitted quite so much.

"Been here long?"

"I only came this afternoon from England. Harry had asked me to stay with him. I hadn't heard."

"Bit of a shock?"

"Look here," he said, "I badly want a drink, but I haven't any cash—except five pounds sterling. I'd be awfully grateful if you'd stand me one."

It was my turn to say "Of course." I thought for a moment and told the driver the name of a small bar in the Kärntnerstrasse. I didn't think he'd want to be seen for a while in a busy British bar full of transit officers and their wives. This bar—perhaps because it was exorbitant in its prices—seldom had more than one self-occupied couple in it at a time. The trouble was too that it really only had one drink—a sweet chocolate liqueur that the waiter improved at a price with cognac—but I got the impression that Martins had no objection to any drink so long as it cast a veil over the present, and the past. On the door was the usual notice saying the bar opened at six till ten, but one just pushed the door and walked through the front rooms. We had a whole small room to ourselves; the only couple were next door, and the waiter, who knew me, left us alone with some caviar sandwiches. It was lucky that we both knew that I had an expense account.

Martins said over his second quick drink, "I'm sorry, but he was the best friend I ever had."

I couldn't resist saying, knowing what I knew, and because I was anxious to vex him—one learns a lot that way—"That sounds like a cheap novelette."

He said quickly, "I write cheap novelettes."

I had learned something anyway. Until he had had a third drink I was under the impression that he wasn't an easy talker, but I felt fairly certain that he was one of those who turn unpleasant after their fourth glass.

I said, "Tell me about yourself—and Lime."

"Look here," he said, "I badly need another drink, but I can't keep on scrounging on a stranger. Could you change me a pound or two into Austrian money?"

"Don't bother about that," I said and called the waiter. "You can treat me when I come to London on leave. You were going to tell me how you met Lime?"

The glass of chocolate liqueur might have been a crystal, the

way he looked at it and turned it this way and that. He said, "It was a long time ago. I don't suppose anyone knows Harry the way I do," and I thought of the thick file of agents' reports in my office, each claiming the same thing. I believe in my agents; I've sifted them all very thoroughly.

"How long?"

"Twenty years—or a bit more. I met him my first term at school. I can see the place. I can see the notice board and what was on it. I can hear the bell ringing. He was a year older and knew the ropes. He put me wise to a lot of things." He took a quick dab at his drink and then turned the crystal again as if to see more clearly what there was to see. He said, "It's funny. I can't remember meeting any woman quite as well."

"Was he clever at school?"

"Not the way they wanted him to be. But what things he did think up! He was a wonderful planner. I was far better at subjects like History and English than Harry, but I was a hopeless mug when it came to carrying out his plans." He laughed: he was already beginning, with the help of drink and talk, to throw off the shock of the death. He said, "I was always the one who got caught."

"That was convenient for Lime."

"What the hell do you mean?" he asked. Alcoholic irritation was setting in.

"Well, wasn't it?"

"That was my fault, not his. He could have found someone cleverer if he'd chosen, but he liked me. He was endlessly patient with me." Certainly, I thought, the child is father to the man, for I too had found him patient.

"When did you see him last?"

"Oh, he was over in London six months ago for a medical congress. You know he qualified as a doctor, though he never practiced. That was typical of Harry. He just wanted to see if he could do a thing and then he lost interest. But he used to say that it often came in handy." And that too was true. It was odd how like the Lime he knew was to the Lime I knew: it was only that he looked at Lime's image from a different angle or in a different light. He said, "One of the things I liked about Harry was his humor." He gave a grin which took five years off his age. "I'm a buffoon, I like playing the silly fool, but Harry had real wit. You know, he could have been a first-class light composer if he had worked at it."

He whistled a tune—it was oddly familiar to me. "I always remember that. I saw Harry write it. Just in a couple of minutes on the back of an envelope. That was what he always whistled when he had something on his mind. It was his signature tune." He whistled the tune a second time, and I knew then who had written it—of course it wasn't Harry. I nearly told him so, but what was the point? The tune wavered and went out. He stared down into his glass, drained what was left, and said, "It's a damned shame to think of him dying the way he did."

"It was the best thing that ever happened to him," I said.

He didn't take in my meaning at once: he was a little hazy with the drinks. "The best thing?"

"Yes."

"You mean there wasn't any pain?"

"He was lucky in that way, too."

It was my tone of voice and not my words that caught Martins' attention. He asked gently and dangerously—I could see his right hand tighten—"Are you hinting at something?"

There is no point at all in showing physical courage in all situations: I eased my chair far enough back to be out of reach of his fist. I said, "I mean that I had his case completed at police headquarters. He would have served a long spell—a very long spell—if it hadn't been for the accident."

"What for?"

"He was about the worst racketeer who ever made a dirty living in this city."

I could see him measuring the distance between us and deciding that he couldn't reach me from where he sat. Rollo wanted to hit out, but Martins was steady, careful. Martins, I began to realize, was dangerous. I wondered whether after all I had made a complete mistake: I couldn't see Martins being quite the mug that Rollo had made out. "You're a policeman?" he asked.

"Yes."

"I've always hated policemen. They are always either crooked or stupid."

"Is that the kind of books you write?"

I could see him edging his chair round to block my way out. I caught the waiter's eye and he knew what I meant—there's an advantage in always using the same bar for interviews.

Martins brought out a surface smile and said gently, "I have to call them sheriffs."

"Been in America?" It was a silly conversation.

"No. Is this an interrogation?"

"Just interest."

"Because if Harry was that kind of racketeer, I must be one too. We always worked together."

"I daresay he meant to cut you in—somewhere in the organization. I wouldn't be surprised if he had meant to give you the baby to hold. That was his method at school—you told me, didn't you? And, you see, the headmaster was getting to know a thing or two."

"You are running true to form, aren't you? I suppose there was some petty racket going on with petrol and you couldn't pin it on anyone, so you've picked a dead man. That's just like a policeman. You're a real policeman, I suppose?"

"Yes, Scotland Yard, but they've put me into a colonel's uniform when I'm on duty."

He was between me and the door now. I couldn't get away from the table without coming into range; I'm no fighter, and he had six inches of advantage anyway. I said, "It wasn't petrol."

"Tires, saccharin—why don't you policemen catch a few murderers for a change?"

"Well, you could say that murder was part of his racket."

He pushed the table over with one hand and made a dive at me with the other; the drink confused his calculations. Before he could try again my driver had his arms round him. I said, "Don't treat him roughly. He's only a writer with too much to drink in him."

"Be quiet, can't you, sir," my driver said. He had an exaggerated sense of officer-class. He would probably have called Lime "sir."

"Listen, Callaghan, or whatever your bloody name is . . ."

"Calloway. I'm English, not Irish."

"I'm going to make you look the biggest bloody fool in Vienna. There's one dead man you aren't going to pin your unsolved crimes on."

"I see. You're going to find me the real criminal? It sounds like one of your stories."

"You can let me go, Callaghan. I'd rather make you look the

fool you are than black your bloody eye. You'd only have to go to bed for a few days with a black eye. But when I've finished with you you'll leave Vienna."

I took out a couple of pounds' worth of bafs and stuck them in his breast pocket. "These will see you through tonight," I said, "and I'll make sure they keep a seat for you on tomorrow's London plane."

"You can't turn me out. My papers are in order."

"Yes, but this is like other cities: you need money here. If you change sterling on the black market I'll catch up on you inside twenty-four hours. Let him go."

Rollo Martins dusted himself down. He said, "Thanks for the drinks."

"That's all right."

"I'm glad I don't have to feel grateful. I suppose they were on expenses?"

"Yes."

"I'll be seeing you again in a week or two when I've got the dope." I knew he was angry; I didn't believe then that he was serious. I thought he was putting over an act to cheer up his self-esteem.

"I might come and see you off tomorrow."

"I shouldn't waste your time. I won't be there."

"Paine here will show you the way to Sacher's. You can get a bed and dinner there. I'll see to that."

He stepped to one side as though to make way for the waiter and slashed out at me. I just avoided him, but stumbled against the table. Before he could try again Paine had landed on him on the mouth. He went bang over in the alleyway between the tables and came up bleeding from a cut lip. I said, "I thought you promised not to fight."

He wiped some of the blood away with his sleeve and said, "Oh, no, I said I'd rather make you a bloody fool. I didn't say I wouldn't give you a black eye as well."

I had had a long day and I was tired of Rollo Martins. I said to Paine, "See him safely into Sacher's. Don't hit him again if he behaves," and, turning away from both of them towards the inner bar (I deserved one more drink), I heard Paine say respectfully to the man he had just knocked down, "This way, sir. It's only just around the corner."

3

WHAT happened next I didn't hear from Paine but from Martins a long time afterwards, reconstructing the chain of events that did indeed—though not quite in the way he had expected—prove me to be a fool. Paine simply saw him to the head porter's desk and explained there, "This gentleman came in on the plane from London. Colonel Calloway says he's to have a room." Having made that clear, he said, "Good evening, sir," and left. He was probably a bit embarrassed by Martins' bleeding lip.

"Had you already got a reservation, sir?" the porter asked.

"No. No, I don't think so," Martins said in a muffled voice holding his handkerchief to his mouth.

"I thought perhaps you might be Mr. Dexter. We had a room reserved for a week for Mr. Dexter."

Martins said, "Oh, I am Mr. Dexter." He told me later that it occurred to him that Lime might have engaged him a room in that name because perhaps it was Buck Dexter and not Rollo Martins who was to be used for propaganda purposes. A voice said at his elbow, "I'm so sorry you were not met at the plane, Mr. Dexter. My name's Crabbin."

The speaker was a stout middle-aged young man with a natural tonsure and one of the thickest pairs of horn-rimmed glasses that Martins had ever seen. He went apologetically on, "One of our chaps happened to ring up Frankfurt and heard you were on the plane. HQ made one of their usual foolish mistakes and wired you were not coming. Something about Sweden, but the cable was badly mutilated. Directly I heard from Frankfurt I tried to meet the plane, but I just missed you. You got my note?"

Martins held his handkerchief to his mouth and said obscurely, "Yes. Yes?"

"May I say at once, Mr. Dexter, how excited I am to meet you?"

"Good of you."

"Ever since I was a boy, I've thought you the greatest novelist of our century."

Martins winced. It was painful opening his mouth to protest. He took an angry look instead at Mr. Crabbin, but it was impossible to suspect that young man of a practical joke.

"You have a big Austrian public, Mr. Dexter, both for your originals and your translations. Especially for *The Curved Prow*, that's my own favorite."

Martins was thinking hard. "Did you say—room for a week?"

"Yes."

"Very kind of you."

"Mr. Schmidt here will give you tickets every day, to cover all meals. But I expect you'll need a little pocket money. We'll fix that. Tomorrow we thought you'd like a quiet day—to look about."

"Yes."

"Of course any of us are at your service if you need a guide. Then the day after tomorrow in the evening there's a little quiet discussion at the Institute—on the contemporary novel. We thought perhaps you'd say a few words just to set the ball rolling, and then answer questions."

Martins at that moment was prepared to agree to anything, to get rid of Mr. Crabbin and also to secure a week's free board and lodging; and Rollo, of course, as I was to discover later, had always been prepared to accept any suggestion—for a drink, for a girl, for a joke, for a new excitement. He said now, "Of course, of course," into his handkerchief.

"Excuse me, Mr. Dexter, have you got toothache? I know a very good dentist."

"No. Somebody hit me, that's all."

"Good God. Were they trying to rob you?"

"No, it was a soldier. I was trying to punch his bloody colonel in the eye." He removed the handkerchief and gave Crabbin a

view of his cut mouth. He told me that Crabbin was at a complete
loss for words. Martins couldn't understand why because he had
never read the work of his great contemporary, Benjamin Dexter:
he hadn't even heard of him. I am a great admirer of Dexter, so
that I could understand Crabbin's bewilderment. Dexter has been
ranked as a stylist with Henry James, but he has a wider feminine
streak than his master—indeed his enemies have sometimes described his subtle, complex, wavering style as old-maidish. For a
man still just on the right side of fifty his passionate interest in
embroidery and his habit of calming a not very tumultuous mind
with tatting—a trait beloved by his disciples—certainly to others
seems a little affected.

"Have you ever read a book called *The Lone Rider of Santa
Fe?*"

"No, I don't think so."

Martins said, "This lone rider had his best friend shot
by the sheriff of a town called Lost Claim Gulch. The story is how
he hunted that sheriff down—quite legally—until his revenge was
completed."

"I never imagined you reading Westerns, Mr. Dexter," Crabbin
said, and it needed all Martins' resolution to stop Rollo saying,
"But I write them."

"Well, I'm gunning just the same way for Colonel Callaghan."

"Never heard of him."

"Heard of Harry Lime?"

"Yes," Crabbin said cautiously, "but I didn't really know
him."

"I did. He was my best friend."

"I shouldn't have thought he was a very—literary character."

"None of my friends are."

Crabbin blinked nervously behind the horn-rims. He said with
an air of appeasement, "He was interested in the theater though.
A friend of his—an actress, you know—is learning English at the
Institute. He called once or twice to fetch her."

"Young or old?"

"Oh, young, very young. Not a good actress in my opinion."

Martins remembered the girl by the grave with her hands over her face. He said, "I'd like to meet any friend of Harry's."

"She'll probably be at your lecture."

"Austrian?"

"She claims to be Austrian, but I suspect she's Hungarian. She works at the Josefstadt. I wouldn't be surprised if Lime had helped her with her papers. She calls herself Schmidt. Anna Schmidt. You can't imagine a young English actress calling herself Smith, can you? And a pretty one, too. It always struck me as a bit too anonymous to be true."

Martins felt he had got all he could from Crabbin, so he pleaded tiredness, a long day, promised to ring up in the morning, accepted ten pounds' worth of bafs for immediate expenses, and went to his room. It seemed to him that he was earning money rapidly—twelve pounds in less than an hour.

He was tired: he realized that when he stretched himself out on his bed in his boots. Within a minute he had left Vienna far behind him and was walking through a dense wood, ankle-deep in snow. An owl hooted, and he felt suddenly lonely and scared. He had an appointment to meet Harry under a particular tree, but in a wood so dense as this how could he recognize any one tree from the rest? Then he saw a figure and ran towards it: it whistled a familiar tune and his heart lifted with the relief and joy at not after all being alone. Then the figure turned and it was not Harry at all—just a stranger who grinned at him in a little circle of wet slushy melted snow, while the owl hooted again and again. He woke suddenly to hear the telephone ringing by his bed.

A voice with a trace of foreign accent—only a trace—said, "Is that Mr. Rollo Martins?"

"Yes." It was a change to be himself and not Dexter.

"You wouldn't know me," the voice said unnecessarily, "but I was a friend of Harry Lime."

It was a change too to hear anyone claim to be a friend of Harry's. Martins' heart warmed towards the stranger. He said, "I'd be glad to meet you."

"I'm just round the corner at the Old Vienna."

"Wouldn't you make it tomorrow? I've had a pretty awful day with one thing and another."

"Harry asked me to see that you were all right. I was with him when he died."

"I thought—" Rollo Martins said and stopped. He had been going to say "I thought he died instantaneously," but something suggested caution. He said instead, "You haven't told me your name."

"Kurtz," the voice said. "I'd offer to come round to you, only, you know, Austrians aren't allowed in Sacher's."

"Perhaps we could meet at the Old Vienna in the morning."

"Certainly," the voice said, "if you are *quite* sure that you are all right till then."

"How do you mean?"

"Harry had it on his mind that you'd be penniless." Rollo Martins lay back on his bed with the receiver to his ear and thought: Come to Vienna to make money. This was the third stranger to stake him in less than five hours. He said cautiously, "Oh, I can carry on till I see you." There seemed no point in turning down a good offer till he knew what the offer was.

"Shall we say eleven then at the Old Vienna in the Kärntner-strasse? I'll be in a brown suit and I'll carry one of your books."

"That's fine. How did you get hold of one?"

"Harry gave it to me." The voice had enormous charm and reasonableness, but when Martins had said good-night and rung off, he couldn't help wondering how it was that if Harry had been so conscious before he died he had not had a cable sent to stop him. Hadn't Callaghan too said that Lime had died instantaneously—or without pain, was it?—or had he himself put the words into Callaghan's mouth? It was then that the idea first lodged firmly in Martins' mind that there was something wrong about Lime's death, something the police had been too stupid to discover. He tried to discover it himself with the help of two cigarettes, but he fell asleep without his dinner and with the mystery still unsolved. It had been a long day, but not quite long enough for that.

4

"WHAT I disliked about him at first sight," Martins told me, "was his toupee. It was one of those obvious toupees—flat and yellow, with the hair cut straight at the back and not fitting close. There *must* be something phony about a man who won't accept baldness gracefully. He had one of those faces too where the lines have been put in carefully, like a makeup, in the right places—to express charm, whimsicality, lines at the corners of the eyes. He was made up to appeal to romantic schoolgirls."

This conversation took place some days later—he brought out his whole story when the trail was nearly cold. When he made that remark about the romantic schoolgirls I saw his rather hunted eyes focus suddenly. It was a girl—just like any other girl, I thought—hurrying by outside my office in the driving snow.

"Something pretty?"

He brought his gaze back and said, "I'm off that forever. You know, Calloway, a time comes in a man's life when he gives up all that sort of thing. . . ."

"I see. I thought you were looking at a girl."

"I was. But only because she reminded me for a moment of Anna—Anna Schmidt."

"Who's she? Isn't she a girl?"

"Oh, yes, in a way."

"What do you mean, in a way?"

"She was Harry's girl."

"Are you taking her over?"

"She's not that kind, Calloway. Didn't you see her at his funeral? I'm not mixing my drinks any more. I've got a hangover to last me a lifetime."

"You were telling me about Kurtz," I said.

It appeared that Kurtz was sitting there, making a great show of reading *The Lone Rider of Santa Fe*. When Martins sat down at his table he said with indescribably false enthusiasm, "It's wonderful how you keep the tension."

"Tension?"

"Suspense. You're a master at it. At the end of every chapter one's left guessing. . . ."

"So you were a friend of Harry's," Martins said.

"I think his best," but Kurtz added with the smallest pause in which his brain must have registered the error, "except you of course."

"Tell me how he died."

"I was with him. We came out together from the door of his flat and Harry saw a friend he knew across the road—an American called Cooler. He waved to Cooler and started across the road to him when a jeep came tearing round the corner and bowled him over. It was Harry's fault really—not the driver's."

"Somebody told me he died instantaneously."

"I wish he had. He died before the ambulance could reach us though."

"He could speak then?"

"Yes. Even in his pain he worried about you."

"What did he say?"

"I can't remember the exact words, Rollo—I may call you Rollo, mayn't I? He always called you that to us. He was anxious that I should look after you when you arrived. See that you were looked after. Get your return ticket for you." In telling me, Martins said, "You see I was collecting return tickets as well as cash."

"But why didn't you cable to stop me?"

"We did, but the cable must have missed you. What with censorship and the zones, cables can take anything up to five days."

"There was an inquest?"

"Of course."

"Did you know that the police have a crazy notion that Harry was mixed up in some racket?"

"No. But everyone in Vienna is. We all sell cigarettes and exchange schillings for bafs and that kind of thing."

"The police meant something worse than that."

"They get rather absurd ideas sometimes," the man with the toupee said cautiously.

"I'm going to stay here till I prove them wrong."

Kurtz turned his head sharply and the toupee shifted very very slightly. He said, "What's the good? Nothing can bring Harry back."

"I'm going to have that police officer run out of Vienna."

"I don't see what you can do."

"I'm going to start working back from his death. You were there and this man Cooler and the chauffeur. You can give me their addresses."

"I don't know the chauffeur's."

"I can get it from the coroner's records. And then there's Harry's girl . . ."

Kurtz said, "It will be painful for her."

"I'm not concerned about her. I'm concerned about Harry."

"Do you know what it is that the police suspect?"

"No. I lost my temper too soon."

"Has it occurred to you," Kurtz said gently, "that you might dig up something—well, discreditable to Harry?"

"I'll risk that."

"It will take a bit of time—and money."

"I've got time and you were going to lend me some money, weren't you?"

"I'm not a rich man," Kurtz said. "I promised Harry to see you were all right and that you got your plane back. . . ."

"You needn't worry about the money—or the plane," Martins said. "But I'll make a bet with you—in pounds sterling—five pounds against two hundred schillings—that there's something queer about Harry's death."

It was a shot in the dark, but already he had this firm instinctive sense that there was something wrong, though he hadn't yet attached the word "murder" to the instinct. Kurtz had a cup of coffee halfway to his lips and Martins watched him. The shot apparently went wide; an unaffected hand held the cup to the mouth and Kurtz drank, a little noisily, in long sips. Then he put down the cup and said, "How do you mean—queer?"

"It was convenient for the police to have a corpse, but wouldn't it have been equally convenient, perhaps, for the real racketeers?" When he had spoken he realized that after all Kurtz had not been unaffected by his wild statement: hadn't he been frozen into caution and calm? The hands of the guilty don't necessarily tremble; only in stories does a dropped glass betray agitation. Tension is more often shown in the studied action. Kurtz had drunk his coffee as though nothing had been said.

"Well—" he took another sip "—of course I wish you luck, though I don't believe there's anything to find. Just ask me for any help you want."

"I want Cooler's address."

"Certainly. I'll write it down for you. Here it is. In the American zone."

"And yours?"

"I've already put it—underneath—in the Russian zone."

He rose, giving one of his studied Viennese smiles, the charm carefully painted in with a fine brush in the little lines about the mouth and eyes. "Keep in touch," he said, "and if you need help . . . but I still think you are very unwise." He touched *The Lone Rider*. "I'm so proud to have met you. A master of suspense," and one hand smoothed the toupee, while another, passing softly over the mouth, brushed out the smile as though it had never been.

5

MARTINS sat on a hard chair just inside the stage door of the Josefstadt Theatre. He had sent up his card to Anna Schmidt after the matinee, marking it "a friend of Harry's." An arcade of little windows, with lace curtains and the lights going out one after another, showed where the artists were packing up for home, for the cup of coffee without sugar, the roll without butter to sustain them for the evening performance. It was like a little street built indoors for a film set, but even indoors it was cold, even cold to a man in a heavy overcoat, so that Martins rose and walked up and down, underneath the little windows. He felt, he said, a little like a Romeo who wasn't sure of Juliet's balcony.

He had had time to think: he was calm now, Martins not Rollo was in the ascendant. When a light went out in one of the windows and an actress descended into the passage where he walked, he didn't even turn to take a look. He was done with all that. He thought, Kurtz is right. They are all right. I'm behaving like a romantic fool. I'll just have a word with Anna Schmidt, a word of commiseration, and then I'll pack and go. He had quite forgotten, he told me, the complication of Mr. Crabbin.

A voice over his head called "Mr. Martins," and he looked up at the face that watched him from between the curtains a few feet above his head. It wasn't beautiful, he firmly explained to me, when I accused him of once again mixing his drinks. Just an honest face; dark hair and eyes which in that light looked brown; a wide forehead, a large mouth which didn't try to charm. No danger anywhere, it seemed to Rollo Martins, of that sudden reckless moment when the scent of hair or a hand against the side alters life. She said, "Will you come up, please? The second door on the right."

There are some people, he explained to me carefully, whom one recognizes instantaneously as friends. You can be at ease with them because you know that never, never will you be in danger. "That was Anna," he said, and I wasn't sure whether the past tense was deliberate or not.

Unlike most actresses' rooms this one was almost bare; no wardrobe packed with clothes, no clutter of cosmetics and greasepaints: a dressing gown on the door, one sweater he recognized from Act II on the only easy chair, a tin of half-used paints and grease. A kettle hummed softly on a gas ring. She said, "Would you like a cup of tea? Someone sent me a packet last week—sometimes the Americans do, instead of flowers, you know, on the first night."

"I'd like a cup," he said, but if there was one thing he hated it was tea. He watched her while she made it; made it, of course, all wrong: the water not on the boil, the teapot unheated, too few leaves. She said, "I never quite understand why English people like tea so."

He drank his cupful quickly like a medicine and watched her gingerly and delicately sip at hers. He said, "I wanted very much to see you. About Harry."

It was the dreadful moment; he could see her mouth stiffen to meet it.

"Yes?"

"I had known him twenty years. I was his friend. We were at school together, you know, and after that—there weren't many months running when we didn't meet. . . ."

She said, "When I got your card, I couldn't say no. But there's nothing really for us to talk about, is there? Nothing."

"I wanted to hear—"

"He's dead. That's the end. Everything's over, finished. What's the good of talking?"

"We both loved him."

"I don't know. You can't know a thing like that—afterwards. I don't know anything anymore except—"

"Except?"

"That I want to be dead too."

Martins told me, "Then I nearly went away. What was the good of tormenting her because of this wild idea of mine? But instead I asked her one question, 'Do you know a man called Cooler?' "

"An American?" she asked. "I think that was the man who brought me some money when Harry died. I didn't want to take it, but he said Harry had been anxious—at the last moment."

"So he didn't die instantaneously?"

"Oh, no."

Martins said to me, "I began to wonder why I had got that idea so firmly into my head, and then I thought it was only the man in the flat who told me so—no one else. I said to her, 'He must have been very clear in his head at the end—because he remembered about me too. That seems to show that there wasn't really any pain.' "

"That's what I tell myself all the time."

"Did you see the doctor?"

"Once. Harry sent me to him. He was Harry's own doctor. He lived nearby, you see."

Martins suddenly saw in that odd chamber of the mind that constructs such pictures, instantaneously, irrationally, a desert place, a body on the ground, a group of birds gathered. Perhaps it was a scene from one of his own books, not yet written, forming at the gate of consciousness. Immediately it faded, he thought how odd that they were all there, just at that moment, all Harry's friends—Kurtz, the doctor, this man Cooler; only the two people who loved him seemed to have been missing. He said, "And the driver? Did you hear his evidence?"

"He was upset, scared. But Cooler's evidence exonerated him. No, it wasn't his fault, poor man. I've often heard Harry say what a careful driver he was."

"He knew Harry too?" Another bird flapped down and joined the others round the silent figure on the sand who lay face down. Now he could tell that it was Harry, by the clothes, by the attitude like that of a boy asleep in the grass at a playing field's edge, on a hot summer afternoon.

Somebody called outside the window, "Fräulein Schmidt."

She said, "They don't like one to stay too long. It uses up *their* electricity."

He had given up the idea of sparing her anything. He told her, "The police say they were going to arrest Harry. They'd pinned some racket on him."

She took the news in much the same way as Kurtz. "Everybody's in a racket."

"I don't believe he was in anything serious."

"No."

"But he may have been framed. Do you know a man called Kurtz?"

"I don't think so."

"He wears a toupee."

"Oh." He could tell that that struck home. He said, "Don't you think it was odd they were all there—at the death. Everybody knew Harry. Even the driver, the doctor . . ."

She said with hopeless calm, "I've thought that too, though I didn't know about Kurtz. I wondered whether they'd murdered him, but what's the use of wondering?"

"I'm going to get those bastards," Rollo Martins said.

"It won't do any good. Perhaps the police are right. Perhaps poor Harry got mixed up—"

"Fräulein Schmidt," the voice called again.

"I must go."

"I'll walk with you a bit of the way."

The dark was almost down; the snow had ceased for a while to fall, and the great statues of the Ring, the prancing horses, the chariots and the eagles, were gunshot gray with the end of evening light. "It's better to give up and forget," Anna said. The moony snow lay ankle-deep on the unswept pavements.

"Will you give me the doctor's address?"

They stood in the shelter of a wall while she wrote it down for him.

"And yours too?"

"Why do you want that?"

"I might have news for you."

"There isn't any news that would do any good now." He watched her from a distance board her tram, bowing her head against the wind, a little dark question mark on the snow.

6

AN AMATEUR detective has this advantage over the professional, that he doesn't work set hours. Rollo Martins was not confined to the eight-hour day: his investigations didn't have to pause for meals. In his one day he covered as much ground as one of my men would have covered in two, and he had this initial advantage over us, that he was Harry's friend. He was, as it were, working from inside, while we pecked at the perimeter.

Dr. Winkler was at home. Perhaps he would not have been at home to a police officer. Again Martins had marked his card with the sesame phrase: "A friend of Harry Lime's."

Dr. Winkler's waiting room reminded Martins of an antique shop—an antique shop that specialized in religious objets d'art. There were more crucifixes than he could count, none of later date probably than the seventeenth century. There were statues in wood and ivory. There were a number of reliquaries: little bits of bone marked with saints' names and set in oval frames on a background of tinfoil. If they were genuine, what an odd fate it was, Martins thought, for a portion of Saint Susanna's knuckle to come to rest in Dr. Winkler's waiting room. Even the high-backed hideous chairs looked as if they had once been sat in by cardinals. The room was stuffy, and one expected the smell of incense. In a small gold casket was a splinter of the True Cross. A sneeze disturbed him.

Dr. Winkler was the cleanest doctor Martins had ever seen. He was very small and neat, in a black tailcoat and a high stiff collar; his little black mustache was like an evening tie. He sneezed again: perhaps he was cold because he was so clean. He said, "Mr. Martins?"

An irresistible desire to sully Dr. Winkler assailed Rollo Martins. He said, "Dr. Winkle?"

"Dr. Winkler."

"You've got an interesting collection here."

"Yes."

"These saints' bones . . ."

"The bones of chickens and rabbits." Dr. Winkler took a large white handkerchief out of his sleeve rather as though he were a conjurer producing his country's flag, and blew his nose neatly and thoroughly twice, closing each nostril in turn. You expected him to throw away the handerkerchief after one use. "Would you mind, Mr. Martins, telling me the purpose of your visit? I have a patient waiting."

"We were both friends of Harry Lime."

"I was his medical adviser," Dr. Winkler corrected him and waited obstinately between the crucifixes.

"I arrived too late for the inquest. Harry had invited me out here to help him in something. I don't quite know what. I didn't hear of his death till I arrived."

"Very sad," Dr. Winkler said.

"Naturally, under the circumstances, I want to hear all I can."

"There is nothing I can tell you that you don't know. He was knocked over by a car. He was dead when I arrived."

"Would he have been conscious at all?"

"I understand he was for a short time, while they carried him into the house."

"In great pain?"

"Not necessarily."

"You are quite certain that it was an accident?"

Dr. Winkler put out a hand and straightened a crucifix. "I was not there. My opinion is limited to the cause of death. Have you any reason to be dissatisfied?"

The amateur has another advantage over the professional: he can be reckless. He can tell unnecessary truths and propound wild theories. Martins said, "The police had implicated Harry in a very serious racket. It seemed to me that he might have been murdered —or even killed himself."

661

"I am not competent to pass an opinion," Dr. Winkler said.

"Do you know a man called Cooler?"

"I don't think so."

"He was there when Harry was killed."

"Then of course I have met him. He wears a toupee."

"That was Kurtz."

Dr. Winkler was not only the cleanest, he was also the most cautious doctor that Martins had ever met. His statements were so limited that you could not for a moment doubt their veracity. He said, "There was a second man there." If he had to diagnose a case of scarlet fever he would, you felt, have confined himself to a statement that a rash was visible, that the temperature was so and so. He would never find himself in error at an inquest.

"Had you been Harry's doctor for long?" He seemed an odd man for Harry to choose—Harry who liked men with a certain recklessness, men capable of making mistakes.

"For about a year."

"Well, it's good of you to have seen me." Dr. Winkler bowed. When he bowed there was a very slight creak as though his shirt were made of celluloid. "I mustn't keep you from your patients any longer." Turning away from Dr. Winkler, he confronted yet another crucifix, the figure hanging with arms above the head: a face of elongated El Greco agony. "That's a strange crucifix," he said.

"Jansenist," Dr. Winkler commented and closed his mouth sharply as though he had been guilty of giving away too much information.

"Never heard the word. Why are the arms above the head?"

Dr. Winkler said reluctantly, "Because He died, in their view, only for the elect."

7

As I see it, turning over my files, the notes of conversations, the statements of various characters, it would have been still possible, at this moment, for Rollo Martins to have left Vienna safely. He had shown an unhealthy curiosity, but the disease had been checked at every point. Nobody had given anything away. The smooth wall of deception had as yet shown no real crack to his roaming fingers. When Rollo Martins left Dr. Winkler's he was in no danger. He could have gone home to bed at Sacher's and slept with a quiet mind. He could even have visited Cooler at this stage without trouble. No one was seriously disturbed. Unfortunately for him—and there would always be periods of his life when he bitterly regretted it—he chose to go back to Harry's flat. He wanted to talk to the little vexed man who said he had seen the accident—or had he really not said so much? There was a moment in the dark frozen street when he was inclined to go straight to Cooler, to complete his picture of those sinister birds who sat around Harry's body, but Rollo, being Rollo, decided to toss a coin and the coin fell for the other action, and the deaths of two men.

Perhaps the little man—who bore the name of Koch—had drunk a glass too much of wine, perhaps he had simply spent a good day at the office, but this time, when Rollo Martins rang his bell, he was friendly and quite ready to talk. He had just finished dinner and had crumbs on his mustache. "Ah, I remember you. You are Herr Lime's friend."

He welcomed Martins in with great cordiality and introduced him to a mountainous wife whom he obviously kept under very strict control. "Ah, in the old days I would have offered you a cup of coffee, but now—"

Martins passed round his cigarette case and the atmosphere of cordiality deepened. "When you rang yesterday I was a little abrupt," Herr Koch said, "but I had a touch of migraine and my wife was out, so I had to answer the door myself."

"Did you tell me that you had actually seen the accident?"

Herr Koch exchanged glances with his wife. "The inquest is over, Ilse. There is no harm. You can trust my judgment. The gentleman is a friend. Yes, I saw the accident, but you are the only one who knows. When I say that I saw it, perhaps I should say that I heard it. I heard the brakes put on and the sound of the skid, and I got to the window in time to see them carry the body to the house."

"But didn't you give evidence?"

"It is better not to be mixed up in such things. My office cannot spare me. We are short of staff, and of course I did not actually see—"

"But you told me yesterday how it happened."

"That was how they described it in the papers."

"Was he in great pain?"

"He was dead. I looked right down from my window here and I saw his face. I know when a man is dead. You see, it is, in a way, my business. I am the head clerk at the mortuary."

"But the others say that he did not die at once."

"Perhaps they don't know death as well as I do."

"He was dead, of course, when the doctor arrived. He told me that."

"He was dead at once. You can take the word of a man who knows."

"I think, Herr Koch, that you should have given evidence."

"One must look after oneself, Herr Martins. I was not the only one who should have been there."

"How do you mean?"

"There were three people who helped to carry your friend to the house."

"I know—two men and the driver."

"The driver stayed where he was. He was very much shaken, poor man."

"Three men . . ." It was as though suddenly, fingering that bare wall, his fingers had encountered not so much a crack perhaps but at least a roughness that had not been smoothed away by the careful builders.

"Can you describe the men?"

But Herr Koch was not trained to observe the living: only the man with the toupee had attracted his eyes—the other two were just men, neither tall nor short, thick nor thin. He had seen them from far above, foreshortened, bent over their burden; they had not looked up, and he had quickly looked away and closed the window, realizing at once the wisdom of not being seen himself.

"There was no evidence I could really give, Herr Martins."

No evidence, Martins thought, no evidence! He no longer doubted that murder had been done. Why else had they lied about the moment of death? They wanted to quiet with their gifts of money and their plane ticket the only two friends Harry had in Vienna. And the third man? Who was he?

He said, "Did you see Herr Lime go out?"

"No."

"Did you hear a scream?"

"Only the brakes, Herr Martins."

It occurred to Martins that there was nothing—except the word of Kurtz and Cooler and the driver—to prove that in fact Harry had been killed at that precise moment. There was the medical evidence, but that could not prove more than that he had died, say, within a half hour, and in any case the medical evidence was only as strong as Dr. Winkler's word: that clean controlled man creaking among his crucifixes.

"Herr Martins, it just occurs to me—you are staying in Vienna?"

"Yes."

"If you need accommodation and spoke to the authorities quickly, you might secure Herr Lime's flat. It is a requisitioned property."

"Who has the keys?"

"I have them."

"Could I see the flat?"

"Ilse, the keys."

Herr Koch led the way into the flat that had been Harry's. In the little dark hall there was still the smell of cigarette smoke— the Turkish cigarettes that Harry always smoked. It seemed odd that a man's smell should cling in the folds of curtains so long after the man himself had become dead matter, a gas, a decay. One light, in a heavily beaded shade, left them in semidarkness, fumbling for door handles.

The living room was completely bare—it seemed to Martins too bare. The chairs had been pushed up against the walls; the desk at which Harry must have written was free from dust or any papers. The parquet reflected the light like a mirror. Herr

Koch opened a door and showed the bedroom: the bed neatly made with clean sheets. In the bathroom not even a used razor blade indicated that a few days ago a living man had occupied it. Only the dark hall and the cigarette smell gave a sense of occupation.

"You see," Herr Koch said, "it is quite ready for a newcomer. Ilse has cleaned up."

That she certainly had done. After a death there should have been more litter left than this. A man can't go suddenly and unexpectedly on his longest journey without forgetting this or that, without leaving a bill unpaid, an official form unanswered, the photograph of a girl. "Were there no papers, Herr Koch?"

"Herr Lime was always a very tidy man. His wastepaper basket was full and his briefcase, but his friend fetched that away."

"His friend?"

"The gentleman with the toupee."

It was possible, of course, that Lime had not taken the journey so unexpectedly, and it occurred to Martins that Lime had perhaps hoped he would arrive in time to help. He said to Herr Koch, "I believe my friend was murdered."

"Murdered?" Herr Koch's cordiality was snuffed out by the word. He said, "I would not have asked you in here if I had thought you would talk such nonsense."

"All the same your evidence may be very valuable."

"I have no evidence. I saw nothing. I am not concerned. You must leave here at once, please. You have been very inconsiderate." He hustled Martins back through the hall; already the smell of the smoke was fading a little more. Herr Koch's last word before he slammed his own door was, "It's no concern of mine." Poor Herr Koch! We do not choose our concerns. Later, when I was questioning Martins closely, I said to him, "Did you see anybody at all on the stairs, or in the street outside?"

"Nobody." He had everything to gain by remembering some chance passerby, and I believed him. He said, "I noticed myself how quiet and dead the whole street looked. Part of it had been bombed, you know, and the moon was shining on the snow slopes.

It was so very silent. I could hear my own feet creaking in the snow."

"Of course it proves nothing. There is a basement where anybody who had followed you could have hidden."

"Yes."

"Or your whole story may be phony."

"Yes."

"The trouble is I can see no motive for you to have done it. It's true you are already guilty of getting money on false pretenses. You came out here to join Lime, perhaps to help him. . . ."

Martins said to me, "What was this precious racket you keep on hinting at?"

"I'd have told you all the facts when I first saw you if you hadn't lost your temper so damned quickly. Now I don't think I shall be acting wisely to tell you. It would be disclosing official information, and your contacts, you know, don't inspire confidence. A girl with phony papers supplied by Lime, this man Kurtz . . ."

"Dr. Winkler . . ."

"I've got nothing against Dr. Winkler. No, if you are phony, you don't need the information, but it might help you to learn exactly what we know. You see, our facts are not complete."

"I bet they aren't. I could invent a better detective than you in my bath."

"Your literary style does not do your namesake justice." Whenever he was reminded of Mr. Crabbin, that poor harassed representative of the British Cultural Relations Society, Rollo Martins turned pink with annoyance, embarrassment, shame. That too inclined me to trust him.

He had certainly given Crabbin some uncomfortable hours. On returning to Sacher's Hotel after his interview with Herr Koch he had found a desperate note waiting for him from the representative.

"I have been trying to locate you all day," Crabbin wrote. "It is essential that we should get together and work out a proper program for you. This morning by telephone I have arranged lectures at Innsbruck and Salzburg for next week, but I must have your consent to the subjects, so that proper programs can be printed. I would suggest two lectures: 'The Crisis of Faith in the Western World' (you are very respected here as a Christian writer, but this lecture should be quite unpolitical) and 'The Technique of the Contemporary Novel.' The same lectures would be given in Vienna. Apart from this, there are a great many people here who would like to meet you, and I want to arrange a cocktail party for early next week. But for all this I must have a few words with you." The letter ended on a note of acute anxiety. "You will be at the discussion tomorrow night, won't you? We all expect you at 8:30 and, needless to say, look forward to your coming. I will send transport to the hotel at 8:15 sharp."

Rollo Martins read the letter and, without bothering any further about Mr. Crabbin, went to bed.

8

AFTER two drinks Rollo Martins' mind would always turn towards women—in a vague, sentimental, romantic way, as a sex, in general. After three drinks, like a pilot who dives to find direction, he would begin to focus on one available girl. If he had not been offered a third drink by Cooler, he would probably not have gone quite so soon to Anna Schmidt's house, and if—but there are too many "ifs" in my style of writing, for it is my profession to balance possibilities, human possibilities, and the drive of destiny can never find a place in my files.

Martins had spent his lunchtime reading up the reports of the inquest, thus again demonstrating the superiority of the amateur to the professional, and making him more vulnerable to Cooler's liquor (which the professional in duty bound would have refused). It was nearly five o'clock when he reached Cooler's flat, which was over an ice-cream parlor in the American zone: the bar below was full of G.I.'s with their girls, and the clatter of the long spoons and the curious free uniformed laughter followed him up the stairs.

The Englishman who objects to Americans in general usually carries in his mind's eye just such an exception as Cooler: a man with tousled gray hair and a worried kindly face and longsighted eyes, the kind of humanitarian who turns up in a typhus epidemic or a world war or a Chinese famine long before his countrymen have discovered the place in an atlas. Again the card marked "Harry's friend" was like an entrance ticket. The warm frank handclasp was the most friendly act that Martins had encountered in Vienna.

"Any friend of Harry is all right with me," Cooler said. "I've heard of you, of course."

"From Harry?"

"I'm a great reader of Westerns," Cooler said, and Martins believed him as he did not believe Kurtz.

"I wondered—you were there, weren't you?—if you'd tell me about Harry's death."

"It was a terrible thing," Cooler said. "I was just crossing the road to go to Harry. He and Mr. Kurtz were on the sidewalk. Maybe if I hadn't started across the road, he'd have stayed where he was. But he saw me and stepped straight off to meet me and this jeep—it was terrible, terrible. The driver braked, but he didn't stand a chance. Have a Scotch, Mr. Martins. It's silly of me, but I get shaken up when I think of it." He said as he splashed in the soda, "I'd never seen a man killed before."

"Was the other man in the car?"

Cooler took a long pull and then measured what was left with his tired kindly eyes. "What man would you be referring to, Mr. Martins?"

"I was told there was another man there."

"I don't know how you got that idea. You'll find all about it in the inquest reports." He poured out two more generous drinks. "There were just the three of us—me and Mr. Kurtz and the driver. The doctor, of course. I expect you were thinking of the doctor."

"This man I was talking to happened to look out of a window—he has the next flat to Harry's—and he said he saw three men and the driver. That's before the doctor arrived."

"He didn't say that in court."

"He didn't want to get involved."

"You'll never teach these Europeans to be good citizens. It was his duty." Cooler brooded sadly over his glass. "It's an odd thing, Mr. Martins, with accidents. You'll never get two reports that coincide. Why, even I and Mr. Kurtz disagreed about details. The thing happens so suddenly, you aren't concerned to notice things, until bang crash, and then you have to reconstruct, remember. I expect he got too tangled up trying to sort out what happened before and what after, to distinguish the four of us."

"The four?"

"I was counting Harry. What else did he see, Mr. Martins?"

"Nothing of interest—except he says Harry was dead when he was carried to the house."

"Well, he was dying—not much difference there. Have another drink, Mr. Martins?"

"No, I don't think I will."

"Well, I'd like another spot. I was very fond of your friend, Mr. Martins, and I don't like talking about it."

"Perhaps one more—to keep you company.

"Do you know Anna Schmidt?" Martins asked, while the whisky still tingled on his tongue.

"Harry's girl? I met her once, that's all. As a matter of fact, I helped Harry fix her papers. Not the sort of thing I should confess to a stranger, I suppose, but you have to break the rules sometimes. Humanity's a duty too."

"What was wrong?"

"She was Hungarian and her father had been a Nazi, so they said. She was scared the Russians would pick her up."

"Why should they want to?"

"Well, her papers weren't in order."

"You took her some money from Harry, didn't you?"

"Yes, but I wouldn't have mentioned that. Did she tell you?"

The telephone rang, and Cooler drained his glass. "Hullo," he said. "Why, yes. This is Cooler." Then he sat with the receiver at his ear and an expression of sad patience, while some voice a long way off drained into the room. "Yes," he said once. "Yes." His eyes dwelt on Martins' face, but they seemed to be looking a long way beyond him: flat and tired and kind, they might have been gazing out across the sea. He said, "You did quite right," in a tone of commendation, and then, with a touch of asperity, "Of course they will be delivered. I gave my word. Good-by."

He put the receiver down and passed a hand across his forehead wearily. It was as though he were trying to remember something he had to do. Martins said, "Had you heard anything of this racket the police talk about?"

"I'm sorry. What's that?"

"They say Harry was mixed up in some racket."

"Oh, no," Cooler said. "No. That's quite impossible. He had a great sense of duty."

"Kurtz seemed to think it was possible."

"Kurtz doesn't understand how an Anglo-Saxon feels," Cooler replied.

9

IT WAS nearly dark when Martins made his way along the banks of the canal: across the water lay the half-destroyed Diana baths and in the distance the great black circle of the Prater Wheel, stationary above the ruined houses. Over there across the gray water was the second bezirk, in Russian ownership. St. Stefanskirche shot its enormous wounded spire into the sky above the Inner City, and, coming up the Kärntnerstrasse, Martins passed the lit door of the Military Police station. The four men of the International Patrol were climbing into their jeep; the Russian M.P. sat beside the driver (for the Russians had that day taken over the chair for the next four weeks) and the Englishman, the Frenchman, and the American mounted behind. The third stiff whisky fumed into Martins' brain, and he remembered the girl in Amsterdam, the girl in Paris; loneliness moved along the crowded pavement at his side. He passed the corner of the street where

Sacher's lay and went on. Rollo was in control and moved towards the only girl he knew in Vienna.

I asked him how he knew where she lived. Oh, he said, he'd looked up the address she had given him the night before, in bed, studying a map. He wanted to know his way about, and he was good with maps. He could memorize turnings and street names easily because he always went one way on foot.

"One way?"

"I mean when I'm calling on a girl—or someone."

He hadn't, of course, known that she would be in, that her play was not on that night in the Josefstadt, or perhaps he had memorized that too from the posters. In at any rate she was, if you could really call it being in, sitting alone in an unheated room, with the bed disguised as a divan, and a typewritten script lying open at the first page on the inadequate too-fancy topply table—because her thoughts were so far from being "in." He said awkwardly (and nobody could have said, not even Rollo, how much his awkwardness was part of his technique), "I thought I'd just look in and look you up. You see, I was passing . . ."

"Passing? Where to?" It had been a good half an hour's walk from the Inner City to the rim of the English zone, but he always had a reply. "I had too much whisky with Cooler. I needed a walk and I just happened to find myself this way."

"I can't give you a drink here. Except tea. There's some of that packet left."

"No, no thank you." He said, "You are busy," looking at the script.

"I didn't get beyond the first line."

He picked it up and read: "*Enter Louise.* LOUISE: I heard a child crying."

"Can I stay a little?" he asked with a gentleness that was more Martins than Rollo.

"I wish you would." He slumped down on the divan, and he told me a long time later (for lovers talk and reconstruct the smallest details if they can find a listener) that there it was he took his second real look at her. She stood there as awkward as himself in a pair of old flannel trousers which had been patched badly in the seat; she stood with her legs firmly straddled as though she were opposing someone and was determined to hold her ground—a small rather stocky figure with any grace she had folded and put away for use professionally.

"One of those bad days?" he asked.

"It's always bad about this time." She explained, "He used to look in, and when I heard your ring, just for a moment, I thought . . ." She sat down on a hard chair opposite him and said, "Please talk. You knew him. Just tell me anything."

And so he talked. The sky blackened outside the window while he talked. He noticed after a while that their hands had met. He said to me, "I never meant to fall in love, not with Harry's girl."

"When did it happen?" I asked him.

"It was very cold and I got up to close the window curtains. I only noticed my hand was on hers when I took it away. As I stood up I looked down at her face and she was looking up. It wasn't a beautiful face—that was the trouble. It was a face to live with, day in, day out. A face for wear. I felt as though I'd come into a new country where I couldn't speak the language. I had always thought it was beauty one loved in a woman. I stood there at the curtains, waiting to pull them, looking out. I couldn't see anything but my own face, looking back into the room, looking for her. She said, 'And what did Harry do that time?' and I wanted to say, 'Damn Harry. He's dead. We both loved him, but he's dead. The dead are made to be forgotten.' Instead of course all I said was, 'What do you think? He just whistled his old tune as if nothing was the matter,' and I whistled it to her as well as I could. I heard her catch her breath, and I looked round and before I could think, is this the right way, the right card, the right gambit?—I'd already said, 'He's dead. You can't go on remembering him forever.' "

She said, "I know, but perhaps something will happen first."

"What do you mean—something happen?"

"Oh, I mean, perhaps there'll be another way, or I'll die, or something."

"You'll forget him in time. You'll fall in love again."

"I know, but I don't want to. Don't you see I don't want to."

So Rollo Martins came back from the window and sat down on the divan again. When he had risen half a minute before he had been the friend of Harry, comforting Harry's girl; now he was a man in love with Anna Schmidt who had been in love with a man they had both once known called Harry Lime. He didn't speak again that evening about the past. Instead he began to tell her of the people he had seen. "I can believe anything of Winkler," he told her, "but Cooler—I liked Cooler. He was the only one of his friends who stood up for Harry. The trouble is, if Cooler's right, then Koch is wrong, and I really thought I had something there."

"Who's Koch?"

He explained how he had returned to Harry's flat and he described his interview with Koch, the story of the third man.

"If it's true," she said, "it's very important."

"It doesn't prove anything. After all, Koch backed out of the inquest; so might this stranger."

"That's not the point," she said. "It means that *they* lied. Kurtz and Cooler."

"They might have lied so as not to inconvenience this fellow—if he was a friend."

"Yet another friend—on the spot. And where's your Cooler's honesty then?"

"What do we do? He clamped down like an oyster and turned me out of his flat."

"He won't turn me out," she said, "or his Ilse won't."

They walked up the long road to the flat together; the snow clogged on their shoes and made them move slowly like convicts weighed down by irons. Anna Schmidt said, "Is it far?"

"Not very far now. Do you see that knot of people up the road? It's somewhere about there." The group of people up the road was like a splash of ink on the whiteness that flowed, changed shape, spread out. When they came a little nearer Martins said, "I think that is his block. What do you suppose this is, a political demonstration?"

Anna Schmidt stopped. She said, "Who else have you told about Koch?"

"Only you and Cooler. Why?"

"I'm frightened. It reminds me . . ." She had her eyes fixed on the crowd and he never knew what memory out of her confused past had risen to warn her. "Let's go away," she implored him.

"You're crazy. We're on to something here, something big. . . ."

"I'll wait for you."

"But you're going to talk to him."

"Find out first what all those people . . ." She said strangely for one who worked behind the footlights, "I hate crowds."

He walked slowly on alone, the snow caking on his heels. It wasn't a political meeting, for no one was making a speech. He had the impression of heads turning to watch him come, as though he were somebody who was expected. When he reached the fringe of the little crowd, he knew for certain that it was the house. A man looked hard at him and said, "Are you another of them?"

"What do you mean?"

"The police."

"No. What are they doing?"

"They've been in and out all day."

"What's everybody waiting for?"

"They want to see him brought out."

"Who?"

"Herr Koch." It occurred vaguely to Martins that somebody besides himself had discovered Herr Koch's failure to give evidence, though that was hardly a police matter. He said, "What's he done?"

"Nobody knows that yet. They can't make their minds up in there—it might be suicide, you see, and it might be murder."

"Herr Koch?"

"Of course."

A small child came up to his informant and pulled at his hand. "Papa, Papa." He wore a wool cap on his head, like a gnome; his face was pinched and blue with cold.

"Yes, my dear, what is it?"

"I heard them talking through the grating, Papa."

"Oh, you cunning little one. Tell us what you heard, Hansel."

"I heard Frau Koch crying, Papa."

"Was that all, Hansel?"

"No. I heard the big man talking, Papa."

"Ah, you cunning little Hansel. Tell Papa what he said."

"He said, 'Can you tell me, Frau Koch, what the foreigner looked like?'"

"Ha, ha, you see, they think it's murder. And who's to say they are wrong? Why should Herr Koch cut his own throat in the basement?"

"Papa, Papa."

"Yes, little Hansel?"

"When I looked through the grating, I could see some blood on the coke."

"What a child you are. How could you tell it was blood? The snow leaks everywhere." The man turned to Martins and said,

"The child has such an imagination. Maybe he will be a writer when he grows up."

The pinched face stared solemnly up at Martins. The child said, "Papa."

"Yes, Hansel?"

"He's a foreigner too."

The man gave a big laugh that caused a dozen heads to turn. "Listen to him, sir, listen," he said proudly. "He thinks you did it just because you are a foreigner. As though there weren't more foreigners here these days than Viennese."

"Papa, Papa."

"Yes, Hansel?"

"They are coming out."

A knot of police surrounded the covered stretcher which they lowered carefully down the steps for fear of sliding on the trodden snow. The man said, "They can't get an ambulance into this street because of the ruins. They have to carry it round the corner." Frau Koch came out at the tail of the procession; she had a shawl over her head and an old sackcloth coat. Her thick shape looked like a snowman as she sank in a drift at the pavement's edge. Someone gave her a hand and she looked round with a lost hopeless gaze at this crowd of strangers. If there were friends there she did not recognize them, looking from face to face. Martins bent as she passed, fumbling at his shoelace, but looking up from the ground he saw at his own eyes' level the scrutinizing cold-blooded gnome gaze of little Hansel.

Walking back down the street towards Anna, he looked back once. The child was pulling at his father's hand and he could see the lips forming round those syllables like the refrain of a grim ballad, "Papa, Papa."

He said to Anna, "Koch has been murdered. Come away from here." He walked as rapidly as the snow would let him, turning this corner and that. The child's suspicion and alertness seemed to spread like a cloud over the city—they could not walk fast enough to evade its shadow. He paid no attention when Anna said to him, "Then what Koch said was true. There *was* a third man," nor a little later when she said, "It must have been murder. You don't kill a man to hide anything less."

The tramcars flashed like icicles at the end of the street: they were back at the Ring. Martins said, "You had better go home alone. I'll keep away from you awhile till things have sorted out."

"But nobody can suspect you."

"They are asking about the foreigner who called on Koch yesterday. There may be some unpleasantness for a while."

"Why don't you go to the police?"

"They are so stupid. I don't trust them. See what they've pinned on Harry. And then I tried to hit this man Callaghan. They'll have it in for me. The least they'll do is send me away from Vienna. But if I stay quiet—there's only one person who can give me away. Cooler."

"And he won't want to."

"Not if he's guilty. But then I can't believe he's guilty."

Before she left him, she said, "Be careful. Koch knew so very little and they murdered him. You know as much as Koch."

The warning stayed in his brain all the way to Sacher's: after nine o'clock the streets are very empty, and he would turn his head at every padding step coming up the street behind him, as though that third man whom they had protected so ruthlessly were following him like an executioner. The Russian sentry outside the Grand Hotel looked rigid with the cold, but he was human, he had a face, an honest peasant face with Mongol eyes. The third man had no face: only the top of a head seen from a window. At Sacher's Mr. Schmidt said, "Colonel Calloway has been in, asking after you, sir. I think you'll find him in the bar."

"Back in a moment," Martins said and walked straight out of the hotel again: he wanted time to think. But immediately he stepped outside a man came forward, touched his cap, and said firmly, "Please, sir." He flung open the door of a khaki-painted truck with a Union Jack on the windscreen and firmly urged Martins within. He surrendered without protest; sooner or later, he felt sure, inquiries would be made; he had only pretended optimism to Anna Schmidt.

The driver drove too fast for safety on the frozen road, and Martins protested. All he got in reply was a sullen grunt and a muttered sentence containing the word "orders." "Gave you orders to kill me?" Martins said and got no reply at all. He caught sight of the Titans on the Hofburg balancing great globes of snow above their heads, and then they plunged into ill-lit streets beyond where he lost all sense of direction.

"Is it far?" But the driver paid him no attention at all. At least, Martins thought, I am not under arrest: they have not sent a guard; I am being invited—wasn't that the word they used?—to visit the station to make a statement.

The car drew up and the driver led the way up two flights of stairs; he rang the bell of a great double door, and Martins was aware of many voices beyond it. He turned sharply to the driver and said, "Where the hell . . . ?" but the driver was already halfway down the stairs, and already the door was opening. His eyes were dazzled from the darkness by the lights inside; he heard but he could hardly see the advance of Crabbin. "Oh, Mr. Dexter, we have been so anxious, but better late than never. Let me introduce you to Miss Wilbraham and the Gräfin von Meyersdorf."

A buffet laden with coffee cups; an urn steamed; a woman's face shiny with exertion; two young men with the happy intelligent faces of sixth formers; and, huddled in the background, like faces in a family album, a multitude of the old-fashioned, the dingy, the earnest and cheery features of constant readers. Martins looked behind him, but the door had closed.

He said desperately to Mr. Crabbin, "I'm sorry, but—"

"Don't think any more about it," Mr. Crabbin said. "One cup of coffee and then let's go on to the discussion. We have a very good gathering tonight. They'll put you on your mettle, Mr. Dexter." One of the young men placed a cup in his hand, the other shoveled in sugar before he could say he preferred his coffee unsweetened. The youngest man breathed into his ear, "Afterwards would you mind signing one of your books, Mr. Dexter?" A large woman in black silk bore down upon him and said, "I don't mind if the Gräfin does hear me, Mr. Dexter, but I don't like your books, I don't approve of them. I think a novel should tell a good story."

"So do I," Martins said hopelessly.

"Now, Mrs. Bannock, wait for question time."

"I know I'm downright, but I'm sure Mr. Dexter values *honest* criticism."

An old lady, whom he supposed was the Gräfin, said, "I do not read many English books, Mr. Dexter, but I am told that yours . . ."

"Do you mind drinking up?" Crabbin said and hustled him through into an inner room where a number of elderly people were sitting on a semicircle of chairs with an air of sad patience.

Martins was not able to tell me very much about the meeting; his mind was still dazed with the death; when he looked up he expected to see at any moment the child Hansel and hear that persistent informative refrain, "Papa, Papa." Apparently Crabbin opened the proceedings, and, knowing Crabbin, I am sure that it was a very lucid, very fair and unbiased picture of the contemporary English novel. I have heard him give that talk so often, varied only by the emphasis given to the work of the particular English visitor. He would have touched lightly on various problems of technique—the point of view, the passage of time—and then he would have declared the meeting open for questions and discussions.

Martins missed the first question altogether, but luckily Crabbin filled the gap and answered it satisfactorily. A woman wearing a brown hat and a piece of fur round her throat said with passionate interest, "May I ask Mr. Dexter if he is engaged on a new work?"

"Oh, yes—yes."

"May I ask the title?"

"*The Third Man,*" Martins said and gained a spurious confidence as the result of taking that hurdle.

"Mr. Dexter, could you tell us what author has chiefly influenced you?"

Martins, without thinking, said, "Grey." He meant of course

the author of *Riders of the Purple Sage,* and he was pleased to find his reply gave general satisfaction—to all save an elderly Austrian who asked, "Grey. What Grey? I do not know the name."

Martins felt he was safe now and said, "Zane Grey—I don't know any other," and was mystified at the low subservient laughter from the English colony.

Crabbin interposed quickly for the sake of the Austrians. "That is a little joke of Mr. Dexter's. He meant the poet Gray—a gentle, mild, subtle genius—one can see the affinity."

"And he is called Zane Grey?"

"That was Mr. Dexter's joke. Zane Grey wrote what we call Westerns—cheap popular novelettes about bandits and cowboys."

"He is not a great writer?"

"No, no. Far from it," Mr. Crabbin said. "In the strict sense I would not call him a writer at all." Martins told me that he felt the first stirrings of revolt at that statement. He had never regarded himself before as a writer, but Crabbin's self-confidence irritated him—even the way the light flashed back from Crabbin's spectacles seemed an added cause of vexation. Crabbin said, "He was just a popular entertainer."

"Why the hell not?" Martins said fiercely.

"Oh, well, I merely meant—"

"What was Shakespeare?"

Somebody with great daring said, "A poet."

"Have you ever read Zane Grey?"

"No, I can't say—"

"Then you don't know what you are talking about."

One of the young men tried to come to Crabbin's rescue. "And James Joyce, where would you put James Joyce, Mr. Dexter?"

"What do you mean put? I don't want to put anybody anywhere," Martins said. It had been a very full day: he had drunk too much with Cooler; he had fallen in love; a man had been murdered—and now he had the quite unjust feeling that he was being got at. Zane Grey was one of his heroes: he was damned if he was going to stand any nonsense.

"I mean would you put him among the really great?"

"If you want to know, I've never heard of him. What did he write?"

He didn't realize it, but he was making an enormous impression. Only a great writer could have taken so arrogant, so original a line. Several people wrote Zane Grey's name on the backs of envelopes and the Gräfin whispered hoarsely to Crabbin, "How do you spell Zane?"

"To tell you the truth, I'm not quite sure."

A number of names were simultaneously flung at Martins— little sharp pointed names like Stein, round pebbles like Woolf. A young Austrian with an ardent intellectual black forelock called out, "Daphne du Maurier," and Mr. Crabbin winced and looked sideways at Martins. He said in an undertone, "Be kind to them."

A gentle kind-faced woman in a hand-knitted jumper said wistfully, "Don't you agree, Mr. Dexter, that no one, no one has written about *feelings* so poetically as Virginia Woolf? In prose, I mean."

Crabbin whispered, "You might say something about the stream of consciousness."

"Stream of what?"

A note of despair came into Crabbin's voice. "Please, Mr. Dexter, these people are your genuine admirers. They want to hear your views. If you knew how they have besieged the Society."

An elderly Austrian said, "Is there any writer in England today of the stature of the late John Galsworthy?"

There was an outburst of angry twittering in which the names of du Maurier, Priestley, and somebody called Layman were flung to and fro. Martins sat gloomily back and saw again the snow, the stretcher, the desperate face of Frau Koch. He thought: If I had never returned, if I had never asked questions, would that little man still be alive? How had he benefited Harry by supplying another victim—a victim to assuage the fear of whom—Herr Kurtz, Cooler (he could not believe that), Dr. Winkler? Not one of them seemed adequate to the drab gruesome crime in the basement; he could hear the child saying, "I saw the blood on the coke," and somebody turned towards him a blank face without features, a gray plasticine egg, the third man.

Martins could not have said how he got through the rest of the discussion: perhaps Crabbin took the brunt; perhaps he was helped by some of the audience who got into an animated discussion about the film version of a popular American novel. He remembered very little more before Crabbin was making a final speech in his honor. Then one of the young men led him to a table stacked with books and asked him to sign them. "We have only allowed each member one book."

"What have I got to do?"

"Just a signature. That's all they expect. This is my copy of *The Curved Prow*. I would be so grateful if you'd just write a little something . . ."

Martins took his pen and wrote: "From B. Dexter, author of *The Lone Rider of Santa Fe*," and the young man read the sentence and blotted it with a puzzled expression. As Martins sat down and started signing Benjamin Dexter's title pages, he could see in a mirror the young man showing the inscription to Crabbin. Crabbin smiled weakly and stroked his chin, up and down, up and down. "B. Dexter, B. Dexter, B. Dexter." Martins wrote rapidly —it was not, after all, a lie. One by one the books were collected by their owners; little half-sentences of delight and compliment were dropped like curtsies—was this what it was to be a writer? Martins began to feel distinct irritation towards Benjamin Dexter. The complacent, tiring, pompous ass, he thought, signing the twenty-seventh copy of *The Curved Prow*. Every time he looked up and took another book he saw Crabbin's worried speculative gaze. The members of the Institute were beginning to go home with their spoils: the room was emptying. Suddenly in the mirror Martins saw a military policeman. He seemed to be having an argument with one of Crabbin's young henchmen. Martins thought he caught the sound of his own name. It was then he lost his nerve and with it any relic of common sense. There was only one book left to sign; he dashed off a last "B. Dexter" and made for the door.

The young man, Crabbin, and the policeman stood together at the entrance.

"And this gentleman?" the policeman asked.

"It's Mr. Benjamin Dexter," the young man said.

"Lavatory. Is there a lavatory?" Martins said.

"I understood a Mr. Rollo Martins came here in one of your cars."

"A mistake. An obvious mistake."

"Second door on the left," the young man said.

Martins grabbed his coat from the cloakroom as he went and made down the stairs. On the first-floor landing he heard someone mounting the stairs and, looking over, saw Paine, whom I had sent to identify him. He opened a door at random and shut it behind him. He could hear Paine going by. The room where he stood was in darkness; a curious moaning sound made him turn and face whatever room it was.

He could see nothing and the sound had stopped. He made a tiny movement and once more it started, like an impeded breath. He remained still and the sound died away. Outside somebody called, "Mr. Dexter, Mr. Dexter." Then a new sound started. It was like somebody whispering—a long continuous monologue in the darkness. Martins said, "Is anybody there?" and the sound stopped again. He could stand no more of it. He took out his lighter. Footsteps went by and down the stairs. He scraped and scraped at the little wheel and no light came. Somebody shifted in the dark, and something rattled in midair like a chain. He asked once more with the anger of fear, "Is anybody there?" and only the click-click of metal answered him.

Martins felt desperately for a light switch, first to his right hand and then to his left. He did not dare go farther because he could no longer locate his fellow occupant; the whisper, the moaning, the click had all stopped. Then he was afraid that he had lost the door and felt wildly for the knob. He was far less afraid of the police than he was of the darkness, and he had no idea of the noise he was making.

Paine heard it from the bottom of the stairs and came back. He switched on the landing light, and the glow under the door gave Martins his direction. He opened the door and, smiling weakly at Paine, turned back to take a second look at the room. The eyes of a parrot chained to a perch stared beadily back at him. Paine said respectfully, "We were looking for you, sir. Colonel Calloway wants a word with you."

"I lost my way," Martins said.

"Yes, sir. We thought that was what had happened."

10

I HAD kept a very careful record of Martins' movements from the moment I knew that he had not caught the plane home. He had been seen with Kurtz, and at the Josefstadt Theatre; I knew about his visit to Dr. Winkler and to Cooler, his first return to the block where Harry had lived. For some reason my man lost him between Cooler's and Anna Schmidt's flats; he reported that Martins had wandered widely, and the impression we both got was that he had deliberately thrown off his shadower. I tried to pick him up at the hotel and just missed him.

Events had taken a disquieting turn, and it seemed to me that the time had come for another interview. He had a lot to explain.

I put a good wide desk between us and gave him a cigarette. I found him sullen but ready to talk, within strict limits. I asked him about Kurtz and he seemed to me to answer satisfactorily. I then asked him about Anna Schmidt and I gathered from his reply that he must have been with her after visiting Cooler; that filled in one of the missing points. I tried him with Dr. Winkler, and he answered readily enough. "You've been getting around," I said, "quite a bit. And have you found out anything about your friend?"

"Oh yes," he said. "It was under your nose but you didn't see it."

"What?"

"That he was murdered." That took me by surprise: I had at one time played with the idea of suicide, but I had ruled even that out.

"Go on," I said. He tried to eliminate from his story all mention of Koch, talking about an informant who had seen the accident. This made his story rather confusing, and I couldn't grasp at first why he attached so much importance to the third man.

"He didn't turn up at the inquest, and the others lied to keep him out."

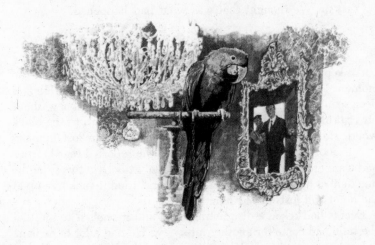

"Nor did your man turn up—I don't see much importance in that. If it was a genuine accident, all the evidence needed was there. Why get the other chap in trouble? Perhaps his wife thought he was out of town; perhaps he was an official absent without leave—people sometimes take unauthorized trips to Vienna from places like Klagenfurt. The delights of the great city, for what they are worth."

"There was more to it than that. The little chap who told me about—they've murdered him. You see they obviously didn't know what else he had seen."

"Now we have it," I said. "You mean Koch."

"Yes."

"As far as we know you were the last person to see him alive."

I questioned him then, as I've written, to find out if he had been followed to Koch's by somebody who was sharper than my man and had kept out of sight. I said, "The Austrian police are anxious to pin this on you. Frau Koch told them how disturbed her husband was by your visit. Who else knew about it?"

"I told Cooler." He said excitedly, "Suppose immediately I left he telephoned the story to someone—to the third man. They had to stop Koch's mouth."

"When you told Cooler about Koch, the man was already dead. That night he got out of bed, hearing someone, and went downstairs—"

"Well, that rules me out. I was in Sacher's."

"But he went to bed very early. Your visit brought back the migraine. It was soon after nine that he got up. You returned to Sacher's at nine thirty. Where were you before that?"

He said gloomily, "Wandering round and trying to sort things out."

"Any evidence of your movements?"

"No."

I wanted to frighten him, so there was no point in telling him that he had been followed all the time. I knew that he hadn't cut Koch's throat, but I wasn't sure that he was quite so innocent as he made out. The man who owns the knife is not always the real murderer.

"Can I have a cigarette?"

"Yes."

He said, "How did you know that I went to Koch's? That was why you pulled me here, wasn't it?"

"The Austrian police—"

"They hadn't identified me."

"Immediately you left Cooler's, he telephoned to me."

"Then that lets him out. If he had been concerned, he wouldn't have wanted to tell you my story—to tell Koch's story, I mean."

"He might assume that you were a sensible man and would come to me with your story as soon as you learned of Koch's death. By the way, how did you learn of it?"

He told me promptly and I believed him. It was then I began to believe him altogether. He said, "I still can't believe Cooler's concerned. I'd stake anything on his honesty. He's one of those Americans with a real sense of duty."

"Yes," I said, "he told me about that when he phoned. He apologized for it. He said it was the worst of having been brought up to believe in citizenship. He said it made him feel a prig. To tell you the truth, Cooler irritates me. Of course he doesn't know that I know about his tire deals."

"Is he in a racket, too, then?"

"Not a very serious one. I daresay he's salted away twenty-five thousand dollars. But I'm not a good citizen. Let the Americans look after their own people."

"I'm damned." He said thoughtfully, "Is that the kind of thing Harry was up to?"

"No. It was not so harmless."

He said, "You know this business—Koch's death—has shaken me. Perhaps Harry did get mixed up in something pretty bad. Perhaps he was trying to clear out again, and that's why they murdered him."

"Or perhaps," I said, "they wanted a bigger cut off the spoils. Thieves fall out."

He took it this time without any anger at all. He said, "We won't agree about motives, but I think you check your facts pretty well. I'm sorry about the other day."

"That's all right." There are times when one has to make a flash decision—this was one of them. I owed him something in return for the information he had given me. I said, "I'll show you enough of the facts in Lime's case for you to understand. But don't fly off the handle. It's going to be a shock."

It couldn't help being a shock. The war and the peace (if you can call it peace) let loose a great number of rackets, but none more vile than this one. The black marketeers in food did at least supply food, and the same applied to all the other racketeers who provided articles in short supply at extravagant prices. But the penicillin racket was a different affair altogether. Penicillin in

Austria was supplied only to the military hospitals: no civilian doctor, not even a civilian hospital, could obtain it by legal means. As the racket started, it was relatively harmless. Penicillin would be stolen and sold to Austrian doctors for very high sums—a phial would fetch anything up to seventy pounds. You might say that this was a form of distribution—unfair distribution because it benefited only the rich patient, but the original distribution could hardly have a claim to greater fairness.

This racket went on quite happily for a while. Occasionally someone was caught and punished, but the danger simply raised the price of penicillin. Then the racket began to get organized: the big men saw big money in it, and while the original thief got less for his spoils, he received instead a certain security. If anything happened to him he would be looked after. Human nature too has curious twisted reasons that the heart certainly knows nothing of. It eased the conscience of many small men to feel that they were working for an employer: they were almost as respectable soon in their own eyes as wage earners; they were one of a group, and if there was guilt, the leaders bore the guilt. A racket works very like a totalitarian party.

This I have sometimes called stage two. Stage three was when the organizers decided that the profits were not large enough. Penicillin would not always be impossible to obtain legitimately; they wanted more money and quicker money while the going was good. They began to dilute the penicillin with colored water, and, in the case of penicillin dust, with sand. I keep a small museum in one drawer in my desk, and I showed Martins examples. He wasn't enjoying the talk, but he hadn't yet grasped the point. He said, "I suppose that makes the stuff useless."

I said, "We wouldn't worry so much if that was all, but just consider. You can be immunized from the effects of penicillin. At the best you can say that the use of this stuff makes a penicillin treatment for the particular patient ineffective in the future. That isn't so funny, of course, if you are suffering from V.D. Then the use of sand on a wound that requires penicillin—well, it's not healthy. Men have lost their legs and arms that way—and their lives. But perhaps what horrified me most was visiting the children's hospital here. They had bought some of this penicillin for use against meningitis. A number of children simply died, and a number went off their heads. You can see them now in the mental ward."

He sat on the other side of the desk, scowling into his hands. I said, "It doesn't bear thinking about very closely, does it?"

"You haven't showed me any evidence yet that Harry—"

"We are coming to that now," I said. "Just sit still and listen." I opened Lime's file and began to read. At the beginning the evidence was purely circumstantial, and Martins fidgeted. So much consisted of coincidence—reports of agents that Lime had been at a certain place at a certain time; the accumulation of opportunities; his acquaintance with certain people. He protested once, "But the same evidence would apply against me—now."

"Just wait," I said. For some reason Harry Lime had grown careless: he may have realized that we suspected him and got rattled. He held a quite distinguished position, and a man like that is the more easily rattled. We put one of our agents as an orderly in the British Military Hospital: we knew by this time the name of our go-between, but we had never succeeded in getting the line right back to the source. Anyway, I am not going to bother the reader now, as I bothered Martins then, with all the stages—the long tussle to win the confidence of the go-between, a man called Harbin. At last we had the screws on Harbin, and we twisted them until he squealed. This kind of police work is very similar to secret service work: you look for a double agent whom you can really control, and Harbin was the man for us. But even he only led us as far as Kurtz.

"Kurtz!" Martins exclaimed. "But why haven't you pulled him in?"

"Zero hour is almost here," I said.

Kurtz was a great step forward, for Kurtz was in direct communication with Lime—he had a small outside job in connection with relief work. With Kurtz, Lime sometimes put things on paper —if he was pressed. I showed Martins the photostat of a note.

"Can you identify that?"

"It's Harry's hand." He read it through. "I don't see anything wrong."

"No, but now read this note from Harbin to Kurtz—which we dictated. Look at the date. This is the result."

He read them both through twice.

"You see what I mean?" If one watched a world come to an end, a plane dive from its course, I don't suppose one would chatter, and a world for Martins had certainly come to an end, a world of easy friendship, hero worship, confidence that had begun twenty years before—in a school corridor. Every memory—afternoons in the long grass, the illegitimate shoots on Brickworth Common, the dreams, the walks, every shared experience was simultaneously tainted, like the soil of an atomized town. One could not walk there with safety for a long while. While he sat there, looking at his hands and saying nothing, I fetched a precious bottle of whisky out of a cupboard and poured out two large doubles. "Go on," I said, "drink that," and he obeyed me as though I were his doctor. I poured him out another.

He said slowly, "Are you certain that he was the real boss?"

"It's as far back as we have got so far."

"You see he was always apt to jump before he looked."

I didn't contradict him, though that wasn't the impression he had before given of Lime. He was searching round for some comfort.

"Suppose," he said, "someone had got a line on him, forced him into this racket, as you forced Harbin to double-cross . . ."

"It's possible."

"And they murdered him in case he talked when he was arrested."

"It's not impossible."

"I'm glad they did," he said. "I wouldn't have liked to hear Harry squeal." He made a curious little dusting movement with his hand on his knee as much as to say, "That's that." He said, "I'll be getting back to England."

"I'd rather you didn't just yet. The Austrian police would make an issue if you tried to leave Vienna at the moment. You see, Cooler's sense of duty made him call them up too."

"I see," he said hopelessly.

"When we've found the third man . . ." I said.

"I'd like to hear him squeal," he said. "The bastard. The bloody bastard."

11

AFTER he left me, Martins went straight off to drink himself silly. He chose the Oriental to do it in, the dreary smoky little night-club that stands behind a sham Eastern façade. The same semi-nude photographs on the stairs, the same half-drunk Americans at the bar, the same bad wine and extraordinary gins—he might have been in any third-rate night haunt in any other shabby capital of a shabby Europe. At one point of the hopeless early hours the International Patrol took a look at the scene. Martins had drink after drink; he would probably have had a woman too, but the cabaret performers had all gone home, and there were practically no women left in the place, except for one beautiful shrewd-looking French journalist who made one remark to her companion and fell contemptuously asleep.

Martins moved on: at Maxim's a few couples were dancing rather gloomily, and at a place called Chez Victor the heating had failed and people sat in overcoats drinking cocktails. By this time the spots were swimming in front of Martins' eyes, and he was oppressed by a sense of loneliness. His mind reverted to the girl in Dublin, and the one in Amsterdam. That was one thing that didn't fool you—the straight drink, the simple physical act: one didn't expect fidelity from a woman. His mind revolved in circles—from sentiment to lust and back again from belief to cynicism.

The trams had stopped, and he set out obstinately on foot to find Harry's girl. He wanted to make love to her—just like that: no nonsense, no sentiment. He was in the mood for violence, and the snowy road heaved like a lake and set his mind on a new course towards sorrow, eternal love, renunciation.

It must have been about three in the morning when he climbed the stairs to Anna's room. He was nearly sober by that time and had only one idea in his head, that she must know about Harry too. He felt that somehow this knowledge would pay the mortmain that memory levies on human beings, and he would stand a chance with Harry's girl. If one is in love oneself, it never occurs to one that the girl doesn't know: one believes one has told it plainly in a tone of voice, the touch of a hand. When Anna opened the door to him, with astonishment at the sight of him tousled on the threshold, he never imagined that she was opening the door to a stranger.

He said, "Anna, I've found out everything."

"Come in," she said, "you don't want to wake the house." She was in a dressing gown; the divan had become a bed, the kind of tumbled bed that showed how sleepless the occupant had been.

"Now," she said, while he stood there, fumbling for words, "what is it? I thought you were going to keep away. Are the police after you?"

"No."

"You didn't really kill that man, did you?"

"Of course not."

"You're drunk, aren't you?"

"I am a bit," he said sulkily. The meeting seemed to be going on the wrong lines. He said angrily, "I'm sorry."

"Why? I could do with a bit of drink myself."

He said, "I've been with the British police. They are satisfied I didn't do it. But I've learned everything from them. Harry was in a racket—a bad racket." He said hopelessly, "He was no good at all. We were both wrong."

"You'd better tell me," Anna said. She sat down on the bed and he told her, swaying slightly beside the table where her typescript part still lay open at the first page. I imagine he told it to her pretty confusedly, dwelling chiefly on what had stuck most in his mind, the children dead with meningitis and the children in the mental ward. He stopped and they were silent. She said, "Is that all?"

"Yes."

"You were sober when they told you? They really proved it?"

"Yes." He added drearily, "So that, you see, was Harry."

"I'm glad he's dead now," she said. "I wouldn't have wanted him to rot for years in prison."

"But can you understand how Harry—your Harry, my Harry—

could have got mixed up . . . ?" He said hopelessly, "I feel as though he had never really existed, that we'd dreamed him. Was he laughing at fools like us all the time?"

"He may have been. What does it matter?" she said. "Sit down. Don't worry." He had pictured himself comforting *her*—not this other way about. She said, "If he was alive now, he might be able to explain, but we've got to remember him as he was to us. There are always so many things one doesn't know about a person, even a person one loves—good things, bad things. We have to leave plenty of room for them."

"Those children—"

She said angrily, "For God's sake stop making people in *your* image. Harry was real. He wasn't just your hero and my lover. He was Harry. He was in a racket. He did bad things. What about it? He was the man we knew."

He said, "Don't talk such bloody wisdom. Don't you see that I love you?"

She looked at him in astonishment. "You?"

"Yes, me. I don't kill people with fake drugs. I'm not a hypocrite who persuades people that I'm the greatest—I'm just a bad writer who drinks too much and falls in love with girls. . . ."

She said, "But I don't even know what color your eyes are. If you'd rung me up just now and asked me whether you were dark or fair or wore a mustache, I wouldn't have known."

"Can't you get him out of your mind?"

"No."

He said, "As soon as they've cleared up this Koch murder, I'm leaving Vienna. I can't feel interested any longer in whether Kurtz killed Harry—or the third man. Whoever killed him it was a kind of justice. Maybe I'd kill him myself under these circumstances. But you still love him. You love a cheat, a murderer."

"I loved a man," she said. "I told you—a man doesn't alter because you find out more about him. He's still the same man."

"I hate the way you talk. I've got a splitting headache, and you talk and talk. . . ."

"I didn't ask you to come."

"You make me cross."

Suddenly she laughed. She said, "You are so comic. You come here at three in the morning—a stranger—and say you love me. Then you get angry and pick a quarrel. What do you expect me to do—or say?"

"I haven't seen you laugh before. Do it again. I like it."

"There isn't enough for two laughs," she said.

He took her by the shoulders and shook her gently. He said, "I'd make comic faces all day long. I'd stand on my head and grin at you between my legs. I'd learn a lot of jokes from the books on after-dinner speaking."

"Come away from the window. There are no curtains."

"There's nobody to see." But automatically checking his statement, he wasn't quite so sure: a long shadow that had moved, perhaps with the movement of clouds over the moon, was motionless again. He said, "You still love Harry, don't you?"

"Yes."

"Perhaps I do. I don't know." He dropped his hands and said, "I'll be pushing off."

He walked rapidly away. He didn't bother to see whether he was being followed, to check up on the shadow. But, passing by the end of the street, he happened to turn and there just around the corner, pressed against a wall to escape notice, was a thick stocky figure. Martins stopped and stared. There was something familiar about that figure. Perhaps, he thought, I have grown unconsciously used to him during these last twenty-four hours; perhaps he is one of those who have so assiduously checked my movements. Martins stood there, twenty yards away, staring at the silent motionless figure in the dark side street who stared back at him. A police spy, perhaps, or an agent of those other men, those men who had corrupted Harry first and then killed him—even possibly the third man?

It was not the face that was familiar, for he could not make out so much as the angle of the jaw; nor a movement, for the body was so still that he began to believe that the whole thing was an illusion caused by shadow. He called sharply, "Do you want anything?" and there was no reply. He called again with the irascibility of drink, "Answer, can't you," and an answer came, for a window curtain was drawn petulantly back by some sleeper he had awakened, and the light fell straight across the narrow street and lit up the features of Harry Lime.

12

"Do you believe in ghosts?" Martins said to me.

"Do you?"

"I do now."

"I also believe that drunk men see things—sometimes rats, sometimes worse."

He hadn't come to me at once with his story—only the danger to Anna Schmidt tossed him back into my office, like something the sea had washed up, tousled, unshaven, haunted by an experience he couldn't understand. He said, "If it had been just the face, I wouldn't have worried. I'd been thinking about Harry, and I might easily have mistaken a stranger. The light was turned off again at once, you see. I only got one glimpse, and the man made off down the street—if he was a man. There was no turning for a long way, but I was so startled I gave him another thirty yards' start. He came to one of those newspaper kiosks and for a moment moved out of sight. I ran after him. It only took me ten seconds to reach the kiosk, and he must have heard me running, but the strange thing was he never appeared again. I reached the kiosk. There wasn't anybody there. The street was empty. He couldn't have reached a doorway without my meeting him. He'd simply vanished."

"A natural thing for ghosts—or illusions."

"But I can't believe I was as drunk as all that!"

"What did you do then?"

"I had to have another drink. My nerves were all to pieces."

"Didn't that bring him back?"

"No, but it sent me back to Anna's."

I think he would have been ashamed to come to me with his absurd story if it had not been for the attempt on Anna Schmidt. My theory when he did tell me his story was that there had been a watcher—though it was drink and hysteria that had pasted on the man's face the features of Harry Lime. That watcher had noted his visit to Anna and the member of the ring—the penicillin ring—had been warned by telephone. Events that night moved fast. You remember that Kurtz lived in the Russian zone—in the second bezirk to be exact, in a wide empty desolate street that runs down to the Prater Platz. A man like that had probably obtained his influential contacts.

The original police agreement in Vienna between the Allies confined the military police (who had to deal with crimes involving Allied personnel) to their particular zones, unless permission was given to them to enter the zone of another power. I had to get on the phone to my opposite number in the American or French zone before I sent in my men to make an arrest or pursue an investigation. Perhaps forty-eight hours would pass before I received permission from the Russians, but in practice there are few occasions when it is necessary to work quicker than that. Even at home it is not always possible to obtain a search warrant or permission from one's superiors to detain a suspect with any greater speed.

This meant that if I wanted to pick up Kurtz it would be as well to catch him in the British zone.

When Rollo Martins went drunkenly back at four o'clock in the morning to tell Anna that he had seen the ghost of Harry, he was told by a frightened porter who had not yet gone back to sleep that she had been taken away by the International Patrol.

What happened was this. Russia, you remember, was in the chair as far as the Innere Stadt was concerned, and the Russians had information that Anna Schmidt was one of their nationals living with false papers. On this occasion, halfway through the patrol, the Russian policeman directed the car to the street where Anna Schmidt lived.

Outside Anna Schmidt's block the American took a hand in the game and demanded in German what it was all about. The Frenchman leaned against the bonnet and lit a stinking Caporal. France wasn't concerned, and anything that didn't concern France had no genuine importance to him. The Russian dug out a few words of German and flourished some papers. As far as they could tell, a Russian national wanted by the Russian police was living there without proper papers. They went upstairs and found Anna in bed, though I don't suppose, after Martins visit, that she was asleep.

There is a lot of comedy in these situations if you are not directly concerned. You need a background of general European terror, of a father who belonged to a losing side, of house searches and disappearances before the fear outweighs the comedy. The Russian, you see, refused to leave the room; the American wouldn't leave a girl unprotected, and the Frenchman—well, I think the Frenchman must have thought it was fun. Can't you imagine the scene? The Russian was just doing his duty and watched the girl all the time, without a flicker of sexual interest; the American stood with his back chivalrously turned; the Frenchman smoked his cigarette and watched with detached amusement the reflection of the girl dressing in the mirror of the wardrobe; and the Englishman stood in the passage wondering what to do next.

I don't want you to think the English policeman came too badly out of the affair. In the passage, undistracted by chivalry, he had time to think, and his thoughts led him to the telephone in the next flat. He got straight through to me at my flat and woke me out of that deepest middle sleep. That was why when Martins rang up an hour later I already knew what was exciting him; it gave him an undeserved but very useful belief in my efficiency. I never had another crack from him about policemen or sheriffs after that night.

When the M.P. went back to Anna's room a dispute was raging. Anna had told the American that she had Austrian papers (which was true) and that they were quite in order (which was rather stretching the truth). The American told the Russian in bad German that they had no right to arrest an Austrian citizen. He asked Anna for her papers and when she produced them, the Russian took them.

"Hungarian," he said, pointing at Anna. "Hungarian," and then, flourishing the papers, "bad, bad."

The American, whose name was O'Brien, said, "Give the goil back her papers," which the Russian naturally didn't understand. The American put his hand on his gun, and Corporal Starling said gently, "Let it go, Pat."

"If those papers ain't in order we got a right to look."

"Just let it go. We'll see the papers at HQ."

"The trouble about you British is you never know when to make a stand."

"Oh, well," Starling said; he had been at Dunkirk, but he knew when to be quiet.

The driver put on his brakes suddenly: there was a roadblock.

You see, I knew they would have to pass this military post. I put my head in at the window and said to the Russian, haltingly, in his own tongue, "What are you doing in the British zone?"

He grumbled that it was "orders."

"Whose orders? Let me see them." I noted the signature—it was useful information. I said, "This tells you to pick up a certain Hungarian national and war criminal who is living with faulty papers in the British zone. Let me see the papers."

He started on a long explanation. I said, "These papers look to me quite in order, but I'll investigate them and send a report of the result to your colonel. He can, of course, ask for the extradition of this lady at any time. All we want is proof of her criminal activities."

I said to Anna, "Get out of the car." I put a packet of cigarettes in the Russian's hand, said, "Have a good smoke," waved my hand to the others, gave a sigh of relief, and that incident was closed.

13

WHILE Martins told me how he went back to Anna's and found her gone, I did some hard thinking. I wasn't satisfied with the ghost story or the idea that the man with Harry Lime's features had been a drunken illusion. I took out two maps of Vienna and compared them. I rang up my assistant and, keeping Martins silent with a glass of whisky, asked him if he had located Harbin yet. He said no; he understood he'd left Klagenfurt a week ago to visit his family in the adjoining zone. One always wants to do everything oneself; one has to guard against blaming one's juniors. I am convinced that I would never have let Harbin out of our clutches, but then I would probably have made all kinds of mistakes that my junior would have avoided. "All right," I said. "Go on trying to get hold of him."

"I'm sorry, sir."

"Forget it. It's just one of those things."

His young enthusiastic voice—if only one could still feel that enthusiasm for a routine job; how many opportunities, flashes of insight one misses simply because a job has become just a job—his voice tingled up the wire. "You know, sir, I can't help feeling that we ruled out the possibility of murder too easily. There are one or two points—"

"Put them on paper, Carter."

"Yes, sir. I think, sir, if you don't mind my saying so" (Carter is a very young man) "we ought to have him dug up. There's no real evidence that he died just when the others said."

"I agree, Carter. Get on to the authorities."

Martins was right! I had made a complete fool of myself, but remember that police work in an occupied city is not like police work at home. Everything is unfamiliar: the methods of one's foreign colleagues, the rules of evidence, even the procedure at inquests. I suppose I had got into the state of mind when one trusts too much to one's personal judgment. I had been immensely relieved by Lime's death. I was satisfied with the accident.

I said to Martins, "Did you look inside the newspaper kiosk or was it locked?"

"Oh, it wasn't exactly a newspaper kiosk," he said. "It was one of those solid iron kiosks you see everywhere plastered with posters."

"You'd better show me the place."

"But is Anna all right?"

"The police are watching the flat. They won't try anything else yet."

I didn't want to make a fuss and stir in the neighborhood with a police car, so we took trams—several trams—changing here and there, and came into the district on foot. I didn't wear my uniform, and I doubted anyway, after the failure of the attempt on Anna, whether they would risk a watcher. "This is the turning," Martins said and led me down a side street. We stopped at the kiosk. "You see he passed behind here and simply vanished—into the ground."

"That was exactly where he did vanish to," I said.

"How do you mean?"

An ordinary passerby would never have noticed that the kiosk had a door, and of course it had been dark when the man disappeared. I pulled the door open and showed to Martins the little curling iron staircase that disappeared into the ground. He said, "Good God, then I didn't imagine him."

"It's one of the entrances to the main sewer."

"And anyone can go down?"

"Anyone."

"How far can one go?"

"Right across Vienna. People used them in air raids; some of our prisoners hid for two years down there. Deserters have used them—and burglars. If you know your way about you can emerge again almost anywhere in the city through a manhole or a kiosk like this one. The Austrians have to have special police for patrolling these sewers." I closed the door of the kiosk again. I said, "So that's how your friend Harry disappeared."

"You really believe it was Harry?"

"The evidence points that way."

"Then whom did they bury?"

"I don't know yet, but we soon shall, because we are digging him up again. I've got a shrewd idea, though, that Koch wasn't the only inconvenient man they murdered."

Martins said, "It's a bit of a shock."

"Yes."

"What are you going to do about it?"

"I don't know. You can bet he's hiding out now in another zone. We have no line now on Kurtz, for Harbin's blown—he must have been blown or they wouldn't have staged that mock death and funeral."

"But it's odd, isn't it, that Koch didn't recognize the dead man's face from the window."

"The window was a long way up and I expect the face had been damaged before they took the body out of the car."

He said thoughtfully, "I wish I could speak to him. You see, there's so much I simply can't believe."

"Perhaps you are the only one who could speak to him. It's risky though, because you do know too much."

"I still can't believe—I only saw the face for a moment." He said, "What shall I do?"

"He won't leave his zone now. The only person who could persuade him to come over would be you—or her, if he still believes you are his friend. But first you've got to speak to him. I can't see the line."

"I could go and see Kurtz. I have the address."

I said, "Remember. Lime may not want you to leave the Russian zone when once you are there, and I can't protect you there."

"I want to clear the whole damned thing up," Martins said, "but I'm not going to act as a decoy. I'll talk to him. That's all."

14

SUNDAY had laid its false peace over Vienna; the wind had dropped and no snow had fallen for twenty-four hours. All the morning trams had been full, going out to Grinzing where the young wine was drunk and to the slopes of snow on the hills outside. Walking over the canal by the makeshift military bridge, Martins was aware of the emptiness of the afternoon: the young were out with their toboggans and their skis, and all around him was the after-dinner sleep of age. A notice board told him that he was entering the Russian zone, but there were no signs of occupation. You saw more Russian soldiers in the Inner City than here.

Deliberately he had given Mr. Kurtz no warning of his visit. Better to find him out than a reception prepared for him. He was careful to carry with him all his papers, including the laissez-passer of the four powers that on the face of it allowed him to move freely through all the zones of Vienna. It was extraordinarily quiet over here on the other side of the canal, and a melodramatic journalist had painted a picture of silent terror; but the truth was simply the wide streets, the greater shell damage, the fewer people—and Sunday afternoon. There was nothing to fear, but all the same, in this huge empty street where all the time you heard your own feet moving, it was difficult not to look behind.

He had no difficulty in finding Mr. Kurtz's block, and when he rang the bell the door was opened quickly, as though Mr. Kurtz expected a visitor, by Mr. Kurtz himself.

"Oh," Mr. Kurtz said, "it's you, Rollo," and made a perplexed motion with his hand to the back of his head. Martins had been wondering why he looked so different, and now he knew. Mr. Kurtz was not wearing the toupee, and yet his head was not bald. He had a perfectly normal head of hair cut close. He said, "It would have been better to have telephoned to me. You nearly missed me; I was going out."

"May I come in a moment?"

"Of course."

In the hall a cupboard door stood open, and Martins saw Mr. Kurtz's overcoat, his raincoat, a couple of hats, and, hanging sedately on a peg like a wrap, Mr. Kurtz's toupee. He said, "I'm glad to see your hair has grown," and was astonished to see, in the mirror on the cupboard door, the hatred flame and blush on Mr. Kurtz's face. When he turned Mr. Kurtz smiled at him like a conspirator and said vaguely, "It keeps the head warm."

"Whose head?" Martins asked, for it had suddenly occurred to him how useful that toupee might have been on the day of the accident. "Never mind," he went quickly on, for his errand was not with Mr. Kurtz. "I'm here to see Harry."

"Harry?"

"I want to talk to him."

"Are you mad?"

"I'm in a hurry, so let's assume that I am. Just make a note of my madness. If you should see Harry—or his ghost—let him know that I want to talk to him. A ghost isn't afraid of a man, is it? Surely it's the other way round. I'll be waiting in the Prater by the Big Wheel for the next two hours—if you can get in touch with the dead, hurry." He added, "Remember, I was Harry's friend."

Kurtz said nothing, but somewhere, in a room off the hall, somebody cleared his throat. Martins threw open a door: he had half expected to see the dead rise yet again, but it was only Dr. Winkler who rose from a kitchen stove, and bowed very stiffly and correctly with the same celluloid squeak.

"Dr. Winkle," Martins said. Dr. Winkler looked extraordinarily out of place in a kitchen. The debris of a snack lunch littered the kitchen table, and the unwashed dishes consorted very ill with Dr. Winkler's cleanness.

"Winkler," the doctor corrected him with stony patience.

Martins said to Kurtz, "Tell the doctor about my madness. He might be able to make a diagnosis. And remember the place—by the Great Wheel. Or do ghosts only rise by night?" He left the flat.

For an hour he waited, walking up and down to keep warm, inside the enclosure of the Great Wheel; the smashed Prater with its bones sticking crudely through the snow was nearly empty. One stall sold thin flat cakes like cartwheels, and the children queued with their coupons. A few courting couples would be packed together in a single car of the Wheel and revolve slowly above the city, surrounded by empty cars. As the car reached the highest point of the Wheel, the revolutions would stop for a couple of minutes and far overhead the tiny faces would press against the glass. Martins wondered who would come for him. Was there enough friendship left in Harry for him to come alone, or would a squad of police arrive? It was obvious from the raid on Anna Schmidt's flat that he had a certain pull. And then as his watch hand passed the hour, he wondered: Was it all an invention of my mind? Are they digging up Harry's body now in the Central Cemetery?

Somewhere behind the cake stall a man was whistling, and Martins knew the tune. He turned and waited. Was it fear or excitement that made his heart beat—or just the memories that tune ushered in, for life had always quickened when Harry came, came just as he came now, as though nothing much had happened, nobody had been lowered into a grave or found with cut throat in a basement, came with his amused deprecating take-it-or-leave-it manner—and of course one always took it.

"Harry."

"Hullo, Rollo."

Don't picture Harry Lime as a smooth scoundrel. He wasn't that. The picture I have of him on my files is an excellent one: he is caught by a street photographer with his stocky legs apart, big shoulders a little hunched, a belly that has known too much good food too long, on his face a look of cheerful rascality, a geniality, a recognition that his happiness will make the world's day. Now he didn't make the mistake of putting out a hand that might have been rejected, but instead just patted Martins on the elbow and said, "How are things?"

"We've got to talk, Harry."

"Of course."

"Alone."

"We couldn't be more alone than here."

He had always known the ropes, and even in the smashed pleasure park he knew them, tipping the woman in charge of the Wheel, so that they might have a car to themselves. He said, "Lovers used to do this in the old days, but they haven't the money to spare, poor devils, now," and he looked out of the window of the swaying, rising car at the figures diminishing below with what looked like genuine commiseration.

Very slowly on one side of them the city sank; very slowly on the other the great cross girders of the Wheel rose into sight. As the horizon slid away the Danube became visible, and the piers of the Reichsbrücke lifted above the houses. "Well," Harry said, "it's good to see you, Rollo."

"I was at your funeral."

"That was pretty smart of me, wasn't it?"

"Not so smart for your girl. She was there too—in tears."

"She's a good little thing," Harry said. "I'm very fond of her."

"I didn't believe the police when they told me about you."

Harry said, "I wouldn't have asked you to come if I'd known what was going to happen, but I didn't think the police were on to me."

"Were you going to cut me in on the spoils?"

"I've never kept you out of anything, old man, yet." He stood with his back to the door as the car swung upwards, and smiled back at Rollo Martins, who could remember him in just such an attitude in a secluded corner of the school quad, saying, "I've learned a way to get out at night. It's absolutely safe. You are the only one I'm letting in on it." For the first time Rollo Martins

looked back through the years without admiration, as he thought, He's never grown up. Marlowe's devils wore squibs attached to their tails: evil was like Peter Pan—it carried with it the horrifying and horrible gift of eternal youth.

Martins said, "Have you ever visited the children's hospital? Have you seen any of your victims?"

Harry took a look at the toy landscape below and came away from the door. "I never feel quite safe in these things," he said. He felt the back of the door with his hand, as though he were afraid that it might fly open and launch him into that iron-ribbed space. "Victims?" he asked. "Don't be melodramatic, Rollo. Look down there," he went on, pointing through the window at the people moving like black flies at the base of the Wheel. "Would you really feel any pity if one of those dots stopped moving—forever? If I said you can have twenty thousand pounds for every dot that stops, would you really, old man, tell me to keep my money—without hesitation? Or would you calculate how many dots you could afford to spare? Free of income tax, old man. Free of income tax." He gave his boyish conspiratorial smile. "It's the only way to save nowadays."

"Couldn't you have stuck to tires?"

"Like Cooler? No, I've always been ambitious.

"But they can't catch me, Rollo, you'll see. I'll pop up again. You can't keep a good man down." The car swung to a standstill at the highest point of the curve and Harry turned his back and gazed out of the window. Martins thought: one good shove and I could break the glass, and he pictured the body dropping among the flies. He said, "You know the police are planning to dig up your body. What will they find?"

"Harbin," Harry replied with simplicity. He turned away from the window and said, "Look at the sky."

The car had reached the top of the Wheel and hung there motionless, while the stain of the sunset ran in streaks over the wrinkled papery sky beyond the black girders.

"Why did the Russians try to take Anna Schmidt?"

"She had false papers, old man."

"I thought perhaps you were just trying to get her here—because she was your girl? Because you wanted her?"

Harry smiled. "I haven't all that influence."

"What would have happened to her?"

"Nothing very serious. She'd have been sent back to Hungary. There's nothing against her really. She'd be infinitely better off in her own country than being pushed around by the British police."

"She hasn't told them anything about you."

"She's a good little thing," Harry repeated with complacent pride.

"She loves you."

"Well, I gave her a good time while it lasted."

"And I love her."

"That's fine, old man. Be kind to her. She's worth it. I'm glad."
He gave the impression of having arranged everything to every-
body's satisfaction. "And you can help to keep her mouth shut.
Not that she knows anything that matters."

"I'd like to knock you through the window."

"But you won't, old man. Our quarrels never last long. You
remember that fearful one in the Monaco, when we swore we
were through. I'd trust you anywhere, Rollo. Kurtz tried to persuade me not to come but I know you. Then he tried to persuade
me to, well, arrange an accident. He told me it would be quite
easy in this car."

"Except that I'm the stronger man."

"But I've got the gun. You don't think a bullet wound would
show when you hit *that* ground?" Again the car began to move,
sailing slowly down, until the flies were midgets, were recogniz-
able human beings. "What fools we are, Rollo, talking like this, as
if I'd do that to you—or you to me." He turned his back and
leaned his face against the glass. One thrust . . . "How much do
you earn a year with your Westerns, old man?"

"A thousand."

"Taxed. I earn thirty thousand free. It's the fashion. In these
days, old man, nobody thinks in terms of human beings. Govern-
ments don't, so why should we? They talk of the people and the
proletariat, and I talk of the mugs. It's the same thing. They have
their five-year plans and so have I."

"You used to be a Catholic."

"Oh, I still *believe*, old man. In God and mercy and all that.
I'm not hurting anybody's soul by what I do. The dead are happier dead. They don't miss much here, poor devils," he added
with that odd touch of genuine pity, as the car reached the plat-
form and the faces of the doomed-to-be-victims, the tired pleasure-
hoping Sunday faces, peered in at them. "I could cut you in, you
know. It would be useful. I have no one left in the Inner City."

"Except Cooler? And Winkler?"

"You really mustn't turn policeman, old man." They passed out
of the car and he put his hand again on Martins' elbow. "That was

a joke, I know you won't. Have you heard anything of old Bracer recently?"

"I had a card at Christmas."

"Those were the days, old man. Those were the days. I've got to leave you here. We'll see each other—sometime. If you are in a jam, you can always get me at Kurtz's." He moved away and, turning, waved the hand he had had the tact not to offer: it was like the whole past moving off under a cloud. Martins suddenly called after him, "Don't trust me, Harry," but there was too great a distance now between them for the words to carry.

15

"ANNA was at the theater," Martins told me, "for the Sunday matinee. I had to see the whole thing through a second time. About a middle-aged pianist and an infatuated girl and an under-standing—a terribly understanding—wife. Anna acted very badly —she wasn't much of an actress at the best of times. I saw her afterwards in her dressing room, but she was badly fussed. I think she thought I was going to make a serious pass at her all the time, and she didn't want a pass. I told her Harry was alive—I thought she'd be glad and that I would hate to see how glad she was, but she sat in front of her makeup mirror and let the tears streak the greasepaint and I wished after that she had been glad. She looked awful and I loved her. Then I told her about my interview with Harry, but she wasn't really paying much attention because when I'd finished she said, "I wish he was dead."

"He deserves to be."

"I mean he would be safe then—from everybody."

I asked Martins, "Did you show her the photographs I gave you—of the children?"

"Yes. I thought, It's got to be kill or cure this time. She's got to get Harry out of her system. I propped the pictures up among the pots of grease. She couldn't avoid seeing them. I said, 'The police can't arrest Harry unless they get him into this zone, and we've got to help!'

"She said, 'I thought he was your friend.' I said, 'He *was* my friend.' She said, 'I'll never help you to get Harry. I don't want to see him again, I don't want to hear his voice. I don't want to be touched by him, but I won't do a thing to harm him.'

"I felt bitter—I don't know why, because after all I had done nothing for her. Even Harry had done more for her than I had. I said, 'You want him still,' as though I were accusing her of a crime. She said, 'I don't want him, but he's in me. That's a fact—not like friendship. Why, when I have a love dream, he's always the man.'"

I prodded Martins on when he hesitated. "Yes?"

"Oh, I just got up and left her then. Now it's your turn to work on me. What do you want me to do?"

"I want to act quickly. You see it was Harbin's body in the coffin, so we can pick up Winkler and Cooler right away. Kurtz is out of our reach for the time being, and so is the driver. We'll put in a formal request to the Russians for permission to arrest Kurtz and Lime: it makes our files tidy. If we are going to use you as our decoy, your message must go to Lime straightaway—not after you've hung around in this zone for twenty-four hours. As I see it you were brought here for a grilling almost as soon as you got back into the Inner City; you heard then from me about Harbin; you put two and two together and you go and warn Cooler. We'll let Cooler slip for the sake of the bigger game—we have no evidence he was in on the penicillin racket. He'll escape into the second bezirk to Kurtz, and Lime will know you've played the game. Three hours later you send a message that the police are after you: you are in hiding and must see him."

"He won't come."

"I'm not so sure. We'll choose our hiding place carefully—where he'll think there's a minimum of risk. It's worth trying. It would appeal to his pride and his sense of humor if he could scoop you out. And it would stop your mouth."

Martins said, "He never used to scoop me out—at school." It was obvious that he had been reviewing the past with care and coming to conclusions.

"That wasn't such serious trouble and there was no danger of your squealing."

He said, "I told Harry not to trust me, but he didn't hear."

"Do you agree?"

He had given me back the photographs of the children and they lay on my desk. I could see him take a long look at them. "Yes," he said, "I agree."

16

ALL THE first arrangements went according to plan. We delayed arresting Winkler, who had returned from the second bezirk, until after Cooler had been warned. Martins enjoyed his short interview with Cooler. Cooler greeted him with patronage. "Why, Mr. Martins, it's good to see you. Sit down. I'm glad everything went off all right between you and Colonel Calloway. A very straight chap, Calloway."

"It didn't," Martins said.

"You don't bear any ill will, I'm sure, about my letting him know about you seeing Koch. The way I figured it was this—if you were innocent you'd clear yourself right away and if you were guilty, well, the fact that I liked you oughtn't to stand in the way. A citizen has his duties."

"Like giving false evidence at an inquest."

Cooler said, "Oh, that old story. I'm afraid you are riled at me, Mr. Martins. Look at it this way—you as a citizen, owing allegiance—"

"The police have dug up the body. They'll be after you and Winkler. I want you to warn Harry. . . ."

"I don't understand."

"Oh, yes, you do." And it was obvious that he did. Martins left him abruptly. He wanted no more of that kindly tired humanitarian face.

It only remained then to bait the trap. After studying the map of the sewer system I came to the conclusion that a café anywhere near the main entrance of the great sewer—which was placed in what Martins had mistakenly called a newspaper kiosk—would be the most likely spot to tempt Lime. He had only to rise once again through the ground, walk fifty yards, bring Martins back with him, and sink again into the obscurity of the sewers. He had no idea that this method of evasion was known to us: he probably knew that one patrol of the sewer police ended before midnight, and the next did not start till two, and so at midnight Martins sat in the little cold café in sight of the kiosk, drinking coffee after coffee. I had lent him a revolver; I had men posted as close to the kiosk as I could, and the sewer police were ready when zero hour struck to close the manholes and start sweeping the sewers inwards from the edge of the city. But I intended if I could to catch him before he went underground again. It would save trouble— and risk to Martins. So there, as I say, in the café Martins sat.

The wind had risen again, but it had brought no snow; it came icily off the Danube and in the little grassy square by the café it whipped up the snow like the surf on top of a wave. There was no heating in the café, and Martins sat warming each hand in turn on a cup of ersatz coffee—innumerable cups. There was usually one of my men in the café with him, but I changed them every twenty minutes or so irregularly. More than an hour passed. Martins had long given up hope and so had I, where I waited at the end of a phone several streets away, with a party of the sewer police ready to go down if it became necessary. We were luckier than Martins because we were warm in our great boots up to the thighs and our reefer jackets. One man had a small searchlight about half as big again as a car headlight strapped to his breast, and another man carried a brace of Roman candles. The telephone rang. It was Martins. He said, "I'm perishing with cold. It's a quarter past one. Is there any point in going on with this?"

"You shouldn't telephone. You must stay in sight."

"I've drunk seven cups of this filthy coffee. My stomach won't stand much more."

"He can't delay much longer if he's coming. He won't want to run into the two o'clock patrol. Stick it another quarter of an hour, but keep away from the telephone."

Martins' voice said suddenly, "Christ, he's here. He's—" and then the telephone went dead. I said to my assistant, "Give the signal to guard all manholes," and to my sewer police, "We are going down."

What had happened was this. Martins was still on the telephone to me when Harry Lime came into the café. I don't know what he heard, if he heard anything. The mere sight of a man wanted by the police and without friends in Vienna speaking on the telephone would have been enough to warn him. He was out of the café again before Martins had put down the receiver. It was one of those rare moments when none of my men was in the café. One had just left and another was on the pavement about to come in. Harry Lime brushed by him and made for the kiosk. Martins came out of the café and saw my men. If he had called out then it would have been an easy shot, but it was not, I suppose, Lime the penicillin racketeer who was escaping down the street; it was Harry. He hesitated just long enough for Lime to put the kiosk between them; then he called out, "That's him," but Lime had already gone to ground.

What a strange world unknown to most of us lies under our feet: we live above a cavernous land of waterfalls and rushing rivers, where tides ebb and flow as in the world above. If you have ever read the adventures of Allan Quartermain and the account of his voyage along the underground river to the city of Molosis, you will be able to picture the scene of Lime's last stand. The main sewer, half as wide as the Thames, rushes by under a huge arch, fed by tributary streams: these streams have fallen in waterfalls from higher levels and have been purified in their fall, so that only in these side channels is the air foul. The main stream smells sweet and fresh with a faint tang of ozone, and everywhere in the darkness is the sound of falling and rushing water. It was just past high tide when Martins and the policeman reached the river: first the curving iron staircase, then a short passage so low they had to stoop, and then the shallow edge of the water lapped at their feet. My man shone his torch along the edge of the current and said, "He's gone that way," for just as a deep stream when it shallows at the rim leaves an accumulation of debris, so the sewer left in the quiet water against the wall a scum of orange peel, old cigarette cartons, and the like, and in this scum Lime had left his trail as unmistakably as if he had walked in mud. My policeman shone his torch ahead with his left hand, and carried his gun in his right. He said to Martins, "Keep behind me, sir, the bastard may shoot."

"Then why the hell should you be in front?"

"It's my job, sir." The water came halfway up their legs as they walked; the policeman kept his torch pointing down and ahead at the disturbed trail at the sewer's edge. He said, "The silly thing is the bastard doesn't stand a chance. The manholes are all guarded and we've cordoned off the way into the Russian zone. All our chaps have to do now is to sweep inwards down the side passes from the manholes." He took a whistle out of his pocket and blew, and very far away here and again there came the notes of the reply. He said, "They are all down here now. The sewer police, I mean. They know this place just as I know the Tottenham Court Road. I wish my old woman could see me now," he said, lifting his torch for a moment to shine it ahead, and at that moment the shot came. The torch flew out of his hand and fell in the stream. He said, "God blast the bastard."

"Are you hurt?"

"Scraped my hand, that's all. Here, take this other torch, sir, while I tie my hand up. Don't shine it. He's in one of the side passages." For a long time the sound of the shot went on reverberating: when the last echo died a whistle blew ahead of them, and Martins' companion blew an answer.

Martins said, "It's an odd thing—I don't even know your name."

"Bates, sir." He gave a low laugh in the darkness. "This isn't my usual beat. Do you know the Horseshoe, sir?"

"Yes."

"And the Duke of Grafton?"

"Yes."

"Well, it takes a lot to make a world."

Martins said, "Let me come in front. I don't think he'll shoot at me, and I want to talk to him."

"I had orders to look after you, sir, careful."

"That's all right." He edged round Bates, plunging a foot deeper in the stream as he went. When he was in front he called out, "Harry," and the name set up an echo, "Harry, Harry, Harry!" that traveled down the stream and woke a whole chorus of whistles in the darkness. He called again, "Harry. Come out. It's no use."

A voice startlingly close made them hug the wall. "Is that you, old man?" it called. "What do you want me to do?"

"Come out. And put your hands over your head."

"I haven't a torch, old man. I can't see a thing."

"Be careful, sir," Bates said.

"Get flat against the wall. He won't shoot at me," Martins said. He called, "Harry, I'm going to shine the torch. Play fair and come out. You haven't got a chance." He flashed the torch on, and twenty feet away, at the edge of the light and the water, Harry stepped into view. "Hands above the head, Harry." Harry raised his hand and fired. The shot ricocheted against the wall a foot from Martins' head, and he heard Bates cry out. At the same moment a searchlight from fifty yards away lit the whole channel, caught Harry in its beams, Martins, the staring eyes of Bates slumped at the water's edge with the sewage washing to his waist. An empty cigarette carton wedged into his armpit and stayed. My party had reached the scene.

Martins stood dithering there above Bates's body, with Harry Lime halfway between us. We couldn't shoot for fear of hitting Martins, and the light of the searchlight dazzled Lime. We moved slowly on, our revolvers trained for a chance, and Lime turned this way and that way like a rabbit dazzled by headlights; then suddenly he took a flying jump into the deep central rushing stream. When we turned the searchlight after him he was submerged, and the current of the sewer carried him rapidly on, past the body of Bates, out of the range of the searchlight into the dark. What makes a man, without hope, cling to a few more minutes of existence? Is it a good quality or a bad one? I have no idea.

Martins stood at the outer edge of the searchlight beam, staring downstream. He had his gun in his hand now, and he was the only one of us who could fire with safety. I thought I saw a movement and called out to him, "There. There. Shoot." He lifted his gun and fired, just as he had fired at the same command all those years ago on Brickworth Common, fired, as he did then, inaccurately. A cry of pain came tearing back like calico down the cavern: a reproach, an entreaty. "Well done," I called and halted by Bates's body. He was dead. His eyes remained blankly open as we turned the searchlight on him; somebody stooped and dislodged the carton and threw it in the river, which whirled it on—a scrap of yellow Gold Flake: he was certainly a long way from the Tottenham Court Road.

I looked up and Martins was out of sight in the darkness. I called his name and it was lost in a confusion of echoes, in the rush and the roar of the underground river. Then I heard a third shot.

Martins told me later, "I walked downstream to find Harry, but I must have missed him in the dark. I was afraid to lift the torch: I didn't want to tempt him to shoot again. He must have been struck by my bullet just at the entrance of a side passage. Then I suppose he crawled up the passage to the foot of the iron stairs. Thirty feet above his head was the manhole, but he wouldn't have had the strength to lift it, and even if he had succeeded the police were waiting above. He must have known all that, but he was in great pain, and just as an animal creeps into the dark to die, so I suppose a man makes for the light. He wants to die at home, and the darkness is never home to *us*. He began to pull himself up the stairs, but then the pain took him and he couldn't go on. What made him whistle that absurd scrap of a tune I'd been fool enough to believe he had written himself? Was he trying to attract attention, did he want a friend with him, even the friend who had trapped him, or was he delirious and had he no purpose at all? Anyway I heard his whistle and came back along the edge of the stream, and felt the wall end and found my way up the passage where he lay. I said, 'Harry,' and the whistling stopped, just above my head. I put my hand on an iron handrail and climbed. I was still afraid he might shoot. Then, only three steps up, my foot stamped down on his hand, and he was there. I shone my torch on him: he hadn't got a gun; he must have dropped it when my bullet hit him. For a moment I thought he was dead, but then he whimpered with pain. I said, 'Harry,' and he swiveled his eyes with a great effort to my face. He was trying to speak, and I bent down to listen. 'Bloody fool,' he said—that was all. I don't know whether he meant that for himself—some sort of act of contrition, however inadequate (he was a Catholic)—or was it for me—with my thousand a year taxed and my imaginary cattle rustlers who couldn't even shoot a rabbit clean? Then he began to whimper again. I couldn't bear it anymore and I put a bullet through him.'"

"We'll forget that bit," I said.

Martins said, "I never shall."

17

A THAW set in that night, and all over Vienna the snow melted, and the ugly ruins came to light again: steel rods hanging like stalactites, and rusty girders thrusting like bones through the gray slush. Burials were much simpler than they had been a week before when electric drills had been needed to break the frozen ground. It was almost as warm as a spring day when Harry Lime had his second funeral. I was glad to get him under earth again, but it had taken two men's deaths. The group by the grave was smaller now: Kurtz wasn't there, nor Winkler—only the girl and Rollo Martins and myself. And there weren't any tears.

After it was over the girl walked away without a word to either of us down the long avenue of trees that led to the main entrance and the tram stop, splashing through the melted snow. I said to Martins, "I've got transport. Can I give you a lift?"

"No," he said, "I'll take a tram back."

"You win, you've proved me a bloody fool."

"I haven't won," he said. "I've lost." I watched him striding off on his overgrown legs after the girl. He caught her up and they walked side by side. I don't think he said a word to her: it was like the end of a story. He was a very bad shot and a very bad judge of character, but he had a way with Westerns (a trick of tension) and with girls (I wouldn't know what). And Crabbin? Oh, Crabbin is still arguing with the British Cultural Relations Society about Dexter's expenses. They say they can't pass simultaneous payments in Stockholm and Vienna. Poor Crabbin. Poor all of us when you come to think of it.